FAERIE OATH

FAE ACADEMY FOR HALFLINGS BOOK 5

BREA VIRAGH

Faerie Oath © Copyright 2023 Artemis Girl Publishing, LLC.

Copyright notice: All rights reserved under the International and Pan-American Copyright Conventions. No part of this book may be reproduced or transmitted in any form or by any means, electronic or mechanical, including photocopying, recording, or by any information storage and retrieval system, without permission in writing from the publisher.

This is a work of fiction. Names, places, characters, and incidents are either the product of the author's imagination or are used fictitiously, and any resemblance to any actual persons, living or dead, organizations, events, or locales is entirely coincidental.

Warning: the unauthorized reproduction or distribution of this copyrighted work is illegal. Criminal copyright infringement, including infringement without monetary gain, is investigated by the FBI and is punishable by up to 5 years in prison and a fine of $250,000.

Cover Artist: Heather Marie Adkins, CyberWitch Press & Graphic Design
www.cyberwitchpress.com

Editor: Deborah Anderson

FAERIE OATH

Using Necromancy comes with a price. But since the dead are keeping secrets, Tavi's ready to pay.

Tavi Alderidge is once again in trouble, and nothing can get her out of it this time. With her mentor, Onyx, out of the picture, and a new and "hairier" shifter problem ready to rise with the next full moon, she needs to focus on finding answers by any means necessary.

The Bureau is on her about what happened to Madam Muerte, the gypsy fortuneteller who foretold great tragedy and somehow ended up worse than dead: murdered. All fingers point to Tavi, and Crown Prince Mike is no longer on her side after discovering one of her own closely guarded secrets.

She's sick of always having to take risks, but the only one who can clear her name is a dead woman. Which means she'll have to turn to the riskiest magic of all: necromancy. But there may be a bigger price to pay than she bargained for when it's not ghosts but very real monsters that start coming out of the shadows...

Fans of Sarah J. Maas, Bella Forest, K.F. Breene, and Zodiac Academy will find themselves enthralled with this dark paranormal romance full of magic and betrayal.

1

Mike reached into his pocket and pulled something out. Keeping eye contact, he laid it gently on the nightstand beside me. "I found this, too," he said. Each word was weighted and landed with the strength of an anvil.

My skin turned to ice. It was my wolf amulet. He'd somehow found the medallion I'd been gifted, emblazoned with the sigil of the halfling shifter gathering, the Claw & Fang.

The red-hot shaft of fear tearing through me made the rest of my wounds seem like nothing. I went hot and cold at the same time, clenching the bedcovering beneath me. The fight with Onyx was nearly forgotten with Mike standing in front of me silently demanding an explanation. The fact that my friend had been under a spell and killed all those pure-blooded Fae sank deeper and deeper in my mind until there was only Mike. Only the damning accusation of that amulet.

"Where did you get that?" I asked.

Mike leveled a serious gaze on me and suddenly he

wasn't my friend anymore. He wasn't the guy who had picked me up on the side of the road when my car broke down. No, the man who stared at me now was the crown prince of Faerie and I knew better than to lie to him.

"This is your necklace, isn't it?" he said softly. "I recognize the chain. I've seen you wearing it a few times and didn't think anything of it until I found it with the rest of your things last night."

Should I bother denying what he already apparently knew? Was it worth a try?

Before I could say anything, he continued, "And I know it's the symbol of the Claw & Fang, a secret society made up of shifters that isn't supposed to exist but does. It does."

I couldn't breathe.

Mike knew.

He knew the truth I'd tried to hide about myself.

"Is there something you want to tell me, Tavi?" he went on. "About why you have this? What *are* you?"

But I didn't have the answers he clearly wanted. I shivered, the cold seeping through my skin all the way down to the bone no matter how tightly I wrapped my arms around my midsection. I thought I'd known fear before? Nothing compared to seeing the betrayal on Mike's face and the response inside of me now. The betrayal, and worse—the sheer terror of the answer I could give him.

"*What are you?*" he repeated.

I swallowed and felt sick and ready to erupt. My secret was out. I sat frozen to the bed with too many emotions inside of me to name. After everything that I'd been through, it had come down to this.

And Mike was staring at me like I was some kind of freak who should have never been born.

Worse than a freak. A *what,* rather than a person who

cared about him. Now I was nothing but a creature to him and something he could barely stand to look at, judging by the expression on his face.

I couldn't lie to him anymore.

"Mike, please—"

"*Please* isn't good enough right now, Tavi," he snapped.

Every lie that I'd told had gotten us to this point, and for what? He knew my secret now. There was no way for me to spin this without digging a deeper hole for myself, and out of everybody in this world, I didn't want to hurt Mike. He was too important to me.

Now I just had to know if he'd ever forgive me for what I'd had to do to survive.

That counted for something, right?

No more lies and no more withholding the truth. I had feelings for him, more than I wanted to admit, and despite everything keeping us apart, I wanted to be with him. I knew it now as if someone had carved the knowledge out of my heart and handed it to me. Which meant I was all in.

It was time to prove it.

At last, I reached out a shaking hand to take the medallion from the nightstand, turning the piece over and over in my palm as though the carved wolf head would somehow give me the courage I needed to finish this.

"I'm a...half shifter," I told him. Even my words shook.

Coward.

I took a deep breath. "My mother was Fae, and my father was a wolf shifter. After they died, my father's brother raised me. He's the alpha of the Alderidge pack where I grew up. I know I'm some kind of abomination who shouldn't have been born, but here I am, and I've been trying to deal with it my entire life."

I didn't want his pity. That was the last thing I wanted,

and I wondered if, looking up, I'd find it written on Mike's face. In those green eyes.

How would I ever be able to face him once I got my story out there in the open? He'd either want me dead or, worse, banished. I'd never talk to him again let alone kiss him, those stolen moments between us reduced to nothing but memories.

"I made it into the Fae Academy for Halflings by tricking the system. I took a potion to hide my shifter side so that only the human portion of me would be visible," I explained. "That's why the test showed me as Fae and human. I paid a witch for the first round of potion." Quickly I stopped myself before I babbled out the rest of the sordid tale.

Mike glanced down at his feet, shaking his head slightly. His blond hair curled around the points of his ears, but I could still see that the tips of his ears had turned a bright crimson.

Finally he raised his head. "Why are you here, Tavi?" The hardness of those words took me by surprise and I winced. "Are you some kind of spy?"

"No!" I blurted out. "I had to go to the Academy. My uncle, the alpha, found my fated mate. Or he found some terrible person and convinced himself that it was my fated mate. But Kendrick Grimaldi is a monster." I shuddered at having to speak his name out loud. "Everything I did was to get away from *him*."

When Mike didn't move, and my shaking threatened to crack bones, I drew in a breath and tried again. "I *had* to escape. Grimaldi is a bloodthirsty bully and a murderer. He's the one who kidnapped me the night of the Wild Hunt. Do you remember? I was waiting for you in the woods and…and…"

Would it even make a difference explaining things to Mike? He was staring at me and although his brows drew together in a scowl, he didn't look like he wanted me to stop.

Or I was reading into things?

I rushed on to tell him about my past life. Who I was, how I'd left it all behind. He barely moved throughout my telling of the story despite the way I verbally vomited all over him. Every last detail spilled to the point where it was information overload even for me.

"Don't you get it?" I asked when I'd finished. "I *want* to be here. I gave up everything to come to Faerie and make a new life for myself. I especially want to be here with you, Mike."

A small muscle near his jaw twitched.

I took that for a good sign, too. Yup, I was delusional, clearly.

If I was going to do this whole baring my heart and being honest thing, then it had to be everything. Anything less would negate the effort. It was all or nothing.

My muscles quaked and my nose began to itch. I swiped it on the back of my sleeve.

"I want to be here *with* you with you. Not just as friends," I continued. "You mean so much to me."

It felt like I was peeling back my soul and showing him the core of me, everything I'd hidden before, and I wished he would say something. Just one little word to let me know I was on the right track or that he even wanted me to keep talking. That he understood.

"I had to keep my shifter side a secret, and this medallion," I paused to sniff, my nose still bothering me, "represented a way to keep that hidden. A way for me to feel like I was really on the right path. Do you understand?"

"I'm not sure," he said at last. "It's a lot for me to take in,

Tavi. You've lied to me from the start. You're not who you said you were. Who you pretended to be."

Ouch. "I had to lie. It was the only way for me to survive."

He looked at me like I'd just told him I'd run over his dog, and it wasn't an expression I wanted to see on his face ever again.

I drifted in place, my body seated but the rest of me having a hard time finding stillness, nose still twitching like someone plucked a hair right out of it. The fight with Onyx had clearly taken its toll. I'd used up too much of my magic, and my body, although I'd been training, hadn't come through the fight in one piece. I'd gotten my ass handed to me by my mentor, who I was dead sure had been placed under a vicious controlling spell.

The healers had done what they could for me but it would take a bit more time than I'd been given to heal entirely from being so battered. Liquid dripped onto my upper lip and I swiped at it, only then realizing my shirt was caked in dried blood.

"Oh, God." Had I had a nosebleed through the entire conversation? And why hadn't Mike said anything?

He must have thought I was absolutely bonkers.

I glanced around for a tissue or a towel or something to stop the flow of blood continuing to drip, but I found nothing except the blankets on the bed.

"I'm sorry," I said, scrambling. "I'm not sure what's—"

"Here."

At once, Mike thrust a handkerchief at me, and I stared at it, blinking, trying to understand and failing. He must have had it hidden in his pocket. But what kind of guy carries an honest-to-goodness old-fashioned handkerchief?

A *prince*, apparently. A Fae prince.

"You're going to have to let me do it. You're really not in a position to help yourself right now, are you?" His voice was hard but something in his face had softened, I noticed when I glanced up at him.

The first touch of the cloth against my sensitive nostrils had me automatically jerking in the opposite direction. Try telling a prince to back off. Try telling *Mike* to back off, I thought as he cleaned my face for me.

The gesture was sweeter than I expected and, if I was being honest, sweeter than I deserved for lying to him all this time. He kept his movements precise and tender, cleaning the blood away with such slowness that tears pricked the corners of my eyes, burning worse than any sort of fire.

This was my punishment. To have the man I loved this close and absolutely devastated by the truth of me. He knew that I was a monster. A monster who wasn't supposed to exist, and this must be our goodbye.

He said nothing about my admissions and nothing about my story. Which of course wasn't finished.

"I've been struggling to find a way to make it work since I got here," I told him. "Between my nature, and these killings, trying to stay ahead in my studies and still work in the kitchen, it's been a struggle. And those Faerie Trials? My mentor was the beast who attacked me. I knew him. He'd been teaching me how to harness the powers I'd never really explored before."

"Wait. You *know* that guy?" Mike asked. "The murderer?"

I nodded, the motion causing a sharp pain to ricochet through my brain. The bleeding had slowed but not entirely stopped. "He was the one trying to teach me about my secondary power."

"Tavi, you're not supposed to *have* a secondary power. What the hell are you talking about? You only have cognitive manipulation. That's what showed up when you tested your innate powers."

Yup, more explaining to do. I shrank further into myself.

"It's a long story. But yeah, there were actually two sigils on the test strip. I manifested shapeshifting powers at the Halfling Academy, in addition to cognitive manipulation. My two sides each manifested a different power. And Onyx was teaching me how to control it so that I could fit in better. We see how well it worked out."

I still remembered what Headmaster Leaves had said when I asked him if it was possible for a student to manifest more than one power.

Quite impossible.

Two would be overkill.

"You survived," Mike clarified. "And your little friend is in custody."

Except I had a feeling that Onyx didn't belong there, but that was another rabbit hole I didn't want to go down with Mike. Not right now.

"Mike—" I broke off when he stared at me. Ah, those eyes. They got me every time. "I want to be here. I hope you know that. *I want to be here.*" Time to go for the gold. "And I want to be with you. As your girlfriend. In a girlfriend-ly way."

His hand fell away.

He was silent for so long that my heart skipped a beat.

I guessed I had my answer, then.

He obviously didn't feel the same way.

The back of my throat burned and my chest hollowed out the longer he refused to speak.

"Are you going to turn me in?" I finally asked.

Mike settled back on his heels with his arms at his sides and the handkerchief clenched in his fist. He wore a thunderous expression, but if I wasn't mistaken his eyes betrayed sadness.

"Do you even know me at all?" he replied quietly.

I wasn't sure that I did, not really. I wasn't sure if I saw what I wanted to see with Mike or if our circumstances had me wearing rose-colored glasses based on everything we'd been through.

"I just need a minute." His hands went to his pockets and he stalked to the door. Taking his blood-covered handkerchief and my heart along with him.

I didn't follow him and I knew he didn't want me to. Better for both of us if we distanced ourselves from the mess of the truth, no matter how it might fracture our friendship.

2

The Faerie Bureau of Investigation called me in for an interview the following morning to talk about Onyx, and I ignored the messages for as long as physically possible. The bed felt like a cloud of everything dreams were made of. As if I'd want to get up anytime soon?

Classes were over until after the Wild Hunt so I had the day off to heal and work in the kitchen, because even a near-catastrophe wasn't enough to get Raelynn to give me a day off from my duties. Still, I had the morning.

I *had* had the morning.

The insistent ding from my phone reminded me what would happen if I ignored the summons completely. They needed my statement about Onyx. When I first woke up, rolling over and rubbing my eyes, checking my pillow for dried blood from my nose, I wondered how they'd gotten this number.

Then I dropped back with a yawn that ended in a scoff. The agents knew everything about me. They probably even had my underwear size on file. For a hot second I debated tossing the phone and pulling my pillow over my head.

Falling back asleep to let my body do what the healers couldn't finish and get me back to rights.

The texts would continue, more than likely followed by a rude wakeup call. And with having to work that afternoon, no rest for me.

Not even during sleep, when nightmares of Mike rejecting me played on repeat. A demented loop until the sun rose.

The same kind of fear I'd first felt at the Bureau returned once I eventually boarded the train to take me across town. The silver bullet traveled inside the expansive magical ring of protection surrounding this town.

Around me, Fae of all shapes and sizes continued with their lives. They spoke and practiced magic. They laughed, lived, and made plans for the future.

I didn't have the luxury of any of those things. Not when I had already put off this meeting with Rooker and Claribel yesterday. They needed to know what had happened and I had to decide what I was willing to tell them. What was pertinent to their investigation into Onyx and what would only dig the hole deeper for him.

It was a fine line to tread.

I refused to believe that he'd been operating under his own wits. Something—or someone—controlled him and forced him to murder those women. To believe otherwise was...unthinkable.

I stepped off the train and onto the platform, then out of the station. The building rose up in front of me. My stomach roiled as I noticed the same plaque with the business name in Fae hieroglyphs just above the door of the deceptive, nondescript exterior. One wouldn't have even known that this was an official government building. At first glance it looked more like some kind of museum with secrets and history waiting inside.

And waiting for *me* at the door? A craggy monstrosity of a creature with skin like rocks. An overly large coat of navy blue with gold buttons hid his chest from view. The gold badge matched the buttons.

Well, crap. Agent Rooker.

He glanced up sharply once I actually stopped walking, as though the silence following my footsteps got his attention more than the movement. His gaze scoured me from head to toe, from my sandals to the black shorts and bright-green shirt that had reminded me so much of Mike's eyes I'd wanted to cry all over again.

I wore the t-shirt anyway.

If Rooker had an opinion about my outfit, he kept his thoughts to himself as he pushed away from the building. "You took your time in coming, Miss Alderidge," he said.

Even his voice reminded me of boulders grinding together during a rockslide. The sun shone overhead, a mockery of what had happened the day before, and the absurdity of the situation washed over me.

"I'm here now," I told him, blinking in the sunlight. Trying to push aside the seething mess in my stomach and the slightly queasy sensation it caused. "Where's your partner in crime?"

Rooker didn't look amused, but then again it was almost impossible to tell with the agent. Not only a fortress but literally made of stone. It made him damn good at his job. Just looking at him intimidated me. "She's inside. Waiting for you," he replied, somehow making me feel worse in only five words.

Without pause, he spun on his heel with surprising grace and pressed in the code for the door. He held it open for me and waited for me to step inside before the locks and the magic re-engaged behind us.

The cathedral-like interior reminded me of the great hall of the academy on the hill. The walls soared toward a ceiling reflecting the image of the sky outside, with arched doorways and a cold stone floor. We passed a front desk ornately carved of living wood and a chair upholstered in velvet on the way to the same small room where they'd interrogated me the first time. No, not the same room. It looked like the same door when I first saw it but the inside had been rearranged.

Now there was no table between us. Only a raised platform with two seats and a single chair waiting on the ground floor in front of them. Like they were two lords and I was the peasant who needed her hand slapped for stealing potatoes.

I should be used to this by now. Shouldn't I? I've been admonished more times since coming to Faerie than in my entire childhood with Will.

Agent Claribel, tall and willowy with Spanish moss dripping from the tips of her hair, had already commandeered the chair on the left. She looked even less amused by my tardiness than Rooker had sounded.

"Sit," she demanded instantly.

And a part of me wanted to peruse the room and take my damn time just to spite her. Sure, like I needed to dig a deeper hole for myself than I already had.

"We need to discuss the murders that took place during the trials." Claribel's voice was a sharp whip of sound that had me ready to react before I thought to school my expression. "The four Fae women were pureblood. Girls roughly between three and six hundred years old. They were all slender, with reddish-hued hair, high cheekbones. Mangled. Claw marks and deep tears on the bodies."

I inclined my head, skin heating at the reminder. *Like I need one.* Onyx had done those things. He'd targeted Fae who looked eerily similar to me, and he'd attacked my teacher from the academy here, Juno Ians. She might not have been able to escape if I hadn't been there to help her.

"Tragedies," I finally agreed.

Onyx had helped me with my transfiguration on multiple occasions. He'd helped me learn how to use my abilities while we sparred, and through it all, I'd had no idea that he was using those techniques to actually kill. And to kill women who looked like me. He'd had me alone plenty of times. Why?

Onyx Grimaldi.

Was it in his blood to be cutthroat, brutal? Should he be defined by the sins of his father...or his own?

There were too many unanswered questions and no way I'd be able to ask him any of them. The court and Bureau probably had him so deep in lockdown, at this point I was sure he'd never see the light of day again.

And I didn't have the brain cells to spare in wondering what I could do about him. I'd get through *this* first, I told myself. Get through today and then I'd figure shit out.

I needed to talk to Selene. If anyone had answers, and a cool logical mind, it was my journalist friend.

Rooker and Claribel stared at me, tense, waiting for me to continue. When I kept my lips zipped, he sighed.

"Your presence throughout these crimes has been labeled as suspicious. On more than one occasion you were within proximity to these scenes. However..." Claribel looked as though her words pained her. "Your classmate, Coral Ferenze, made a statement on your behalf. You have been cleared of any wrongdoing in association with the pureblood murders by that alone."

I sat up straighter in my chair. "What? Coral helped me?"

Why would she do that? She didn't do anything without a reason. Coral was the classic mean girl and part of Mike's Elite Academy friend group, a snooty upperclassman with bright red lips, hazel eyes, long straight nose. Slender and curvy and absolutely *perfect*. Selfish, entitled—

And Onyx had gone after her, too.

There was enough of a strange similarity between us that she'd been made a target and, honestly, at one point during the trials I wasn't sure she'd survive. When had they even gotten a chance to talk to her?

"Did you not hear me, Miss Alderidge?" Claribel asked. Her eyes narrowed. "You've been cleared in the pureblood murders but there are still questions. Coral, in her statement, indicated that it seemed as though you knew the beast. Onyx Grimaldi."

"What do you know about the halfling shifter?" Rooker leaned forward, and although it was almost impossible to tell his expression, he seemed aggravated. "What can you tell us about the monster?"

Crap. I had to think fast. No sense denying our friendship now.

"I, ah, met him in a coffee shop. The one close to the apartment that my friend rents," I said on the fly. "I went out for coffee with my best friend, Melia, and met Onyx there by chance. He was attractive and kind and we seemed to hit it off. So we chatted."

It was the best I could come up with and close enough to the truth that it didn't sound like a complete fabrication.

"Oh, so you're dating?" Rooker wanted to know.

I started. "Uhhh, no. Not dating."

Onyx had asked but...no. I'd said no. I'd refused him because my heart already belonged to someone else, and if that made me closed off, then so be it. Onyx and I were better as friends. Or at least that was what I'd told myself at the time.

"You're not dating him, but you got to know him well enough to recognize him in his halfling warrior form." Claribel was not buying this act. Not one bit. "What can you tell us about your friend?" she pressed.

She placed special emphasis on the last word and I wondered if she knew what went on inside my head. Did she see what I had to hide from them? I had the gift of mental manipulation but I knew it was against the law to use it during these types of perfunctory conversations.

Right?

Or maybe I was just making shit up.

I hesitated. Should I tell them that I thought Onyx was being controlled by magic? That he wasn't responsible for any of those murders?

That would mean admitting that I did know him just as well as they accused me of knowing him.

"What's going to happen to him?" I asked instead. "I mean, I know he's been taken into custody, but what kind of punishment is he facing?"

The two of them shared a look and I wished I hadn't been there to see it. "He'll stay in custody until his trial," Rooker told me, in the softest voice I'd ever heard him use before. "Then he will go before the Elder Council and more than likely sentenced to death. Murder brings an immediate death sentence."

Immediate? "Wait a minute!" I gasped. "What about his trial? Surely he'll be allowed to explain—"

"The Elder Council's word is law," Claribel snapped. "Once they reach a decision, that is the blade of justice. There will be no chance to refute their judgment."

No judges. No juries. No defense. The government was the law here, judge and executioner in one.

That left things open for so much corruption. Who maintained order within the Elder Council? Who was there to make sure things were balanced and fair?

And wasn't the king on the Elder Council too?

"You have a right to be worried about a death sentence, considering you are still under investigation for the murder of Madam Muerte," Claribel continued.

"You are still a person of interest in another case, however," Rooker added.

Didn't I know it.

"There is no evidence to prove I had anything to do with Madam Muerte," I argued, already knowing what he referred to. Because I hadn't done a damn thing. I'd been waiting in the garden for Mike to return when I heard a scream and just happened to be the unlucky person who found the body.

I found a lot of bodies.

It was definitely a curse. Or a gift. Or maybe both.

They continued trying to nail me to the wall with their questions until it seemed they were both satisfied. It was impossible to tell time but it felt as though several hours had passed since I first stepped off of the train.

The conversation always turned to Madam Muerte, I thought as I pushed out of the building, exhausted.

My heart sank into the pit of my stomach. I hadn't even *tried* to clear Onyx's name. I'd done the best I could to keep my own head above water without raising suspicion. Because I knew in doing so I'd only put myself at risk too.

And I'd been through enough.

However, if Onyx died for those crimes he had been forced to commit, then his blood would be on my hands, too. Not to mention I needed to figure out who *really* killed Madam Muerte.

Else I might end up on the gallows right beside him.

3

The more time that passed throughout the day, the angrier the entire situation made me feel until the blood in my veins seemed to change to acid and everything boiled inside. My hands curled into fists to the point where my nails dug grooves into my skin. My tendons ached when I finally managed to straighten my fingers out.

Still a suspect in Madam Muerte's murder when there was nothing to tie me to the death itself. The bureau was never going to leave me alone, and this stuff with Onyx sealed my fate.

Work was no picnic, either, though for a time it actually felt like a little respite, being down there in the kitchens doing routine tasks. I'd hoped the constant low-level background chatter would take my mind off of the insane pressure in my life that seemed to have no end in sight.

Today, I went to work in a rage that made the other workers steer clear of me. My thoughts never calmed down. If anything, the mindlessness of the tasks, the repetition, gave me more time to feed that rage.

I wrenched the apron over my head and tied it around

my waist as I glared at one of the new girls at the bread station, the one I preferred working at, until she squeaked and shifted away to do something else.

Why couldn't the authorities leave me alone? Actually do their jobs and find the real culprit? Or how about they focused on the spells that had manipulated Onyx? Anything besides bothering innocent people like me to the point where I was about to crack.

"Someone is in a bit of a snit today."

Raelynn sidled up behind me just as I made to grab a plate, trying to push it out of my way—only to break it. It slammed against the mixing bowl with such force it broke into two pieces.

An accident. Just me working while feeling a bit too rage-y.

"Oh hell."

But when I glanced over at the butter-yellow haired Fae in charge of the kitchen, Raelynn was glaring at me.

"Do we have a problem, Tavi?" she asked.

Her lilting accent made everything she said come out like a song but I wasn't having it.

"I'm fine," I snapped. "It was an accident."

"If this continues, then we *are* going to have a problem." Her voice held more than a hint of warning. "Get yourself together. I'll not have you coming in here and upsetting people with your bad attitude."

"I'm *fine*," I insisted.

She grabbed the bowl of dough away a split second before I reached for it, holding it against her chest with all the protection of a mother with her baby.

Over one mixture of flour, yeast, salt, and water? Seriously?

For some reason that made me madder than when I'd

walked through the door. Once again I'd been branded as an enemy. Okay, well, maybe not that serious, but at the very least a threat.

A threat to the safety of a loaf of bread for the king's table.

I yanked the bowl of dough away from her and slammed it down on the countertop then drove my hands down into it without washing them. Pissed at her for even suggesting there was a problem. *I* didn't have a problem. I was here to work. Here to do the job I'd been assigned to do.

"You know what?" Raelynn said. "No. No, this is unacceptable."

"What's unacceptable?"

"You and your attitude right now. Girl, get the hell out of my kitchen, because I'm not dealing with your attitute or you right now."

I gawked at her, my eyes wide. "Are you kidding me?"

"Absolutely not. You come in here breaking things and throwing everyone into a frenzy. Take yourself to your room until you've calmed down. I don't want to see you until tomorrow."

She pointed at the door until I had no choice but to storm out. Feeling like a damn idiot. I didn't even take off the apron. I practically heard everyone let out an audible breath once I left.

Fine. I didn't need Raelynn to be pissed and against me right now too. It wasn't high on my priority list to make more enemies, or even on the list period. Something was seriously bubbling and brewing inside of me.

I kept my head down for the most part, rushing through the hallways trying to get back to my room along with my "attitude." Raelynn didn't understand. It wasn't that I wanted to be this way. But shit piled on top of other shit tended to put a person in a foul mood. Now I wasn't going to be able to work, which meant more time trapped in my own mind listening to my repetitive and circular thoughts.

I wasn't watching where I walked, of course, and knocked into something solid and muscled on my way up the stairs.

"I'm sor–"

Oh. *Shit*. I hadn't just run into *some*one. Not just *any* someone, I realized once recognition clicked into place. The *worst kind* of someone.

King Tywin Thornwood stood with his shoulders thrown back and one salt-and-pepper eyebrow lifted. Reducing me to a puddle with a single look.

I hurried to excuse myself while alternately trying to ignore the serious side-eye as he passed, continuing on his way. Urgent business, then. He had to have urgent business otherwise I'd be on the receiving end of yet another tongue-lashing from the king.

I'd never had a civilized conversation with the man and I doubted that would ever change for us. He wasn't exactly on my side, and for someone like him to be in a squarely opposite position... Well, there were too many people who possessed much more power than I did who wanted to keep an eye on me.

My stomach lurched and bile seemed to pop and fizzle its way up to the back of my throat while I hustled to put serious distance between me and the king. The second I walked through the door to my room, I ripped the apron off and tossed it in a pile on the floor.

I needed to get out of the castle, not just up to my room. Because honestly I felt like I was literally going crazy. My skin itched and a swell of heat made its way along my limbs until my fingers tingled.

I stalked back and forth, with my fingers blazing trails through my hair and the strands ready to pop out of my skull.

Not good.

Where was the brain booster powder when I needed it? Because the way things had been going, whenever I took too much and forgot everything, I might have used a little oblivion. A little break from reality.

Not a good way to solve problems, I knew that.

I almost wished for it, although that sounded insane. What else was new? My entire existence was insane. But I had control over one thing: I could leave this room. After hurrying to change clothes, I drew on a pair of sneakers and I was out of the castle and striding across the courtyard in minutes. Trying not to look like I was running for my life.

I remembered how overjoyed I'd been when I first came to Faerie, staring around at this entirely new world with wonder. A kid on Christmas morning who'd never seen a pile of presents so large. I remembered the train ride through the tunnel, and all the spells in place to keep undesirables away from the castle. Supposedly, according to Mike, only those with pure intent would be able to pass through the spells or else they'd be frozen in place.

No access to the king's town.

So how the hell did the person who took control of Onyx get into Eahsea? It had to be someone who lived here. Maybe even someone I knew because the town wasn't exactly a hopping place.

Now the sloping cobblestone streets lined with copper-roofed cottages, smoking chimneys, and more flowers than a garden center seemed normal to me, I thought as I marched. Familiar, even. I knew exactly how the sharp spiral spires of the castle would look thrusting into the blue sky, how the winding valley paths all lead toward the palace.

The magic had gone out of this place for me—and not just because of living here. Everything that had happened with Onyx had tainted the experience.

Same with the constant bubbling thunderheads ringing the outskirts of the valley, ready to drop their heavy burdens and punish the land when they did. This wasn't the busiest place in Faerie but we always had visitors in the town and at the academy. The stormy weather had been keeping some away while it brought others: scholars wishing to study why this normally placid place had suddenly become a hotbed for weird weather phenomena.

Mentally, I raised my hand. My bad.

The entire land of Faerie was alive, and the earth itself fed and replenished the power of the people who lived here. Anyone with fairy blood had access to that magic, and when things went wrong, when the land rebelled...

Thunderstorms.

There were bigger places out there in the world of Faerie. Bigger cities, rugged wilderness. Would it be so bad to run again? To get the hell out of here? The urge captured me so strongly I fought the physical need to step off the sidewalk and bolt. Every part of me yearned to break free. Surely there was a big enough city in Faerie where I could hide out there for the rest of my life.

To disappear and be done with all of this bullshit heaped on my shoulders.

Except...

Mike.

The tiny smile on my face disappeared as though it had never existed.

Mike was here.

Even angry with each other, even unsure whether he'd keep my secret, the thought of leaving him hurt so badly I lifted a hand to rub a sudden pain in my chest. Leaving him, never knowing what might have happened between us...was devastating.

Melia's apartment was nestled downtown in an attic with a sloping ceiling and barely large enough for furniture. She'd rented a place close enough to the castle that I'd always know she was near. Just like the king would always know where I was, although I didn't miss the tracking device he'd once implemented.

I climbed the stairs to the attic and knocked on the rickety door before making myself at home: I let myself inside and called out a brief hello to the woman who had once been my mentor.

"Is that my bestie I hear knock, knock, knocking on my chamber door?" Melia bounced off of the bed and quickly accosted me with the warmest hug I'd ever received.

One I mirrored back to her.

I sneezed when her wild brown curls went straight up my nose, but her dusky-gold arms maintained a grip on me.

"Are you okay?" she asked. "You don't seem like you're okay, and I've been meaning to reach out to you about the whole thing, girl, but you needed space. At least, I told myself you needed space."

I nodded against her as I let her talk. Melia processed things verbally, by working through them out loud, and whenever she was upset she tended to babble. The familiar feeling of her arms, her scent, wound around me and a knot of tension in my chest began to loosen.

"I'm fine," I assured her. "A little beat up and more emotional than I've been since puberty, but fine. What about you?"

"I'm not sure. I'm still trying to process and it seems like none of the pieces are coming together, girl. Like everything is kind of fragmented," she replied. "I really liked Onyx, and although he wasn't always the loudest person in the room, he never struck me as the worst. You know what I mean?"

Finally she released me from the hug and we shifted over to sit on her bed.

"He always struck me as a nice guy despite his past being full of secrets. Like yours." She lifted golden eyes to meet mine. "I never got a bad vibe off of him, and I like to think that my intuitive juju is on point."

"It always has been," I said, dropping my gaze to the floor. She wasn't saying anything new, or anything I hadn't thought of already. Good to know we were on the same page.

Melia opened her mouth, then paused and lifted a hand and a buzz of magic erupted from her palm, enclosing us in a bubble of silence to keep anything we'd say between us. Safer that way. It bugged me that I hadn't thought of it first.

"What he did is completely out of character," she continued with a groan. She dropped her head, clasped her hands between her knees. "It's not like him. He wanted to stay under the radar. He wanted to live a life where he could do what he wanted rather than living on the run or in fear. Why would he do something so high profile? I mean, get real. The Onyx we both knew would never kill anyone. He never even swatted a spider!"

"What do you think about the possibility of someone else controlling Onyx?" I asked her with a forced mild tone. "Knowing what kind of beast lurked inside of him, how much sense would it make for someone on the outside to take over and *force* him to do what they want?"

Melia thought about it for approximately half a second

before she nodded emphatically. "Yeah. Yeah, that makes much more sense! Onyx wasn't the type to just go loco for no reason. You saw something, didn't you?" Her eyes widened. "You saw something. Tavi?"

"I did," I admitted, biting my lip. "It really did look like he was under a spell and he came out of it at exactly the wrong time. Onyx was being used. He was the fall guy. There was magic in the air that didn't belong to either one of us."

Melia pushed to her feet and paced in the eleven feet of clearance she had. "I found out where he's being held. A little bit of digging, no big deal." Her eyes widened at my expression. "Don't worry. No one will even know I sent my probes out for information. I've gotten good at covering my tracks. But he's being held in a prison hospital. He's...well, he's in bad shape."

My chest tightened painfully. "Could you see if he was going to make it?" I asked. "How did he look?"

"The information in his charts isn't public, but from what I've been able to see, he has a long road ahead of him. He pushed himself to the brink while he was in halfling form and drew way more magic than he'd ever done before, which took a tremendous toll on his body. It's all uphill but the healers are doing their best so that they can prosecute him for the murders. They *want* him alive—"

I filled in the rest. "So that he can suffer."

"They want him alive *for now*, let me clarify. Surely he'll be put to death once they get a confession out of him. I'm guessing they want to study him and understand his motives. He does need a few things. I managed to go in and pretend to be his cousin to speak to the nurse. She has a list of things that will make Onyx a little more comfortable." Melia stopped, paused, her hands propped on her hips and her attention fixed on the opposite wall. "I have to work tonight. I was going to take care of it tomorrow." Her mouth turned down. "He has no one, Tavi. He has no one, so I figured I'd help him."

"He was my mentor." I stood up. "I'm the one who put him in the hospital. I'm the one who hurt him so badly." And I'd forever feel guilty for it, even though I'd had to fight for my own life.

"You want to go to his house and get the things he needs and take them to him? Are you sure you can handle going there? Seeing him?"

I shrugged. "It's not like it's going to kill me."

This time.

4

It probably wasn't the smartest idea in the world but I let myself into Onyx's place later that day. More than likely the Bureau watched it in case someone else tried to break in but I didn't sense any kind of protection or monitoring spells when I opened the door. If they were there, then whoever put them up did a damn good job of camouflage.

It was a small cottage that fit in nicely with its surroundings, lattice work with climbing vines and bright purple flowers hiding most of the windows from sight. Average. Ordinary.

Only the occupant had been extraordinary. And my friend.

One of several halfling shifters hiding in plain sight when our kind wasn't wanted, wasn't accepted. We weren't supposed to exist and yet we did, right under the nose of the king. More of us than I'd ever guessed and all of us on the run from something in our lives. Onyx and I bonded because we'd both been trying to escape the same person.

His father.

I had the key to the front door because he'd given it to me after a few training sessions, like it was a token of trust. Funny, no one had asked me about that. They had no reason to suspect that I was closer to Onyx than they saw on first glance.

Casting a silencing bubble around me after Melia pounded it into my head to constantly watch my back, and making sure there was no one around to see, I stepped inside.

Immediately I was floored by the quiet hush.

The place smelled of him. And at once, it felt almost impossible for me to reconcile my mentor with Kendrick Grimaldi, Onyx's father and my supposed fated mate, the one I'd tried so desperately to get away from, an older fellow kept young by black magic. And blood, I thought. Black magic and blood.

A true monster—and someone had cruelly turned his son into the same thing. It wasn't fair.

I shook my head to clear it, forcing one foot in front of the other until I stood in the center of the neat living room. Onyx had once knocked me on my ass and sent me through the coffee table, then repaired it with a single magical word. It stood brand new now. Taunting me with its wholeness.

He'd helped me more than I'd ever be able to repay.

When had he become the target? When had someone started to control him?

Being here triggered more than just memories. Questions piled on top of one another. Urgency to find the answers pushed me into the kitchen.

We'd shared coffee there. He knew exactly how I liked mine—warm, with whipped milk and a splash of cinnamon and honey—and we'd laughed at some of the ridiculous spells other Fae had cast on themselves to change their physical appearance. We'd discussed the king and his ridiculous witch hunt against me in regards to the murder of Madam Muerte. The only thing we hadn't been able to talk about was Mike.

Now I'd lost both of the major men in my life and it wasn't as if I had them to spare.

But Onyx... Had the control over him started with the first pure-blood murder? Or did it go further back than that?

There I went, getting off track again. From my pocket I grabbed the list of things he'd asked Melia to fetch and stared at it. They seemed like the smallest, most innocent things. For instance he'd asked for a watch, because the one he'd been wearing broke.

A watch.

And a change of clothes because he wanted to wear something besides a hospital gown.

Were they treating him decently? Probably not, considering what he'd done.

Crap. *I hate this.*

I drew to a sudden halt in the bedroom. The sheets were still rumpled from the last time he'd slept there. Clothes were strewn across the floor and a pile of books teetered on the nightstand.

"Okay," I said out loud, needing to hear something besides the frantic rat-a-tat of my own heart. "A bag. He's got to have one somewhere. Who wouldn't have a bag?"

I found a black duffel in his closet and threw a change of clothes in there first. The watch, on the other hand, was going to be a bit of a hassle.

Luckily for me, Onyx had always been an organized person. I found a plain wooden box on top of his dresser and inside were tidy rows of watches, amulets, and rings. I grabbed every watch I could find, not knowing which one he wanted, and brought the handful up for a perusal.

In my haste a ring came along with the watches. The ring now dangling from the tip of my index finger boasted a familiar pack crest.

Kendrick Grimaldi's pack crest, to be precise.

I shook it off as though it had burned me, my pulse ratcheting up into dangerous territory and my lungs seizing. The gold crest glinted up at me and demanded my attention.

No.

I forced myself to stare at it rather than looking away as I wanted to do. The insignia was a stark, painful reminder of my past. Where I'd come from and what I was trying so desperately hard to escape.

How strange, though, that my arch enemy from the human realm still had a hold on me here. And his son had become a sort of villain here in the Fae realm. The parallels made my skin itch.

"It's okay," I said out loud to calm myself. "It's all going to be okay."

I threw the watches into the duffel bag and used the side of my hand to scrape the unnerving ring back into the jewelry box, then slammed the lid of the box shut, grabbed the bag, and headed out.

Melia had given me directions to the location where they were keeping Onyx while he recovered. I hadn't called ahead to let them know that I planned to visit, but I had his things; hopefully they wouldn't give me too much trouble.

And if they did, I'd channel my inner Raelynn and burst through the doors anyway.

The Fae hospital looked more like a Victorian gothic revival mansion done in taupe- and brick-colored stone, with a turreted slate roof and stained-glass windows. Located about a mile away from the Elite Academy, it stood out among the other stone cottages on the quiet street. The hospital had been built on a slight rise to give it a view of the rolling city but not high enough to impede on the school's vista.

My nerves ate at me as I walked through the front doors.

"I'm here to see Onyx Grimaldi," I told the Fae at the front desk.

She blinked six eyes at me before glancing down at the book in front of her. "He is not seeing visitors currently."

"Well, I'm Tavi Alderidge." I said my name like it somehow made a difference. At least, I crossed my fingers it did. "And I'm not leaving here until I see Onyx. I have his personal things he asked for."

I shifted the bag on my shoulder, heavy enough to cause an ache.

Now the Fae woman's eyes were wide, all six of them.

It had to mean something. I'd kinda been banking on the fact that, as a person of interest, the hospital would at least be aware of me in connection to the case.

For what felt like the first time in a long time, my hunch paid off.

"One of the guards will escort you to the room." The woman jerked her chin and under that silent command, one of the guards I'd definitely missed walking through the door came closer and took the bag from me.

The fellow was tall and broad-shouldered, with a pair of horns curling over his ears and disappearing into his hair. For a second he reminded me of Magnus Crackenbush, the officiator of the games. But it must have just been the horns because this guy said nothing and glared at me whenever he caught me staring.

Eventually he brought me up to the third floor and stopped in front of a closed door with a nondescript glyph burned into the wood.

"Stop here," he grumbled.

Urgency pushed at me. "Why?"

"You can't be alone in the room with him. There is a dividing wall separating the viewing area from the patient. Stay on your side of the wall and there won't be a problem."

The guard practically dared me to argue with him. I simply nodded. "Fine. Whatever it takes."

Finally he squeezed his eyes shut and pushed a palm flat against the wood and muttered something. The same magic word as the glyph on the door, apparently, to give him access to the quarters.

When he finally opened his eyes, he gestured for me to take the knob. The moment my hand closed around it, a shock of electricity pulsed through me and I jumped back.

His dry chortle made my hackles rise.

"Just making sure you are who you say you are," he told me. "The magic recognized your energy signature."

"And if I hadn't been the actual Tavi Alderidge?" I asked.

"Then you'd be dead."

He made it sound so simple.

Shivering, I left the guard behind laughing at his little version of a joke and walked inside, stopping at the half wall with Onyx on the other side. They'd bound him to the bed to keep him from trying to escape. Bandages wrapped around his wounds and the side of his head while an IV hooked in his arm fed him a constant stream of fluids.

It killed me not to be able to go to him. To be on the other side of the bars seeing him, small and broken, pale and wan.

But awake.

He was awake.

And he greeted me with an uneasy smile. "I wasn't sure you'd come to see me," he said weakly. "I'd hoped, but I knew better than to expect anything."

I swallowed over a boulder-sized lump in the back of my throat.

"I brought you some things. I'm sure the guards are checking to make sure I didn't sneak something in that would help you escape," I replied, forcing myself not to look back.

"You don't want me to escape. It's safer for you while I'm tied to this bed." He lifted a bound wrist for emphasis.

I shook my head at the pain in his voice. "I, ah, didn't know which watch you wanted," I said instead. "So I brought all of them." I didn't mention the ring, or how his house had affected me. Much like seeing him now caused a hitch in my breathing.

With my hands on the bars, I stared at him; our gazes caught and held.

"Why?" I finally had to ask.

"Why did I do it?" Onyx shook his head, the movement causing him to wince. "That's what you want to know, right?"

I didn't answer him but he knew.

"I don't remember anything. I'm sorry, Tavi. I'm sorry that I hurt you. It wasn't me. You have to know I wouldn't hurt you."

"Do you have any idea who made you commit those murders? Or why?"

"No. And I tried to tell the Bureau about it when I made my statement. They didn't want to listen."

I snorted. "Be serious. When have you ever known them to listen?"

The teasing tone dissipated a bit of the tension between us and the grin he cracked helped even more. I'd told the cops my suspicions too. So maybe now, with both of us saying the same thing, the seed was planted.

Maybe.

What else could I do? Standing there watching him, I felt helpless. It wasn't the first time in my life but this time it felt like things were bigger somehow. "Do you think your wounds will heal? I'm surprised that they haven't already," I said out loud. Because the silence threatened to strangle me and things had never felt this awkward between us.

"I hope so. They were too extensive for magic. The healers tried everything they could but only time will tell," Onyx answered with a tiny attempt at a shrug.

I sighed, hissing out a breath. I'd done that to him. I'd wounded him so badly that even the healers couldn't do anything. How would I ever be able to make it up to him? I had to try.

If he lived long enough.

That thought wormed its way to the forefront of my mind and I struggled to force my expression to be blank. Onyx didn't need any more bad news.

"Will you ever be able to forgive me for hurting you so badly?"

Onyx stared at me for a moment longer before glancing away. "If I'd killed you, I never would have forgiven *myself*." He swallowed hard. "You did what you had to do, Tavi. I don't blame you."

I still felt terrible, though.

Was there anything that I could do to help him? *Really* help him, and not just bring him a change of clothes and his damn watches? I pondered as I made my way back to the castle. I had already failed him when I'd spoken to Rooker and Claribel. Or rather, what I *hadn't* said.

My legs carried me into the castle by muscle memory, up the steps toward my room.

There had to be a way to get us both out of it. But if I somehow managed to get him out without the king and Elder Council clearing his name, where would we go? It wasn't as if we could just find a new world.

And damn it, I didn't want to run anymore. I didn't want to have to keep one step ahead of chaos just so that I had a chance at surviving.

Lost in thought, I pushed open the door to my room and then froze, seeing a woman with burnished red hair seated on my bed.

Coral captured my gaze the moment she saw me.

"I know you're a werewolf," she said immediately.

My stomach plummeted.

Then she nodded. "And I am, too."

5

I slammed the door, rushed over to her and slapped my hand against Coral's mouth, shushing her firmly. "You freaking psychopath!" I hissed out. "People are out there. They'll overhear you."

She had to be lying. This was one of her stunts, something she was doing for attention or to make up for what had happened to her the other day when Onyx attacked.

She didn't try to push me away or remove my hand. Scrutinizing eyes scoured mine, back and forth, her nostrils flaring. This was the closest I'd ever been to Coral, considering how nasty she usually treated me at school.

That alone spoke volumes—her willingness to let me touch her. Normally she wouldn't be caught dead in my general presence, not without Mike around. She'd sought me out and planned this.

Finally, when I was sure she wouldn't say anything else to damn us both, I released my hold on her. "And how the hell do you know? You *aren't* a shifter. I would have noticed by now." I sent my magic out in a wave and scanned for any kind of spell she might have put in place to record me. When I found none, I wrapped us in a silencing bubble.

Her hands went to her hips, becoming at once as haughty as she usually acted. "Well, I'm sorry, but I know what I know, Tavi. That's why I had to come and talk to you," she declared. "You have answers I need."

"How do you know what you know?" I tried hard not to roll my eyes at her tone.

"Okay, so, during the Trials? When I was in and out of consciousness during your fight with Onyx?" she posed, looking ready to tap her foot in impatience, classic mean-girl style.

I scoffed. "I thought you were dead then. You're supposed to be in critical condition now." That was the story I'd been told.

Funny, Coral didn't look critical. She looked like her usual self: armed, loaded, and ready to antagonize. Selene had told me to be prepared for the fallout, but Coral stating brazenly that she was a werewolf?

Not the kind of fallout I'd anticipated.

"You're not the only one who can tell a story, Tavi." Even my name sounded like an insult. "My parents told the press I was critical. Once I woke up and gave my story, they hired a personal healer and got me out of that healing center as soon as possible."

I rubbed the scar on my side without thinking.

She pointed at me. "I defended your honor!"

"So that you could come here and make up crazy stories about werewolves?" I asked with a snort.

Completely unlike Coral, she nodded, not a single snarky comment on her lips. "I was actually conscious enough to see you shift into a wolf. That's how I know your secret. I saw you."

Shock coursed through me. Crapballs. I'd really been banking on her being unconscious. To have this sprung on me— "But you didn't tell anyone. Why?"

Which was the most fantastic break of my life. Not the fact that I was half Fae, half wolf shifter and making my way in life. Not the fact that I'd made it to another world by way of good grades and old-fashioned stubbornness. No, it was Coral Ferenze keeping a secret that didn't belong to her, one that would get me killed if anyone found out.

I'd thought she wanted me dead.

"You hate me," I said simply, blinking at her. We stood facing each other as though neither one of us dared move and break this tentative truce. "Why didn't you turn me in?"

Coral simply shrugged. "I guess you saved my life or something. I owe you."

My mouth dropped open before I thought to keep it zipped. Any sign of weakness in front of Coral usually amounted to a world of torment with her attitude. She always acted as though she were the best of all of us. She backed it up with her magic, too.

And now she feels like she owes me? No. That was even more astounding and nothing Coral would say on her own. Had she been coerced?

I glanced around again as if the room would somehow reveal clues that I'd missed. "Why are you in my room? Why would you come to me?"

"I'm healing in a weird way and you're the one who can show me what to do. Okay?" She still wouldn't mock me. Things must really be dire in her world for her to be here and not utilize all of this prime ammunition to bury me. Had the attack messed with her head?

I stared at her, waiting for a punch line that never came, my insides absolutely wrecked.

"Look, some really strange things have been happening to me," she said, then pointed down to my messy bed. "I need to sit. Do you mind?"

"Sure, go ahead."

She pushed aside the bunched-up sheets and multitude of books taking up residence without even a snort of derision. "I'm a vegetarian. I have been for years. I can't stand the thought of consuming something that used to be alive and walking around and feeling. Lately, *all* I've wanted is red meat." Groaning, Coral dropped her head down into her hands, her red hair fanning out around her knees when she hunched forward. "I'm craving uncooked red meat. It's like I have to have it or else I'm going to go nuts."

"Maybe you've got a vitamin deficiency," I offered unhelpfully.

Even without her looking up, I felt her glaring at me. "There's more. My sense of smell is outrageous. I can literally smell *everything*. Your room is surprisingly clean-smelling despite how messy it is, Tavi, which is super weird. I can tell you what kind of soap you used in your shower and the notes in your perfume. I also can't wear any of my silver jewelry anymore."

And here I'd thought Fae were naturally averse to silver anyway. Trust Coral to be the one to wear it and discipline her mind into thinking it was perfectly okay. Until now.

"There's gotta be an explanation for all of those things," I replied. "Maybe whatever the healers did caused a chain reaction. Your body is still trying to right itself."

She shook her head. "I'm more active during the full moon, and I've noticed some small patches of hair in places...well, in places they don't belong. Hair that doesn't want to magic away when I try to spell myself." Now she openly glared at me, pushing hair behind her ear so I got the full effect of the old Coral. "Get it?"

I held my hands up in front of me like a shield. "Don't blame me for your hormonal imbalances. Most shifters don't have those kinds of hair problems unless there are underlying issues."

And then I wanted to kick myself. Because I shouldn't be talking about shifters with Coral. Not when she was more likely to go back to her band of cool kids once classes started back. Not when she could tell Arlyss and Lane and the others all about me being a shifter.

"It took a lot to get me to come to you. Don't just dismiss me," she said, slicing a hand through the air. "I've been doing a lot of research about this. I'm becoming a werewolf, and I'm sure of it." She absently rubbed the area where Onyx's claws had wounded her. "Your friend did this to me. I have no one else to turn to, so yes, I broke into your room to ask you a few questions. I know you'd never want to openly talk to me about this otherwise. And we *do* need to talk."

"There's a good reason not to talk openly," I replied. I pressed a palm to my own squirming gut, then scoffed. "You can't *become* a werewolf, though. You're born a wolf shifter. There's no way around it. I've never heard of anyone being turned against their will before."

And wouldn't that be something Uncle Will taught to the youngsters in the pack? The necessity of being careful not to infect others?

"Are you sure? Like one hundred percent sure?" Coral pressed.

"*If* it's possible, then no one ever speaks about it. It would be a pretty important topic in the shifter community if it were a thing. Trust me. Wolves are born, not made."

She pushed to her feet. "That asshole wolf bled all over

my open wounds and it got into my system. I know it. Something happened and I'm changing. Isn't that how vampires are made? An exchange of blood?" She sounded desperate for answers, ones I had no ability to provide.

As far as I knew, and as far as Uncle Will had told me, there was no such thing as a *made* wolf. That was the bottom line.

I could only imagine how awful it would be for one, should they exist, because things were bad enough for a halfling. To be a *made* wolf would be seen as practically undead.

"First of all, vampires aren't real, are they?" I asked her.

Eyes wide, Coral simply shrugged without answering.

"Secondly..." I trailed off. Finally I gestured for her to sit again and joined her on the edge of the bed, exhausted. "Pack life is remote and tight. Strangers are never brought in. Ever. Bloodlines and lineages extend back in time for centuries. Could it be possible for someone to be *changed into* a werewolf? Maybe." My throat suddenly burned, dry and itchy. "So I'm sorry, but I don't actually know. Magic is magic, after all."

It was so strange for me to sit there with Coral, who, rather than wearing her usual sour and superior expression, looked uncharacteristically scared.

New territory for both of us, I thought. And I prayed she wasn't turning into a wolf. That it wasn't a *thing*. Because I had no idea what to do.

"Look, I just don't know what to do and you're the only halfling wolf I know," she said at last.

I jerked at how her words strangely echoed my internal monologue.

"So will you help me? Or not?"

I threw up my hands. "Help you *what*?"

Coral dropped her head back with a loud and put-out groan. "Are you being purposely slow or are you really this dimwitted? Come on, Tavi. If I'm turning into a you-know-what, then I need you to help train me on how to deal with this crap. There's no way I can make it on my own without people finding out."

"I'm not dimwitted," I said, baring my teeth at her. My hackles rose the longer I looked at her and every instinct I possessed told me it was a bad idea to get involved. Coral wasn't the type of person I'd call *trustworthy*.

She had connections and money in Faerie. If anything happened to her, or she decided I'd given her wrong information or stepped out of line, she would ruin me.

I already had enough people queued up for that particular pleasure, and it didn't matter that she'd defended my honor after the business with Onyx. The possibility remained.

But there we sat, with Coral the closest I'd ever seen to pleading, and I knew.

I knew I'd never be able to say no. I'd have to see this thing through not only to cover my own ass but if something *had* happened, if she *was* changing, then she needed help.

I'd been in her position not that long ago, trying desperately to stay afloat and navigate this new world on so many levels. Onyx stepped up to help me, one of the only half shifter, half Fae I'd known before Selina and her group took me under their wing.

Bad idea.

"Fine," I agreed at last. And definitely against my better judgment considering my own mentor had nearly just murdered Coral.

Now it seemed I had a mentee of my own, one who brought out *my* murderous tendencies. Coral responded with little fanfare, merely nodding her head in satisfaction before rising from the bed.

"You made the right choice," she replied finally.

"Oh, like I had a choice?" I tossed back.

Coral waved once, the gesture looking strangely like she was flipping me off despite my having just agreed to help her. Then she disappeared out of the room as quickly as she'd arrived.

Wow. I had a fun summer ahead, it seemed. Like walking a tightrope with a pit of daggers beneath me. Keeping my balance would be crucial.

What had I just gotten myself into?

6

Onyx remained laid up in the hospital on medical rest, which put his future on hold. There was no official date as to when he would be brought before the Council, and only a notation for the public that the criminal investigation case was ongoing. Fat load of good it did for Onyx except that it gave us time.

Time to figure out what happened.

I hated to consider this a silver lining but I also wasn't prone to ignoring good things that happened, even if they were tied up with the bad. With the judgment temporarily postponed, I had a chance to actually focus on some other important things, for once.

Things like dealing with Coral.

Academy classes were on break, thanks to the summer solstice and the annual activities planned during this season. The time off gave me a little reprieve from the hard work of classes and studying with Juno in my spare moments.

Better yet, things had even mellowed in the kitchens since my little breakdown two days ago.

When I showed up for my next shift, the girls all seemed to tiptoe around me like I'd explode at any moment. I kept my head down and kneaded bread like the champ I'd become. At least Raelynn refused to treat me any differently. She had her own little rage habits that gave her away and after two shifts of us ignoring each other, we got back on semi decent terms without speaking.

Everything came up roses for me.

For approximately two more days.

Two.

Then I received a text on my phone from an unknown number, although the message made it clear who'd sent it: Coral.

I'd always appreciated that she was one hundred percent out in the open about things she wanted. Coral always went in directly for the kill rather than skirting around the real issue or trying to manipulate people into giving in to her. It seemed rather odd for Fae, who in general delighted in manipulating those around them.

Maybe it had something to do with her wealth. Coral came from near-royalty, her family among the wealthiest of Eahsea. They were just a step below the rest of the courtiers who always hung around the castle in hopes of attaching themselves to the king's coattails. Wealthy enough to command respect and dominate those around them but not able to hold an official title.

Meet me at the summer cabin. Outside of town.

She followed her text with an address and left me no wiggle room to make an excuse.

Ah, okay, so she didn't want me going to her actual house. Coral's family lived a few blocks outside of the main courtyard within view of the palace. *This* address, if I believed my phone, was outside of town.

"Great," I said out loud as I stared at the phone. "Sounds perfect."

A free afternoon always cost more than I thought it would in the end. However, I'd agreed to help, so I was duty-bound. Dragging on a fresh shirt and my yoga pants—much better for moving around—I followed the directions on the phone, walking to the place rather than taking the train.

It gave me time to think.

As usual it was a perfect day in town. Flowers bloomed, birds chirped, and the sun shone down in golden rays of light if you ignored the thunderheads near the hills. I wondered if anyone else got tired of perfection or if it was just me, today. No one even looked up at me as I passed them and soon enough, thanks to the insanely walkable cobblestone streets, I found myself on a side street nestled into the hills themselves. The houses were scattered here, with more acreage between them.

Eventually I stopped in front of a richly decorated cottage. "Summer home," I muttered. Right. It was just as large as the mansion where I'd grown up.

Coral must have been waiting at the door because she threw it open as soon as I arrived. She flipped her hair over her shoulder for effect before curving her lips in a sardonic smile.

"There you are. Took you long enough to get here," she chided.

"It's great to see you, too." I used my chin to gesture toward the front porch and the gold-plated columns keeping the slanted roof aloft. "Why did you want to meet here?"

"It's farther away from the palace and my mom is out. So we have the entire place to ourselves. Make sense now?"

I shrugged. "Sure, it makes sense." I struggled with a tight smile of my own because I wanted this to go well.

Teaching her would be much less painful if we weren't at each other's throats all the time.

"Well, come inside. Let's get down to it."

I couldn't tell if she was pleased to see me or not.

What I did notice, however, was the paleness of her usually made-up face, and lines of strain around her eyes that she'd normally never allow anyone to see. Coral was clearly nervous and not taking any great pains to hide it from me. *Good.* That made two of us. I'd rather wrestle a rampaging elephant barefoot than spend any one-on-one quality time with Coral in a foul mood.

Yet there we stood in the grand foyer of her summer "cabin."

"Do you want something to drink?" she offered. "A soda or whatever? You look a little thirsty." Even nervous she still managed to sound put-out.

"Some water would be great," I said.

She nodded, pursing her pink lips, and headed off toward what I assumed would be the kitchen, with me wondering whether I should trail behind her or not. When she returned with a glass of water so cold condensation had already begun to form on the surface, she swept her arm out grandly toward the living room to the left. It looked surprisingly normal without any of the usual Fae accouterments I was used to seeing. The grandeur certainly rivaled that of the palace, but a TV with a large black screen took up most of one of the walls, with a plush sofa facing the thing.

It was an entirely different vibe than her house in the city. There, even I'd felt small and insignificant, and I came from a wealthy family myself.

I took a seat on the edge of the couch and tried not to notice Coral sitting as far away as she could possibly get and still be in the same room.

"So, what do you know about shifters?" I began, taking a sip of water.

She cleared her throat and straightened her already perfect posture, shot me an easy, go-to-hell grin. "You mean besides the fact that they're brutal and disgusting and practically animals?"

"Okay," I replied slowly, "the first one might be true, depending on the person, but not the last two. And again, the personality of the shifter in question determines how they act."

I corrected her firmly even as my thoughts drifted toward Kendrick Grimaldi.

Coral thought shifters were brutal? She needed to meet my fiancé.

"Keep in mind this is brand new territory for both of us," I continued. "I've never heard of a turned shifter so we're both going to have to learn as we go. But a few things on shifter abilities before we start."

I set my glass down and rubbed my hands together, wondering *how* to start. It wasn't like I had any experience on a crash course for new wolves. I'd grown up in the pack. We were a family and a tight-knit unit even when the only person related to me by blood was the Alderidge alpha, Uncle Will.

Coral gestured for me to continue with her perfectly manicured nails. How much would change, I wondered, if she really did turn out to be a *made* wolf? She might be the first of her kind. I wished I had a manual for this.

"Come on, Tavi. Lay it on me," she demanded. "I need to know everything so that I can be prepared. What should I expect?"

I wanted to see her wounds. Did that make me crazy? I wanted to see where Onyx had slashed her but knew logically there would be no marks on her skin. Fae healed quickly. So did wolves. My own scars were an exception because of the irreparable damage he'd inflicted.

"As shifters, we're able to change shape whenever we want," I told her, "though the force of the full moon does impact us. We're strongest during the full moon, and oftentimes with the pack there's a gathering of all members where we change shape and run through the forest as one unit. Most packs own their own land, their territory, and stick together while they defend the boundaries of that territory."

Coral nodded, listening intently. Thankfully, she didn't interrupt.

"Your wolf, if you have one, won't be a separate entity from you. It's a part of you, and any instincts you may feel when you're in that shape are *your* instincts, just melded with those of the beast you become. You can expect to be frightened. It's an entirely different world and especially different from Fae glamour. You're not just *convincing* others that the wolf is you—the wolf really *is* you. It's an entirely different set of abilities. You'll be stronger, faster. There's magic in being a shifter. And you'll have three forms." I paused and held up my fingers. "Human, wolf, and warrior form which is a cross between the two and is the strongest of the three. The only thing that can stop your warrior form is another wolf or a really strong Fae."

"Or a silver bullet?" she supplied dryly.

"Having never experienced that myself, I'll say yes. But I feel like that would stop pretty much anyone," I said with a tiny smirk. Then, swallowing past the lump in my throat, I asked the burning question: "Have you...ah...shifted yet?"

Coral glanced down at her lap and smoothed out several nonexistent wrinkles in her flowery pink sundress. "Um..."

Shit, this was serious if she had to think about it. "No, not yet. Just kind of sprouting fur and lengthening canines out of nowhere. Especially if I'm stressed out."

A shiver trailed icy fingers down my spine. A part of me had seriously hoped she'd been joking about the whole thing. Or if not exactly joking, blowing it out of proportion based on nerves or whatever.

"Okay, well, that's our first goal then." I sounded way too chipper, to try and make up for my own nerves. "We're going to see if you can change, and then I can help you learn to control your urges so that you don't accidentally wolf out in front of the wrong people."

"That can happen? I mean, wolfing out? Like I'll just suddenly change into an animal at Elite?" she asked, wide-eyed.

I grimaced, almost feeling pity for her. "Yeah. It's absolutely a thing and it tends to happen with a lot of the younger pups after they experience their first change. It takes practice to learn how to control yourself, because let me tell you, there's such freedom in being the wolf." Personally, I missed it terribly. "It might also help for you to come to the halfling meetings with me."

Was I going there, really?

Was I going to tell her about the Claw & Fang?

"There's a group here in Faerie made up of half shifters, and there are a few other halfling wolves who can help you through this transition," I hurried to say.

Coral shook her head. "Nope. I don't want to associate with riffraff."

"Is that what you think of halfling shifters? If so, let me remind you that *you* are riffraff now."

She had nothing to say to that, only offering me a slight narrowing of her eyes and a thinning of her lips. There was no way around it. If she really was shifting, then this would be her new reality, and the sooner she learned to accept that the better for everyone involved. And certainly better for me because I'd have others around to help me navigate these treacherous waters.

"Come on," I said. "There has to be some place for us to practice shifting where no one is going to see us."

"Duh. This place is protected by magic. There's an entire yard that is invisible to the outside world."

"And what do you do in your invisible backyard paradise?"

"Wouldn't you like to know."

I followed her outside. "Actually, I would."

Maybe she and Arlyss, or Arlie-bear, made out back there and that was why she wanted to keep it hidden. Or maybe her family made sacrifices to the spirits of the land.

Coral led the way out the back and the rear glass door opened up onto a vista of gardens rivaling those at the palace.

"We need more space. I'm afraid that if you shift and freak out, you'll destroy your fountain." I glanced over at the towering water feature as tall as some of the trees. "Or trash one of the flower beds or something."

Coral scoffed, exasperated, and continued walking down one of the winding stone paths. Butterflies flitted in the air around the flowers like winged crystals. Magic. I wasn't sure I'd ever get used to living in Faerie, or the feeling of the air here.

Eventually the path opened up into a meadow clearing ringed by tall trees that blocked the view even if the area hadn't been magically protected.

"Will this meet your exacting specifications?" she asked, her tone acidic and biting.

I ignored her and took my sweet time inspecting everything from the tree bark to the grass. "Sure, this will do." Eventually I rounded on her, planting my feet on the ground and adjusting my stance for better balance, the way Onyx taught me.

Only we weren't going to spar. Not today. Eventually I'd have the chance to knock Coral on her ass and I'd take whatever opportunity presented itself. Today had to be about getting her oriented enough to embrace the change. But right now, with her glaring at me, I knew neither of us was comfortable with the other yet. I wondered if we ever would be, or if every meeting would be like this.

"The first thing we're going to do is work on breathing," I told her, even as I struggled to remember what Uncle Will had taught me on the night of my first shift.

Coral scoffed, a short and harsh exhalation. "I know how to breathe, Tavi."

Keep it together. Try not to kill her yet.

"I'm not talking about regular breathing. Think of it more like a meditative state. I'm trying to get you out of your thoughts and into your body. This kind of magic doesn't come from your head or any kind of spell. It's all about grounding and accessing what's already inside of you," I told her. "I'm sure you've learned about breathing techniques before. A lot of people in the mortal world do them before big tests or whenever they're stressing out hardcore."

Coral mimicked my posture intuitively, and I watched her chest rise and fall. "I don't need to psych myself out before tests. I'm naturally gifted. I can retain information even when I haven't studied much."

"Wow, it must be amazing to be you." I lifted my hands in front of me, inhaling deeply, before pushing them down with a loud exhale.

"You could say that. I've lived a charmed life."

We continued with the breathing exercise until I saw her shoulders relax. "And it's never bothered you? That you've lived in this cocoon of money and power?" I asked. "Sorry if this seems weird, but you've always been kind of a jerk in school and I figured it had to do with your upbringing."

Wow, I was on an honesty kick lately.

And I kinda liked the way her eyes went wide. Still, Coral kept breathing deeply. "My upbringing has been a blessing and a curse. Okay?" she said, though her tone had lost a little of its edge.

Once I got lightheaded from my own breathing, I moved her into a few stretches to get her muscles limber. It would help her with the change and honestly help make her even calmer.

"You mean the great Coral Ferenze isn't as perfect as she seems to be?"

"I mean that nothing is ever as easy as it looks on the outside. And if it looks easy from a distance then that speaks to the hard work going into the charade." She puffed her cheeks, holding in a breath while she stretched her calves. "My entire life I've known that the world is watching and judging and if I'm not perfect then there are consequences," she finished.

"From who?" I wanted to know.

"From everyone. Especially my father. He isn't content to just be wealthy. He wants more and he always has. I wouldn't be surprised if he arranged a match for me and forced me down the aisle."

"Now *that* I understand. Better than you think," I muttered dryly.

Unless I missed my mark, Coral wasn't as put-together as she seemed. The pain in her eyes looked achingly familiar to me because I'd seen the same look staring at me from the mirror. The hard exterior hid trauma she wasn't ready to unpack, I realized as her walls continued to drop lower and lower.

"Okay, now clear your mind and focus on how it feels to be solidly on two feet," I told her.

"Not four feet?" she joked.

I smiled at that. "Not yet. We're working up to it. Now that we're all warmed up we can start to focus on what's beneath the skin. How did you feel when you suddenly started to sprout fur and fangs?"

Coral made a face before saying, "Terrified. Lost. I didn't want anyone to see me but I was in the middle of class and the teacher continued to lecture. I felt alone."

"It can be a sobering experience if you're not around people who understand you."

"Please," she scoffed. "That's been the story of my life. I'm used to it at this point." She shook her head.

"I get it, I really do. But—"

"Hello! Coral? Are you out here, baby?" a soft, feminine voice called out from the house.

The two of us nearly jumped out of our skin and Coral went ghost-white.

"My mom's home," she hissed. "She's not supposed to be home yet!"

"Well, you better say something or else she'll get suspicious." I glanced around for somewhere to hide.

When I caught sight of Coral again, she no longer looked nervous. She looked the way she did every time I saw her in the hallway: poised and in control. The mask slipped down over her so easily I wondered at any hint of vulnerability I might have seen before.

"God, Mom, I have to let you know every move I make?" she yelled back. "We're out in the garden!"

"We?" Coral's mom asked.

"Me and a friend from Elite." Coral gestured for me to fall into step beside her.

I leaned in close to whisper, "You called me a friend. She'll clearly see that's a lie."

"Not if you act like a normal Fae." She made it sound like an insult.

I'd gotten pretty good at hiding but nowhere near the level of mastery Coral exhibited. We made it back to the house and her mom stood on the rear deck with a large smile plastered across her face. Dark hair cascaded in effortless waves down to the small swell of her hips, cheeks and lips were tinted to match, and her eyes were a dazzling shade of turquoise.

Damn. I almost stopped in my tracks. Something about the woman felt oddly familiar to me but not in any way I'd be able to explain.

"Mom, this is Tavi, and she was just leaving," Coral huffed out. "Tavi, say goodbye to my mom, Nixa."

"Oh, Tavi, you don't have to leave on my account. I just got back from the market." Nixa turned her attention to her daughter, the similarities between them evident in every line of their bodies. The way they stood, the small movements they made, the little quirks. "I thought we'd spend the afternoon shopping. Doesn't that sound nice?"

Coral turned to me, her smile brittle. "Catch you later, then."

"Sure," I replied with forced ease. "See you in school."

Yet on my walk back to the castle, I couldn't shake the feeling that I knew Coral's mom.

And that I should be very worried.

7

When I woke in the morning with an empty schedule, I didn't know what to do with myself. An entire day just for me? *Inconceivable.* Stretching my arms overhead, I let sleep leave me slowly rather than leaping up and getting started with the day. What did *I* want to do? Really?

Whatever I want?

My thoughts automatically drifted to the grotto where I used to go to read. And the last time I'd been there. With Mike. And Mike's lips on mine.

Remembering Mike brought a flash of pain and I placed my hand over my stomach. I still hadn't heard from him and it was driving me crazy. He needed time, so I'd stopped myself from reaching out, but it hurt.

No.

I shook my head like it would somehow knock those thoughts loose and they wouldn't bother me anymore. Rising with a groan, I shuffled over to my private bathroom and showered. What I really wanted was to talk to Mike and explain why I wasn't a bad person, even though I'd lied to him. It wouldn't really get us anywhere, because I knew I had hurt him, but it didn't stop me from wanting.

I hadn't seen Melia for a few days. Maybe I should head to her apartment and see what she was up to.

It would be nice to get outside, too, and away from the castle. Although no matter where one went in town, the looming specter of the palace was visible.

Mind made up, I threw on a flowing emerald green jumper and a black tank top and headed out of my room. On my way through town, past one of the bustling cafes, the wind caught a brightly colored flyer from the side of the building and it smacked me in the face.

Grunting, I ripped it off of my cheek and stared at the now scrunched paper.

"What the hell?"

Come to the Solstice Carnival!

The bold headline brought a wave of sadness, and those thoughts I'd worked to suppress now rose with renewed force. Well, damn. Last year Mike had chauffeured me around the carnival. He'd gotten me all kinds of treats I'd never tasted before, laughing and joking and acting like my boyfriend although we hadn't been dating.

Now we weren't even talking.

This year, I'd skip the thing. It would be nothing but bad memories of how Madame Muerte's murder had been ruining my life for a year now. Not to mention all the good memories of my date with Mike and how, for a brief moment, I'd thought we could actually be something.

Something wonderful and real.

I shoved the flyer into the nearest trashcan and kept walking.

At least none of the palace guards had broken down my door to cart me off to prison for being a shifter. So Mike hadn't ratted me out. I was safe on that end, even though I still faced suspicion over what happened to Madam Muerte.

With the unexpected time off, clearing my name shot to the top of my priority list. And who knew? It would probably be easier to help Onyx clear *his* name when I wasn't a suspected murderer, too. Especially with how corrupt the whole law and order thing appeared to be in this kingdom.

I'd thought things would be different here.

Better.

Easier, certainly...yet look where I'd landed: on top of a larger heap of trouble than the one I'd used to catapult myself into this new world. My old trouble even followed me once I stepped through the portal.

Melia wasn't at the apartment when I knocked but a quick round of texting, something I should have done before I even started this trek, got me on the right path toward one of the cafes in town. And there sat my best friend in the whole world with her hair wild around her shoulders and a book clasped in her slender brown hands. She glanced up at my approach, a smile lighting her face and her eyes crinkling at the corners.

"Hey! I'm glad you could make it out today. I didn't want to bother you so I just took myself out on a little mini date." She stood up and wrapped her arms around me. "Isn't it just the most spectacular day? I mean, come on, how could I stay inside on a day like today!"

I returned the hug. "I'm just happy we both have some time off without me burning the candle at both ends and you working your butt off," I said.

Melia scoffed. "I don't really have a butt to work off anymore, do I? Too skinny."

"But gorgeous. Like a willowy Amazon huntress."

She burst out into full-fledged laughter, then motioned for me to join her at the table.

"Sure, I'll take that. I've never been one to turn down a compliment." The sun glinted off the gold highlights in her curly hair, emphasized the planes of her cheekbones and the richness of her caramel-colored skin. "So what's up?" Melia asked. "You've got something on your mind, I can tell. You're not just here for coffee."

"I definitely do. You've always been able to read me like a book." I glanced up at the winged Fae manning the counter and she returned my grin, heading over to grab my order. Once I figured out what I wanted to drink, I turned back to Melia, happy to have my own coffee brewing. Not something I'd ever turn down. Not even on my worst day.

"That's what a good mentor does, isn't it? I know your tells and your facial expressions," she said.

I crossed one leg over the other, getting comfortable. "We're not at the Fae Academy for Halflings anymore, Mel."

"Doesn't matter. Mentor for life."

Warmth spread from my heart through the rest of my body. I'd really won the lottery when Melia was assigned to be my guide at the Halfling Academy. I might have gotten paired off with someone who didn't understand me, or, worse, someone who refused to understand me.

Instead, I'd been given this breathtaking woman who was not only smart but funny, who'd stood by my side and gotten herself into trouble with me more times than I could count. How would I ever repay her?

"I'd rather you just be my friend," I replied.

"Oh, well, done. Of course. But spill the beans. What's going on in that brain of yours today? Or do you need some caffeinated courage before we dive into the juicy parts?"

I knew what I wanted to say. I'd thought about the direction of my focus on the walk over here. Still, it was hard to get the words out.

"Girl, no need to wait. Look." Melia glanced over at the server's arrival, a woman with an apron and a glamour to make her arms appear the texture of alligator skin.

She placed the steaming mug of vanilla latte in front of me and I dove in. Not even caring that I burned my tongue and sported a foam mustache when I finally leaned back.

"I've decided that I'm going to try to clear my name on this whole Madam Muerte thing," I said carefully. "For real this time."

"I get it, so I'm not telling you to let this drop. But you're sure this is the best time to focus on these things? I mean, there is so much going on. Everything with Onyx—"

"It's a lot. I don't know where to start. I only know that I need to start." I leaned in close and whispered, "How can we help him if I can't help myself?" A spotlight on me wouldn't help him in the long run.

"Well, if it were up to me, I'd try to find out more about the woman herself. Madam Muerte was a very public figure. Well-known. She always traveled the circuits and she never missed a Solstice Carnival. Until this year. But it's not your fault and we know that," she hurried to say.

I groaned, dropping my head into my hands. "Now I feel worse." The taste of coffee went from sweet to bitter in my mouth.

"Don't feel worse. Plan your attack. Since she *was* a public figure then there has to be information about her out there that we can access. Fae version of the internet. There's also sure to be articles written about any feuds she might have had. Enemies or people who didn't like her. You know, the kind of people who would want her dead."

Melia always knew best.

"You make a good point."

"Of course I make a good point." She looked pleased with herself.

"That's a really good place to start, Mel. You always have good ideas."

She took a sip of her coffee before saying, "I'm surprised you didn't think about that before now. Then again, you have been super busy. And it can't be easy to live in the palace the way you do, constantly under King Tywin's thumb, with the Bureau sniffing at our feet—"

I held up a hand to stop her. "Okay, I get it. I live it," I said with a smile. And I loved the way she said *our*.

"You know, you might also be able to get your hands on the guest list for last year's Solstice Ball. The odds are good that the killer's name will be on it. That's when she died, right? At the Solstice Ball. And only guests had access to the private gardens around the ballroom." She leaned even closer so that our foreheads practically touched now. "If it *were* up to me—and I've given this a lot of thought—I'd start there. It won't be easy to access, but once you do then you'll have a better place to start. At least, better than scrambling around in the dark. There are a lot of citizens in Eahsea but not all of them had access to the palace grounds."

Oh. *Damn.*

She was absolutely on the money.

Melia laughed at whatever expression she saw on my face. "That's what I'm here for, Tavi. To think about all the things you aren't able to figure out because you've been in this for so long. You're tired. You're stressed. Like an albatross around your neck. So I'm just offering you a fresh perspective."

"You're right again," I replied through numb lips. "And you're amazing."

She grinned. "Thank you." She glanced around the café, scrutinizing the clientele and narrowing her eyes. "But let's continue this back at my place. Okay? We'll have a little more privacy, and if I stay here I'll keep spending money. Coffee after coffee. You know?"

"Agreed."

Melia and I chugged the rest of our drinks, and then we hightailed it back to her apartment for the relative privacy there.

I didn't trust a thing. Well, I trusted Melia, but surely Rooker and Claribel were keeping an eye on her since we were good friends. If anything about her popped up on their radar then she'd come under scrutiny, and that was the one thing I refused to let happen.

The moment we locked ourselves in her cramped attic space, Melia booted up her laptop with a spell that she assured me would hide our online activity from public view. Not that I trusted it implicitly, by any stretch. But we were being as safe as possible while we searched. Because what else could we do?

I wondered about how well the spell would work, all things considered, but settled at her side as the first of the search results began to load. Melia was a whiz kid when it came to technology. And luckily for us, she'd hit the nail on the head when she made the comment about Madam Muerte being a public figure. I hadn't even thought about starting there and seeing what the faerie web had to say about the gypsy woman.

There were so many entries it would take us a long time to get through them. Some were biographical and others scandalous.

"Ooh, look at this one," I said, pointing to an article

halfway down the page. "*Madam Muerte's Predictions Spark Controversy.*"

Melia nodded. "We can start there, but I'm actually leaning toward this one a little lower. It's a personal blog, but from this comment it appears to be someone who is clearly pissed off at whatever they heard and seems to know her personally." Melia hovered the pointer over the website. "Some guy named Elias Hawthorne?"

"Click on it."

The more we read, the clearer it became that Elias hated Madam Muerte for a number of reasons. He'd written a bunch of scathing articles regarding interactions he'd had with her in the past, as well as compiling interviews with past recipients of her predictions.

"*She's a fraud, a charlatan, a shyster out for money who should no longer be allowed to spew her false predictions for coin,*" Melia read out loud. "*She needs to be stopped.*"

Those words settled like lumps of stone in my stomach. My mouth went dry.

Could Elias Hawthorne have wanted to stop her badly enough to silence her forever?

8

I needed a copy of the Solstice Ball guest list. That was the next logical step, to check and see if Elias Hawthorne had been there at the ball during the murder. Unfortunately, I couldn't ask Mike for help since he was still avoiding me. My gut ached again the way it always did when his name popped into my head.

How in the blue blazes of all things holy would I get my hands on a copy of last year's list? Crapballs.

Where would the palace even keep such things? Probably with the social secretaries of the king and queen, since they would be in charge of the festivities, or perhaps now the list was already archived. Was there an archive assistant I could approach?

None of them would talk to me, I felt sure. I didn't have access to those people and places, and without Mike as even a friend at this point I was dead in the water.

My hands curled into fists and I shoved them deep into my pockets as I paced my room a few hours after hanging out with Melia.

I only had one person who might be able to get me

access to that list: Selene Montrosse. As a journalist, she had connections far beyond my own. She might be able to at least point me in the right direction. And luckily for me, I had a meeting with the group tomorrow night.

A meeting I was determined to drag Coral to, whether she liked it or not.

I sent her a text, one I didn't expect her to answer, before taking the train over to the station nearest her summer cabin and trekking it the rest of the way. She answered the door when I knocked and scowled at me, then stepped aside reluctantly to give me space to walk inside.

"Tavi, this is really inconvenient. I have an appointment to get my nails done tonight."

That was the basic gist of her excuses, ones she threw at me without hesitation and hoped would stick. When none of them did, and when I refused to leave without her, she gave up her pity party and went straight into frustration, forcing me to follow her as she stomped up to her bedroom to change clothes into something "more appropriate," which she made sound like a curse.

Typical Coral.

At least some things remained the same.

"But *why*?" she whined, slipping into a pair of stretchy jeans. "I don't want to do this. I especially don't want to make the acquaintances of other half shifters. It's better if you go alone."

"I'm not leaving here without you. This is your world now, and the sooner I make introductions the better it will be for you."

She changed into designer sneakers and slipped on more jewelry than one person should before she dragged her feet down the stairs once again.

"But they're gross!"

"As I keep insisting, if *they* are gross then *you* are gross. You'd better get used to it. These people can help you. Life isn't going to be the same for you going forward," I insisted as we walked.

A warm, clear night and a new meeting place announced only an hour ago. The wolf medallion had glowed a half second before the notation materialized inside my journal, magicked so that even the protections around the castle couldn't keep the spell from taking root.

Giving me just enough time to get changed, put away my research on Madam Muerte and Elias Hawthorne, then head out to collect the truculent Miss Ferenze. Who at the moment looked about two seconds away from stomping her feet and turning out a full tantrum, toddler-style but with the finesse of a socialite.

"I know you don't want to go tonight," I continued soothingly, "but this will be good for you. To make friends. To talk to people who are in your situation and understand how important it is to keep a low profile."

"I *have* friends."

Her insistence went in one ear and out the other. I hurried my steps, impatient to get to the meeting place on the outskirts of town to ask Selene about the guest list. Good thing this time we weren't meeting on the cliffs in our usual spot. There was no way I'd be able to get Coral there. She didn't have the same kind of power that I did, or my friend Bronwen. We were both able to shift into any kind of animal form, and I could even become inanimate objects, although that was a much harder skill to master.

Coral, once she embraced her new reality, would change into a wolf and, I supposed, her warrior halfling form. And she was nowhere near ready to do either of those things, so we were hoofing it.

Tuning out the constant drone of Coral explaining to me that she had the best friends in the world and why she considered them so, we navigated the winding streets of the private neighborhood until we came to the edge of the king's town, with the wild forest beckoning us forward. There weren't a lot of people out at this time of night, the middle of the week, although there was always a celebration somewhere if one looked hard enough.

Finally we reached the turning point and I cut left into the woods after making sure no one followed us. The Claw & Fang hadn't exactly been my first choice of secret societies when I first came to Faerie. I'd hoped to avoid all hooks like that altogether. Unfortunately for me, things didn't quite turn out the way I wanted, and *they* found *me*. Then the group opened their arms to me. I found an old friend from my own wolf pack that I hadn't seen since I was a child.

And I found people who were like me. Hiding. Some on the run. Outcasts all.

Coral had a lot to learn about her new reality and this group was her fast track.

Eventually we passed through several magical wards that she surely felt, though she made no indication. The air thickened, tingling against my skin.

We were almost there.

Once the wards accepted us and let us through, we stepped through the last of the trees into the small clearing outlined by giant stone monoliths. A sacred place, I realized. And much closer than I'd imagined.

"Tavi! There you are. I was waiting for you." A familiar voice reached me through the darkness and a moment later Bronwen stepped out from behind a towering tree trunk.

My friend from years ago, Bronwen Minuti had been part of the Alderidge wolf pack before she and her family disappeared. I'd asked Uncle Will countless times what happened to them but he had no information for me. Fast forward to my move to Faerie and the weird-ass crow that kept showing up on my windowsill. A crow that I'd had no idea was actually Bronwen in her shifted state.

She reached out her arms for a hug and I stepped into them willingly. She stood a good head shorter than me which made her perfect hug height.

"Hey, Bronwen, you don't think Selene and the others will mind that I brought a friend, do you?" I broke the hug and gestured over my shoulder to where Coral—what else was new—stood with her nose haughtily in the air. "She's having a little bit of a hard time with her transition."

"What do you mean her transition?" Bronwen asked. She eyed Coral from head to toe and the look on her face told me she'd taken the other girl's measure accurately enough. She lowered her voice to a whisper. "Isn't she kind of a bitch? I remember you complaining about her before."

And Bronwen, apparently, also had a damn good memory and keen observation skills.

"Onyx wounded her during the Trials. She's...changing." I tried, not quite succeeding, to keep skepticism out of my voice.

Coral might have been desperate to convince me but I guess I still wasn't one hundred percent certain. Too many years of having it drummed into me that wolves were not *made*.

"Coral Ferenze, this is my good friend, Bronwen Minuti," I said for introductions.

Coral sniffed. Then pushed past us both and proceeded into the glowing ring of light cast by a small lantern in the middle of the clearing ahead.

"Wow," Bronwen whispered.

"I'm sorry. She's not usually—"

Bronwen sliced her hand through the air to stop me. "Save it. I know her type, even if I didn't let your opinions influence me. All the kids who go to Elite think their shit doesn't stink. I've also had my fair share of interactions with bullies and I can sniff them out from a mile away."

"Coral isn't a bully." And I wasn't sure why I wanted to come to her defense.

"Yeah? We'll see."

Bronwen kept one arm loose around my waist as we walked toward the lantern and followed Coral into the clearing, where the rest of the members of the Claw & Fang stood in a ring around the lantern. A dome of magic kept the light from being discovered by anyone who might happen to get too close to our wards.

These were good people. People who had the same issues I did and only wanted to make a better life for themselves. Like Buzz and Lisbet. Like Selene.

I'd have to be careful from now on, though, because I saw a definite possibility of Coral and Bronwen at each other's throats. Then I caught sight of Selene near one of the massive pillars of stone and those worries evaporated from the front of my mind, replaced with different ones.

I left Bronwen with a pat to her shoulder in a small reassurance and crossed to Coral. "The black-haired woman," I murmured. "That's Selene. She's my contact. I've got to talk to her for a minute."

Coral scrutinized the other, older Fae and I half expected her to sniff again. To show her disapproval for anyone gathered here tonight. And, true, they were all staring at her as well, but finally she shrugged and said, "I've seen her around. The Faerie Trials. She was reporting."

I raised a warning finger. "Don't say anything, okay? And

don't go anywhere. I'm going to talk to her about a different topic and I'll be right back."

"Suit yourself. You're the one who forced me to come along with you. I guess it's only typical that you abandon me immediately." And there was the sniff.

"You'll be *fine*," I assured her.

She started to protest but I darted away as fast as my legs could carry me, anxiety swirling in my chest.

Selene glanced over Buzz's head at the sight of me hightailing it toward her, though her smile remained tight at the edges. When I finally made it to her side, she grabbed my wrist in warning. "The next time you decide to bring someone to one of our meetings, someone who isn't vetted, *don't you fucking dare*. Got me?" she snapped.

Buzz took that as his cue to bolt and disappeared into the crowd.

"I'm sorry," I apologized automatically. "She needs our help. She doesn't understand what's going on with her ever since Onyx—"

Selene jerked me closer with a hiss. "Tavi, for God's sake, don't say his name. Not tonight."

I blinked at her, surprised. "Okay, I'm sorry. But Coral is in my class at Elite and she needs help. She's trustworthy. She's been experiencing some changes since she was attacked."

"How do you know?" Selene pressed. "How do you know she's trustworthy?"

"Because she has to be. She won't risk her or her family's reputation by letting her condition be known."

"Well, I don't trust her." Selene glanced over my head to where Coral stood doing her best not to look out of place yet standing out dreadfully.

"I'm not sure that I do, either, but I know what it's like to be the odd man out in a new place. She needs our help and I thought she might find people to talk to her. To show her how to make it through this." I wasn't sure how to make her understand this weird feeling I had that Coral needed to be here.

Just as badly as I needed to talk to Selene about the other matter.

After a few tense moments where I barely breathed, Selene finally nodded, her black hair bobbing around her chin. "Fine. She can stay. But this is the last favor you get from me, Miss Alderidge. I've done enough for you already without jeopardizing the safety of the others in the Claw & Fang."

I cleared my throat before saying in a small voice, "Actually, I need something else. Sorry."

"How did I somehow know this?" She groaned, rolling her eyes and dropping her hold on me. "You've brought a heap of shit to my doorstep tonight, it seems, and now you want more?"

I wanted to bring up the shit she'd dropped on me during the Trials, and her insistence through the whole ordeal. I wanted to bring up a lot of things but knew better. *Tread lightly.*

"Well, as you know, I'm still a person of interest in the Madam Muerte murder." I did my best not to worry my fingers or drag my feet along the forest floor like a naughty child even though the way Selene looked at me made me feel exactly that. "But I have a new theory I'd like to explore and it involves whoever was on the guest list the night of the Solstice Ball."

Selene arched a delicate brow. "The Solstice Ball?"

"I'd hoped that you would be able to get me access to

that list so I could study the names and see who is on it," I finished. Lamely, I might add.

"What's in this for me?" she asked.

"What?"

"I mean, if I help you, what's in this for me? If you're asking me to do something risky then I need to be compensated."

"Not just done out of the goodness of your heart?"

She crossed her arms over her chest. "Things don't work that way in the world."

"There will be more of me to go around once my name is cleared," I explained. "I'll have more freedom to come and go. Less heat coming down on my head that may impact *you* by association."

She scoffed as though she was above reproach but I knew that she had a giant secret to keep, too. Not one person in this clearing tonight needed more attention brought to them. I understood her worry there.

"Let's even see if this is possible, first," Selene finally said with a growl, baring her teeth at me. She whipped her phone out of the back pocket of her pants and brought up a tab on a secure server. Did she use the same spells that Melia did? "The good thing about being a journalist is that I can get my hands on pretty much anything." Her eyes narrowed. "It's good to have a lot of friends in high places."

"It must be nice," I grumbled. I could use a few friends in those high places rather than nemeses in them.

"The guest list for the Solstice Ball..." She trailed off, her fingers flicking along the screen faster than I could follow as she typed out a message and searched at the same time. "Yes, it shouldn't be too hard to find. Not that I want you to get your hopes up."

Just before I dove off the edge into a freak-out because

getting the guest list was probably going to be impossible, Selene smiled. "Got it. I'll forward it to you."

A fire kindled inside of me. "Are you kidding?"

"Would I kid you?" Her smile was full of meaning. "Now you owe me."

"I'll add you to my list," I said with an answering smile of my own. "Thank you for that. Once I've cleared my name with this case, I'll be able to help On—my friend."

"Oh? Why would you want to help someone like that?"

"Because I don't think he committed the murders on his own. I think he was manipulated. Actually, I could use help there, too."

"I'm sorry." Selene shook her head, her attention already on the rest of the members arriving in the clearing for our meeting. "Your *friend*, as you call him, is a criminal. He's on his own."

"But—"

She held up a warning finger, her nails long and sharp-pointed. "No more buts on this. Leave the matter alone. You're already knee-deep in a handful of other matters. Leave the criminals to the Bureau to deal with." She strode off toward the others but fired over her shoulder: "He'll get what he deserves."

9

"All right!" Melia rubbed her hands together, a sly smile lighting her face. "Let's see what we've got here."

"Be proud of me. I somehow managed to not look at this list until today," I told her. "I waited for you."

"My hero. I *am* proud of you. Now hand it over and let's see what we're working with. I'm anxious enough these days."

Tell me about it.

We sat together on her bed the following day with the copy between us and my fingers itching to pick up the pages we'd freshly printed. There were a lot of them, tons of names. Then again, the Solstice Ball was a big affair in the realm. Melia and I decided to do this together and see if between the two of us we would be able to decipher any clues.

"I didn't think the printer would ever stop. And she got this for you in how many seconds?" Melia asked.

"Ten, if I had to approximate."

Her lips rounded in a low whistle. "It *does* pay to have friends in high places."

I'd already told her what Selene relayed to me in all the gory detail, although the rest of the meeting—and Coral's presence—I kept to myself.

Right away I saw a lot of familiar names on the list of attendees. Pretty much everyone that I knew from Elite Academy and working in the castle had been there that night. I guessed that living in the palace had perks. Correction: being with Mike had its perks.

"Ugh." I swallowed over a wave of revulsion.

"What?" Melia leaned closer. "Who?"

"Arlyss Clearwater. He's such a tool. You remember me telling you about him?" And Coral still thought the guy walked on water, a good second choice if she couldn't get her claws into Mike.

"Well, we know it wasn't him in the garden. So let's keep looking," Melia urged.

It took us another page before one name stood out from all the others.

"Holy shit! Look, Melia. It's Elias Hawthorne," I cried. "Just like you said."

She grabbed the paper and held it up close to her face even though she didn't need glasses at all. "The guy who wrote the blog article. I had a gut feeling he'd found a way into that party but I didn't want to say it out loud in case I was wrong. What are the chances he stayed by the banquet tables the entire time," she mused, "stuffing his face."

"Let's hope the chances are slim and he's the guy." The fellow who wrote so scathingly about Madame Muerte online would make a perfect suspect. Did Rooker and Claribel know about him?

Well, this was another mark against him, in my book. He was probably the killer after all.

And had anyone taken him in for questioning? I wanted to know badly.

"Do we know what he does? Besides blog about people that he hates?" I asked.

"We don't yet, but we easily can find out. Especially since we found the connection between them and we know he had motive and opportunity. Plus you said you heard a man's voice in the gardens, right?" Melia pressed, flipping from one page to another.

I drew in a breath. For the first time in a long time, a sliver of hope kindled inside of me. Hope that I might actually be able to clear my name and prove the king wrong, since he so desperately wanted me to be guilty.

"Maybe we could email him and see if we can set up a time to meet," I suggested. "That way it won't look like we're creeping around trying to get the scoop on him. As a journalist he's bound to be the suspicious type. If we keep this out in the open, he'll be more trusting of our motives."

Melia looked wary. "Yeah, but if he's the killer, then it's dangerous to get close. You're basically shining a massive spotlight on yourself saying *here I am, come murder me now*."

"It's a risk I have to take," I said with a shrug, a knot in my gut tightening. "Otherwise I might never get a chance to talk to him face to face. And besides, I'm not Madame Muerte. I'm nobody."

It didn't even sound like an insult when I said it to myself. I *wanted* to be a nobody these days. I craved it because I'd spent every waking moment since my eighteenth birthday trying to find a place where I could feel safe. And look where it got me.

"Yeah, Tavi, I get it. But you're trying to expose her real

killer!" Melia rolled her eyes before saying, "That automatically puts you in more danger than the average stalker."

I rubbed the side of my head in a desperate attempt to relieve some of the pressure there. Not a chance. "Okay, fine. I've got another idea."

Melia groaned and let her head drop back on her neck. "Please don't do anything stupid."

I pressed my hand to my chest. "Me? Are you kidding?"

"Yes, *you*." She shot me a side-eye like it was her job. "You really ought to leave the idea stuff to me. I'm at least trying to save our hides."

I had a plan in mind that may or may not land my ass in hot water. So what? Probably would, but what did I have to lose at this point? That was what I told myself as I held my palms out to Melia.

"This is going to work," I assured her. "Trust me."

"Don't take this personally, but…no."

I ignored her and dragged over my laptop, sending out an email and reading the words out loud as I typed.

"To whom it may concern," I began. "I am a student journalist working with the esteemed Selene Montrose. I'm currently doing an exposé on Madam Muerte." Melia groaned but I kept going. "I would love to meet you, as I found your write-up online and I believe it would be a good element for my piece. Get back to me as soon as possible, please. Thank you for your time."

I clicked send and closed the laptop like a punctuation.

"And we're off to the races."

She stared at me with concern evident in her face. "I hope you know what you're doing."

"This will work," I insisted brightly.

Famous last words.

I remembered last year's Solstice Carnival in every detail, like a dream where everything I'd ever wanted had been mine. A balmy night in Faerie after working so hard to get here. And Mike at my side, a prince come to life.

He hadn't looked at me like I was a freak or anyone or anything out of the ordinary. He'd looked at me with interest as he showed me around the festivities. All the delicious things to eat, the colorful people, the tents with their ornate displays...

All of it had changed for me now.

Every single bit of it.

Which made showing up to work instead of enjoying myself at the carnival a little easier to swallow. At least in work I'd be able to bury myself in preparations for food for the ball the king would surely throw, instead of immersed in memories of times best forgotten. It sounded morose even to me, but what other choice did I have?

Plus Raelynn needed me.

She'd given me plenty of time to change my mind about going, and when I insisted that I had no better place to be than the kitchens, she nodded and threw a sack of flour into my arms. "If you've got time to feel sorry for yourself then you can help me with some of the ancient grain loaves. Got it?"

I nodded, hauling the flour over to my station and getting to work the way she'd taught me.

Making it all of fifteen minutes before a commotion had the girls around me scattering, one of the fire sprites so close she almost singed off a lock of my hair.

"What in the blue blazes of the Underworld is this about?" Raelynn muttered.

A glance over my shoulder showed none other than Coral standing in the doorway to the kitchen. Which was something that had never happened before and I would have bet my life would never happen period.

Her gaze landed on me and her eyes narrowed.

And then, in a resonant, bell-like tone of voice, came my name from her mouth. "Tavi Alderidge!"

"Whatever this is, Tavi—" Raelynn began, already furious.

I held up a flour-covered hand to stop her from finishing the threat. "I'll take care of this. I'm sorry. I'm sorry! I wasn't expecting a visitor."

Hustling forward, I grabbed Coral by the elbow, much to her outrage, and tugged her into the hallway so that we could shut the door behind us.

"Are you crazy?" I hissed at her. "What are you doing here?"

She glanced back and forth with a look of pure disgust on her face. "I want to go to the carnival today."

I shook my head, confused. "You don't need me or my permission to go to the carnival," I replied.

"I don't trust myself with all these weird things happening to me." Now she stared at me like I was an idiot and she was about two seconds away from snapping her fingers in my face to get me to keep up. "I need you to watch me and make sure I don't do anything bad."

"Well, as you can see, I'm pretty busy at work."

"I *need* you," she implored in the whiniest voice I'd ever heard her use.

"And I really don't want to go." My hands went to my hips. A white print remained on Coral's elbow. She might be stubborn but I'd gotten used to her enough to know that if I cracked even a little, she only pressed harder.

Normally I'd think twice or three times about getting into an argument with her. Today was not a normal day for me, though.

"Why would you not want to go?" Coral mimicked my posture. "There's food and boys and fortune tellers."

I shuddered at that last part. "There are too many memories for me there." Not to mention Mike. He was bound to be somewhere around. There was no way I wanted to run into him right now with things so strained between us.

A finger rose and pointed right at my face and I saw that she had, indeed, gotten her nails done. "I'm not taking *no* for an answer. You are going to the carnival with me and that's the end of the story. I need this, you need this. I mean, think of what being seen with me will do for your reputation. It's not like it would be a hardship for you to make new friends."

"I have friends," I muttered under my breath. Sounding eerily similar to her last night, which made me feel a little sick. "I mean, I don't need the kind of people you call friends in my life."

In the end, to avoid a screaming match in the castle hallways, Coral won because that was what Coral did. She won.

"Fine." I dragged the apron off of my neck and bunched it in my hand. "Fine, I'll go with you."

Her self-satisfied smirk almost had me changing my mind just to be obstinate.

"Great. Come on."

"Literally right now?" I asked.

She tapped her foot on the cold stone. "Yes, right now. You're coming home with me so that we can get you dressed in something cuter. Plus your makeup needs help." Her gaze scoured my face. "A lot of help."

Gee, that made me feel a whole hell of a lot better.

Luckily Raelynn would rather send me on my way than deal with me and Coral combined, and within ten minutes I was trailing after Coral toward her house a few blocks over from the castle.

Going along with her was much less work than trying to fight her, I hated to admit. Even as my stomach dropped and the rest of me felt sick and clammy. Being alone with Coral wasn't my idea of a party or a picnic, especially considering everything we'd been through. She'd always struck me as big-headed and two-faced in the best of circumstances, not to mention the way she alternately flirted with Mike and stayed up Arlyss's ass.

She barely spared a look behind her as she headed up the curving gold-railed stairs to her room.

Her room was about as massive as the entire floor I stayed on in the castle.

"Sit." She pointed to her bed with all the authority of the queen herself.

"Are you going to tell me to stay, too?" I grumbled.

"Only if you give me a hard time." She turned to me again, this time with a clinical stare while she considered what to do with me. Was she as uncomfortable as I was?

She didn't look it, but I had to wonder if she found this strange. Not what was happening to her, but talking to me like a peer instead of an enemy or a bug ready to be squashed beneath her feet. She crossed to her closet with a small hum under her breath and dragged out a couple of hangers.

"These should look good on you. You're larger than I am, of course. Everywhere except your bust."

"You're really not helping me."

"Trust me, I'm going to help you. Honesty is the best

policy." She held up a purple sundress against me, checking the tone against my skin and hair before tossing it away. "You want me to be honest, don't you?"

"I'd rather not be here at all. Since we're being honest."

"Too damn bad, Tavi. We're helping each other. I think something green. For today," she clarified. "It will help bring out the color in your eyes."

She dressed me like a doll before sitting me down at her vanity, larger than my desk, and drawing out a container of lipstick that looked exactly like the shade she wore.

I studied her while she applied each new item of makeup on me. "Why are you doing this?"

Her lips pursed in concentration. "What?"

"Why are you so concerned with how I look right now? Is it because you don't want me to reflect badly on you *even though you need me*?"

"Duh. You looking good serves me on multiple levels." She leaned back and smacked her lips in a clear indication for me to do the same. "Okay, now close your eyes. It's time for some mascara. Do you normally wear mascara?"

I shook my head. "Not really. Sometimes, for special occasions. I got dolled up for that party Mike made me go to." The one at her house where we got into a huge fight. My stomach soured.

"Yeah, that party wasn't exactly the best of times. You looked so embarrassed," she said with a chuckle. I squeezed my eyes closed against her laughter.

"Thanks."

"I'm sorry about that, by the way."

"Why are you sorry? Because I ruined your party?"

"Because no one should have a crowd of people see your private issues. There. Look at me."

I blinked up at her and a small smile played in her mouth and eyes.

"Tolerable," she allowed.

I shrugged and replied, "Okay, I'll take it."

By the time she found a pair of shoes that fit my feet—so much wider than Coral's, she told me—my stomach had become like a solid pile of iron chains. Each footstep I took had them clanking together.

But we made it to the carnival eventually, though now I was dealing with not only Coral but her friends too, who met us at the entrance posts. They weren't the best kind of people by a long shot. They were the golden guys and girls of the Elite Academy who only gave me attention when they wanted to make fun of me for something. Or when they wanted to go old-school and knock my books out of my arms for giggles.

They stared at me now and the blood in my veins turned to ice. What kind of pranks would they pull on me *this* time?

Lark raised an eyebrow but didn't say anything as we walked in, falling into step beside me.

"She must have some serious dirt on you for you guys to be together. What is she holding over your head?" he muttered.

I swept my gaze along every nook and cranny of the meandering walks between tents. "It's nothing like that," I assured him.

But I had to be on my guard, always. I had to make sure that no one took me by surprise. Being back here hurt. Just as much as I'd expected it to hurt.

Arlyss sniggered from where he sauntered ahead, bumping occasionally into Coral like he knew how the contact made her titter. "She's just trying to fit in," he said sarcastically.

Out of place was an understatement. After several minutes of their company, I couldn't breathe. I couldn't think, and I didn't want to act like the loser they all thought I was.

"Sorry, I'm gonna go get a drink," I told them.

Not that anyone paid any attention to me.

Just a little break, a reprieve from the "popular kids." How did Coral manage it all the time? It wasn't quite a mask that she wore, but she wasn't always the person I saw when her friends were around. Wasn't it exhausting for her?

I collided with someone in the crowd and automatically held out my hands to steady myself. "Pardon me—"

"Tavi?"

The blood in my veins went from ice to pure fire when I glanced up at Mike's familiar face. Not scowling, no. Worse.

Filled with confusion. And fear.

10

My heart, still broken from the last time we'd been in the same space together, began to crack along the lines I'd thought had scabbed over.

Especially with the way he now looked at me.

Mike stared, his eyes wide and his pointed ears twitching, but he didn't move away from me.

I cleared my throat. It felt drier than before and yet all thoughts of getting a drink were forgotten.

"Mike, h-hi." My voice came out as a squeak and I cleared my throat a second time, hoping I didn't sound as though I'd choked.

Shit. I'd expected that I would see him here, but the drastic scenarios in my imagination did not hold a candle to how bad it felt in reality.

I shouldn't be this weird around him, considering I'd known I'd probably run into him today. So I followed with something equally embarrassing as heat rose to my cheeks. ""How are you? I didn't expect to see you here." *Liar.*

He shifted from foot to foot, but I gave him credit: He

didn't take his eyes off me, even if he did look like he wished to be anywhere but standing in front of me.

"I've been good." He spoke haltingly, his hand gripped around a plate of food that looked surprisingly like a funnel cake. An inhale brought with it the scent of fried food, sugar, and thunderstorms over a forest.

Oh, Mike...

My toes curled in my borrowed heels.

"I'm glad to hear that."

Conversation had never been this stilted between us, not even once I found out his real identity. My heart ached in my chest, thudding as though to remind me how painful it had been when he ran away from me.

Mike learned the secret of who—*what*—I was and ran away.

A flush crept up my neck, heating all the way up to my cheeks and forehead. His eyes narrowed as he took me in but instead of saying anything Mike thrust the funnel cake at me.

"I know this is one of your favorites," he said low under his breath.

The world shrank and contracted until it was only the two of us and that fried food goodness. My nostrils widened, stomach growling, and I took a piece of it from the side. Ripping it off and holding it just above my lips.

"Thank you?" I coughed. "I mean, yeah, thank you, Mike."

He stared at me for another achingly long second before he said, "Look, I'm sorry. Truly. That doesn't make it any better, and we've got a lot of people around right now, but I want you to know that. I had hoped to run into you today to tell you."

I jerked, staring at him. "Really?"

"Yeah. Tavi, you're my *friend*." The word felt loaded and yet a whisper of anticipation flickered through my veins. A whisper that spoke of salvaging what we once had. "You mean a lot to me. And I *am* sorry for how I reacted. But..."

His hesitation inferred that now was not the right time to talk about it.

Okay, so it wasn't exactly the make-up that I'd had in mind. Not by a long shot. But as his eyes caught mine and held, as the sounds of the carnival slowly returned, the edges of my lips tugged north in an approximation of a smile. I slid the bite of funnel cake between my lips and the sugar burst on my tongue.

Mike chuckled at my swoon. "I thought you would like it. Do you wanna take a walk with me?"

Coral would probably be pissed at me for ditching her. But she would be fine with her friends. They were her comfort zone. As long as nothing crazy or out of the ordinary happened to provoke her, she'd be calm enough to keep herself under control. She really didn't need me. And if anyone knew how to keep a mask on, it was Coral.

"Sure. As long as we keep away from gypsies and fortune tellers," I told Mike.

He grimaced, shaking his head so that his golden hair slid over his pointed ears, and agreed with a "*Fuck* yeah."

The longer we walked, the more even-keeled I felt. Like we were getting back to somewhat normal together again. I'd missed him more than I wanted to admit, I realized. More than my mind even comprehended, because standing next to him, with his familiar scent winding through my senses and branding itself in my bones, I was home.

"Please tell me that you're having the same kind of trouble with classes that I am," Mike said.

"You're having trouble?"

"Yup. Again. It doesn't matter what school I'm in or what kind of tutors I have. I'm always a step behind, much to my father's perpetual disappointment."

"I'm sure you're doing better than I am," I admitted. "I've been creeping by. Juno is ready to tear her hair out with our private lessons." I didn't mention the meetings with the Claw & Fang. Mike wouldn't understand and this tentative peace between us was too new for me to shatter.

"You're still working with Juno?" Mike asked as we passed a vendor selling carved rune stones for seeing the future.

I cringed, not wanting anything to do with scrying or prophecies or anything of a supernatural nature, and hustled to get past.

"Trying to. It's been a little hard balancing everything at once."

"What else is going on?"

I chuckled and asked, "Do you really want to know?"

Mike shrugged. "I wouldn't have asked if I didn't want to know. Tell me."

Relief flooded through me. "Well, I've been trying to figure more out about what really happened to Madam Muerte. And you've heard about everything with Onyx, so it's helping me to focus on really clearing my name."

"I'm not sure it's such a good idea," he said. Pausing for such a long period of time while he chewed his piece of cake that I wondered if he had to really work to find something nice to say about that. "But if you want, I'm here to help. Maybe I need something to get my mind off of classes. An anti-focus."

"You'd really help? With everything?"

"I know I've been a shit friend lately but you have to know that I'm here. Right?"

I mulled that over.

"Come on. Give me something to do. I can help," Mike pressed, nudging me with his arm.

And there were the tingles. Back after so long. "Okay." My voice came out tinny and strangled. "Maybe you could take a look at the list of ball attendees last year? See if you have any input? I've been talking to Melia about it and we both agree that the murderer has to be on there."

Mike shot me a side-eye. "You have the list with you?" He offered me the funnel cake again and I ripped off another bite and chewed while I fumbled in my bag for the list.

"Yeah. Uh, it's right here." I dragged it out and Mike took it, his moss-green eyes scanning the pages.

"You might want to cross-check the list with the members of that secret society of yours, Tavi," he suggested. "That halfling wolf club of yours?"

Like I needed clarification. "You're still blaming the wolves for what happened?" I asked him.

Mike blinked at me but his lips thinned out into a straight, terse line.

"Wow." I huffed out a chuckle. "Wow, that is unreal."

"What's unreal is that you hid something that big from me," he hissed.

"Like I had any choice? You've proven that you would have been oh so supportive."

His brow furrowed before he said, "And you can't blame me for being shocked. I've been told my entire life that wolves are the enemy and yet here you are and there's a secret society—"

I reached up and slapped a hand over his mouth. "Why don't you shout it out for everyone to hear?"

"Don't." Mike peeled my hand away, his expression darkening into a glower. "Don't do that."

I took a step away from him. The Crown Prince, who I'd touched like I wasn't one of his subjects. He'd touched *me* like I was not one of his subjects. But apparently that was different.

And just like that, our tentative truce crumbled into dust.

"Here, I'm not hungry anymore." I shoved the funnel cake back at him and turned on my heel.

"You're just going to walk away?" Mike didn't raise his voice. Didn't cause alarm and disrupt the rest of the carnival attendees. Yet his voice struck through me like an arrow.

"I'm taking a page out of your book," I muttered, hoping he would catch my every word.

A glance over my shoulder, seeing the way he stiffened, assured me that he had. Mike might be royalty but he had no right to talk to me the way he did, no right at all. I stopped in the middle of the main walk between tents, my shoulders stiff and my stomach squirming.

Return to Coral and the shit-show with her friends and risk running into Mike again since they were his friends too...or go back to the castle.

Back to my room and the relative safety of the four walls there.

I scoffed, my feet making the decision for me and taking me home. Each step through the flower-scented air and my head spun higher, dizzy with everything that had happened today. Safe in the castle, *right*. I'd never be safe under the king's roof, not ever.

No matter how golden the bars, it was still a cage.

~

THE SUMMONS HIT EARLY the next morning with the rising of the sun and came in the form of a fist pounding on my door. Seconds later, a letter slid underneath the wood with the official stamp of the King of Faerie. I pushed the hair out of my face and stared at it with bleary eyes for a long moment. An acidic taste coated the back of my throat.

Whatever it was, whatever words were written on that paper, it would not be good.

My stomach dropped and the rest of me followed it down through the floor into the grottos below. Not literally, although I'd done that before—become part of the walls thanks to my power.

Another secret that Mike knew nothing about.

Gritting my teeth, I stumbled over and grabbed the letter with numb fingers, breaking the seal apart into two pieces.

"Your presence is requested by His Eminence, King Tywin Thornwood, the Glorious Coming of the Morning Sun in These Lands," I read out loud.

He wanted me to come to a meeting in his private parlor a few doors down from the throne room. And I had less than thirty minutes to get down there.

Stomach rumbling like it knew I wouldn't have time to get breakfast, I hustled into the shower to wipe the sleep from my eyes. From my mouth. From the rest of my body. Even the steady pulse of hot water and jasmine-scented soap did nothing to erase my unease.

Nothing good ever came from standing in front of the king. He was the one who'd insisted I be investigated for the death of Madam Muerte. He was the one who'd brought me into the castle, keeping me under his watchful gaze—and his thumb. He was the one who tracked me and watched my very move. And for what?

What could possibly come out of this meeting now?

My footsteps rang hollow on my way down to the main floor of the castle. Living here wasn't weird anymore, if I ignored the guards posted on every corridor. Those Fae warriors tasked with keeping the royal family and everyone who worked here safe from threats.

Including the Unseelie.

And Dorian Jade.

I pushed those thoughts to the very back of my head as I approached the wooden door to the king's parlor, thick enough that it would take a battering ram to get through and held together with iron spikes. I'd dressed in a navy-blue button-up shirt with a pair of black pants and black ballet flats. The classic picture of a serious student.

Footsteps sounded behind me and my heart did a neat little flip up into my throat as Mike approached.

He did his best to hide his own shock at seeing me but his ears twitched.

"Brace yourself," he said under his breath as he knocked on the door.

Tywin's booming voice bade us enter, with all the regal pompousness of a dictator.

My heart stayed lodged in my throat as a burst of magic dragged the door open and Mike glanced down at me, his expression silently urging me to hold my tongue. He didn't have to warn me.

He knew something was up, too. Had he known about it yesterday, or was the call to meet a surprise to Mike, too? I wondered but had no opportunity to ask. Mike took a long, bracing breath and led the way into the study through the towering open door.

I did my best to set aside any indication of just how

nervous I felt, especially when the door shut itself behind me.

No looking back.

No wishing I'd stayed out of Faerie in the first place and dealt with my problems in the mortal realm.

I wasn't sure what I'd expected, but King Tywin's study took up the length of the throne room, just as expansive, and the only difference came from the lack of a cathedral ceiling here. To the left and right, bookshelves rose to the ceiling, packed to bursting with books and artifacts. Some of them resonated magic while others were hidden behind panels keyed only for the king's access. The room extended to a wide stone balcony surrounded by ferns and neon-pink bougainvillea, and heavy red velvet curtains, tied back to the wall, would no doubt block the light whenever Tywin wished for privacy.

The king himself sat behind a massive oak desk littered with papers and glass ornaments. He straightened his shoulders, waiting for us to pass beyond the bookshelves to stand in front of him.

"Michael. Tavi Alderidge." His cool amber eyes fixed on us, his tone business-like and short.

I refrained from squirming beneath the weight of that stare, wondering how many people in the city of Eahsea had gotten a glimpse of this room. This was where the king spent his days. The Elder Council oversaw most of the day-to-day activity in Faerie while the king and queen maintained authority simply by existing, their magic without question and their grip strong.

Or so we'd been told.

No doubt things were very different here from the pack structure I'd grown up understanding; councils and circles within circles, so many people holding on to the illusion of power while the main hierarchy always came back to Tywin.

Mike inclined his head. "Father," he said, halting a couple of steps away from the desk. "You wanted to see us?"

My tongue seemed to swell to three times its normal size and I said nothing.

Tywin drummed his fingers on the desktop. "I wanted to let you both know, personally, that you will be expected to begin tutoring together to prepare for next semester. Effective immediately. I've received reports of your individual progress at the Elite Academy and I'm not pleased with what I've seen. Your next semester will be more intensive. Hands-on work. I want the two of you to help bolster each other."

Mike stiffened beside me. "That doesn't make any sense. Why would you want us to tutor together? Is Tavi not already receiving guidance from Professor Juno Ians?"

Tywin glanced over at me and then his eyes narrowed on his son. "Please, Michael, tell me. Am I beholden to you? Am I to explain myself to you in any way?"

The temperature in the room seemed to plummet and I shivered. Mike's posture stiffened even more under the reprimand.

"No, Father, of course not," Mike answered eventually. "I only wanted to know why you'd want us to work together, as Tavi and I are closely matched in our classes."

It really didn't make any sense, and the look on Mike's face, the disgust he wore out in the open, would only aggravate his father further.

If Mike didn't watch himself then he would regret it. As it was, Tywin's face revealed nothing, but that didn't mask the fact that he was a potential bomb waiting to explode. "You will work together and begin your training immediately. You are in the same classes and you live under the same roof. As loath as I am to admit it, you have a connection between you that I believe may help you both advance if given the proper stimulation."

His tone indicated that this was the end of the story. We had answered his summons, heard him tell us what he wanted us to do, and he demanded that we kneel and obey. I bristled at the expectation, having never liked Tywin and his high-handed nature. If he were a wolf, without a shadow of a doubt I would have seen him as a rival. But I'd heard about what the king did to those he perceived as a threat.

He'd worn his crown for too many centuries now to act in any other way.

"I will be observing your sessions to make sure that all is going according to plan," said the king.

"Oh, will you?" Mike asked tightly.

Tywin's narrowed gaze shifted to me and I knew he saw my barely controlled anger thrumming through my veins. No amount of magic was able to hide it from him.

Tension rippled between the three of us.

"Is there anything else you'd like to throw in my face before you take your leave?" Tywin waved a hand at Mike. "Consider this your permission, *son*."

The last word fell with an unexpected amount of venom.

A warning.

Mike shook his head, not quite meekly but no longer rebellious. "No, sir."

Tywin snapped his fingers. "Dismissed."

I didn't dare breathe until we'd left the study, and only then did my lungs expand painfully, my chest aching.

"I'm sorry, Tavi," Mike whispered before heading down the hall in the opposite direction from where I'd come only minutes earlier.

Had it been mere minutes?

Shit. Now I'd have to spend time with Mike under Tywin's watchful gaze. Which wasn't exactly lying low and listening until I could get myself and this murder business sorted. No, this was worse.

An asshole monarch breathing down my neck, just waiting for me to make a mistake.

11

I shifted from foot to foot, with unease raising the fine hairs on the back of my neck. "Are you *sure* no one is going to walk in on us back here?" I asked Coral again. It felt so public, so out in the open, like we stood in a park rather than a private backyard.

She huffed, her hands going to her hips in her classic I'm-in-charge stance, only this time I knew better than to think she was arrogant. She was clearly nervous. Her knuckles had gone white, and there were dark shadows beneath her expressive eyes that she hadn't been able to cover with makeup, although she'd tried.

"Are you not convinced that I'm telling the truth?" she threw back at me. "Like I would risk my reputation! No one is going to see us. If anyone is stupid enough to trespass on this private property then Daddy will kill them. Done."

"I'm not sure what you're willing to do but wolves are always cautious. Even mutant half-wolf creatures like you."

Her indignant squawk had a smile tugging at my lips as I bent down, adjusting the tie in the laces of my sneakers. Too easy, really.

Tavi a month ago would never tease Coral about anything. She made it impossible to get close to her at the academy, based in part by her friends but mainly by her crap attitude. Not that getting to know her in this setting was a walk in the park but at least now a small crack had been opened in the wall between us. We were starting to understand each other if not like each other.

I wondered if I would ever like her.

Understanding was a good start. Mutual respect was too much to ask for.

"Okay, well, if you're sure..." I trailed off, glancing dramatically left and right to see if an audience lurked in the rose bushes.

"Can you just show me how to shift again?" she asked.

When I turned back to her, she was studying her fingernails, her long auburn hair loose and flowing down to the small of her back. This was the girl most people looked up to, the one they wanted to be, and *she'd* come to *me* with a problem.

"I want you to go into wolf form. You're not ready for halfling warrior form yet." I held up my hand to stop her before she had a chance to resurrect the argument where she maintained that she was strong and I stood my ground that she needed more time to get used to her new reality.

And pretty soon, our little under-the-radar training sessions would have to stop. Otherwise I'd be spread too thin and King Tywin would know that something was up once my grades slipped in class again. I didn't want to drag Coral into that mess.

Her life was already much more complicated than she knew.

"Wolf form for now, Coral. Halfling form is your strongest form and it takes a lot more energy to hold. If you can master being in your wolf form for five minutes, then you won't have such an issue with warrior form. It will be no problem," I finished.

Coral scoffed, tossing her hair over her shoulder. "Of course I'll be able to master it. Like any other new skill, Tavi. It only takes me a little bit to learn and then I'm good for a lifetime."

"Sure, whatever you say."

Her teasing didn't bother me much; already frustrated, I knew it wasn't Coral bothering me, but the conversation with King Tywin. More like a steamroll than a conversation. And I wondered whether it was a punishment for me having to be around Mike, or Mike having to deal with me. Probably a punishment for both of us with one fell swoop so that Tywin didn't have to waste much more time on us.

Except he'd said he would sit in with us to watch us train, or study, or whatever it was he wanted to see us do. A little dance for him either way. He might as well dress us up like marionettes with strings around our wrists and ankles.

"Hey!" Coral lifted her voice to get my attention. "Hello? We're here to focus on *me*."

I blinked and, unless I missed my mark, saw a hint of concern in her eyes.

"Yeah, I'm sorry, I'm just a bit...distracted." I sighed and tried to give her all my attention. "Now let's see you change form. Just remember what I talked you through earlier. Nice and easy. Not forceful. This is natural, the way your body wants to move and react. Okay?"

She took a deep breath, then let it out and closed her eyes, widening her stance so that her feet were hip-width apart, her shoulders relaxed, and her arms loose at her sides. Her heartbeat evened out in a few seconds and mine struggled to match her slow, easy rhythm. There was still too much on my mind and my focus was scattered.

When was it not?

I lived my entire life scattered.

Closing my own eyes, I brought my breathing in line with Coral's. I'd hated my life in the pack before. Okay, well, *hate* was a strong word, but I'd been discontented. Definitely discontented. I'd spent my time trying to sneak out to talk to Elfwaite, my purple-skinned pixie friend in the park. I'd worked for Uncle Will at his law firm and gossiped with Dawn, waiting to see if Jason would ask me out or not. Easy and simple things where my greatest concern was what outfit to wear to my eighteenth birthday party.

Before the days of Kendrick Grimaldi, my fated mate who was not, and my life on the run from him.

Fuck.

My fingers clenched and I blew out an audible breath. When I cracked open my eyes I saw Coral.

But *not* Coral.

She'd grown several feet, her arms muscled, and thick hair the same color as on her head poked out through her skin. Iron-strong claws burst from her nail beds, her fingers long and curved, her haunches thick. A few more seconds and...a wolf stood in front of me, much larger than a normal lupine, with extra muscle and a knowing glint in her eyes.

As close to a pureblood form as I'd ever seen, and the breath dissolved in my lungs just staring at her. If I'd still possessed even a shred of doubt about her changes, it was all gone now. Disappeared. She'd been right: Onyx infected her.

And...

...and it *was* possible for Fae to be changed into shifters.

"Wow!"

The word slipped out and she smiled at me. White canines glinted inside her mouth.

"Well? What do you think?" Her voice came out in a guttural garble as though she wasn't used to speaking through all those teeth yet. She'd get there.

We'd get there together.

Laughter bubbled up inside of me and my own wolf pressed closer to the surface in a desire to join Coral. It had been so long since the last time I'd run. Since I'd really let myself stretch and feel the full power of that form. And the last time I'd gone into my own halfling warrior form against my friend.

"I think you did a really great job. I'm proud of you," I said softly. "You look magnificent."

Coral opened her mouth to answer but a soft female voice sounded from just behind us. "What are you girls up to out here? I have a feeling you *aren't* preparing for classes to start again."

Panic ripped through me and left a trail of ice in its wake.

"Shit!" Coral exploded into action, crouching down to use the bushes to cover her while she desperately tried to shift back to human form. "It's nothing, Mom!"

"Well, your tone of voice says otherwise, sweetie pie."

Nixa Ferenze poked her head through the hidden walkway in between pink rose bushes and stared at me, her smile dropping away by the moment.

"It's really nothing, we're fine," I told her, wrapping my arms around my chest, stuffing my own wolf down deeper inside of me and away from the surface. "It's nothing at all."

Her eyes narrowed in typical mom suspicion. Or at least what I assumed was typical. "Are you sure? Now you're starting to worry me. And what are you doing in the bushes, Coral? My goodness! You're crawling around in the dirt."

Coral scrounged around, half-hidden by blooming foliage, and for a moment I forgot how to breathe. When she finally dragged herself into a standing position, she'd returned to her normal shape, if not a little worse for wear. "Everything is fine, Mom." She flipped her hair over her shoulder and managed to sound both relieved and put-out at the same time. *She's back*. "What do you want? You're bothering us."

Nixa held up her hands. "Sorry, love bug. I just heard a little commotion and I wanted to come out and check on you." She turned to me, her eyes kind and most of the suspicion banished. "Would you like something to drink, Tavi?"

"No, thank you, Mrs. Ferenze," I answered with a smile. "But I appreciate your asking. I'm fine."

Coral tapped her foot impatiently while Nixa crossed to her daughter and placed an affectionate kiss on her forehead. "Well, I'll be inside if you need anything. Study hard, girls. Although I'm not sure how you're doing it *without books*." She left that little zinger hanging in the air and made her way back to the house.

Coral and I waited until we no longer heard the sound of her footsteps, neither of us daring to breathe, and finally she sank to the ground, legs folding beneath her.

"Oh, my God." She tugged at her hair this time, pulling it away from her face and sucking on her teeth. "She almost caught us."

I didn't want to remind her of the gut feeling I'd had about our privacy being disrupted today.

"She'd never understand. *Never*. She'd kick me out and disown me."

"Calm down," I urged. "She loves you. It might not be as awful as you imagine."

Coral lifted her face to mine and I was surprised to see her eyes wet and tears streaming down her cheeks. "You don't get it, Tavi. My mom *won't* love me anymore when she finds out about this. And...who am I kidding?" She sniffed and swiped furiously at her tears. "I'm a fool for trying to hide this from her. It's only a matter of time until she finds out and then it's all going to be over for me. She'll hate me."

"She won't hate you."

"She won't understand, though. I know it. And Mom shuns what she doesn't understand. I'm nothing but a monster." Coral stared at her palms like they held the secret to becoming something else. Anything else. "I'll lose my mom..."

I dropped to my knees in front of her, only inches away, careful not to touch her. "She loves you. It's clear to me that she does. You won't lose her even if it does take her a while to come around. We're going to do our best to make sure she doesn't find out while you learn to navigate this new lifestyle."

Coral glared at me. "You don't know what it's like to have to earn your parents' love. Or what it would be like to no longer have the one person who has always been in your corner. I—" Much to my all-encompassing surprise, she snapped her lips closed on whatever she'd been about to say. "But you *do* know. Don't you?" She grew solemn. "You don't have parents."

The fire inside of me, aching for a good fight so that it would have an exit, extinguished as I shook my head. "No, I don't have a mom. Or a dad. My Uncle Will raised me, and he did the best he could with a kid but it wasn't the same." It was never the same.

We sat for the longest time together in that garden, with the sun warm overhead and the breeze bringing with it the scent of myriad flowers. I turned my face to the sky, Somewhat uncomfortable with the sudden understanding between the two of us. Okay, so we'd never be besties. I wouldn't even call this budding thing between us a friendship, because no one annoyed me like Coral did. She'd never be the first one I turned to when I needed a shoulder or an ear or backup.

Yet something had changed between us. We now had a more solid foundation.

"I'm not really sure I'm up to doing more today," Coral said at last.

"That's fine. I've got some other things to work on anyway. Maybe you should—"

"If you're about to suggest I have a little mommy and daughter bonding time then I'm going to literally throw up in my mouth," Coral retorted.

Just like that, we were back to the dynamic we both were accustomed to. Only now, I smiled. "Whatever you say, Princess."

I grabbed my bag and headed back to the castle, avoiding the train. The walk would do me good. The winding cobblestone streets remained unchanged even though a year had gone by. The summer carnival, the solstice, they brought in a crowd and filled the sidewalk cafes and parks.

Thornewood Castle loomed large on one side of the city, with the Elite Academy a miniature mirror on the opposite hillside. My legs ached by the time I walked through the main gates of the palace with the guards barely blinking at my arrival.

Once upon a time, armed guards in matching livery

might have seemed weird to me, even after the muscled security I'd grown up used to in the wolf pack—those protector wolves one step below my Uncle Will as the Alpha. And today seemed to be chockfull of memories about the past. I tapped the side of my head on my way up the stairs, hoping to dislodge the melancholy but having no luck.

Would my mom have done what Coral feared about her mom? If she'd found out something secret about me, would she have judged and shunned me, or would she have been open? Would she have told me to sit down and discuss it with her?

Useless thoughts, considering how long she'd been gone and the impossible chance of getting her back.

Inside my room, I dropped the bag on the floor and headed over to the desk and the work I'd set aside to spend time with Coral. I pulled up my email and the first entry was from an unfamiliar address.

Curious, I clicked on it, and my eyes widened.

Tavi, thanks so much for your interest. I'm happy to help out in any way possible. Meet me tomorrow at my office. Come prepared. Come alone. Off the record.

Best Regards,

Elias Hawthorne.

12

Usually, I didn't trust when people wanted me to go anywhere alone. Strength in numbers and all that jazz, and people surprised you in the worst ways, usually. It was rare to meet anyone who had your best interests at heart.

Yet my fingers paused above the keyboard and the automatic message I wanted to type out to Melia, to let her know that our trick had worked. I'd made contact with Elias Hawthorne and he wanted to meet with me.

Tomorrow, he'd said. It didn't give me much time to figure out a plan of attack but it seemed best to play by his rules.

I slowly withdrew my hands, shoving them into my pockets to keep from typing and drawing Melia into this any further. It would only bring more danger to her doorstep which was something I didn't want to do. And sending a message even through an encrypted line still left a trail.

I'd go alone, the way Elias wanted, and I'd take notes the old-fashioned way and find a place to hide them if anyone came prying. Right now the name of the game had to be putting my trust in no one while keeping Melia as safe as possible.

Leaving my pack behind had left a certain hole in my life. Melia was my new pack. She might not realize it but this mess was mine to clean up alone.

Way too much had happened this past week for me to logically think about.

I slept fitfully that night, nightmares and dreams mingling in my subconscious until I woke up in the morning with grit in my eyes and a stomach ache. Elias hadn't given me a time but I figured the earlier the better.

I managed to tame my hair into a semblance of order, braiding the strands so that the dual French braids hung down my back. Since I'd written pretending to be a student journalist, and using Selene as my "in," I needed to look the part. I needed to be confident. And if the feeling refused to come naturally, then I'd fake it à la the most confident person I'd ever met:

Persephone Glaski, the mean girl of the Fae Academy for Halflings who'd made my life hell and had the whole blonde, perfect, blue-eyed, and curvaceous thing going on. With Persephone in mind, I grabbed a pair of navy-blue slacks from my wardrobe. They were wrinkled and smelled slightly of cedar but I doubted Elias would mind much.

Student journalist. I had a distinctive picture in mind of how I wanted to look.

Coupled with a white shirt and a blue blazer that would have fit in at *any* academy, I stared at myself in the mirror. The hollows of my cheeks stood out along with my pale skin but it was a pretty studious look for me. Not bad, all in all.

This is a win, I reminded myself. This *was* a win and I had to take it as such.

"Show time," I murmured.

Or so I thought until I saw the letter slid beneath my door complete with the king's seal. My stomach dropped as I bent down to grab it, knowing my plans for the morning were about to be shot to hell and feeling it in every fiber of my being.

Training session. Rear gardens. 9 am.

Well, it seemed the king's aides liked to keep their messages short and to the point.

A glance at the clock showed that I had five minutes to change my clothing and get my ass downstairs. Not even enough time to mentally and emotionally prepare to see Mike again.

"Shit!" I shucked my flats off and the pants followed, changing from business casual to ready-to-kick-a-little-Fae-ass in two point seven. Or whatever would come up for us in today's training session.

I had to take retaliation off the table, especially with the king there watching, and keep it light and casual. Nothing that spoke of the mess of emotions seething inside of me when it came to the crown prince.

With only a couple of minutes left, I bolted down the hall, arms pumping and sneakers making no noise. I arrived in the rear gardens out of breath and with such an explosion of motion that Mike and the guard turned to face me with varying expressions, of surprise on the former and disgust on the latter.

"The little halfling barely made it in time," the guard muttered under his breath.

My imagination, or had he been counting on my tardiness?

"I'm sorry I'm late."

"It's fine." Mike wore a loose pair of black pants and a matching t-shirt, the dark color bringing out the golden tone of his skin and throwing his pale hair into stark relief. My mouth watered as I stared at him. But no, no, that was wrong. He'd been a complete ass to me recently and a little eye-candy moment wasn't about to make me change my mind and forget everything.

"I did the best I could, considering the summons arrived with less than five minutes to spare," I told the guard as sweetly as possible. "At least I'm already warmed up. Where is the king?"

Tywin didn't want to bring himself out here for these training sessions that *he* mandated? Coward. This was his punishment but I supposed he thought himself above such things.

The guard straightened, his legs pressing together and his chest thrown out, eyes ahead. "His Majesty has many other important obligations this morning. He does not have a moment to spare on paltry training sessions."

Mike and I both heard what the guard did *not* say: that we were so far beneath the king's notice. Even his only son.

"Oh, yes." Mike crossed his arms over his chest. "Paltry training sessions with his less-than-average student of a son. I'm just making sure I understand the direction you're attempting to go with your words."

The guard kept his gaze on the lawn ahead though we both noticed the tightening in his lips.

I turned to face Mike, crossing my arms over my chest and adopting a similar posture to his and hoping the prince didn't notice the tension crackling between us, suddenly there in an instant. Not quite the storms that erupted when I first came to Faerie but the same kind of power, bringing with it the same mixed sense of unease and pleasure. We were explosive together, and it only took standing in the same area for those energies to manifest.

"I hope you're ready for this," I said, my voice tight.

"For what?" Mike quirked an eyebrow at me. "What do you think is going to happen today?"

I felt rather than saw the guard's attention on me. "You already know." I shook out my hands. "Whatever it is we're supposed to do. You want to tell me what classes you had trouble in, and we can focus there? Right now it looks like physical education." I gestured toward an assortment of training tools set on a red-velvet blanket near the base of the rear patio. "Or defense arts, maybe?"

Mike grimaced, shaking his head so hard that his hair fell across his forehead.

"What's wrong?" I asked.

He cut his gaze toward our audience and the warning was clear. "Now really isn't the time to talk."

"Then *when* would the time be? This space is supposed to be used for mutual tutoring. Or do you think you have nothing to learn from me?" I reached out for a long sword and swung it around in a circle as if I knew how to test its weight and balance and see if it was a good one. On second thought I set it back down on the blanket.

A weapon in my hand when it came to Mike was a bad idea. Not that I'd actually hurt him. But if the likelihood was there I might very well take my aggression out on whoever was closest.

"On the contrary. I think you have a lot to learn from *me*," Mike retorted.

The crackling tension ratcheted up a notch as I lifted a brow. "Are you serious? I'm not the one falling behind in classes. You told me so yourself. I already have someone from Elite helping me."

We circled each other, both glaring, my anger and frustration and sadness growing the longer I looked at him.

He scoffed. "You're constantly falling behind. That's probably why my father forced us to work together."

"Do you have another little toy in your pocket to try and bolster your powers?"

Lightning crackled around his fingertips. "What's your problem, Tavi?"

"*My* problem? You're joking."

Mike twitched and his magic flared brightly. "Why would I be joking? You're clearly pissed at me. You looked like you wanted to skewer me with that sword."

"Oh, you think I have a problem? After everything you've said to me? Or how about your disappearing act after that —" I stopped, hissing out a breath. Too easy, I realized, to unleash on him and let everything that had been festering inside of me explode.

The way I'd assumed it would.

Mike, the scum, looked like he was about an inch away from throttling me with his bare hands, and I noticed that he'd shifted to keep his back to the weapons.

"Are we actually going to practice our magic, or do you want to stand out here in the sun talking to me all morning?" Mike asked. "Father won't be pleased to see us wasting time."

And his tone was enough to make me snap.

"You want magic? That's great. I'll give you magic." I called up a whirlwind to blow around me, mingling with his lightning. I'd never shown an aptitude for the air element until I started working with Juno.

Mike blinked, narrowed his eyes against the dust and debris stirred by my windstorm. "You call that magic?" he said. "What are you going to do, knock me over with a gentle breeze?"

"Better than the ridiculous little sparks you've got going on."

It was one of his best skills, I thought as we rounded each other. Talking shit when he didn't have the mettle to back up his words. No one talked shit like Mike. And I supposed it was to be expected, considering his bloodline, because I knew no better shit-talker than a politician. His dad stood at the top of the heap.

Deep down, though, I didn't mean to make light of Mike's magic. Not really. Logic seemed to have fled with him staring at me the way he did.

"Stop me, then," Mike said slowly. "Stop my lightning before it can manifest any further. A little push and I can burn a trail down the lawn." He leaned closer. "I *have* been practicing in my spare time."

He wanted a physical magic duel? Then I'd oblige him. The wind might not be strong enough to combat his pure energy, which I'd never seen Mike handle before, but I had a few tricks up my sleeve thanks to Melia and her tutoring. Thanks to Juno and *her* tutoring. And thanks to poor Onyx.

Things I'd never wanted to use on Mike before but had been a little too willing to practice when it came to the attack during the Faerie Trials.

No more talk.

I gave in to the gaping pit of the dark abyss inside of me, the pit that tied my soul to the elemental magic of the Fae and had only grown since I moved to this land.

I pivoted, spinning on my heel to feint to the right before coming at him from the left in a combination attack. Physical *and* magical. I swung a fist up coated in pure ebony darkness that absorbed the light, sucking it into myself. My fist cracked home on his cheekbone and his skin split. Power spilled out from the wound and trickled down his arms, lashing around his wrists and stopping his lightning from coming at me in a counter attack.

"Shit!" Mike lifted a hand and cupped his bleeding cheek, his eyes wide. "Tavi—"

Mired in my feelings, I hit him again, this time with a punch to the gut that had him doubling over. My night-wrapped fist made contact with him a third time and Mike held up a hand to get me to stop.

Why did he have to act like that? High and mighty but also smug. He knew my secrets and he wasn't making this easy on me. I wasn't in the wrong, I thought, gathering more strength. I wasn't in the wrong because I had done what was necessary to survive.

And standing out in the sun and talking? We weren't able to *talk* to each other because he was too busy jumping down my throat with his attitude and I was too busy trying to defend myself. I lashed out again. And again.

It wasn't until I saw the real pain in his eyes that I actually did stop. I dropped my arms to my sides, along with my connection to my magic.

"Are you *insane*?" he croaked out, still bleeding. "We're supposed to be working together. You're trying to beat the crap out of me!"

My powers guttered out. "I'm s-sorry—"

"Save it," he interrupted hotly as his spine stiffened.

"I'm trying to apologize to you," I added. Sounding less like I was sorry and more like I barely restrained myself from hitting him again.

"I don't want your apology, Tavi."

"Sir, are you all right?" The guard wasn't supposed to break his composure. Or interfere.

I scoffed, torn between fury and heartbreak. "Sure. He's fine. Not like I hit him *that* hard, anyway."

Mike took a moment to compose himself. The cut on his cheek was already healing. "I'm fine. But this *training* is over for the day."

"Agreed." I swallowed over a lump in my throat.

The moment I turned away from him, the tears I'd been holding at bay burned the corners of my eyes and slid down my cheeks. I rubbed at them and hoped the fabric of my shirt absorbed everything. No way in hell I wanted Mike and that horrible guard to see me cry. No way I wanted anyone to see me as weak.

The tears refused to stop. It literally only took me two steps to break down in a sob. I hadn't gotten very far, had I?

13

My bag went back over my shoulder, and on the way out of the castle I stopped by the kitchens to grab a scone and an apple from Raelynn directly.

She swung a slotted spoon at me. "Are you coming in to work today or not? I can't keep track of you these days."

I deftly jumped out of the way. "Later," I assured her. "I'll be in later. I promise."

"You'd better. Because I'm not about to track you down and make you do your job—" Her warning rant followed me out to the castle gates and beyond when I swore I still heard her voice in the wind.

Elias had included the address to his place of work, only a few shops down from the cafe Melia and I liked to frequent. Which meant it would be easy to find. And a lot of people around in case things went wrong.

With me, things going wrong seemed to be the main course on the table every day. I survived on a steady diet of it, actually.

I clutched the strap of my shoulder bag as I walked, the

soles of my shoes clicking against cobblestone, trying to mentally push aside the session with Mike while preparing for whatever discussion Elias had in mind.

So much for enjoying the time off from classes.

So much for doing whatever I wanted.

I walked past the place three times before I realized what I'd done and had to backtrack. No plaques marked the outside of the building but I checked the gold hammered numbers on the door against what I'd seen in the email and rapped three times against the wood. No answer came, not even when I tugged the string on the magically enchanted bell.

The doorknob tingled against my palm as I pushed inside, glancing left and right in the gloom. "Hello? Mr. Hawthorne?"

My voice echoed back to me and a rustle of papers sounded from the rear of the main room.

"Who is it?" a male voice called out.

"It's Tavi Alderidge! I sent you the email? We were supposed to meet today."

And none of this was what I'd expected. If anything, it was like stepping into a cave, piled high with formations of things even my sensitive eyes had difficulty making out in the gloom. Was Elias Hawthorne a hermit?

He'd known I was coming, right?

"Yes! Um, I'm in the rear of the house. The parlor—*shit!* —is down the hall toward the atrium. Just come on through. Make yourself at home and pardon the mess."

I slowly made my way down the winding hall toward the source of light from the windows in the back.

This was not really an office, then, so much as his house, and in the fancy quarter of town, too. He was right on the edge of the touristy section that was notoriously hard to get into real-estate-wise. I knew this because Melia had looked at places there and we'd both lost our minds. Too expensive.

So there was more to Elias Hawthorne than met the eye. He wasn't just an internet troll or reporter. He wasn't just a man who ran a blog.

Already wary, I went into downright paranoia-land—how did he have enough money to live this way?

I carefully picked my way through the piles of books and the furniture laden with the same. The low lighting didn't bother me; my wolf sight noted each obstacle. But the air smelled of dust and old paper and beeswax. I found Elias in the "parlor," as he'd said—actually an old greenhouse turned into an office with his laptop and, again, more piles of books.

He glanced up from behind the laptop screen, his black hair sticking out at all angles like he'd just pulled his finger from a light socket. Bug eyes stared at me in surprise even though he knew I'd arrived, made larger yet by the giant, thick lenses of his glasses. A smattering of facial hair covered the strong set of his chin.

His eyes might be buggy but they saw everything and narrowed as they took in my outfit.

"Who are you?" he grunted out.

I offered him a smile and said, almost squirming out of my skin, "I'm the one who reached out to you about meeting to talk. My name is Tavi. I work under Selene." In a manner of speaking, anyway; not a full-fledged lie.

It took him a few seconds to make the connection entirely, his synapses apparently firing at last. Pushing his glasses back up his nose, Elias finally smiled. Okay, he was younger than I'd expected. Then again, it was hard to judge age by Fae standards. He might be forty or four hundred. Everything about him looked humanoid until he stood and a pair of translucent dragonfly wings unfolded from against his spine, completely natural and not some kind of physical addition. They flared out in a halo behind him and caught the sun coming in through the greenhouse glass.

How did those delicate wings hold up a man of his size? Elias Hawthorne might be skinny but damn, his shoulders were the width of a linebacker's back in the human realm. Did he only work out the top half of his body?

"Tavi, yes. You said you were doing an exposé on Madam Muerte." Elias broke eye contact and riffled through a series of papers in a manilla folder next to his laptop. "Yes, I remember now. I said we would meet to discuss—" He turned apologetic. "I'm a little lost in my own world right now."

"You said you wanted to meet today, as well," I reminded him. "I'm sorry if I've interrupted something important. Your email never specified a time."

"Everything is important." For a brief second he sounded grumpy at the intrusion, but when he stared at me again, his eyes crinkled, lit by some inner mirth. "Sometimes I can use a little respite from work. My own world might be important but it never pays to sink too deeply into it, not when there is so much more happening on the outside. You know what I mean?"

I blew out a breath. "Don't I ever."

"Clear off a seat and I'll be happy to discuss my findings with you." He held out a hand toward the front of his desk. "Go on."

Clear off a seat? Sure.

Only a single ladder-back chair, and it was piled with books covered in so much dust and the like that it would take a miracle to clean. With only half a thought for my dark pants, I moved the books on the seat aside and plopped down, keeping a death grip on my messenger bag.

"Just like that?" I questioned. "You're willing to discuss what you've found about the murder with me? You don't even know me."

I winced. Like I needed to remind him that I was a stranger. Or give anything away to indicate I wasn't exactly Selene's journalist mentee.

"Sure. Why not?" Elias asked. He found whatever he was looking for and returned to his seat as well, without so much as a handshake for an introduction. Just like that we were going to dive in. "I know Selene's reputation. She's a beast in the field and very thorough in any story she chooses to cover. She's released several doozies over the years. Any student she's decided to take on is going to be a force. It's better that we introduce ourselves now than wait until we're on opposing ends of a juicy article."

Squirming a little at his praise, hoping my reaction didn't give me away, I motioned with my chin toward the folder he held. "Do you keep everything in written form?"

"Oh, yes. I like to keep these as a backup. I retrieved them from my safe once I replied to your email. This is everything I've managed to compile on the murder. Not that it's anything compared to what the Bureau has in their files but I do my best with my resources."

Elias settled himself in his seat before fixing his attention on me, looking for all the world like he saw beneath the surface to every secret I tried to hide. Damn. Hopefully he wouldn't be another Juno, whose uncanny ability to delve beneath the surface brought her into my own inner circle in terms of trust. Not like I'd had much of a choice in the matter, though.

I knew from the start I'd have to keep my wits about me

with Elias.

Drawing my own pad and magically enchanted pen from my bag, I did my best to bestow him with the same look he gave me. Jovial and friendly but with a steel core of strength that showed I meant business.

"If you don't mind, I'd like to discuss why exactly you hated Madam Muerte," I said, once again channeling Persephone. Elias would have no choice but to talk to me and tell me what he knew, the enchanted pen writing down everything he said word for word. That way there would be no chance of me remembering things inaccurately. "Your blog posts held nothing back and you went to the trouble of finding personal accounts from other people who also appeared to have a problem with her."

Elias set his elbows on the desk and steepled his exceedingly long fingers together in front of him, tapping his chin. "Let me be clear. My interest in her had nothing to do with the woman as a person but rather her profession and how she chose to use her so-called gifts." He shook his head. "As someone familiar with my work, I'm sure you're aware that I covered several other traveling charlatans who professed to have a calling for psychic arts. None of them were nearly as prolific, or drew such drastically parallel reactions, as Muerte."

"Parallel reactions?"

"People either loved her or hated her. She was either entirely spot-on or so damn wrong it elicited a visceral reaction from those who received her prophecies," Elias continued. "I focused my attention solely on Muerte and her seeing prowess."

"How did she choose to use those gifts, in your opinion?" I asked.

"She chose to exploit those around her. She had a touch

of the true sight, don't get me wrong." Elias grew a bit louder, more passionate, as he spoke. He made it sound so simple. "But outside of the Oracle herself, having true sight is a rarity among the Fae, which is why none of the other psychics drew the same crowds as she did. It's been bred out of most ancient seer bloodlines. Madam Muerte used the speck of gift she actually possessed to find the weaknesses in those around her and gain whatever she could from exploitation." He scowled.

Remembering what the carnival gypsy had said to me a year ago, I wanted it to be true. I wanted her words of doom and gloom to be false, because otherwise the alternative was unthinkable.

I remembered how Mike had insisted he pay for a reading because she'd said some wild things to him and he thought I would be amused. Muerte had gone into convulsions immediately upon reaching into my future, her hand gripping mine to the point of pain while she spouted off about me being a catalyst to the end.

Something about stormy skies.

And the fulfillment of the Faerie Prophecy.

"It sounds as though you were personally involved with one of her *predictions*." I used air quotes on the last word, thinking that Elias would appreciate it.

"Yes, you might say I was personally involved with one of her more scandalous predictions. You may not guess this when you look at me, but I'm a retired Bureau Investigator."

My blood turned to ice at his revelation.

He was going to figure me out. He probably saw through me right now and only bided his time while the rest of his old friends and buddies made their way here to take me into custody.

Trying not to act affected, I crossed one leg over the

other, my pen magically dancing above the paper to record his words. "Excuse me for saying it, but you don't strike me as the type," I finally said with a tiny grin.

He waved a hand. "Never could tolerate all the rigid rules," he confessed. "Madame Muerte *predicted* corruption in the Bureau itself, stating that our organization would turn out to be the enemy of the king, or something crazy like that. I have the exact wording here." He pointed to the folder.

"Why would she say something like that?"

Didn't Muerte know better than to make an enemy of the Bureau? They were powerful beyond measure, probably second only to the Elder Council itself.

Elias shrugged. "I'm not sure, but that was the beginning of the end for my career. I went down the rabbit hole, so to speak, tracking down others she'd spoken to and recording any predictions of hers I could get. If you ask me, whoever offed her really did us in Faerie a favor."

"You think that someone took her out because she said something they didn't like?" I repeated dully.

That night in the garden there had been a male voice in addition to Madam Muerte's, someone angry.

Elias nodded along with my thoughts, almost as though he could hear them. "I absolutely do think so. The Bureau hated her. I hated her. I'm not sure what else I can tell you. She made some powerful enemies."

Like someone else I know.

"Anything you want to offer is greatly appreciated," I said.

I spent the next twenty minutes with Elias, the pen jotting away and my thoughts wandering. And I left his place wondering if Madam Muerte had been right about one thing after all: the Bureau and their corruption.

14

Sleep came but not easily, and once I did manage to catch a little shut-eye, my dreams were enough to have me *wanting* to wake up again. More nightmares than dreams actually, with thunderous skies overhead and shadow monsters snapping at my heels.

Monsters named Rooker and Claribel, if I had to hazard a guess. Monsters wearing Madam Muerte's face and grabbing at me from the shadows while telling me about how I'd be the end to life in Faerie as everyone knew it now.

I was still reeling about Elias's revelation about the prophecy regarding the Bureau when I woke up to scratching noises at my bedroom door. Although I shrugged off sleep easily, the worry remained, fear that he'd send someone after me because I knew about the prediction that may or may not have been bogus.

The scratching noises were not just a part of my dream, though.

I scrubbed my eyes and still heard the sound of fingernails scraping over wood. Heart thudding out a dangerous beat, I sat straight up.

Something was out there at my door and trying to get my attention.

Forcing myself to swallow over the lump in my throat, I pushed the covers aside and grabbed the candlestick from my desk for a weapon, going old-school. Colonel Mustard in the library. Absolutely. My mouth went dry as I crept over to the door on my tiptoes. I'd get the better of them and I'd bash some brains in before they had a chance to do the same thing to me.

I wrenched it open with one hand and brought the candlestick down with the other in attack.

"*Whoa!*" Mike raised his arms at the last instant to intercept the hit and I stopped just short of braining him.

"Damn it." My arm dropped like it was made of lead, my pulse high enough to make me dizzy and the rest of me turning to jelly. "Are you kidding me, Mike? You know you can't just sneak up like that. It's the middle of the night."

"I wasn't sneaking. I was—"

"Scratching," I supplied.

"I'm sorry. I wanted to talk to you but I didn't really want to wake you up. That was my way of accomplishing both at the same time, I guess." From the anxious set of his shoulders, more than likely he'd been hoping I *wouldn't* wake and he might slink off back to his room. Whatever it was he wanted to say had to be important.

I shook my head and he reached out to take the candlestick from me, prying each finger off until he held it instead.

"How about I keep this? In case you get any ideas," he said. "Judging from the way our first training session went, I'd say you have quite a few of them."

I opened the door further to him and he stepped past me into the bedroom without another word. The door closed behind us and I fixed a silencing bubble around us to keep the rest of the castle from overhearing whatever it was he had to say. Although I routinely swept my room for bugs, I wouldn't put it past the king to have other spying methods in place.

Nowhere was safe.

But Mike...Mike was here, taking up all the oxygen in the room. Mike wanted to talk. To me.

"What's up?" I asked with forced nonchalance.

Let me be perfectly clear: I'd never been cool around Mike. Not once, even before I knew he was the prince. First he'd been a suspected serial killer, stalking me through the night when my car broke down on the side of the road. Then he'd been just a nice boy in my class helping me. Then a prince. And through it all I'd found him to be the most handsome man I'd ever seen in my life. Not traditionally, the way an All-American Boy Next Door would look. Or a Tall, Dark, and Handsome Alpha-hole type.

He was just Mike.

And I thought he'd been mine once.

He stood in the middle of the bedroom floor like he wasn't sure where to go and finally turned to fix me with his green-eyed stare.

"You were crying," he stated. "When you left training this morning. I saw you."

I could go with the classic I-had-something-in-my-eye bit and blow him off. But if he was here in the middle of the night then he deserved the truth, and so did I. "Yes, I was crying," I agreed. And suddenly realizing I only wore a tank top and tiny sleep shorts, I hustled to the bed and grabbed a blanket to wrap around my shoulders.

Mike noticed. "That hurt me more than what you did with your magic. To see you that way. To see you so undone.

Even through everything, you've never cried in front of me before," he said.

He wanted to talk about being undone? Anytime I was around him, with the two of us breathing in the same air, that was what he did to me. He burrowed beneath my defenses without even trying. And it wasn't because of his status. I could give a crap about Mike being a prince. It was everything else that made him unique. His quirky sense of humor and the way he always tried his best but somehow fell a step behind. It was his realness and the wholesome way he looked at life, without a hint of the coldness of his father.

But until we sorted out what we meant to each other, *really* meant to each other, I kept those thoughts to myself.

I shrugged indifferently, or at least I attempted indifference. "I'm fine. There's nothing for you to worry about. Me crying is not your concern."

"Except I think it is." He took a step forward, the candlestick still gripped in one hand and his other reaching for me before he thought better of it. He stopped and cleared his throat. "I want you to know. This back-and-forth thing that we have going on? It's not always easy for me."

He was telling *me*? I'd spent way too much time on this roller coaster to think anything between us was ever easy in general. We were either meant to be together, or incredibly toxic for each other, and I hadn't figured out which one of those was the truth yet.

"What's *really* going on?" I asked him, huddling deeper into my blanket.

"What do you mean?"

"With us," I clarified. "*Why* do we have this back and forth? One minute we're on, and the next I feel like you're a stranger who wants nothing to do with me." Not to mention he hadn't said another word about finding out my secrets.

And maybe I'd *wanted* to hurt him, a bit, with my magic. To show him that I wasn't some weakling he could set aside and blame his problems on, that I was a person.

That I was a woman.

I wanted to be *his* woman.

"I never want to see you cry," Mike said gently. "I never want you to hurt, period. That's all I know. As to what's really going on...I've been trying to figure that out since the Trials. Finding your medallion threw me for a loop and left me struggling to process a few things about you, about who you really are. I still don't have any answers but...I miss you."

Something thawed messily inside my chest. "I miss you too." I took a step toward him before I realized what I'd done. Before I realized that Mike had done the same and now only a scant few inches separated us.

"I understand why you had to keep secrets."

"I understand why you needed time to process," I said, in a show of vulnerability that I hoped would demolish the last of the distance as well and help us heal. "I *don't* understand why you can't give me an answer as to what's going on with us."

"Because it isn't normal, Tavi. Nothing between us has been normal from the start. And you're right, the back and forth is pure bullshit," he replied.

"Then just tell me what you want."

He pushed his hair behind his ear, uncomfortable. "I don't have an answer for you."

So we continued to spin in circles. But pushed to the edge the way these last few weeks, few months, had pushed me? I was done spinning.

"Mike, I—" I broke off, bowed my head, then raised it again to look directly at him. "I can't keep doing this."

My words shocked both of us and his eyes widened.

"Can't keep doing what?" he asked.

"This." My hand swirled between us. Against all better judgment and logic, against every instinct for self-preservation I possessed and with my blood close to simmering, I went with the big guns and told him: "I'm in love with you."

"Y-you...what?"

A reality bomb dropped and my shock at having admitted what I'd felt this whole time did not stop me from speaking again.

"I've been in love with you since our first semester at the Halfling Academy." There was a very real desire to pull the blanket over my head and finish this out through the safety of the fabric. "But every time I turn around, there is something driving us apart. Murderers or monsters or wolves. Your dad or the Bureau or magic. Your confusion. With everything that has happened, is still happening, the only thing I'm *not* confused about in this world is how I feel about you. And you're running hot and cold. I don't know where I stand with you."

He stared at me for a long moment before closing the distance in two steps and drawing me into his arms. No passion, no heat. Just understanding and comfort.

"You love me." He huffed out a laugh. "You really do."

"I don't see how that's a funny thing," I murmured against him.

But the longer I breathed, the more I relaxed into his embrace, the familiarity of him, despite the way he wouldn't answer me.

Until he spoke again and I stiffened.

"I have to admit I'm confused by my feelings for you.

Since you're being honest with me I know I've got to do the same. And as much as I want to say the words back to you, I don't know if I can. The only thing I do know is that I want to be around you. All the time. I never want to be away from you."

"If that's true, then what's going on between us? Really?" I asked. "Please give me an answer." *Even if it hurts.*

Mike stared down at me. "You're right about something always driving us apart. That's been a big part of why I needed to take some extra time. It makes me think our timing just isn't right. No one said that romance is easy, but seriously? No one else has the problems that we have. I don't know, Tavi, but I want to try. Okay?"

"Try what?" I pressed. "Giving this a shot?"

My heart leapt at the possibility, and then plummeted at his hesitation. He didn't answer for the longest time and I knew better, I *knew* better, than to attempt to fill in the words for him.

When Mike finally nodded, pressing me closer to his chest, his hold on me unbreakable, it felt unreal. A big cosmic joke and the punch line would leave me reeling.

"I'm not sure what's going to happen to us if we do give this a try, but I know I'll lose you if we don't," he said.

It wasn't a *yes*. Not the full-fledged, whole-bodied agreement I wanted. Needed.

I started to push away but he gripped me tighter yet.

"I want you to know this, and know that I'm telling you the truth. I trust you, Tavi. I really do. Even with all the secrets, I know *why* you had to keep them from me. I trust you more than I trust my own family."

I jerked my head up to look at him. "You can't mean that."

"I do. That's part of the problem, and the main reason

why I hesitate to get into this. Something is up with my father. And I don't trust what's going on with him," Mike continued. "He's been cagey, aloof. Hostile."

"More than his usual?" I allowed myself a tiny smirk at King Tywin's expense. Yet my interest was piqued in a way it definitely shouldn't have been when I desperately needed to keep my head down. "What is he doing? What's changed?"

Mike loosened his hold only enough to trail one hand up my spine and leave delicious heat tingling in the wake of his touch. "He's acting concerned. And I know better than to trust any words of his when he's shown time and again that they mean nothing," he said.

His fingers continued to slide over the line of my spine, caressing the area below my neck. I shivered and arched closer to him. "Concerned about what?"

"That's what I don't know. But I do know he's taking extra security measures whenever he leaves his library, which he rarely does these days. He's engrossed in something serious but he won't tell anyone what's going on." He smoothed my hair with a gentle caress. "And I want to say that I'm sorry for implying that the shifters were to blame for the pure-blood murders."

I stiffened at that. "You *want* to say or you're *saying* it?" I pressed.

"You're right." Mike chuckled. "I'm saying it. I'm sorry. There are plenty of other people who might have been controlling Onyx, but instead of believing you, I turned against you. I let my family's prejudice color what I know and what I've seen of you. It wasn't right or fair."

Finally. One of the massive walls between us started crumbling down brick by brick. It felt huge, his revelation. Not only belief but trust.

"There are bad shifters out there," I told him. "Just like

there are bad Fae out there. But I had nothing to do with Onyx or the spells forcing him to kill. He was my friend. Is," I corrected. "He is my friend. And he needs my help to clear his name."

Mike shifted, his probing fingers continuing their trail of fire up my arm before he took hold of my chin to still me. His gaze found mine and I shivered. "That's something I've always admired about you. You're so willing to go to bat for your friends."

I grimaced. "It's a bad thing."

"No, it's not a bad thing. It's wonderful. That's why I trust you, Tavi. Because I've gotten to know you and I know that you'll always step up for the people you love. You have my back."

It was everything I wanted from him.

Yet—

I paused as his thumb brushed over my bottom lip. "Do you have mine?" I asked, needing to know the answer. "Do you have my back, Mike?"

"Yes."

He dipped his head and kissed me, stealing my next breath. Oh, it had been too long since he'd last kissed me. The shivers were back and the world narrowed so that in the hush of this room, we were the only two people alive. We were the only ones who mattered.

His lips massaged mine gently, reverently.

"I'm here for you. And I'm terrified of what that means because of my father," Mike whispered against me. "I don't want to put you in danger."

I looped my arm around the back of his neck to draw him closer to me. Wanting to wrap my body around his in the same way. This kiss was the apology I'd desperately craved.

Yet—

This might be the first step in making up, but we still had a long road ahead of us. Starting with the King and whatever doom he'd bring down on our heads. Guillotine-sharp and just as unmerciful.

15

The morning loomed ahead with the sun rising in dazzling gold and peach above the hills over the city. Despite my lack of sleep, and my early morning interruption in the form of the man of my dreams and his amazingly talented lips, I felt decent when I rose.

Better than decent.

A knot of tension had released inside of my chest, as opposed to the chains in my gut which stayed with me no matter what, and I felt much better having the air cleared with Mike. To the point that, when the letter arrived summoning me to my next royal study session, I didn't balk or complain.

Verbally, at least.

The time and location on the note gave me enough of a window to head out and grab a fancy coffee—as opposed to the kitchen where I'd be cornered about work—before meeting with Mike in the library. I'd stopped myself from getting one for him though, knowing that the guard would report anything untoward to King Tywin. Such as buying things for his son that might mean we have anything deeper than what we'd shown him.

Not like I wanted to give the king access to every part of me.

Tywin had no place in the growing relationship between me and Mike. Rather, his growing feelings. I loved him and now he knew.

Surprise had me gasping and nearly dropping my biodegradable magic coffee cup when I saw Mike standing beside not the guard but Tywin himself. The ruler wore his usual gold crown perched cockily atop his head, with his amber eyes hot and searing into mine.

"My sources tell me you have tardiness issues. I'm pleased to see you've only arrived thirty seconds late this time around, Miss Alderidge," he said to me. "From what I've been told, this is a vast improvement."

My automatic reaction of *I aim to please* stilled on my tongue. I didn't dare look at Mike.

"Apologies, Your Highness." I bowed my head. "I left the palace grounds to grab some—"

He cut me off with a wave of his hand. "I care less about your predilections for caffeinated beverages and more about how you and the crown prince may help each other improve your skills." He gestured toward a stack of tomes already waiting for us at a long, polished wood table. "I've taken the liberty of arranging a selection of important books for your sessions. Surely you'll get through them in no time and the improvements shall be immediate. Perhaps studying the archaic origins of defensive magic will help you prepare a little better."

The last bit was a pointed, dagger-like blow aimed at Mike and I knew it was because of what had gone down at our last training session.

I bit my lip hard enough to bleed in order to stay silent and not look at Mike, who stiffened at my side.

"You are supposed to be learning to be a better Fae, to contribute to the strength of your society. Instead I have to hear about how my son stayed open and allowed an attack without any form of retaliation. Perhaps tears are a weakness of his," Tywin continued.

He looked inordinately pleased with himself for putting together this situation.

What I wanted to do was use the same magic on the king but doubted I'd make it far.

There was no such thing as a fair fight when it came to King Tywin. Or any sort of fairness. I cast a glance at Mike who gestured sharply to the table and the massive tower of books waiting there. Elias Hawthorne would probably go crazy for this library, considering the state of his own house.

I thought about what Mike had told me this morning regarding his father and I tried to look at the king through a new lens. What was really going on that had him acting in a way that got Mike's back up?

"You will sit there quietly for approximately thirty minutes until I've deemed you ready to begin quizzing each other," King Tywin said with a soft laugh. "You may begin."

Like we were on some kind of game show where every second counted.

I grabbed the chair beside Mike in the dim hush of a place where I'd always been comfortable. Amid the giant bookcases and the plush window seats with their velvet cushions, I'd escaped from my reality multiple times.

Now Tywin watched my every move, monitored and stored them away, and my skin itched.

"So," Mike hissed from the corner of his mouth, "what do you want to do?"

A cough from Tywin had me flinching and when I glanced up with my face pulled tight, the King glared at me from his perch across the room, four Fae guards manning his sides.

"About what?" I asked in a whisper.

"Our next move. You know what I mean." Mike tried to surreptitiously plan our next step and I gave him credit for the attempt. But the sound of his fingers flicking through the old rustling papers did nothing to cover the low tenor of his voice.

"This is really not the time to talk about it." I stared down my nose at the book and then up to Mike. "We've got to focus."

"We're never going to get ahead on clearing your name if we have to study defensive magic from fifteen thousand years ago," Mike said pointedly.

I frowned. "We won't with your dad watching us, either."

Mike understood but that didn't make the task in front of us any easier.

"It's weird, right?" I asked him once we all settled into our roles for the day. "How certain parties are so intent on us working together? Especially considering how *he* feels about me."

Mike arched a single golden brow. "You mean, how he hates you?"

I nodded, biting down on my lower lip. I knew that the king hated me but hearing it from his son's lips still stung more than a little.

"You might think he does, but I refuse to believe it," Mike continued. "There has to be another reason he keeps pushing us together."

I flipped through one page and on to the next, page after page, the lines of text blurring together in a single unbroken smudge of black on tea-colored paper. "You're entitled to your opinion, and I'm entitled to mine," I retorted.

King Tywin shifted, clearing his throat, and I pressed my nose a little closer to the book spine.

"We're never going to get to talk here. You're right. Meet up later?" Mike asked. "In town?"

"Away from the castle," I agreed.

"Fuck yes."

"Can I invite Melia?"

I caught the tail end of Mike's smile before he grabbed another book from the stack. "*Good.*"

LIKE OLD TIMES, I thought as I settled at the café table with a large glass container of bubbling coffee over a heatless flame at the center, something new that the place wanted to try to gain customers. So far, I hadn't tasted a sip, but the presentation was satisfying. I might have sat there with my chin balanced on my hands watching it bubble for the rest of the day.

Especially given my headache from all that reading.

Melia had ordered our favorite appetizer of deep-fried squash blossom, and the steaming platter rested alongside the coffee with our three matching espresso cups ready to fill. The server with the alligator skin assured us that once the chocolate-colored bloom in the center of the bubbling coffee opened, it would be ready.

"I haven't seen that look on your face for a long time," Melia said, picking at one of the blossoms and finding it too hot to eat, her fingers scalded.

"What look?" I asked.

"You're happy. After the shit-storm that's followed since

we met, it seems like you haven't had an opportunity to really be yourself in a long time." She trailed her eyes from me to Mike and back again. "I think I can guess the source of the change."

He didn't seem bothered in the slightest at her insinuation, only sat back in his chair with his arms folded over his chest.

"You're not wrong." The moment the bloom opened, I grabbed the coffee pot and doled out the dark roast with chicory and several spices only found in Faerie.

"It's good to have the gang back together even if it's still for a kind of shit-storm subject," Mike agreed. "It's been too long since things felt normal."

That was a good word for it. *Normal.* We could pretend, for a few hours anyway, that we were students and our greatest worry was an exam or two.

Melia reached across the table and placed her hand over mine. "If the gang is really back, then we're going to get to the bottom of this and figure out a way to solve the murder once and for all." Her smile turned nuclear. "Trust me. There's no better team!"

She looked so self-assured that I automatically wanted to believe her. Melia always had that air about her: smart and studious but the kind of person who lit up a room when they entered. She'd made a great mentor and an even better friend. It did feel good, too.

Being back together put me on top of the world, and confident.

Plus Mike resting in his seat beside me, shifting now so that his arms crossed behind his head and his knee brushing mine. It filled me with relief. Warm, delicious relief that things were almost back to the status quo between us. Add Melia in and the circle really was complete.

"What did you find out from your meeting with Elias the other day?" Melia asked.

Mike shot me a questioning look and I filled him in on what had happened with the journalist and his connection to Madam Muerte.

"He was certain that only a handful of people within the Bureau heard her prediction and quickly shoved it under the rug," I finished.

"Because of what she said?" Mike asked.

"Apparently so. It was bad enough that they closed ranks and tried to keep it on the down low. Elias didn't get into the details of why he *retired*—and you can imply the air quotes there—but I wonder if it doesn't have something to do with this whole thing."

Melia shook her head, troubled. "I really don't like the implication that the Bureau is involved in the murder in any way. What are we going to do about that?"

I'd been asking myself the same question.

"I'm not sure what we can do," I said with a shrug. The coffee went a long way toward thawing the chill in my bones at the thought of dealing with the Bureau in this capacity but not all the way.

"Is there any way for us to figure out exactly what they know about the case? Do they have their files digitized into a system we can hack?" Mike braved the heat and popped an entire squash blossom into his mouth.

Melia shook her head. "I did a little bit of reading about the Bureau's formation after they first brought Tavi in for questioning. They only make handwritten accounts and all of their evidence is sealed away in a nether space between worlds, accessed with keys attuned to each agent's magic."

"So that's a no?" Mike clarified.

"There might be a way if we steal a key." Melia sounded

way too at ease with the thought of not only breaking and entering but stealing a key, much like the one used to get back and forth to Faerie.

"You say that like it's a walk in the park," I replied. "We don't know the layout of the inside and I doubt that's going to be online anywhere." Personally I wanted to get my hands on whatever prediction Muerte had made, to see the exact wording.

"None of this is going to be easy. We all know that, so there's no sense in lamenting it. I'm being objective here," Melia added. "It's better if we start at the bottom instead of getting caught up in the details."

"Tavi's got powers that none of the rest of us do. If anyone has a chance of getting one of those keys, it's her." Mike apparently had more confidence in me than I did.

"Are you talking about my cognitive manipulation? Or my transfiguration?" Or anything else I'd rather not have him talking about in public? We had to be careful what we talked about and who might find it strange that the crown prince met with two nobodies. We'd forgone the silencing bubble to not stand out but now I worried we'd made a mistake.

"It seems like this is a little sudden," I put in. "Like we're rushing things."

"Of course we're rushing things. But that doesn't mean it isn't the right move to make," Melia responded.

I felt insanely unprepared for something that big. Which was not to say that I hadn't done equally stupid things before in the past, with just as little preparation time. I'd broken into a secure wing of the castle and stolen a magical artifact.

I'd almost died.

This was a step beyond that. The Bureau was one of the

most magically protected places in the kingdom outside of the king's own bedchamber, I'd bet.

"What if," I wondered, "aside from the keys they really don't have excellent security?"

"I believe they call that a false sense of complacency." Melia offered me a grin that said she knew I'd get to that point eventually.

"Yeah. I'm not sure how we can figure that out without trial and error, and I've had my share of error." I cut a glance to Mike. "Do you know of anything that might be of help?"

"I've been trying to dig up anything I can on them, considering what's been happening with your, ah, buddy. But like Melia said, there really isn't much," he replied. "I know they have a record room somewhere on the first floor."

Okay, so we'd limit our search to the first floor, once we got inside. *If* we got inside. My head spun.

"I've, ah—" Melia stopped and twirled a curl around her finger. "I've been practicing my skills in terms of cyber security. I can probably access the street cameras around the place and see what I see."

"There are street cameras?" I was a million miles behind. In so many ways.

"Are we sure this is the route to take?" Mike asked. "Elias Hawthorne might still be a suspect. He knows too much."

I shook my head. "He hated Madam Muerte but he wasn't organized enough to pull off a stunt like that. Not and get away with it." I hesitated to tell them that I hadn't gotten a dangerous vibe off of Elias. Not that my senses counted for much these days. I didn't want to hang my hat on something like a *feeling*. Elias wasn't the one we needed to look at, and I wasn't sure how I knew that, but I knew.

"He used to work for the Bureau," Mike finished.

"And I'm betting he wasn't the only one who heard

about her prophecy calling out the Bureau and all the employees for shady dealings. Someone held a grudge, and boom. One dead gypsy." I hated to sound so flippant about it but my gut told me not to focus on Elias. He wasn't our guy.

"So we ultimately need to turn our sights to the Bureau. It makes sense," Melia said with a decisive nod.

And only one way to do it, too. We would have to break in and hope we didn't get caught.

16

We decided there wasn't any time to waste, with the king closing in on us and everything else going on. Once classes started again then things would be worse still. We'd have even less time and even more eyes. So later that evening, once the sun went down and the cloak of night would hopefully hide our sins a little better, I pushed open the creaking door to the hall and poked my head through. Left, right.

Nobody in sight.

I closed it again but didn't flip the lock.

It had been a long time since I'd used my transfiguration abilities for anything this complicated. Not since getting stuck in the walls, which was not an experience I wanted to repeat in my lifetime.

Standing in the middle of the bedroom, I closed my eyes, focusing on the well of magic inside of me that lived separately from my wolf. It spread through me with a tingling wave like sparks flying away from a fire, my access to that deep pit limitless. I held the picture of the figure I wanted to become in my mind and let my body do the rest of the hard work.

The tingle spread out through my core, my arms shrinking, my legs bending backward, and only a small measure of pain accompanying the change. A pain I knew well and recognized. My teeth shifted to little points, whiskers bursting from my cheeks.

Half a breath later a small spotted tabby cat stood where my human body had. I blinked in the darkness until the world sharpened and I saw everything, down to the last detail, the dust bunnies and clumps of hair among my piles of laundry.

Yuck.

No time for distractions. I had to focus.

Disguised, I trotted out of the room and wound my way through the darkened hallways toward the gardens.

In the tiny cat body, my worries seemed *less*: less insurmountable, less insane. Everything came down to black and white, forward or behind. My goal lay ahead of me so I didn't spare a moment thinking about the rest.

A male body separated itself from the shadows at the end of the giant stretch of lawn. Hidden beneath the towering trees marking the border of the forest, Mike had his arms crossed as he glanced back and forth looking for me.

I wound around his legs, purring in the back of my throat, until he realized there was something there and jumped out of the way.

The pounding of his heart sounded overly loud to my sensitive ears.

"Christ. Don't do that," he warned.

I let out a chirruping meow and eventually he bent to

run a hand along my back, all the way down to my twitching tail.

His touch sent a tingle through me. If he thought it was weird, at least he didn't stop. And his touch felt so damn good.

"Are you going to change back anytime soon, or—"

I swatted him with a paw but kept my claws sheathed. It was better for us not to be seen together, especially with the cameras on the streets. But Mike with a cat might be dismissed.

He finally got the message and we took off without any further delay.

Melia had managed to gain access to the street cameras around the Bureau. The office building was located in a high traffic area of town, and we'd learned that the agency was open twenty-four hours a day. This late at night, however, we might have a chance of running into fewer agents.

Especially since there was no way for us to legitimately gain access. Although no one explicitly stated what I'd have to do, I understood: the wall bit. Again. It was the only way to get inside without being noticed, and every part of this plan hinged on my powers not conking out at the worst possible moment.

Which was asking a lot, I thought as I trotted beside Mike, trying to keep up with his long-legged strides. We turned a corner a block away from the office and Melia separated herself from the flower-covered pergola she'd been hiding beneath.

"You guys took long enough," she said. "I was starting to worry."

"No need," Mike replied. "Better safe than sorry, so we took our time."

I sat down in front of Melia and blinked up at her, waiting until she noticed me and chuckled.

"You could have gone for something even more inconspicuous, you know." She tickled me under the chin before straightening to face Mike. "We need her to use her abilities to get through the wall. Once she's inside, she can open the door and let us in. There are cameras only in the interrogation room. At least that's what all the information states. The rest of the halls aren't patrolled that way. There are special keycards to access the archives only, so once we're inside we'll have to find one."

"The information? What information?" Mike asked.

Melia waved that away. "Don't question my methods here, Princeling. I've done my research."

"Stick with the plan and we're all going to be just fine. Right?" He sounded like he wanted a promise and no one offered one.

"More like follow my lead," Melia corrected.

We tried to stick to the areas that the perimeter cameras wouldn't pick up but only Melia knew their placement. She guided us along the sidewalks until she turned right sharply, heading down the narrow alley between buildings. Another block over she stopped and gestured toward a vague door-shaped outline on an otherwise blank wall.

"This should be it," she whispered. "Hidden by a cloaking spell, but this is the entrance not open to the public. Tavi, will your magic allow you to become a part of the door and the spell itself without triggering alarms?"

I guessed we would see.

I pressed a paw to the building and closed my eyes, sending a wave of power against the material to sense its make-up. Steel. Wood. And a compound that felt eerily similar to Magnasterium, familiar yet not.

I could become anything I saw in my mind as long as I held the picture of it there with utter conviction. I had to believe without a shadow of a doubt to become one with the wall in order to walk through it. It didn't matter that I really didn't want to do this.

This wasn't my first time, at least, I told myself as reassurance against a sudden wave of terror. It wouldn't help to wonder what would happen once I made it to the other side, or who or what would be waiting for me there. Or the cost to my power.

A few seconds, a few steadying breaths, and the wall absorbed me as I stepped forward.

I set aside every hint of desperation inside of me while I maintained the picture of the wall. The feeling of it, the reality of it. A large thrust of power sent me into the wall entirely and I became part of the wood and metal.

And magic.

As I absorbed the magic of the wall inside of me, pain became my world, attacking my nervous system because it was the only part of me still left able to feel. I was on fire. I was ice. I was nothing but pain.

Despite the agony, I came out the other side very much in human form, albeit with blood trickling from my nose.

The tingle of the magical wards remained inside of me, in my blood, lighting every nerve and creating steady pain that did not dissipate. Well, shit. I hadn't used that much magic in too long, apparently. My power had been strained, muscles tensed and frozen as my body transformed from cat to wall then back to its normal form.

No more walls, I'd vowed once, and I renewed that vow now. But I'd accomplished what I set out to do. I was inside. I peeled open my eyes, blinking away the double vision. I waited for the alarms to sound and about a thousand agents to come raining down on me like hellfire.

When nothing happened, I exhaled my held breath and looked around. The room I found myself in was plain, with gray painted walls and no clue to help me identify where I might be. I stared at the door straight in front of me. Okay, no time to worry about what lay beyond that door. I'd gotten this far without being seen—a small miracle—so I turned around and found the handle to the hidden outside door and tugged it open. The wards recognized me as part of them and dissolved without me having to do anything to try and break or unravel them.

I considered it a perk of the transfiguration but knew better than to count on getting lucky again.

With the spells null, no one would detect Melia and Mike stepping inside.

We kept our footsteps light and our inhalations small as the three of us squeezed inside and faced the inside door as a single unit. Mike clapped me on the shoulder and pressed his fingers to my skin gently before releasing me. *A job well done*. It was all the praise I'd get.

I held a hand out for them to wait while I tried the inside door, pulling it open and peeking around it at the long open hallway ahead. Nowhere to hide. My stomach sank a little further. That wasn't going to help us keep hidden. No cameras inside but that didn't mean that people wouldn't walk by at any moment, or sense our energy signatures. We'd done our best to cloak them with spells, but without a potion I had my doubts.

My days of stealing ingredients from the kitchen pantry were long over.

What other choices did we have? Gesturing for them to follow, I led as the three of us made our way down the hallway, glancing left and right, searching for agents in the area.

None of this felt right. One wrong breath would send us spiraling.

A skeleton crew, I told myself. There were only a few agents in the building at this hour, and surely if they were here this late they were all too busy working on cases.

A shadow of a body shifted in the hallway ahead and I ducked back and made myself as small as possible.

I had no idea where we were going. I only knew that we didn't have much time. The records room was on the first floor and my doubts at having one of the locked doors in this hall be the one we sought were tripling by the second.

We had to be in and out before anyone discovered our presence—and we still had to find the right room. Still find a keycard that would open said room. I wouldn't risk telling Melia and Mike, but this felt like a ridiculously stupid idea all of a sudden, like a slap in the face reminding me that we'd been rash.

Once the figure of the agent ahead of us disappeared into another room and the coast cleared, we crept further into the building. My heart jettisoned into my throat and stayed lodged there so that each breath hurt. My focus lay ahead on the hall, on the crew still present in the building. As if a countdown ticked to the moment when they would inevitably find us.

We'd rushed this. I knew it in my gut. We'd rushed getting in here and now that we had, we were floundering.

My head spun and I had to pinch myself to focus again. I didn't hear the others creeping behind me but I felt them. The fine hairs on the back of my neck rose.

We could do this.

We *had* to do this.

The alternative was unthinkable.

I tried the doorknob to the room on my left and found it locked. A placard on the door had the name of the agent etched on it. Not one I recognized, either, so I was willing to guess they weren't involved with Madam Muerte. I needed to find Claribel's office. Or Rooker. Surely they'd have something in connection with Madam Muerte's original prophecy.

Glancing to the right, I saw more names of agents, more offices. We turned the corner and I hissed out a breath when my gaze landed on the turned back of an agent. My arm whipped behind me to keep the others from barreling into me while we waited. The agent mumbled something to himself before he walked forward and turned a corner. The main expanse of the Bureau building stretched like some distorted hall of mirrors in front of us, impossibly large.

I was ready to turn the corner and proceed when suddenly Mike grabbed the back of my shirt and hauled me off my feet.

I dangled for a split second with my arms and legs tensing until he set me down and pointed in the opposite direction. I'd thought that was a dead-end hall upon first glance—until I noted the haze of illusion magic. And through the haze, a door made of oak and iron and beset with so much magic that whatever was on the other side had to be something big.

Not an office or a dead end, no, but an official records room?

I stared back at Mike and Melia and nodded once, the message clear. We hustled forward and I pressed my hand against the illusion magic. We didn't have a key card. There was no way to get one unless—

The spell snapped and crackled before allowing us

entry. Correction: allowing *me* entry. I reached out to grab Mike's hand, hoping he'd form a chain with Melia, because the wards in this palace still seemed to recognize me from when I'd been part of the wall and absorbed the hidden door magic.

My heart thudding fast enough to make me go blind, I reached out for the doorknob and tugged. *The records room was only accessed by a key...*

Except *I'd* somehow become the key we needed. The spells allowed me to slip through them with ease, and Melia and Mike in turn since they were linked to me through touch.

Holding my breath, I turned the knob and pulled the door open slowly. The hinges made no sound. The moment we bolted inside, the moment we closed the door behind us, the silence became deafening. Rows of filing cabinets looked like something I'd see in Uncle Will's office rather than an official government building where magic existed. They towered overhead into the endless expanse of ceiling.

There was no magic here, I thought, tiptoeing forward and tugging at the handle of the first cabinet. Only the magic that had to be used to access the place. Inside it was a different story, no spells to protect these files from outsiders because outsiders were not allowed to be here.

We weren't supposed to be inside these four walls.

"Hurry," Melia whispered, her voice a hiss.

She didn't need to tell me.

Mike took his own cabinet while Melia moved to the far end and the three of us searched. File after file, and if there was any order to these things, I couldn't figure it out. My fingers raced over the folders, tingling with what might have been anticipation.

Or my nerves were just shot.

Everything was shot, especially since this was the one chance I had to get the information I needed. If this ended badly I was done.

Worse than done. I was dead.

I almost missed the name, what with my eyes blurring and my fingers flying way too quickly. Until a spark snapped at me and I stopped to draw in a breath. To get myself centered. And slowly backed up until I found the folder I'd been searching for.

Muerte.

Death. It really did seem appropriate.

Before I had a chance to call out, the door swung open.

A spotlight fell on me. And at that moment, I blanked. I froze as adrenaline coursed through every piece of me. Mike and Melia were on the other side of the room, hidden from sight, so the man in the doorway wouldn't see them.

But he would see me.

In the split second before he twisted his head and caught me in his gaze, I reacted.

The change ripped through me, and the first thing I saw in my mind became my reality. It probably should have been a puddle. Instead, feathers exploded from me. My arms shrank and warped.

The folder slipped from my beak and the sound drew the agent's attention.

"What the hell?" He narrowed yellow-slitted eyes on me. "Get out of here! Shoo! How did you get in here?"

A regular bird. Not a halfling in disguise. It did nothing to calm my absolutely shot nerves as I dove for the folder.

And the agent dove with me.

His hand collided with my body and sent me flying in the opposite direction. Mike and Melia were on the other side of the room, hidden from sight. Thank God. That was my only thought. Thank God they weren't visible, the open door shielding them from the agent.

The agent in question had his arms up in front of his face, waving them wildly like a mad man.

"Get the fuck out of here!" he screeched.

I somehow managed to gain control over my little body before I hit the opposite wall but lost my grip again on the folder in the process.

"Must have snuck in when the door was open, dumb-shit bird."

I changed course and flew out of the room with my heart beating a painful tattoo in my chest. The agent followed, shooing me toward a window and opening it ahead of me with his magic.

A glance behind showed Mike and Melia grabbing the folder and sneaking out of the door while the agent kept his focus on me. Melia shoved it into the confines of her jacket and nodded to me before they bolted.

I flew through the window as fast as my wings were able to carry me, away from the Bureau building. Having to put a lot of faith in the fact that my friends would find the exit and make it through.

I made it into the neighboring alley where we'd first gathered and dropped like a stone. Nestled between the ground and the wall. For half a heartbeat I sat there to get my breath back. In the next I called my magic, shifting back into my normal body.

Only to wait.

Wait while it felt like the sky fell around me and it wasn't a warning or a drill. It was the real deal. Too much time passed. They'd been caught; they must have been, because this was taking too long. How the hell was I going to get them out?

I never heard their footsteps approaching. One moment I was alone, and the next Mike and Melia turned the corner with their arms linked.

Two friends out for a midnight stroll.

Melia saw me first and her shoulders hunched as she collapsed on herself.

Mike cast a silencing bubble but his dark eyes gave none of his thoughts or emotions away.

"You made it out." Melia grabbed me in a hug tight enough for me to feel the way she shook.

"So did you." I hugged her back, my lifeline, infinitely grateful for her presence. "And you got the folder?"

"Yeah, of course. Not like we were going to leave without the goods. Girl, that took decades off my life," Melia said with a nervous chuckle.

"Agreed," Mike grunted.

Melia drew the folder out of her jacket and held it in front of me. My fingers trembled as I took it and flipped through.

"Wow, this is a lot of information," I said, leafing through the papers in the folder. "At least they've been thorough."

"I would hope so. They've spent enough time looking into this case. Looking in the wrong direction, more like," Melia said with a low, slow exhale. "It's good to know that they're doing their job, and if they would actually target the right suspect, they'd get this solved immediately."

I remembered what Elias said about her prophecy, about a crack in the Bureau. I wondered if they would have a copy of her exact words in the folder. I felt like it would really help if we had a direction, a clue. It would be a colossal waste of time to start covertly looking into every single agent that had ever worked for the Bureau.

"There's nothing here," Mike said, looking over my

shoulder. "It's just a bunch of dates. Who she spoke to in the few days leading up to her death."

"I wonder if they wrote down what she said to you? Since, you know..." Melia shrugged. She didn't need to finish that thought.

Flipping through the pages, I reached the end of the document and went to close the folder. Until I realized that the last page numbered 257. And the page my thumb landed on, two back from the last, numbered 200.

"What the hell?" I mumbled, leafing back and forth.

"There are pages missing. A *lot* of pages." Melia picked up on things right away. She craned closer, her eyes scanning the documents.

198, 199, 200—257.

"A lot of them," Mike agreed.

A chill skittered through me.

Someone had taken them and no one would convince me otherwise. Someone was purposely hiding information about the Muerte murder...and pinning it on me.

17

Rooker and Claribel were the lead agents assigned to the case. They would be the best place to start. Surely they had information written down, personal notes and similar stuff, that hadn't made it into these files. Hadn't been *stolen* from the files, more than likely.

"I'm going back in. I have to search their desks," I said, snapping the folder closed. "There's obviously a bunch of information taken from the file and one of them will know something about it."

"Hell no! Are you out of your mind?" Mike hissed. "Going back in there is suicide, Tavi. We barely made it out and we wouldn't have if it wasn't for you tricking the wards."

"It's way too dangerous. You're going to get caught. We'll probably not make it out of here as it is," Melia added. In the dim hush of the early morning blackness, even she looked pale.

But we were here.

I had to make good on whatever luck got us this far.

"I'm going. You guys wait here and I'll go alone. I can shift into a bug or something and go unseen. You can't," I said.

"This is a really bad idea. You won't find anything that hasn't made it into the file. If someone stole these papers then what makes you think they haven't already stolen the rest? Anything having to do with Muerte?" Mike tried to get me to see the insanity of my plan.

"We're in this deep. And without the missing pages then we won't know how to handle this threat. We don't even know what the threat is. I have to go back." And I was the only one, they both knew that, no matter what kinds of worries darkened their minds.

I pushed the folder into Melia's arms and shifted back into a cat before either of them tried to stop me. My nerves were shot but I focused on getting the missing information. Getting back in and digging around. Someone called after me but I tuned them out, sprinting back to the Bureau building.

This time when I pushed my paw to the wall and forced my mind to change my shape again, the spells sucked at me to draw me deeper. They welcomed me, and the pain of the change, the agony of becoming the wall again, seemed more like a welcome than any kind of punishment.

Not easier, no. But at least it was a pain that I knew, and one I anticipated. That didn't lessen it to any extent. My cells warped and froze, torn apart and put back together in that same unnatural form.

When I popped out on the other side, once again human, the dizziness forced me to my knees. I sucked in great gasps of air until my chest tightened and ached like iron banded around me. Each moment I wasted trying to bring myself back would cost me later and I knew it. Yet every muscle twitched and pain pinged through me in an excrutiating wave.

Once it ebbed enough for me to breathe without wanting to cry, I stood up straight, hands on my hips. And dove back into the lion's den.

I already knew the entry hall from this back entrance held nothing but offices and none of them of use to me.

Rooker and Claribel... Where were their offices? Or did they operate out of cubicles? Sort of old-school cop bullpen kind of deal? I had no idea and no opportunity to find out without risk. I pulled open the interior door and glanced around to see if the agent who'd chased me out of the records room still lurked around waiting for the return of the errant bird.

I wasn't sure if I had enough energy to shift again. My knees trembled, my arms felt like pulled taffy, and the rest of me was just along for the ride at this point. Good thing the hall was still empty.

I tiptoed along, making as little sound as possible and feeling like I was made of rubber. Around the corner, the rest of the main hall loomed ahead and agents milled, some in groups and others with their noses pressed to the pages of the folders they held. I wouldn't get anywhere this way, trapped like a rat in a maze. Luckily for me, the Fae were inordinately fond of living, growing things.

Large terra cotta pots held towering ferns and palms.

None were close, though. I'd have to sprint from one potted plant to another and hope that no one saw me. I sent a pulse of magic out from the place inside of me and managed to shrink down, way too slowly for comfort, into a mouse.

My discomfort tripled despite my small size. Exhaustion crashed down, threatening to send me unconscious right then and there.

That endless well seemed a little hard to access right then, about a million miles away and blocked. I pushed myself forward, scurrying around the corner when one of the agents of the nearest group broke away.

She slogged toward me with heavy footsteps I felt through my body, and I swerved closer to the wall to avoid being squished. My heart continued to race as I jogged. One inch, two. And finally the shade of the plant hid me from view. From this angle it looked like the Sears tower and nearly impossible to climb.

My nose twitched, assaulted with the stagnant scents of too many Fae in one space. The group of agents broke apart with a laugh and went off in their separate directions.

I saw a straight path from one plant to the other between their open legs. A risk I had to take. I darted out from my hiding place and bolted toward the other plant.

"Fucking disgusting!"

Another female agent stomped her foot directly next to my face. I squeaked. Leaping up into the air, adrenaline and terror spurring me forward so that I not only made it to the plant but halfway up the side of the pot in one jump. I climbed into the dirt and huddled beneath one of the saw-toothed bottom leaves.

Too much, this was too much, and too many obstacles for me to come out of this unscathed. I'd almost gotten squashed! Someone had seen me.

I waited several beats, each second feeling like an eternity to my senses, then I peered over the edge of the pot. The group had disbanded and only a few agents milled around the main hall. With no one around to smash me flatter than a pancake, and with every instinct I possessed telling me to make haste, I scurried out of the pot, dropping to the floor.

None of the names on the plates affixed to the doors were familiar to me. None of them indicated anything I needed to stop and check out.

Eventually I made it to the opposite end of the hall and had to double back to check the names on the other side. Still no luck.

My gut sank and dipped, spinning in circles and making me sick. Did mice throw up? I was about to find out.

With a little squeal of frustration, I headed into another wing of the Bureau building, one I hadn't checked before. Rooker and Claribel had to be around here somewhere. And if they weren't on night duty then they had to have a base of operations.

I drew in a deep breath and tried to pick out their scent among the rest. It was like pulling a needle out of a haystack.

More offices down that hallway. I searched the names, and the more time I spent without an audience the more at ease I felt. Which was a terrible idea but it didn't stop me from scurrying out in the open and staring up at each of the names for half a breath.

Until I found a room with rows of desks and a very familiar piece of Spanish moss draped over an equally familiar blazer.

Okay, clue one fit.

The exhaustion ebbed a little more underneath the weight of my curiosity, my need to find out more about the two agents who kept giving me a hard time. There were several other agents stationed in the room, definitely giving me bullpen vibes except the view through the windows showed the shadowy impressions of more flowers and trees. So they had a view of the garden, which had to make work better for them.

I shook my head, whiskers twitching again, and shifted into my normal form. Each inch I gained cost me more than I wanted to pay. The change took triple the time it normally did, and by the time I stood on two legs instead of four, I keeled over, hands slapping against the top of the nearest desk to keep from falling face-first onto the floor.

Holy shit. I'd have to sleep for three days to get over this.

My heart pounded out an erratic beat that surely signaled a heart attack on the horizon and I forced myself to turn to the desks. Sure enough, the nameplates showed the names of my two favorite agents.

This was where they worked. Maybe they weren't high up enough to warrant their own offices yet. Either way, once I tuned into the energies, Rooker and Claribel's scents stood out like a slap in the face, one like a swamp in sunshine and the other like a desert after the rain.

I made sure no one stood in the door before pushing myself to a standing position, wobbly and unsteady. Time to investigate. Nothing untoward popped out at first. Nothing that screamed "*I have something to do with the murder and not you.*"

Although Claribel apparently had some strange hobbies.

A collection of antique hand and school bells lined the perimeter of the workspace she'd claimed for her own.

I'd known an elder in our pack who chose to collect dolls, and another who spent most of their time tracking down old cars. People were collectors.

But it was still weird. Something to do with her name,

perhaps. I reached out to trail my fingers over the edge of one of the golden school bells but stopped short. Leaving a trace was asinine no matter how badly I wanted to touch it. I couldn't risk leaving my scent behind in case the security breach was noticed.

Rooker's space was clean of debris and anything personalized except for a photograph of a landscape from a place I didn't recognize. He always did seem like the one who kept things professional. He didn't give in to his emotions the way Claribel often did when we were in the interrogation room. Which was not to say he was innocent in all of this, just that he'd be tougher to figure out..

I pulled open one drawer after another, skimming through the papers and assorted odds and ends in each and finding nothing with my name on it. Nothing related to Madam Muerte, either. Frustrated, I moved over to Claribel's desk, careful not to disturb her bell collection.

Her drawers were less organized than Rooker's had been. No paperwork, either. She must have another space for her files because they weren't in this desk, that was for sure. I pulled back, standing up straight and taking in a deep breath.

Okay, *think*.

Who would have a reason to take those missing pages from the file? Who would have access, and when did they take all those pages?

Those weren't questions I'd be able to answer tonight, but for some reason finding nothing in the desks stoked a fire burning beneath my sternum and all the way down to my hips. I definitely didn't have enough power left to shift, so maybe I could—

"You've made my night, Tavi Alderidge. Made. My. Night."

Rooker's voice sounded from the doorway and I froze, caught in the act and too terrified to turn around.

My fate was sealed.

18

The deep silence in the interrogation room was designed to keep any suspects unfortunate enough to be there on edge. I told myself it wouldn't work for me again, as it had once, but I had to admit it unnerved me. The silence, and the exhaustion. Everything combined to enhance my discomfort while they left me sitting there.

Especially because the Bureau was up to their old tricks. I sat *alone* in the room waiting for an agent to come talk to me. Rooker had pushed me into the cell-like space and promptly locked the door behind him. Hours ago.

A power move, and part of me wondered if I deserved it for breaking in.

Until I remembered those missing pages. That had me dragging every stray emotion back inside of me and locking it in a mental vault where no one would be able to gain access, no matter how hard they pried.

More hours went by until Rooker and Claribel burst into the room with their interrogative lasers focused directly on me. Through me. Spearing me in place with that look alone.

"Surprising, Miss Alderidge, to see you back here so soon. It seems we can't get rid of you." Claribel's smile turned viperous. "And at such a late hour, too."

"Without an invitation," Rooker added.

"It left us wondering how you managed to get so deep into the Bureau in the first place. It's not an easy feat and one has to wonder why you would go to so much trouble to get inside." She pressed her hands to the table in front of me and leaned in. "Were you looking for something in particular?"

Clearly they'd both been on the late shift and were more than a little tired. Not that Rooker's normal rough exterior gave anything away but his shirt and tie were disheveled and his eyes weren't as sharp as usual. Claribel's hair was limp behind her ears and there were lines around her eyes that spoke of the same kind of exhaustion I felt.

"What can I say? I really like you guys," I told them before busting out in a yawn. "I just had to see you."

They turned to each other with a similar look on their faces, one that screamed exasperation. Like they'd been hoping all my hours alone would have caused some cracks.

In fact that had only made me more determined not to give them anything.

"I really thought we were done with you for the time being, but it seems to me you can't keep your nose out of trouble for long. We should have guessed," Rooker continued. "Never in my wildest dreams would I imagine you'd be foolish enough to break into this building."

"It's nothing," I assured them. Or tried to.

Claribel grabbed the chair across from me and yanked it back with such force it screeched over the floor. Oh, she was *pissed* to catch me for some reason. I would have thought that she'd be almost victorious, Seeing as I'd been prowling in their desks.

"What are you doing here?" Claribel glared at me.

"Absolutely nothing," I insisted.

Claribel smirked. "You expect us to believe that? You must have had a reason to purposely break into a highly warded facility, which leads me to think that you had a specific goal in mind," she said. Her fingers tightened around the back of the chair but neither of them sat. What were you looking for?"

"Nothing."

Rooker shook his head and sank into the other seat opposite me, finally sitting. "How did you manage to get inside this building, Miss Alderidge? What did you do to break through the protection spells?"

Claribel's next question came out in a hiss. "What kind of magic did you work?"

Rooker shook his head morosely. "The last person who broke into the Bureau illegally was punished so severely no one remembers his name. Or his face."

The interrogation went on for another half hour or so, with Claribel too agitated to do anything but pace back and forth while Rooker just sat across from me and stared.

"You're only going to make this harder for yourself if you don't give us the answers we want," she insisted. "What's wrong with you, girl? Tell us the truth and we might be able to help you."

I closed my mouth until my lips were a thin line, an unbroken seam. These two would be no help to me. I knew that from personal experience with them.

She clucked her tongue at me before leaning over the table and baring her teeth. At once, the Spanish moss of her hair looked eerily similar to snakes. "You must be some kind of stupid, then. That's all I can say."

"I'm not stupid!" The words exploded out of me.

"Then you must be delusional," Claribel sneered. "Because only an idiot would be caught in the act. If you were going to trouble yourself then the least you could have done was evade detection. You've really shot yourself in the foot this time, Alderidge. There's no way out of this. And instead of helping yourself, you're just making it worse. Good job." She offered me a slow clap.

"I really thought she was smarter," Rooker added.

Claribel turned to her partner. "You gave the girl too much credit, clearly. Her halfling nature makes her weak and stupid. Pitiful humanity at its finest."

"*I'm not stupid*," I repeated.

"Then how else do you explain what you've done tonight?" Rooker glanced at his watch. "Pardon me. This morning. You've wasted your time and ours, and for what?"

"Fine!" I snapped, pushed to the edge. "I was trying to learn more about Madam Muerte's death."

Rooker might have smiled. I was too incensed to see him clearly. Red overtook my vision and crept along the edges until everything went a shade of burgundy. "Tell us more," he pressed.

And once I started, there was no stopping me, it seemed. "I wanted to find out more information because there is definitely *more* going on than meets the eye. It's right in front of all of our noses and no one is doing a damn thing about it. Seems all you guys are capable of doing is pinning it on me for being in the wrong place at the wrong time."

"Oh, like right now? Is that what you're saying?"

My hands tightened into fists. "I'm saying that I'm the only one who is actually trying to do something here. Because if you're looking at me as a suspect, you're looking at the wrong person. The only thing I'm guilty of doing is breaking into the Bureau because I wanted answers. Nothing else."

Claribel leaned closer yet so that her face was inches from my own. "We know that you met with the retired agent Elias Hawthorne. We know that you're stepping on way too many toes and digging into places where you don't belong. Now, do you want to ask me how I know all these things?"

Rather than letting her see my fear, I showed her rage instead. "At least I'm trying to find out what really happened with Madam Muerte's murder, which is more than I can say for you two. Maybe you should concentrate on finding the real killer rather than focusing on me."

Seething, Claribel pushed away from the table and paced. After a long moment she left the room without a backwards glance and let the door slam shut behind her.

Rooker, oddly enough, winced at the sound.

"Come on, then, girl." He rose to his feet. "Let's escort you back to the palace where you belong."

"You're releasing me?"

"We have to tell the king that you were caught breaking into the Bureau."

My heart gave a heavy, panicked thud. Rooker looked at his watch again, this time with a hint of longing, and I wondered if he was thinking about his bed the way I was. It had been a long night.

"Someone from the palace is expecting you," he informed me.

"What do you mean?"

"I mean we've alerted the proper channels that you are on your way home."

Oh goody.

Claribel remained behind at the Bureau to process the paperwork associated with my break-in while Rooker left with me to personally make sure I returned to where I belonged. My legs went from jelly to pure wood, my knees unbendable. Rooker tipped his head to the other agents filtering into the building for the start of the early morning shift, directly behind me.

"Please," I begged him as we walked. "Don't tell on me. Don't tell the king what happened."

He stared straight ahead, unmoved. "You and I both know that isn't possible."

"I think there's someone in the Bureau who has gone rogue." What did I have left to lose? I was in deep shit on this one. The kind of shit that I wouldn't be able to claw my way out of. And if this was the end, then I might as well put all the cards on the table. "I think the rogue is the one who killed Muerte. Not me. They're using me as a scapegoat to cover it up. Someone messed with the papers in the case file, too."

Rooker didn't slow or give any indication that he'd heard me outside of a small, barely noticeable tic in his rocky jaw. "Impossible."

"It's *not* impossible! Elias told me about Muerte's prediction of a traitor in the agency," I told him doggedly.

"You're crazy. No one in the Bureau would take out a civilian without just cause. We protect. We do not attack."

"But that's what Madam Muerte herself predicted! That the Bureau would go bad. There really is more going on than you think there is, if only you'd open your eyes—"

"I refuse to believe that nonsense," Rooker said with a grimace.

And there it went. My last chance, shot down. Each step felt like I'd dragged my feet through wet cement but there was no way Rooker would let me go. He'd haul me before the king if it was the last deed he accomplished in his career.

We walked in silence after that, with only the night creatures around us for comfort and even they sounded dimmer than usual, more distant. Like they were trying to find anywhere else to be. The guards manning the front gates of the castle acknowledged Rooker when he flashed his badge at them and stepped aside to allow him to pass. This time of night, surely they didn't get a lot of action. This would be the talk of the town.

"Don't you think we should wait until morning to alert the king?" I tried. "He needs his beauty rest. He has an entire world to run. There's really no urgency to do this right now."

"A message has already been dispatched. He'll be waiting for you inside." Rooker stared straight ahead.

I stumbled and he reached out at the last instant to catch me by the back of my shirt before I face-planted.

This really was the end, no joke. There would be no more second chances. There were already too many things not adding up, and once the king heard about my latest disaster, he'd flip.

Death. Surely it would be death.

I barely knew where I was, barely knew how to open my eyes or make my body cooperate. I might have sunk down to the ground if Rooker hadn't held me upright.

"You're going to have to go through with this," he admonished.

Like I had any other choice. Even running away was off the table now, because they'd simply dispatch people to find me and bring me back. No, I'd brought this on myself, and it was time to face the consequences.

"I did break into the office because I wanted to know about the prophecy, and the file. That's the only thing. I stole the file on Madam Muerte and tried to find more in your desks. Please don't take me to King Tywin. Please?"

Rooker shook his head. "It's too late. But thank you for your honesty." *At last.*

"Please!"

He escorted me ahead although he'd released his hold on me. Several guards materialized out of the faint dawn light to bring us not to the quiet office where Mike and I had met with the king to discuss our training but to the throne room itself. The ceiling soared, and yet the solitary figure dwarfed by the throne at his back kept my attention like nothing else. Held it in a way that made frostbite seem warm and welcoming.

He said nothing for the longest time. Only waited there for our approach. Waited for me to prostrate myself in front of him.

Tywin didn't say my name. He did not tear his gaze from mine until I stopped at the foot of the dais with the guards behind me. Rooker remained near the door as still as a statue. He might as well have disappeared into the walls for all he moved.

And soon, under the weight of the king's attention, everything else in the world faded away. It was the worst kind of tunnel vision.

"Do you understand what you've done?" he finally asked. His index finger twitched once where he had his hand curled around the armrest and then lay still. "You broke into the Bureau. Illegally. That is irrefutable. So save your breath if you have an urge to defend your actions. I find I'm rather done with your excuses."

I hung my head, an ache in the back of my neck a sudden warning that he might decide to chop off my head and be done with it. I'd caused so many problems already.

And the fact that we were alone here, that the queen or even Mike hadn't been involved...

A good thing, I told myself.

Mike needed to stay far away from this shit-show.

"One more offense—listen to me well because I won't be repeating this to you—one more offense and you will be expelled from school permanently."

It seemed a small price to pay. Too small, and I glanced up at him. He must have seen something on my face I wasn't aware of because Tywin's eyes narrowed.

And his expression went sharp, nearly feral.

"Not only school. Not only cast out from the Elite Academy, but from Faerie itself. The door will close, your access will be revoked, and you will be banished from this place and these people for the rest of your natural born days."

I stared at him through wide, burning eyes, my insides sharp and uncomfortable. "*No.*" The word came out in a whisper.

"You've been warned not to cross me. Repeatedly you thwart the authority of those around you, given chance after chance after chance." His hold on the arm of the throne tightened each time he spoke. "If the threat of banishment is not enough to wake you up, I don't know what is."

He waved a hand not just with regal authority but with a heavy touch of disgust. I was dismissed. And as I turned to leave, I wondered if my legs would carry me away from the royal presence before my knees buckled and I collapsed from sheer shock.

19

Banishment.

No more wiggle room. Not even room to breathe and try to dispel some of this sharpness in my gut, this box of spikes pressing closer and closer with each mistake.

There was someone in my room waiting for me after the king finished his verbal flaying. I shouldn't have been surprised to see Mike there, but the way he surged to his feet from the bed, the way his worried gaze fell on me, *surprise* was the only emotion left.

"Tavi! What happened? When an hour had passed and you didn't return, I sent Melia home then I came straight here to wait for you," he said, his tone urgent even when hushed. "I was worried that something went wrong."

I didn't have the energy to work the silencing bubble around us. And I didn't trust my magic at this point, either. For a second I floundered, with my mouth working but nothing coming out.

Mike got the message when I didn't speak and immediately raised a fist. The silencing shield formed around us and cut off all outside noise.

"Are you okay?" he asked softly.

No, not okay. Not even a little okay.

I burst into tears and Mike didn't waste another moment before stepping up and gathering me into his arms. "It's okay now," he soothed. "It's all going to be fine. You're here. You're alive."

"For how long?" I managed to get out.

He ran a hand along my spine before moving me to the edge of the bed. He dropped down at my side and cradled me against him.

"It will all be fine," he repeated.

I huffed but it came out more like a hiccup. "You have no idea how wrong you are." Did he know I'd just met with his father? Or had he been in here the entire time?

Safe.

I should be happy that he and Melia were safe. Why wasn't I happy? Because I was out of control and spiraling. Yet Mike's soothing went a long way toward helping me compose myself.

I told him what happened. All through the interrogation with Rooker and Claribel, up to the moment with King Tywin.

When the king—

I lost my voice, my breath. The tears returned with a vengeance and I buried my face in Mike's shirt.

"He threatened to kick me out of Faerie for good," I sobbed.

Mike stilled as he held me, his fingers twitching along my skin before he gathered me closer yet. His arms banded around me with such force I thought he'd grind my ribs together.

"We're going to figure this out, Tavi," he said gently. "I'm not going to let anything happen to you."

"There's nothing you can do. If that's what your father wants—"

When Mike spoke again, his voice sounded hard. Unyielding. And, I hesitated to think, just like his father's had earlier. "I don't give a shit what he wants. I'm not going to let anything happen to you. That's a promise."

The tears fell harder now, against my will, raging to get out of me. I pushed away from him, sniffling. Ducking and hiding my face so that he didn't see everything I needed to keep from him.

"I'm going to take a shower."

Not only did I feel filthy, but a shower would help me regain my bearings before I did anything else. Before I could *think* again. The rawness of the emotions, the feelings inside of me all battling for supremacy, the lack of sleep—it combined to leave me reeling and the only certainty I knew was that I wanted Mike to keep touching me, holding me.

Which was a bad idea.

Mike stared at me before nodding, rising and seeming to tower over me. "Come on."

He pressed against the small of my back with his fingers and guided me toward the bathroom.

Once inside, I shut the door, leaving Mike on the other side, and slowly stripped out of my sullied clothing. Stepping under the spray of the hot water in the shower, I let myself go numb. I pressed my palms flat against the tile wall and closed my eyes. Wanting to lose myself in the spray swirling down the drain, taking with it all stress, all worry, all fear.

I might have stayed like that forever if the glass door hadn't opened. And I didn't need to look up to know that Mike stood there. He'd peeled off his clothes and then stepped into the shower with me. Close enough to touch but not touching me, not making a move because he didn't want to spook me. Rather than running his hands along my skin, he stepped close enough to share the shower spray and grabbed the soap from the ledge. He ran the bar along my spine, down my arms. Along my hips and the swell of my rear.

Almost clinical in a way, except my body knew he was there. Knew if I arched even a little, I'd come into contact with him, with everything I'd wanted from him but hadn't allowed myself to have.

He finished washing my body and moved on to my hair, lathering up the strands with a floral shampoo that left us both sweetly scented. Then he reached around to cut off the water. I stood there, heart pounding and eyes closed, his chest pressed to my back. A moment later he wrapped me in a soft towel, leading me out of the shower. Another towel for my wet hair, then Mike wrapped a towel around his hips, leaving him bare from the waist up.

He led me to my bed and urged me to lie down. When I did, he followed me, sliding next to me and enfolding me in his arms.

Should I have been nervous? Maybe. But I was still numb, and the numbness didn't want to let go. It kept its claws in me even as he held me without expectation, without pressure of any kind, only the compassionate contact of skin against skin.

"Do you feel better now?" Mike asked.

I shook my head and, going on instinct, turned to cuddle against his chest, close enough to press my forehead to his chin.

"I can't go back," I whispered. "I can't go back to that

world. And I can't imagine life without you. I won't leave you, Mike."

He slid his hands along my shoulders and up to my damp hair, spreading the strands. "You'll never leave me, Tavi."

I clung to him. "Never."

The numbness gave way to something even more terrifying: frenzy. Panicked, freaked-out frenzy where my subconscious showed me what life would be like without this man at my side. Too awful to imagine.

When his lips found mine, I didn't think. I reacted.

I erupted.

His hands fisted in my hair to keep me close while he changed the angle of the kiss, deepening it and sliding his tongue between my lips. I wanted to melt into him as I arched to bring my body closer to hisHe stole my breath.

"Tavi—"

I didn't give him a chance to finish whatever he was about to say The king might threaten expulsion but there was no way I'd allow him to take me away from Mike.

I tugged his lips to mine again, my hands caressing, demanding. His touch heated me further until it was a wonder the towels, the very bed itself, didn't disintegrate into ash. Mike leaned me back so that my head was cushioned by the pillows and then slowly—*excruciatingly slowly*—he removed the towels until we were both naked.

And suddenly my body was on full display for him. For the first time.

Color pinked my cheeks.

He didn't shy away from me. If anything, it seemed that Mike looked closer. His gaze traveled over my clavicle, down to my breasts to the hard nubs of my nipples, and lower to the small thatch of auburn hair at the juncture of my thighs. Every part of me tingled and came alive.

I slowly opened my legs to him and he shifted between them, on his knees. Reared over me like some kind of golden god where I practically saw the strength of his magic crackling around him.

His facial expression held the question of whether I wanted this or not. There was one clear direction we were headed and we both knew there would be no going back once we made that leap.

This was inevitable.

And not just because I wanted him. I *needed* him.

Emotions burned beneath my sternum that I needed him to banish, to ground me in my body in a way we'd never experienced before. Or at least not in any way *I* had.

I reached out to him, dragging him down to me and clinging to him. Our lips crashed together and the last of the reservations disintegrated. He slid a hand between us to palm my breast. Hesitant at first, until I arched into him in a clear demand. *More.*

Mike squeezed, massaging the globe before pinching my nipple between his thumb and forefinger, making me gasp. His weight settled partially on top of me, one arm propping him up as if he feared crushing me underneath him.

I bear-hugged his chest to mine to show him I would not be crushed, that I craved the weight, the closeness, the...*intimacy*. When I shifted my hips just enough to bring me into contact with his groin, the last remaining walls between us tumbled down.

It was fire and passion and like nothing I'd ever experienced before. Mike moved his fingers from my breast down the flat plane of my belly toward the apex between my legs. The moment his fingertip trailed along my slit for the first time, I nearly erupted, nearly jumped out of my skin.

I didn't want to be upset anymore. I didn't want to feel anything except him. It became impossible to hold back my desire, and my heart fluttered happily, a living entity desperate to get what it wanted.

Mike.

"I want you," I whispered. "I've always wanted you. There is nothing about you I don't want."

Heat pooled in my abdomen and stoked my desire hotter yet.

"And I want you," Mike admitted between kisses, his touch light and feathering. "I'll do anything for you."

I grinned. "Talk is cheap. Show me."

I slid my hand along his spine, memorizing the feel of his strength and those hard muscles, the curve of his ass. I nipped at his chin as he brought his index finger in line with my core, his thumb pressed to my—

Holy shit!

He pressed directly on my clit and sensation erupted from the area all the way through me. This was what I'd wanted. The alone time with Mike I'd craved. My insides quivered and my core clenched around the finger he slid inside of me.

I wanted him more than anything else in my life, after so many years of toeing the line, watching him and being unable to be with him thanks to the limitations in my life.

Now there was nothing else between us. Only skin.

Desperate for more, I slid my hand between us and gripped him for the first time. That long, hard length of him already straining for me the way I strained for him.

"I don't know what I'm doing," I warned him.

When I caught his eyes, his were dark and hooded and

blurred. "I'd say you're doing a fine job," he replied with a grunt.

He was so soft and hard at the same time, his skin like velvet over that steely core.

I wasn't lying when I admitted I had no idea what I was doing, truly. I'd only ever kissed before. Only ever teased into my own pleasure but never with another person.

Mike took my lips as he circled my clit with his thumb, the movement of his fingers in and out of me matched by the way I worked him. He lifted his hand to my chest and squeezed one breast and then the other. I panted. I melted. My next breath in brought to me the scent of our combined arousal and apparently Mike had the same thought, as his cock jumped in my hand. My nipples tweaked harder.

And the look in his eyes when he reared back...

"I'm sorry for everything, Tavi," he whispered to me.

The thrumming of my body didn't dispel the other unpleasant emotions the way I'd wanted it to. My tears were much too close to the surface for comfort and my bottom lip trembled as the tears finally gave way.

"Don't cry. Please, Tavi." His movements on my core didn't slow or pause while he spoke. "I can't stand it when you cry."

I widened my legs to accommodate him in a clear demand, electricity building as he worked me.

I'd never been the instigator for things between us, not really. I hadn't wanted Mike to do anything he didn't want to do. It somehow felt like this choice didn't belong to either one of us. Only a natural progression.

And I refused to back down. No more space between us, no more tiptoeing around each other. I needed this, and he did too just as badly.

He continued to play with me until the orgasm grew and

built and ripped through me like his lightning. I came apart in his hands, throwing my head back with a yell. Mike nibbled the side of my neck and grabbed my hips, hitching me into the right position so that his erection slapped against my core.

His tongue drew along my skin. "Don't cry," he said again.

Anticipation grew and he pressed me back into the bed, stealing my eye contact again the way I wanted him to steal other things.

Not steal, no. I *gave* him everything willingly. No longer shy, and on the verge of giving in to my freak-out, I knew of only one way to banish the demons for tonight. He angled against me, working himself until I felt the way he strained against my moist heat.

"Are you sure you want this?" he asked. "You're not in your right mind. You're upset."

I dragged my own tongue along the side of his neck and down to his collarbone, loving the way he jumped at the touch. His words tapered off into a groan, my body clenching in anticipation. I opened myself wider to show him that I wanted this. The head of his erection pressed to me and felt impossibly large.

He was so damn powerful and delicious. There were no words left to describe how I felt about him, or what he did to me. I wrapped my legs around him and squeezed to keep him against me. His next exhale left sharply when I clenched, wanting to be filled.

Lined up with my still spasming core, he watched me, memorized my reaction, and tentatively slid home.

—*Oh!*

It was a completely different sensation than anything else, even his fingers. I moaned at the intrusion, and Mike clamped a hand around the base of my neck as he thrust slowly home, burying himself inside of me. A quick flash of pain accompanied the movement while my body adjusted to the massive intrusion, stretching and accommodating. He began to undulate his hips, a slow, easy rhythm to get me used to being filled.

This was... I had no words to describe it.

It wasn't the same flash of heat as the orgasm, but a low and constant pleasure from the way our bodies fit together.

So damn good and so right, being there with him. The beat of his heart went faster to meet my own.

What would happen if I—

I bent my knees on either side of his hips and the movement brought him deeper yet. Mike's eyes were close to crossing and his movement became erratic, his thrusting spasmodic.

And suddenly I felt enlightened with a certain rush of power. I wasn't a spectator. I wasn't out of control here. I was the one in control, his pleasure in my hands. Or, rather, in my body.

This was what I wanted for my reality. This was the fantasy I wanted to live every day in my life, where I got to bask in my feelings for this man and everything he represented. How had I managed to live this long without him?

We were made for each other. If that sounded clichéd, I didn't care.

His body inside of mine was paradise, the missing piece, my...mate? I wasn't sure how it was supposed to feel when you met your mate, but this was closer to what I imagined than I'd ever experienced with anyone else in my life. Not that I'd been with any other man this way. Mike claimed that gift alone.

I clenched around him and a strangled groan erupted

from his throat. He pulled out so that only his engorged head was still inside of me before he thrust home again.

"Yes. *Yes*."

My words spurred him on, coupled with the insistent lift of my hips to urge him to go faster. To give me more. *Harder*.

He slipped his fingers up from the base of my neck to wrap in my hair and draw my head back as he drove into me faster yet and without mercy.

"Yes!" And I said the word with each thrust, like he knocked it out of me. I arched my back to bring myself into better alignment with him, squeezing him through each thrust. He used his knees to push my legs open further, and my mouth went dry when I looked up at him.

This man...he just *knew*. There was no other way to describe it. I never wanted him to stop, never wanted to be without his body driving into mine. He kept me in place while he sought his own pleasure, both of us panting, the pace suddenly demanding and rough.

Each thrust sent me closer to another edge, just as potent as the first one. Our bodies smacked together and I slapped a hand to his back and dug my fingernails along his skin, no doubt leaving a mark.

"Oh my fucking God, *Tavi!*"

And I didn't shy away from the roughness of our coupling, not once I knew what to expect. My own cries took on a moaning, keening quality, my back pressed to the mattress to keep up with his frenzied movements.

His hips jerked again and at once he stilled, his dick pulsing inside of me, his own orgasm sneaking up on him while my core filled with heat.

Surreal. It was all surreal.

And wonderful.

We stayed there once we'd finished, clinging to each

other just as hard as I'd clung while I cried. Mike cradled my head to his shoulder.

"I'm sorry," he said against my ear.

I shook my head. "Sorry for what?" The fact that I could speak at all was a small miracle. I felt wrung out and spent, but deliciously so.

The first golden rays of light cut through my windows and cast gilded patches on the floor. Morning already.

I stroked his hair. "I'm okay, Mike."

He pulled out of me, reaching for one of the discarded towels before I had a chance to look at him. He wrapped it around his waist, with his attention focused on the windows.

The familiar tingle of magic wrapped me in a warm embrace, centering on the heat in my core until it melted away.

"They teach it in health classes at the academy, you know," Mike said almost casually as he reached for his clothing and tugged his shirt over his head. "A way to prevent pr—" Suddenly shy, he swiped a hand through his sweat-slicked hair, his cheeks flushed. "I won't leave you in a bad way. I've made sure of it."

My afterglow faded second by second. Mike pulled on his pants then sat on the edge of the bed to put his shoes on. I wanted to crawl on his lap, not wanting this interlude to end. But something about his posture told me there would be no cuddling, no hugs. The bond between us that had flared so alive and hot before guttered out, and confusion replaced those good feelings.

"Wait a minute—" I'd been open about my feelings from the beginning, but Mike?

"I'm sorry," he repeated, then went out the door without so much as a glance back at me. He disappeared as quickly as he'd arrived and left me lying alone on the bed that still smelled of our lovemaking.

He left me.

Every freak-out emotion shifted into an awful kind of shame and heartbreak. Had he made love to me because he wanted to...or because he felt bad for me? Was it *pity*?

His actions, the ones I'd told him spoke more than words, told me a different story now. That he'd done what he had to do in order to get my mind off of my possible banishment. Except instead of making me feel better, I felt a thousand times worse, with hot tears closing in like hungry animals.

20

A sense of the surreal colored my every movement in the next few hours, after what little sleep I managed to carve out for myself. All through work at lunchtime, I felt mechanical, going from one chore to another by routine rather than any sense of presence.

I acted like nothing had changed—even though *everything* had changed for me.

I'd had sex for the first time. With Mike.

Mike, the same man who'd filled my head and heart and sent my dreams spiraling with thoughts of *what if*.

He'd made love to me and I remembered every detail. He'd made love to me and then left me in the next breath. Left me without so much as a kiss goodbye.

Had he made love to me because he wanted to?

Or because he felt bad for me?

Those were the two main questions circling in my head. Love or pity? Pity or love? The more I thought about it and remembered his face on the way out the door, the angrier I got. My fatigue didn't help matters, either.

My mind was splintered into a thousand directions and

none of them really made sense to me. I had to try to act normal, whatever normal really was. Yet all I could do was think about Mike. It really sucked.

"Christ, Tavi, you're going to burn that towel if you leave it too close to the flames!" Raelynn admonished, her sharp tone dragging me out of my self-absorption. "Where's your head these days? It's like you're not even here."

"You don't want to know where my head is," I murmured as I raced to grab the hand towel I'd tossed on the counter just a hair too close to the open flames of the stove. "Sorry," I added.

When I turned back to Raelynn, she had her hands on her ample hips and her eyes full of vinegar and acid. "I don't care what's going on in your little brain. I need you to *focus*. There's no way we're going to get dinner ready if you're in here mucking it up. Do you understand? You've hardly worked at all during your break from school and when you are here, you're a million miles away! What's going on, girl?"

"I'll try to do better." What else could I say? Raelynn wasn't the type of Fae to accept any kind of excuse from me. And I didn't want anyone knowing what had happened last night.

I went back to one of the only jobs that Raelynn trusted me with: making bread. I gathered ingredients and mixed them, setting the bowls of dough aside and sealing them with a little push of magic. They'd rise for a few hours before they were ready to knead. One after the other. Bowl after bowl until we had enough bread to feed the entire castle.

"Tavi!"

Raelynn belting out my name brought me back to my senses and I realized I'd mixed an entire bowl of dough with cornstarch rather than flour. The difference in texture hadn't even alerted me.

"Shit. I'm sorry! It was a simple mistake." I looked around for the trash and dumped the entire bowl out.

Would this add to the king's ire, if he found out that I'd wasted ingredients? That his guards wouldn't have the bread they needed for their sandwiches? He'd *surely* kick me out and send me back to the human realm for that. He'd condemned me for Madam Muerte's murder even when I had nothing to do with it, since I hadn't helped my case by breaking into the Bureau.

The *corrupt* Bureau.

Moving to the sinks, I rinsed out the bowl. I'd still not found the wording for that prophecy, and Claribel had been so damn angry at me during the interrogation. Did they act the same way around Onyx? Who knew, because nobody I'd talked to gave a single care about the poor guy. No one at the meeting had been willing to step up and help him.

Worry for him gnawed at me, even with everything else going on.

On and on my mind went, turning over everything and landing on nothing concrete.

"Mix a new batch or I'm going to have you on dish duty for a month," Raelynn threatened. I caught the echo of her foot tapping on the floor. It went along perfectly with the tongue-clucking. "Do you really want to get thrown in the pit for good?"

That was what she affectionately called the corner where the hot water ran constantly by magic, always recycled so nothing was wasted, and little minions like myself worked to clean up the mess of everyone else in the castle.

"I'm expecting an answer, Tavi."

The demand followed her threat and I wouldn't say

either one surprised me. Once, I'd thought that doing work for my uncle at his law firm was strenuous. Office management type of stuff. I'd thought it beyond me. I was also seventeen at the time.

Now I knew better.

"I don't want to work the dish pit. I'll do better. Promise." I tapped the side of my head. "My brain is just a little mushy today. I didn't get a lot of sleep last night and I'm feeling a little woozy."

"Keep it in your cranium and out of my kitchen," she said. "We can't afford to throw out any more ingredients because of you. The guard is made of hungry Fae who won't wait."

I got it, I really did. I spared a glance at the wretched, steaming area of the kitchen where the dishes never ceased, and shuddered. Point taken. I'd be more careful.

Punching the dough in front of me would only ruin it and not help my ire one bit. I purposely slowed down and worked it the way I'd been taught before moving on to the next. Then the next and the next.

Mike, Mike, Mike.

Obviously I was losing it. Just like I'd lost—

I stopped, blew out a breath. Time to face it: I'd lost my virginity to the person my wolf wanted to claim for her own and who brought a whole mess of trouble along with him. Not that I needed help in the matter, either. It was only natural to keep thinking about it, right? To wonder about what had changed in me aside from the obvious. Or if anyone else saw those changes.

"Tavi, I swear on everything holy, this is it for you, young lady. This is the fucking end and I am not joking!"

I glanced up sharply when Raelynn called my name *again*, just in time to duck when she threw something at my face. It bounced off of my shoulder and fell with a hard clunk in front of me. My stomach sank fast.

"Someone stole all of the brain boost powder," she said through gritted teeth. The color of her face became fuchsia.

I shook my head, feeling the blood leach from my own face. "It wasn't me!"

"Like hell it wasn't you." Raelynn looked like she wished for something else to throw at me, anything that would do damage. "I regret ever turning you on to the brain boost powder, and now it's all gone? You've got to be kidding me! *Dammit.*"

"I swear by everything holy, Raelynn, it wasn't—" I hissed out a breath and ducked again when she launched every empty plate on the shelf behind her at me with a wave of magic.

"Get out! I never want to see your face here again. Do you understand me? You're banned from the kitchens, lass, and if I see you, you will regret it."

It felt like my stomach flipped itself out of my body. "*No,*" I tried to say, but the word fell from my lips as a mere whisper. I took a deep breath and tried again. "It wasn't me, Raelynn. I swear."

"I don't want to hear your excuses! You're fired for good this time," she finished, pointing to the door. "Get out of my sight now before I do something drastic."

The other kitchen workers went painfully still, their gazes volleying between us while they waited for the fallout. This was happening because of my background. Because I'd used the drug before and those blackouts caused me nothing but trouble. Because I didn't know.

Arguing would do no good. The entire kitchen remained silent, waiting for someone to explode first. I wouldn't give them the satisfaction. Even when my lower lip trembled so much that I had to bite down hard, I said nothing.

With as much dignity as I could muster, I tugged off the apron and tossed it aside, then held my head high as I left the kitchens.

But that was just an act. I felt the shame like poison in my blood. And it didn't help matters that I'd brought this on myself.

I spent most of the afternoon in the gardens waiting for something to change and fate to smile down on me. I waited in vain. The time came for my training with Mike, something that the king would not budge on and that baffled me. He thought me such a horrible influence but kept putting me together with his son for these training sessions where nothing happened.

We weren't getting better.

We weren't getting stronger.

We were just going in circles.

I wanted to see Mike more than anything. But I still fretted about how he'd left me earlier. And how the hell was I going to tell him about what happened in the kitchens today? The only obvious explanation was that someone had stolen that brain boost powder.

Someone had taken the brain boost powder knowing that I'd be the prime suspect. I was being framed. Did this fit in with what had happened at the Bureau? Or was this some new hell unleashed upon me? How did it all connect?

Each step heavy and wearying, I made my way out to the rear lawn and found Mike waiting for me with only a single guard. Mike looked over at my arrival but kept silent, kept his arms at his sides and didn't reach for me the way I wanted him to.

"What happened?" he asked the moment I stopped in

front of him. Dark circles smudged beneath his eyes and his skin looked extra pale.

"What makes you think something happened?" I countered.

"Dad isn't here. You can talk to me, Tavi. Are you okay? You look ready to erupt."

His guard shuffled to the side, his attention focused elsewhere. Nevertheless I kept my voice low. "You mean you actually want to talk to me? You actually give a shit?"

He had the gall to look hurt. "That's not fair."

"Fine. You want to know what happened? I'll tell you." So I did, and my anger surged anew at the retelling until my chest tightened and made it hard to breathe. My eyes suddenly began to sting. Tears were going to be the death of me. Having Mike so close made it all seem much worse, much closer, much more world-ending. "I didn't steal anything," I insisted. "I think someone is setting me up."

"Why would you think that?" he asked.

"It's too big of a coincidence that this happened right now, so soon after everything else. What if...what if the rogue Bureau agent found out through the grapevine that we're onto him? Or her? That I got caught sneaking into the Bureau? I told Rooker about the archives, you know."

Mike looked like he wanted to go nuclear. "You did *what*?"

"I revealed to Rooker that I was the one who'd broken into the records room, because I thought it would help me get out of being taken to your father. Which means that the whole Bureau could know by now!"

"You need to take a breath," Mike insisted, raising his hands like a shield. "Really think about this and what you're saying. Those are big accusations."

I shook my head. "I've done nothing but try to breathe

all afternoon, since I got fired. Breathing is doing nothing for me. And no one is helping me!" I paced back and forth, ready to set the lawn on fire with my footsteps. This was all wrong.

Instead of being there for me, Mike stood back like an outsider, everything in his demeanor changed since he left my room that morning. The area between my legs throbbed like a reminder of what now felt like his intrusion.

"You're not thinking clearly. This isn't urgent, Tavi. Take a moment to ground yourself and then we'll see if we can work this through. If you react as if this is the end of the world, then you jump to conclusions and only hurt yourself."

I felt like I was a top, spinning and wobbling and about ready to fall over. Another moment wasn't going to kill me, true, but damn if this didn't *feel* like an emergency.

"I, ah..." Mike cleared his throat. "I think we should talk about what happened this morning. I really think we need to discuss...things."

Immediately I wanted to be anywhere else. My fears surged forward, louder than the voice in my head. "We really don't," I insisted, holding tightly to my torso.

Please don't let my fears be true.

Embarrassment curdled my stomach. If he had only been with me because I was upset and he felt bad for me, then saying it to me now would be like the final nail sealing my coffin.

I couldn't handle it.

"No, I think we do. What I did...what we did together..." Mike trailed off and glanced at the guard.

"Look, let's just do what we're here to do. Okay?" I asked.

In what might have been the first break of my day, he

must have heard the plea in my voice and eventually nodded, dropping the subject.

And after a few hours, after doing my best to push all of my fears away and focus on the moment in front of me, I stumbled through the door back into my room.

I felt empty. My stomach, my mind, my spirit, all of me. Hollow. I wondered if sleep would come easily to me or not. Would I toss and turn, replaying and examining every moment, or would I be granted the comfort of sweet oblivion if only for a few hours?

I dropped down on the bed, my fingers curling in the sheets. Would they still smell like Mike? Would each inhalation be a reminder of what we'd done? Fetal position time. I pulled the blankets around me cocoon-tight and tried to let the rest of my life slowly fade as the sun began its descent. Day bled into night, and although my stomach growled for food, I couldn't eat. I didn't even want to eat.

Crapballs. This wasn't how I'd wanted things to be with the two of us. Whatever magic we'd discovered together wore off in the cruel light of day. Now someone was framing me? How had they gotten into the castle? Or were they already in the castle to begin with?

A caw sounded from the window a split second before a shining black beak tapped on the glass. Dark beady eyes peered in at me from a cocked and feathery head. Despite everything, a small smile twitched at my lips. I knew that bird.

I hurried across the room and threw open the window to let Bronwen inside. The moment I flipped the latch, she shifted back into her human form, whirling around like a ball of energy to grab me in the hug I desperately needed.

"Hey, you!" She practically bounced on her toes, the top of her head coming up to my chin.

"Hey yourself. I didn't get a chance to say bye to you after the meeting!" I exclaimed.

"I know, I know. I've been pretty distracted. I've just been *so* busy lately! I thought it might be a good idea to come check in on you."

Embarrassingly, my eyes teared up, and Bronwen leaned back far enough to scan my face.

"Uh oh," she said. "Something has happened. What is it?"

I swiped at my eyes to clear them. "Actually, a *lot* of things have happened."

"Well, good thing I have time, then." She tugged me with her and we sat together on the edge of my bed. "Tell me everything, and don't leave anything out. You're clearly upset and I must know why."

For the second time that day, and in a lot more detail than I'd given to Mike—because he knew the gist of a lot of what had been happening already—I walked Bronwen through my misery. The walls inside me came crashing down and for a brief moment I felt seen. Validated in a way I usually only felt with Melia.

Bronwen interjected occasionally with comments, at first angry, then incredulous.

"I'm at an impasse on what to do about Madam Muerte," I said. "I'm not sure if I even should be doing something or just lying low. What if the brain boost frame-up was a warning for me to stop what I'm doing?"

Bronwen was on her feet in an instant and pushing away from the bed with her usual endless energy. "Of course you should do something! Are you crazy? Solving her murder will solve all of these other problems you're having. Why don't you just reanimate the old bitch and ask her yourself what happened?"

I blinked at her. "Uh... Excuse me?"

She rolled her eyes but not unkindly. "*Necromancy.*" Bronwen paced back and forth, like she had too much energy inside of her to be contained. "It's dark magic." She glanced my way. "And it's illegal."

"Yeah, of course." I shivered with that someone-just-walked-over-your-grave feeling.

"*But*...it's possible. We just need the right supplies." Bronwen looked determined. "It really is the only thing to do at this point. If you want answers, then I can only think of one woman who would have them. She'd not only be able to tell you what she said in the prophecy, but who killed her. It's a no-brainer."

"*And* we have to not get caught," I supplied.

"Duh. Also it requires a blood sacrifice," she added. "I feel I should mention that."

My insides stilled. "Like...like cutting myself?"

"No. Like death."

21

Death. It sounded like such a foreign and huge thing for some reason, that eventuality at the end of every life magical or otherwise. For shifters, death loomed closer than most due to our animal instincts. Our very nature brought us hand in hand with death and there was no escaping what would happen. A cycle, we'd been taught, even as wolf pups. A cycle where we were born of the flesh and we eventually returned to the ground that fostered us through our lives.

A blood sacrifice, though... Was that going to be the cherry on top of this terrible and illegal idea?

I didn't want to die, but Bronwen further explained that necromancy wouldn't require my actual death but a sacrifice, a symbol with actual blood. In other words, we'd have to find an animal to sacrifice to complete the spell.

What other choice did I have?

It seemed so stupid to add one more illegal activity to my long list of sins. My sins, at this point, were only leading me down one path. This would either work and take me off that path, or I'd join the old gypsy woman in a casket.

I wouldn't tell Mike or Melia about this next step I'd decided to take, since I'd already involved them way too much. Reanimating Madam Muerte was something I'd have to do without them. Not to mention they'd both try to talk me out of doing it.

Bronwen, as a half shifter, understood a little better what drove me.

We both knew that sometimes you had to get dirty to do the right thing.

Although a little twinge of guilt colored my emotions, I'd killed enough small animals during my existence as a wolf shifter. I wasn't overly worried about one more, which sounded horrible, but that part of the whole dark magic thing didn't bother me as much as it might have others. Fresh blood was life. It was a cycle, and my wolf leaned into it willingly in order to reach our end goal.

It was the all-too-human part of me that held tight to my reservations and blasted those ideas inside my head. That this was illegal. Definitely, unequivocally illegal.

That if I got caught doing one more thing outside the bounds of King Tywin's laws I'd be done for good. Thrown right back into Kendrick Grimaldi's grasp and left with no way to help myself or Onyx.

More to the point, how would Melia look at me if she ever found out about this? How would Mike? My semi-boyfriend would not be happy to know that I'd performed dark magic.

Even knowing that necromancy would be the right thing didn't stop me from having night terrors that evening. I slept like a rock, though my mind was busier than ever, conjuring up all kinds of images of stalking monsters and mystery figures reaching out for me.

I was the blood sacrifice in my dreams.

I MET Bronwen down the street from the castle the following evening just before midnight. Without giving myself a chance to chicken out, I shifted into crow form, the same way she did whenever we'd first re-established our friendship. Better that way. The guards wouldn't report that they'd seen a crow flying overhead, but they'd surely tell the king if they saw me sneaking out.

Worry continued to gnaw at me from the inside out.

I landed on an arbor beside Bronwen and cawed to get her attention. She glanced up, took one look at me, and her expression hardened. She nodded and shifted in the same breath. The two of us took off, matching each other beat for beat, while Bronwen led the way down the slope toward the graveyard.

She was more prepared than I gave her credit for on such short notice. Not that Bronwen ever presented herself as flaky. But this was dark magic, serious shit by any account and in any world. The fact that she not only wanted to help but that she'd suggested it in the first place? It was hard not to see her in a slightly different light.

She landed on a gravestone, shifting as she did so that she perched there with her short legs kicking out in front of her.

I followed a second later and stood at her side, staring out at the eerie scenery.

"How do you know she's here?" I asked.

A chill crept inside of me and took up residence. I had no way to shake it off, either, although I hunched deeper into the black jacket I wore. Loose leggings and black boots completed the look and I felt every inch the grave robber I was supposed to be. A chill in the middle of summer. Right.

Although...was it technically robbing a grave if we were only waking up the occupant using the dark arts? It wasn't like we wanted to take her anywhere.

I might have laughed if this wasn't so ridiculous. And also terrifying.

"Most Fae, when they die, are returned to the land by the element of their choice. Burned, and their remains are given back. Murder victims? It isn't so simple. She wasn't burned, Tavi," Bronwen said as she hopped off the gravestone. "Which means she'll be here along with others like her."

I stared out across the sea of stone markers in the cemetery. "*All* murder victims?"

"Or those who died dishonorably over the years. It amounts to the same thing in the eyes of the king." Bronwen shrugged like this was old news and I wondered how much of the dark underbelly of Faerie I knew nothing about.

"And you knew where to find her?"

"It pays to scout ahead. This is serious shit, Tavi. We really don't have any room to mess up. You know?" Bronwen nibbled her lower lip. "She's just up ahead. Near the tree."

A gnarled tree wound dark limbs eerily into the black sky, but at least it was a good marker. Bronwen shouldered the bag with all of our supplies, tightening her hold on the strap, and gestured with her head toward the tree. Slowly we tramped farther into the graveyard.

It should have been freaky in the middle of the night and enough to send me spiraling right back into those nightmares. I thought I did a decent job of shoving those nerves aside until a dove's coo echoed from her bag. The sound had me jumping and clutching at my chest.

"What is that?" I asked Bronwen.

She'd been oddly silent about what was needed for this

little bit of necromancy. She kept walking now without slowing her pace.

"Pure white dove," she answered, her voice hollow.

Our fresh blood.

"It had to be a dove?"

"Pure white. If you want the magic to work."

I shook my head. "I still have no idea how you knew about this. It doesn't exactly seem like this should be in your wheelhouse, Bron."

"Sadly, it was part of my education once I came here. And, of course, all of the knowledge came with a warning not to use and abuse the magic. There's always a price to pay."

I narrowly avoided rolling my eyes. When was there not a price to pay? That was all I'd done my entire life. Pay and pay. There were good things, too. So many good things that came from the pain and the fight, but I wanted a break. Needed a break.

So tonight I'd pay again and hope that I hadn't created an overdraft.

"I really appreciate you doing this with me."

Bronwen stopped near the tree, her smile wan. "What are friends for?" she asked.

"This goes above and beyond friendship and I think you know that."

She froze at whatever she heard and turned before holding out a hand. I waited for a moment before reaching out and taking it.

"I don't have a lot of people that I care about in my life. I'm not doing this as a favor. I'm doing this because I genuinely care about you and I know you're innocent. If I can help you this way, then I will. Otherwise you'll muck this up."

"I wouldn't know what to do, you're right," I admitted. "I wouldn't have even attempted this on my own."

Sane people wouldn't.

"I understand. This is witch stuff, not what they teach in schools, and I happen to know the current monarchy has tried really hard to push all this stuff underground and pretend like it doesn't exist." She stopped, gnawing the inside of her cheek as she scouted for the right spot to set up. "Now comes the fun part."

"The rest of this isn't fun?" My tone went full-on sardonic.

"We have to dig her up."

Bronwen broke her hold on me to reach out and grab a branch from the tree. A pulse of magic rose from her palm in a green corona and shifted the branch so that it formed a handle and spade.

"We can use magic to make a shovel but we can't use magic to lift her coffin?"

Bronwen's smile was grim. "Yup, that's about it. Like I said, the fun part. It shows our willingness to complete the task. Think of magic like cheating, in this case."

I grabbed my own limb from the tree and although my magic wasn't nearly as seamless or forceful as Bronwen's, I soon had a shovel in hand. I stared at the rocky ground beneath the shadow of the tombstone, the moon a sliver overhead but casting enough light for this to be the most ominous picture of my life.

Madam Muerte had been dead for a year.

Neither of us spoke as we dug, and soon a pile of dirt was heaped as high as the stone marker in front of us. The tip of Bronwen's shovel hit the coffin and we shared a look.

"Easy," she said, swiping at a sheen of sweat on her brow.

She had her hair pulled back but small strands still escaped. "I told you. This was nothing."

"Sure, sure."

The dove cooed again and goose bumps rose along my skin. None of this was easy, not from start to finish. I crouched down and scraped the last layer of dirt away from the wood, fingertips brushing over the heads of the steel nails used to keep the coffin lid in place. Somehow the two of us managed to maneuver the head part of the wooden box out of the dirt to give ourselves enough purchase to pry it open.

The smell hit first.

The rancid smell of rotting meat.

"Damn." I pinched my nose shut but it did nothing to help. "Didn't anyone use a spell on her to keep her from stinking so badly?"

"It's part of the natural decaying process. Like I told you before, things are done differently for murder victims." Bronwen's voice was muffled by the sleeve of her shirt.

You'd think they'd be treated with a little more respect than simply left to rot in the ground. Maybe whoever had been in charge of the funeral hated Muerte just like everyone else seemed to hate her.

But I wasn't about to ask questions, not when the stench had my eyes watering. A glance down showed fraying strands of hair and teeth peeking out from her desiccated lips, the skin over her skull pulled tight.

"Well," I said, "let's start the ritual."

Bronwen and I climbed out of the hole quickly and she opened her bag. "Agreed. We don't have any more time to waste," she replied.

Time, the one thing I didn't have in abundance. Trouble? Now that I had plenty to spare.

Bronwen drew out the bird and cupped it in her palms. Oddly docile for being toted around in a bag. She placed the white dove down on the ground and removed several black tapered candles and a mason jar of what looked like salt. An assortment of crystal points followed and she set those out in a grid.

She drew a line of salt around the two of us and I mimicked her posture once she settled on the ground with her legs crossed and palms open.

A flicker of thought had the candle tapers lighting.

Bronwen closed her eyes. I kept mine open. Call it morbid curiosity but I wanted to watch everything.

"We call upon the energy of this world to cast sacred circles. One around me, one around Tavi, and one around the both of us, to protect us in this moment," Bronwen intoned.

The wind picked up immediately.

"In this dark hour, we use the energy of the earth to help in our search for answers and justice. We cast our grounding roots deep into the core, our attention traveling down our spines and into those roots. Deeper and deeper until we tap into the crystalline core at the center of the earth," she continued. "Tavi. Grab the dove."

I reached out for the bird, its body still but its little heart beating like crazy against its delicate ribs.

I'm sorry.

The poor thing had no idea what was in store for it. Or maybe it did, and that was why it stayed so still in my hands while Bronwen continued to chant.

An answering swell of power rose up inside of me at her words although I recognized only a handful of them. It didn't matter whether I knew them or not. The circle of salt glowed around us despite the wind ripping through the cemetery. The once clear sky filled with clouds blacker than the night itself, boiling thunderheads with lightning slashing in their depths.

"Bronwen..."

She didn't hear me. Or if she did, she didn't stop whatever words she gave back to the earth in exchange for the power we drew. A low moan sounded and it took me way too long to realize it was the wind, howling through the trees and the tombstones. Lightning crackled overhead but the air felt dry. No hint of rain on the horizon.

This was the realm, I realized. Faerie itself reacting to this dark magic.

I knew it. My gut sank as I remembered how bad it had been when I first got here. I was a dark spot in this place, and now I was doing something even worse than just existing.

"A pin through its heart," Bronwen told me. "Now."

I hadn't even realized I held the pin in my fingers until I glanced down to see the sharp point an inch away from the dove.

"I'm sorry," I muttered, too low to be heard over the raging wind. And without waiting for another sign, I pierced the dove's heart.

Much more than just existing—I was killing a bird to do dark magic. The moment felt pregnant with foreboding.

Once the pin slid home and the bird breathed its last, the wind picked up to such lengths my hair whipped into my face and debris began to lift from the ground. The salt circle disappeared immediately.

"Bronwen, how close are we?" I asked. I had to nearly scream for her to react to my voice.

"Too close to stop now!" she yelled in return.

She continued with the chant until the magic inside of

me rose to an almost painful level. It pressed against my skin and burned from the inside out, seeking relief. Seeking a vessel. I squeezed the dead bird hard before the magic left my body in a whoosh. At the same time a tree branch whipped up and slammed right into the side of Bronwen's head, sending her prostrate to the ground with her eyes closed and blood trickling from her face.

22

"Bronwen!" Her name left me in a panicked rush and I dropped the dead bird, scrambling over to help my friend. The limb had slashed her across the temple and split her skin; blood trickled from her wound and trailed down to the collar of her shirt.

She was out cold. Her eyes were closed and her lashes way too dark against the paleness of her skin.

I fumbled for a pulse amid the howling wind and threat of rain, finding it at the base of her neck. Thin but there. Reedy, I'd heard it called. I pressed my palm to her cheek and smoothed the hair away from her face before I drew her into my arms and sent whatever was left of my power toward her.

"Come on," I muttered. "Wake up. Please, wake up!"

She didn't respond.

"I can't do this without you." Fear turned me into a human icicle, but with my hands occupied I couldn't drag my jacket tighter around us. I could only hold Bronwen and hope that some of our body heat might be shared between us. She felt like a little icicle herself, her breathing shallow and her chest fluttering like the bird's had done.

The temperature dipped suddenly to the point where my breath clouded in front of my face. I patted Bronwen's cheek repeatedly, cradling her close like I could somehow shield her body with my own even though that was ludicrous.

A small tornado stole the last of the candles, their flames long guttered out, and sent them flying off into the blackness never to be seen again.

"You've got to wake up! Whatever we did, we did it wrong. It didn't work. Bronwen, please. I have no idea what to do," I screeched.

This was my fault too. All of it, the crazy weird weather and what happened to Bronwen. Because I'd done dark magic. Because I'd tried to escape to this place where I didn't belong.

It wasn't like I went out of my way to make that connection, either. I'd done this as surely as I'd chosen to take a shower that day. *Dark magic*. The weather continued to beat at us like it had a personal vendetta, lashing out at me as the rain finally dropped in hard pellets, icy and ready to slice through skin.

"Come *on*, Bronwen!"

This wasn't how things were supposed to go. Not by a long shot. And the thought of the weather responding to my doing any kind of magic was ridiculous. Yet there we crouched, with the wind and rain beating at us and debris flying everywhere. Something smacked the back of my head and I winced at the flash of pain.

I held up a hand and tried to draw on my magic, only to find it stuttering inside of me for some reason. A cold engine needing to warm up. Or worse: I'd used too much trying to raise a corpse and the necromancy had drained me.

But no. I'd been at the bad end of being overtired before. This was different. This was a blockage purposely keeping me down.

Bronwen felt way too small and too vulnerable for this kind of thing. How was I going to get her out of here if I couldn't even draw a shield between us and the weather?

The tenor of the wind shifted and changed, the moan deepening. I flinched, wanting to cover my ears with my hands. I was still bent over Bronwen when the moan sounded again, louder this time, directly beside me.

I finally turned around and my eyes widened, gut dropping, as Madam Muerte crawled out of her open grave.

The old psychic gave new meaning to *horror*. Newly animated, her skin peeled away from her face while the remnants of her desiccated eyes stared at me in their yawning sockets. She reached out a clawed hand, her fingernails curling out of the bone. Sloughing skin, pure white teeth. She moved like a ghastly nightmare, what was left of her old vocal cords grinding together horrendously. The sound dug directly beneath my skin.

Wind, rain—nothing stopped her. They whipped at her body while I stayed frozen. My own body refused to move.

It had worked.

Fuck, it *worked*, and the sight was more terrifying than I'd bargained for. I tried to scramble back, keeping my hold on Bronwen, anything to put distance between me and the corpse I'd called up. If dark magic did this, then I vowed to stay away from it after tonight. I'd never mess with the stuff again.

"You. The one."

I screamed, and still my limbs refused to obey when

everything inside me urged flight. I sat there like an idiot screaming my head off because zombies were real, and I'd raised this one.

"*It's you. The light...in the dark.*" Madam Muerte's voice was a nightmare come to life and elemental in the same vein as the weather. "*Light in the dark.*"

"No!" It was the only word I could form. It was the only word that came to mind. "No! *No!*" I scrambled again, my arms around Bronwen's shoulders and my feet digging into the ground like I'd somehow be able to force myself back. All in vain.

What was she saying?

"*...Born to rip the Fae apart...*"

Okay, yeah, she definitely knew it was me. Because that was part of the Faerie Prophecy.

"*Secrets and storms! At 'croaching light of black moon morn, a shifter child shall be born—*"

I continued to back us away as far as I was able until I hit the nearest gravestone, the heels of my sneakers digging deep grooves in the mud.

This was what we'd been trying to do. Wasn't it? I struggled to get my pulse under control, to wet my lips and my dry mouth in order to speak.

"Madam Muerte...who killed you?" I demanded. Okay, I had to try again. That came out all garbled. I cleared my throat and, as loud as physically possible, said, "Who killed you?"

"*Stormy skies, secrets, great prophecies.*" The corpse shook her head like it was a struggle to get her thoughts together and it hurt her to try.

I pulled myself together enough to realize it was the same thing that she'd told me at the Solstice Carnival a year ago. I'd been freaked out then, when she grabbed my wrist to keep me close while the words of the Prophecy rolled off her tongue.

I had no clue then what it *really* meant to freak out.

"Please, talk to me!" I begged her. "Who killed you? Who was it in the garden with you the night you died? What kind of prophecy did you make about the Bureau and the corruption there?"

She shook her head again as if in confusion, and inches of decaying skin peeled away from the bone with her movement. The urge to puke rose up strong.

"*The age of the Prophecy—*" Muerte broke off.

If I didn't know any better, I'd say she was pleading with me and begging me to understand what she wanted to say.

I tamped down the horror of being face to face with a real reanimated corpse and focused on the information I wanted. "You have to tell me who killed you. That's the only way we can help you and help ourselves. You know who it was, don't you?" I pressed. "You know who killed you and how to make this right. You really were a Seer, and just as powerful as the Oracle. Weren't you?"

She kept shaking her head, the wind raging around the three of us. Until a burst of unnatural speed brought her right in front of my face and my terror stole the last of the air in my lungs.

Madam Muerte grabbed me with a surprisingly strong grip. "*Not all rings are pure. The peal—*"

Madness danced along the decaying lines of her arms and face and in the empty sockets of her eyes, as if lighting them from within.

"What does that mean?" I begged.

"*The clear tolling can herald a celebration, or the knell of death.*"

None of it made sense to me. And the harder I tried to

figure it out, the more I racked my brain for some ways those clues stacked together, the picture stayed out of focus, just out of reach.

"Tell me who murdered you and I can try to help you. A name, please. Give me a name and we can put you back in the ground." I went for a smile and failed. "We can give you the burial that you deserve. But you have to work with me. With us. A name, Madam Muerte, please! Help me catch a murderer."

That was the whole reason we were out here in the first place. The whole reason for bringing Muerte back to life and attempting dark magic we had no business doing.

She cocked her head to the side. "*Murder*." The word was a growl in the back of her dead throat.

"Yes. Please, tell me."

I had no time to react before she attacked. So startled I had no chance to defend myself.

Madam Muerte took me down, on top of me, tearing into my flesh and silencing my scream.

I hit the back of my head hard enough to see stars, Madam Muerte's overly long fingernails ripping at my skin. Terror warred with agony and blood poured from the gashes she inflicted. Bronwen fell out of my arms the moment the zombie had me down but at least she toppled away to a safe distance rather than become a shield between us.

The zombie loomed over me with her mouth gaping open and dirt and ooze dripping from between her teeth.

"*Listen—*" she groaned.

I reacted on instinct, kicking out and sending the corpse flying over my head. She landed on the gravestone and plummeted down. I had two seconds to react, to drag Bronwen back away from the hole of the open grave before

Madam Muerte rose, shook herself out, crouched on her heels.

She faced me with a growl and her teeth bared like an undead bear. *"You need to find the light. Listen—listen for the ring to herald..."* She trailed off as if still confused.

My arms ached and with the storm raging, it would be a tough maneuver to get her back in the coffin right now. Especially with the need to protect the unconscious Bronwen. Rather than fighting her, I decided to run. It was me she was focused on, so I hoped she would follow and leave Bronwen alone. I hauled myself to my feet, determined to put whatever distance between us that I could.

But before I'd taken a single step, Madam Muerte closed the distance between us with that same preternatural speed. She grabbed my ankle and yanked.

I slammed down onto my stomach and screeched as she dragged me toward her, covering my body with her own and biting down on my shoulder. Those teeth tore through the skin and added more of my blood to the graveyard dirt, her claws pinning my arms down.

It burned.

I'd been bitten several times during a full-moon run. Sometimes the wolf pups got a little too playful, or the teenagers too rowdy and not in full control of their powerful bodies. This was different. Her bite burned like nothing I'd ever felt before.

The pain helped me disassociate but that thought stuck out in my mind. Her bite burned like someone putting salt on an open wound and grinding it in deep. I refused to even think about the implications of that bite, and despite the pain my rage swirled. Grew. Intensified. I focused it on the corpse on my back.

Somehow I managed to buck hard and put enough

space between us to shift our positions. I rolled over, knowing I'd have to try and surprise her to stay one step ahead of whatever freaky magic gave her preternatural strength.

"Not this time, you bitch." My knee came up to the small of her back hard enough to crack her bones. I did hear an actual, distinct crack, and a second kick sent her catapulting overhead.

Once I had her dislodged, I grabbed the tree-branch-turned-shovel and slammed it down on her head.

She dropped once again but didn't stay down long. Not that I expected her to.

"Why can't you just tell me who killed you?" I yelled in her face as she rose again to face me. I was a panicked, bloody maniac, but at this point it was either her or me and I wasn't that far gone to give up now. "I'm trying to help you!"

And then it was clear I'd made a big mistake trying to reason with the dead.

Madam Muerte launched herself at me the way a big cat predator would, and although I sidestepped at the last moment, one of her arms wrapped around my midsection and took me with her.

I lost my grip on the shovel.

She wrapped her hand around my throat and squeezed, pushing me down and slamming my skull into the ground once, twice, as many times as necessary to render me unconscious. Stars danced while black encroached on my vision. Her bite on my shoulder burned more fiercely with her proximity.

This was it. I had to find a way to defeat her or I was a goner.

I had no experience with zombies. Or any undead, for

that matter. Was there a way to get her back in her grave *and keep her there*?

I choked, closer to blacking out. Desperation powered a final struggle, and I kicked up with my knee. Three times—and she barely budged. My lungs ached and the rest of me seemed to go up in flames; no matter how hard I tried to push her off, even calling on my wolf and using every bit of the physical strength left in me—

And suddenly a burst of magic sprang from that dark, deep place inside of me that felt previously inaccessible. It laced my veins with lightning and slammed out of my palms and into the zombie, sending her flying back on a shriek.

The blast cost me more than I wanted to admit. And with my wolf still missing in action, still blocked because of whatever we'd done with the dark magic spell, I had no defenses left when the zombie recovered before I did. I managed to kick her in the face but that only slowed her pursuit momentarily. She was relentless, growling and lashing out at me with both arms. I landed a punch to her jaw and sent the lower bone flying off.

Her empty eye sockets glowed white with some kind of horrifying unholy light I didn't have a moment to process before she had me down again.

"*You're the light!*" she howled, grimacing down in my face. I wasn't sure where the voice came from, since she now had no lower jaw.

It didn't stop her from going in for the kill and trying to take a chunk out of my neck.

Pinned again.

Energy depleted. I was done.

An audible *thwak* sounded over the noise of the raging storm and an instant later Madam Muerte fell away, with her skull smashed in.

Bronwen stood over her, a large rock gripped in her hands. Her shoulders sank the moment she knew the zombie was down, her fingers holding the rock releasing and letting it fall to the wayside.

"Tavi?" Her voice trembled. "Are you okay?"

It took me way too long to get my breath back and each inhalation sent more pain spiraling through me. Slowly I closed my eyes, the constant drip of rain on my face both a blessing and a curse. I nodded to Bronwen and she crumpled at my side.

"It worked," she said, sounding surprised.

"It worked too well," I responded, my voice a thin growl of sound. Clearing my throat didn't help. "We've got to rebury her."

"Did you get your answers?"

"Not exactly. She was out of her mind." I pushed up, every part of me feeling steamrolled and achy.

Together we worked to rebury Madam Muerte, although the rain didn't slow and turned the dirt mound to mud. The wind continued to tear at us and sent each rain droplet into our skin, needle-like.

"The weather has gotten worse since we started," Bronwen remarked.

A glance showed her pale-faced with dark circles beneath her eyes but she didn't stop.

"It's my fault," I told her.

"Oh, come on."

"The weather in this realm has been shit since I came. And I'm worried that whatever we did tonight made it worse."

I shoveled mud back on top of the coffin, hyper-vigilant for a resurgence. Maybe the old gypsy was still determined to come after me and take her chunk of flesh.

Bronwen laughed. "There are plenty of half shifters in this world. And plenty of people who use dark magic. That's crazy talk."

"It's really not."

"You've let this whole thing go to your head."

"Mike told me, when I first got here, that they haven't had bad weather for years. Then I showed up," I said, leaving the assumption evident.

We scooped the last of the mud on the grave, and Bronwen, still a little woozy on her feet, waved a hand to smooth the surface of the ground. Although even that little bit of magic cost her, she had much more left in her bank than I did, and soon the ground looked undisturbed.

No signs of a scuffle. No signs of anything unusual.

"It's called paranoia," she replied, looking ready to drop. "Sure, the weather has been a little crazy, but it's a coincidence. Nothing more. Okay?"

I wanted to take her word for it but a little voice inside of me said not to discount the connection.

We stood for a moment longer with funnels of wind forming and dying around us.

"Are you going to be all right?" she asked.

I nodded, using my uninjured arm to push sopping wet hair out of my eyes. "I'll be fine," I assured her. "Please let me know when you get home."

"I'd hug you but you're covered in zombie slime."

I graced her remark with a self-conscious chuckle. "I get it. Thank you. For everything."

She dipped her head in acknowledgement before using the last of her power to shift. The crow took off and within seconds she blended so well with the night I lost track of her. I didn't have that luxury. Standing in the graveyard, I tried to call on my shifting power. Even wolf form would get me back to the castle faster.

No such luck.

I was stuck in human form.

The storm worsened during my trek to the castle and left me frozen down to my core. If Mike saw me now...

He'd *really* regret sleeping with me. And there would be no more pity fucks in the future. It would have been nice to know he did those things because he felt about me the same way I felt about him.

Funny how exhaustion had me going straight into my feelings. Each step seemed to last a millennium and my legs felt as if they weighed about a thousand pounds apiece. Luckily for me, the rain and the wind helped hide me from the two guards manning the rear entrance to the castle. Neither saw much outside of the rainwater dripping from their helmets.

I managed to sneak around them and drag myself up the stairs, my bones and muscles protesting. In the dim light of the hallway sconces, the gash on my arm looked worse than it had when I'd gotten it. I trudged up to my room knowing I left a trail behind me. If anyone came to question, I'd just tell them that the storm bothered me and I wanted to get an up close and personal look to make sure the roof wasn't about to blow off. It was late enough there would be no one out of their beds. Hopefully after a few hours of sleep I'd have enough of my power back to erase the marks.

It was a big if, though.

A throat cleared at my approach to my room and when I glanced up from the floor, Claribel waited at my door with a pair of handcuffs dangling from her spidery fingers.

Her expression twisted into a satisfied smirk. "I'd ask

what you're doing out at this hour, Miss Alderidge, but it no longer matters," she told me with way too much pleasure.

I opened my mouth to ask her what this was about then snapped it shut. I knew.

"The king has ordered your banishment from Faerie."

"*What?*"

"I'm here to carry out your punishment." She jingled the handcuffs. "You've been formally accused of thievery of the castle's supply of brain boost powder. Therefore you've been officially ejected from Faerie. You can make this easy on yourself or difficult. Either way, you'll be gone before dawn and never coming back."

23

"I didn't do it," I protested, my lips feeling numb. "I didn't steal the powder."

"You've been caught in the act and you're still trying to deny your involvement," Claribel responded with a self-satisfied huff. "Imagine that. I'm not surprised in the least."

She stood there, no need to move to cut off my exit because she knew as well as I did: There was nowhere to run anymore.

My shoulders sagged. Shame coursed through me because what with all the surprises of the day, I couldn't even be shocked by this one. I didn't have the energy to fight back or to tell her what I really thought. And at the moment, if I tried to bolt, she'd make this hurt. I'd had enough of hurting.

"You're silent now. I'm taking it for as much an admittance of guilt as you're capable of making. There is no way out and you know this. I know this. It's better for everyone if you come with me quietly and without fuss."

Did I pack a bag? Did I shove every inch of my life here

into a suitcase and take it with me to the mortal realm as a reminder? I shuffled from foot to foot, unsure of myself.

I'd fought so hard to prevent this, and yet there I stood, and all I felt was numb. All those emotions that had beaten at me for the last two days disappeared entirely.

"Can't I say goodbye to my friends?" I asked her. My tongue seemed swollen, making speech difficult. "There are people here I care about. I'd like to see them one last time before I go."

"If you really cared about them then you would have tried to stay out of trouble." Claribel cocked her head to the side while she stared at me, still not quite sure what to make of me. Did she see the spark that petered out to nothing inside of me? "I'm curious what you were doing tonight. You stink of graveyard dirt."

Her eyes narrowed. "But it doesn't matter, not anymore. You've lost your chance to remain a citizen and King Tywin is done with you. Come with me now without a fuss. This doesn't have to be painful for anyone. A quick exit and the realm can return to its normal state."

Without me in it. I got it. I'd always understood I was an interloper here.

I woodenly held out my arms to her, sucking in a breath when she slammed the cuffs down on my wrists. Binding magic coursed through me and tamped down whatever spark of power still flickered inside. Numbness spread down from the top of my head through my limbs and into my center to cut me off from everything I'd felt my entire life. Leaving me empty, blank.

"Let's go." She pushed my shoulder to get me moving in the opposite direction and, like Rooker had, stayed a foot behind me while we walked.

We made our way slowly down the main stairs into the

entrance hall and out the front doors. Surprisingly there were no guards around at this hour. The cuffs must guarantee that I wouldn't kick up a fuss. Why would they need to see me off? It wasn't like they wanted me around.

If anything, the guard as much as their leader wanted to see me out of their castle and their lives. It made things easier. Claribel had me well in hand on her own.

I hung my head as she herded me into a vehicle parked just outside of the palace gates. The wind did nothing to dispel a thick gray mist hanging over the river near the outer wall. I barely glimpsed the water beneath it and when I did, I saw that it ran sluggish and black.

"How did the king know?" I asked. "That I was out tonight?" Had he known the entire time?

Just like him, I thought, no energy left to even bristle. He'd probably known I would make a move and had his spies watching me, spies who had seen me take off into the graveyard.

Claribel remained silent. She got me set up in the back of the vehicle, with the cuffs biting into my wrists a little more with each inhalation. It was the first vehicle I'd seen since coming to Faerie, outside of the train, and was probably only for the use of the agents. I didn't see an insignia on the side of it but that meant nothing.

"Why did he send *you* to get me? To upset me, right?" I shook my head and squeezed my eyes shut. "He knew it would bother me the most to see you."

The last I hissed out beneath my breath, and if she heard me, Claribel made no sign of it.

"What portal are we using? You can tell me that at least."

Once again Claribel ignored my questions. She settled in the front seat of the vehicle that looked surprisingly like a four-door sedan in the mortal world, then inserted a clear quartz point into a slot in the dashboard. The car roared to life and took off without her having to press her foot to the gas.

Holy fuck, this was it. The end of everything. Shame eventually gave way to horror. Everything I'd worked for, everything I'd tried so hard to accomplish, and all for nothing. I'd never see Melia again. Or Mike.

I wouldn't be able to help Onyx. God, poor Onyx. I hadn't been to see him since that first day in the hospital. He had no idea what was going on, how hard I'd tried to get my name cleared so that I would be able to have a clear path to help him—

It sounded selfish now.

"Agent Claribel," I tried again, swallowing over a lump in my throat, "it wasn't me. There's something else behind all of this. None of this was me, and tonight, the graveyard...I have an explanation."

She focused her attention ahead without so much as a twitch to let me know she'd heard me.

"There's someone in the Bureau behind all of this. Madam Muerte—" I lurched forward as the vehicle ran over some kind of pothole. "She made a prophecy. Right? About dissension in the Bureau? Someone who heard the prophecy, another agent perhaps, was the one who killed her." Another thought struck me then. "They might even be behind the pure-blood killings! They'd have the might and the power to frame Onyx for the crimes when he had nothing to do with them, either. Please. You have to listen to me!"

Claribel still didn't react. She didn't have the excuse of a barrier, either, like one in a taxi or a cop car. Nothing separated us from each other. She either placed a vast amount of faith in those cuffs or she knew that I wasn't going to fight anymore.

Every last bit of hope left to me died sometime during the long drive. The storm made our progress slow, with a magical halo keeping the rain from the windshield. No amount of magic was able to stop the howling wind, though. It battered the vehicle and threatened to send it sliding across the cobblestone road leading out of the city and into the wilderness that surrounded the valley.

I lost track of how long we drove. Eventually I closed my eyes, focusing on the sensation of the cuffs and pushing everything else aside. My mind remained blank. There was no escape plan.

No plan period.

Nothing that would get me out of this car until Claribel decided to end the torment of her silence. Finally, in the deep dark nowhere, she pulled over to the side of the road and removed the crystal from the dash to cut the engine.

Still quiet, she got out of the vehicle and into the driving rain. The back door opened and she reached inside to pull me out, guiding me ahead of her away from the road and into the darkness with the rain driving cold needles of moisture into my skin. It seeped through my jacket and deeper.

"What's going on?" I asked, my teeth chattering.

"Walk." She bit out the word, and the surprise of hearing her speak had me stumbling over my feet in whatever direction she pushed.

Tree trunks swayed with the force of the storm, and limbs shivered overhead though leaves still clung stubbornly to most of the branches. Claribel stayed close enough to touch me if she had a need. I walked. I thought. I worried, and tried not to cry although she wouldn't see it if I did. The rain did enough to hide my face and wash away any evidence of my breakdown.

Kenrick Grimaldi.

Would he sense that I was coming, through whatever mistake of fate had made a match between us?

Was he lying in wait for me, knowing I was at my lowest point, and ready to pounce? To claim his prize?

My shivering deepened until my teeth clacked together and the bite on my shoulder throbbed.

This forest was not like the one around Eahsea. Not like the one where I ran during the Wild Hunt, thinking that Mike would be the one to come and find me, to claim me. These trunks were thicker and wilder. Older than those around the king's castle and city, as though he hadn't dared exert his power over them. They were gnarled and untamed in a way that spoke to the wolf at the core of me.

This time my shiver wasn't one of cold or fear but wanting. I'd irrevocably lost the chance to run through these woods.

Claribel drew me to a stop, maneuvering me so that my back pressed to the trunk of one of those wild old trees hard enough to send pain spasming through my wound.

"Where's the portal?" I asked her. "Why didn't we use the one outside of the train station?"

"Because you're not going back to the Fae Academy for Halflings. Haven't you figured it out?" she asked. Her tone said she expected a response from me.

I just couldn't figure out what that response should be. Suddenly I remembered how warm and welcoming this place had felt when I first arrived. Now everything felt cold. It was late in the night but the woods seemed darker than ever.

The discomforting sensation of something monumental,

something portentous, heading my way grew exponentially stronger by the second. The scent of pine and wet leaves tickled my nose as the sensation grew and I tried very hard to focus my attention on the agent.

"Well?" Claribel pressed. "You're not going back to the human realm period." She snapped her fingers in front of my face when my attention seemed to go in every direction at once. "Tell me. Speak up."

"But I thought..." I trailed off as I glanced around.

I thought we were walking to a portal to send me back to a place closer to my actual home with Uncle Will. No? Something was wrong. Very wrong.

Claribel called up her magic, and ropes twined around her made from the Spanish moss of her hair. She directed the ropes around my body with her magic. My eyes popped wide and I struggled against the ropes as a wave of foreboding crashed down on my head and threatened to drown me. The intensity had me gasping and I glanced around at the forest, trying to decide if this was illusion or terrible reality.

"Hold still!" she demanded. "Make this easier on yourself."

"What are you doing?" I shrieked.

This wasn't right on any level. Not because she was banishing me, but because my gut told me there were worse things that waited for me.

"I said hold still." Claribel slammed her fist into the side of my head hard enough to send me spinning. "If you'd just kept your fucking nose out of things, then this wouldn't be happening!"

"Wait—"

She hit me again when I didn't do as she asked and only the ropes around me kept me from sagging down to my knees. My head spun and the rest of the forest with it, a gray-black swirl of confusion.

The stars were back with a vengeance and when I swept my tongue along my teeth, I tasted blood.

"Shut up," she demanded. I shook my head and Claribel spat out something in a Fae tongue I didn't understand.

"Tell me what's going on," I got out somehow. "What are you doing?"

The ropes tightened enough that they forced the breath out of my lungs and I was right back in that graveyard with Madam Muerte. I sucked in as much air as my screaming lungs allowed when the truth hit me harder than those fists.

That was what Madam Muerte's zombie had meant by her cryptic "bell ringing" statements. Peals and tolling...they all related to the bells, like the ones on Claribel's desk. Like her name. How could I have missed it? When it was right in front of my face the entire time?

Too late. It was too late. The ropes bound me tightly. I was trapped.

"It was you the entire time," I managed to get out. "*You* killed the gypsy fortune teller."

Claribel whipped around to face me, her eyes inscrutable.

"You're the one behind all of it!" It was all so clear to me now.

The glint in her eyes was evident despite the weather, her facade of concerned agent falling away to reveal the rotten core underneath.

"*Yes*, okay? Yes. I was there that night in the garden."

"But I...I heard a man's voice."

She scowled at me. "You heard what you wanted to hear. There are all sorts of spells in place that can distort a person's voice. Do you think this is my first show, Tavi?

Honestly, you kids. You make me sick. You stumble into things and think you deserve a gold medal for being right."

She manipulated the ropes around me to bind tighter but still kept a good distance between us.

That night in the garden I'd heard Madam Muerte arguing with who I'd thought was a man, yelling about this being her show and the other person was just the side act. Claribel's statement cemented what I already knew.

"Why?"

The word barely left me before Claribel lifted her hands and her magic sparked in the dark night. "I did what I had to do. What Dorian Jade tasked me to do," she replied.

I started. "Dorian Jade!"

"You've figured out this much, girl. You tell me why the most powerful Fae would place me in this court. Put the rest of the story together and let me see how much you've managed to dig up."

"You're a plant from the Unseelie."

A weight seemed to lift the moment I said it, although Claribel wasn't aware. Even I wasn't aware for the longest time. I inhaled sharply, my chest expanding while the rest of my body shrank and tensed.

And the cuffs loosened. I had no idea what happened, amid the storm and the tumble of debris from the trees, but I wasn't about to stop fighting. I'd come too close to give up now. And I'd been right.

Right about all of it.

Claribel was the rogue agent, and she was also Unseelie.

Claribel clapped slowly in my face as thunder boomed, a backdrop to the smirk she'd adopted once again. "You couldn't leave well enough alone. You got too close. Is it any wonder that you're here tonight? You're the only one to blame."

The well of magic inside of me was not replenished, but it wasn't cut off the way the cuffs usually worked. I'd thought so at first, that initial blanket of nulling power so shocking to my system.

But there was a place in me that the cuffs couldn't access.

The exhaustion lifted enough for me to reach my wolf. The shifter side of me that always bubbled just beneath the surface. Those cuffs were supposed to work for shifters, because they'd worked on Onyx, hadn't they? In my human form, however, I leaned hard into that magic, something completely apart from my Fae side. And the swelling of my muscles with the change burst the cuffs and the moss ropes right off of me.

I slammed my half-shifted claws into Claribel's face and hoped she'd go down in one blow.

She did not.

24

She lashed out at me with more magic than I'd seen her use before. I slammed back against the tree trunk with the ropes keeping me pinned and powerless. I pushed several of them away from my face while the others wrapped around my ankles, the cuffs jangling around my wrists with each movement.

"I don't want to kill you," Claribel stated.

No, just hurt me. I focused every bit of magic left to me on dealing with the ropes, sending a pulse out and disintegrating them. Which worked for approximately two seconds before Claribel summoned more and pushed me back a second time. The air exploded forcefully from my lungs.

The dregs of my magic felt a little too far away for me to access with any kind of ease. Instead, I closed my eyes and went not for the pool of power but as close as I was able to get. The cuffs kept a blanket of numbness around me but if I could just find a way through that, to my shifter magic—

There.

A glow in the darkness.

I saw the picture in my head and held it as tightly as

possible when it wanted to change and become something else. My limbs shortened so that the ropes had no purchase and in place of my human body floated a sparrow, the cuffs dropping to the forest floor.

I had to get away as far as possible. Claribel might not want to kill me but she'd made it clear she wanted to take me down and keep me there.

Without hesitation I darted up into the tree limbs, with Claribel's ropes following, reaching, only inches behind me.

A quick shift to something smaller did the trick but only briefly. Heart beating hard enough to crack my ribs, I flew closer to the tree trunk, hoping to hide.

"Do you understand *anything* that's happening?" Claribel called out after me. "You've muddled your way into too much truth, but do you truly understand what's going on, Miss Alderidge?"

I found it funny that she called me by my last name now. At this point? After everything?

"Come on out, little girl. Make this easier on yourself. Fighting it is only prolonging the inevitable. I'm not here to kill you, as I've said. Come out, come out."

The woods around us fell silent outside of the wind and rain while Claribel bided her time.

"Dorian Jade has plans for you, girl."

Her voice sounded directly next to my head and I bolted forward, slamming into the tree trunk hard enough to knock myself back. The bird's eyes saw enough but not with fear driving me the way it did.

Claribel floated above one of the large limbs and reached out to grab me. And when she did, she squeezed, her teeth flashing white in the darkness.

"Such big plans," she continued, her voice still loud even

when she dropped it low. "You have more power than any of us thought, and this proves it to me."

She squeezed again and breath exploded from my body, pain taking its place.

I reacted on instinct then, the picture in my head one that I saw in the mirror every day. Claribel didn't expect me to shift back to human form. She quickly dropped her hold and I pivoted as the change completed, kicking off of the tree trunk and using the momentum to hurl myself at the agent.

We collided in a crash that sent us both hurtling down to the ground. I landed on top of Claribel, driving her head into the tree roots.

Her hands came around my neck and squeezed as her power sent her rope hair jettisoning out toward me.

"You and Dorian Jade can go eat a brick," I grunted out, forced to divide my attention between her and those ropes.

If they gained any purchase then I'd go unconscious and I didn't need to be psychic to understand that.

Claribel would stop at nothing.

She focused her attention on my upper body rather than my lower. Instead of forcing her to let go, I fell back, the ropes binding us taking her with me so that she reared overhead, her eyes wide in surprise. And that was when I kicked her in the side.

She keeled over, the ropes falling away and giving me a moment to scramble onto my hands and knees. I lurched to my feet, only to have Claribel punch her power at me. Enough to have me scrambling backwards.

"Power, yes," she continued, shoulders hunched and chest heaving, "but untrained."

"I have a mentor. Two of them, actually, and they're both better people than you are."

She punched out again and I blocked her, though the hit sent a shock wave through me from the top of my head to the soles of my feet.

I threw up a hand and blocked Claribel's next hit with a halo of magic. Our two powers clashed and sparks flared to life between us, crackling in the rain. Ozone singed the inside of my nose with each inhalation.

Magic built up inside of me now that the cuffs were off, the magic of survival, and I let it flow up. Flow out. Hotter and stronger and better than any kind of power I'd used before. Every part of me trembled with the effort of holding such strength so I sent it flying toward Claribel.

She rose off the ground, spun, and deflected all of that power.

It hit the car, some of it absorbed and a line of it reflected back. I directed it toward her and the magic lassoed around her wrist to tug her off of her feet.

With her free hand, Claribel swung her own magic in a circle overhead and aimed. It hit a tree behind me and set the whole thing on fire.

With the time in this fight ticking down too fast, I poured all of my energy into my next hit. If she didn't go down, what with the downpour and my exhaustion, then I didn't want to think about what would happen.

Day after day I'd been exhausted and toeing a line, neither of which seemed to ever end, I thought as I drew up my power. The midnight darkness in my hands shimmered with sparks of red and gold bursting to life like mini supernovas, the magic beating inside of me like my pulse.

And Claribel blocked me with her Spanish moss before I had a chance to let it loose. The power guttered and sparked before it fell away to darkness, her ropes cutting off my air supply.

"Shit," I managed to get out. Punching at her and aiming for her torso but coming up short.

Claribel's hair was a wet and wild mass on her face. She shot me a disgusted look, the ropes binding me to the gnarled old tree, where thankfully the heavy rain had extinguished the fire. "You think you can go up against the biggest threat there is," she ground out. She cracked her knuckles against the side of my head. "Stupid, stupid child. You have no idea what you're doing and that's how you've gotten yourself in this situation."

The magic inside of me guttered and it seemed to me that the tighter the ropes became, the harder it was for me to think. The lack of oxygen had my brain turning to mush.

Claribel wrapped me like a mummy so that only my eyes showed, since she knew about the shifting now.

And once she was satisfied that she'd done the job well, once she knew without a doubt that I wouldn't be able to attack her again, she chuckled.

"You put up one hell of a good fight." She rubbed her jaw. "And a few good hits in there to boot. It's too bad you're *lazy*."

I tried to repeat the word back to her as a question, but no sound came out. I coughed when my next inhale brought with it fibers of the moss rope rather than fresh air.

"Lazy and untrained and willful. In any other circumstances I might have actually admired you," she admitted, pushing a lock of Spanish moss behind her ear. "In these circumstances? You are a thorn in my side that will soon be eradicated. Enjoy your last breaths."

Then she left me.

Alone in the dark and stormy night with rain lashing at my eyes, unable to move, barely able to take a breath.

I'm dead.

This was it. It had to be the end for me.

I'd always tried not to give in to those kinds of thoughts although I had them often, and it seemed that now, after a rough night and more injuries than I could count—first with the zombie, and then with Claribel—my struggle to remain hopeful reached an end point.

After Claribel disappeared and the sound of the vehicle taking off down the road disappeared with her, I struggled against the bindings. I twisted for a long time to get a little leeway but she'd bound me too tightly.

Something about the way she'd in effect mummified me against the tree kept me from not only accessing my power but being able to shift at all.

Panic wore me down faster than anything else and when the adrenaline ran its course, I passed out.

The dark of unconsciousness held nothing for me, though. Nothing but more pain and an endless, sweeping tiredness written into my very bones. When I finally regained consciousness, I wasn't sure how much time had passed, but the rain never ceased and the sky hadn't lightened.

I tried to move and hissed out a frustrated breath at the tightness of the ropes and whatever Claribel had done to them to keep me paralyzed in this cocoon.

But that little power nap had allowed a tiny period of rest, and with the increase in energy came something else.

A renewed determination to survive.

Gritting my teeth, I struggled, bucking and swiveling to fight against the prison.

If Claribel and Dorian Jade got their way, they'd destroy the people I cared about. And if I didn't get out of this prison, then no one would be able to tell Mike and the others that their enemies gathered and would come for them.

Sooner than anyone expected.

My struggle did nothing for the longest time and my frustration grew to unbearable proportions, biting at me as surely as the coarse fibers.

That horrible woman! She had the nerve to charge after me this whole time knowing full well she was the one to blame.

I twisted harder.

She was the one who had done all of this to us and left me here to die, left me here for the elements to take.

The fury inside of me burned hotter than the exhaustion and hotter than any power out of my reach. With a roar, I somehow managed to shift. Not fully, and not into my pure halfling warrior form.

Something in between.

Some kind of monster created out of pure rage and countless injustices. A monster determined to fight no matter how bad the circumstances, and as fur sprouted along the lines of my trapped arms, a new kind of strength was born from the abyss of knowing I'd do whatever it took to survive.

The force and might of the wolf form allowed me to fight harder against the bindings. The ache in my bones faded away as they slowly loosened with my amplified strength.

Bucking, yanking, trying to get some leeway. Eventually I scraped through the ropes around my face, the fibers peeling back skin and scratching deep, and I could breathe at last.

The rain washed the blood away but I tasted it on my tongue.

Almost there. Only a little further and I'd be able to—

A fierce roar cut over the sound of the storm and sent the leaves scattering across the clearing. When I glanced up, a giant creature stalked out of the gloom toward me, eyes glowing red.

Dorian Jade's champion had come to finish me off.

Try as hard as I might to be strong, fear curdled my insides, and I wondered if I'd survived the ordeal with Claribel only to face a worse end.

25

The creature was like nothing I'd ever seen before. He towered over me, towered over my bastardized wolf form which were some of the strongest forms I'd ever seen. A halfling warrior could pretty much take on anything, and yet the creature before me gave me serious pause.

Standing with arms at its sides, chest heaving, its height reached halfway up the trunk of the nearest tree. Red eyes fixed on me, the same deep red color as the heart of a forge with a strong-armed blacksmith working the bellows. It seemed a strange amalgam of creatures from claws befitting a lion, to a body the size of a horse, with the muscular chest of an ox, and the sleek torso and hind legs of a wolf.

Keeping eye contact, it crept closer, saliva glinting among its canines. Closer and closer until my struggle against those bonds became very real and very frantic. Even in my full warrior form I'd be no match for this beast and we both knew it.

The monster swaggered forward on all fours and

stopped when it was close enough for me to smell its breath. Foul and fetid and stinking of death.

No, *no*.

I didn't dare speak or make any kind of noise, only kept up my struggling against the bonds that held me.

Closer still, towering over me. The beast lifted its front paw and swiped down without mercy. A scream erupted as its claws dug deep furrows in my side.

But they also cut through the bindings.

The rest of the ropes fell away and I sagged forward, with the monster dropping onto me half a beat later. With an unmatched ferocity it bit down into my shoulder, the one that Madam Muerte hadn't tried to take a chunk out of, and blood poured from the punctures.

My screams continued without end until even my own ears wanted to rupture from the sound. And the *pain*—unlike anything. It burned. It *burned*. My strength ebbed to a dangerous level.

Yet—

My brain still worked, thankfully, and I realized something about this creature that I wouldn't have guessed from looking at it the first time.

Him, I corrected, my thoughts getting dimmer even as I tried to maintain focus. He was a direwolf. And he'd been sent by Dorian Jade.

Any more blood loss and they'd accomplish the job, we both knew it. I kicked at the underside of the creature before my feet shifted into the paws I needed. The sharp dagger-like talons I needed to gain purchase on his sensitive belly. Although my cuts were only skin-deep, the surprise of a counterattack had the direwolf letting go of my shoulder.

I'd learned to take advantage of those small moments. The ones that made all the difference in the long fight.

He caged me between his arms but there was enough space for me to shift. For me to reach for my powers and allow the change to sweep through me. I grew beneath the direwolf into my halfling form, muscles bulging and dark fur sprouting along my arms and legs and back. I lurched up and knocked into the beast to get him off-balance.

A growl tore from the back of his throat as he rounded on me, looking entirely unsurprised to see another monster staring at him rather than a human girl. A strange sort of intelligence showed on his animal face but it didn't stop him from attacking again before I drew my next breath.

We came together in a clash of fury, the direwolf going for the wounds on my shoulders while I dove for the gouges on his stomach. I tried to avoid his teeth and claws but my next hit felt like hitting a brick wall. His muscles did not budge.

I swatted at him with my power next, accompanying the hit with a swift kick from my rear legs straight into the creature's ribs.

I fought for my survival, for the world Dorian Jade wanted to tear apart, and for everyone in it. I fought even knowing I was too tired and overmatched to win. I could barely see the beast through the rain as we battled with built-in weapons and magic.

He reared over me with a bloody muzzle and his eyes were feral.

Fierce.

I leaped out of the way as he charged at me and managed to put the tree between us this time. The rain thickened between us and it seemed that we fought outside of time. Desperate and enraged. Surrounded by nature and rivalries older than ourselves.

He swiped at me and those claws whizzed by my head,

taking a sizable slice out of the tree. Splinters erupted from the hit and peppered my face.

I called up my power even in this form, bringing one of the fallen limbs from a tree behind me and sending it, spear-sharp, to try and impale the direwolf. The makeshift spear went across the line of his spine and trailed blood behind it but did not stop him. Did not even slow him down.

He clawed at the slippery ground to propel himself forward and hit me in the middle of my back when I spun to bolt. I hit the ground hard enough to rattle the teeth in my elongated jaws. A quick pulse of magic placed a shield between our two bodies and the direwolf snapped at the barrier. Bellowed in frustration when it didn't give out although his rear legs still pinned me down and made escape impossible.

How much longer would I be able to keep this up, I wondered as he battered against my measly defenses. Going on the offensive seemed impossible, and my strength for defense was ebbing fast.

I managed to carve out a path between his thick front legs and rose. Unsteadily, yet I rose. To my dying breath I'd do my best to end this so that no one else would be hurt. The direwolf stayed behind, biting at the shield as I attacked this time with everything I had left in me.

Snapping at the back of his neck until my teeth slid through the skin, I latched on. He roared, rearing back and slamming me into the tree where Claribel had tied me. When the first hit didn't dislodge me, he slammed me backwards a second time and my head cracked on the unyielding trunk. I saw stars and an encroaching darkness.

Slowly I slid off of him and crumpled, whimpering.

I'd fought plenty in my time. Even the fight with Onyx hadn't been smooth or easy. This was something else entirely, like a gnat beating itself against a ship hoping to change its course. The direwolf overpowered me in every way, and all I could do now was try to stay out of its way.

I put as much distance between us as my failing strength allowed, yet he kept pushing forward, trying to corral me. The boundaries of the trees around the clearing seemed to crowd forward as well in a completely different type of cage.

"Why do you want to hurt me so badly?" I called out, my voice deeper and garbled in this form. "Tell me."

The thing growled in response and the fury in his red gaze deepened. Whatever made this creature the way it was, he hated me with everything inside of him. No magic, true, but with his brute strength he didn't need any.

The crown needed to know about this. *If* I made it out of this clearing in one piece. Even a few pieces would be a better option than death.

With a feral roar of my own, we both charged at the same time and his paw collided with my face, snapping my head back on my neck. The pain was intense but it was nothing compared to my chest and the tightness there when his body covered mine and he pushed me to the ground. Pushed me *into* the ground a few inches beneath the surface.

The immovable pressure of his body against mine demolished the last of my hard-won hope. It disintegrated bit by bit leaving me empty inside. The power keeping me shifted into my halfling warrior form stuttered and died until I shifted back to human form beneath the creature.

Weak and defenseless.

The direwolf wasn't confused by the change, or if he was he didn't show it. He only bent his massive head to the side of my neck and sniffed like he wanted to draw my essence inside of him.

A desperate cry erupted from the back of my throat against my will and I squeezed my eyes shut as though that would somehow help me find if not hope, then a little internal fortitude. That same will to survive I'd felt with Claribel.

Except she'd been a Fae capable of reasoning. Maybe she refused to reason but at least I knew I could speak to her.

The direwolf? Was a different story entirely.

"Please," I whispered. "Whoever sent you here to kill me, you don't have to do this. I'm not your enemy."

My words didn't seem to penetrate his animal mind whatsoever.

I felt his growl against my skin, spreading terror through me like fire. His eyes burned like coals and those teeth continued to gleam. Those teeth were death, coming for me, his only reason for being here. I sucked in a final breath—

A crack of lightning flashed overhead, splitting the sky and illuminating the clearing enough for me to make out the individual whiskers protruding from the direwolf's snout. The crack grew louder, morphing into the sound of splintering wood, and in the next instant, a large tree limb dropped from overhead and cracked against the creature's spine.

He fell with a yelp, pinning me with enough force to grind my bones into dust. My scream mingled with his whine of pain.

I lifted my hands between us automatically and pushed against his chest to make some room for myself. The tree limb, larger than my torso, kept the wolf down while I scrambled. The heels of my sneakers dug into the earth but it wasn't enough to get me out of there. And trying to move the wolf was no use. The ground had more yield than his body.

With the limb keeping him down, keeping him disoriented, I somehow managed to maneuver my body enough to turn over onto my belly and claw and dig my way out. He dropped into the space my body had vacated, growling and craning his neck to snap at the wood and dislodge it.

Thank God for mother nature.

I sat for the briefest moment against the trunk of a neighboring tree, attempting to calm myself and get my breath back, staring at the direwolf. Now was my chance to run and pray for escape.

Even with the rain hiding my scent, my wounds would make it impossible for me to get far, and any kind of trail I made, he'd be able to follow. Too exhausted to move, I could only stare as the direwolf lurched a long arm forward.

His claws buried into my ankle and yanked me forward. The tree limb over his back toppled to the side, and he reared above me. A flash of triumph turned his eyes gold before they settled back into that familiar red glow. My heart plummeted.

Oddly enough, my fear faded away as my body automatically attempted to shift into any form other than my own. But no, nothing. Not so much as a tuft of fur as I bled from more places than I could count.

The direwolf roared in my face and spittle flew.

He pinned me beneath him again, with his claws flexing above my heart, pausing as if making sure I knew the end was near. Five seconds from certain death and I was out of options.

The weight pushed me into the rain-soft ground and a pitiful whimper erupted from my own throat. Those claws would rip out my heart, and those teeth would shred me in an instant.

I knew how my blood would taste to him.

Hot and metallic. And delectable. Irresistible.

He'd gobble me down like a—

26

My *cognitive manipulation power.*

I hadn't tried that yet. A fresh wave of adrenaline spiked through me. I might not have my shifting powers but I hadn't tried that one since the cuffs came off. Surely I wasn't still blocked, right? By anything other than my own exhaustion.

In fact I hadn't tried cognitive manipulation for the longest time. And I'd never attempted it on an animal before. Not as if I'd had many opportunities, or the need. But it worked on people... Could it work on animals, too? Even on magical Fae animals that were abnormally large and horrifying?

Despite the danger and despite not knowing if this would even work, I had nothing to lose at this point. Nothing *left* to lose, anyway. If I didn't at least make the attempt then I'd be dead for sure. It was inevitable.

In a way, my cognitive manipulation power was very much like my transfiguration power. It only worked so long as I knew that what I wanted to happen actually *would* happen. At the Halfling Academy, I'd convinced my teachers they were seeing fantastic things, like the desks turning into lions.

What would this creature see? What did I want him to *believe* he was seeing? And would I be able to reach into his mind in time to stop his claws from tearing through my ribs?

With a tremendous effort I pushed all my doubts and worries and panic aside and focused on what I wanted the direwolf to experience, to believe entirely. The growl echoed low in his throat, his gaze piercing through me. Ignoring him *and* his fangs, I muttered the spell under my breath, something I'd memorized long ago that was designed to hone my focus and my magic. My shifting might have gone out like a guttered candle inside, but the deep well of magic power lay resting. Waiting...f only I could access it.

In my head I held the image of what I wanted the creature to see, down to the last detail. Sight, smell, feeling, texture, all of it. I had to manipulate all of those things in order to get him to comply. Once I held that image firmly, I reached out for his mind and tapped into the energy of the creature.

Blocking out my fear, blocking out the forest around me and the rest of the world. I held his mind in my metaphorical hands and centered all of the last of my power on him.

Trust me. Let me live.

The spell allowed me to see his energy signature clearly, pulsating around the massive and somewhat deformed body. The direwolf glowed with the colors of the forest, with a thick spiral of black close to his head. Then I speared my influence straight into that spiral along with the rest of my magic.

"I am not your enemy. I'm your friend," I said out loud, holding his gaze and trying desperately to reach him. "You are *my* friend. Not only my friend, but you love me. You would never want to hurt me. The *last* thing you want to do is hurt me. You would do anything in your power to protect me."

Another push toward him. He had to be made afraid of what would happen to me for this to work. For him to believe I told the truth. No questions, either. If I introduced even the slightest bit of doubt in his mind then my manipulation would not take.

"You know me," I continued. "You would die for me. And you are going to stop this right now because this has all been a mistake and you feel awful about hurting me. You're going to let me go and never bother me again. You will never hurt me again as long as you live, no matter what anyone else says or tries to get you to do."

I sent every last bit of my magic into the mind of the direwolf. And then I saw the barrier. That was the black spiral around his head. A barrier set in place by whoever it was who'd sent him here to attack me. It took every bit of strength I had left inside of me to break through that barrier, whatever it was that had been put in place to keep me out.

His master wanted me out.

Except this was life or death for me…and eventually I found a crack in that wall and wormed my way through. Once the barrier shattered, the direwolf was an open book. A story waiting for me to write it, and if I'd had more magic, it would have been so easy for me to break him from the inside. But no. I held myself back from that and stopped as the last of my energy drained away.

The direwolf grunted and at once his weight left me.

I felt almost criminal. When I manipulated the faculty at the Halfling Academy for my magic test, that had been different. They knew what I was doing. It was their choice to test my power. This creature had been forced to kill against his will, and even my going in to eradicate that order seemed wrong.

This beast wasn't a dog to be controlled. He was a gorgeous creation, a weapon meant to kill. Whoever had broken him initially—because I had no doubt the barrier had come with a measure of breakage to begin with—was the true monster in this case.

My stomach roiled and I wanted to sink further into the ground and disappear. The moment I saw that the direwolf was not going to attack again, or rather the moment his claws drew back into his fur and he released his hold on my chest, I sucked in a breath and let it out in a long, slow sigh. Within moments he was under my control, sitting down a foot away from me, completely docile. I pushed myself up into a seated position with the direwolf still across from me.

My head spun and the rest of me ached. Nothing new, but this time felt especially potent. I'd been wrung out entirely.

"Well," I said out loud to the direwolf, "here we are. I have no idea what we should do now, though." I scratched the side of my head. "I never had a chance to think this through."

He tilted his head to the side and stared at me with a question in its eyes, all hints of his former frenzy gone. I got a much better look at him and the long, powerful lines of his body. A gorgeous killing machine was putting it mildly.

"You're good. I don't want to call you a good boy but I'm so tired. I just...you're a good boy."

His tongue lolled out of the side of his snout through those teeth, almost panting like a dog, and the picture was so at odds with the murder-wolf he'd been before that I wanted to laugh. He wouldn't hurt me now, I assured myself.

Had to keep assuring myself because it felt a little wrong to be sitting across from him like we were the friends I'd convinced him we were.

This handsome, wild creature. Tamed.

The two of us stayed there in relative silence, the quiet hush of the forest trying to sooth me but I was too wound up. Too keyed to do anything. The storm had run its course, at least, though my clothing had soaked through.

Another glance at the docile direwolf and my exhaustion almost pulled me under. I took the chance to rest even though I knew it might cost me. Until the sound of something tramping through the woods caught my attention.

I pushed up to my feet and almost toppled over when my ankle didn't want to hold me anymore. Eventually I straightened, putting more weight on the opposite leg.

"I don't know your name, boy, but protect me," I ordered the direwolf. "Protect me from the intruders. Don't let them come any closer."

He got up much slower than I had, but once he gained his feet my fear rose anew and I had to work to ignore it. *He's safe...because he's mine.* The direwolf turned toward the newcomers and growled in warning before launching himself in attack, ready to tear off and rip whoever it was limb from limb.

Too late. I realized too late that I recognized the mop of golden blond hair that peeked out from between damp tree branches. *Mike.*

"Stop!" I screamed out the word when the figures of Mike and his mother separated from the foliage. "Stop right now! Don't hurt them."

Much to my surprise—although why should I be surprised?—the direwolf obeyed immediately and backed down, only inches away from tearing into Mike.

Mike jerked in the opposite direction as color leached from his face, the dark collar of his jacket turned up to protect him from the rain. He hadn't backed down, though. He stood tall and strong, with one arm swept out to shove the queen behind him as he prepared to shield her with his body.

Although the direwolf whined at being stopped, although he remained tense and poised, ready for action, he made no further move toward the two of them.

"Tavi." Mike's voice remained a calm undertone but didn't waver. "What the hell is this?"

I gestured tiredly toward the direwolf. "*This* is a problem that I handled." I wanted to drop to my knees at his feet and thank him for coming to find me. How had he managed it? But he was here, he'd brought his mom, and it was going to be all right.

All right.

A foreign concept these days.

"How did you find me?" I asked.

For the longest while, I stayed rooted to the spot despite the desire to run to him and throw myself into his arms. No sudden movements with the direwolf, I reasoned, and especially not with the two of them staring at me like they'd seen a ghost.

"You've been gone for hours," Mike said. "We panicked. I went to check on you in your room."

"So you came looking for me," I filled in.

Mike reached into his pocket and removed a piece of cloth. "I had this. And I used it to track you." He glanced behind him at his mother. "Well, Mom used it to track you. We had to be careful, though, and not let anyone know what we were doing."

The Queen of Faerie. She stood half shielded behind

her son, her hand on his shoulder, a steadying presence even as she stared at the direwolf.

I stared at the cloth Mike held, shook my head, mouth opening but the question seemed stuck in the back of my throat. "You still have the handkerchief?" I managed finally.

The same one he'd used to clean my bloody nose. And he'd used it to track me with his mother's help. My gasp of surprise had the direwolf raising his hackles and growling again.

Queen Laina lifted a hand to shush me before I said anything else. She'd used blood tracking to find me, but blood tracking wasn't Fae magic. That was one of the lessons Professor Hawthorne drummed into us from the beginning in his History of Magic class.

It was *witch* magic.

Which meant that the royal queen of Faerie was a witch. At least a part of her. Somewhere in her history someone with powerful magic had practiced, and the knowledge, the ability, passed through her and into the royal line.

What did that mean for Mike?

"No one knows about my heritage," she told me with a genial smile. It looked entirely out of place in this situation. "That's why I rarely leave the palace. But you're important to Michael and I knew we needed to help you."

"Will you call down your—" Mike motioned toward the creature.

I cleared my throat before saying, "Direwolf. He's a direwolf."

"He hurt you?"

I glanced down at the scratches along my legs and arms and the marks on my shoulders and hissed out a breath. "No more than I'd already had the shit beat out of me tonight. It's really been fucked up." Then I remembered that it was the queen standing in front of me, the queen who Mike had tasked to help him tonight and I winced. "I'm sorry for my language, Your Majesty."

She shook her head and stepped forward, past the wolf. "I'd say you're entitled to curse as much as you want and as loudly as you are able. You're entitled to rage and throw a fit. You've been through too much. I don't need to know the details to see that."

She didn't spare another look at the creature before she reached out to take my hand. After a brief hesitation, I lifted the least-injured arm and placed my hand in hers. Then jumped when Mike seemed to suddenly materialize at my side and press a kiss to my temple. It was like pure sunlight on a cool day, thawing through the ice of my skin in a way I hadn't realized I needed.

"You're okay?" he asked.

I nodded, taking in a deep breath when Laina sent a wave of healing magic into my hand. And there came the fire, sizzling up my arm and rapidly coursing throughout my entire body.

She closed her eyes, her power assessing, probing, but not in the way I expected. There was nothing overpowering about her magic. Comparing her and Tywin would be like standing in a gentle spring drizzle compared to a monsoon.

"Michael?" Laina asked. "Will you join me? It's going to take some work to help her out of here. She's lost a lot of blood."

She kept her hold on me while holding out her opposite hand to her son. He took it and the power grew in a green halo around them.

The same color as their eyes.

"Unseelie direwolves aren't just wolves," she told me while they worked on healing my wounds. I closed my eyes, leaning into the sensation. "They're magical creatures. They come from the land the same way that the Fae do. Once broken, though, they can be used, as they consume other Fae and take that person's special abilities and magic into themselves. They then return to their handler where the magic can be siphoned off and used by the handler for whatever purpose they have in mind."

It felt like the ground beneath my feet suddenly disappeared. "Wait. What? I don't get it."

"Whoever sent the wolf to you did so because they want your powers," Mike filled in for me.

I nodded because now it made sense. "Dorian Jade," I told them.

Neither of them moved but their reaction was absolute in the stillness. They'd expected the name and yet it still shocked them.

I rubbed my temple with my free hand. "Why would Dorian Jade want my powers? Why does he even know who I am?"

"I'm sorry, sweet girl, but I don't have the answers for you. This is a war you've stepped into where we are all floundering around in the dark doing the best we are able." Queen Laina sent another healing pulse of her magic into me and although the exhaustion remained, the worst of the aches and pains faded into nothingness.

I blew out a sigh of relief. "That is so much better. Thank you."

A smile twitched across Mike's lips. "I've been learning from my mother. I'm still not able to do it on my own but one day I might. One day I *will*," he corrected. "Mom's a really good teacher."

"I promise you I am going to stand up for you, Tavi. Nothing that has happened has been your fault. I know this." Laina finished her healing and gently dropped my hand.

I rotated my ankle where the direwolf had grabbed me. It still twinged a little but the ache was nothing compared to what it had been a few minutes ago. "How do you know, though? How do you know I'm innocent of what I've been accused of?" What had Mike told her?

She stared at me, staring beneath the surface, her gaze assessing yet without judgment. "I can see the truth outside of what my son tells me. I know that you are a bright girl. He wouldn't get involved with you if you were not deserving. He knows much better than to trust his company to those who are unworthy. We're going to figure out what really happened and clear your name. You have my word."

Her word? Did she have enough authority? How much could I trust her? And what would it cost for this kind of help? But with her and Mike standing this close, I wanted to trust them both so badly my teeth ached.

"What if Claribel really was telling the truth, though? About the king casting me out of Faerie for good because of the brain boost powder?" I pressed. "I didn't steal it. I didn't steal anything. It wasn't me."

"Agent Claribel wasn't telling you the truth," Laina insisted. "That never happened. Tywin has made no official proclamation on the subject. Your status here is safe."

It seemed so strange to hear her talk about the king of Faerie in a conversational way. This was the woman who slept beside him at night, I remembered, a little freaked out.

"We'll find whoever really took the brain boost powder," Mike told me. "Just like we'll make sure that the right party is prosecuted for the Madam Muerte murder."

"It was Agent Claribel from the Bureau," I told them.

"She admitted it to me. Right before she tied me to a tree and left me for a direwolf's snack."

It also felt wrong that the two of them took my word on it so easily, without a million questions. It was simply the truth, and they bobbed their nearly identical heads at me.

"Then we'll find Claribel and bring her to justice. I promise you that," Laina added. She pulled the sides of her black robe tighter around her and I finally noticed that a spell must have kept the rain from touching her skin.

Mike wasn't faring so well on that count.

I sighed. "There are an awful lot of promises being thrown around."

I looked up at Mike when his fingers began trailing delicious sensation along my bicep. He was looking back at me in a way he hadn't looked at me since before we slept together. It nearly brought me to my knees. Oh, gosh. That man...he was going to be the death of me.

I swallowed. "Claribel is working for Dorian Jade," I found myself saying, without breaking eye contact. "He orchestrated all of this. She was his agent this entire time."

"And then he sent the direwolf to kill you and collect your power." Laina looked over her shoulder to where the wolf sat waiting. For what, none of us knew. "It seems he's been thwarted once again."

"You've been through hell tonight." Mike gathered me against him, and although I stayed stiff at first, the longer he held me the more I melted into him. His pulse echoed through the side of my face that I kept pressed to his chest. "Come on. Let's get back to the castle."

"I still can't believe you guys found me. How did you even know I needed help?"

"I had a feeling I couldn't ignore, and when I went to check your room, you weren't there. There was, however, a rather incriminating and alarming trail of water and mud in the hallway. I just *knew* that you were in trouble and I had to do something to find you.."

And he'd gone to his mom for help. I wasn't sure what to make of that, whether to give in to the insistent dread ready for my acknowledgement or the even more insistent hope. Hope felt better. Hope that maybe this nightmare was over at last.

Then again, an even greater nightmare loomed ahead. One where Dorian Jade played a dark and depraved puppet master.

Mike guided me in the direction he and Laina had come and had to slow his stride to stay with me. My legs didn't want to work properly.

Leaves and twigs cracked behind us and when I glanced around, I saw the direwolf only a few paces back.

"Oh, no. No way." I tried to shoo it away. "You...go on. Go home to your master. You did a good job."

The massive beast dropped to his haunches, head cocked to the side as he listened to me. A low whine sounded in the clearing.

"I said go on, now!" No matter how hard I tried to wave my arms in his face to get him to go, he just sat there staring. Whining. Pleading with me in a way that he knew I understood. "The damn thing is acting like a dog," I grumbled.

"Well, I guess you have a new pet now, Tavi," Mike said with a chuckle.

"What? No. I can't— H-he's not *mine*."

"Have you told him that?"

I glanced at the direwolf and the acknowledgment had him taking a few steps toward me, still whining. Oh God, what was I going to do with him? I had no place to keep him in my room. Did the king have a stable or a menagerie for magical pets? That wasn't fair, either. The direwolf deserved an open forest to run free. Where no one would ever bother him again.

"You're seriously not going to leave?" I said to him.

The longer I looked at the direwolf, though, the more I thought it might not be so bad to have his muscle on my side. An ally who would do what I asked...*maybe*. At this point, with so many people out to get me, the more teeth I had at my disposal the better.

27

We went straight from the forest into a waiting carriage, one that magically expanded to accommodate the three of us plus my new direwolf. He looked adorable clambering up the steps and into the velvet-lined confines. But he didn't kick up a fuss when I told him to be easy. All he did was come over and rest his head on my lap once I made myself comfortable.

Then I passed out.

Mike roused me when we approached the same Faerie hospital that held Onyx, and had to guide me through the hallways to a private room. The little bit of sleep I'd gotten on the ride back to Eahsea made me loopy, disoriented, and I only had enough wherewithal to tell the direwolf to go wherever Mike directed and not to worry about me. My protector didn't go easily, but eventually one of the hospital orderlies took me in hand, a woman with kind eyes, and Mike and the queen took off back to the castle with the direwolf.

Hopefully they'd treat him nicely. I tried to tell them that before the nurse got me situated, but as soon as my head hit the pillow, I was out like a light again.

I didn't wake up until the sun had set over the mountains just visible out my window. The bed beneath me wasn't as soft as my own but it was comfortable enough, safe enough, to have me finally feeling ready to release the tension I held knotted in my muscles.

A nurse walked in and checked on me, lighting another bowl of incense on my bedside table and chanting low under her breath before her eyes popped open and she nodded. All must be well, then, because she left with as much talk as she'd arrived, which was none.

She'd left me a fresh glass of water, for which I was grateful. I grabbed the water and chugged the entire glass. Damn, that was good. And the incense herbs smelled fantastic. Lavender and sage and something with citrus.

I reached up to rub my eyes, the wounds on my arms pink and beginning to scab over. Every part of me hurt, and I knew I had a better chance of growing wings than of getting out of this bed anytime soon, as much as I wanted to move and be free.

I was alive.

The healing in the forest had only taken me so far, but *I was alive*.

I relaxed into my pillows, my arms and legs feeling leaden and heavy, dragging me into the comfort of the sheets once again.

Alive *and* safe, I mentally amended. Those two things usually didn't go together. Did they? How long would it last?

A sort of scuffle sounded outside the door to my room and I knew it was about me. Much to my surprise, the person who entered was not Mike, or Melia, or anyone I'd count as a friend.

It was Queen Laina herself.

She addressed the entourage behind her. "Give us privacy, please."

Dusk turned her blonde hair to molten gold, and the pale curve of her cheeks was stained a blushing pink that echoed the opals in her crown. She closed the door behind her right in the face of the four guards trailing her, and when she lifted her hand, a protective barrier formed.

My gut sank. *Shit*. Why would she throw up a silencing bubble?

"Please don't kill me," I whispered.

She raked her sympathetic gaze down my battered body. "Tavi, honey, no one is coming to kill you. I gave you my word."

"I'm sorry, but words don't mean anything to me." I wanted to be honest with her.

I knew her secret. Her son knew mine.

It left us at an impasse.

"As distressed as I am to hear your trust has been abused, this is a private conversation, and there is no need for curious ears to take what we have to say back to anyone interested in gossip. Do you mind if I come to sit with you?" she asked in her usual delicate manner.

She'd helped me when I needed someone. Although trust didn't come easily, I reluctantly offered some of it to the queen and nodded.

"I spoke with my husband earlier today. I advocated for you."

I glanced at her sharply and regretted the movement when pain ripped down my neck and spine.

Laina caught my wince as she settled herself at the edge of my cot with her hands folded across her lap. She wore a gown of cornflower blue with ivory lace around the bodice and her wrists. A genuine ball gown that showed off her features to their best effect. I looked and felt like mud beside her.

"I told Tywin that I believe we are seeing the beginning of the Faerie Prophecy play out. The beginning of the end of everything we've known." She stared at her slender fingers. "I don't believe you have anything to do with it, despite several interested parties maintaining the opposite. However, I believe you will have a part to play, as will we all."

My heart dropped right along with my stomach. "Thank you for believing me." My lips were numb. What else could I say? I had no words.

The queen had no idea that I was a half-shifter, right? So while her statement and the earnest sincerity behind it meant so much to me, she was wrong.

"I just want to say that if you ever need anything, please don't hesitate to talk to me. I'm on your side," she insisted.

"That's really not necessary," I countered.

"Why not?" she questioned. "My son clearly has feelings for you. The type of feelings that— Ah, you're in no position to discuss them. Pardon me. Michael would call it my motherly instinct. I don't know when to back off. But please, Tavi, know that I'm here should you need assistance. You've done your land a great service and those with good hearts need to stick together. Don't you think?"

She rose without a sound and fixed me with a look so kind, so potent, it nearly stopped my heart. Mike had a really good mother. And Faerie had a better queen than it had a king. At least in my opinion.

Her son had feelings for me. I repeated it several times to myself although my brain refused to process it. She knew about Mike, about us. The *us* that didn't exist, not really. Except *something* must be there for the queen herself to see it, to comment on its existence. I wasn't sure whether to be warmed with joy or terrified.

Both, probably.

With my head fuzzy and the rest of me nothing but a mass of aches and pain, I waited until the queen left, taking her massive amount of magic with her, before relaxing into my pillows.

I'd just had a private audience with the queen and she was on my side. On *my* side. I wondered how her husband really felt about that or if he'd disagreed with her desire to come here and talk to me. How had she explained her late night jaunt into the woods to him?

Or did he not know?

Too many questions buzzed around my head, and the longer I tried to find answers, the more tired I felt.

And I wasn't alone for long. The guards at the door, two who had remained behind when the queen left, stood to attention and I sat up straight. Just in time to see Rooker flash his badge at the two of them and the guards step aside to allow him entry. He stood a good head taller than the guards with his expression giving nothing away.

"Miss Alderidge?" His craggy voice set my teeth on edge until I saw his eyes. Or whatever was visible of his eyes in between the rocks that made up his entire being.

But he seemed subdued somehow. More than usual. Had he slept at all last night?

What if Claribel had gone back to him and fed him more lies? Now he was he here to really take me away?

No, the queen told me I was safe. So why would Rooker want to—

"Is this a bad time?" he asked gently.

"I don't have anything else on my schedule." My attempt at a joke resulted in a small chuckle sounding two pebbles rubbing together and Rooker stepped fully into the room.

He shut the door behind him, effectively sealing the guards out, and my heart thumped painfully, my breath quickening. Nothing good came from being trapped in a room alone with a Bureau agent.

"Should I worry?" I asked as he cast a silencing bubble around us.

"Precautions." Rooker spared me a look over his shoulder. "I'm the one that should worry, Miss Alderidge. Trust me." He took his time in grabbing a chair and sliding it over to my bedside before settling down. The thing looked ready to crack at any moment beneath his weight. "This won't take long," he continued.

"It's fine," I assured him, even though I was totally wrung out.

"I met with the king and the prince this morning. And I see you've just been visited by Her Royal Highness."

Those words had me sitting up a little straighter despite my body feeling like one giant scab ready to burst. "Yeah?"

"I wanted to personally assure you that you're no longer a person of interest in the Madam Muerte murder. I thought you'd feel a little better hearing from me. You're officially cleared."

More good news? It felt awkward to me, like some cosmic trick. "How does that work, exactly?" I asked.

"Don't ask any more questions," he warned, lifting a finger. "You get into too much trouble when you ask questions. For once, I need you to sit there and listen to me carefully." It was hard to tell, but I'd have sworn Rooker looked a little uncomfortable.

I gulped. "There's more?"

This was a completely different Rooker from the one I'd known during any of my interrogations, and I wondered if it was because of how much had changed or because he no longer felt like he was the one in control. In those rooms, he'd been calling the shots. He'd wanted answers out of me. Now he was the one supplying the answers and it obviously wasn't in his nature to do so.

"Claribel is MIA. She disappeared after she attacked you. I wonder what you know. Did she say anything during your encounter?" He paused for only a moment, not giving me time to respond, before barreling on. "I haven't been able to stop thinking about the prediction regarding the Bureau corruption. You made mention of it and it got me thinking, even before what happened last night. I wonder about what you witnessed the night of the murder, and how it all fits together. It seems like there are too many things that aren't adding up for me, and the more I think about it, the less it makes sense."

"This isn't going to be easy for you to hear, then," I tried to tell him.

He shook his head before saying, "I don't care. I need to know what you know."

I kneaded the sheets nervously. "Is this in an official capacity?".

Rook paused for only a moment before he said the one word I'd hoped for but didn't expect. "No."

So I told him everything that had happened, from start to finish. About the fight, about Claribel working with Dorian Jade, about the direwolf. Everything I'd been too scared to talk about before just poured out of me, and through it all Rooker looked bothered. Hurt. He looked angry, and I wondered if it was directed at me or at himself.

I'd tried to tell him about the corruption but he hadn't been willing or able to hear me. Now? He'd apparently changed.

Rooker took notes and kept his lips shut until I'd finished. His mouth formed a thin crack in his exterior while he mulled over everything.

"The queen and Mike were there. They can corroborate everything, if you need that." My throat hurt from talking. "If you still don't trust me."

Rooker held up a hand, his pen continuing to write for him. "Thank you for your statement. I do appreciate it. You've given me a lot to consider, and my superiors will be interested in the new angles this brings to the situation."

My eyes bulged. "I thought you said that this was off the record?"

"Your *statement* will be off the record but I'm hoping that what you've said will help us work out a stronger case against Claribel." He winced. "And against Dorian Jade in turn. I'm sure you're aware that the Bureau is dedicated to taking down the Unseelie king and his entire court."

"I figured as much."

"Well." He put away his pen and notebook, then clapped his hands on his thighs and stood, whatever he had for bones snapping together at his movement. "Get well soon, Tavi. And—"

I stared after him as he made his way to the door. "And...?"

He hesitated. "I'm going to put this out there whether you like it or not." My gut sank at that. "You should think about becoming an agent one day. Put those skills of yours to good use. The answers might not always be easy, but I think your tenacity would be just what we need."

Rooker left me with that statement hanging in the air and no clue how to feel about it. Me? An agent?

What fresh hell did he want to unleash on his coworkers? Despite myself, I chuckled, falling back onto my pillows with a sigh. Me as an agent!

28

It took days for me to feel like myself again. Most of the time, even with my physical wounds completely healed and the scars erased, the rest of me still went up in flames at random times. I still hurt. If given the chance, I would have stayed in bed for another week without moving or even getting up to go to the bathroom.

The world didn't wait for me and neither did Coral.

I left the Fae hospital with a clean bill of health from the nurses and a headache from hell, only to get back to my room to see that I had a dozen missed messages from Coral asking where I'd gone and when I planned to continue our training, messaging repeatedly until my phone felt like the enemy.

I whipped off a quick response assuring her that I was alive, not that she'd asked, and I'd meet with her tomorrow. Then I showered for about an hour, changed into my comfiest t-shirt and shorts combination, and set off to find my direwolf.

Mike met me on my walk and brought me out to a makeshift

pen that he'd had set up at the end of the great lawn, far away from anyone who might accidentally wander too close. We chatted lightly through the walk, our fingers brushing with each stride, and the direwolf was so happy to see me that it immediately brightened the rest of the storms in my head.

The following night, I met Coral for more training.

Slowly, of course, taking care not to push myself beyond my abilities. This would be all Coral, I vowed. Let her show me what she could do now, what she'd learned. I'd be there for moral support and to help calm her down if things got out of hand but I think I'd earned a little respite after everything.

I forced myself to walk, though, instead of hiring something to take me over to her summer house. Call it pride or ego or whatever.

Or maybe I just didn't want to get in another vehicle again after what happened with Claribel. Not for a long time. Except I made it to the front gate of the palace only to find Coral there waiting for me, her foot tapping out a prissy rhythm on the ground.

"Took you long enough," she said the moment she spotted me. "My God, it almost feels like you've been avoiding me."

"Why are you waiting for me? And what do you want me to say? Sorry for almost dying, I didn't mean to put you out?" Except it *was* almost nice to see her. And there might have been something close to disquietude in her eyes when she looked at me.

"Because I thought you'd back out," she replied. "Clearly. I was about a second away from calling in a favor to get me into the palace itself. My dad knows people, you know. It would have been easy enough to walk right in."

Only Coral managed to sound concerned and put-out at the same time.

"I'm fine, by the way, thank you for asking." I fell into step beside her. "You seriously thought I was going to back out?"

"No, duh. I know you. You might act like you're put-out but if you give your word then you'll always follow through."

"Well, thank you for the escort, I guess. It's good to know that you care." I knocked her with my shoulder and winced when pain zinged from the area.

That damn zombie bite. The evidence might be gone but I swore I still felt Muerte's teeth lodged in my skin.

"I *don't* care. I'm only trying to protect our arrangement," she replied testily.

For some reason, Coral knowing about me didn't bug me the way it once would have. In fact it felt easy. It felt like *pack*.

Sadly, Coral *had* become a part of my pack—*sadly* because she wasn't the type to be an insta-bestie. Not in the least. She was more the kind of person that tested you constantly but you put up with it because you knew wasn't a lost cause. But she was here, and she was getting stronger, and one day I'd look back on all of this and—

"Oh. My. God! Look at this. Trash day came early." A familiar, snide female voice came at us from the opposite side of the street.

I didn't need to look up to know that Persephone was headed in our direction. The stomp of multiple footsteps heralded the arrival of her fan club only a few feet behind her.

"Tavi," Persephone purred.

When I finally turned in her direction, both her hands

were on her hips and her pretty, pouty lips twisted in a sneer.

"What are you doing out here at this time of night? Trying to stick to the shadows so that no one will see your face and have nightmares? And who is your little friend?"

Persephone looked ready for a verbal beat-down like she'd been aching for a good one for way too long. She'd consider this her Christmas come early.

Coral simply held out her hand and a blast of magic pushed Persephone and her gaggle of meanions back a step, the soles of their shoes skidding across cobblestone.

"Pass," Coral said breezily and without slowing her step.

Persephone squawked but we were already halfway down the street before she recovered her composure. I let out a breath as we turned the corner.

And Coral turned that same hand to me to stop me from speaking. "Don't thank me," she drawled. "People like that really piss me off. It's only right that we put them in their place so that they don't think they can keep acting like fools in front of us."

"Like you were any different when we first met?"

She flicked her gaze my way but said nothing for the rest of the walk. My hands went into the pockets of my shorts. Huh. Coral had defended me from Persephone rather than making an excuse for us being seen together. Fancy that.

Finally we made it to her backyard, passing through her gate and into the garden now colored with the shadows of twilight.

"Are you going to tell me what happened or will you make me beg for it?" she asked once we'd cast the silencing bubble around us.

I set my stance to move through some yoga positions while we warmed up our physical bodies. Coral immediately mirrored my movements, standing in front of me. "Bad things," I told her.

"Oh, right, because that's really detailed." Her voice was dry.

So I told her everything, about the Bureau and even about the direwolf. I gave Coral credit; she only broke form once. When I finished, she shook her head.

"I don't know how you manage to get into such trouble," she told me.

I shrugged. "I'm a magnet for the stuff. Remind me to never taunt the universe to give me whatever it can again."

"Is that what you did?"

"I must have, but I don't remember."

"Why didn't you tell me?" A thread of anger wound through her tone. "I could have helped."

Reaching across, I grabbed Coral by the arm to halt her movements. "Thank you," I said. "Direwolves are dangerous creatures and I'm not entirely sure you would have been a help instead of a hindrance, but thank you. It means a lot that you'd even offer."

She sounded exhausted as she said, "People continuously underestimate me. Don't do that. Okay?"

"Okay." I chuckled. "Next time I'm in a bad situation where I'm about to die, I'll make sure you're there to have my back."

She nodded decisively. "Good."

"Are you ready to shift completely into your halfling warrior form?" I asked her, rubbing my hands together in anticipation.

This would be the first night she changed and stayed that way for more than a few minutes. I wasn't ready to lead her through the woods yet, but if she managed to hold her wolf for five or more minutes then she'd be ready for our next session where we actually ran through the woods on four legs. After that, I'd test her reflexes and have her fight me. I only asked for five minutes where she didn't lose focus and start shifting back to human or get distracted by the new smells around her and take off.

Coral fixed me with a look that showed she meant business. "Is it weird that I'm excited?" She bounced from foot to foot. "I mean I've changed before but this feels different somehow. Like I've passed some kind of test and this is the next step."

"I'll be right there with you," I assured her. And mentally crossed my fingers that the telepathy between packmates while in wolf form would be there between us, too. It would help me to guide her better once she had her wolf form.

I mentally crossed a second set of fingers that I had enough of my power replenished through the healing that I'd be able to keep up with her.

"Thank you, Tavi," she said softly.

"Don't thank me yet."

I pushed my low-level exhaustion aside, focusing on the change. Feeling it tingle from my fingers all the way up my arm and down to my feet. Okay, that was a good start. Damn good start. And once I started, it all went much easier than the first initial push. Wiggling my toes in my sneakers, I let the wolf rise. Let her take over control until my bones cracked and my jaw lengthened.

I peeled open my eyes to see Coral bent at the waist, with dark fur thrusting out of her arms. Claws lengthened from the tips of her curved fingers and her back legs bent. The first hint of her tail began to grow.

Pride. That was the sensation. Pride that something awful, an accident, had resulted in another beautiful wolf and another Halfling learning to navigate the world. We weren't monsters. We weren't the enemy that the other Fae made us out to be. We were here, alive.

"*Coral!*"

Nixa's sharp cry pierced the haze of the change and I immediately snapped upright, fangs bared in a snarl at her silent approach. Coral's mother stood under the arbor of roses with her hands covering her mouth and her long red hair standing out against her icy pale skin.

My blood went Arctic-cold.

Coral remained half shifted and turned to her mother in horror. "No!" The strangled word ripped from her throat. She pushed the change aside, agonizingly slow, while she tried to compose herself when her nature would demand she follow through.

When a fully human Coral stood there, she burst into tears.

"Mom, no. No!" She ran forward but stopped a foot away from Nixa and lifted a hand before dropping her arm to her side, fingers flexing. "Please. Please!"

Nixa simply stared, her eyes rounded in a combination of agony and…something else. Something I couldn't begin to put a name to as I forced my own wolf down.

What could I say? What could I do? Horror flashed through me, keen and bright and impenetrable.

Coral flipped out, her chest heaving and tears staining her cheeks.

"Mom, please don't tell the cops. Please! Don't turn me in. It was an accident. I got hurt, I changed. It wasn't my fault." Coral pointed to me. "Tavi is helping me control it but she's good. She's not a threat. What they say about halflings, it's…it's not true. There are good halflings out there, good people. Like me! Mom, I won't hurt anyone, I swear, just please don't tell the Bureau about me. Please!"

Much to my surprise, Nixa grabbed Coral around the shoulders and dragged her in for an unbreakable hug.

I forgot to breathe as I watched them. Nixa clenched her daughter to her chest and Coral grabbed hold of her mom's shirt, crying for all she was worth.

"My baby," Nixa whispered. Softly, but I heard her. After a long moment, Nixa leaned back, swiping auburn-colored hair away from her daughter's face. "Coral, honey. Breathe. You've got to breathe."

Coral wouldn't let go of Nixa's shirt. The material bunched in her fists.

"What? I can't!" she screamed. Definitely not breathing. "I can't, I can't."

Nixa continued to soothe her, running a steady hand along Coral's hair, her demeanor at once calmer than either of us expected.

"How could I not love you? I promise, Coral. I will *never* not love my daughter because of something that happened to her. If it was an accident then you should have come to me and we would have fixed it together. You wouldn't have had to do it alone."

Coral renewed her sobbing and tears stung my own eyes.

"Look, honey. My own *sister* fell in love with a werewolf. A long time ago. Somewhere out there, I have a halfling niece I've never met. You grow fur. So what?" Nixa said as she held her daughter closer. "I'm used to this, to tell you the truth. You're my daughter and I will love you more than life itself, no matter what happens."

"Your sister?" Coral asked, her voice muffled.

"Yes. She's back in Faerie now, hiding, so we still don't have much contact with each other. I guess you could say that we all have secrets that we've kept. And now I'll keep yours. Both of yours." Nixa smiled over Coral's head, her gaze meeting mine. Her smile was for me.

My heart stopped beating. Dead in my chest.

The air left my lungs in a whoosh and I dropped to my knees, black spots in front of my vision.

That was why, I realized distantly, my mind fracturing. That was why Nixa seemed so familiar to me. Because she looked and acted just like my own mom.

Sisters.

Nixa was my aunt.

And my Mom was alive. Alive and hiding out in Faerie.

THE END

Continue the Fae Academy for Halflings novels with *Faerie Hunted.*

For author updates and free books, sign up for Brea's newsletter
www.breaviragh.com/newsletter

ALSO BY BREA VIRAGH

Fae Academy for Halflings

Faerie Marked

Faerie Gift

Faerie Prophecy

Faerie Trials

Faerie Oath

Bad Wolves

Never Prey

Never Submit

Never Tamed

Bad Wolves: The Complete Collection

Cinnamon Bay Romance

Love on the Boardwalk

Jewel of the Bay

Haunting on Seafoam Street

Celebration on Seafoam Street

Boardwalk Beginnings

Boardwalk Bliss

Control the Burn

Fight the Burn

Vienna Blue Novels

Blue Persuasion

Colossal We Come

Until Forever Ends

The Dark Half

Shadows Come

Rise

The Cavaldi Birthright

Fate Walks

Morning's Light

In the Dark

Twilight Sun

Small-Town Contemporary Romance

Sugar and Gold

Your Hand in Mine

Last Christmas Angel

Stand Alones

Wake the Dream

Rose and Bane

[Courageous, She Loves (A Dark and Twisted Snow Queen Retelling)](Courageous, She Loves)

[Fated, She Flies (A Dark and Twisted Swan Princess Retelling)](Fated, She Flies)

Shifter by Christmas

Beneath my Skin

Midnight Skies

ABOUT THE AUTHOR

BREA VIRAGH is a USA Today bestselling romance author based in the Blue Ridge Mountains. She is a proud Gryffindor, a graduate of Brakebills, and a member of Fairy Tail. When she isn't writing and daydreaming about her newest project, her hobbies include binge-watching HGTV, scouring thrift shops for goodies, and maintaining her alpha status among her puppy and three cats.

Read More from BREA VIRAGH
www.breaviragh.com

Printed in Great Britain
by Amazon

HENRY BRADSHAW SOCIETY

Founded in the Year of Our Lord 1890 for the editing of Rare Liturgical Texts

SUBSIDIA · VII

PUBLISHED FOR THE SOCIETY
BY
THE BOYDELL PRESS

HENRY BRADSHAW SOCIETY

for the editing of rare liturgical texts

PRESIDENT

Abbot Cuthbert Johnson, OSB

HONORARY VICE-PRESIDENTS

Professor Dr Helmut Gneuss, FBA
Miss Barbara Harvey, CBE, FSA, FBA
The Revd Professor Richard W. Pfaff, DD, FSA

OFFICERS OF THE COUNCIL

Professor Susan Rankin,, FSA, FBA (Chairman)
Dr N. Bell (General Secretary)
Dr Rosalind Love (Publications Secretary)
Dr M. B. Moreton (Treasurer)

Enquiries concerning membership of the Society should be addressed to the Hon. General Secretary, N. Bell, Music Collections, The British Library, London NW1 2DB

THE DIVINE OFFICE
IN ANGLO-SAXON ENGLAND
597–*c*.1000

Jesse D. Billett

LONDON
2014

© Henry Bradshaw Society 2014

All Rights Reserved. Except as permitted under current legislation no part of this work may be photocopied, stored in a retrieval system, published, performed in public, adapted, broadcast, transmitted, recorded or reproduced in any form or by any means, without the prior permission of the copyright owner

First published for the Henry Bradshaw Society 2014
by The Boydell Press
an imprint of Boydell & Brewer Ltd
PO Box 9, Woodbridge, Suffolk IP12 3DF, UK
and of Boydell & Brewer Inc.
668 Mt Hope Avenue, Rochester, NY 14620–2731, USA
website: www.boydellandbrewer.com

Paperback edition 2019

ISBN 978 1 90749 728 5 hardback
ISBN 978 1 90749 735 3 paperback

ISSN 1352–1047

A CIP catalogue record for this book is available
from the British Library

The publisher has no responsibility for the continued existence or accuracy of URLs for external or third-party internet websites referred to in this book, and does not guarantee that any content on such websites is, or will remain, accurate or appropriate

Typeset by the author using the X₃TEX Typesetting System

For Jill

Contents

TABLES	ix
ILLUSTRATIONS	x
PREFACE	xi
NOTE ON USAGE	xv
ABBREVIATIONS	xvi
MANUSCRIPT SIGLA	xix

Part I. *The Historical Development of the Divine Office in England to c.1000*

1. TOWARDS A 'NEW NARRATIVE' OF THE HISTORY OF THE DIVINE OFFICE IN ANGLO-SAXON ENGLAND — 3
2. THE DIVINE OFFICE IN THE LATIN WEST IN THE EARLY MIDDLE AGES — 13
   - The typical secular and monastic forms of the Office — 13
   - The Office under the 'rule' of monastic tradition — 23
   - The Roman Office and its development — 30
   - 'Secular' and 'monastic' Offices in the ninth-century Frankish Church — 52
   - Conclusions — 77
3. THE DIVINE OFFICE IN ENGLAND FROM THE AUGUSTINIAN MISSION TO THE FIRST VIKING INVASIONS, 597–*c*.835 — 78
   - The Office under the *uita regularis* in English minsters — 78
   - The teaching of John the Archcantor — 91
   - The liturgical decrees of the Council of *Clofesho* (747) — 98
   - Evidence for the Roman Office *horarium* in Anglo-Saxon sources — 102

	Evidence for the Roman division of the psalter	109
	The Ushaw lectionary fragment	121
	Chant texts in Alcuin's *De laude Dei*	126
	Conclusions	132
4.	THE DIVINE OFFICE IN ENGLAND FROM THE FIRST VIKING AGE TO THE ABBACY OF DUNSTAN AT GLASTONBURY, *c*.835–*c*.940	133
	The ninth-century decline and its liturgical implications	134
	Evidence for liturgical continuity through the ninth century	139
	Restoration and innovation under Alfred and his heirs	142
	Conclusions	148
5.	THE DIVINE OFFICE AND THE TENTH-CENTURY ENGLISH BENEDICTINE REFORM	149
	Glastonbury and the Aachen texts (940×946–957)	153
	Continental contacts (*c*.950–963)	164
	The movement spreads (963–*c*.970)	169
	Regularis concordia (*c*.970)	179
	Evidence for Benedictinization	186
	Conclusions	195

Part II. Manuscript Evidence for English Office Chant in the Tenth Century

6.	A METHODOLOGY FOR THE STUDY OF ANGLO-SAXON CHANT BOOKS FOR THE OFFICE	199
	The *moyen court* of Gabriel Beyssac and its development by Victor Leroquais	200
	Hesbert's *Corpus antiphonalium officii*	203
	A more flexible approach to analysing Office *ordines*	211
	Adaptation to the analysis of early fragments	217
7.	TWO WITNESSES TO THE CHANT OF THE SECULAR OFFICE IN ENGLAND IN THE TENTH CENTURY	220
	Codicological setting and liturgical contents	220
	Liturgical *ordo* and Continental affiliation	227
	Date of transmission and place of reception	231
	Conclusions	233

8. A FRAGMENT OF A TENTH-CENTURY ENGLISH
    BENEDICTINE 'BREVIARY'   252
    Materials and preparation   253
    Script and decoration   255
    Liturgical contents and book type   262
    Liturgical *ordo*   267
    Conclusions   282

9. A FRAGMENT OF A TENTH-CENTURY ENGLISH
    BENEDICTINE CHANT BOOK   301
    Materials and preparation   302
    Script and decoration   304
    Liturgical contents and book type   313
    Liturgical *ordo*   323
    Conclusions   334

10. CONCLUSION: WAYS OF MAKING A BENEDICTINE
    OFFICE   348

Appendices

A. Transcription Conventions   353

B. London, British Library, Royal 17. C. XVII, fols. 2, 3, 163–6
   (Text)   356

C. Oxford, Bodleian Library, Rawl. D. 894, fols. 62–3
   (Text)   374

D. London, British Library, Burney 277, fols. 69–72, and Stowe
   1061, fol. 125 (Text)   380

BIBLIOGRAPHY   389

INDEX OF MANUSCRIPTS   419

INDEX OF LITURGICAL FORMS   425

INDEX OF BIBLICAL REFERENCES AND LITURGICAL
   READINGS   444

GENERAL INDEX   446

Tables

2.1	The distribution of psalms and canticles in the secular *cursus*	16
2.2	The distribution of psalms and canticles in the monastic *cursus*	18
2.3	The three nocturns of the Night Office on Sundays and feast days in the secular and monastic *cursus*	21
2.4	The nocturn(s) of the Night Office on ferial days and simple feasts in the secular and monastic *cursus*	22
2.5	A tentative reconstruction of the psalmody of the Roman monastic Office in the later fifth century	38
2.6	The probable distribution of psalms in the Roman Office in the time of St Benedict (530s)	39
5.2	Chronology of Continental contacts during the first twenty years of the English Benedictine reform	165
6.1	Two different 'Benedictinizations' of the same secular responsory series for the second Sunday in Lent	210
7.1	Responsories for the Book of Tobit in Durham, Cathedral Library, A. IV. 19 and Cambridge, Corpus Christi College 41	227
7.2	Responsories for the four Sundays of Advent added to Durham, Cathedral Library, A. IV. 19 and Cambridge, Corpus Christi College 41	235
7.3	Sources in *CAO* with Advent responsory lists identical to that in Durham, Cathedral Library, A. IV. 19	239
7.4	Key to Hesbert's shorthand for *CAO* Advent responsories and verses included in Tables 7.5–7.8	241
7.5	Responsories and verses of Advent I in sources related to Durham A. IV. 19 and Corpus 41	244
7.6	Responsories and verses of Advent II in sources related to Durham A. IV. 19 and Corpus 41	246

7.7	Responsories and verses of Advent III in sources related to Durham A. IV. 19 and Corpus 41	248
7.8	Responsories and verses of Advent IV in sources related to Durham A. IV. 19 and Corpus 41	250
8.1	Responsories assigned to Monday, Tuesday, and Wednesday in Holy Week in Royal 17. C. XVII	268
8.2	Responsories for Palm Sunday (arrangement 1)	286
8.3	Responsories for Palm Sunday (arrangement 2)	292
8.4	Antiphons for the Benedictus and Magnificat during Holy Week	295
8.5	Holy Week antiphon *ordines* related to Royal 17. C. XVII	299
9.1	Psalms assigned to the Night Office of St Lawrence	321
9.2	Responsories for the feast of St Lawrence (arrangement 1)	336
9.3	Responsories for the feast of St Lawrence (arrangement 2)	342
9.4	Night Office antiphons for the feast of St Lawrence	345

Illustrations

8.1	London, British Library, Royal 17. C. XVII, fol. 164r Reproduced with the permission of the British Library Board. All rights reserved	259
9.1	Oxford, Bodleian Library, Rawl. D. 894, fol. 63r Reproduced by permission of the Bodleian Library, University of Oxford	308

Preface

This book attempts an overview of the history and development of the liturgy of daily prayer, the Divine Office, as it was performed in England from the Augustinian mission to the end of the tenth century. It is not exhaustive. The treatment of the early period, while intended to be complete as far as extant liturgical sources go, has not extended to the full range of potentially relevant literary and architectural evidence. The end date of *c*.1000, chosen as more or less the end of the first generation of monastic reform in England, has meant the exclusion of most of the comparatively abundant eleventh-century manuscript evidence, which remains mostly unedited and unstudied. The conclusions reached are therefore necessarily provisional. But I hope that they will provide a useful framework for future study of the Divine Office in English liturgical and literary sources, study that will enrich our understanding of the influences and aspirations that shaped Anglo-Saxon ecclesiastical and monastic culture, and especially of the distinctive ideology and praxis of the tenth-century English Benedictine reformers and their successors.

A number of the ideas and conclusions in the book were first presented in conference papers that have since been published. The substance of the tables in Chapter 7 was first published in D. Rollason, C. Leyser, and H. Williams (eds.), *England and the Continent in the Tenth Century* (Turnhout, 2011) – and here I would note my gratitude to the proof-reader of that volume, Deborah A. Oosterhouse of DAO Editorial Services, whose attention to detail prevented several unfortunate errors from remaining in the tables. An account of the distinctive Palm Sunday responsories discussed in Chapter 8 was included in my contribution to M. Diesenberger, Y. Hen, and M. Pollheimer (eds.), *'Sermo doctorum': Compilers, Preachers, and their Audiences in the Early Medieval West* (Brepols, 2013). I thank the British Library for permission to reproduce Royal MS 17. C. XVII, fol. 164r, and the Bodleian Library for permission to reproduce Rawl. MS D. 894, fol. 63r.

In the ten years that it has taken to bring this work from inception to publication, I have incurred debts of gratitude to a great many people. Chief among them is Susan Rankin, who when she accepted me as a doctoral student in 2003 could not have known that she was taking on the role of midwife in a long and painful labour. I had the benefit not only of her brilliant insight and creativity and of the example of her rigorous attention to detail in the analysis, interpretation, and presentation of the sources of our knowledge, but also of her generosity, patience, and genuine pastoral care, upon which the success of the project seemed so often to depend. Since my graduation in 2009 she has been an ever ready advocate and counsellor in all the doubts, disappointments, and occasional little victories that figure so large in a young scholar's early career. I am very grateful to her.

Next I must mention the late David Chadd. His work inspired the methodology developed in the second part of this book, which was improved through his perceptive suggestions and selfless sharing of laboriously collected data. His untimely death in 2006 cut short a conversation about the history of the Divine Office in England, and the use of computers in investigating it, that I had hoped would continue for many years.

Rosamond McKitterick supervised the M.Phil. dissertation that laid much of the groundwork for the doctoral research out of which this book arose, and always made herself available to help with specific and general questions. David Ganz generously assisted me on points of palaeography (including letting me read an early version of his essay on Square minuscule, which has since appeared in the first volume of *The Cambridge History of the Book in Britain*), as well as sharing his extensive knowledge of the literary and documentary sources of the early Middle Ages. Helmut Gneuss kindly shared unpublished information relating to MS Rawl. D. 894. Tom Licence, Michael Reeve, and Michael Lapidge helped with difficulties of Latin translation. I was fortunate to have two of my former teachers as Ph.D. examiners, Tessa Webber and Thomas F. Kelly, who read the original dissertation with care and offered helpful suggestions for its improvement. Rosalind Love and Michael Lapidge, in their capacity as members of the Publications Committee, first recommended my dissertation for publication by the Henry Bradshaw Society and shepherded its early progress. I am grateful to them for their efforts, and to the Society, of which I have been a member for nearly a decade but whose publications I admired even as an undergraduate. Nicolas Bell and Rosalind Love brought their remarkable erudition to the correction of the proofs. The meticulous care they bestowed on that task was profoundly humbling for the author. Eleanor Giraud was commissioned by the Society to prepare the indexes, which she did carefully and expertly. Her efficiency has allowed the book to come to publication much sooner than it would have if this essential work had been left in my hands. Nicolas Bell, Susan Rankin, and David Ganz offered various suggestions for the improvement of the indexes.

It goes without saying that no one who has assisted me in my research, writing, or proof-reading is responsible for any errors that remain. This conventional disclaimer is urgently relevant in this case, because I myself have produced camera-ready copy using the X$\exists$TEX document preparation system, a descendant of the LATEX system in which my dissertation was originally written. The author is therefore responsible for every jot and tittle in the book. That is a frightening thought in itself, but all the more so given that the book includes both dense numerical tables and heavily annotated semi-diplomatic editions of three difficult manuscript fragments. Nevertheless, I will confess that once a research grant from the Social Sciences and Humanities Research Council of Canada (SSHRC) enabled me to purchase a computer powerful enough to deal with the software, tinkering with the book became a source of immense satisfaction. I am grateful to the staff of the Boydell Press for being willing to trust this important work to an amateur, and for the guidance and correction that I have received from them along the way. As I grappled with the the extremely complex markup and coding that the text required, I had continual recourse to the generous and resourceful online TEX community. The most important interventions, however, came from a polymathic friend, David Allsopp, who distinguished himself by his keen enthusiasm and good humour in the face of frequent conundrums and occasional disasters.

Financial support for my doctoral research was provided by King's College, Cambridge, which awarded me the Augustus Austen Leigh Studentship and met many small costs and shortfalls besides. I also had the benefit of a choral scholarship between 2001 and 2004, which, while modest in financial terms, was one of the richest gifts I have ever received. The choir's Director of Music, Stephen Cleobury, kindly included me in projects where my scholarly work could be put to practical use. At King's I also benefitted from an ORS Award from Universities UK, a grant from the Cambridge Commonwealth Trust, a grant from the Bibliographical Society, and the Mary Le Messurier Scholarship from the Canadian Centennial Scholarship Fund, administered by the Canadian Women's Club of London. A generous grant from a discretionary fund administered by the late Rev. Prof. Peter J. Gomes at the Memorial Church, Harvard University, made it possible for me to go to Cambridge in the first place. In 2006 I was elected to a Research Fellowship at St John's College, Cambridge, where I completed my dissertation and made the first revisions for publication under the most favourable of circumstances, and with the leisure to pursue other projects and to teach. The College also contributed generously to various research expenses. In 2010 I returned home to Canada to take up a SSHRC post-doctoral fellowship at the Centre for Medieval Studies in the University of Toronto, which allowed me to continue with my academic work through a period of considerable strain and uncertainty. In 2012 I took up an assistant professorship at Trinity College, Toronto, and found there the stability and collegial support without which this book would probably have been abandoned. In that connection I must thank the then-Provost of Trinity, Andy Orchard, now Rawlinson and Bosworth Professor of Anglo-Saxon in the University of Oxford, who also served as my research adviser during my SSHRC fellowship and who has offered timely advice on matters both scholarly and practical.

Under the category of financial support, I must mention the late Peter Avery, OBE, of King's College, Cambridge, a student of Persian history and literature who for two years employed me as his amanuensis. Taking dictation from him in his College rooms opened my eyes to new worlds of learning and beauty. In the preface to my doctoral dissertation, I wrote that his friendship had changed my life. It was a sweet sorrow to present him with a copy of that preface at Addenbrooke's Hospital during his final illness. On reading it, he said to his assembled friends, 'I think I deserved that.' He did. Another departed benefactor is Dr Mary Berry, CBE, who taught me how to sing Gregorian chant *properly* and quietly gave me bursaries to attend chant and liturgy events organized by the Schola Gregoriana of Cambridge.

It remains only for me to thank my wife, Jill Aitken, whose love and support have been a constant encouragement. She deserves most of the credit for the completion of this book. She has carried me through many periods of doubt and torpor with characteristic discipline and tenacity, both before I finished my doctorate, when the happy arrival in 2007 of our daughter Margaret afforded me every opportunity to procrastinate, and after the birth of our two beautiful sons James (2009) and William (2011), who have conspired to allow me to typeset only under cover of darkness. The dedication of this book is but a token of my love and gratitude.

J. D. B.

Trinity College, Toronto
In festo S. Bedae Venerabilis
27 May 2014

Note on Usage

I use upper case 'O' when referring to the Divine Office as a single entity ('the Office'), and lower case 'o' when referring to specific services ('the office of Vespers', 'the daytime offices'). The second sense is sometimes communicated by the synonym 'hour' ('the lesser hours of Terce, Sext, and None'). I have tried to make clear from the context when the fourth-declension noun *cursus* should be read as a plural, without resorting to a macron (*cursūs*).

In the early Middle Ages, the midnight office was referred to as 'Nocturns' (*ad nocturnos*), and the morning office as 'Matins' (*matutina*). Eventually, Nocturns came to be called 'Matins', and Matins became 'Lauds', from the daily *Laudate* Psalms, 148 and 150. I have used a conflation of early and late medieval terms (Night Office and Lauds) to avoid confusion. Some (e.g. the Carthusians) use 'Night Office' to refer to Nocturns and Lauds together. I use it to refer only to Nocturns.

In the second part of the book I follow David Chadd in using the term *ordo* in a specific technical sense to denote the distinctive selection and arrangement of chants in any one source.

When an edition of a text includes a facing translation ('ed. and tr.'), I quote from the facing translation unless otherwise indicated, giving the original language in a footnote. Otherwise, unless another published translation is explicitly cited, translations are my own.

In palaeographical descriptions I use the terminology defined in M. B. Parkes, *English Cursive Bookhands 1250–1500* (Oxford, 1969; rev. repr. London, 1979), p. xxvi, and in Parkes's *Their Hands Before Our Eyes: A Closer Look at Scribes* (Aldershot, 2008); see especially the glossary, pp. 149–55.

In Latin transcriptions, I have preferred consonantal *i* and *u*; but all Latin quotations reproduce exactly the orthography of the editions from which they are drawn, including *j* and *v*. In the diplomatic editions in the appendices, scribal distinctions between *u* and *v* are reproduced (most commonly *capitalis* 'V' as a *littera notabilior*). In the appendices I have largely followed the transcription conventions proposed in Parkes, *English Cursive Bookhands*, pp. xxviii–xxix.

Abbreviations

Andrieu	*Les Ordines Romani du haut Moyen Âge*, ed. M. Andrieu, 5 vols., Spicilegium sacrum Lovaniense 11, 23, 24, 28, 29 (Louvain, 1931–61).
BCS	*Cartularium Saxonicum: A Collection of Charters relating to Anglo-Saxon History*, ed. W. de G. Birch, 3 vols. and Index (London, 1885–99); cited by number assigned by Birch to each charter.
Bede, *Historia ecclesiastica*	Bede, *Historia ecclesiastica gentis Anglorum*, ed. C. Plummer, *Venerabilis Baedae Opera historica*, 2 vols. (Oxford, 1896). Translation: B. Colgrave, in J. McClure and R. Collins, *Bede: The Ecclesiastical History of the English People, The Greater Chronicle, Bede's Letter to Egbert* (Oxford, 1999), pp. 1–295.
BL	London, British Library
BnF	Paris, Bibliothèque nationale de France
CAO	*Corpus antiphonalium officii*, ed. R.-J. Hesbert, 6 vols., Rerum ecclesiasticarum documenta, Series maior, Fontes, 7–12 (Rome, 1963–79).
CCCM	Corpus Christianorum, Continuatio medievalis
CCM	Corpus consuetudinum monasticarum (Siegburg, 1963–).
CCSL	Corpus Christianorum, Series Latina
CLA	*Codices Latini antiquiores: A Palaeographical Guide to Latin Manuscripts Prior to the Ninth Century*, ed. E. A. Lowe, 12 vols. (Oxford, 1934–71).
EEMF	Early English Manuscripts in Facsimile
EETS	Early English Text Society original series
EHD I	*English Historical Documents*, I: *c. 500–1042*, ed. D. Whitelock, 2nd edn (London, 1996).
Gamber, *CLLA*	K. Gamber, *Codices liturgici Latini antiquiores*, 2nd edn and *Supplementum* (with G. Baroffio), 3 vols., Spicilegii Friburgensis subsidia 1, 1a (Freiburg, Switzerland, 1968–88).

ABBREVIATIONS

Gneuss, *Handlist*	H. Gneuss, *Handlist of Anglo-Saxon Manuscripts: A List of Manuscripts and Manuscript Fragments Written or Owned in England up to 1100*, Medieval and Renaissance Studies 241 (Tempe, AZ, 2001).
Haddan and Stubbs, *Councils*	*Councils and Ecclesiastical Documents relating to Great Britain and Ireland*, ed. A. W. Haddan and W. Stubbs, 3 vols. (Oxford, 1869–78).
Hartzell, *Catalogue*	K. D. Hartzell, *Catalogue of Manuscripts Written or Owned in England up to 1200 Containing Music* (Woodbridge, 2006).
HBS	Henry Bradshaw Society
Ker, *Catalogue*	N. R. Ker, *A Catalogue of Manuscripts Containing Anglo-Saxon* (Oxford, 1957; repr. 1990 with supplement originally ptd in *Anglo-Saxon England* 5 (1977), 121–31).
MGH	Monumenta Germaniae historica
Cap.	Legum sectio II: *Capitularia regum Francorum*, ed. A. Boretius and V. Krause, 2 vols. (Hanover, 1883–97).
Conc.	Legum sectio III: Concilia (Hanover, 1883–).
Epp.	Epistolae in quarto, 6 vols. (Berlin, 1891–1939).
SRG	Scriptores rerum Germanicarum in usum scholarum (Hanover, 1871–).
SS	Scriptores in folio, 30 vols. (Hanover, 1824–1924).
PL	*Patrologiae cursus completus: Series Latina*, ed. J.-P. Migne, 221 vols. (Paris, 1841–64).
Plummer	*Venerabilis Baedae Opera historica*, ed. C. Plummer, 2 vols. (Oxford, 1896).
Regularis concordia, ed. Symons	*Regularis concordia Anglicae nationis monachorum sanctimonialiumque*, ed. and tr. T. Symons, *The Monastic Agreement of the Monks and Nuns of the English Nation*, Nelson's Medieval Classics (Oxford, 1953). All quotations and translations (unless otherwise indicated) are from this edition.
Regularis concordia (CCM)	*Regularis concordia Anglicae nationis*, ed. T. Symons and S. Spath (with M. Wegener and K. Hallinger), in *Consuetudinum saeculi X/XI/XII monumenta non-Cluniacensia*, ed. K. Hallinger, CCM 7.3 (Siegburg, 1984), pp. 61–147. This text, which includes a much fuller critical apparatus, is not quoted, but its section and page numbers are given in parentheses.

ABBREVIATIONS

RSB   *Regula S. Benedicti*, ed. J. Neufville, in A. de Vogüé, *La Règle de Saint Benoît*, 7 vols., Sources chrétiennes 181–6, vol. 7 *extra seriem* (Paris, 1971–7), I–II. Translation: *RB 1980: The Rule of St. Benedict in Latin and English with Notes*, ed. T. Fry (Collegeville, MN, 1981).

S   Numbered charters in P. H. Sawyer, *Anglo-Saxon Charters: An Annotated List and Bibliography*, Royal Historical Society Guides and Handbooks 8 (London, 1968).

Manuscript Sigla

A44   Albi, Bibliothèque municipale Rochegude, 44 (antiphoner, written at Albi for an unknown church, s. ix ex., *c.*890); ed. J. A. Emerson and L. Collamore, *Albi, Bibliothèque Municipale Rochegude, Manuscript 44: A Complete Ninth-Century Gradual and Antiphoner from Southern France* (Ottawa, 2002).

Alb   BL C.110.a.27 (printed breviary, use of Benedictine abbey of St Albans, 1532).

B   Bamberg, Staatsbibliothek, Lit. 23 (antiphoner, Bamberg, s. xii); ed. Hesbert, *CAO*.

Bec   BnF lat. 1208 (Bec consuetudinary with additional liturgical matter, Priory of Notre-Dame de Bonne-Nouvelle, Rouen, s. xiii/xiv); ed. M. P. Dickson, *Consuetudines Beccenses*, CCM 4 (Siegburg, 1967).

BnR   Rouen, Bibliothèque municipale, 254 (*olim* A. 226) (antiphoner, Priory of Notre-Dame de Bonne-Nouvelle, Rouen, s. xiv).

Brn   BL Burney 277, fols. 69–72, with BL Stowe 1061, fol. 125.

C   BnF lat. 17436 ('Antiphoner of Charles the Bald', Compiègne, 860×880); ed. Hesbert, *CAO*.

Cbr   Cambrai, Bibliothèque municipale, 38 (*olim* 40) (antiphoner, Cambrai Cathedral, *c.*1230–*c.*1250); indexed by B. Haggh, K. Glaeske, and L. Collamore in the 'CANTUS Database'.

Cdm   BL Harley 4664 (breviary, Coldingham Priory, Berwicksh., cell of Durham Cathedral Priory, s. xiii).

Cht   Oxford, Bodleian Library, Lat. liturg. e. 6, e. 37, e. 39, and d. 42 (partially dismembered breviary of Chertsey Abbey, Surrey, *c.*1320).

Clu   BnF lat. 12601 (noted breviary, use of the abbey of Cluny, Burgundy, s. xi ex.).

Cor1   BnF lat. 11522 (breviary, Corbie, s. xi/xii).

Cor2   Amiens, Bibliothèque municipale, 115 (noted breviary, Corbie, s. xii med.).

MANUSCRIPT SIGLA

D	BnF lat. 17296 (antiphoner, monastery of Saint-Denis, Paris, s. xii); ed. Hesbert, *CAO*.
E	Ivrea, Biblioteca Capitolare, CVI (antiphoner, Ivrea, s. xi); ed. Hesbert, *CAO*.
Ely	Cambridge, University Library, Ii. 4. 20 (breviary-missal, Ely Cathedral Priory, s. xiii).
Evm	Oxford, Bodleian Library, Barlow 41 (*pars hiemalis* of a breviary of Evesham Abbey, Gloucestershire, s. xiii).
F	BnF lat. 12584 (antiphoner, Saint-Maur-des-Fossés, s. xi/xii); ed. Hesbert, *CAO*.
Féc	Fécamp, Musée de la Bénédictine 186 (ordinal, Fécamp, s. xii ex.), supplemented with Rouen, Bibliothèque municipale, 245 (*olim* A. 190) (antiphoner, s. xiii in.), and Rouen 244 (A. 261) (noted breviary, s. xii ex.); ed. D. Chadd, *The Ordinal of the Abbey of the Holy Trinity, Fécamp (Fécamp, Musée de la Bénédictine, MS 186)*, 2 vols., HBS 111–12 (Woodbridge, 1999–2002).
Flr	Orléans, Bibliothèque municipale, 129 (*olim* 107) (ordinal, Fleury, s. xiii); ed. A. Davril, *Consuetudines Floriacenses saeculi tertii decimi*, CCM 9 (Siegburg, 1976).
G	Durham, Cathedral Library, B. III. 11 (antiphoner, France, s. xi); ed. Hesbert, *CAO*.
Glo	Oxford, Jesus College 10 (diurnal and hymnal from a breviary of Gloucester Abbey, s. xii–xv).
Gnt	BL Add. 29253 (breviary, Ghent, s. xiv).
H	St Gall, Stiftsbibliothek, 390–1 (antiphoner, St Gall, s. x/xi); facsimile: *Antiphonaire de Hartker: Manuscrits Saint-Gall, 390–391*, Paléographie musicale, 2nd ser., 1 (Solesmes, 1900); new edn ed. J. Froger (Berne, 1970); text ed. Hesbert, *CAO*.
Hyd	Oxford, Bodleian Library, Rawl. liturg. e.1* (breviary, Hyde Abbey, Winchester, s. xiii/xiv); ed. J. B. L. Tolhurst, *The Monastic Breviary of Hyde Abbey, Winchester*, 6 vols., HBS 69, 70, 71, 76, 78, 80 (London, 1932–42).

MANUSCRIPT SIGLA

L   Benevento, Archivio Capitolare, 21 (antiphoner, S. Italy, Beneventan script, attributed by Hesbert, without documentation, to the abbey of San Lupo, s. xii ex.); ed. Hesbert, *CAO*.

M   Monza, Basilica S. Giovanni C. 12/75 (antiphoner, Monza, s. xi); ed. Hesbert, *CAO*.

Mch   BL Add. 43405–6 (breviary in two volumes, Muchelney Abbey, Somerset, s. xiii)

MoR   Private collection, 'Antiphoner of Mont-Renaud'; facsimile: *Antiphonaire du Mont-Renaud*, Paléographie musicale 16 (Solesmes, 1959; 2nd edn 1989).

Nor   BnF lat. 1276 (breviary, unidentified Norman monastery, s. xiv)

OuR   Rouen, Bibliothèque municipale, 252 (*olim* A. 486) (antiphoner, St-Ouen, Rouen, s. xiv).

Par   BnF lat. 15181 and 15182 (noted breviary, two volumes, Notre-Dame Cathedral, Paris, *c.*1300); indexed by S. Kidwell, with editorial assistance from C. Downey, in the 'CANTUS Database'.

Pet   Cambridge, Magdalene College, F. 4. 10 (antiphoner, Peterborough Abbey, s. xiv).

R   Zurich, Zentralbibliothek, Rheinau 28 (antiphoner, Rheinau, s. xiii); ed. Hesbert, *CAO*.

Roy   BL Royal 17. C. XVII, fols. 2–3, 163–6

Rwl   Oxford, Bodleian Library, Rawlinson D. 894, fols. 62–3.

S   BL Add. 30850 (antiphoner, Silos, s. xi); ed. Hesbert, *CAO*.

Tro   BnF lat. 13241 and 13242 (breviary, Troarn, s. xv).

V   Verona, Biblioteca Capitolare, XCVIII (antiphoner, Verona, s. xi); ed. Hesbert, *CAO*.

Vst   Arras, Bibliothèque municipale, 465 (*olim* 893) (antiphoner, St-Vaast, Arras, s. xiv); indexed by K. Glaeske, C. Downey, and L. Collamore in the 'CANTUS Database'.

Wcb   Valenciennes, Bibliothèque municipale, 116 (breviary-missal of Winchcombe Abbey, Gloucestershire, *c.*1140).

Wor   Worcester, Cathedral Library, F. 160 (composite book including antiphoner, Worcester Cathedral Priory, s. xiii[1]); facsimile: *Le Codex F. 160 de la bibliothèque de la cathédrale de Worcester: Antiphonaire monastique (XIIIe siècle)*, 2 vols., introduction and facsimile, Paléographie musicale 12 (Tournai, 1922); 2nd edn, facsimile only (Solesmes, 1997).

MANUSCRIPT SIGLA

Wul Cambridge, Corpus Christi College 391 ('Portiforium of St Wulfstan' with breviary-style Offices, Worcester Cathedral Priory, s. xi med.); ed. A. Hughes, *The Portiforium of St Wulstan*, 2 vols., HBS 89–90 (Leighton Buzzard, 1958–60).

Yor-M Cambridge, St John's College D27 (ordinal and customary, St Mary's Abbey, York, s. xv); ed. The Abbess of Stanbrook [L. McLachlan] and J. B. L. Tolhurst, *The Ordinal and Customary of the Abbey of Saint Mary, York*, 3 vols., HBS 73, 75, 84 (London, 1936–51).

Part I

The Historical Development of the Divine Office in England to *c.*1000

1

Towards a 'New Narrative' of the History of the Divine Office in Anglo-Saxon England

This book is about the Divine Office and its performance in Anglo-Saxon England. The Divine Office comprises the several non-sacramental services of psalmody, lections, and prayers recited daily by religious communities (usually of monks, nuns, or canons), and by individuals otherwise bound to do so. Unlike research into the Mass, work on the Divine Office has historically been the preserve of priests and religious, intended for a clerical audience.[1] In recent decades, however, a number of important studies and research tools have appeared that have made the Office more accessible to the wider scholarly community.[2] Research on the Divine

---

[1] The disparity is vividly demonstrated in Cyrille Vogel's classic work *Introduction aux sources de l'histoire du cult chrétien au Moyen Âge*. The only serious treatment of the liturgy known widely among non-specialists, the revised and expanded English version devotes just six pages to the Divine Office: C. Vogel, *Medieval Liturgy: An Introduction to the Sources*, rev. and tr. W. Storey and N. Rasmussen (Portland, OR, 1986), pp. 363–8.

[2] In particular, two valuable surveys of its development and regional variation: P. Bradshaw, *Daily Prayer in the Early Church: A Study of the Origin and Early Development of the Divine Office*, Alcuin Club Collections 63 (London, 1981); R. Taft, *The Liturgy of the Hours in East and West: The Origins of the Divine Office and its Meaning for Today*, 2nd rev. edn (Collegeville, MN, 1993). And also convenient, reliable, and insightful handbooks for understanding the minutiae of Office liturgy and Office books: A. Hughes, *Medieval Manuscripts for Mass and Office: A Guide to their Organization and Terminology* (Toronto, 1982); J. Harper, *The Forms and Orders of Western Liturgy from the Tenth to the Eighteenth Century: A Historical Introduction and Guide for Students and Musicians* (Oxford, 1991). The electronic CANTUS Database continues to offer new students the chance to become intimately familiar with the music books of the Office, the antiphoner and the noted breviary, through preparing digital indices of manuscripts for inclusion in the database: 'CANTUS: A Database for Latin Ecclesiastical Chant', currently hosted by the University of Waterloo <http://cantusdatabase.org> last visited 5 April 2013. The appearance in 2000 of an important collection of essays showed that the Divine Office was finally beginning to receive the attention it deserves from medievalists of many disciplines: M. E. Fassler and R. A. Baltzer (eds.), *The Divine Office in the Latin Middle Ages: Methodology and Source Studies, Regional Developments, Hagiography* (Oxford, 2000).

Office in Anglo-Saxon England has enjoyed the benefit of earlier scholars' dedication to the production of authoritative and accessible editions of English liturgical manuscripts.[3] Apart from editions, the literature has fallen largely into two categories: 'descriptive' studies, concerned with the cataloguing and editing of texts and the identification of references to the Office in narrative sources and booklists,[4] and 'functional' studies, exploring how the Office can provide the key to the correct interpretation of material not itself directly connected with the performance of the liturgy (such as vernacular literary works).[5]

The study of the Office in Anglo-Saxon England has been largely contained to the tenth and eleventh centuries, the period best attested in surviving manuscripts. Most of these manuscripts (and they are largely fragmentary) present the liturgical situation in England in the wake of the Benedictine reform movement of the second half of the tenth century. In much that has been written about the Anglo-Saxon Office, there may be discerned a set of prevailing assumptions that the tenth- and eleventh-century situation may be read back into the poorly documented seventh, eighth, and ninth centuries. These assumptions are based on a traditional narrative of the history of the Office in England that might be dubbed the 'Benedictine Hypothesis'.

Inquiry into the liturgy of the Divine Office as it was performed in the first 350 years of Anglo-Saxon Christianity has for over a century been subsumed into the larger subject of Anglo-Saxon monastic life in general, which has until recently been centred on the question of when the *Regula S. Benedicti* was first introduced to England. As shall be seen in more detail in Chapter 2, the *Regula S. Benedicti* lays down a very distinctive

---

[3] First in the publications of the Surtees Society and later in those of the Henry Bradshaw Society 'for the editing of rare liturgical texts', whose work is ongoing: most recently, *The Durham Collectar*, ed. A. Corrêa, HBS 107 (London, 1992), which, in addition to an edition of the manuscript, includes discussion of the evolution of composite books for the Office.

[4] H. Gneuss, 'Liturgical books in Anglo-Saxon England and their Old English terminology', in M. Lapidge and H. Gneuss (eds.), *Learning and Literature in Anglo-Saxon England: Studies presented to Peter Clemoes on the occasion of his Sixty-fifth Birthday* (Cambridge, 1985), pp. 91–141, with the books of the Office described at pp. 110–27; R. W. Pfaff (ed.), *The Liturgical Books of Anglo-Saxon England*, Old English Newsletter, Subsidia 23 (Kalamazoo, MI, 1995), especially pp. 45–85.

[5] S. Rankin, 'The liturgical background of the Old English Advent lyrics: A reappraisal', in Gneuss and Lapidge, *Learning and Literature*, pp. 317–40; and in the same volume, M. McC. Gatch, 'The Office in late Anglo-Saxon monasticism', pp. 341–62, discussing the link between the vernacular sermons of Ælfric of Eynsham and the annual cycle of biblical readings at the Night Office.

manner in which the Divine Office is to be performed. If the point at which English monks were following the *Regula S. Benedicti* could be determined, so the hypothesis goes, it would be known what form of the Office they were using. Writing in 1888, Henri Logeman articulated three possibilities: (a) the Rule arrived in 597 with Augustine of Canterbury and his companions (Logeman's preference); (b) it was introduced in the time of Bishop Wilfrid, in the latter half of the seventh century; or (c) observance of the Rule could not be discerned anywhere in England before the time of Saint Dunstan and the monastic reform of the tenth century. All students of the question were 'agreed in attributing a high character and a great authority to the Rule in England when once introduced'.[6]

The last major attempt to claim St Augustine of Canterbury for the Benedictine Order was made by Cuthbert Butler in 1882, arguing, based on supposed allusions in the writings of Gregory the Great to the text of the *Regula S. Benedicti*, that Gregory's monastery dedicated to St Andrew on the Coelian Hill in Rome, of which St Augustine had been 'prior', followed the Rule.[7] Ultimately, however, this tradition rests solely on Gregory's authorship of a biography of St Benedict, which formed the second book of his *Dialogi*.[8] If Gregory knew the text of the Rule, which seems likely, it does not necessarily follow that it governed his own monastic life or that Augustine himself studied it, though Augustine may have absorbed its teachings through Gregory, who as his abbot was his first teacher in the patrimony of monastic tradition.[9] And there is nothing to indicate that any monastery in Rome was strictly 'Benedictine' before the tenth century.[10] Yet despite the circumspection shown by later authors, the traditional view that Augustine was a Benedictine has proved tenacious, as

---

[6] *The Rule of S. Benet: Latin and Anglo-Saxon Interlinear Version*, ed. H. Logeman, EETS 90 (London, 1888), p. xvi.
[7] C. Butler, 'Was St. Augustine of Canterbury a Benedictine?', *Downside Review* 3 (1882), 45–61 and 223–40.
[8] Gregory I, *Dialogi* (*Dialogorum libri IV*), II, ed. A. de Vogüé, *Grégoire le Grand: Dialogues*, II: *Livres I–III*, Sources chrétiennes 260 (Paris, 1979), pp. 120–249; tr. C. White, *Early Christian Lives* (London, 1998), pp. 161–204.
[9] P. Wormald and T. Charles-Edwards, addenda to J. M. Wallace-Hadrill, *Bede's Ecclesiastical History of the English People: A Historical Commentary*, Oxford Medieval Texts (Oxford, 1993), p. 217.
[10] K. Hallinger, 'Papst Gregor der Grosse und der hl. Benedict', in B. Steidle (ed.), *Commentationes in Regulam S. Benedicti*, Studia Anselmiana 42 (Rome, 1957), pp. 231–319; G. Ferrari, *Early Roman Monasteries: Notes for the History of the Monasteries and Convents at Rome from the V through the X Century*, Studi di antichità cristiana 23 (Vatican City, 1957), pp. 379–407.

in Bertram Colgrave's judgement (reprinted in 1985) that 'The rule of St Benedict was of course introduced to England by St Augustine and his fellow-monks in 597. The monastery he established, was probably the first Benedictine house outside Italy'.[11] St Augustine has remained firmly Benedictine in the imaginations of many non-specialists.

Whatever doubts persisted about Augustine, none doubted that the Venerable Bede was a true follower of the *Regula S. Benedicti*. Butler considered him 'assuredly a typical Benedictine'.[12] J. M. Wallace-Hadrill indirectly revealed that he was of the same opinion when he wrote of St Augustine and his companions, 'Had they been followers of St Benedict, Bede would surely have recorded it,' because, in Wallace-Hadrill's thinking, Bede was obviously a Benedictine himself.[13] David Knowles considered that the Northumbrian monasteries were the first in England to accept the Rule from their foundation, although he recognized that the discretion of the abbot would have been important in its application.[14]

So far as the liturgy of the monastic Office in England has been considered at all, it has been against this backdrop of an assumed dominance of the *Regula S. Benedicti*. For Charles Plummer, the Office sung at Wearmouth in the time of Benedict Biscop was obviously that of the Rule.[15] The view that English 'Benedictines' of Bede's time were using a Benedictine Office liturgy is implicit in David Knowles's case for a complete extinction of English monasticism under the pressure of Viking raids during the ninth century.[16] In a discussion of the celebrated 'Worcester Antiphoner', Worcester, Cathedral Library, F. 160 (Worcester, s. xiii),[17] Knowles observed that Worcester had not been a monastic church before

---

[11] See Colgrave's edn of Stephen of Ripon's *Vita S. Wilfridi: The Life of Bishop Wilfrid by Eddius Stephanus*, ed. and tr. B. Colgrave (Cambridge, 1927), p. 161.
[12] 'Was St. Augustine of Canterbury a Benedictine?', p. 59.
[13] Wallace-Hadrill, *Bede's Ecclesiastical History*, p. 36. But see the addenda to this comment by Wormald and Charles-Edwards, cited in n. 9, above.
[14] D. Knowles, *The Monastic Order in England: A History of its Development from the Times of St Dunstan to the Fourth Lateran Council, 940–1216*, 2nd edn (Cambridge, 1963), pp. 22–3.
[15] *Venerabilis Baedae Opera historica*, ed. Plummer II, 364.
[16] See his Appendix I, *The Monastic Order*, p. 695.
[17] *Le Codex F. 160 de la bibliothèque de la cathédrale de Worcester: Antiphonaire monastique (XIIIe siècle)*, 2 vols., text and facsimile, Paléographie musicale 12 (Tournai, 1922); 2nd edn, facsimile only (Solesmes, 1997). The volume containing an introductory text to the first edition includes an extended essay presenting the 'traditional' view, now to be rejected, of the introduction of Gregorian chant to England by Augustine of Canterbury, written by Laurentia McLachlan, abbess of Stanbrook (pp. 99–110). The second edition gives the facsimile with only such introductory material as pertains to the manuscript directly.

its reform under St Oswald, and therefore, 'even if some of the old books had survived [the ninth century] they would not have contained the full monastic office, nor would a tradition of chant have survived the period of decadence with all the purity of the Worcester *Antiphoner*'.[18] In other words, in Knowles's thinking, any books from a monastic church of the eighth or ninth century would be expected to contain the Benedictine Office. Worcester lacked them only because it had not previously been a Benedictine foundation.[19]

The traditional 'narrative' underlying the writings cited above, which remains popular today, can be summarized as follows. St Augustine of Canterbury, like his patron, Pope Gregory I, was a Benedictine monk. After arriving in England, he and his companions continued to pray the Divine Office according to the pattern given in the *Regula S. Benedicti*. This use spread throughout the monasteries of England, supplanting the customs taught by a separate wave of Irish missionaries. Benedictine liturgy especially flourished in an eighth-century 'golden age' in Bede's Northumbria. Pure Benedictine monasticism was wiped out in the ninth century through the combined effects of foreign invasions and native laxity. True monasticism, together with monastic liturgy, was only restored to its pure original form in the middle of the tenth century as part of the revival led by St Dunstan, St Æthelwold, and St Oswald. This was accomplished by importing teachers and liturgical books from reformed monasteries on the Continent, since the native English tradition had entirely disappeared. The sources of this restoration, however, were themselves sufficiently pure that the reformed monastic Office liturgy was substantially identical to what had been performed at Wearmouth-Jarrow in the eighth century, and indeed at Canterbury in the seventh.

Most students of Anglo-Saxon history, even those without special knowledge of the liturgy, would reject this model today. Not one statement in this narrative should now be accepted as true. It seems likely that this set of assumptions has gone unchallenged from the nineteenth century down to the present day only because it has never been articulated so baldly. Except for oblique inferences and tangential comments that reveal that they hold these assumptions, most authors describing Anglo-Saxon monasticism have been generally silent about the Office.

The main problem with the 'Benedictine Hypothesis' is that it fails to

---

[18] Knowles, *The Monastic Order*, p. 554.
[19] To call the chant of the Worcester Antiphoner 'pure' presents its own problems.

distinguish between three very different questions to do with the *Regula S. Benedicti*: When was the Rule introduced to England? Did English abbots govern their monks according to the Rule's directions? And if so, did they feel obliged to obey the Rule's liturgical code as well? The traditional narrative of the 'Benedictine Hypothesis' assumes that the answer to the second and third questions would be 'Yes' as soon as the Rule was introduced into England. It conflates Benedictine liturgy with Benedictine monastic piety and discipline.

During the past forty years, the shaky structure of assumptions underlying this view of Anglo-Saxon monasticism and liturgy has been completely dismantled. Even Cuthbert Butler had been forced to admit that the 'Benedictines' of seventh- and eighth-century England were not the same as Benedictines of later centuries; indeed, he suggested that opposition to his argument would arise mainly from 'the application to those early days of modern ideas, then unknown, about religious orders, and the hard and fast distinctions between them'.[20] Scholars have taken care not to read later medieval models of monastic life back into earlier centuries, and particularly not into the lives of prominent English churchmen.[21] The Latin word *monasterium* and its Old English equivalent *mynster* are now seen to denote not merely communities devoted to an enclosed, contemplative religious life, but also ecclesiastical foundations of varying composition, some of whose members were involved in the active life of pastoral care.[22] A minster might include a mixture of priests, monks, lesser clerics, and nuns; secular clergy are often mentioned in the seventh- and eighth-century sources as residents of *monasteria*, under the authority of some kind of superior. These 'minsters' were the hub of their pastoral activities.[23]

Initial attempts to determine the place of these early medieval minsters in the development of the parochial system of later medieval centuries were dogged by controversy, earning the pejorative epithet of 'the Minster

---

[20] Butler, 'Was St. Augustine of Canterbury a Benedictine?', p. 240.
[21] P. Wormald, 'Bede and Benedict Biscop', in G. Bonner (ed.), *Famulus Christi: Essays in Commemoration of the Thirteenth Centenary of the Birth of the Venerable Bede* (London, 1976), pp. 141–69. C. Holdsworth, 'Saint Boniface the monk', in T. Reuter (ed.), *The Greatest Englishman: Essays on St Boniface and the Church at Crediton* (Exeter, 1980), pp. 47–67.
[22] S. Foot, 'Anglo-Saxon minsters: A review of terminology', in J. Blair and R. Sharpe (eds.), *Pastoral Care before the Parish* (Leicester, 1992), pp. 212–25.
[23] C. Cubitt, *Anglo-Saxon Church Councils c.650–c.850* (London, 1995), p. 116.

Hypothesis'.[24] There is now little disagreement, however, that England's 'monastic landscape' in the seventh, eighth, and ninth centuries embraced a panoply of forms, some of which are only mentioned in the narrative sources so that they may be criticized. As John Blair has recently put it:

> The reality is likely to have been a spectrum containing a rich and varied mixture of forms, and if some were spiritually unappealing and pastorally supine when viewed from the moral heights of Jarrow, it need not follow that they were socially or culturally useless to the laity around them.[25]

The implications of the new 'minster model' of the early Anglo-Saxon Church for the liturgy of the Divine Office are substantial. That no one surviving monastic rule seems to have been imposed on monasteries means that it is unsafe to construct a general picture of Anglo-Saxon Office liturgy based on the few references to the customs of individual houses that are scattered throughout the narrative sources. The ground for a major reassessment of the evidence has been prepared by Sarah Foot in her fine study of early English monasticism.[26] From letters, saints' lives, and Bede's *Historia ecclesiastica,* Foot has culled an impressive array of references to the various hours of prayer observed in different minsters. As liturgical scholars are only too aware, contemporary authors record very little about the liturgy, probably because there was no need to explain liturgical details to their audiences, who were often vowed religious themselves. Hagiographers would be more likely to mention the personal devotions of saints beyond the shared liturgical round of the community.[27] The same problem arises in liturgical books, where the most fundamental texts are often omitted as too familiar to need explanation, leaving the modern researcher, who can never attain a personal, practical experience of the medieval monastic liturgy, to supply the missing information through informed guesswork. Such guesswork

---

[24] E. Cambridge and D. Rollason, 'Debate: The pastoral organization of the Anglo-Saxon Church: A review of the "Minster Hypothesis" ', *Early Medieval Europe* 4 (1995), 87–104. This criticism elicited a useful defence, moderating some aspects of the new interpretation: J. Blair, 'Debate: Ecclesiastical organization and pastoral care in Anglo-Saxon England', *Early Medieval Europe* 4 (1995), 192–212. These two articles cover most of the earlier bibliography on the subject.
[25] J. Blair, *The Church in Anglo-Saxon Society* (Oxford, 2005), p. 81.
[26] S. Foot, *Monastic Life in Anglo-Saxon England, c. 600–900* (Cambridge, 2006), pp. 191–205.
[27] Foot, *Monastic Life*, p. 199.

is rendered extremely difficult by the variety that must have prevailed in Anglo-Saxon liturgical observance. Foot's cautious refusal to read later practices or Continental documents into the early Anglo-Saxon context forces her to conclude that much of early Anglo-Saxon liturgical custom is unknowable beyond the broad outlines that emerge from the consensus of her sources: 'Bearing in mind the impossibility of reconstructing precisely how the office was celebrated in any one house, it is probably unwise to attempt to read too much into these isolated references.'[28] As shall be shown in subsequent chapters of this study, however, a good deal more can be said about the sources that survive than Foot was able to pursue in what was only a small section of a larger work.[29] The liturgy of the Office as sung in English minsters was no doubt influenced by many different liturgical traditions – Italian, Irish, Frankish, Spanish. A certain amount of eclecticism probably characterized even those houses that would have identified themselves as strictly 'Roman' or 'Irish' in ethos, classifications belying the interwoven strands of English monastic and liturgical custom.[30] Gregory the Great had, after all, advised Augustine to take whatever he thought beneficial from the non-Roman liturgies he encountered, even if observers like Bede may have taken a narrow view of whether anything truly beneficial was to be found outside the Roman heritage of the English Church.[31] Nevertheless, despite the severe lack of surviving liturgical books and the large chronological spread over which the scant available evidence is scattered, it is possible to make certain assertions about the Office as it was sung in at least the larger, better established minsters of England. This is the subject of Chapter 3 of this study. Chapter 4 examines the effects on Office liturgy of the Viking invasions and the decline in learning of the ninth century, as well as the revival under King Alfred. Chapter 5 assesses the sources and impact of the tenth-century Benedictine reform.

---

[28] Foot, *Monastic Life*, p. 197.
[29] That Foot's interpretations of the evidence have occasionally been revised or contradicted in these pages should not in any way be seen as a denigration of the contribution she has made. Moreover, Foot's survey contains valuable information not covered here, particularly about parallel questions such as who participated in the Office in Anglo-Saxon minsters.
[30] Blair, *The Church in Anglo-Saxon Society*, p. 81; P. Sims-Williams, *Religion and Literature in Western England, 600–800*, Cambridge Studies in Anglo-Saxon England 3 (Cambridge, 1990), pp. 87–143.
[31] Gregory's second *responsio*, in Bede, *Historia ecclesiastica*, I. 28, ed. Plummer I, 49. See P. Meyvaert, 'Diversity within unity: A Gregorian theme', *Heythrop Journal* 4 (1963), 141–62, repr. as ch. VI in his *Benedict, Gregory, Bede and Others* (London, 1977).

Without attempting to provide a comprehensive history of the Divine Office in England up to the Conquest, this book shall propose a new 'narrative' to replace the untenable assumptions behind much thinking on the Anglo-Saxon Office to date. It will be useful to advertise here, in broad outline, the conclusions that will be reached. The form of the Office introduced by the Augustinian mission cannot have been 'Benedictine' in the later medieval sense. It was probably an early form of the Office sung by monastic communities attached to the major basilicas in Rome, a precursor to what would later be called the 'secular' Office, sung by priests and clerks. This Roman form of the Office gradually found favour with English abbots and abbesses, who were not bound to follow the liturgical prescriptions of any one monastic rule. Significantly, there was in the early centuries no distinction between the Offices sung by secular clergy and vowed monastics, just as there was no clear distinction between 'secular' and 'monastic' churches or communities. The Viking invasions of the ninth century, coinciding with a decline in English learning and a secularization of religious communities, may have done violence to English ecclesiastical culture; but the liturgy of the Office was not entirely lost, nor was there total discontinuity with the past. The reform of learning under King Alfred reinvigorated the old traditions and introduced more recent Continental developments, including, it would seem, a 'Gregorian' (Romano-Frankish) form of the Roman Office. In the middle of the tenth century, pursuing a fundamentalist interpretation of the *Regula S. Benedicti*, a small but influential group of reformed monasteries began to sing the Office according to a strictly Benedictine pattern, the first time this had ever been done in England. The secular clergy continued to sing the Roman or 'secular' Office. While a significant number of the reformed houses, chiefly those connected with Bishop Æthelwold, did seek to imitate exactly what they found in the Office books of reformed Continental houses, other communities, and it seems that these were affiliated with St Dunstan, adapted books already in their possession – books arranged for use with the Roman form of the Office – to be used with the new Benedictine pattern.

This new narrative can be reduced to two essential points. First, although the *Regula S. Benedicti* was known and studied in early Anglo-Saxon England, the Benedictine form of the Office was not used in England before the monastic reform of the tenth century. Second, once this reform took place, it was not absolutely necessary for monasteries to apply to the Continent for books suitable for the new Office liturgy, even if one influential group of houses seems to have done so. The first point is elaborated in the historical discussions in Chapters 3 to 5, taking into account contemporary Continental liturgical developments, discussed in Chapter 2. Evidence for the second point is adduced in the studies of individual manuscript fragments that make up Chapters 7, 8, and 9, making use of both conventional palaeographical and codicological approaches and a comparative liturgical methodology that is developed in Chapter 6.

2

The Divine Office in the Latin West in the Early Middle Ages

The history of the Divine Office as it was performed in Anglo-Saxon England cannot be considered in isolation from the history of the Office on the Continent. In the present chapter, a few Continental themes of special importance to the Anglo-Saxon situation are explored, beginning with a brief account of the familiar classification of the medieval Office into two typical forms, one 'secular' and the other 'monastic'. This classification is inadequate to describe the liturgical situation on the Continent and in England in the early Middle Ages. Instead, the role of monastic tradition, written and unwritten, in governing Office liturgy must be considered, particularly in the Office as it was sung from an early stage in the monasteries of Rome. The origin of the system of separate forms of the Office for secular clergy and monks must be sought in the imposition of the Roman Office on the Frankish Church in the eighth century followed by the adoption by Frankish monks, beginning in the ninth century, of a different form drawn from the *Regula S. Benedicti*.

The typical secular and monastic forms of the Office

For the greater part of the Middle Ages in the West, the Divine Office was celebrated according to one of two fixed patterns, or *cursus*. One was the secular *cursus*, sometimes called the 'Roman' or 'cathedral' *cursus* (not to be confused with the 'cathedral Office' of late antiquity, which was something altogether different), the other the monastic *cursus*, also called the Benedictine *cursus*. Any student of the Divine Office must be able to tell the difference between the two. The secular *cursus* was the Office sung in secular cathedrals, collegiate churches, and, in the later Middle Ages, by the mendicant orders of friars (Franciscans and Dominicans).[1] The secular *cursus* lacks an early 'foundation document'. The earliest systematic description of the secular Office, with only slight differences from its classic later medieval form, is found in the writings of Amalarius of Metz (d. *c.*853).[2] The 'monastic *cursus*' is the pattern of the Divine Office used in Benedictine monasteries ('black monks'), and in those of related orders (Cistercians, Carthusians, etc.). This pattern is based on the prescriptions in the *Regula S. Benedicti*, which are in turn based largely on a form of the Divine Office sung in Rome in the sixth century, with which St Benedict was familiar. The monastic *cursus* of the Middle Ages, however, included musical and textual elaborations not foreseen by St Benedict.[3]

Both forms are, on the surface, similar in many ways. They make use of the same eight daily offices: the Night Office (sometimes called Vigils or Nocturns, and later known as Matins), Lauds (originally called Matins), Prime, Terce, Sext, None, Vespers, and Compline. In both *cursus*, the whole of the book of Psalms is sung through completely in the course of a single week, though the psalms are distributed in different ways. The secular and monastic *cursus* share many common texts in addition to the psalter.

Some of the differences between the two *cursus* are very slight. Both begin the Night Office with the versicle and response *Domine labia mea aperies, et os meum annuntiabit laudem tuam* (Ps. 50:17). But this is said three times in the Benedictine *cursus*, and only once in the secular.[4] Oft

---

[1] The breviary promulgated in 1568 by the Council of Trent, whose liturgy, with occasional minor alterations, was normative for all Roman Catholic clergy until 1911, was also of this type: *Breviarium Romanum: Editio princeps (1568)*, Edizione anastatica, ed. M. Sodi and A. M. Triacca, Monumenta liturgica Concilii Tridentini 3 (Vatican City, 1999). The papal bull *Quod a nobis* permitted existing local breviaries to continue to be used when it could be shown that they had been in constant use for at least two hundred years prior to 1568. These local diocesan breviaries also followed the secular *cursus*, differing from each other only in superficial details.

[2] Amalarius of Metz, *Liber de ordine antiphonarii*, cc. 1–7, ed. J.-M. Hanssens, *Amalarii episcopi Opera liturgica omnia*, 3 vols., Studi e testi 138–40 (Vatican City, 1948–50) III, 13–224, at pp. 18–37. This work of Amalarius, known only from an early printed edition of a single manuscript, now lost, is somewhat controversial. The antiphoner it describes, the result of Amalarius's own collation of Roman and Frankish books, has left no descendants, so the extent to which Amalarius's comments can be applied to the Frankish situation generally is questionable. The fundamental pattern of the Office, however, was not the subject of any of Amalarius's revisions. Amalarius also treats the Office, sometimes in more detail, in his universally popular *Liber officialis*, IV. 1–17, ed. Hanssens II, 403–65.

[3] *RSB* 8–18.

[4] *RSB* 9:1; Amalarius of Metz, *Liber de ordine antiphonarii*, c. 1. 2, ed. Hanssens III, 19.

repeated texts like this are seldom recorded in early Office books. The major differences between the monastic and secular *cursus* are to be sought in two areas: the distribution of the 150 psalms over the course of a single week, and the number and arrangement of the musical pieces that accompany the psalms and the readings from the Bible and the Fathers. The differences in the organization of the Office in the Benedictine and Roman traditions have been dealt with in many books.[5]

The differences in how each *cursus* distributes the psalms over the week are most easily appreciated through inspection of Tables 2.1 and 2.2.[6] Both distributions are clearly based on the ideal of reciting all 150 psalms in numerical order. This is somewhat obscured in the monastic *cursus*, which begins the Sunday Night Office with Psalm 20, the first nineteen psalms having been transferred to the office of Prime. The monastic *cursus* also differs from the secular in allowing certain longer psalms to be divided into two, counting as two separate psalms for the purpose of St Benedict's prescribed framework for each hour. Both patterns share the principle of never repeating a psalm in more than one office, though some psalms, because of their appropriateness to certain times of the day, are repeated daily in a fixed place (for example, Psalms 148–50 at Lauds).

---

[5] The clearest and usually most reliable treatment is in Harper, *The Forms and Orders of Western Liturgy*, which is far more useful than the 'introduction' it claims to be. Other useful summaries may be found within D. Hiley, *Western Plainchant: A Handbook* (Oxford, 1993), pp. 25–30. Taft, *The Liturgy of the Hours in East and West*, pp. 134–8, discusses only the Benedictine arrangement, as, more thoroughly, does J. B. L. Tolhurst, *Introduction to the English Monastic Breviaries*, HBS 80 (London, 1942), pp. 7–18 (vol. 6 of *The Monastic Breviary of Hyde Abbey*). Descriptions of the medieval secular *cursus* other than Harper's are fewer and less reliable (see n. 7 below). Vogel's *Medieval Liturgy* includes no material at all on the *cursus*.

[6] Similar tables may be found in P.-M. Gy, 'La Bible dans la liturgie au Moyen Age', in P. Riché and G. Lobrichon (eds.), *Le Moyen Age et la Bible*, Bible dans tous les temps 4 (Paris, 1984), pp. 537–52, at pp. 546–9, and A. de Vogüé, *La Règle de Saint Benoît*, Translation, Notes, and Commentary, with Latin text and critical apparatus by J. Neufville, 7 vols., Sources chrétiennes 181–6, vol. 7 *extra seriem* (Paris, 1971–7) I, 102–3. Vogüé's table for the Roman Office is a hypothetical reconstruction of sixth-century Roman practice, and does not represent what would become standard in the medieval period. Vogüé's table for the Benedictine *cursus* has one error: the psalms at the Night Office (*Vigile*) on Monday should read '36/1 36/2', not '35 36'. Ps. 35 is used on Monday at Lauds. P.-M. Gy's tables, on which the tables given here are based, have one error in Table 1: on Wednesday, the Night Office (*Matines*) should not include Ps. 53, which is sung daily at Prime. These are typographical errors, and do not represent factual mistakes on the part of the authors. It is hoped that the tables offered here have escaped similar slips.

Table 2.1 The distribution of psalms and canticles in the secular *cursus*

	Sun	Mon	Tue	Wed	Thu	Fri	Sat
Night Office	94	daily as Invitatory					
Nocturn I		**Single nocturn on weekdays**					
1–3;	26^a–37	**38**–41	**52**	**68**–79	**80**–8	**97**–108	
6–14		43–9	54–61			93;95;96	
Nocturn II	15–17		51	63;65;67			
Nocturn III	18–20						
Lauds	$92\,(50)^b$	50 daily on weekdays					
	99 (117)	5	42	64	89	142	91
	62+66	daily					
	Cant.^{c}	Cant.	Cant.	Cant.	Cant.	Cant.	Cant.
	148–50	daily					
	Benedictus^d	daily					
Prime	21–5^e						
	53	daily on weekdays and feast days					
	$117\,(92)^f$						
	118:1–32	daily on weekdays and feast days					
Terce	118:33–80	daily					

16

Sext	118:81–128	daily
None	118:129–76	daily
Vespers	**109**–13	114–16 121–5 126–30 131–2 137–41 143–7
		119–20 134–6
	Magnificat[g]	daily
Compline	4; 30:2–6; 90; 133; *Nunc dimittis*[h] daily

[a] Figures in bold type denote psalms given the highest grade of decoration according to the 'liturgical divisions' in the Vespasian Psalter, BL Cotton Vespasian A. I (St Augustine's, Canterbury, 720s?). Ps. 1 is missing from the manuscript. Pss. 17 and 118 receive mid-grade decoration.

[b] From Septuagesima to Palm Sunday, Pss. 92 and 99 are replaced by Pss. 50 and 117.

[c] A different Old Testament canticle is sung each day at this point in Lauds. Sun: *Benedicite* (Dan. 3:57–88); Mon: *Confitebor* (Isa. 12:1–6); Tue: *Ego dixi* (Isa. 38:10–20); Wed: *Exultauit* (1 Sam. 2:1–10); Thu: *Cantemus* (Exod. 15:1–19); Fri: *Domine audiui* (Hab. 3:2–19); Sat: *Audite caeli* (Deut. 32:1–43).

[d] Luke 1:68–79.

[e] Most medieval books assign Pss. 21–5 to Sunday Prime. In the late medieval Roman Curial Office, they were omitted outside the period from Septuagesima to Palm Sunday. In the Tridentine *Breviarium Romanum* of 1568, whose distribution was normative until 1911, Pss. 21–5 were redistributed over the ferial days at Prime as a variable psalm following Ps. 53 (Mon. 23; Tue. 24; Wed. 25; Thu. 22; Fri. 21).

[f] Ps. 92 replaces Ps. 117 from Septuagesima to Palm Sunday (moved here from Lauds). Notice that Ps. 99 does not need to be reassigned during this period because it also occurs in the Saturday Night Office, the only psalm duplicated in the distribution.

[g] Luke 1:46–55.

[h] Luke 2:29–32.

Table 2.2 The distribution of psalms and canticles in the monastic *cursus*

	Sun	Mon	Tue	Wed	Thu	Fri	Sat
Night Office	3	daily as 'waiting psalm'					
	94	daily as Invitatory					
	Nocturn I	**Nocturn I**					
	20–5	**32**[a]**–4**	**45–49**	**59–61**	**73–4;76**	**85–6**	101–2
		36a–b[b]	51	65	77a–b	88a–b	103a–b
		37		67a–b	78	92–3	104a–b
	Nocturn II	**Nocturn II**					
	26–31	**38–41**	52–5	**68a–b**	79–84	**95**–100	105a–b
		43–4	57–8	69–72			106a–b
							107–8
	Nocturn III	(No third nocturn on weekdays)					
	3 canticles[c]						
Lauds	66	daily as 'waiting psalm'					
	50	daily					
	117	5	42	63	87	75	142
	62	35	56	64	89	91	Cant. a
	Cant.[d]	Cant.	Cant.	Cant.	Cant.	Cant.	Cant. b
	148–50	daily					
	Benedictus	daily					

Prime	118:1–32	1;2;6	7–8 9a	9b 10–11	12–14	15–16 17a	17b 18–19
Terce	118:33–56	118:105–28	**119**–21	daily Tue. to Sat.			
Sext	118:57–80	118:129–52	122–4	daily Tue. to Sat.			
None	118:81–104	118:153–76	125–7	daily Tue. to Sat.			
Vespers	**109**–12	113–14 115+116 128	129–32	**134**–7	**138**a–b 139–40	**141** 143a–b 144a	**144**b 145–7
	Magnificat	daily	daily				
Compline	4;90;133						

[a] Figures in bold type denote psalms given the highest grade of decoration according to the 'liturgical divisions' in the Bosworth Psalter, BL Add. 37517 (prov. St Augustine's, Canterbury, s. x^2). The non-liturgical decoration of Pss. 1, 51, and 101 is not noted here.

[b] *RSB* 18:21 requires that longer psalms be divided to achieve twelve units of psalm in every Night Office without specifying which psalms. The division marked 'a' and 'b' in this table reflect medieval usage. The Rule specifies divisions for Pss. 138, 143, and 144 at Vespers, and says that Pss. 115 and 116 are to be joined as one psalm (*RSB* 18:16–17).

[c] *RSB* 8:6 leaves the choice of three Old Testament canticles to the abbot. Various sets are found appended to monastic psalter manuscripts.

[d] The Roman canticles of the secular *cursus* are used (see *RSB* 13:9–10), the only difference being that the Saturday canticle is divided into two parts. Sun: *Benedicite* (Dan. 3:57–88); Mon: *Confitebor* (Isa. 12:1–6); Tue: *Ego dixi* (Isa. 38:10–20); Wed: *Exultauit* (1 Sam. 2:1–10); Thu: *Cantemus* (Exod. 15:1–19); Fri: *Domine audiui* (Hab. 3:2–19); Sat: *Audite caeli* (Deut. 32:1–21 and 22–43).

Although their characteristic distributions of the psalms constitute a fundamental difference between the secular and monastic *cursus*, these can sometimes be difficult to discern in medieval Office books, where familiarity with the psalmody of the Office is often taken for granted. More obvious differences may be sought in the musical pieces (antiphons and responsories) used in any one office, as well as in the biblical and patristic/hagiographical lessons (as found in a lectionary or a plenary breviary). These differences are most apparent in the Night Office on Sundays and feast days, as is illustrated in Table 2.3. In each *cursus*, the Night Office on these days is divided into three nocturns. Each nocturn in the secular *cursus* has three readings and responsories (nine in total), while each nocturn in the monastic *cursus* has four (twelve in total). The antiphons and psalms of the Night Office are likewise differently organized. Each nocturn of the secular festal Night Office has three antiphons and three psalms, except on Sundays, when the first nocturn has twelve psalms and each of the three antiphons governs a group of four psalms.[7] The first two nocturns of the monastic festal Night Office have six psalms each. The number of antiphons assigned to these nocturns can vary, depending on the liturgical rank of the day. In the third nocturn of the monastic festal Office, however, three canticles (poetic texts from the Old Testament outside the psalter) are sung under a single antiphon.[8] The single antiphon for

---

[7] Earlier secular practice seems to have been to sing the psalms of the first nocturn with no antiphons: Amalarius of Metz, *Liber officialis*, VIII. 1, ed. Hanssens II, 442. The psalmody of the Sunday Night Office is given incorrectly in L. Collamore, 'Charting the Divine Office', in Fassler and Baltzer (eds.), *The Divine Office in the Latin Middle Ages*, pp. 3–11, at pp. 4–5, where only three psalms are assumed to be sung in the first nocturn instead of the correct twelve. Collamore's omission arises from her dependence on the indices of antiphoners stored in the CANTUS Database: since the indices record only the antiphons, she did not notice that four psalms were sung under each of the three antiphons provided for the first nocturn. Hughes (*Medieval Manuscripts*, pp. 50–80) offers an authoritative, and occasionally overwhelming, discussion of the Office based on a close study of mainly late medieval sources; but what seems to be a typographical error on p. 55, figure 4.3, puts twelve psalms into each of the three nocturns of the secular *cursus*, instead of just the first. In Hughes's shorthand, the three nocturns ought to read: '(P4A)3 (PA)3 (PA)3'.

[8] *RSB* 11:6. St Benedict, writing in the early sixth century, actually prescribed that the canticles should be sung with the refrain *Alleluia*. In the surviving medieval Benedictine antiphoners, however, antiphons using various texts are found, with *Alleluia* used in the Easter season. The choice of which canticles were sung was left to the abbot. Sets of canticles copied in medieval psalters may be grouped into several families. See J. Mearns, *The Canticles of the Christian Church, Eastern and Western, in Early and Medieval Times* (Cambridge, 1914), pp. 81–93, and H. Schneider, *Die altlateinischen biblischen Cantica*, Texte und Arbeiten 29–30 (Beuron, 1938), pp. 134–8.

Table 2.3 The three nocturns of the Night Office on Sundays and feast days in the secular and monastic *cursus*

Secular	Monastic
First nocturn	**First nocturn**
3 groups of 4 psalms, with 3 antiphons (Feasts: only 3 psalms, 3 antiphons)	6 psalms with 6 antiphons
Versicle and Response	Versicle and Response
Pater noster, Absolution	*Pater noster*, Absolution
Blessing, Lesson & Responsory 1	Blessing, Lesson & Responsory 1
Blessing, Lesson & Responsory 2	Blessing, Lesson & Responsory 2
Blessing, Lesson & Responsory 3 (+*Gloria patri*)	Blessing, Lesson & Responsory 3
	Blessing, Lesson & Responsory 4 (+*Gloria patri*)
Second nocturn	**Second nocturn**
3 psalms with 3 antiphons	6 psalms with 6 antiphons
Versicle and Response	Versicle and Response
Pater noster, Absolution	*Pater noster*, Absolution
Blessing, Lesson & Responsory 4	Blessing, Lesson & Responsory 5
Blessing, Lesson & Responsory 5	Blessing, Lesson & Responsory 6
Blessing, Lesson & Responsory 6 (+*Gloria patri*)	Blessing, Lesson & Responsory 7
	Blessing, Lesson & Responsory 8 (+*Gloria patri*)
Third nocturn	**Third nocturn**
3 psalms with 3 antiphons	3 Old Testament canticles under 1 antiphon
Versicle and Response	Versicle and Response
Pater noster, Absolution	*Pater noster*, Absolution
Gospel verse	Gospel verse
Blessing, Lesson & Responsory 7	Blessing, Lesson & Responsory 9
Blessing, Lesson & Responsory 8	Blessing, Lesson & Responsory 10
Blessing, Lesson & Responsory 9 (+*Gloria patri*)	Blessing, Lesson & Responsory 11
	Blessing, Lesson & Responsory 12 (+*Gloria patri*)
Te deum laudamus	*Te deum laudamus*
	Gospel of the Day
	Te decet laus
	Kyrie, *Pater noster*, Preces
	Collect

the canticles is among the more useful indices for determining to which *cursus* a manuscript belongs. A single antiphon labelled *antiphona ad cantica* in the third nocturn indicates a monastic book.

The ferial Night Office is less helpful in distinguishing the secular *cursus* from the monastic (see Table 2.4). Both *cursus* include three lessons

Table 2.4 The nocturn(s) of the Night Office on ferial days and simple feasts in the secular and monastic *cursus*

Secular	Monastic
Single nocturn	**First nocturn**
12 psalms with 6 antiphons	6 psalms with 6 (or 1 or 3) antiphons
(Simple feast: 9 psalms & 9 antiphons)	
Versicle & Response	Versicle & Response
Pater noster, Absolution	*Pater noster*, Absolution
Blessing, Lesson & Responsory 1	Blessing, Lesson & Responsory 1
Blessing, Lesson & Responsory 2	Blessing, Lesson & Responsory 2
Blessing, Lesson & Responsory 3	Blessing, Lesson & Responsory 3
(+*Gloria patri*)	(+*Gloria patri*)
	Second nocturn
	6 psalms with 6 (or 1 or 3) antiphons
	Chapter
	Versicle and Response
	Kyrie, Pater noster, Preces
	Collect
	Benedicamus domino

and responsories on ferial days. They differ in other respects – not least in the presence of a daily second nocturn in the monastic *cursus* – but these tend to be common texts, seldom included in the contents of antiphoners and breviaries. Looking at a small manuscript fragment preserving only a ferial Night Office, it might be impossible to tell whether it was from a secular or a monastic book.

Numerous other clues are to be found in antiphoners and breviaries.[9] At Lauds and Vespers, the monastic *cursus* has a short responsory (*responsorium breue* after the short lesson (*capitulum*); the secular *cursus* does not. But the secular *cursus* has a short responsory after the *capitulum* in the lesser hours of Prime, Terce, Sext, None, and Compline; the monastic *cursus* does not. Vespers in the secular *cursus* has five psalms with five antiphons; monastic Vespers has only four. In secular Compline, the psalms are sung under an antiphon; in monastic Compline they are sung *directanei*, without an antiphon. Also at Compline, the secular *cursus* includes the Gospel canticle *Nunc dimittis*, which is omitted in

---

[9] Contrasting descriptions should be sought in Harper, *The Forms and Orders of Western Liturgy*.

monastic Compline.

So much, then, for the secular and monastic forms of the Office as they were known through the greater part of the Middle Ages. But this classification did not obtain in the liturgical situation of the early Middle Ages.

The Office under the 'rule' of monastic tradition

By the sixth century there was throughout Western Europe a widely shared understanding of the basic defining characteristics of monasticism. The abbots of some monasteries kept this tradition without writing down a definitive rule of life (Lérins, Réôme, Brou), while others committed their teachings to writing (Caesarius and Aurelian of Arles, the anonymous 'Master', St Benedict).[10] Whether written monastic rules were used or not, there was a broad consensus about what constituted 'true monasticism', and it was possible to speak of 'true monks'.[11] This consensus first emerges in the decrees of the early ecumenical councils of the Church, coinciding with the explosion of monasticism in the fourth century. One explanation of the Latin terms used to describe the monastic life, *regulariter* and *iuxta regulam*, is that they do not refer to 'a rule' as such, but rather translate the Greek for life according to the 'canons' (*kanones*).[12] The Ecumenical Council of Chalcedon held in 451, for example, promulgated a number of decrees relating to monks and nuns, in which may be seen an emerging consensus around the threefold monastic qualities of poverty, celibacy, and obedience (though such a clear formulation did not emerge until the later Middle Ages).[13]

---

[10] M. Deanesly, *Augustine of Canterbury* (London, 1964), pp. 134–5.
[11] There is a long tradition of monastic literature dedicated to the question, with the first chapter of the *Regula S. Benedicti* a relatively late representative: see *RB 1980: The Rule of St. Benedict in Latin and English with Notes*, ed. T. Fry (Collegeville, MN, 1981), ed. Fry, pp. 313–21.
[12] Ferrari, *Early Roman Monasteries*, pp. 382–3.
[13] *Decrees of the Ecumenical Councils*, I: *Nicaea I to Lateran V*, ed. N. P. Tanner (London, 1990); see canons 3, 4, 7, 8, 16, 24. On the threefold profession, see *RB 1980*, ed. Fry, pp. 457–66. A belief that the early ecumenical councils offered sufficient guidance for community life is found in the prologue of the *Regula canonicorum* of Chrodegang of Metz, composed *c*.755, ed. and tr. J. Bertram, *The Chrodegang Rules: The Rules for the Common Life of the Secular Clergy from the Eighth and Ninth Centuries* (Aldershot, 2005), pp. 27 and 52: 'Were the discipline of the Three Hundred and Eighteen [fathers of the Council of Nicaea] still in force, with that of the other holy Fathers, were clergy and bishops still living

The earliest monastic writings, however, identify *regula* with the person of the abbot. As early as the letters of Jerome and as late as the *Dialogi* of Gregory the Great, to 'live *sub regula* means to live under an abbot, he being the living rule of the monastery'.[14] From John Cassian onwards, *regula* could also mean the catholic consensus of all cenobitic communities, a tradition believed to have originated with the apostles and which was subsequently under the guardianship of 'qualified superiors' ('abbot, cellarer, deans, ancients').[15] Finally, the universal monastic tradition found concrete expression in the specific rules of individual communities or groups of monasteries, which might or might not be written down. Each local rule was consciously 'a product and a particular crystalization' of the wider tradition.[16] St Benedict's description of his work as a 'small rule for beginners' acknowledges the existence of a higher standard of the monastic life, in the scriptures, the writings of the Fathers, and in monastic tradition.[17] Both the *Regula S. Benedicti* and the slightly earlier 'Rule of the Master' (*Regula Magistri*), from which Benedict borrows extensively, frequently refer to the joint authority of the written Rule (as an expression of the monastic tradition) and the abbot as mediator, trustee, and arbitrator of that tradition, using variants of the phrase *sub regula uel abbate*, with the abbot always in second position.[18]

The form of the Divine Office used by a monastic community was similarly governed by the universal monastic tradition as mediated by the customs of a particular monastery and interpreted by its abbot. In a monastery whose abbot did not impose any particular written monastic rule, or perhaps wrote down a new rule incorporating teachings from various sources, the Divine Office could conceivably take any number of forms within a broadly accepted basic framework. John Cassian (d. *post*

according to the pattern of conduct they laid down, it would be superfluous for us, insignificant as we are, to make any further comment, or say anything, as if it were new, about a subject which has been so well treated.' ('Si trecentorum decem et octo reliquorumque sanctorum patrum, canonum auctoritas inviolata perduraret, et clerus atque episcopus secundum eorum rectitudinis normam viverent, superfluum videretur a nobis exiguis minimisque, super hanc rem tam ordinate dispositam aliquid retractari, et quasi quiddam novitatis adici.') On the work and influence of Chrodegang, see p. 52 and n. 137 below.

[14] A. de Vogüé, 'Sub regula uel abbate: A study of the theological significance of the ancient monastic rules', in M. B. Pennington (ed.), *Rule and Life: An Interdisciplinary Symposium*, Cistercian Studies 12 (Spencer, MA, 1971), pp. 21–64, at p. 26.
[15] Vogüé, 'Sub regula uel abbate', p. 27.
[16] Vogüé, 'Sub regula uel abbate', p. 29.
[17] Vogüé, 'Sub regula uel abbate', p. 30.
[18] Vogüé, 'Sub regula uel abbate', pp. 23–4 and n. 7.

430) reported that there were nearly as many different ways of reciting the Office as there were monasteries that he had visited.[19] Most surviving monastic rules say little about how the Office was performed. The carefully delineated Office liturgy of the *Regula S. Benedicti* is unusual for its kind. In the monastic rule composed by Ferreolus of Uzès (d.581), monks were to strive to sing the entire psalter each day in numerical order from beginning to end. This was to be accomplished both at specific hours of communal prayer, when the psalms were recited aloud, and throughout the rest of the day, when the psalms were recited silently as a private discipline. Only two hours of communal prayer are mentioned: a morning hour (*ad matutinas*) and a night hour (*ad nocturnas*), to which occasional nocturnal vigils are sometimes to be added.[20] While the Office described by Ferreolus could be seen to imitate the twofold Office of the Egyptian 'Desert Fathers' of the fourth century, described by Cassian,[21] it is more likely that Ferreolus assumes a more complete liturgical observance that needs no explanation, a 'communal *cursus* of psalmody of the Lord' (*publicus psallendi cursus dominicus*).

If Ferreolus chose to defer to an existing tradition rather than impose something of his own devising, he would be entirely in harmony with monastic attitudes. John Cassian judged that excessive liturgical diversity arose mainly from monks' ignorance of truly authoritative precedents for

---

[19] John Cassian, *Institutiones* (*De institutis coenobiorum*), II. 2, ed. and tr. (French) J.-C. Guy, *Jean Cassien: Institutions cénobitiques*, Sources chrétiennes 109 (Paris, 1965), pp. 58–9.
[20] Ferreolus of Uzès, *Regula ad monachos*, cc. 12–13, *PL* LXVI, 964: 'XII. Ut omni tempore psalmi usque ad finem Psalterii in ordine decantentur: sibi tamen secretius propter propriam mercedem; excepto publico psallendi cursu dominico, quantum per singulos dies, Deo tamen scienter laudes offerat occulta ruminatione. Similiter etiam convenerit oratione subjuncta noctibus psalmorum frequentia vigilare, ut impleatur illud: *In die clamavi et nocte coram te* [Ps. 87:2]; et illud: *In lege ejus meditabitur die ac nocte* [Ps. 1:2]. XIII. Quotiescunque vigilia nocturna propter exorandum Deum, aut devotione petitur, aut festivitate debetur, nullus monachorum, praeter aegritudinem certam aut necessitatem, si praesens fuerit, absens esse praesumat. Ne interiori taedio gravius laborare consuescens vivente carne spiritalis anima moriatur: sed potius promissi illius cupidus quaerere simul et invenire contendat, qui dixit: *Diligam eos qui diligunt me: et qui mane vigilant ad me invenient me* [Prov. 8:17]. Et in psalmo etiam continetur: *Tunc quaerebant eum, et convertebantur, et ante lucem veniebant ad eum* [Ps. 77:34]. Nam ut quotidie ad matutinas omnes omnino surgant, si non censetur superfluum, commonemus: ad nocturnas vero cunctis diebus ita omnes celeriter pariterque consurgant, ut cunctis simul concurrentibus nullus inveniatur venisse posterior. At vero qui contrarius huic deprehenditur statuto, tot diebus solus jejunet, quot horis cum fratribus vigilare non voluit.'
[21] See Taft, *The Liturgy of the Hours*, pp. 57–73.

how the Office should be sung (which for Cassian meant the Office of the Desert Fathers). Deference to precedent is a hallmark of monastic thought, receiving its definitive formulation in St Benedict's great discourse on humility (an apt example since it is based almost entirely on the earlier *Regula Magistri*, which in turn drew on Cassian's *Institutiones*):

> The eighth step of humility is that a monk does only what is endorsed by the common rule of the monastery and the example set by his superiors.[22]

As the monk was to obey the abbot as the representative of Christ, so the abbot himself was to obey scripture and tradition as Christ obeyed his Father.[23]

All liturgy tends towards conservatism, and monasticism's strong deference to tradition meant that deviation from established norms was especially frowned upon, above all when it came to the Divine Office, the central activity of any monastery.[24] In theory, an abbot could alter the Divine Office at will. In practice, abbots seem to have exercised this prerogative by choosing a form of the Office from a limited number of existing traditions of recognized historical or spiritual authority. An anonymous treatise *Ratio de cursus qui fuerunt eius auctores* ('An account of the *cursus*: Who were its authors?') written some time before 767, apparently by a monk in a Continental house of Irish observance, lists all the forms of the Divine Office known to its author and traces the historical pedigree of each.[25] According to this treatise, only three varieties of the Divine Office were in use in Gaul. The Roman Office (*cursus Romanus*), says the writer, was first sung by disciples of St Peter and introduced at Lyons

---

[22] *RSB* 7:55: 'Octavus humilitatis gradus est si nihil agat monachus, nisi quod communis monasterii regula vel maiorum cohortantur exempla.' Cf. John Cassian, *Institutiones*, IV. 39. 2, ed. Guy, p. 180, where this is the sixth of ten degrees of humility.

[23] Cf. *RSB* 2:4, and its definition of the antithesis of the good abbot at 64:3. See also Vogüé, *La Règle de Saint Benoît* VII, 135, comparing the two sayings of Christ concerning obedience in Luke 6:16 and John 6:38.

[24] The Carolingian reforms of the ninth century were hampered by this monastic conservatism; see the section 'The limited influence of Benedict of Aniane's reforms', beginning on p. 69 below.

[25] *Ratio de cursus qui fuerunt eius auctores*, ed. J. Semmler, in *Initia consuetudinis Benedictinae: Consuetudines saeculi octavi et noni*, ed. K. Hallinger, CCM 1 (Siegburg, 1963), pp. 77–91. The text survives in a single manuscript source, BL Cotton Nero A. ii, fols. 37r–42r (N Italy, s. viii/ix). See P. Jeffery, 'Eastern and Western elements in the Irish Monastic prayer of the Hours', in Fassler and Baltzer, *The Divine Office in the Latin Middle Ages*, pp. 99–143, at pp. 131–4. I have adopted Jeffery's translation of the title.

in the second century. The Irish Office (*cursus Scottorum*), with which the writer is most familiar, is linked to St Mark the Evangelist. The Gallican Office (*cursus Gallorum*) originated with St John the Evangelist. The *cursus Scottorum* referred to may be that laid down in the *Regula monachorum* of Columbanus; something like a Gallican Office is perhaps represented in the monastic rules of Caesarius and Aurelian of Arles.[26]

The writer goes on to mention three forms of the Office of which he has only second-hand knowledge. There is an Eastern Office (*cursus Orientalis*), 'which is not observed in the custom of the Gauls' (*quae in Gallorum consuetudine non habetur*), associated with several notable saints, including St Athanasius, one of the Nicene Fathers. After this is mentioned a *cursus* composed by St Ambrose. This is probably to be identified as the use of Milan, still sometimes called the 'Ambrosian Rite'. Last of all, the author mentions the *cursus* of the *Regula S. Benedicti*.

The historical arguments put forward are, of course, nonsense. The treatise does nevertheless inadvertently reveal how important it was that liturgical forms be supported by the authority of tradition. There is nothing to indicate that this author disbelieved his own testimony. It is reminiscent of the 664 Synod of Whitby, where Bishop Colman made a similar argument in defence of the Irish method of calculating the date of Easter.[27] (At Whitby, as later in Gaul, the authority of St Peter proved insurmountable.) The importance of authority and precedent in liturgical traditions militates against any argument – made necessarily from absence of evidence – that early medieval abbots would be inclined to devise their own systems of Office liturgies independently. Local variety (for instance in the observance of particular saints' days or the selection of particular chants) would of course remain the norm, but only within the stable outline of the chosen tradition.

Most important, the abbot could choose to follow any liturgical tradition, and was not bound to follow the dictates of any one monastic rule. The comments of the anonymous author of the *Ratio de cursus* about the Benedictine Office are very instructive on this point:

---

[26] Columbanus, *Regula monachorum*, c. 7, ed. and tr. G. S. M. Walker, *Sancti Columbani Opera*, Scriptores Latini Hiberniae 2 (Dublin, 1954; repr. 1970), pp. 128–33. On the Office in Irish monastic traditions, see Jeffery, 'Eastern and Western elements', pp. 99–127. Aspects of the Gallican Office may be represented in the monastic rules by Caesarius (d.542) and Aurelian (d.551) of Arles; on the various traditions of the Office in Gaul, see Taft, *The Liturgy of the Hours*, pp. 96–113.

[27] Cf. Bede, *Historia ecclesiastica*, III. 25, ed. Plummer I, 183–9.

There is yet another *cursus*, which was composed by the blessed Benedict. He composed it with but little difference from the Roman *cursus*. You may find it written in his Rule. But nevertheless, the blessed Gregory, bishop of the city of Rome, as it were in a privilege for monks, affirmed this *cursus* by his own authority in the Life of St Benedict in the book of Dialogues, where he said: 'This holy man, the blessed Benedict, could not teach otherwise than he lived himself.'[28]

This description comes last in the list of Office forms known to the author of the *Ratio de cursus*, which suggests that he had as little practical experience of it as of the Eastern and Milanese rites that precede it. Just as the Eastern *cursus* was most likely known to the author through the writings of John Cassian, and the Milanese by his own admission from the writings of St Augustine of Hippo,[29] so the Benedictine *cursus* is known to him through the written *Regula S. Benedicti*, and not through personal experience of having heard the Office sung according to the Rule's pattern. Moreover, according to the *Ratio de cursus*, the Benedictine Office derives its authority not from being included in the *Regula S. Benedicti*, nor indeed from St Benedict's personal sanctity, but from the endorsement of Gregory the Great in the *Dialogi*.[30] The similarity of the Benedictine Office to the Roman Office is also evidently important as proof of the legitimacy of the Benedictine form. The writer's obvious preference for the 'Irish *cursus*' coupled with his awareness of the *Regula S. Benedicti* as a written document could indicate that he belonged to a house following a *regula mixta* combining the *Regula monachorum* of Columbanus with the *Regula S. Benedicti*.

---

[28] *Ratio de cursus*, ed. Semmler, p. 91: 'Est et alius cursus beati Benedicti qui ipsum singulariter pauco discordante a curso Romano conposuit quem in sua regula repperis scriptum. Sed tamen beatus Gregorius urbis Romae pontifex quasi priuilegium monachis ipsum sua auctoritate in uita sancti Benedicti in libro dialigorum [*sic*] adfirmauit ubi dixit: Non aliter sanctus uir docere poterat nisi sicut ipse Benedictus uixit.'

[29] Augustine, *Confessionum libri XIII*, IX. 7 (§ 15), ed. L. Verheijen, CCSL 27 (Turnhout, 1971), pp. 141–2; cf. Paulinus of Milan, *Vita sancti Ambrosii*, c. 13, *PL* XIV, 27–46, at col. 31.

[30] See p. 5 n. 8 above. All the more so in the *Ratio de cursus* if the phrase *sed tamen* (translated as 'But nevertheless' above) retains its Classical sense of a limit or correction of something already said before a parenthetical interruption. This would make possible the paraphrase: 'This *cursus* is found only in the Rule of St Benedict, but it is nevertheless valid because of Pope Gregory's authority.' But it would be unwise to credit this author with too much grammatical precision.

To conclude, under the 'rule of monastic tradition', the abbot of a community was free to devise any liturgy for the Divine Office that he thought appropriate. Most abbots, however, probably gave strong consideration to the weight of tradition, and would have hesitated to introduce novelties. Documents such as the *Ratio de cursus* acknowledge only a handful of Office liturgies as authoritative, and most early written monastic rules say little about the form the Office should take. A written rule containing detailed liturgical instructions could be valued for its teaching without any implication that its *cursus* was binding. A house governed by a *regula mixta* recognizing both the *Regula S. Benedicti* and the *Regula monachorum* of Columbanus would have to make a choice, since both these rules give detailed liturgical directions. And the choice would not be limited to the *cursus* described in these rules, but could extend to the Roman *cursus* or the Gallican custom of perpetual psalmody (*laus perennis*). Early medieval monasticism made a clear distinction between the specific teachings of a monastic rule on the recitation of the Office (*cursus*) and its more general teachings on the monastic life (*regula*).[31]

So far as the *Regula S. Benedicti* is concerned, it is possible that some early medieval houses would have tried to implement the Rule's liturgical code in its entirety, but there is no surviving evidence for this. Indeed, after the sack of Benedict's own foundation at Monte Cassino by the Lombards, some time between 568 and the composition of Gregory's *Dialogi* in 593, it would be difficult to prove that the Office of the Rule was being sung in any European monastery before Monte Cassino was restored by Petronax of Brescia around 717. Even after this date, there is no evidence for what form of the Office was sung at St Benedict's own monastery. It cannot be guessed what the Anglo-Saxon pilgrim Willibald would have learned there when he arrived in 729.[32]

---

[31] See A. W. Robertson, *The Service-Books of the Royal Abbey of Saint-Denis: Images of Ritual and Music in the Middle Ages* (Oxford, 1991), p. 21, with an analysis of an A.D. 666 privilege of Drauscius, Bishop of Soissons, in favour of the nunnery of Notre-Dame de Soissons, no. 355 in *Diplomata, chartae, epistolae, leges aliaque instrumenta ad res Gallo-Franciscas spectantia*, ed. J. M. Pardessus, 2 vols. (Paris, 1843–9) II, 138–41, at p. 139; also ptd *PL* LXXXVIII, 1184.

[32] Hugeburc of Heidenheim, *Hodoeporicon (Vita S. Willibaldi)* [written c.770], c. 5, ed. O. Holder-Egger, in *Vitae aliaeque historiae minores*, MGH SS 15.1 (Hanover, 1887), pp. 86–117, at p. 102; tr. C. H. Talbot, *The Anglo-Saxon Missionaries in Germany* (London, 1954; repr. 1981), pp. 153–77, at pp. 172–3. It has been suggested that Willibald may have been instrumental in restoring the Office of the Rule at Monte Cassino: *RB 1980*, ed. Fry, p. 104. This would rely on the unsound assumption that 'Benedictine' monasticism was normative for Anglo-Saxon monks in the eighth century.

The Roman Office and its development

It was an unwritten, local tradition of the *cursus* that had the greatest impact on Western Office liturgy. As has been mentioned, before the tenth century monks in Rome followed no one monastic rule, and neither did they write down directions for their traditional form of the Office. At Rome, no liturgical distinction was made between monks and secular clergy when it came to the Divine Office. Every Roman basilica was served by at least one monastery, and usually more. The resident monks were responsible for the daily recitation of the Divine Office in its entirety. As Guy Ferrari pointed out in his fundamental study of Roman monasteries, 'practically without exception the foundation of monasteries around the major basilicas, and most of the minor ones also, was due to the wish of some pope to insure the due recitation of the divine office in the basilica'.[33] Priests and deacons might attend and assist at certain hours, especially Lauds and Vespers, but they were chiefly responsible for saying Mass and for performing pastoral duties (especially baptisms). The biography of Pope Gregory III (731–41) in the *Liber pontificalis* gives a good illustration of how monks and secular clergy shared the liturgical round between them on a feast day: 'Let vigils be celebrated by the monks, and the solemnity of Masses by the weekly duty priests.'[34]

The first systematic description of the Roman Office was made in ninth-century Carolingian Gaul by Amalarius of Metz.[35] The development of the Roman Office in earlier centuries must be reconstructed from indirect or incomplete evidence, the most important witnesses being the *Regula S. Benedicti*, and the somewhat earlier *Regula Magistri*. Both base their instructions for the Divine Office on contemporary Roman practice. The 'Master' was familiar with Roman monasticism of *c*.500, Benedict with that of about a quarter of a century later. Although St Benedict's is the later work, he seems to have been far more conservative in his departures from the Roman model.

The seminal work on this subject was done in the 1920s and 1930s by Camille Callewaert, who noticed that the pattern of the Office in the *Regula S. Benedicti* was modelled on the Roman monastic Office known to Benedict in the early sixth century. When Benedict departs from the

---

[33] Ferrari, *Early Roman Monasteries*, pp. 372–4; quotation at p. 374.
[34] *Liber pontificalis*, ed. L. Duchesne, 3 vols., vol. 3 ed. C. Vogel (Paris, 1886–1957) I, 421: 'a monachis vigiliae celebrentur et a presbiteris ebdomadariis missarum solemnia'.
[35] See p. 14 above.

familiar Roman practice of his day, he uses a different 'tone of voice', giving careful instructions. But when he assumes that Roman practices will be followed, he passes over these with little comment.[36] For example, on Saturdays at Lauds, the Rule prescribes that the canticle from Deuteronomy (*Audite caeli*, Deut. 32:1–43) is to be divided into two parts (*qui diuidatur in duas glorias*), because of its length.[37] But on the other days of the week, 'a Canticle from the Prophets is said, according to the practice of the Roman Church.'[38] As may be seen in the notes to Tables 2.1 and 2.2 above, *Audite caeli* is also sung on Saturdays in the secular *cursus*, but undivided. The other canticles sung on weekdays are identical in the secular and the monastic *cursus*. St Benedict's willingness to divide longer psalms and canticles was itself an innovation apparently unknown in the Roman tradition of his day.[39] By 'listening' to the Rule in this way, Callewaert was able to confirm the hypothesis of Suitbert Bäumer, who had argued that the Roman Office already existed in a largely complete form in St Benedict's time; this overturned the rival hypothesis of Pierre Batiffol, who held that the Roman Office developed relatively late, perhaps in imitation of the *Regula S. Benedicti* itself.[40] But Callewaert went further in arguing that the sixth-century Roman Office known to Benedict must have differed in many respects from the *cursus* found in the official 'Tridentine' Roman breviary.[41]

In the reconstruction of the early Roman Office, much remains unresolved. Three topics are considered here for their particular relevance to the Anglo-Saxon sources that will be addressed in Chapter 3: the daily *horarium* in Roman monasteries, the development of the distribution of

---

[36] C. Callewaert, *De breviarii Romani liturgia*, 2nd edn (Bruges, 1939), pp. 52–5 (=vol. 2 of his *Liturgicae institutiones*).
[37] *RSB* 12:9.
[38] *RSB* 13:10: 'Nam ceteris diebus canticum unumquemque die suo ex prophetis sicut psallit ecclesia Romana dicantur'.
[39] Divided psalms were finally incorporated in the Roman Office when a new distribution of the psalter was promulgated by Pius X in 1911. For the effect of Pius's reforms on the distribution of the psalms, see J. Pascher, *Das Stundengebet der römischen Kirche* (Munich, 1954), pp. 64–5 and comparative tables on pp. 88–91; see also Callewaert, *De breviarii Romani liturgia*, pp. 97–100.
[40] The debate between Bäumer and Batiffol is summarized in S. Bäumer, *Histoire du bréviaire*, tr. R. Biron, 2 vols. (Paris, 1905) I, 293–305. Cf. P. Batiffol, *History of the Roman Breviary*, tr. A. M. Y. Baylay [from the 3rd French edn] (London, 1912), p. x.
[41] Callewaert's *De breviarii liturgia Romani* presents in summary his findings published in a number of articles investigating specific questions, most of which are reprinted in his collected papers, *Sacris erudiri*, ed. the Monks of St Peter of Aldeburg (Steenbrugge, 1940).

the psalms throughout the course of the week, and the gradual addition of extra nocturns to the Sunday Night Office. As will be argued in Chapter 3, the Anglo-Saxon evidence suggests that elements characteristic of the early Roman tradition were known and imitated in England.

The sevenfold horarium *of the Roman Office*

Like the Benedictine Office, the Roman Office comprises eight daily 'hours' of prayer: the Night Office, Lauds, Prime, Terce, Sext, None, Vespers, and Compline. But in a number of medieval sources, both Continental and English (especially Anglo-Saxon), the Roman Office is said to comprise only seven hours. The contradiction is only apparent, as was made clear to Roman Catholic seminarians trained before the 1970 reform of the breviary:

> The Divine Office consists of seven canonical hours, namely: Matins and Lauds (counted as one hour), Prime, Terce, Sext, None, Vespers, and Compline. ... Matins and Lauds together theoretically form the first of the canonical hours of the Divine Office. Practically, however, they are two separate hours, and this justifies us in considering each by itself.[42]

The grouping together of the Night Office and Lauds as a single hour is partly to be explained as an exegetical rationalization of Psalm 118:164, 'Seven times a day have I praised you' (*septies in die laudem dixi tibi*). When John Cassian described the creation of a new hour of prayer at sunrise (a *nouella sollemnitas*) in the *cursus* followed by monks in Bethlehem, he noted that in expanding their *cursus* from six existing hours to seven the monks fulfilled this Davidic rule of prayer.[43] *Septies in die* was likewise linked to the number of offices in the daily *horarium* in a

---

[42] B. A. Hausmann, *Learning the Breviary* (New York, 1932), pp. 39 and 43. See also F. L. Cross and E. A. Livingstone (eds.), *The Oxford Dictionary of the Christian Church*, 3rd edn rev. (Oxford, 2005), under 'Hours, Canonical'.

[43] John Cassian, *Institutiones*, III. 4, ed. Guy, pp. 102–6. This *nouella sollemnitas* has been variously interpreted as a form of Lauds or Prime; see Taft, *The Liturgy of the Hours in East and West*, p. 79. The confusion arises because Cassian only explicitly names five other hours in the Bethlehem *cursus*. We are either to understand the Night Office to comprise both 'Vigils' and Lauds, or the monks' customary communal prayer before retiring to count as Compline (IV. 19. 2, ed. Guy, p. 146). Cassian seems to speak of two different hours of 'matins' (*matutina*), the second of which is the recently introduced *sollemnitas*. This suggests that the Night Office and Lauds are treated under a single umbrella term. Guy prefers the Compline solution (p. 105 n. 1).

commentary on the psalms by Cassiodorus, written after 548. The seven hours known to Cassiodorus are given as *matutinum* (meaning Lauds), Terce, Sext, None, *lucernaria* (meaning Vespers), Compline, and Nocturns.[44] The office of Prime was not part of the *cursus* known to Cassiodorus when he first published his *Expositio*; but Prime is mentioned in some manuscripts of the *Expositio* that may represent a second edition produced during Cassiodorus's lifetime.[45]

These first authors to apply *Septies in die* to the number of hours in the *cursus* were therefore familiar with forms of the Office that comprised exactly seven hours. But we know from the *Regula S. Benedicti* and the *Regula Magistri* that both Prime and Compline were well established in the early sixth-century Roman monastic Office. This created a problem for monastic authors within the Roman tradition who wished to apply this passage of scripture to their own Office, which was in reality eightfold. St Benedict's terminological solution was to link Psalm 118:164 to the daytime hours only, and to justify the Night Office by reference to Psalm 118:62: 'In the middle of the night I arose to give you praise' (*media nocte surgebam ad confitendum tibi*).[46] Chrodegang requires the separation of the Night Office and Lauds found in the *Regula S. Benedicti*, his *Regula canonicorum* being in many respects an adaptation of the Rule for communities of secular clergy.[47] Descriptions of the Roman Office as sevenfold are absent from texts connected with the Frankish ecclesiastical reforms of the ninth century.

Benedict's solution was not adopted by other authors. Some commentators were apparently untroubled by the problem. Alcuin, writing on the Continent before 798×802 (perhaps during his retirement at Tours), quoted Cassiodorus verbatim in his own treatment of Psalm 118:164.[48]

---

[44] Cassiodorus, *Expositio psalmorum*, 118. 164, ed. M. Adriaen, *Magni Aurelii Cassiodori Expositio psalmorum*, 2 vols., CCSL 97–8 (Turnhout, 1958) II, 1132.
[45] Vogüé, *La Règle de Saint Benoît* V, 514 n. 12.
[46] *RSB* 16:4; see Vogüé, *La Règle de Saint Benoît* V, 511–18.
[47] Chrodegang, *Regula canonicorum*, c. 5, ed. J. Bertram, *The Chrodegang Rules*, p. 32.
[48] Alcuin, *Expositiones in psalmos poenitentiales, in psalmum 118, et in psalmos graduales*; the most recent edition is that of Frobenius Forster (1777), repr. *PL* C, 570–639, with the commentary on Ps. 118 at cols. 597–620 (verse 164 is treated at cols. 617–18.) On the authenticity of this work, and for bibliography, see M.-H. Jullien and J. Perelman (eds.), *Clavis scriptorum Latinorum medii aevi: Auctores Galliae, 735–937*, II: *Alcuinus*, CCCM extra seriem (Turnhout, 1999), pp. 168–70. See also D. A. Bullough, *Alcuin: Achievement and Reputation* (Leiden, 2004), pp. 257–8. Alcuin also cites *Septies in die* in a kind of layman's book of hours that he compiled for Charlemagne's personal use. Here, however, the hours are given as *prima, secunda, tertia, sexta, nona, vespertina*, and *duodecima*, appar-

Amalarius of Metz took *Septies in die* to refer to all the hours except Compline, which he regarded as the fulfilment (*perfectio* and *consummatio*) of the first seven.[49] But as Callewaert noted, it was the interpretation classing the Night Office and Lauds as two parts of a single hour that was widely accepted from the beginning ('haec interpretatio passim deinceps admissa fuit').[50]

The roots of this interpretation of *Septies in die* may be sought in the historical development of the liturgy. The Night Office and Lauds grew out of the combination of different ways of celebrating the same, single hour: 'the bipartite office called matutinal in certain rites, nocturnal in others, and "Matins" by us', as Jean-Michel Hanssens put it.[51] The exact nature of the evolution of the Night Office and Lauds remains a controversial question; but there is basic agreement that the two offices arose through the combination of the monastic midnight office with the praise psalms of 'morning prayer' in the the fifth-century 'cathedral Office', a service attended by the clergy and the laity. Both offices served the same function; the monks simply began earlier in the night and sang more psalms.[52] Vestiges of the common origin of the Night Office and Lauds were preserved in the Roman monastic Office more than in any other tradition. The Roman Night Office lacks any concluding matter, such as a litany, dialogue, or collect, and Lauds follows it directly, without a gap, as Amalarius learned from the Roman archdeacon Theodore:

I asked whether the teachers of the Romans recite anything in the

---

ently adjusted for the schedule of a king. But he also advises three nocturnal hours, bringing the total to ten, which he compares to the laws of Moses. (*Officia per ferias*, PL LI, 509–612, at col. 509.)

[49] Amalarius of Metz, *Liber de ordine antiphonarii*, c. 7. 1, ed. Hanssens III, 35. Amalarius may have been influenced here by Gregory the Great's numerological treatment of the numbers seven and eight. See Gregory I, *Moralia in Iob*, XXXV. 8, ed. M. Adriaen, 3 vols., CCSL 143, 143A and 143B (Turnhout, 1979) III, 1785, specifically his interpretation of Eccles. 11:2: 'give portions to seven, and likewise to eight'.

[50] Callewaert, *De breviarii Romani liturgia*, p. 20. Callewaert did not cite particular examples, but indicated that evidence was to be found in the works of Bede, Isidore, Hrabanus Maurus, and others. A detailed account of the spread of this interpretation remains a *desideratum* of liturgical studies. A good starting point for such an enquiry would be the remarks on the subject by Alardus Gazaeus, the seventeenth-century commentator on the *Institutiones* of John Cassian; see *PL* XLIX, 129–31 (notes).

[51] J.-M. Hanssens, *Aux Origines de la prière liturgique: Nature et genèse de l'office des matines*, Analecta Gregoriana 57 (Rome, 1952), p. 3: 'L'office biparti appelé matutinal dans certains rites, nocturnal dans d'autres, matines par nous-même, et continué dans le rite romain par le couple de l'office nocturne, nommé aujourd'hui matines, et de laudes.'

[52] See Taft, *The Liturgy of the Hours in East and West*, pp. 191–206.

space between Nocturns and Lauds. He [Theodore] replied to me, 'Nothing; rather, after the nocturnal office they say immediately, *Deus in adiutorium meum intende* [the opening versicle of Lauds]. ... They often finish the nocturnal office with the eight responsories and nine lessons.[53]

The Roman Night Office thus had no conclusion of its own. This is also attested indirectly by the ninth-century commentator on the *Regula S. Benedicti* Hildemar of Corbie, who considered the absence of an interval in the Roman Office between the Night Office and Lauds to contradict the teachings of the Rule.[54]

The primitive link between the Night Office and Lauds is apparent even in the *Regula S. Benedicti*, in which both hours are treated as 'nocturnal'. Prime and the rest of the day hours are considered together as a group.[55] The ambiguity is even greater in the slightly earlier *Regula Magistri*. Moreover, the 'Master' used *Media nocte surgebam* (Ps. 118:62) merely to justify the time of night when monks should rise to sing the Night Office, and not (as in the *Regula S. Benedicti*) as a scriptural authority for a further eighth hour beyond the seven hours implied in *Septies in die* (Ps. 118:164).[56]

A further indication that the Night Office and Lauds were joined together in the Roman monastic Office is found in the custom of the 'second sleep'. Having risen in the middle of the night to recite the Office, monks in many traditions would return to bed until sunrise.[57] At Rome, when monks rose from their second sleep they did not sing Lauds, but Prime, as related in the *Passio S. Eugeniae*, thought to describe Roman customs of the fifth and sixth centuries.[58] Likewise, *Ordo Romanus XVIII* lists Prime as the first office of the day, indicating that it should be sung in the

---

[53] Amalarius of Metz, *Liber de ordine antiphonarii*, prologus §§ 6–7, ed. Hanssens III, 14: 'Interrogavi si aliquid dicerent magistri Romanorum interstitium nocturnalis officii et matutinalis; responsum est mihi: Nihil, sed continuo post nocturnale officium dicunt: "Deus in adiutorium meum intende". ... Saepe in octo responsoriis et novem lectionibus finiunt nocturnale officium.'

[54] See p. 70 and n. 189 below.

[55] *RSB* 17:1; see Vogüé, *La Règle de Saint Benoît* V, 409.

[56] *Regula Magistri* 33:1, ed. and tr. (French) A. de Vogüé, *La Règle du Maître*, 3 vols., Sources chrétiennes 105–7 (Paris, 1964–5) II, 176. See also Vogüé, *La Règle de Saint Benoît* V, 409 n. 38.

[57] On this custom in a number of European monastic traditions, see Vogüé, *La Règle de Saint Benoît* V, 427–31.

[58] *Passio S. Eugeniae*, preserved in the fifteenth-century *Sanctuarium seu Vitae sanctorum* of Boninus Mombritius, ed. two anonymous monks of Solesmes, 2 vols. (Paris, 1910) II,

dormitory, not in the monastery church (with the same arrangement for Compline).[59] In both cases, the Night Office and Lauds will have been sung together before the second sleep. St Benedict eliminated the second sleep for his monks, but the *Regula Magistri* recommends a second sleep after Lauds during the summer, when the nights are shorter; Prime is always to begin 'when the rays of the sun have already pierced through'.[60] Some Roman monasteries, like the one whose customs were imitated in *Ordo Romanus XVIII*, seem to have allowed for the second sleep to occur after the Night Office and before Lauds during the longer nights in winter.[61] This concession may have arisen from the need for a smaller community to devote considerable time to manual labour, which was not a concern of the major basilican monsteries in Rome.[62] The testimony of Amalarius makes no allowances for a separation between the Night Office and Lauds in the Roman basilican liturgy at any point during the year. It is conceivable, however, that Roman monasteries may have observed different schedules in winter and summer. The *Regula Magistri* says that in winter the Night Office must be completed before 'cockcrow' (*pullorum cantus*), but that in summer the monks wait until cockcrow to rise for the Night Office.[63]

To summarize, the Roman Office may be described as 'sevenfold' because the Night Office and Lauds are counted as a single hour. This view, traditional from an early stage, was based in part on the primitive unity of the Night Office and Lauds and in part on the 'scriptural' number of the offices given in Psalm 118:164 (*Septies in die*). That the Night Office and Lauds were celebrated as one continuous service is seen in the evidence given by Amalarius and in the custom of the 'second sleep'.

391–7, at p. 397 lines 54–5. See the *Regula Magistri* 33:18, ed. Vogüé II, 180 and n. 18; see also his *La Règle de Saint Benoît* V, 428–9.

[59] *Ordo Romanus XVIII*, ed. Andrieu III, 205–13; see §§ 1, 3, and 10. Vogüé disproves Andrieu's contention that these provisions describe a Gallican monastery following the use of Luxeuil. See n. 58 above.

[60] *Regula Magistri* 34:5 and 33:15–18.

[61] *Ordo Romanus XVIII*, § 19, ed. Andrieu III, 207. Cf. *Regula Magistri* 33.

[62] Andrieu, *Les Ordines Romani* III, 198, argues that *Ordo Romanus XVIII* was intended for a small community, since it refers only to a prior, not to an abbot.

[63] *Regula Magistri* 33:3–14.

The Roman distribution of the psalter

The Roman distribution of the psalms throughout the week, first described in detail by Amalarius, was the product of centuries of development and modification. Camille Callewaert was the first to propose a reconstruction of the Roman distribution as St Benedict might have known it in the first half of the sixth century.[64] Callewaert's reconstruction has been revised in various ways by later scholars, chiefly Joseph Pascher.[65] As Adalbert de Vogüé has so thoroughly demonstrated, the relationship between the Benedictine Office and the Roman Office is not always so straightforward, even if Benedict was firmly within the Roman liturgical tradition.[66] The Rule nevertheless remains an important clue to recovering earlier states of development of the Roman distribution of psalms. This subject will be of importance in Chapter 3, where it will be argued that certain early Anglo-Saxon sources seem to point to the use in England of a Roman distribution of the psalms pre-dating that described by Amalarius.[67]

In the earliest recoverable phase of the history of the Roman Office (perhaps datable to the fifth century), the psalms seem to have been divided between just two daily hours, the Night Office and Vespers (see Table 2.5). Psalms 1–108 were assigned to the Night Office, Psalms 109–150 to Vespers. As in all later versions of the Roman distribution, twelve psalms were sung at the Night Office on weekdays, the 'angelic number' of the Egyptian Office. This would have left thirty-six psalms to be sung on Sunday.[68] Joseph Pascher has argued that daily Vespers originally had six psalms, not the later five, perfectly dividing the 42 psalms

---

[64] Callewaert, *De breviarii Romani liturgia*, p. 56. Callewaert's distribution is reproduced without critical comment in M. Righetti, *Manuale di storia liturgica*, 4 vols., vols. 1–3 3rd edn, vol. 4 2nd edn (1959–69) II, 627, and in Taft, *The Liturgy of the Hours in East and West*, p. 136.

[65] In addition to the studies cited specifically below, see J. Pascher, 'Das Psalterium der Apostelmatutin', *Münchener theologische Zeitschrift* 8 (1957), 1–12; idem, 'Sinneinheiten in der Verteilung der Psalmen des Breviers: Ein weihnachtlicher und ein österlicher Typus', *Münchener theologische Zeitschrift* 8 (1957), 190–205; and idem, *Die Methode der Psalmensauswahl im römischen Stundengebet* (Munich, 1967).

[66] Vogüé, *La Règle de Saint Benoît* V, 383–643 *passim*, and especially pp. 637–43.

[67] A similar summary, but couched in a description of the sources of the Benedictine Office, may be found in Bradshaw, *Daily Prayer in the Early Church*, pp. 135–49. Bradshaw's summary, like that given here, depends in the main on the outstanding synthesis of Adalbert de Vogüé. The development of the Roman monastic Office, not to mention its final medieval form, is almost completely ignored in Taft, *The Liturgy of the Hours in East and West*.

[68] Bradshaw, *Daily Prayer in the Early Church*, p. 138.

Table 2.5 A tentative reconstruction of the psalmody of the Roman monastic Office in the later fifth century

	Sun	Mon	Tue	Wed	Thu	Fri	Sat
Night Office	1–36	37–48	49–60	61–72	73–84	85–96	97–108
Lauds	50; 62; 66; 148; 149; 150 (daily)						
	Benedictus? (daily)						
Terce/Sext/None	118? (daily)						
Vespers	109–14	115–20	121–6	127–32	133–8	139–44	145–50
	Magnificat? (daily)						

over seven days.[69] In addition to the 'current psalmody' (*psalmodia currens*) of the Night Office and Vespers, six invariable psalms suitable for daybreak seem to have been sung daily at Lauds.[70] The Gospel canticles *Benedictus* and *Magnificat*, first attested in the *Regula Magistri* (*Euangelium* or *Canticum de euangelia*), the *Regula S. Benedicti*, and *Ordo Romanus XII*, may already have been well established,[71] as may the use of Psalm 118 daily at Terce, Sext, and None.

Several significant changes were introduced to the Roman distribution before the composition of the *Regula S. Benedicti*. A plausible reconstruction of this middle phase is given in Table 2.6.[72] Variable psalms and canticles were introduced to the invariable psalmody of Lauds.[73] Around the same time, the current psalmody of the Night Office and Vespers was revised to exclude psalms that were already being sung at Lauds and at the lesser day hours. The exclusion of these psalms reduced the number

---

[69] J. Pascher, 'De psalmodia vesperarum', *Ephemerides liturgicae* 79 (1965), 317–26.

[70] J. Pascher, 'Der Psalter für Laudes und Vesper im alten römischen Stundengebet', *Münchener theologische Zeitschrift* 8 (1957), 255–67.

[71] Vogüé, *La Règle de Saint Benoît* V, 493 and n. 24.

[72] The reconstruction in this table is essentially the same as that given in Vogüé, *La Règle de Saint Benoît* I, 102.

[73] It would seem that the canticles were identical to those found in the later secular Office (see Table 2.1, p. 16 above). Cf. *RSB* 13:10: 'sicut psallit Romana ecclesia'. It is possible, but it seems unlikely given their suitability for their assigned days in the secular distribution, that Psalms 142 and 91 originally appeared in numerical order, as they do in *RSB* 13:8–9; Bradshaw, *Daily Prayer in the Early Church*, p. 147.

Table 2.6 The probable distribution of psalms in the Roman Office in the time of St Benedict (530s)

	Sun	Mon	Tue	Wed	Thu	Fri	Sat
Night Office							
	94 (daily as Invitatory) ···						
	1–3	26–37	38–41	52	68–79	80–8	97–108
	6–25		43–49	54–61		93; 95; 96	
			51	63; 65; 67			
Lauds							
	92?	50 (daily) ···					
	117	5	42	64	89	142	91
	62+66 (daily) ···						
	Cant.^{a}	Cant.	Cant.	Cant.	Cant.	Cant.	Cant.
	148+149+150 (daily) ···						
	Benedictus (daily) ···						
Prime							
	53; 118:1–16; 118:17–32 (daily) ···						
Terce							
	118:33–48; 118:49–64; 118:65–80 (daily) ···						
Sext							
	118:81–96; 118:97–112; 118:113–28 (daily) ···						
None							
	118:129–44; 118:145–60; 118:161–76 (daily) ···						
Vespers							
	109–13	114–16	121–5	126–30	131–2	137–41	143–7
		119–20			134–6		
	Magnificat (daily) ···						
Compline							
	4; 90; 133 (daily) ···						

^{a} The canticles were probably those of the later secular *cursus* (see Table 2.1).

of psalms recited daily at Vespers to five. Lauds was also reorganized to have five units of psalmody: the six invariable psalms were collapsed into three units (50, 62+66, 148–50), leaving room for one variable psalm and also a variable Old Testament canticle.[74] Twelve psalms continued to be recited at the Night Office on weekdays; but fewer psalms were left to get through in the Sunday Night Office.

[74] Vogüé, *La Règle de Saint Benoît* V, 485–6.

Evidence for the psalmody of the Sunday Night Office during this middle phase in the evolution of the Roman *cursus* was uncovered by Raymond Le Roux in his study of the 'psalmic responsories'.[75] These responsories were sung, in the medieval secular Office, during the season of variable length between Epiphany and Septuagesima.[76] Unlike most of the large repertory of responsories, the psalmic responsories draw their texts entirely from the psalms, and not from the texts of the biblical, patristic, or hagiographical readings of the Night Office. The psalmic responsories may represent the oldest layer of responsory texts.[77] They seem to have been used on any occasion that did not have its own proper responsories.[78]

So far as they are relevant to the development of the Roman *cursus*, Le Roux's conclusions may be summarized in three points. First, except for later compositions, the psalmic responsories assigned to a given day of the week are always drawn from the psalms recited at the Night Office on that day.[79] Second, an older layer within the tradition, with the widest circulation, may be distinguished from later additions that arose in particular localities.[80] Finally, within this older layer the responsories assigned

---

[75] R. Le Roux, 'Les répons "De Psalmis" pour les matines de l'épiphanie à la septuagésime', *Études grégoriennes* 6 (1963), 39–148, with two fold-out tables.

[76] Amalarius reports that at Rome they were sung with the readings from the summer lessons in the weeks following Pentecost: *Liber de ordine antiphonarii*, prologus §§ 4–5, ed. Hanssens III, 13–14; for the Frankish placement, see *Liber de ordine antiphonarii*, c. 27. 1, ed. Hanssens III, 61. See also Le Roux, 'Les répons "De Psalmis"', p. 40. On the post-Epiphany period, see Hughes, *Medieval Manuscripts for Mass and Office*, pp. 9–10 and 44–5. Since this season had no special liturgical provisions of its own, it was often the point at which 'standard' ferial material was given at length in Office books; see R. W. Pfaff, 'The "sample week" in the medieval Latin Divine Office', in R. N. Swanson (ed.), *Continuity and Change in Christian Worship*, Studies in Church History 25 (Woodbridge, 1999), pp. 78–88.

[77] Though, as Brad Maiani has pointed out, there is nothing to distinguish the surviving melodies of the psalmic responsories from the supposedly later responsories with non-psalmic texts; see his 'Readings and responsories: The eighth-century Night Office lectionary and the *Responsoria prolixa*', *Journal of Musicology* 16 (1998), 254–82, at pp. 265–8.

[78] As, for example, in *Ordo Romanus XVI*, § 53, ed. Andrieu III, 154.

[79] Le Roux, 'Les répons "De Psalmis"', p. 41. Brad Maiani's illuminating study of the responsories refers to their occurrence in numerical order as a possible indicator of their antiquity ('Readings and responsories', p. 256). But because the psalms of the Night Office are always recited in numerical order, the apparent numerical arrangement of the psalmic responsories is in fact a product of their liturgical order. Maiani does not cite Le Roux's study, and seems to have been unaware of it when he wrote his article.

[80] Le Roux, 'Les répons "De Psalmis"', pp. 49–50.

to Sunday draw their texts from Psalms 1–25.[81]

Using different kinds of evidence, Joseph Pascher argued for an early form of the Sunday Night Office in which Psalms 1–25 were sung.[82] He suggested, moreover, that Psalms 4 and 5 were at first included in the Sunday Night Office, despite their use elsewhere (at Lauds on Monday and at Compline daily). An entry in the Ivrea Antiphoner seems to indicate that when a psalm was removed from the current psalmody of the Night Office, it was 'replaced' by singing a neighbouring psalm twice.[83] If this bizarre compromise solution enjoyed any currency at Rome, it seems to have had no influence on the *Regula S. Benedicti*, which accepted (and extended) the principle of removing from the psalmody of the Night Office and Vespers those psalms deployed elsewhere in the *cursus*.

The views of Callewaert and Pascher notwithstanding, Psalm 94 was probably sung daily as an Invitatory in Rome by St Benedict's time.[84] The fixed psalms of the little hours were also probably in place: Psalm 53 was sung daily at Prime in addition to two sections from Psalm 118, the remainder of which was divided between Terce, Sext, and None. Three psalms (4, 90, and 132) were sung daily at Compline, by this time too familiar to need naming in the *Regula Magistri*.[85]

Some difficulty attends the use of Psalms 92 and 99 in Sunday Lauds.[86] In St Benedict's distribution, both are found in the current psalmody of the Night Office, which might suggest that they had no special place in the Roman distribution as it stood in the 530s. Their place in the medieval secular *cursus* is itself complicated by seasonal variations.

---

[81] Le Roux, 'Les répons "De Psalmis"', p. 47; see also his large tables.
[82] J. Pascher, 'Zur Frühgeschichte des römischen Wochenpsalteriums', *Ephemerides liturgicae* 79 (1965), 55–8.
[83] Hesbert, *CAO* I, 3 (under MS 'E'). Pascher, 'Zur Frühgeschichte', p. 56, contains a most unfortunate typographical error: the series of psalms given from the 'Codex Eporediensis' should read '1 2 3 4 6 7 7 ...', instead of the printed '1 2 3 4 5 7 7 ...'. The series of psalms given in the Ivrea Antiphoner would seem to indicate that Ps. 5 was omitted but Ps. 4 was not. Ps. 7 was sung twice to preserve the same number of psalms.
[84] Vogüé, *La Règle de Saint Benoît* V, 435 n. 4. Cf. Callewaert, *Sacris erudiri*, pp. 135–44, arguing that it was borrowed into the Roman Office from the *Regula S. Benedicti*; Pascher, 'Zur Frühgeschichte', held the same view, but revised Callewaert's theory about how the removal of Ps. 94 affected the current psalmody of the Night Office. In support of Callewaert and Pascher, there remains the disconcerting presence of Ps. 94 in the main body of psalmody of the Night Office of Epiphany.
[85] *Regula Magistri* 37:1. Cf. *RSB* 18:19; Vogüé, *La Règle de Saint Benoît* V, 527–43, esp. p. 542.
[86] O. Heiming, 'Zum monastischen Offizium von Kassianus bis Kolumbanus', *Archiv für Liturgiewissenschaft* 7 (1961–2), 89–156, at p. 150 n. 59.

Outside the period from Septuagesima to Holy Saturday, Psalms 92 and 99 are the first two psalms of Lauds on Sunday. (See Table 2.1 on page 16 above.) In Septuagesima and Lent, however, Psalm 92 is relegated to Prime, replaced by Psalm 50, the more penitential text that opens ferial Lauds. Psalm 99 is removed altogether during this time, replaced by Psalm 117, itself normally used at Prime in the secular *cursus*; but Psalm 99 is unique in having retained its place in the current psalmody of the Night Office for Saturday despite being sung at Lauds. An attractive solution would see Psalm 92 assigned to all Sundays from the early sixth century, Psalm 50 being judged unsuitable for the weekly celebration of the Resurrection. Only later, out of a desire to emphasize the penitential character of the season from Septuagesima to Holy Saturday,[87] did the custom arise of reverting to Psalm 50. Perhaps at the same time, Psalm 99 was added to Lauds as a psalm suitable for Sundays outside the penitential season; but its place in the Night Office on Saturday was retained, to maintain the recitation of the whole psalter weekly even when Psalm 99 was not sung at Lauds. Militating against this hypothesis is St Benedict's failure to include Psalm 92 in his own scheme for Sunday Lauds. But even if Benedict drew his scheme for Lauds more directly from Roman practice than from the *Regula Magistri*,[88] he nevertheless followed the 'Master' in giving no place to Psalm 62 in daily Lauds, and so he may also have imitated the *Regula Magistri* in preferring to retain Psalm 50 at Lauds on all Sundays, irrespective of the contemporary Roman custom (especially if the use of Psalm 92 was a recent innovation).[89]

The distribution shown in Table 2.6 cannot account for the variation that doubtless existed in the practices of different monasteries within Rome itself. Certain features in it may have appeared before others. Both the *Regula Magistri* and the *Regula S. Benedicti* bear witness to a period of great liturgical development and creativity.[90] This reconstruction does, however, demonstrate the three fundamental traits of the Roman distribution in the time of St Benedict: (a) all 150 psalms were sung over the course of the week; (b) most of the psalms were 'got through' in the current psalmody of the Night Office and Vespers; and (c) psalms assigned

---

[87] A character already evident in both the *Regula Magistri* and the *Regula S. Benedicti* in their abstention from saying 'Alleluia' during this time: *RSB* 15; cf. Vogüé, *La Règle du Maître* I, 55–6.
[88] See Vogüé, *La Règle de Saint Benoît* V, 491.
[89] Vogüé, *La Règle de Saint Benoît* V, 490 n. 16.
[90] Vogüé, *La Règle de Saint Benoît* V, 486–7 and n. 8.

to Lauds and the little hours because of the appropriateness of their texts were not repeated elsewhere in the distribution.

Between the sixth century and the ninth, the Roman distribution attained its permanent form as described by Amalarius (Table 2.1). By at least the later eighth century, when the practice was imitated at Monte Cassino, the complicated system of seasonal alternation of Psalms 50, 92, 99, and 117 at Lauds was established.[91] Compline was expanded by the addition of Psalm 30:2–6 (chosen for verse 6, *In manus tuas commendo spiritum meum*) and the canticle *Nunc dimittis*, whose use here was apparently unknown to St Benedict.[92] The psalmody of the Sunday Night Office was further reduced by the removal of Psalms 21 to 25 to Prime.[93] This left just eighteen psalms at the Night Office: Psalms 1–3 and 6–20.[94] Amalarius does not mention the presence of Psalms 21–25 in his description of Prime. This may simply be because he saw no opening for an allegorical explanation of their position in Prime; but it could also indicate that this change in the distribution of psalms was not yet firmly established in ninth-century Frankish practice. Once these changes had been made, the Roman distribution of psalms remained fixed until the revisions made to the breviary of the papal Curia in the thirteenth century, extended by the Tridentine revision of 1568.[95]

---

[91] *Ordo Casinensis II dictus Ordo officii* (prob. 778×797), § 19, ed. T. Leccisotti, in *Initia consuetudines Benedictinae*, ed. Hallinger, CCM 1, pp. 113–23, at p. 122, under MS 'A'. I owe my awareness of this text to Jeffery, 'Eastern and Western elements', p. 142 n. 89. Although not sanctioned in the *Regula S. Benedicti*, the substitution of at least Ps. 92 for Ps. 50 on certain occasions was standard in later monastic practice; see Tolhurst, *Introduction to the English Monastic Breviaries*, p. 196.

[92] The possibility of a late entry of the *Nunc dimittis* into Compline was proposed long ago by Suitbert Bäumer, who saw here an intervention by Gregory the Great (*Histoire du bréviaire* I, 364). Callewaert (*De breviarii Romani liturgia*, pp. 56 and 199) was uncomfortable with this idea.

[93] As Bradshaw has pointed out (*Daily Prayer*, p. 148), St Benedict also used Prime as a repository for psalms that did not fit into the current psalmody of the Night Office, which he held strictly to twelve psalms per night.

[94] Amalarius of Metz, *Epistola ad Hilduinum*, § 55, ed. Hanssens I, 341–63, at p. 351.

[95] See S. J. P. Van Dijk and J. H. Walker, *The Origins of the Modern Roman Liturgy: The Liturgy of the Papal Court and the Franciscan Order in the Thirteenth Century*, (Westminster, MD, 1960). Prof. Peter Jeffery informs me that some medieval development confined to Rome itself may also be observed in the two surviving 'Old Roman' antiphoners, though I have not been able to pursue this.

The number of nocturns in the Sunday Night Office

Table 2.6 does not show how Psalms 1–25 were divided among the nocturns of the Sunday Night Office in the sixth century. That St Benedict's pattern for the Night Office on Sunday uses three nocturns could be taken as evidence that the Roman Office of his day also used three nocturns. St Benedict's third nocturn, however, seems to derive from a separate source, albeit a Roman one (with antecedents at Milan and even Jerusalem), namely a vigil in commemoration of the Resurrection made up of three psalms and a gospel reading (or possibly a canticle).[96] This vigil pattern is similar in structure to St Benedict's third nocturn, which includes three canticles and the reading of the gospel for the day by the abbot.[97] The Roman observance of three psalms and a gospel reading was a special 'vigil', not to be confused with the daily midnight office of psalmody (the Night Office).[98]

One way to reconstruct the pattern of the Roman Sunday Night Office in its earlier phases is through the development of the number of readings (and the responsories that accompany them). In the time of Amalarius, the Roman Office had nine readings and eight responsories (the last reading having no responsory). But this pattern may not have obtained in the sixth century. The Night Office described by St Benedict and the all-night vigil of the *Regula Magistri* are so different from each other, even though both rules reflect Roman practices to varying degrees, that it seems likely that the Roman Night Office for Sunday, which may also have included a separate all-night vigil beginning on Saturday evening, did not offer these two monastic legislators a model suitable for adaptation.[99] The readings of the Night Office seem generally to have been treated with greater flexibility than the psalmody. Whereas the number of psalms to be sung in the Egyptian monastic Office was established by an angelic intervention, Cassian is careful to explain that the number of lessons read by the Egyptian monks (two at each hour) was a human ordinance, established by the Desert Fathers on their own initiative.[100] A letter to Charlemagne from Theodemar, abbot of Monte Cassino, defends Benedict's lenient arrange-

---

[96] Vogüé, *La Règle de Saint Benoît* V, 474–9, citing, among various pointers to early Roman practice, a vigil imposed on the monks of St Peter's by Gregory III (731–41) in 732; *Liber pontificalis*, ed. Duchesne I, 422, lines 32–3.
[97] *RSB* 11:6–10.
[98] Bradshaw, *Daily Prayer in the Early Church*, p. 138.
[99] Bradshaw, *Daily Prayer in the Early Church*, p. 138.
[100] John Cassian, *Institutiones*, II. 6, ed. Guy, p. 68.

ment for the summer Night Office, which on weekdays requires just a single short lesson recited by heart, by asserting that the Roman Night Office of St Benedict's time had no scriptural readings at all. Long readings, he contends, were only introduced later, by Gregory I or by Honorius.[101] Theodemar can hardly have had reliable information about the nature of the Roman Night Office in the sixth century, and in any case he describes weekdays rather than Sundays. But he reveals that even in the eighth century it was recognized that the readings of the Night Office were less fixed by ancient tradition than the psalmody.

The *Liber diurnus*, a book of templates for letters and declarations drafted in the papal chancery, includes a form called *Cautio episcopi* in which a bishop just consecrated by the pope promises to recite daily vigils (*uigiliae*) with his clergy. These vigils are to comprise three lessons, three 'antiphons', and three responsories in summer; 'four lessons with their antiphons and responsories' in winter; and 'nine lessons with their antiphons and responsories' on all Sundays of the year.[102] This text was composed no later than 559.[103] It has sometimes been interpreted uncritically as the scheme of readings current in the Roman Night Office at this time,[104] or even as the only public form of the Office used in Rome at all.[105] There is obviously some relationship between the number of readings given in the *Cautio episcopi* and the eventual form of the secular Office, with nine readings on Sundays and three on weekdays.[106] The augmentation of the Office during the winter finds a parallel in the *Regula Magistri*, and the use of four lessons on winter weekdays could be seen as the inspiration for St Benedict's Sunday Night Office, with four readings

---

[101] Theodemar, *Epistola ad Karolum magnum* (787×797), ed. E. Dümmler, MGH Epp. 2 (Berlin, 1895), pp. 509–14, at p. 511: 'sive a beato papa Gregorio sive, ut ab aliis adfirmatur, ab Honorio.' On this letter, see also p. 59 below.
[102] *Liber diurnus*, III. 7 (no. 74), ed. T. Sickel (Vienna, 1889), pp. 77–8: 'Illud etiam prae omnibus spondeo atque promitto, me omni tempore per singulos dies a primo gallo usque mane, cum omni ordine clericorum meorum vigilias in ecclesia celebrare; ita ut minoris quidem noctis, id est a Pascha usque ad aequinoctium XXIV^a die mensis Septembris, tres lectiones, tres antiphonae atque tres responsorii dicantur: Dominico autem in omni tempore novem lectiones cum antiphonis et responsoriis suis persolvere Deo profitemur.' Excerpts tr. Bradshaw, *Daily Prayer in the Early Church*, p. 137.
[103] Vogüé, *La Règle de Saint Benoît* V, 468 n. 59.
[104] J. D. Crichton, 'The Office in the West: The early Middle Ages', in C. Jones, G. Wainwright, E. Yarnold, and P. Bradshaw (eds.), *The Study of Liturgy*, rev. edn (London, 1992), pp. 420–9, at p. 421.
[105] Batiffol, *History of the Roman Breviary*, pp. 37–9.
[106] Vogüé, *La Règle de Saint Benoît* V, 472.

in each nocturn. But the *Cautio episcopi* was intended to apply to suburbicarian bishops and their clergy. The priests of at least one church protested against this daily burden.[107] It says nothing about the Office as it was recited by the monks attached to the greater basilicas. Moreover, as Paul Bradshaw points out, the *Cautio episcopi* describes a vigil, beginning at cockcrow and lasting until dawn (*a primo gallo usque mane*), not the midnight office of psalmody that developed into the secular Night Office.[108] As for St Benedict's use of four readings, this could equally have arisen from a desire to have both psalms and readings arranged in sets of twelve.[109]

The Roman basilican Office known to St Benedict in the sixth century seems to have differed from other monastic liturgical traditions in lacking a weekly great night vigil beginning on Saturday evening.[110] Certain letters of St Jerome allude to a practice, apparently widely accepted in the late fourth and early fifth centuries, of rising at midnight to recite psalms and then rising a second time to read the scriptures and to pray.[111] It is difficult, however, to discern what the relationship might have been between the Night Office of Roman monks and any custom of vigils on Sundays or feasts. Before the ninth century, certain feast days, notably Christmas, seem to have been marked by having two nocturnal offices: an office proper to the feast, perhaps with nine lessons, and the usual ferial office of the day, in which the psalms and lessons of the occurring weekday were recited (but with further chants appropriate to the feast).[112] These two offices were eventually conflated into a single festal Night Office, with the omitted psalms and antiphons allocated to the octave of the feast.[113]

When it came to the non-festal Sunday Night Office, the Roman monks gave it greater solemnity, not, it would seem, by adding a vigil,

---

[107] *Codex iuris canonici*, ed. E. Friedburg (Leipzig, 1879) I, 316.

[108] Bradshaw, *Daily Prayer in the Early Church*, p. 138.

[109] Vogüé, *La Règle de Saint Benoît* V, 480.

[110] Vogüé, *La Règle de Saint Benoît* V, 456. (Some traditions had a vigil beginning on Friday evening.) Vogüé further suggests (p. 462) that the wording of the *Regula Magistri* may indicate a reaction against a tendency in Rome to abandon these vigils. Bradshaw rejoins that Rome never knew an all-night vigil and that the vigil in the *Regula Magistri* must be an innovation based on other monastic traditions (*Daily Prayer*, p. 143).

[111] See Bradshaw, *Daily Prayer in the Early Church*, pp. 134–5.

[112] *Ordo Romanus XII*, §§ 4 and 23–4, ed. Andrieu II, 460–1 and 465–6.

[113] The double office is no longer present in *Ordo Romanus XV*, §§ 7–11. See R. Le Roux, 'Aux origines de l'office festif: Les antiennes et les psaumes aux matines de Noël et de la Circoncision', *Études grégoriennes* 4 (1961), 65–170 and fold-out table.

but by increasing its psalmody: 36 psalms in the reconstructed fifth-century arrangement (a tripling of the ferial number of 12), 23 (or 25) psalms in the early sixth century (a doubling).[114] The number of readings in the early Roman Night Office can be determined only indirectly. Raymond Le Roux's work on the psalmic responsories suggests that behind the layer of eight responsories (for nine lessons) in widest circulation there is a still older set of only five responsories (for six lessons).[115] If the later pattern of three lessons to each nocturn can be taken as a model, this earlier version of the Sunday Night Office would appear to have had only two nocturns. An early form of the Night Office with only two nocturns is also suggested by Le Roux's analysis of the psalms and antiphons of Christmas, and behind this two-nocturn form an even earlier state with just one nocturn and three lessons.[116] Here we may notice that in the classic Roman tradition the Night Office of Easter has only one nocturn of three lessons; but notwithstanding Anton Baumstark's second 'law of liturgical evolution', which holds that 'primitive conditions are retained with greater tenacity in the more sacred seasons of the liturgical year',[117] it cannot be relied upon that this arrangement is archaic.[118]

What emerges in the development of the Roman Sunday Night Office is a gradual increase in the number of readings and a gradual decrease in the number of psalms.[119] The evidence does not permit any definite assertions about the chronology of these developments. It would be imprudent to insist that increases in readings coincided exactly with a decrease in psalmody. But something like the following framework would make sense:

---

[114] Vogüé, *La Règle de Saint Benoît* V, 457 n. 17.

[115] Le Roux, 'Les répons "De Psalmis"', p. 49. The gradual increase in the number of responsories is illustrated in a table on the same page (column D reflects the further development that took place in the 'Old Roman' antiphoners, a pattern not found in earlier Frankish books).

[116] Le Roux, 'Aux origines de l'office festif', pp. 119–25; *idem*, 'Les répons "De Psalmis"', pp. 46–9 and 143–4.

[117] *Comparative Liturgy*, tr. F. L. Cross from the 3rd rev. French edn, ed. B. Botte (Westminster, MD, 1958), p. 27.

[118] Early descriptions of the Easter Office are rare and vague; see *Ordo Romanus XIIIB*, § 6, ed. Andrieu II, 500.

[119] Vogüé, *La Règle de Saint Benoît* V, 480.

	5th cent.	6th cent.	8th cent.
Psalms:	36	23	18
Lessons:	3	6	9
Nocturns:	1	2	3

The one remaining question is how the psalms were divided between the nocturns of the middle phase. The five psalmic responsories linked with this middle phase by Le Roux are *Domine ne in ira* (Ps. 6), *Deus qui sedes* (Ps. 9), *Notas mihi fecisti* (Ps. 15), *Diligam te domine* (Ps. 17), and *Domini est terra* (Ps. 23).[120] If the responsories were drawn from the psalms appropriate to each of the two nocturns, the first nocturn will have included Psalms 6, 9, and 15. The second nocturn will have included Psalms 17 and 23. The second nocturn would therefore begin with either Psalm 16 or Psalm 17. The number of verses in Psalms 1–3 and 6–16 is almost exactly equal to the number of verses in Psalms 17–25.[121] It is interesting, therefore, to find in the twelfth-century Ivrea Antiphoner, which preserves a number of apparently archaic features relating to the psalmody of the Night Office, that the versicle for the second nocturn on Sundays (in what is now a three-nocturn form) is Psalm 17:29: *Quoniam tu illuminam (sic)*.[122] Psalm 17 is also the longest psalm recited in the Sunday Night Office. These facts might justify a revision of Table 2.6 to divide the Sunday Night Office into two nocturns, the first comprising Psalms 1–3 and 6–16, the second Psalms 17–25.

The reconstruction of the sixth-century Office proposed above is fragile, based partly on the internal evidence of the medieval secular Office itself, and partly on the evidence of earlier Roman practice that can be gleaned from indirect witnesses like the *Regula S. Benedicti* and the *Regula Magistri*. It cannot even be said that this form of the Office was

---

[120] Le Roux, 'Les répons "De Psalmis"', p. 49.

[121] About 173 in the first group, 169 in the second. These reflect the 'sung' verse divisions of breviaries and choir psalters (and, following this model, the verse numbers in the psalter of the Anglican Book of Common Prayer). The verse numbering system found in printed editions of the Vulgate often assigns separate verse numbers to the *tituli psalmorum* and groups under single verse numbers texts that in performance would be split into two balanced verses. The exact number of 'sung' verses will also have depended on how many times the *Gloria patri* was recited in the course of the psalmody.

[122] Hesbert, *CAO* I, 87–9 (MS 'E' § 36). This was first observed by Adalbert de Vogüé, *La Règle de Saint Benoît* V, 471 n. 66. To this reference may be added two more. Amalarius of Metz gives this versicle as an alternative to the 'standard' second nocturn versicle, *Media nocte surgebam* (Ps. 118:62); *Liber officialis*, IV. 9. 17, ed. Hanssens II, 446. It also appears in the Tridentine Breviary: *Breviarium Romanum: Editio princeps*, p. 42.

celebrated in all Roman monasteries. This reconstruction may represent the practice of only one Roman institution. Of the four major Roman basilicas, the basilica of St Peter at the Vatican was the most important liturgically.[123] When Pope Gregory III (731–41) founded the monastery of St Chrysogonus in Trastevere, he ordered the monks there to recite the offices 'secundum instar officiorum ecclesiae beati Petri apostoli'.[124] More important, Gregory III gave precisely the same instructions when he refounded the monastery of St Pancratius at the Lateran, ordering that the Office be observed in the Lateran just as it was in St Peter's 'diurnisque nocturnisque temporibus'.[125] It was to St Peter's that Frankish liturgical reformers looked when they sought an authoritative model for their own Office liturgy and monastic regulations. *Ordines Romani XVIII* and *XIX* both refer to 'the monasteries of St Peter' in their titles.[126]

In the seventh century St Peter's was served by three monasteries, SS. John and Paul, St Martin, and St Stephen Major; a monastery of St Stephen Minor was added in the eighth century.[127] As was mentioned earlier, these monasteries were responsible for the maintenance of the daily Office in the basilica. A passage in *Ordo Romanus XIX* gives some idea of the liturgical authority ascribed to the abbots of the monasteries of St Peter's. At the end of *Ordo XIX*, the eighth-century Frankish redactor has appended a list of authoritative figures said to have been instrumental in shaping the chant and liturgy of the Roman Church. He first lists seven popes: Leo, Gelasius, Symmachus, John, Boniface, Gregory, and Martin. Pope Martin's reign ended in 657. These are followed by three abbots, judged *bien mysterieux* by Michel Andrieu:

> Post istos quoque Catalenus Abba, ibi deserviens ad sepulcrum S. Petri, et ipse quidem anni circuli cantum diligentissime edidit. Post hunc quoque Maurianus Abba, ipsius S. Petri Apostoli serviens, annalem suum cantum et ipse nobile ordinavit. Post hunc vero Domnus Virbonus Abba et omnem cantum anni circuli magnifice ordinavit.[128]

---

[123] The others being the Lateran, St Mary Major, and St Paul.
[124] *Liber pontificalis*, XCII. 9, ed. Duchesne I, 418; see Ferrari, *Early Roman Monasteries*, p. 399.
[125] *Liber pontificalis*, XCII. 10, ed. Duchesne I, 419; see Ferrari, *Early Roman Monasteries*, p. 366.
[126] Ed. Andrieu III, 205 and 217.
[127] Ferrari, *Early Roman Monasteries*, pp. 367–8.
[128] *Ordo Romanus XIX*, § 37, ed. Andrieu III, 224.

Ordo Romanus XIX survives in a single St Gall manuscript of the later eighth century.[129] Andrieu considered this list to be an invention of the Frankish redactor, whom he suspected to have had no first-hand experience of Roman customs.[130] It is striking, however, that the list of popes ends in 657 and that the last abbot is addressed with the respectful title *Domnus*, which would suggest that he was still alive when the list was first composed.[131] It is impossible to attribute to these abbots any specific liturgical or musical innovations; but their inclusion in this list, which may be an excerpt from a seventh-century Roman document, underscores the importance of the monasteries serving St Peter's Basilica in shaping the Roman liturgy.

The notice in the *Liber pontificalis* of the foundation of the monastery of St Stephen Minor by Pope Stephen II (752–7) refers to a reform of the Office sung in St Peter's:

> Meanwhile the blessed pope, ever reflecting on the things of God, had the nighttime offices, which had become slack for a long time, carried out in the hours of night, and in the same way he restored the daytime office as it had been of old. To the three monasteries which since ancient times perform this office at St Peter's he added a fourth, and there he established monks who might thenceforth join together in the office, and he ordained an abbot over them. There he bestowed many gifts, both everything necessary for the monks in the monastery, and estates outside; he established even to this day that with the other three monasteries they should chant in St Peter's, the prince of the apostles.[132]

---

[129] St Gall, Stiftsbibliothek, 349, pp. 104–18.

[130] Andrieu, *Les Ordines Romani* III, 12–15. He was here concerned to refute the ingenious hypothesis of Carlo Silva-Tarouca that *Ordo Romanus XIX* was a composition of John the Archcantor; 'Giovanni "Archicantor" di S. Pietro a Roma e l'"Ordo Romanus" da lui composto (anno 680)', *Memorie*, I.1, Atti della Pontificia Accademia di Archeologia, Serie 3 (Rome, 1923), pp. 159–219.

[131] Batiffol, *History of the Roman Breviary*, p. 54 n. 2; *Die Gesänge des altrömischen Graduale: Vat. lat. 5139*, ed. M. Landwehr-Melnicki with an introduction by B. Stäblein, Monumenta monodica Medii Ævi 2 (Basel, 1970), pp. 54*–7*. Stäblein's theory that Maurianus, Catolenus, and Virbonus were involved in the creation of the 'Gregorian' repertory of plainchant is now rejected.

[132] *Liber pontificalis*, XCIV. 40, ed. Duchesne I, 451: 'Sed interea idem beatissimus papa, semper quae Dei sunt meditans, officia quod per multo tempore relaxati fuerant nocturno tempore nocturnis horis explere fecit et diuturno officio similiter restauravit ut ab antiquitus fuerat. Et a tribus monasteriis qui prisco tempore in ecclesia beati Petri apostoli eundem officium persolvuntur adjungens quartum, ibidem monachis qui adhuc in ipso coniungere-

The passage affirms the central liturgical importance of the monasteries attached to St Peter's. But we can only speculate about whether this reform of the Night Office included any substantive structural changes (such as the addition of a third nocturn to the Sunday Night Office). This text is a later addition to the main material in the *Liber pontificalis*, and if the tradition it reports is authentic, it may refer simply to an effort that was made to get the monks to sing the Night Office at night, rather than anticipating it the day before or delaying it until morning. It is nevertheless a provocative thought that the *Liber pontificalis* should link a reform of the Office with the pontificate of Stephen II, whose visit to Saint-Denis in 754, with Chrodegang of Metz as his escort, has so long been seen as a watershed in the Romanization of the Frankish liturgy.[133]

The addition of nocturns to Sunday and festal Night Office probably occurred in stages, beginning with the great solemnities of the year and gradually extending the same dignity to all Sundays. The earliest evidence for the use of a Night Office of nine lessons is perhaps the description of the *Triduum sacrum* in *Ordo Romanus XXXA*, which is probably a Frankish composition of the second half of the eighth century.[134] *Ordo Romanus XII*, another Frankish text composed somewhat later, seems to assume the use of nine lessons on most feasts; but its description of the Night Office for the Octave of Easter and other Sundays and feasts reveals that the situation may still have been unstable.[135] The Roman Office had already attained its enduring medieval form, with three nocturns in the Sunday Night Office, when the earliest Frankish Office antiphoners were copied. But some of the discrepancies between the Roman and Frankish Office books inspected by Amalarius in the first half of the ninth century, and the variation that he reported between churches in Rome itself, would be unsurprising if Chrodegang had undertaken to imitate at Metz a form of the Roman Office that was still in a state of flux. Earlier, independent local Frankish initiatives to imitate Roman customs will have further

---

tur officio instituit, atque abbatem super eos ordinavit. Et multa dona ibi largitus est, tam universa quae in monasterio necessaria sunt monachis, quamque foris immobilia loca, qui in psallentio beati apostolorum principis Petri cum supradictis tribus monasteriis usque in hodiernum diem constituit.' Translation: R. Davis, *The Lives of the Eighth-Century Popes (Liber Pontificalis): The Ancient Biographies of Nine Popes from AD 715 to AD 817*, Translated Texts for Historians 13 (Liverpool, 1992), pp. 68–9. Davis's translation gives 'real estate' instead of 'estates'.

[133] See p. 52 n. 137 below.
[134] Ed. Andrieu III, 455–8.
[135] *Ordo Romanus XII*, § 20, ed. Andrieu II, 464.

complicated the eighth-century situation.

'Secular' and 'monastic' Offices in the ninth-century Frankish Church

A sequence of events begun in the eighth century resulted in the eventual adoption of Rome's local monastic Office tradition as the normative Office liturgy of all secular clergy in the West and the resurrection of the Benedictine Office as the sole Office of monks. Two stages must be discerned, both of which are linked with the reform of the Frankish Church undertaken by the Carolingian kings in the eighth and ninth centuries. The first stage occurred in the reigns of Pippin III (751–68) and Charlemagne (768–814). Sources long familiar to historians speak of a major legislative effort to impose Roman liturgy, including the Roman Office, on all Frankish churches, whether served by communities of secular canons or by monks. In the second stage, beginning under Louis the Pious (814–40), the *Regula S. Benedicti* was promoted as the only appropriate model for monastic life, and under a strict interpretation, urged by Benedict of Aniane, it was argued that the Office should be performed by monks exactly as it was laid down in the Rule.

The imposition of the Roman Office on the Frankish Church under Pippin III and Charlemagne

What is today called the 'secular Office' originated when the Office as it was sung by monks in the greater basilicas of Rome was adopted as the sole form of the Office to be used in Frankish cathedrals and monasteries.[136] This came about largely through the influence of Chrodegang, bishop (later archbishop) of Metz (d.766), who imposed the recitation of the complete Roman Office on the community of canons in his cathedral. It was he who arranged the visit of Pope Stephen II to the court of Pippin III at Saint-Denis in 754.[137] This visit gave Pippin the opportunity to hear

---

[136] The process was sketched out by Pierre Salmon in his consideration of the history of the obligation for all clergy to recite the Office; see *The Breviary through the Centuries*, tr. Sister David Mary [from *L'Office divin: Histoire du formation du bréviaire*, Lex orandi 27 (Paris, 1959)] (Collegeville, MN, 1962), pp. 1–11.

[137] Paul Warnefrid ('the Deacon'), *Gesta episcoporum Mettensium*, ed. G. H. Pertz, MGH SS 2 (Hanover, 1829), pp. 260–70, at p. 268. See C. Vogel, 'Saint Chrodegang et les débuts

the Roman liturgy sung by Stephen's entourage, prompting the king to supplant the Gallican liturgy with the Roman, as Walahfrid Strabo wrote in the middle of the ninth century:

> In fact, when Pope Stephen came into Francia to Pippin, Emperor Charles the Great's father, to seek justice for St. Peter against the Lombards, his clergy brought the more perfect knowledge of plain-chant (*cantilena*), which almost all Francia now loves, to Pippin at his request. From that time onward its use was validated far and wide.[138]

This *cantilena Romana* or *cantus Romanus* should not be construed solely as a musical repertory: the terms *cantus* and *cantilena* encompass all texts recited in the course of the liturgy, and the music of the Roman liturgy, including the music of the Divine Office, had no identity separate from the liturgical texts.[139]

Of the 'Gallican Office' – probably a collective reference to many different local practices – and the process whereby it was displaced, little is known. Perhaps the earliest evidence of Pippin's policy regarding the Office is found in the *Ratio de cursus*, composed at the latest a year before Pippin's death.[140] As has already been seen, the author's aim was to defend both the Gallican Office (*cursus Gallorum*) and above all an 'Irish Office' (*cursus Scottorum*), perhaps to be identified with the *cursus* in the *Regula monachorum* of Columbanus, by showing them to date back to apostolic times. Scholars have questioned the true extent of Pippin's (and indeed Charlemagne's) liturgical reforms, suggesting that substantial change was not to occur until the ninth century and that existing Gallican

---

de la romanisation du culte en pays franc', in *Saint Chrodegang: Communications présentées au colloque tenu à Metz à l'occasion du douzième centenaire de sa mort* (Metz, 1967), pp. 91–109. For a critical survey of work on Chrodegang's activities and influence, see J. Barrow, 'Review article: Chrodegang, his rule and its successors', *Early Medieval Europe* 14 (2006), 201–12.

[138] Walahfrid Strabo, *Libellus de exordiis et incrementis quarundam in observationibus ecclesiasticis rerum* [written before 842], c. 26, ed. and tr. A. Harting-Correa (Leiden, 1996), p. 167: 'Cantilenae vero perfectiorem scientiam, quam iam pene tota Francia diliget, Stephanus papa, cum ad Pippinum patrem Karoli Magni imperatoris in Franciam pro iustitia sancti Petri a Langobardis expetenda venisset, per suos clericos petente eodem Pippino invexit, indeque usus eius longe lateque convaluit.'

[139] Vogel, 'Saint Chrodegang et les débuts de la romanisation', p. 97.

[140] See p. 26 above.

customs were sometimes passed off as Roman.[141] But the defence in the *Ratio de cursus* of non-Roman Office traditions, together with the apparently firm establishment of the Roman Office in Frankish monasteries by the first half of the ninth century (for which see below), suggests that the Roman Office was adopted with some enthusiasm by the Frankish Church in the eighth century, with or without the encouragement of an official royal programme.

The earliest royal document in which the Roman Office is officially promoted for use throughout the Frankish kingdom is Charlemagne's *Admonitio generalis* of 789 (*capitulum* 80):

> To the whole clergy. That they learn the Roman chant (*cantus Romanus*) fully, and that it be performed in an orderly way throughout the liturgy of the night and day (*per nocturnale uel gradale officium*),[142] as our parent of blessed memory, King Pippin, strove to accomplish when he did away with the Gallican [chant] in favour of unity with the holy apostolic see and for the peaceful concord of the holy Church of God.[143]

Charlemagne took a special interest in the Night Office, commissioning Paul Warnefrid (Paul the Deacon) to compile a lectionary of patristic readings appropriate to the seasons and festivals of the ecclesiastical calendar:

> Furthermore, inflamed by the examples of our father Pippin of venerable memory, who by his own endeavour adorned all the churches of Gaul with the chants of the Roman tradition, we, with watchful consideration, are no less taking care to endow these same [churches] with a series of special readings [i.e. the homiliary].[144]

---

[141] See Y. Hen, *The Royal Patronage of Liturgy in Frankish Gaul to the Death of Charles the Bald (877)*, HBS Subsidia 3 (London, 2001), chapters 2 and 3.

[142] On the translation of this phrase, see H. Hucke, 'Graduale', *Ephemerides liturgicae* 69 (1955), 262–4.

[143] Ed. A. Boretius, MGH Cap. 1 (Hanover, 1883), pp. 52–62 (no. 22), at p. 61: 'Omni clero. Ut cantum Romanum pleniter discant, et ordinabiliter per nocturnale vel gradale officium peragatur, secundum quod beatae memoriae genitor noster Pippinus rex decertavit ut fieret, quando Gallicanum tulit ob unanitatem apostolicae sedis et sanctae Dei aeclesiae pacificam concordiam.'

[144] Charlemagne, *Epistola generalis* [786×800], ed. A. Boretius, MGH Cap. 1 (Hanover, 1883), pp. 80–1 (no. 30), at p. 80: 'Accensi praeterea venerande memoriae Pippini genitoris nostri exemplis, qui totas Galliarum ecclesias romanae traditionis suo studio cantibus decoravit, nos nihilominus solerti easdem curamus intuitu praecipuarum insignire serie lec-

One report of the successful implementation of the Roman Office survives in a letter of Leidrad, archbishop of Lyons, to Charlemagne, written in 813 or 814:

> And so, when at your command I had taken upon myself [the governance of] the aforementioned church [i.e. Lyons], in proportion to my humble abilities I laboured with all diligence to the end that it might be possible to have clerics to perform the liturgy (*clerici officiales*),[145] which through God's favour I now possess to a great

---

tionum.' Copies of this letter were distributed together with Paul's Homiliary, for which see R. Gregoire, *Les Homéliaires du Moyen Âge: Inventaire et analyse des manuscrits*, Rerum ecclesiasticarum documenta, Series maior, Fontes 4 (Rome, 1966), and by the same author, *Homéliaires liturgiques médiévaux*, Biblioteca degli 'Studi medievali' 12 (Spoleto, 1980). No modern critical edition of Paul's Homiliary has ever appeared; the text printed in *PL* XCV, 1159–1566, includes many later interpolations. The best single manuscript witness is Karlsruhe, Bad. Landesbibliothek, Aug. perg. XXIX and XIX (St Gall, s. ix$^{1/4}$); Gamber, *CLLA*, no. 1660*. See A. G. Martimort, *Les Lectures liturgiques et leurs livres*, Typologie des sources du Moyen Âge occidental 64 (Turnhout, 1992), pp. 87–8; and C. L. Smetana, 'Paul the Deacon's patristic anthology', in P. E. Szarmach (ed.), *The Old English Homily and its Backgrounds* (Albany, NY, 1978), pp. 75–97.

[145] *Clerici officiales*: the meaning is somewhat obscure. The 'Abavus Glossary' (s. viii/ix), so named because of its first lemma, gives three word-equivalents for *officialis*: *agaro* (*-so*), in classical usage a contemptuous term for a servant, 'lackey'; *minister*, a servant, attendant, or inferior official; and *lictor*, an attendant granted to a magistrate as a sign of official dignity, also responsible for executing sentence; ed. J. F. Mountford in *Glossaria Latina*, ed. W. M. Lindsay et al., 5 vols. (Paris, 1926–31) II, 23–121, at p. 92. From this, *clerici officiales* might be translated 'subordinates' or 'deputies'. Du Cange (C. du Fresne), *Glossarium mediae et infimae Latinitatis*, new edn by L. Favre, 10 vols. (Niort, 1883–7) VI, 35, for *officiales*, gives 'clerici ac sacerdotes qui ecclesiam deserviunt' ('clerics and priests who render service [or officiate?] in a church'); this same definition is given as one possibility in F. Arnaldi et al. (eds.), *Novum glossarium mediae Latinitatis ab anno DCCC usque ad annum MCC* (Heidelberg, 1957–): 'qui dessert une église', followed by a citation of this very passage in Leidrad's letter. The context within the letter itself, however, is primarily liturgical. A parallel usage is found in Amalarius, who cites a rubric found 'in nostris libris officialibus', by which he clearly means the various books used in the liturgy; *Liber officialis*, IV. 29. 3, ed. Hanssens II, 496 (the title of the work itself is, of course, relevant to this question). The same use of *officialis* is found in Agobard of Lyons, *De antiphonario (ad cantores ecclesiae Lugdunensis)*, c. 19, ed. L. van Acker, *Agobardi Lugdunensis Opera omnia*, CCCM 52 (Turnhout, 1981), pp. 335–51, at p. 351: 'Quapropter, auxiliante Dei gratia, omni studio pietatis instandum atque obseruandum est, ut, sicut ad caelebranda missarum sollemnia habet Ecclesia librum mysteriorum fide purissima et concinna breuitate congestum, habet et librum lectionum ex diuinis libris congrua ratione collectum, ita etiam et hunc tertium officialem libellum, id est antiphonarium, habeamus omnibus humanis figmentis et mendaciis expurgatum.' ('Wherefore, with the help of God's grace, it must be insisted upon and observed with all pious endeavour, that, just as for celebrating Masses the church has a book of mysteries [the sacramentary] constructed with pure faith and elegant

degree. And therefore you were indeed pleased, in your pious kindness, to grant to me at my request one of the clerics of the church of Metz, through whom – with God's help and your generous approval – the order of psalmody (*ordo psallendi*) has been restored in the church of Lyons to such an extent that, so far as our abilities permit, whatever the *ordo* demands for the complete discharging of the Divine Office (*divinum officium*) is now performed, in part, according to the rite of the holy palace.[146]

The promotion of the Roman liturgy, to judge from Leidrad's letter, proceeded through the imitation of models first established at Metz and, though the legislative documents do not say so, at Charlemagne's palace chapel in Aachen.[147]

To judge from subsequent effects, the programme was successful throughout the Frankish kingdom. By the middle of the ninth century, the issue was no longer whether the Roman form of the Office was to be used, but whether the Frankish performance of the Roman Office ought

---

brevity, and has a book of readings collected from the holy books with agreeable reason, even so also this third "book of the liturgy" (*officialis libellus*), that is, the antiphoner, we ought to hold pure from all human inventions and lies.') In this example, three books of the liturgy, the sacramentary, the lectionary, and the antiphoner, are described as *libri officiales*. This sentence could be interpreted to refer only to books used at Mass, but all the examples quoted by Agobard earlier in the treatise are antiphons and responsories of the Office. *Officialis* used adjectivally must have as one of its meanings 'pertaining to the liturgy', and this seems the likely meaning in *clerici officiales* in Leidrad's letter.

[146] Ed. E. Dümmler, *Epistolae Karolini aevi*, II, MGH Epp. 5 (Berlin, 1895), pp. 542–4 (no. 30): 'Denique postquam secundum iussionem vestram supra dictam ecclesiam suscepi, iuxta vires parvitatis meae omni industria egi, ut clericos officiales habere potuisset sicut iam Deo favente ex magna parte nunc habere videor. Et ideo officio quidem vestrae pietatis placuit, ut ad petitionem meam mihi concederetis unum de Metensi ecclesia clericum, per quem Deo iuvante et mercede vestra annuente ita in Lugdunensi ecclesia restauratus est ordo psallendi, ut iuxta vires nostras secundum ritum sacri palatii nunc ex parte agi videatur quicquid ad divinum persolvendum officium ordo deposcit.'

[147] R. McKitterick, 'Royal patronage of culture in the Frankish kingdoms under the Carolingians: Motives and consequences', in *Committenti e produzione artistico-letteraria nell'alto medioevo occidentale*, 2 vols., Settimane di studio del centro italiano di studi sull'alto medioevo 39 (Spoleto, 1992) I, 93–135, at pp. 123–4: 'One went to court if one had a good voice and musical sense and … one learnt to sing music in the emperor's chapel of a quality to be experienced nowhere else in the kingdom.' See also the account of monks from Jerusalem having learnt to sing the Nicene Creed at Charlemagne's palace, with the controversial addition of *filioque* that outraged neighbouring Greek monks: R. Haugh, *Photius and the Carolingians: The Trinitarian Controversy* (Belmont, MA, 1975), p. 66; R. G. Heath, 'The Western schism of the Franks and the "filioque"', *Journal of Ecclesiastical History* 23 (1972), 97–113.

to conform exactly to contemporary custom in the city of Rome itself, not just in structure but in specific content. Amalarius of Metz, prior to editing his own version of the Office antiphoner (apparently of very limited influence and now lost, but reconstructed to an extent by Jean-Michel Hanssens),[148] undertook a comparison of the antiphoners in use in Metz in his time with an antiphoner given by the pope to Abbot Wala of Corbie in 825. In the Prologue to his own antiphoner (*c.*831), he remarked upon the many differences he found,[149] and throughout his *Liber de ordine antiphonarii* (*c.*840), he listed many of these discrepancies, indicating that sometimes he had preferred the Roman custom, and at other times had preserved Frankish texts and arrangements. Amalarius's remarks provoke many questions about just how closely the Frankish Church had succeeded in imitating Rome (or had even sought to do so) in the particulars of the liturgy (questions vigorously debated especially by musicologists), but the form of the Office – its arrangement of psalms and readings – seems to have been accepted universally. The antiphoner devised by Amalarius was to be used with the Roman *cursus*. And while the contents of Amalarius's antiphoner were attacked as unsound and lacking in authority by Agobard of Lyons in his *De antiphonario* (838),[150] Agobard's own antiphoner was for use with the same Roman form of the Office, differing only in the texts of its antiphons and responsories.

The use of the Roman Office by Frankish monks

Because it conforms so closely to the expectations of most historians about how the Roman liturgy was introduced into Francia, the brief summary just given of the imposition of the Roman Office is unlikely to arouse serious objections, so long as the question is limited to the form of the Office – the *cursus* – and not to the specific texts and melodies that went along with the recitation of the psalms and biblical readings in their

---

[148] See the tables in Hanssens III, 110–224.
[149] *Prologus antiphonarii a se compositi*, cc. 2–4, ed. Hanssens I, 361–3, at p. 361. On the work of Amalarius, see M. Huglo, 'Les remaniements de l'antiphonaire grégorien au IXe siècle: Hélisachar, Agobard, Amalaire', in *Culto cristiano, politica imperiale carolinga: 9–12 ottobre 1977*, Convegni dei Centro di studi sulla spiritualità medievali (Università di Perugia) 18 (Todi, 1979), pp. 87–120; R.-J. Hesbert, 'L'Antiphonaire d'Amalaire', *Ephemerides liturgicae* 94 (1980), 176–94; C. A. Jones, *A Lost Work by Amalarius of Metz: Interpolations in Salisbury, Cathedral Library MS 154*, HBS Subsidia 2 (Woodbridge, 2001).
[150] For full reference, see above, n. 145.

distinctive Roman arrangement, a subject that awaits further explanation. Few scholars, however, have given due consideration to the origins of the 'monastic Office' based on the *cursus* laid down by St Benedict in his Rule.[151] When the Roman Office was imposed as part of Pippin and Charlemagne's liturgical programme, it was not the cathedrals and secular churches alone that were expected to comply, but the monasteries as well. This was compatible with the spirit of the *Regula S. Benedicti*, a text that exerted more and more influence in Francia over the course of the eighth century. Although eleven chapters of the Rule are devoted to a careful explanation of how the Office ought to be performed, Benedict allowed for some discretion when it came to the *cursus* of psalms:

> Above all else we urge that if anyone finds this distribution of the psalms unsatisfactory, he should arrange whatever he judges better, provided that the full complement of one hundred and fifty psalms is by all means carefully maintained each week, and that the series begins anew each Sunday at Vigils.[152]

Benedict's own arrangement of the psalter relied heavily on the Roman *cursus*, so it is no surprise that the Roman Office is compatible with this provision. Indeed, Benedict may have had the Roman Office specifically in mind when he added these verses. The phrase translated as 'begins anew' (*a caput reprendatur*) could be more literally rendered as 'taken again from the beginning'. The Sunday Night Office (Vigils), the chronological beginning of the cycle of each week, actually begins with Psalm 20 in Benedict's arrangement, but with Psalm 1 in the Roman.[153]

During a visit to St Benedict's original monastic foundation at Monte Cassino in 787, Charlemagne apparently saw a manuscript of the Rule supposed to have been St Benedict's autograph, and desired to receive a copy of it. A copy was prepared and sent to the king – the now lost exemplar of St Gall 914 – together with a covering letter composed by Paul the Deacon in the name of Abbot Theodemar. This letter provides valuable early evidence that Frankish monks were using the Roman Office, and that this Office was thought to be perfectly compatible with the Rule:

---

[151] A notable exception is the very fine account in Robertson, *The Service-Books of the Royal Abbey of Saint-Denis*, pp. 19–49 (esp. pp. 34–42).

[152] *RSB* 18:22–3: 'Hoc praecipue commonentes ut, si cui forte haec distributio psalmorum displicuerit, ordinet si melius aliter iudicauerit, dum omnimodis id adtendat ut omni ebdomada psalterium ex integro numero centum quinquaginta psalmorum psallantur, et dominico die semper a caput reprendatur ad uigilias.'

[153] Vogüé, *La Règle de Saint Benoît* II, 534 n. 23.

Concerning the division of singing the psalms throughout all the days of the week, if something seems better to anyone than what the blessed father himself established, he has permission from him to sing what he judges to be better. If it should thus be pleasing to your most wise heart, it is not required that [your] monks, who now are singing in the Roman manner, should be compelled to divide the psalms according to the holy Rule. Instead, if it seems appropriate to you, they are able to receive the pattern of a stricter life, while still singing in their accustomed manner.[154]

Theodemar mentions earlier in the letter that the monks of Monte Cassino themselves had adopted some Roman customs not included in the Rule for their recitation of the Office, namely the use of three long lessons in the Night Office on ferial days during the summer, where Benedict, noting the shortness of the nights, had given the indulgence of a single short lesson recited by heart.[155] The guideline suggested by Theodemar is that departures from the Rule's liturgical code are acceptable so long as any additions arise from the desire to praise God even more.[156]

Charlemagne's request for an authoritative copy of the *Regula S. Benedicti* is reminiscent of his earlier requests to Pope Hadrian for authoritative copies of the 'Gregorian' sacramentary and the *Collectio Dionysiana* of canon law, and the Rule figures prominently as a standard for monastic

---

[154] Theodemar, *Epistola ad Karolum magnum*, ed. Dümmler, p. 511: 'Nam et de psalmorum canendorum per singulos septimane dies divisione si cui melius fuerit, quam ipse beatus pater instituit, ab ipso habet licentiam, ut melius aestimaverit, canere. Nec debent cogi monachi, si tamen vestro sapientissimo cordi ita placet, qui nunc Romano more psallunt, iuxta institutionem sacre huius regule psalmos dividere; sed possunt, si vobis ita videtur, solito more canentes, arcioris vite normam suscipere.' The authenticity of this letter was challenged by its most recent editors, K. Hallinger and M. Wegener (*Initia consuetudines Benedictinae*, ed. Hallinger, CCM 1, pp. 137–75, at pp. 152–4), who thought the contents of the letter to reflect ninth-century concerns. But the attribution to Theodemar, with Paul the Deacon seen as the true author, is strongly defended in J. Neufville, 'L'authenticité de l'"Epistula ad regem Carolum de monasterio sancti Benedicti directa et a Paulo dictata"', *Studia monastica* 13 (1971), 295–309.
[155] See *RSB* 10.
[156] Ed. Dümmler, p. 511: 'Nec enim credendum est hoc beato patri Benedicto displicere: sed potius gratum ei esse, si quis supra id, quod ille in Dei laudibus instituit, propter Dei amorem adiciendum esse curaverit.' ('Neither must we believe that this would be displeasing to our blessed father Benedict. On the contrary, it would be acceptable to him if anyone, for the sake of the love of God, should take care to add above and beyond what he [Benedict] instituted for the praise of God.')

life in legislative texts from 789 onwards.[157] The Annals of Lorsch report that at the great Aachen Synod of 802 the whole of the *Regula S. Benedicti* was read out and expounded to the abbots and monks who were present. The capitulary issued at that synod decrees that abbots are to live with their monks as the Rule requires and that all monks are to keep the Rule 'steadfastly and valiantly' (*firmiter ac fortiter*).[158]

Nevertheless, none of the legislation from Charlemagne's reign speaks of the recitation of the Divine Office according to the Rule. Only the *Chronicon Moissiacense*, composed some time after 818, suggests that the 802 synod required that all bishops and their clergy should perform the Office according to the custom of the Roman Church and that all monks following the Rule of St Benedict should perform the Office according to the teaching of the Rule.[159] Such a provision seems extremely unlikely. The synod seems rather to have been an occasion for a volatile disagreement between two leading abbots, Adalhard of Corbie and Benedict of Aniane, precisely over the extent to which the letter of the Rule's directions could be modified to respond to contemporary conditions – a disagreement ultimately only resolved by the death of Benedict of Aniane

---

[157] Beginning with the *Duplex legationis edictum* (23 March 789), ed. A. Boretius, MGH Cap. 1 (Hanover, 1883), pp. 62–4 (Karoli Magni capitularia, no. 23). See J. Semmler, 'Benedictus II: Una regula – una consuetudo', in W. Lourdaux and D. Verhelst (eds.), *Benedictine Culture 750–1050*, Mediaevalia Lovaniensia, ser. 1, 11 (Leuven, 1983), pp. 1–49, at p. 4 and n. 21.

[158] *Annales Laureshamenses*, s.a. 802, excerpt ed. A. Boretius, MGH Cap. 1 (Hanover, 1883), p. 105: 'Similiter in ipso synodo congregavit universos abbates et monachos qui ibi aderant, et ipsi inter se conventum faciebant et legerunt regulam sancti patris Benedicti, et eam tradiderunt sapientes in conspectu abbatum et monachorum.' *Capitulare missorum generale*, c. 12, ed. A. Boretius, MGH Cap. 1 (Hanover, 1883), pp. 91–9, at p. 93: 'Ut abbate, ubi monaci sunt, pleniter cum monachis secundum regula vibant adque canones diligenter discant et observent; similiter abbatissae faciant'; c. 17 (p. 94): 'Monachi autem, ut firmiter ac fortiter secundum regula vivant'. cf. *Capitulare missorum item speciale* (802?), cc. 32–5 (pp. 102–4, at p. 103); Semmler, 'Benedictus II', pp. 4–5.

[159] *Chronicon Moissiacense* (*post* 818), s.a. 802, ed. G. H. Pertz, MGH SS 1 (Hanover, 1826), pp. 282–313 (pp. 306-7): 'Mandavit autem, ut unusquisque episcopus in omni regno vel imperio suo, ipsi cum presbyteris suis, officium, sicut psallit ecclesia Romana, facerent. ... Similiter et in monasteriis sancti Benedicti servantibus regulam, ut officium ipsius facerent, sicut regula docet.' ('He commanded that every bishop in all the kingdom or his own jurisdiction, together with his priests, should perform the Office as the Roman Church sings it. ... Likewise also that in monasteries observing the Rule of St Benedict they should perform the Office as the Rule teaches.') See J. Semmler, 'Reichsidee und kirchliche Gesetzgebung bei Ludwig dem Frommen', *Zeitschrift für Kirchengeschichte* 71, 4th ser. 9 (1960), 37–65, at pp. 64–5.

in 821.[160] As we shall shortly see, a few monasteries, adopting the rigorist position urged by Benedict of Aniane, must have begun independently to recite the Office according to the Benedictine *cursus* early in the ninth century. But most, maintaining existing traditions, will have continued to follow the Roman *cursus*, as is presumed in the letter of Theodemar.

The use of the Roman Office in Frankish monasteries, even in those where the *Regula S. Benedicti* was accorded pride of place in matters of governance and spiritual direction, has not been widely noticed or commented upon at any length.[161] Several of the early *Ordines Romani* quite clearly reflect this early fusion between Benedictine monastic life and Roman liturgical custom. *Ordo Romanus XVI* begins:

> In the holy name of our Lord, Jesus Christ, here begins the Instruction of ecclesiastical order regarding how those faithfully serving the Lord in monasteries ought, with the Lord's help, to celebrate Masses, the feast days of the saints, and the Divine offices day and night throughout the year, both according to the authority of the catholic and apostolic Roman Church, and according to the provisions and Rule of St Benedict, just as it was passed on to us by very wise and venerable fathers in the Roman Church.[162]

Ordo Romanus XVII, which incorporates material from *Ordo XVI*, likewise begins by stating that it shows how to perform the Roman liturgy in the context of Benedictine monastic life.[163] Andrieu dates *Ordo XVI* to the

---

[160] Semmler, 'Benedictus II', pp. 10–11, 41 n. 57, and 48 n. 2; D. Ganz, *Corbie and the Carolingian Renaisance*, Beihefte der Francia 20 (Sigmaringen, 1990), pp. 23 and 26.

[161] A. Angenendt, *Monachi peregrini: Studien zur Pirmin und den monastischen Vorstellungen des frühen Mittelalters*, Münstersche Mittelalterschriften 6 (Munich, 1972), pp. 213–15. J. Semmler, 'Pippin III. und die fränkischen Klöster', *Francia* 3 (1975), 88–146, at pp. 139–42. R. McKitterick, *The Frankish Kingdoms under the Carolingians, 751–987* (Harlow, 1983), p. 113. M. de Jong, 'Carolingian monasticism: The power of prayer', in R. McKitterick (ed.), *The New Cambridge Medieval History*, II: *c.700–c.900* (Cambridge, 1995), pp. 622–53, at p. 632.

[162] Ed. Andrieu III, 145–54, at p. 147: 'In nomine sancte domini nostri Iesu Christi incipit instruccio ecclesiastici ordinis, qualiter in coenubiis fideliter domino servientes tam iuxta auctoritatem catholice atque apostolice romane ecclesie quam iuxta dispositione et regulam sancti Benedicti missarum solemniis vel nataliciis sanctorum seu et officiis divinis anni circoli die noctuque, auxiliante domino, debeant celebrare, sicut in sancta ac romana ecclesia a sapientibus ac venerabilibus patribus nobis traditum.' On the *ordines*, in addition to Andrieu's monumental edition, see Vogel, *Medieval Liturgy*, pp. 135–224; and A.-G. Martimort, *Les 'Ordines', les ordinaires et les cérémoniaux*, Typologie des sources du Moyen Âge occidental 56 (Turnhout, 1991), pp. 20–47.

[163] Ed. Andrieu III, 173–93, at p. 175.

third quarter of the eighth century, and *Ordo XVII* to the end of the eighth century. The Office liturgy envisaged in *Ordo XVI* conforms quite clearly to the Roman *cursus*, not the Benedictine. The feast days of the saints are to be observed with nine lessons and responsories at the Night Office,[164] and the Night Office of Christmas is specifically said to have nine psalms and antiphons.[165] (If the Benedictine *cursus* were being followed, twelve lessons and responsories, and twelve psalms with three canticles would be have been expected.) *Ordo XVI* does include a nod towards Benedictine liturgical practice; it mentions, for example, that the lesser doxology, *Gloria patri*, should only be added to the third responsory of each nocturn in the Night Office, whereas Roman custom adds the *Gloria* after each responsory (§ 15). But even this does not acknowledge that the Benedictine *cursus* requires four responsories in each nocturn on Sundays and feast days, not three as in the Roman *cursus*. A similar situation may be seen in *Ordo Romanus XVIII*, also of the late eighth century.[166] It is intended for a community in which passages from the *Regula S. Benedicti* are to be read aloud daily (§ 4), but the Office follows the Roman *cursus*: the versicle *Domine labia mea aperies* is recited only once at the beginning of the Night Office, not three times as in the Rule, and it is followed immediately by the Invitatory, Psalm 94, whereas Psalm 3 would be expected first in the Benedictine *cursus* (§§ 16–17). No attempt is made in *Ordo XVIII* to incorporate even these easily added surface details of the Benedictine *cursus* into an exclusively Roman scheme for the Office.

Theodemar's letter to Charlemagne and the *Ordines Romani* just cited show how, even where the *Regula S. Benedicti* was adopted as the guide for monastic life, the Roman Office was still promoted and used. It is impossible to speak of a 'monastic Office' distinct from a 'secular Office' during the reigns of Pippin III and Charlemagne. The Roman form was used by both monks and secular clerics. There certainly seems to have been no question of different liturgical books for monks and secular clergy. As has already been mentioned, Wala, abbot of Corbie, obtained a copy of the Roman Office antiphoner, presumably for use in his monastery.[167] And Helisachar, variously attested as abbot of Saint-

---

[164] *Ordo Romanus XVI*, § 12, ed. Andrieu III, 148; cf. *Ordo Romanus XVII*, § 78, ed. Andrieu III, 186.
[165] *Ordo Romanus XVI*, § 25, ed. Andrieu III, 150; cf. *Ordo Romanus XVII*, § 10, ed. Andrieu III, 177, which also specifies nine lessons.
[166] Ed. Andrieu III, 203–8.
[167] See above, p. 57.

Riquier and of Saint-Aubin in Angers, undertook a major editorial revision of the Roman antiphoner while he was archchaplain at the court of Louis the Pious. A letter introducing his work (dated between 814 and 822 by Edmund Bishop) shows that he was aware of only one kind of antiphoner, originally composed in Rome, so it was believed, but corrupted over time by foolish copyists:

> Certain things in them are distorted by writers' errors, others by the mistakes of the unskilled, and some are due to inappropriate combinations. From which it is clear that the antiphoner of the night office, which was properly edited by its author at Rome, has been considerably corrupted by those just mentioned.[168]

Perhaps the best illustration of the use of the Roman Office by Frankish monks in the reign of Charlemagne is furnished by the book known as 'Charlemagne's Psalter' (BnF lat. 13159), copied at an unknown scriptorium between 795 and 800 for use at the abbey of Saint-Riquier. It was probably commissioned by the lay abbot of Saint-Riquier, Angilbert, on the occasion of Charlemagne's visit to the newly completed abbey church at Easter in 800.[169] The psalter was intended for liturgical use: in addition to its *Gallicanum* psalter text, it includes hymns and canticles for the Office, the *Laudes regiae* (litanies for the benefit of the king, sung after the Gloria at Mass), and a tonary of Mass chants. A liturgical function is also revealed by the psalter's decoration, which is organized according to 'liturgical divisions' (for which see further on page 111 below). The psalms receiving the highest grade of decorated initial, which often takes

---

[168] Helisachar, *Epistola Nidibrio Narbonensis archiepiscopo*, ed. E. Dümmler (after E. Bishop), *Epistolae Karolini aevi*, III, MGH Epp. 5 (Berlin, 1899), pp. 307–9 (Epistola variorum, no. 6), at p. 308: 'Quoniam quędam in eis scriptorum vitio depravata, quę imperitorum voto ablata, quę etiam sunt admixta. Unde liquido patet, quod antiphonarius bene apud urbem Romanam ab auctore suo editus in nocturnalibus officiis, ab his quos supra memoravimus magna ex parte sit violatus.' Translation: K. Levy, 'Abbot Helisachar's antiphoner', in his *Gregorian Chant and the Carolingians* (Princeton, NJ, 1998), pp. 179–86, at p. 181 (originally published in the *Journal of the American Musicological Society* 48 (1995), 171–2 and 177–84). See E. Bishop, 'A letter of Abbat Helisachar', in his *Liturgica Historica: Papers on the Liturgy and Religious Life of the Western Church* (Oxford, 1918), pp. 333–48; and also Huglo, 'Les remaniements'.

[169] F. Masai, 'Observations sur le Psautier dit de Charlemagne (Paris lat. 13159)', *Scriptorium* 6 (1952), 299–303; Huglo (tr. S. Boynton), 'The cantatorium: From Charlemagne to the fourteenth century', in P. Jeffery (ed.), *The Study of Medieval Chant: Paths and Bridges, East and West* (Woodbridge, 2001), pp. 89–101, at pp. 89–92; and see the notice of relevant literature on p. 90 n. 6.

up the whole page, are Pss. 1, 26, 38, 52, 68, 80, 97, 109, and 143.[170] As may be seen from Table 2.1, these are the first psalms recited at the Night Office on each day of the week, and at Vespers on Saturday and Sunday, in the Roman (secular) *cursus*. The church at Saint-Riquier was built at around the same time as the palace chapel at Aachen, using similar materials and following a nearly identical octagonal plan.[171] From the liturgical divisions in BnF lat. 13159, it would appear that in the new churches at Aachen and Saint-Riquier, similarities in architecture went along with similarities in (Roman) liturgy. Here we may recall that Leidrad of Lyons likewise reformed the liturgy at Lyons *secundum ritum sacri palatii*.[172] It would be surprising if Angilbert, the intimate friend and counsellor of Charlemagne, were any less dedicated in implementing Charlemagne's liturgical programme.

The psalter in BnF lat. 13159 was later partly adapted for use with the Benedictine *cursus*. In several of the longer psalms that are divided into two parts in the Benedictine Office, the end of the first part has been indicated with a cue for the *Gloria patri* in red ink, and the beginning of the second part has been indicated with a clumsy large red initial.[173] It is to the story of why such a change would be made that we now turn.

Louis the Pious, Benedict of Aniane, and the 'monastic Office'

It was the great reforming councils led by Benedict of Aniane at Aachen in 816 and 817 that first mandated the use of the Office of the Rule in all Frankish monasteries:

> They [the monks] are to celebrate the Office according to what is contained in the Rule of St Benedict.[174]

This measure had the personal support of the new emperor, Louis the Pious.[175] Benedict of Aniane sought to establish *una regula, una*

---

[170] The whole manuscript has been digitized at 'Gallica: Bibliothèque numerique', Bibliothèque nationale de France <http://gallica.bnf.fr> last visited 15 April 2013.
[171] Huglo, 'The cantatorium', p. 90.
[172] See p. 56 above.
[173] Pss. 9:20; 17:26; 36:27; 67:20; 68:17; 88:20; and 103:25. No divisions have been marked where they would be expected in Pss. 77, 104, 138, 143, and 144.
[174] *Synodi primae Aquisgranensis decreta authentica* (23 August 816), c. 3, ed. J. Semmler, in *Initia consuetudinis Benedictinae*, ed. Hallinger, CCM 1, pp. 457–68, at p. 458: 'III. Ut officium iuxta quod in regula sancti Benedicti contineatur celebrent.'
[175] De Jong, 'Carolingian monasticism', pp. 630–3.

consuetudo: monks were to live under one Rule, and to observe the Rule with one interpretation and one ceremonial.

The same councils produced legislation for secular clergy (canons) living in communities. These too were now organized into a clearly defined 'order' within the hierarchy of the Church, an *ordo canonicus*, strictly differentiated from the *ordo monasticus*. The *Institutio canonicorum* promulgated by the councils, which duplicated many of the provisions in Chrodegang's *Regula canonicorum*, enjoined on canons the recitation of their own Office.[176] It is clear that the Office referred to in the legislation followed the Roman arrangement, although it is never explicitly named as 'Roman'. This is a further indication of how widely accepted the Roman form of the Office had become.[177]

With their liturgical prescriptions for the *ordo monasticus* and the *ordo canonicus*, the Aachen *capitula* of 816 contain the first expression of the idea of two parallel forms of the Office, one for monks and one for secular clergy.[178] Up to this point, the boundary between the canonical and the monastic states had itself been indistinct. The clear division made between monks and canons seems to have been part of an evolution in thinking about the nature of the Carolingian empire as a Christian society in which every citizen had his proper place. The division of monks and canons into *ordines* imitated the class system of ancient Rome. The traditional division of Roman society around the time of Cicero was threefold, with citizens assigned to the *ordo senatorius*, the *ordo equester*, or simply to the *populus*, though there were, of course, more subtle distinctions (for example, the *ordo scribarum*). The Christian society envisaged by Louis the Pious also included at least three *ordines*: the *ordo canonicus*, the *ordo monasticus*, and the laity. Only when every citizen was obedient to the calling of his *ordo* could harmony and justice flourish. This is demonstrated succinctly in a passage from the poem in praise of Louis the Pious by Ermoldus Nigellus, composed between 826 and 828. In a speech attributed to Louis following his consecration by the pope in 816, Ermoldus articulates the emperor's desire for the good ordering of his realm:

---

[176] On editions and studies of Chrodegang's *Regula canonicorum*, see Barrow, 'Review article: Chrodegang'.
[177] *Institutio canonicorum*, ed. A. Werminghoff, *Concilia aevi Karolini (742–842)*, 2 vols., MGH Conc. 2.1–2.2 (Hanover, 1906–8) I, 308–421. The material relating to the Office is found in cc. 126–31 (pp. 406–8), taken directly from Chrodegang's *Regula canonicorum*, which in turn quotes from Isidore's *De ecclesiasticis officiis*.
[178] But see the account of the 802 Synod of Aachen in the *Chronicon Moissiacense* (p. 60 n. 159 above).

That the holy rule of the fathers may be binding upon the order of the clergy (*ordo clerum*), and that the venerable law of the fathers may unite the people (*populus*); and that the order of monks (*monachorum ordo*) may flourish in the teaching of Benedict, that by good deeds and a holy life it may attain the heavenly pastures; that the rich may apply the law, and the poor may obey the same, without respect of persons.[179]

The reference to the 'holy rule of the fathers' alludes to the opening sentence of the *Regula canonicorum* of Chrodegang, though this passage was not quoted in the *Institutio canonicorum*.[180] The use of different forms of the Divine Office by secular canons and monks was just one of several ways in which the distinction between the two *ordines* was to be emphasized. Other differences included norms of dress and attitudes towards private property. Canons were not to wear the monastic cowl; monks could own no property.

The abbots assembled at Aachen in 816 evidently knew that the Benedictine *cursus* would not be embraced unquestioningly by all monks. The anonymous *Statuta Murbacensia*, a commentary on the first draft of the Aachen decrees written by one of the abbots present at the council, acknowledge that the use of the Roman Office had been part of the shared inheritance of Frankish monasticism:

This chapter [on the use of the Office of St Benedict] is intended to be observed by all who thus far have been accustomed to carry on using the Office of the Roman Church while wearing the monastic habit. We ourselves, indeed, lived under the same disposition [i.e. the Roman Office] as it were from our very cradles, brought up [in it] by our elders. But whatever comes to mind that negligence (*negligentia*) has overlooked, amendment of life (*emendatio*) will be obliged to make good: namely ...[181]

---

[179] Ermoldus Nigellus, *In honorem Hludowici carmen*, Book II, lines 954–9, ed. and tr. (French) E. Faral, *Ermold le Noir: Poème sur Louis le Pieux et Épitres au Roi Pépin* (Paris, 1964), p. 76: 'Regula sancta patrum constringat in ordine clerum, | Et populum societ lex veneranda patrum; | Et monachorum ordo Benedicti dogmate crescat, | Moribus et vita pascua sancta petat; | Dives agat legem, pauper teneatur eadem, | Nec personarum sit locus atque modus.'

[180] See note 13 above.

[181] *Actuum praeliminarium synodi primae Aquisgranensis commentationes sive Statuta Murbacensia*, c. 3, ed. J. Semmler, in *Initia consuetudinis Benedictinae*, ed. Hallinger, CCM 1, pp. 441–50, at p. 442: 'Quod capitulum illis obseruandum conuenit, qui actenus Romanae

There follows a detailed list of changes that a monastery using the Roman Office would have to make to conform with the synod's decree (such as singing Compline without antiphons). This passage is fascinating in that it evidently comes from a monastery that was in the vanguard of the Anianian reforms: it had abandoned the Roman *cursus* some time before the 816 synod, but within the living memory of a community that had been trained in the old dispensation. It also reveals the underlying motive for such a change. Perfect monastic conversion, the commentator argues, means total submission to the Rule in its entirety. The Latin of the last sentence of this passage (*quicquid menti occurrit, quod neglegentia pretermisit emendatio subplere debebit*) is very similar to a sentence in the chapter in the Rule on 'mistakes in the oratory', that is, mistakes made in the performance of the Office (*RSB* 45:1–2):

> Nisi satisfactione ibi coram omnibus humiliatus fuerit, maiori uindictae subiaceat, quippe qui noluit humilitate corrigere quod neglegentia deliquit.
>
> (If he does not use this occasion to humble himself, he will be subjected to more severe punishment for failing to correct by humility the wrong committed through negligence.)

The term *emendatio* is used in the Rule for the satisfaction that a brother must make after he has departed from the Rule (or, indeed, from the monastery itself, through excommunication or wilful absence), 'following his own evil ways'.[182] As Adalbert de Vogüé has observed, *emendatio*, as St Benedict uses it, does not usually mean an externally imposed punishment ('châtiment'), but the monk's willingness to make good a shortcoming in himself ('le fait de se corriger d'un défaut').[183] When read against this background, the words of the commentator of the *Statuta Murbacensia* seem to imply that the use of the Roman Office by monks qualifies, on a spiritual level, as a 'mistake in the oratory', and that the true monk will be humble enough to see that he has been disobedient to the Rule,

---

ecclesiae officio sub monachico habitu degentes usi sunt. Nos uero qui ab ipsis pene cunabulis a maioribus nostris eruditi in eadem dispositione uiximus, quicquid menti occurrit, quod neglegentia pretermisit emendatio subplere debebit: id est ...'
[182] *RSB* 29:1.
[183] Vogüé, *La Règle de Saint Benoît* V, 825. See also *RB 1980*, ed. Fry, p. 435: 'Its predominant meaning is reformation or correction of one's behaviour as a result of an internal change of attitude.' Hildemar's commentary on the Rule (for which see p. 69 n. 187 below) identifies penitence as the necessary quality of *emendatio*; *Expositio Regulae*, c. 29, ed. Mittermüller, p. 366: 'ille veraciter emendat vitium, qui poenitentiam veraciter agit.'

if only through ignorance, and will make amends. Smaragdus, abbot of Saint-Mihiel, in his commentary on the Rule, apparently written shortly after the 816 council, also expresses the view that humility and trust in the teachings of St Benedict are the proper attitudes for monks when it comes to the Office:

> Blessed Benedict has left this distribution of the psalms, but not the whole office, to the judgment of a discerning person, while giving this advice especially, that he who wants to keep this distribution of the psalms according to his arrangement should do so; but he who decides that another distribution is better may leave aside the former and observe the latter without fault. For our part, we exhort the one who has promised to live according to this Rule to hold firmly to it and keep it as far as he can; let him trust in the mercy of God and believe that the heavenly kingdoms will be open to those who keep it.[184]

Nevertheless, the commentator of the *Statuta Murbacensia* goes on to indicate that certain Roman practices could be accommodated in the Rule's distribution of the psalms:

> Concerning those things that have been added to the Rule's distribution of the psalms from the custom of the Roman Church, but which are not held in use in certain monasteries, we have decided that we should retain them for the moment, until our elders advise either that they should be done away with or that they should be more definitely retained.[185]

---

[184] *Smaragdi abbatis Expositio in Regulam S. Benedicti*, c. 18, ed. A. Spannagel and P. Englebert, CCM 8 (Siegburg, 1974), pp. 207–8: 'Hanc autem psalmorum distributionem, non totum officium, beatus Benedictus in iudicantis posuit arbitrium, hoc praecipue monens ut qui vult hanc psalmorum distributionem secundum suam tenere dispositionem teneat; qui autem aliter melius iudicaverit, illam tenens istam sine culpa dimittat. Nos autem hortamur eum qui secundum hanc promisit se vivere regulam, in quantum valet firmiter teneat et conservet eam, et confidens de dei misericordia credat quia custodientibus eam patebunt caelica regna.' Translation: D. Barry, *Smaragdus of Saint-Mihiel: Commentary on the Rule of Saint Benedict*, with intr. essays by T. Kardong, J. Leclercq, and D. M. LaCorte, Cistercian Studies 212 (Kalamazoo, MI, 2007), p. 331.

[185] *Statuta Murbacensia*, c. 3, ed. Semmler, p. 443: 'Ea uero quae in regulari distributione psalmorum de usu Romanae ecclesiae addita sunt et in quibusdam coenobiis in usu non habentur, adhuc nobis retinenda censuimus, donec consultu meliorum aut dimittantur aut ad tenendum certiora reddantur.' The Roman alteration of the Sunday psalms of Lauds during Lent might be meant here. See n. 91 above.

That the *Statuta Murbacensia* had to justify, in strong terms, the absolute necessity of using the Benedictine *cursus* for perfect monastic obedience probably means that considerable resistance to this innovation was expected. And as the passage just quoted shows, even those who agreed that monks should use a 'Benedictine' Office liturgy could disagree about what exactly this entailed.

The limited influence of Benedict of Aniane's reforms

The reforms instigated by Benedict of Aniane were not readily accepted by all monks. The new legislation extended not just to the liturgy, but to every aspect of monastic life, and provoked objections, especially from those communities that preserved ancient traditions. Many who would formerly have defined themselves as monks found that their pattern of life did not match the requirements of this new Benedictine monasticism. The result was that the inmates of many 'monasteries' chose instead to define themselves as secular canons. This was the decision of most of the monks of St Martin of Tours in 817.[186] The difference between monks and canons in this new Carolingian mindset was actually very slight, the chief distinction being that canons made no vow of poverty and could own property. Both groups lived in community under a written rule and were devoted to singing the Office, though the forms of the Office used by the two groups were now to be distinct.

While some monks, like those at Tours, made a deliberate decision to align themselves with the *ordo canonicus* rather than the *ordo monasticus*, many communities of monks seem simply to have ignored those reforms with which they disagreed, especially the injunction that only the Benedictine Office was to be sung. That many monasteries still considered themselves 'monastic' even though they used the Roman Office is evident from the criticisms levelled at them by monks who had been persuaded that no monk worthy of the name would sing anything but the Benedictine Office. The commentary on the Rule dating from *c.*845 by Hildemar of Corbie, based on his *viva voce* teaching in the monastic school of Civate, records the distaste of strict reformed Benedictines (like himself) for those monks who were still using the Roman Office.[187] In his comments on the

---

[186] De Jong, 'Carolingian monasticism', p. 632.

[187] The text of this commentary survives in three main recensions. The longest, attributed in the manuscripts to Hildemar himself, is available only in the edition by Rupert Mittermüller, *Vitae et Regula SS. P. Benedicti una cum expositione Regulae*, III: *Expositio Regulae*

eighteenth chapter of the Rule, where St Benedict gives permission to use a distribution of psalms other than his own, Hildemar argues that Benedict was not being literal, but was rather adopting the rhetorical humility commonly found in the writings of the doctors of the Church. He tries to prove this by arguing that even if the Roman distribution of psalms were permitted, the rest of the Roman Office would not conform to Benedict's prescriptions:

> And by this [permission], what do you – who have abandoned the Office of the Rule – do about the interval that the blessed Benedict ordered should be used for study? What do you do about the hymns, and what about the readings, when there are supposed to be twelve of them read, and what about the three canticles that are then to be sung? And again, if you perform the Roman Office, you sing fewer psalms than are contained in the Rule; for during the week after Easter, which is called *Alba*, and in the week of Pentecost, the whole psalter is not sung. But the Rule orders that the psalter is to be sung every week, together with the canticles; and if it happens not to be sung, the service of monastic devotion is shown to be extremely lazy, that is, negligent. Especially so, for ought not monks to labour more in their offices than canons? For canons are sometimes not able to prolong their Office because of the crowd of the people, including women and children. But monks are free from these impediments, and go lightly armed.

ab Hildemaro tradita et nunc primum typis mandata (Regensburg, 1880). A shorter version was long attributed to Paul the Deacon, on the strength of a title added to a manuscript held in Monte Cassino, published as *Pauli Warnefridi diaconi Casinensis in sanctam Regulam commentarium* (Monte Cassino, 1880). The third recension survives under the name of 'Abbot Basilius'. It has not received its own edition, but the texts unique to this version have been printed in P. W. Hafner, *Der Basiliuskommentar zur Regula S. Benedicti: Ein Beitrag zur Autorenfrage karolingischer Regelkommentare*, Beiträge zur Geschichte des alten Mönchtums und des Benediktinerordens 23 (Münster, 1959), pp. 116–43. See also K. Zelzer, 'Überlegungen zu einer Gesamtedition des frühnachkarolingischen Kommentars zur Regula S. Benedicti aus der Tradition des Hildemar von Corbie', *Revue Bénédictine* 91 (1981), 373–82; and M. de Jong, 'Growing up in a Carolingian monastery: Magister Hildemar and his oblates', *Journal of Medieval History* 9 (1983), 99–128. What is known of Hildemar's life was first established by Ludwig Traube, *Textgeschichte der Regula S. Benedicti*, 2nd edn, ed. H. Plenkers (Munich, 1910), pp. 40–4 and 107–8. Much valuable comment is to be found in M. A. Schroll, *Benedictine Monasticism as Reflected in the Warnefrid–Hildemar Commentaries on the Rule*, (Columbia University) Studies in History, Economics, and Public Law 478 (New York, 1941), although the author's uncritical acceptance of the apocryphal attribution of one of the recensions to Paul the Deacon introduces some problems of dating and context.

Therefore, when you do thus – that is, when you sing the Roman Office – you do not seem to be lovers of the holy Rule, but rather breakers of it; for those who love our way of life do not wish to sing any Office but that of the Rule.[188]

Hildemar's critique points out certain requirements of the Benedictine Office not satisfied by the Roman Office as it was known to him: the Roman Office did not allow for an interval between the Night Office and Lauds, a time set aside for study in the Rule;[189] hymns were not sung in the early medieval Roman Office, but are stipulated in the Rule;[190] Sundays and feast days require twelve lessons and responsories in the Rule, not the nine provided in the Roman Office; the Roman Office used no Old Testament canticles in the third nocturn on Sundays; and the Roman Office reduced the amount of psalmody during the octaves of Easter and Pentecost, an apparent contravention of the Rule's insistence on the complete recitation of the whole psalter each week. Hildemar, apparently unaware that the Office being sung by the secular clergy was originally itself monastic, explains the reduced psalmody of these major festivals as a concession for clergy who must be entangled in worldly affairs. A monk worthy of his vocation, Hildemar argues, will desire to follow the Rule to the letter when it comes to the Office. Like the anonymous author of the *Statuta Murbacensia*, Hildemar says that to neglect the Benedictine *cursus* is to be 'negligent' (*negligens*). Hildemar's strong attack probably indicates that the Roman Office was more widely recited in monasteries than the

---

[188] Hildemar, *Expositio Regulae*, c. 18, ed. Mittermüller, pp. 312–13: 'Ac per hoc vos, qui relinquitis officium regulare, quid facitis de intervallo, quod B. Benedictus praecipit meditatione inservire? quid facitis de hymnis et de lectionibus, quando duodecim leguntur, et de tribus canticis, quae tunc canuntur? Et iterum si romanum officium facitis, minus psallitis, quam regulae officium contineat; nam in hebdomada post Pascha, quae vocatur alba, et in hebdomada Pentecosten, in quibus totum psalterium non canitur, quod praecipit regula per unamquamque septimam omnimodo esse canendum cum canticis suis, quia, si non fuerit cantatum, nimis iners h[oc] e[st] negligens ostenditur esse devotionis monachorum servitium, maxime cum plus debent monachi quam canonici in officiis laborare? Canonici enim aliquando propter populorum turbam et feminarum atque infantum non possunt prolongare suum officium, a quibus impedimentis monachi liberi et expediti existunt. Et ideo cum ita agitis, i.e. cum officium romanum facitis, non videmini amatores esse sanctae regulae sed transgressores; quia illi, qui amatores hujus vitae sunt, nolunt aliud officium canere quam regulare.'
[189] *RSB* 8:3: 'Quod vero restat post uigilias a fratribus qui psalterii vel lectionum aliquid indigent *meditationi inserviatur*.' [emphasis added] ('In the time remaining after Vigils, those who need to learn some of the psalter or readings should study them.')
[190] The term used in the Rule for metrical hymns is *ambrosianum*; e.g. *RSB* 9:4.

reformers of the first half of the ninth century would have liked to admit. Even where the Aachen decrees of 816 were readily obeyed, a fully Benedictine Office observance could not be established overnight. Some light is thrown on the process by the case of the permission given by Abbot Hilduin of Saint-Denis *c*.836 for the translation of some of St Denis's relics to Fleury on the condition that the Office of St Denis be sung there *more monastico*, that is, using the revised twelve-lesson version of the office that he had recently made at Emperor Louis's request.[191] This was probably the first strictly 'Benedictine' Office observed at Saint-Denis, and perhaps also at Fleury. The Benedictine *cursus* may in some cases have been introduced piecemeal, with *libelli* giving all that was necessary for individual feast days. The earliest example of this phenomenon may be the twelve-responsory feast of the Translation of St Benedict preserved in the 'Compiègne Antiphoner', BnF lat. 17436 (860×877).[192] The otherwise exclusive use of the secular *cursus* in BnF lat. 17436 has obscured the book's probable monastic origins – Jacques Froger suggested, based on its liturgical contents, that it was copied for the monastery of Saint-Médard of Soissons.[193] The oldest chant book known to me with a fully Benedictine arrangement of chants is Trier, Stadtbibliothek, 1245/597, a composite book containing the *Regula S. Benedicti*, a martyrology, a set of homilies, a collectar, and (fols. 107r–127r) what commentators have called a *Chorbuch*, a highly organized list of Office chants that could be described as a Benedictine antiphoner in incipit.[194] The hymnal is datable to *c*.860, and the *Chorbuch* is in a contemporary hand.[195] The different parts of the manuscript were bound together some time before the whole

---

[191] See the analysis in Robertson, *The Service-Books of the Royal Abbey of Saint-Denis*, pp. 41–2.

[192] *CAO* I, § 1024.

[193] J. Froger, 'Le Lieu de destination et de provenance du "Compiendiensis"', in J. B. Göschl (ed.), *Ut mens concordet voci: Festschrift Eugène Cardine* (Sankt Ottilien, 1980), pp. 338–53, at pp. 346–7; and see Robertson, *The Service-Books of the Royal Abbey of Saint-Denis*, pp. 36–7.

[194] P. Siffrin, 'Der Collectar der Abtei Prüm im neunten Jahrhundert (Trier, Stadtbibliothek 1245/597, Bl. 129ᵛ–138ᵛ)', in *Miscellanea liturgica in honorem L. Cuniberti Mohlberg*, 2 vols., Bibliotheca 'Ephemerides liturgicae' 22–3 (Rome, 1948–9) II, 223–44, at pp. 225–6; W. Haubrichs, *Die Kultur der Abtei Prüm zur Karolingerzeit: Studien zur Heimat des althochdeutschen Georgsliedes*, Rheinisches Archiv 105 (Bonn, 1979), p. 91 n. 39 and p. 101; *The Durham Collectar*, ed. Corrêa, pp. 54–63, at pp. 55–6. I am indebted to the Keeper of Records in the Stadtbibliothek, Dr Reiner Nolden, for clarification about the manuscript's origin and provenance.

[195] *The Durham Collectar*, ed. Corrêa, p. 55 and literature in n. 72.

book was given to the Abbey of St Martin in Trier in 899. The *Chorbuch* could possibly be seen as a re-organization for the Benedictine *cursus* of the contents of a secular antiphoner, without any of the texts given in full. Of 'complete' antiphoners, the Office antiphoner portion of the tenth-century 'Mont-Renaud manuscript', currently in a private collection, has a mix of twelve- and nine-lesson Night Offices.[196] The famous 'Hartker Antiphoner', St Gall, Stiftsbibliothek, 390 and 391, copied at St Gall by the recluse Hartker, dates from around the year 1000.[197] Although the antiphons, psalms, and canticles in this antiphoner are arranged, with certain important exceptions, according to the Benedictine *cursus*, the provision of responsories is insufficient for a festal and Sunday Night Office of twelve lessons as required by the Rule. Hartker preserved a Roman pattern of only nine lessons.[198] An abbot of St Gall elected with Louis's support in 817, Gozbert, probably attended the Aachen synods of 816–17. He was a favourite of the emperor, winning a royal immunity for St Gall in 818.[199] If St Gall was among the houses that sincerely embraced the new Benedictine ideal, it is instructive that an Office antiphoner of St Gall still did not fully conform to the Benedictine *cursus* over 180 years after the Aachen synods.

Benedict of Aniane's immediate impact on Carolingian monasticism seems therefore to have been relatively limited. In the second half of the ninth century, conditions were not favourable for a consolidation of what gains had been made by the reformers. This was especially so in northern Francia, where, as in England, ecclesiastical foundations were harassed by Viking raiders. Elsewhere in the Frankish kingdoms, political instability prevented the furtherance of a movement whose success had depended absolutely on royal support. Although the power struggle between the sons of Louis the Pious and the fracturing of the Carolingian empire were not so calamitous and destructive as has often been thought,[200] the disappearance of central imperial authority meant that a unified Carolingian monastic policy was no longer enforced by royal legates (*missi*). Their inspections, recorded in charters from Louis's reign, had been essential to

---

[196] *Antiphonaire du Mont-Renaud*, facsimile ed. the Monks of Solesmes, Paléographie musicale 16 (Solesmes, 1955; 2nd edn 1989); see Robertson, *The Service-Books of the Royal Abbey of Saint-Denis*, p. 44 and pp. 425–34 (esp. p. 427).
[197] *L'Antiphonaire de Hartker: Manuscrits de Saint-Gall 390–391*, facsimile, Paléographie musicale, sér. 2, 1 (Solesmes, 1900; new edn ed. J. Froger, 1970).
[198] Hesbert, *CAO* I, pp. vi–ix.
[199] For this information I am indebted to Julian Hendrix.
[200] McKitterick, *The Frankish Kingdoms*, pp. 124–5.

securing the compliance of many monasteries.[201] Some houses that had been reformed in the first half of the ninth century had become communities of canons by the tenth.[202]

The precarious state of reformed monasticism at the beginning of the tenth century is depicted vividly in the Life of St Odo of Cluny written by John of Salerno in 943. While a young canon in Tours, Odo chanced to find in the community's library a copy of the *Regula S. Benedicti* and was inspired to follow its teachings.[203] According to the Life, he and a companion, Adhegrinus, sought a monastery where the Rule was observed, but could find none in all of Francia. Discouraged, Adhegrinus resolved to go to Rome; but passing through Burgundy, he came upon the abbey of Baume, whose abbot, Berno, had instituted there the customs of Benedict of Aniane (called 'Euticius' in the Life).[204] There the two friends took the monastic habit. Berno would later become the first abbot of Cluny. Baume owed its knowledge of the Aachen customs to Saint-Martin in Autun, whence Berno had been sent. Saint-Martin, in turn, had been reformed by monks from Saint-Savin near Poitiers, which had been given to Benedict of Aniane by Louis the Pious.[205]

John of Salerno's dramatic image of a landscape almost devoid of Benedictine monasticism is obviously a literary exaggeration, though it is striking that Benedict of Aniane seems no longer to have been known by name (perhaps 'Euticius' is a corruption of his birth name, Witiza). That the customs of reformed Carolingian monasticism were preserved only in a single house is not quite credible, seeing that the texts promulgated at Aachen in 816–17 were to inspire other reform movements independent of Cluny, specifically those led by Gerard of Brogne and John of Gorze. The texts of reformed monasticism were obviously preserved in a number

---

[201] McKitterick, *The Frankish Kingdoms*, p. 119.
[202] McKitterick, *The Frankish Kingdoms*, pp. 119 and 279.
[203] John of Salerno, *Vita sancti Odonis abbatis Cluniacensis secundi*, I. 15, ed. J. Mabillon (1685), repr. *PL* CXXXIII, 43–86, at col. 50.
[204] John of Salerno, *Vita sancti Odonis*, I. 22–3, *PL* CXXXIII, 53–4.
[205] Ardo Smaragdus, *Vita Benedicti abbatis Anianensis et Indensis*, c. 33, ed. G. Waitz, in *Vitae aliaeque historiae minores*, MGH SS 15.1 (Hanover, 1887), pp. 198–220, at p. 214: 'Alium demum illi monasterium gloriosimus rex dedit, ubi, ut reor, 20 monachos misit abbatemque illis constituit. Situm vero est monasterium illud in territorio Pictavense et dedicatum in honore sancti Savini; in quo positi fratres dum in piis studiis vigilanter desudant, turba monachorum non parva eis adiungitur.' Cluny later cherished a tradition, fabricated in the ninth century and later reported by St Hugh of Autun and Rodolphus Glaber, that Saint-Savin was founded by monks first trained by St Maurus, a disciple of Benedict of Nursia himself.

of institutions, even if not implemented in a living practice, before the 'rediscovery' of reformed monasticism in the tenth century.

Implications for the history of the Benedictine Office

For all its limitations, the reform instigated by Louis the Pious and Benedict of Aniane was largely successful in one of its aims: the *Regula S. Benedicti* won near universal acceptance as the one code of legislation appropriate for monks. But the counterpart of *una regula*, Benedict of Aniane's cherished *una consuetudo*, was not realized.[206] The Benedictine Office was not to become normative on the Continent until the end of the tenth century.

It is currently impossible to say whether even those houses directly reformed by Benedict of Aniane, such as Saint-Savin or Inde, granted to him by Louis the Pious, ever sang the Office exactly as it was envisaged in the Aachen legislation at any point in the ninth century, let alone the tenth. It does seem that at least the Benedictine division of psalms was used at Inde: a Life of Benedict of Aniane mentions that the monks there recited the Roman version of the daytime offices as an extra devotion in addition to the Office of the Rule.[207] More definite assertions may be possible once all the fragments of antiphoners and breviaries known to have survived from the ninth and tenth centuries have been edited and analysed.[208] What does seem probable is that the transition to a strictly Benedictine form of the Office would be among the last changes effected in a reformed monastery. This seems finally to have happened at Saint-Denis, for instance, only during the brief abbacy of Odilo of Cluny (994–8).[209] As grounds for resisting change, reluctant monks could point to the long-standing custom using the Roman Office alongside the Rule.

In a monastery where a switch to the Benedictine Office was welcomed in principle, it would still take some time to learn and teach the new forms, to acquire, copy, or somehow create the correct books, and to train the monks in their use. Even at Monte Cassino, where, as Theodemar's

---

[206] De Jong, 'Carolingian monasticism', p. 633.

[207] Ardo Smaragdus, *Vita Benedicti Anianensis*, c. 38. 3, ed. Waitz, p. 216; tr. A. Cabaniss, *The Emperor's Monk: Contemporary Life of Benedict of Aniane by Ardo* (Ilfracombe, 1979), p. 89.

[208] For information, albeit incomplete, on fragmentary survivals, see Gamber, *CLLA* II, 495–500 and 606–12, and Suppl. pp. 126–7 and 164–6.

[209] Robertson, *The Service-Books of the Royal Abbey of Saint-Denis*, pp. 44–5.

letter to Charlemagne implies, the Benedictine *cursus* seems to have been followed, it is apparent that the community's Office antiphoners were still organized for the Roman *cursus*. In a letter to Charlemagne's *comes* Theodoric, Theodemar explains that the Roman *cursus* is followed on Monte Cassino during the last three days of Holy Week. Otherwise, he says, the psalms are chanted in accordance with the Benedictine *cursus*. But this sometimes requires creative compromise:

> Except for the three days before Easter that I have already mentioned, we always chant the psalms in the manner required by the Rule. And on Sundays we always act in accordance with the Rule, singing twelve lessons and psalms as it is enjoined for us. ... But on those days when, following the Roman practice, we only chant the nine psalms appointed for the feast, such as Christmas and Epiphany, the Ascension, St. Peter, and other saints like Martin and Benedict, we divide the last three psalms into two 'Glorias' each, and so make up twelve psalms.[210]

It would seem that on major feast days the monks of Monte Cassino chanted the psalms appointed for the feast (*psalmos congruentes*) as they found them in their Roman books. Instead of adding three further appropriate psalms, as later Benedictine monks would do,[211] they nodded to the letter of the Rule by dividing the last three psalms into two parts.

No doubt similar compromises were made in newly reformed Frankish monasteries until the proper books were obtained. And it would take more than books to establish the new liturgy as a self-sustaining, living practice. If a house were subsequently to align or realign itself with the *ordo canonicus*, then this fledgling Benedictine Office tradition would be lost, and the secular Office resumed.

---

[210] Theodemar, *Epistula ad Theodoricum gloriosum*, c. 12, ed. J. Winandy and K. Hallinger, in *Initia consuetudines Benedictinae*, ed. Hallinger, CCM 1, pp. 125–36, at p. 132: 'Psalmos vero, praeter tres noctes ut praemissum est, ante Pascha, semper regulariter psallimus. In diebus autem dominicis secundum sanctam regulam semper facimus duodecim lectiones canentes sicut nobis praecipitur psalmos .... Si quando autem novem psalmos secundum Romanum morem diebus congruentes canimus, ut in die Natalis Domini sive Epiphaniae, in Ascensione Domini sive beati Petri vel etiam sanctorum Martini ac Benedicti, tres posteriores psalmos in duas dividimus *Glorias*, ut omnino duodecim fiant.'
[211] See Table 9.1, p. 321 below.

Conclusions

From this investigation of the history of the Office in the West before the establishment of the classic medieval pattern of a 'secular' and a 'monastic' *cursus*, several important facts have emerged. First, the Roman Office was in a state of continual development throughout the early Middle Ages. Second, at no time before the ninth century was the *Regula S. Benedicti* promoted as the sole authority, or even a preferred authority, for monastic Office liturgy. Third, the notion of a 'Benedictine Office' that all monks ought to sing was first mooted in the monastic reform movement of Louis the Pious and Benedict of Aniane. Fourth, this movement was limited in influence and short-lived: its liturgical principles only obtained widespread currency through a second wave of monastic reforms on the Continent in the tenth century.

It is therefore at the very least unsafe to assume that the 'Benedictine' Office liturgy that eventually became normative for Western monks was practised in England before it was first established on the Continent through the reforms of Benedict of Aniane and Louis the Pious in the first half of the ninth century. While it can be argued that some liturgical customs ultimately of Roman origin may first have reached the Franks through the Anglo-Saxons,[212] there is nothing to suggest that the strict adherence to the Rule's liturgical code encouraged by Benedict of Aniane was first taught by Anglo-Saxon missionaries on the Continent. Indeed, as shall be made clear in Chapter 3, the fundamental principle of the Continental reforms, namely the separation of monks and canons into two discrete *ordines* with distinctive liturgical traditions, is very difficult to discern in the English Church at any time before the middle of the tenth century.

---

[212] See Y. Hen, 'Rome, Anglo-Saxon England and the formation of the Frankish liturgy', *Revue Bénédictine* 112 (2002), 301–22. This idea has long been proposed in broad terms, e.g. J. McKinnon, 'The emergence of Gregorian chant in the Carolingian era', in *idem* (ed.), *Antiquity and the Middle Ages: From Ancient Greece to the 15th Century*, Man and Music 1 (Basingstoke, 1990), pp. 88–119, at p. 116.

3

The Divine Office in England from the Augustinian Mission to the First Viking Invasions, 597–*c*.835

Despite the almost total absence of surviving early Anglo-Saxon Office books, there is nevertheless evidence of various kinds for how the Office was sung in a few houses, as well as some evidence for the ideal to which the leaders of the English Church aspired when it came to Office liturgy. As shall be seen in the present chapter, this ideal was the Roman monastic Office. This may be seen in the manuscript and literary evidence for the sevenfold Roman Office *horarium* and the Roman weekly distribution of the psalms. Evaluating the available evidence for the readings and chants of the Office, however, requires some adjustment of how the term 'Roman' is to be applied to the early English liturgy, where Irish and especially Gallican liturgical traditions exerted considerable influence.[1] What is quite clear, however, is that there is no evidence for the use of the monastic Office as laid down in the *Regula S. Benedicti*, despite the esteem in which the Rule was held. The evidence rather points to the joint recitation of a single Office by both monks and secular clergy.

The Office under the uita regularis *in English minsters*

Before examining the evidence for the use of any particular form of the Office in early Anglo-Saxon England, it will be useful to assess the context of its performance, namely minsters governed without the absolute authority of any one monastic rule whose inmates could include secular

---

[1] See C. Cubitt, 'Unity and diversity in the early Anglo-Saxon liturgy', in R. N. Swanson (ed.), *Unity and Diversity in the Church: Papers Read at the 1994 Summer Meeting and the 1995 Winter Meeting of the Ecclesiastical History Society* (Oxford, 1996), pp. 45–57.

clergy as well as contemplative monastics, both groups using the same form of the Office.

As was seen in Chapter 2, monastic life in the Middle Ages, including the Divine Office, was ultimately ordered not through the rigid application of written rules, but by a common consensus on what it meant to live *regulariter*. In its narrowest interpretation, this meant living in obedience to the canons of the Church. With one possible exception, no manuscript of canon law copied in England survives from before 800; but the influence of the Anglo-Saxon missionaries is evident in a number of Frankish canon law manuscripts, and it is likely that Italian canon law collections were introduced to Francia, at least in part, via Anglo-Saxon England.[2] That the canons of the Council of Chalcedon were known and applied to monastic governance in England is seen in the decrees of the Council of Chelsea (*Celichyth*), convened by Archbishop Wulfred (805–32) in 816.[3]

---

[2] R. McKitterick, 'Knowledge of canon law in the Frankish kingdoms before 789: The manuscript evidence', *Journal of Theological Studies* 36 (1985), 97–117, at pp. 111–17. The one possible exception is Cologne, Dombibliothek, 213, copied by a Northumbrian scribe, but probably on the Continent (*CLA* VIII, 40 and 66; *CLA* Suppl., p. 62). This is a copy of the *Collectio Sanblasiana*, a collection of conciliar decrees arranged chronologically. It was compiled at the beginning of the sixth century in Italy, possibly in Rome, by an unknown author who made use of the earlier *Collectio Dionysiana* of Dionysius Exiguus (d.537×555), written in Rome *c*.500. L. Kéry, *Canonical Collections of the Early Middle Ages (ca. 400–1140): A Bibliographical Guide to the Manuscripts and Literature*, History of Medieval Canon Law (Washington, DC, 1999), pp. 29–31. The *Collectio Sanblasiana* includes the decrees of the Council of Chalcedon. F. Maasen, *Geschichte der Quellen und der Literatur des canonischen Rechts im Abendlande*, I: *Die Rechtssammlungen bis zur Mitte des 9. Jahrhunderts* (Graz, 1870), pp. 504–12.

[3] Ed. Haddan and Stubbs, *Councils* III, 579–85, at p. 582 (c. 24): 'monasteria, quae semel dedicata sint cum consilio Episcoporum, et in primis statuitur regularis vita, seu etiam abbas vel abbatissa ab Episcopo benedicatur, sic in perpetuo permaneant monasterias [sic]. ... quia hoc capitulum nullus estimat noviter a nobis constitutum; sed si quis desiderat, in synodo Calcidanesse repperire non pigiat.' ('Monasteries, when once they have been dedicated with the consultation of bishops, and the monastic life (*regularis vita*) has in the first place been established, and an abbot or abbess has been blessed by the bishop, should always continue as monasteries. ... No one should judge that this decree is our own innovation. If anyone so desires, it should not irk him to seek it in the Synod of Chalcedon.') The Chalcedon canons were also invoked at a much earlier synod, convened at Hertford by Archbishop Theodore in 672, though canons regulating monasteries are not mentioned in Bede's account of it (*Historia ecclesiastica*, IV. 5, ed. Plummer I, 214–17). Bede gives the year as 673, but see W. Levison, *England and the Continent in the Eighth Century* (Oxford, 1946), pp. 266–7. Plummer (II, 38–9) would argue that Bede's primary source itself may have been incorrect, though he saw no problem with the date as Bede gives it (II, 212). Theodore may have had the *Collectio Dionysiana*, as Plummer suggested (II, 212), but it could equally have been one of the later compilations based on Dionysius's work.

Bede argued that councils convened by bishops were essential to root out what he considered the false monasticism of aristocratic minsters.[4]

As on the Continent, however, ultimate authority for interpreting and teaching the monastic life rested with the abbot of the community. Benedict Biscop famously based his rule of life for Wearmouth on his knowledge of the customs of seventeen different monasteries on the Continent.[5] For Bede, the monks of Wearmouth and Jarrow were disciples, spiritual children, not of an abstract monastic ideal, but of a man, Biscop.[6] The same theme emerges in a letter of Alcuin written to the monks of Wearmouth and Jarrow in 793, in which the monks are urged, 'Keep most diligently the observance of the monastic life (*regularis uita*) that the most holy fathers Benedict and Ceolfrith established among you.'[7]

Eanmund, the first abbot of the unknown monastery celebrated in Æthelwulf's *De abbatibus* (803×821), obtained from his bishop an expert teacher of the monastic tradition: 'He was a priest who laid down monastic laws and, unrolling the scrolls of the ancients, which the creator spirit had brought down from heaven, he gave instruction to the novices.'[8]

---

[4] Bede, *Epistola ad Ecgbertum episcopum*, § 13, ed. Plummer I, 405–23, at p. 415: 'Quae nimirum caecitas posset aliquando terminari, ac regulari disciplina cohiberi, et de finibus sanctae ecclesiae cunctis pontificali ac synodica auctoritate procul expelli, si non ipsi pontifices magis huiusmodi sceleribus opem ferre atque astipulari probarentur.' ('Such blindness could certainly be ended at any time, confined by the discipline of regular monastic life and expelled far beyond the borders of the holy Church by joint episcopal and conciliar authority, if only the bishops did not show themselves to be aiding and abetting in these offences.') Translation: J. McClure and R. Collins, *Bede: The Ecclesiastical History of the English People, The Greater Chronicle, Bede's Letter to Egbert* (Oxford, 1994), pp. 343–57, at p. 352.

[5] Bede, *Historia abbatum*, c. 11, ed. Plummer I, 364–87, at pp. 374–5; also the anonymous *Vita Ceolfrithi* (*Historia abbatum auctore anonymo*), c. 6, ed. Plummer I, 388–404, at p. 390.

[6] Homily on Benedict Biscop, *Homeliarum euangelii libri II*, I. 13, ed. D. Hurst, *Bedae Opera homiletica*, CCSL 122 (Turnhout, 1955), pp. 88–94, at p. 93: 'Nos namque sumus filii eius quos in hanc [monachicae deuotionis] domum pius prouisor induxit; nos sumus eius filii quos diuersis carnaliter editos parentibus in unam sanctae professionis familiam spiritaliter fecit adgregari; nos sumus filii eius, si iter uirtutum eius imitando tenemus, si non a semita regulari quam docuit torpendo deflectimus.' ('For we are his sons, whom our blessed provider led into this house of monastic devotion. We are his sons whom, though born of various parents according to the flesh, he caused to be gathered into one family of holy profession according to the spirit. We are his sons if we hold his way of virtue for imitation. We are his sons if we turn not aside into sluggishness from the monastic path that he taught.') My emendation 'monachicae deuotionis' replaces Hurst's 'monachiae'.

[7] Alcuin, *Epistola 19*, ed. E. Dümmler, *Epistolae Karolini aevi*, II, MGH Epp. 4 (Berlin, 1895), pp. 53–6, at p. 54: 'Regularis vitae observationem quam statuerunt vobis sanctissimi patres Benedictus scilicet et Ceolfridus, diligentissime custodite.'

[8] Æthelwulf, *De abbatibus*, V, lines 110–12, ed. and tr. A. Campbell (Oxford, 1967), p. 10:

Eanmund seems not to have used a written rule, but rather committed this teaching to memory.⁹ Even though these English abbots remained the final arbiters of monastic tradition in their houses, both Benedict Biscop and Eanmund seem to have exercised this authority not through innovation but through the careful evaluation of the existing traditions enshrined in written rules and the customs of other houses.

The *Regula S. Benedicti* is the only surviving rule known with any certainty to have been copied and studied in England.¹⁰ It was studied and glossed at Canterbury by students of Archbishop Theodore (668–90) and Abbot Hadrian, who were familiar with the so-called *textus interpolatus* version of the Rule that may have originated in Rome *c*.600.¹¹ Bishop

---

'presbiter ille fuit, statuens monastica iura, | instituitque nouos ueterum munimenta reuoluens | hic monachos, caelo tulerat que spiritus auctor'. The house was founded 705×716, probably at Crayke, north of York. See M. Lapidge, 'Aediluulf and the School of York', in his *Anglo-Latin Literature, 600–899* (London, 1996), pp. 381–98 (originally published in A. Lehner and W. Berschin (eds.), *Lateinische Kultur im VIII. Jahrhundert: Traube-Gedenkschrift* (St Ottilien, 1990), pp. 161–78). The reference to scrolls inspired by the Holy Spirit could be from John Cassian's *Institutiones*, which were studied in the school of Theodore and Hadrian at Canterbury, as shown by Old English glosses of its text preserved in the 'Leiden Glossary'; see M. Lapidge, 'The School of Theodore and Hadrian', in his *Anglo-Latin Literature, 600–899*, pp. 141–68, at pp. 151 and 156 (originally published in *Anglo-Saxon England* 15 (1986), 45–72). Alcuin made use of Cassian in his *De anima ratione*, *PL* CI, 639–50; see M. R. Godden, 'Anglo-Saxons on the mind', in Lapidge and Gneuss, *Learning and Literature*, pp. 271–98, at p. 272.

⁹ Æthelwulf, *De abbatibus*, V, lines 106–8, ed. and tr. Campbell, p. 10: 'mystica uerba pii pre sensu discit acuto. | insuper arripiens memori narranda relatu, | sensibus in cordis conplectit cuncta rimatus;' ('He [Eanmund] apprehended the mystic words of the pious man because of his sharp discernment; seizing upon them, furthermore, to narrate them in a retentive account, he examined them and enclosed them all in his inner thoughts.')

¹⁰ The oldest surviving copy of the *Regula S. Benedicti* was written in England: Oxford, Bodleian Library, Hatton 48 (s. vii–viii, prov. Worcester), no. 4118 in the Bodleian Summary Catalogue; *CLA* II, 2nd edn, *240; see E. A. Lowe, *English Uncial* (Oxford, 1960), p. 20 and Plate XX. *The Rule of St Benedict: Oxford, Bodleian Library, Hatton 48*, facsimile ed. D. H. Farmer, EEMF 15 (Copenhagen, 1968). The *RSB* is the only monastic rule ever quoted or alluded to in English literary sources: P. Wormald, 'Æthelwold and his Continental counterparts: Contact, comparison, contrast', in B. Yorke (ed.), *Bishop Æthelwold: His Career and Influence* (Woodbridge, 1988), pp. 13–42, at p. 18 and refs. in n. 13.

¹¹ As Michael Lapidge has ingeniously demonstrated, the 'Leiden Glossary', copied at St Gall *c*.800, preserves Old English glosses made at Canterbury in the seventh century ('The School of Theodore and Hadrian', pp. 150 and 158–60). Early copies of the Rule belong to three textual families, the *textus purus*, represented by St Gall, Stiftsbibliothek, 914 (copied by two monks of Reichenau *c*.820), a *textus interpolatus*, whose oldest witness is Hatton 48, and a *textus receptus* that emerged in the Carolingian monastic reforms of the ninth century that combines the two other families, with some new variants of its own: Traube, *Textgeschichte der Regula S. Benedicti*; P. Meyvaert, 'Towards a history of the textual trans-

Wilfrid's biographer seems to suggest that Wilfrid brought the Rule northward after a sojourn in Kent around the year 665.[12] If this date is correct, the Rule must have been part of monastic observance in Canterbury even before the pontificate of Theodore.

The dominance of the *Regula S. Benedicti* in England has led some commentators to assume that it was enforced strictly in all monasteries. But that Benedict Biscop insisted that his successor should be elected 'according to the Rule of St Benedict' does not prove that Wearmouth and Jarrow were strict Benedictine houses.[13] Alcuin's letter to the monks of Wearmouth and Jarrow recommends that the Rule be read to the brethren:

> And let the Rule of St Benedict be read more often in the assembly of the brothers, and explained in their own tongue so that it may be understood by all. Let each one correct his life according to its teaching; so that you may keep inviolate the vow that you made to God at the altar, as the prophet says, 'Make a vow and pay it to the Lord your God.' For a false promise (*infidelis promissio*) displeases God.[14]

This seems to describe the Rule's procedure for admitting a novice, which requires the placement on the altar of a written *promissio*.[15] But the monks of Wearmouth and Jarrow may have promised something like the 'stability, fidelity to monastic life, and obedience' that the Rule rather vaguely requires, without ever submitting themselves solely to this one written document.[16] The one surviving detailed account of the admission of a novice to an English monastery does not correspond to the

---

mission of the *Regula S. Benedicti*', *Scriptorium* 17 (1963), 83–110; *RB 1980*, ed. Fry, pp. 102–12. See *The Rule of St Benedict*, ed. Farmer, p. 11. The *textus interpolatus* glossed at Canterbury differed in certain word variants from Hatton 48 (Lapidge, 'The School of Theodore and Hadrian', p. 159).

[12] Stephen of Ripon, *Vita S. Wilfridi*, c. 14, ed. and tr. Colgrave, *The Life of Bishop Wilfrid*, pp. 30–1; Colgrave's comment, protesting that Wilfrid must have been exposed to the Rule on his earlier Continental journeys, is on p. 161.

[13] Bede, *Historia abbatum*, c. 11, ed. Plummer I, 374–5.

[14] Alcuin, *Epistola 19*, ed. Dümmler, p. 54: 'Saepiusque regula sancti Benedicti legatur in conventu fratrum et propria exponatur lingua, ut intellegi possit ab omnibus. Ad cuius institutionem unusquisque suam corrigat vitam; ut, quod Deo vovitis ante altare, inviolabiliter custodiatur a vobis; dicente propheta: 'Vovete et reddite domino Deo vestro'. Displicet enim Deo infidelis promissio.'

[15] *RSB* 58:17–19.

[16] See *RB 1980*, ed. Fry, pp. 457–66.

Rule's instructions.[17] As John Blair has remarked, 'Some founders, most famously the great Northumbrian nobleman-abbots Wilfrid and Benedict Biscop, constructed rules based heavily on St Benedict's, but they did so by choice rather than obligation, and in an eclectic spirit.'[18] The *Regula S. Benedicti* was respected as an authoritative compendium of monastic tradition, but it was no substitute for a living rule of life, as at Lindisfarne, where between 664 and 676 St Cuthbert, then the community's prior, 'arranged our rule of life which we composed then for the first time and which we observe even to this day along with the Rule of St Benedict'.[19]

The *Regula S. Benedicti* enjoyed such prestige because it was viewed as part of the English Church's Roman inheritance. St Benedict and his Rule were popularly associated with Rome in English and Continental writings from the early seventh century onwards, with Benedict described as the 'Roman abbot' (*abbas Romensis*).[20] Bishop Wilfrid invoked his advocacy of the Rule as proof of his Roman orthodoxy:

> Was I not the first, after the death of the first elders who were sent by St Gregory, to root out the poisonous weeds planted by the Scots [i.e. the Irish]? Did I not change and convert the whole Northumbrian race to the true Easter and to the tonsure in the form of a crown, in accordance with the practice of the Apostolic See, though their tonsure had previously been at the back of the head, from the top of the head downwards? And did I not instruct them in accordance with the rite of the primitive Church to make use of a double choir singing in harmony, with reciprocal responsions and antiphons? And did I not arrange the life of the monks in accordance with the rule of the holy father Benedict which none had previously introduced there?[21]

---

[17] Hugeburc, *Hodoeporicon (Vita S. Willibaldi)*, c. 1, ed. Holder-Egger, p. 88; see M. de Jong, *In Samuel's Image: Child Oblation in the Early Medieval West* (Leiden, 1996), p. 54.
[18] Blair, *The Church in Anglo-Saxon Society*, p. 80.
[19] Anonymous, *Vita S. Cuthberti*, III. 1, ed. and tr. Colgrave, *Two Lives of St Cuthbert* (Cambridge, 1940), pp. 60–139, at pp. 94–7: 'nobis regularem uitam primum componentibus constituit, quam usque hodie cum regula Benedicti obseruamus.'
[20] J. Wollasch, 'Benedictus abbas romensis: Das römische Element in der frühen benediktinischen Tradition', in N. Kamp and J. Wollasch (eds.), *Tradition als historische Kraft: interdisziplinäre Forschungen zur Geschichte des früheren Mittelalters* (Berlin, 1982), pp. 119–37. The title *abbas Romensis* first appears in a letter from Venerandus, founder of the monastery of Altaripa, to Constantius, bishop of Albi, dated to the mid-620s; ed. Traube, *Textgeschichte der Regula S. Benedicti*, pp. 87–8.
[21] Stephen of Ripon, *Vita S. Wilfridi*, c. 47, ed. and tr. Colgrave, *The Life of Bishop Wil-*

The authority attached to the *Regula S. Benedicti* throughout Western Europe depended to a large extent on the biography of Benedict in the *Dialogi* of Gregory the Great. Aldhelm of Malmesbury (d.709) seems to have felt that England's monastic tradition could be connected to St Benedict only via Gregory:

> He [Benedict] was the first to set forth in the struggle of our life the way in which the monasteries might hold to a desired rule, and the way in which a holy man might hasten, ascending by the right path, to the lofty heights of the heavens. Pope Gregory once described his renowned life, revealing it in documents [i.e. in Gregory's *Dialogi*] from the beginning to the time when this blessed man departed to the heavenly citadel. In the number of his pupils we are gathered together rejoicing, whom fertile Britain bears in its bosom as citizens; it is from him that the grace of baptism flowed to us, and from him a venerable throng of teachers hastened [to us].[22]

Here, the *Regula S. Benedicti* is numbered among Gregory's gifts to England, along with baptism and teachers. In the estimation of early English monks, the Rule was but one part of a larger Roman tradition.

All this shows that the common assumption that Anglo-Saxon monasteries sang the Office according to the Benedictine *cursus* is unsound. Christopher Holdsworth has proposed the only text ever identified as

---

frid, pp. 98–9: 'Necnon et ego primus post obitum primorum procerum, a sancto Gregorio directorum, Scotticae virulenta plantationis germina eradicarem; ad verumque pascha et ad tonsuram in modum coronae, quae ante ea posteriore capitis parte e summo abrasa vertice, secundum apostolicae sedis rationem totam Ultrahumbrensium gentem permutando convertem? Aut quomodo iuxta ritum primitivae ecclesiae assono vocis modulamine, binis adstantibus choris, persultare responsoriis antiphonisque reciprocis instruerem? Vel quomodo vitam monachorum secundum regulam sancti Benedicti patris, quam nullus prior ibi invexit, constituream?' Wilfrid was here facing deprivation of part of his see at the hands of King Aldfrith, Archbishop Berhtwald, and the Council of *Ouestrafelda* (*c*.703).

[22] Aldhelm, *Carmen de virginitate*, lines 870–80, ed. Ehwald, *Aldhelmi Opera*, MGH AA 15 (Berlin, 1919), pp. 350–471, at p. 390: 'Primo qui statuit, nostrae certamine vitae | Qualiter optatam teneant coenubia normam | Quoque modo properet directo tramite sanctus | Ad supera scandens caelorum culmina cultor. | Cuius praeclaram pandens ab origine vitam | Gregorius praesul cartis descripserat olim, | Donec aethralem felix migraret in arcum; | Huius alumnorum numero glomeramur ovantes, | Quos gerit in gremio fecunda Britannia cives; | A quo iam nobis baptismi gratia fluxit | Atque magistrorum veneranda caterva cucurrit.' Translation: M. Lapidge and J. L. Rosier, *Aldhelm: The Poetic Works* (Cambridge, 1985), p. 122.

possibly referring to the use of the Benedictine Office in England during the early Saxon period, found in Willibald's Life of St Boniface:

> Hanc enim ita omnibus in commune viventibus et maxime suo, sub regulari videlicet disciplina, abbati monachica subditus oboedientia praebebat, ut labore manuum cottidiano et disciplinali officiorum administratione incessanter secundum praefinitam beati patris Benedicti rectae constitutionis formam insisteret, omnibusque exemplum bene vivendi in verbo, in conversatione, in fide et castitate se praebens, ut omnes de fructu eius perciperent et omnium mercedis aeternae perciperet portionem.[23]

The Latin could be construed in several ways. The standard translation by C. H. Talbot does not mention the Office at all:

> Such obedience as befits a monk was given by the saint to all the members of the community, and particularly to the abbot, and he applied himself assiduously, as the Rule of St. Benedict prescribes, to the daily manual labour and the regular performance of his duties (*officia*). In this way he was an example to all both in word, deed, faith and purity. All could profit by his good deeds, whilst he on his side shared in their common eternal reward.[24]

Christopher Holdsworth, however, considered this to be a direct reference to the Benedictine Office: 'Wynfrith strove to work every day with his hands and to perform the offices in an orderly manner ... according to the prescribed shape of the regulated law of the blessed father Benedict.'[25] But the most natural translation would see the adverbial phrase *secundum praefinitam* ... as modifying Wynfrith's efforts in both *opera manuum* and *officia*. In other words, Boniface fulfilled the duties of a monk described in the Rule: the performance of manual labour and the observance of the daily Office – neither unique to Benedictine monasticism.[26] The passage

---

[23] Willibald, *Vita Bonifatii*, c. 2, ed. W. Levison, *Vitae Bonifatii archiepiscopi Mogutini*, MGH SRG 57 (Hanover, 1905), pp. 1–58, at p. 10.
[24] *The Anglo-Saxon Missionaries in Germany* (London, 1954), pp. 23–62, at pp. 30–1.
[25] Holdsworth, 'Saint Boniface the monk', p. 56.
[26] It is significant that the passage also emphasizes Boniface's obedience towards the other members of the community, another traditional monastic virtue found in the *Regula S. Benedicti* (chapter 71) but not limited to it (cf. John Cassian, *Institutiones*, IV. 30. 1, ed. Guy, p. 164). The editors of a reprint of Talbot's translation remark, 'This passage provides a good example of how difficult it is to determine exactly what monastic rule was in force. The Latin has "secundum praefinitam beati patris Benedicti rectae constitutionis formam,"

therefore says nothing about the specific form of the Office sung at Crediton, which will have been decided by the abbot's interpretation of the monastic tradition.

An important aspect of the Office liturgy of early English minsters was the cooperation of monks and clerks in its performance. From the Augustinian mission until Æthelwold's expulsion of the clerics from Winchester's Old Minster in 964, such evidence as survives indicates that there was no liturgical or canonical reason why monks and secular clergy could not sing the Office together. Augustine, who had spent his whole adult life as a Roman monk, modelled his new church at Canterbury on the plan of a Roman basilica served by a liturgical community of monks dwelling in a separate monastery: his cathedral had the same dedication as the Lateran basilica ('Jesus Christ the Holy Saviour'),[27] and he provided it with a monastery, dedicated to SS. Peter and Paul, just outside the city walls. Pope Gregory expected close cooperation between the cathedral's monks and secular clergy in the performance of the Office: clerics in minor orders could marry and live apart, but they were nevertheless to 'attend to the chanting of the psalms' (*canendis psalmis inuigilent*).[28] The cathedral and

---

a remarkable circumlocution that probably means that Boniface particularly liked some aspects of Benedict's Rule, not that he actually lived in a monastery uniquely governed by that Rule.' (T. F. X. Noble and T. Head (eds.), *Soldiers of Christ: Saints and Saints' Lives from Late Antiquity and the Early Middle Ages* (London, 1995), pp. 107–40, at pp. 113–14 n. 15.)

[27] N. Brooks, *The Early History of the Church of Canterbury: Christ Church from 597 to 1066* (Leicester, 1984), pp. 103–5. The Lateran was only linked with St John the Baptist (from the dedication of its baptistery) and St John the Evangelist (from an oratory in the baptistery) in the Middle Ages.

[28] Gregory I, *Responsiones*, c. 1, in Bede, *Historia ecclesiastica*, I. 27, ed. Plummer I, 48–9: 'Sed quia tua fraternitas monasterii regulis erudita seorsum fieri non debet a clericis suis in ecclesia Anglorum, quae auctore Deo nuper adhuc ad fidem perducta est, hanc debet conuersationem instituere, quae initio nascentis ecclesiae fuit patribus nostris; in quibus nullus eorum ex his quae possidebant aliquid suum esse dicebat, sed erant eis omnia communia. Siqui uero sunt clerici extra sacros ordines constituti, qui se continere non possunt, sortire uxores debent, et stipendia sua exterius accipere; quia et de hisdem patribus, de quibus praefati sumus, nouimus scriptum, quod diuidebatur singulis, prout cuique opus erat. De eorum quoque stipendio cogitandum atque providendum est, et sub ecclesiastica regula sunt tenendi, ut bonis moribus uiuant et canendis psalmis inuigilent, et ab omnibus inlicitis et cor et linguam et corpus Deo auctore conseruent.' ('Because you, brother, are conversant with monastic rules, and ought not to live apart from your clergy in the English Church, which, by the guidance of God, has lately been converted to the faith, you ought to institute that manner of life which our fathers followed in the earliest beginnings of the Church: none of them said that anything he possessed was his own, but they had all things in common. If, however, there are any who are clerics but in minor orders and who cannot be continent, they should marry and receive their stipends outside the community; for we know that it is writ-

monastery were less than four hundred yards apart, a distance no obstacle at all to joint participation at the Divine Office by the cathedral community and the monks. This cooperation meant that Bede was able to speak of the cathedral and monastery as a single church, an *ecclesia Cantuariorum*.[29] The clergy and the monks were clearly participating in the joint recitation of a single form of the Office. The canons of the 747 Council of *Clofesho*, discussed in more detail below, suggest that this was the common practice, enjoining both seculars (*ecclesiastici*) and monks (*monastici*) to use the same form of the Office (the Roman *cursus*),[30] and admonishing priests, most of whom seem to have resided in minsters, to be faithful assistants to their abbots (or abbesses!).[31]

The Carolingian conception of separate *cursus* for clerks and monks may have been known in England in the early ninth century. Two charters of Archbishop Wulfred (805–32) in favour of Christ Church have usually been interpreted as evidence that he imposed Chrodegang's *Regula canonicorum* on the secular clerics there.[32] The first (*c*.813) requires clergy to attend the recitation of the daily Office, to take their meals together in a refectory, to sleep in a common dormitory, and to live 'according to the rule of monastic discipline of life' (*juxta regulam monasterialis disciplinae vitae*). The second (*c*.825×832) provides for the care of elderly and infirm clerics residing in the community.[33] The first charter dates from the same year in which several Continental synods ordered cathedral canons to live in regulated communities, which suggests that Wulfred may have been acting in imitation of contemporary Continental

---

ten concerning those fathers whom we have mentioned that division was to be made to each according to his need. Care must also be taken and provision made for stipends and they must be kept under ecclesiastical rule, living a moral life and attending to the chanting of the psalms and, under God's guidance, keeping their heart, their tongue, and their body from all things unlawful.') Translation: Colgrave, p. 42. On the authenticity of the *Responsiones*, see Meyvaert, 'Diversity within unity'. The cathedral community perhaps comprised some of the original Roman missionaries who had taken major orders, some Frankish clergy who joined the mission before it arrived in England, and the first men to have been ordained from among the English converts (Brooks, *The Early History*, pp. 87–91).

[29] Bede, *Historia ecclesiastica*, praefatio, ed. Plummer I, 6; Brooks, *The Early History*, p. 92.
[30] Quoted below, p. 99.
[31] Council of *Clofesho*, c. 8, ed. Haddan and Stubbs, *Councils* III, 360–76, at p. 365.
[32] Haddan and Stubbs, *Councils* III, 576 n. a; and Brooks, *The Early History*, p. 156.
[33] S 1265 (BCS 342) and S 1268 (BCS 380). Cf. *Regula canonicorum*, cc. 5–8 (recitation of the Office); cc. 21–4 (common table); c. 3 (common dormitory); and c. 28 (care of the infirm).

developments.[34] As Brigitte Langefeld has argued, however, all of Wulfred's reforms could have been inspired by parallel passages in the *Regula S. Benedicti*.[35] This would not require, as Langefeld seems to imply, that Wulfred reformed Christ Church as a monastic priory.[36] Wulfred could instead have aimed to restore the communal life of the cathedral as described in Bede's *Historia ecclesiastica*. According to Alcuin, York had been reformed along similar lines a century earlier under Bishop Bosa (678–86 and 691–705):

> This father of the church enriched its worship (*decoravit cultum*) and made its clergy live a life apart from the common people, decreeing that they should serve the one God at every hour (*omnibus horis*): that the mystical lyre should sound in unbroken strain, that human voices, forever singing heavenly praises to the Lord, should beat upon the heights of Heaven; regulating every hour with alternate duties: now a reading, now a holy prayer. Whoever wished to proclaim the Lord's praise by his treatment of the flesh he commanded swiftly to satisfy his physical needs: that all should sleep but little and take what food was to hand, that no one should claim lands, food, houses, money, clothes, or anything as his private property, that everything should always be shared.[37]

---

[34] In particular the Council of Mainz, c. 9, and the Council of Tours, c. 23, ed. Werminghoff, *Concilia aevi Karolini* I, 259–73 and 286–93, at pp. 262 and 289; neither decree mentions any specific rule for cathedral canons, whereas both councils refer explicitly to the *Regula S. Benedicti* in provisions for monks (Council of Mainz, c. 11, p. 263; Council of Tours, c. 25, p. 290.)

[35] B. Langefeld, '*Regula canonicorum* or *Regula monasterialis uitae*? The Rule of Chrodegang and Archbishop Wulfred's reforms at Canterbury', *Anglo-Saxon England* 25 (1996), 21–36.

[36] See the critique in Barrow, 'Review article: Chrodegang', p. 202 n. 6: '*monasterialis* need not refer to a specifically monastic community, since *monasterium* in the earlier Middle Ages was used indiscriminately for all sorts of ecclesiastical communities, not only those observing a monastic rule.' It should be noted that the 805 charter S 1259 (BCS 319) that Barrow takes as evidence that Wulfred had established a *mensa* (common table) for the canons at Christ Church was in fact issued by his predecessor, Æthelheard.

[37] Alcuin, *Versus de patribus regibus et sanctis Euboricensis ecclesiae*, lines 857–70, ed. and tr. P. Godman, *Alcuin: The Bishops, Kings, and Saints of York*, Oxford Medieval Texts (Oxford, 1982), pp. 70–3: 'Hic pater ecclesiae cultum decoravit et illam | moribus a plebis penitus secernit et uni | deservire Deo statuit simul omnibus horis: | ut lyra continuo resonaret mystica plectro, | aethereas Domini decantans laudibus odas | vox humana quidem superum pulsaret Olympum, | omnia dispensans alternis tempora causis: | lectio nunc fieret, sed nunc oratio sacra. | Quisque Dei laudes praeferret corporis usu, | iusserat hunc raptim complere negotia carnis: | omnibus ut fieret parvus sopor, esca sub ictu, | non terras vic-

This imposition of a communal life and shared ownership of property on the clerks of York, some fifty years before Chrodegang penned his *Regula canonicorum*, suggests that no such Continental model would be needed in Wulfred's Canterbury either. If it were accepted that Wulfred reformed Christ Church as a community of secular canons governed by Chrodegang's *Regula canonicorum*, this would imply the use of the secular *cursus* for the Divine Office in the cathedral. There is nothing to suggest that Wulfred also introduced the monastic *cursus* anywhere. There is in any event nothing in the 813 charter to indicate that Wulfred made a rigid distinction between clerks and monks, referring to the community simply as 'the brothers' (*fratres*). An eleventh-century account in the 'F' manuscript of the Anglo-Saxon Chronicle, admittedly designed to support the rights of the monastic chapter after the Conquest, tells of how secular clerics and monks cooperated in the recitation of the Office at Christ Church following the devastation of the (supposedly monastic) community in an epidemic in 870.[38] If the

tusque, domus, nummismata, vestes, | nec quicquam proprium sibimet iam vindicet ullus, | omnia sed cunctis fierent communia semper.' I have modified the translation to read 'enriched its worship' where Godman gives 'endowed its fabric'.

[38] *The Anglo-Saxon Chronicle: A Collaborative Edition*, VIII: *MS F*, ed. P. S. Baker (Cambridge, 2000), pp. 67-9: 'Þa ferde Æðered cing to 7 Ælfred his broðer 7 naman Æðelred Wiltunscire biscop 7 settan hine to arcebiscope to Cantuarebyri, forðan he wæs ær munec of ðan ylcan mynstre of Cantwarebyri. Eal swa hraðe swa he com to Cantuarbyri, 7 he warð getremmed an his arcestole, he ðohte hu he mihte ut adræfan ða clericas þe þar binnan wæran þa se arcebiscop Ceolnoð þarbiforan sette far swylcre neode ged[ ] swa we seggan wyllað. Þas forman geares þe he to arcebiscope geset was, þa wearð swa mycel mancwealm þæt of eallan ðan munecum þe he þar binnan funde na belifan na ma þonne fif munecas. Þa far þare[ ] he his handpreostas 7 eac sume of his tunpreostan þæt hi scoldan helpan þan feawan munecan þe ðar belifen wæran to donne Cristes ðeowdom, forðan he na mihte swa færlice munecas findan þa mihtan be heom sylfum þone ðeowdom don, 7 far ðissan he het þæt ða preostas þa hwile, eal þæt God giefe sibbe on þis lande, þan munecan helpan scoldan. To þan ylcan timan was þis land swyþe geswent mid gelomlican feohten, 7 farþi se arcebiscop na þar embe beon mihte, farðan ealne his timan was gewinn 7 sorhge ofer Englaland, 7 forþi belifan þa clericas mid ðan munecan. Nas næfre nan tima þæt þar næran munecas binnan, 7 æfre hefdan þone hlafordscipe ofer ða preostas. Eft se arcebiscop Ceolnoð þohte, 7 eac to þan ðe mid him weran sæde, "eal swa hraþe swa God gifþ sibbe on þisan lande, oððe þas preostas scelan munecas beon, oððe * * * elles hwar munecas eal swa fela don binnan þan mynstre wylle * * * þæt magan þone ðeowað ðe heom sylfan don, farðan God wat ðat ic" * * *.' (Square brackets and asterisks denote illegible or damaged text. Other diplomatic marks in the edition have not been reproduced.)

Latin version: 'Tunc Æþeredus rex et Alfredus frater eius dederunt Æþelredo episcopo de Þiltunscire archiepiscopatum Cantię, eo quod fuit monachus eiusdem ecclesię. Cum autem uenisset cantuariam, statim cogitare cepit, quomodo possit eicere clericos de Ecclesia christi, quos Ceolnoðus pro tali necessitate compulsus ibi posuit. Primo igitur anno ordina-

account is spurious – and the inclusion of defensive asides, in particular the assurance that the monks 'ever had lordship over the priests', could suggest the embellishment of a genuine tradition[39] – it at least seems to accept without surprise that the monks and clerks would have sung the same form of the Office.

tionis suę tanta mortalitas facta est in Ecclesia Christi ut de tota congregatione monachorum non remanerent nisi quinque. Qua de causa, quia ita subito non potuit inuenire tot monachos, qui ibi seruitium Dei facere possent, ex simplicitate cordis precepit capellanis clericis suis, ut essent cum eis usquequo Deus pacificaret terram, que tunc nimis erat turbata propter nimias tempestates bellorum. Accepit etiam de uillis suis presbiteros, ut essent cum monachis, ita tamen ut monachi semper haberent dominatum super clericos. Cogitauit idem archiepiscopus et sepe suis dixit, quia "statim cum Deus pacem nobis dederit, aut isti clerici monachi fient aut ego ubicumque monachos inueniam, quos reponam. Scit enim Deus", inquid, "quod aliter facere non possum". Sed numquam temporibus suis pax fuit in Anglia, et ideo remanserunt clerici cum monachis, nec ullo tempore fuit ecclesia sine monachis. Sed nec iste Æðeredus archiepiscopus aliter potuit facere.' ('Then went king Æthered and Ælfred his brother, and took Æthelred, bishop of Wiltshire, and appointed him archbishop of Canterbury, because he had formerly been a monk of the same monastery at Canterbury. As soon as he came to Canterbury, and he was firmly settled in his archiepiscopal chair, he thought how he might drive out the clerks who were therein, whom the archbishop Ceolnoth had before placed there, for such need as we shall relate. The first year that he was appointed archbishop there was so great a mortality, that of all the monks that he found there within, no more than five monks remained. Then [for this reason, out of the simplicity of his heart,] he commanded his private priests, and also some of his vill-priests, that they should help the few monks who remained to do Christ's service, because he could not so readily find monks who might by themselves do the service; and for this he commanded that the priests the while, until God should give peace in the land, should help the monks. At the same time this land was greatly harassed by frequent conflicts, and on that account the archbishop could not attend to this object; for all that time there was strife and sorrow over England; and therefore the clerks remained with the monks. Nor was there ever a time that monks were not there within, and they ever had lordship over the priests. Again the archbishop Ceolnoth thought, and also said to those who were with him: 'As soon as God shall give peace in this land, either these priests shall be monks, or .... elsewhere I will place within the monastery as many monks as may do the service by themselves; for God knows that I ...' [Latin version concludes: 'But neither was Archbishop Æthelred able to do otherwise.']) Also printed in *Two of the Saxon Chronicles Parallel: A Revised Text*, ed. C. Plummer (based on the edition of J. Earle), 2 vols. (Oxford, 1892–9) I, 283–5 (Appendix B). Translation: *The Anglo-Saxon Chronicle according to the Several Original Authorities*, ed. and tr. B. Thorpe, 2 vols., Rolls Series 23 (London, 1861) II, 60–1.

[39] Other examples of reformed monastic tampering with older Christ Church texts include the adaptation of Æthelheard's 805 charter in favour of the Christ Church *familia* to refer specifically to 'monks' (*monachi*) rather than 'brothers' (*fratres*) when it was entered into the cathedral's thirteenth-century cartulary (London, Lambeth Palace Library, 1212): BCS 320, altering BCS 319 (S 1259).

The teaching of John the Archcantor

It is natural to suppose that Augustine and his companions brought to Canterbury a form of the Roman Office, and established it as the normative form of Office liturgy in the churches that they founded. But it cannot be proved that this Office could be recognized as the monastic Office used in the Vatican Basilica, which evolved into the medieval secular *cursus*.[40] Within Bede's lifetime, however, the opportunity arose for direct liturgical transmission from St Peter's in Rome to northern England in the person of John, abbot of the monastery of St Martin and *archicantor* of St Peter's Basilica, who came to England accompanied by Benedict Biscop in 678, remaining two years, 'in order that he might teach the monks of his monastery [Wearmouth] the mode of chanting throughout the year as it was practised at St Peter's in Rome'.[41] Bede speaks of John's teaching in mostly general terms: 'the yearly *cursus* of singing as it was done at St Peter's in Rome'; 'the order and rite of singing and reading'; 'and committing to writing those things required for the celebration of festal days over the whole cycle of the year'.[42] John's monastery in Rome shared the duty of reciting the Office daily in St Peter's, and he seems to have taught the whole content of the Divine Office: both the 'order of psalmody' with its musical technique, and the more elaborate individual musical pieces sung in the Office, the antiphons and responsories: Bede says quite clearly that John taught 'the order of singing (*cantandi*), of "psalming" (*psallendi*), and of ministering in the church according to the manner of the Roman arrangement'.[43] Bede the singer is specific in including the word *psallendi*

---

[40] See p. 49 above.

[41] The teaching of John the Archcantor during his sojourn at Wearmouth in 679–80 is described by Bede in his *Historia abbatum*, § 6, ed. Plummer I, 369, and in his *Historia ecclesiastica*, IV. 18, ed. Plummer I, 240–1 (whence the quotation). An account is also given in the anonymous *Vita Ceolfrithi*, § 10, ed. Plummer I, 391. See also Rankin, 'The liturgical background'. It has long been believed that Bede's *Historia abbatum* is a revision of the anonymous *Vita Ceolfrithi*; but, as Ian Wood will argue in a commentary on a new edition of the texts by Christopher Grocock, it seems much more likely that the *Vita Ceolfrithi* was written as a reaction to Bede's *Historia abbatum*.

[42] Bede, *Historia ecclesiastica*, IV. 18, ed. Plummer I, 240–1: 'cursum canendi annuum, sicut ad sanctum Petrum Romae agebatur'; 'ordinem uidelicet, ritumque canendi ac legendi'; 'et ea quae totius anni circulus in celebratione dierum festorum poscebat, etiam litteris mandando'.

[43] Bede, *Historia abbatum*, § 6, ed. Plummer I, 369: 'ordinem cantandi psallendi atque in ecclesia ministrandi iuxta morem Romanae institutionis'.

where the anonymous *Vita Ceolfrithi* has only *cantandi*.[44] *Psallere* can mean simply 'to sing', but its juxtaposition here with *cantare* reveals a more technical meaning. While the *Regula S. Benedicti* is not absolutely rigid in its use of verbs to do with singing, using *psallere, cantare, canere,* and even *dicere* to indicate that a text should be sung,[45] instances of the word *psallere* nevertheless appear predominantly in the context of singing psalms, with or without an antiphon.[46] *Cantare*, by contrast, appears most often in relation to more complicated music, which in the Office usually means responsories.[47] The distinction is important because psalmody is an activity of the whole community: psalms are intoned by members of the community in order of seniority, beginning with the abbot.[48] The more specialized tasks of 'singing and reading' (*cantare autem et legere*), however, are reserved for those monks of any rank who are skilled in liturgical singing and who will 'edify' their hearers.[49] Bede, intimately familiar with the language of the Rule,[50] makes it clear, in a way that the *Vita Ceolfrithi* does not, that John taught the Roman Office in its entirety: both the more complicated, melodic chants of the liturgy, which varied throughout the year (*ordo cantandi*), and the basic, unchanging pattern of psalmody in the Office, requiring only simple skills (*ordo psallendi*). Bede is the first author to speak of a system of chants 'for the whole cycle of the year', suggesting a fully developed system of 'proper' chants for the feasts of the year.[51]

---

[44] Cf. *Vita Ceolfrithi*, § 10, ed. Plummer I, 391.
[45] *RB 1980*, ed. Fry, p. 403.
[46] For example, *RSB* 11:6; 13:10; 17:6; 18:9; 18:23; 18:24; 43:11.
[47] For example, *RSB* 9:5–6; 11:3.
[48] *RSB* 47:2.
[49] *RSB* 38:12; 47:2–3. The Rule's implied distinction between *cantores* and *psalmistae* is also found generically in Isidore of Seville, *Etymologiae* (*Etymologiarum siue originum libri XX*), VII. 12. 24–6, ed. W. M. Lindsay, 2 vols., Oxford Classical Texts (Oxford, 1911), and is made explicit in the monastic context in the ninth-century commentary on the Rule by Hildemar, *Expositio Regulae*, c. 8, ed. Mittermüller, p. 275. On Hildemar's commentary, see p. 69 n. 187 above.
[50] A. G. P. Van Der Walt, 'Reflections on the Benedictine Rule in Bede's homiliary', *Journal of Ecclesiastical History* 37 (1986), 367–76.
[51] J. McKinnon, *The Advent Project: The Later-Seventh-Century Creation of the Roman Mass Proper* (Berkeley, CA, 2000), p. 92. The Council of *Clofesho*, c. 12, seems to point to a recognized set of proper chants, which, if priests are not able to sing them, are nevertheless to be read out (ed. Haddan and Stubbs, *Councils* III, 366): 'Ut presbyteri saecularium poetarum modo in ecclesia non garriant, ne tragico sono sacrorum verborum compositionem ac distinctionem corrumpant vel confundant, sed simplicem sanctamque melodiam secundum morem Ecclesiae sectentur: qui vero id non est idoneus adsequi, pronunciantis modo

Bede tells us nothing about the specific content of John's musical and liturgical teaching, merely indicating that a written version of his instructions had been made available for other monasteries to copy. But something of the character of John's teaching is communicated in the famous story of how, after a plague had carried off almost all the skilled singers at Jarrow, Abbot Ceolfrith and 'one small boy' (almost certainly Bede himself) maintained by themselves the tradition of singing the Office antiphons that had been taught to them by John until new singers could be trained.[52] Ceolfrith initially abandoned the use of antiphons at the lesser hours, but was so distressed by this that he reinstated them.[53] The context suggests that Ceolfrith was fearful that Jarrow would lose the oral tradition that he had worked so hard to establish. For the anonymous biographer of Ceolfrith, therefore, the distinctive element of John's teaching was the oral repertory of antiphons and responsories.

What John taught is sometimes referred to, unhelpfully, as 'antiphonal singing' (not a term used by Anglo-Saxon authors). The term is unhelpful because it conflates two separate issues: the literary form of the sung text and the mode of execution whereby the text was performed.[54] In the earliest monastic psalmody, the psalms were sung by soloists to a highly ornamented reciting tone. This practice is known as 'direct psalmody'. Sometimes the soloist's singing would be interrupted periodically with repeated refrains (antiphons) sung by the listening congregation.[55] The

---

simpliciter legendo, dicat atque recitet quicquid instantis temporis ratio poscit.' ('Priests are not to prate away in the church after the fashion of worldly poets, neither should they spoil or jumble together with a dramatic voice the proper arrangement (*compositio*) and correct phrasing (*distinctio*) of the sacred words. Rather, let them follow the simple and holy melody according to the custom of the Church. If anyone is not capable of attaining this, he should speak and recite simply, in the style of one reading aloud, whatever the present circumstance requires.')

[52] *Vita Ceolfrithi*, § 14, ed. Plummer I, 393. The plague occurred in 686. On the identification of this boy with Bede, see Plummer I, pp. xi–xiii. If the *Vita Ceolfrithi* is indeed dependent on Bede, and not the other way round, then it can hardly mean anyone but Bede himself.

[53] Patrick Wormald perceptively noticed that Ceolfrith acted in conformity with *RSB* 17:6 ('Bede and Benedict Biscop', pp. 143–4).

[54] I am here following O. Cullin, 'De la psalmodie sans refrain à la psalmodie responsoriale: Transformation et conservation dans les répertoires liturgiques latins', *Revue de musicologie* 77 (1991), 5–24. See also J. Claire, 'Saint Ambroise et le changement de style de la psalmodie: Traces importantes de transformation de la psalmodie sans refrain en psalmodie avec refrain dans le Carême milanais', *Études grégoriennes* 34 (2006–2007), 13–57.

[55] J. Dyer, 'Monastic psalmody of the Middle Ages', *Revue bénédictine* 99 (1989), 41–74; *idem*, 'The singing of psalms in the early-medieval Office', *Speculum* 64 (1989), 535–78, at

use of refrains gave the text a 'responsorial' literary form. So far as the earliest practice can be reconstructed – and for this we depend on vestigial traces in much later sources – it would appear that the recitation tones of the soloist and the refrains of the congregation made use of the same kinds of more or less elaborate musical phrases.[56]

In the course of the fifth and sixth centuries monastic psalmody underwent a radical change. The psalmody of the Office had at first been understood as a kind of liturgical reading to which the assembled monks would listen, responding with compunction in silent prayer. But by the time of the *Regula Magistri* and the *Regula S. Benedicti*, psalmody was coming to be understood as vocal prayer in itself: the psalms were no longer addressed by God to the listening monks, but by each monk to God with his own lips. As a result of this new understanding, monks began to sing the psalms together, chorally.[57] This new choral psalmody was served by a much simpler manner of recitation; the stark, unadorned psalm tones of later Milanese, or 'Ambrosian', chant may preserve something of the utter simplicity of the choral psalmody that had emerged by the seventh century and later evolved in to the somewhat more decorated 'Gregorian' psalm tones of Romano-Frankish chant.[58] Also, apparently from its earliest beginnings, choral monastic psalmody was distinguished by the division of the monks into two choirs that answered each other verse by verse. This is the practice that is properly called 'antiphonal singing'. Thus, antiphonal psalmody too could be either 'direct' or, by the addition of a refrain, 'responsorial'.[59] How the refrains were sung (soloists or choir?) and how they were divided between the two sides of the choir remains an unresolved question.[60] To the endless confusion of scholars, however, the term *antiphona* came to be applied to the refrains that were intercalated in psalms sung chorally by two alternating choirs: already in the *Regula S. Benedicti* an 'antiphon' can be a psalmic refrain.[61]

---

pp. 542–6. On the use of *Alleluia* as the refrain, see G. Oury, 'Psalmum dicere cum alleluia', *Ephemerides liturgicae* 79 (1965), 97–108.

[56] Cullin, 'De la psalmodie sans refrain', p. 23.

[57] P. Jeffery, 'Monastic reading and the emerging Roman Chant repertory', in S. Gallagher, J. Haar, J. Nádas, and T. Striplin (eds.), *Western Plainchant in the First Millennium: Studies in the Medieval Liturgy and its Music* (Aldershot, 2003), pp. 45–103, at pp. 77–9.

[58] T. Bailey, 'Ambrosian psalmody: An introduction', *Rivista internazionale di musica sacra* 1 (1980), 82–99, at pp. 97–8.

[59] Cullin, 'De la psalmodie sans refrain', p. 24.

[60] See E. Nowacki, 'The performance of Office antiphons in twelfth-century Rome', in *Cantus planus: Papers Read at the Third Meeting* (Budapest, 1990), pp. 79–91.

[61] E.g. *RSB* 9:4: 'deinde sex psalmi cum antiphonas'; Cullin, 'De la psalmodie sans refrain',

The distinction between 'antiphons' and two-choir singing is an important one. For although the *Vita Ceolfrithi* emphasizes the oral repertory of antiphons and responsories, for most Anglo-Saxon authors the distinctive feature of 'Roman' ecclesiastical music was the performance of the psalms standing in two choirs. Wilfrid's list of his catholic credentials in his defence at *Ouestrafelda* included teaching the Northumbrians to sing responsories and antiphons standing in a 'double choir' (*binis adstantibus choris*) 'according to the rite of the primitive Church' (*iuxta ritum primitivae ecclesiae*),[62] by which Wilfrid probably means Rome, implying, rightly or wrongly, that the Irish missionaries active in Northumbria, whose differing customs Wilfrid so despised, did not use two-choir psalmody or, it would seem, antiphons and responsories.[63] Benedict Biscop managed to continue to sing the Office during his final illness by having some of his monks come to his bed to sing the psalms 'in two choirs' (*duobus in choris*).[64] The practice is also mentioned several times in the writings of Aldhelm:

> May antiphons strike the ear with pleasing harmonies and the singing of psalms (*psalmorum oda*) reverberate from twin choirs (*classibus geminis*); may the trained voice of the precentor resound repeatedly and shake the summit of heaven with its sonorous chant!

p. 24.

[62] Stephen of Ripon, *Vitae S. Wilfridi*, c. 47, ed. and tr. Colgrave, *The Life of Bishop Wilfrid*, pp. 98–9. See above, p. 83.

[63] Perhaps difficult to accept, since the performance of psalms with antiphons is mentioned in the *Regula monachorum* of Columbanus (*c.*543–615), c. 7, ed. Walker, *Sancti Columbani Opera*, p. 131 and n. 1. Two apparent references to double choirs have been found in Irish hymns. See J. B. Stevenson, 'Hiberno-Latin hymns: Learning and literature', in P. Ní Chatháin and M. Richter (eds.), *Irland und Europa im früheren Mittelalter: Bildung und Literatur / Ireland and Europe in the Early Middle Ages: Learning and Literature* (Stuttgart, 1996), pp. 99–135, at p. 113. Stevenson identifies two early hymns from the 'Irish *Liber hymnorum*' that seem to refer to singing with alternating choirs. The first is Cu Cuimine's Marian hymn, *Cantemus in omni die*, strophe 2, ed. J. H. Bernard and R. Atkinson, *The Irish Liber Hymnorum*, 2 vols., HBS 13–14 (London, 1989) I, 33–4 (text), II, 124–5 (notes): 'Bis per chorum hinc et inde | collaudemus Mariam | Ut uox pulset omnem aurem | per laudem uicariam' ('Let us praise Mary doubly, with a choir on this side and on that, so that the voice may strike every ear with reciprocal praise.') The second is attributed to St Patrick: *Ecce fulget clarissima*, strophe 9, ed. Bernard and Atkinson I, 160 (text), II, 222 (notes): 'Psallemus Christo cordibus | alternantes et uocibus' ('Taking turns, let us sing unto Christ with hearts and voices'). Isidore considered antiphonal singing, which he defined as reciprocal singing by two choirs (*vox reciproca duobus scilicet choris alternatim psallentibus*), to have been a Greek innovation (*Etymologiae*, VI. 19. 7).

[64] Bede, *Historia abbatum*, § 12, ed. Plummer I, 376.

Brothers, let us praise God in harmonious voice, and let the throng of nuns also burst forth in continual psalmody! On these feast-days let us all chant hymns and psalms and appropriate responds beneath the roof of the church (*subter testitudine templi*), intoning the melodies with the continuous accompaniment of the psaltery; and let us strive to tune the lyre with its ten strings – just as the psalmist urges us to 'praise (the Lord) with ten strings' [Ps. 32:2]. Let each one of us adorn the new church with his singing, and let each lector – whether male or female – read the lessons from Holy Scripture.[65]

(*Carmen ecclesiasticum III*, lines 46–58)

When the fourth cockcrow – as if it were the fourth vigil of the night – had roused the slumbering masses with its clarion calls, then standing in two responding ranks we were celebrating matins and the psalmody of the Divine Office.[66]

(*Carmen rhythmicum*, lines 123–30)

[On St Benedict's holy life and appropriate name:] My mediocre talent too, supported by the authentic authority of ancient writers,

---

[65] Aldhelm, *Carmen ecclesiasticum* III, lines 46–58, ed. Ehwald, *Aldhelmi Opera*, pp. 14–18, at pp. 16–17: 'Dulcibus antifonae pulsent concentibus aures | Classibus et geminis psalmorum concrepet oda; | Ymnistae crebro vox articulata resultet | Et celsum quatiat clamoso carmine culmen! | Fratres concordi laudemus voce Tonantem | Cantibus et crebris conclamet turba sororum; | Ymnos ac psalmos et responsoria festis | Congrua promamus subter testitudine templi | Psalterii melos fantes modulamine crebro | Atque decem fidibus nitamur tendere liram, | Ut psalmista monet bis quinis psallere fibris; | Unusquisque novum comat cum voce sacellum | Et lector lectrixve volumina sacra revolvant!' Translation: Lapidge and Rosier, *Aldhelm: The Poetic Works*, pp. 48–9. The translators' suggestion (pp. 236–7 n. 26, and repeated by Foot, *Monastic Life*, p. 191) that the singing was accompanied by a musical instrument (the 'psaltery') should be disregarded; the passage translated as 'the accompaniment of the psaltery' might be more simply rendered as 'the melody of the psalter'.

[66] Aldhelm, *Carmen rhythmicum*, lines 123–30, ed. Ehwald, *Aldhelmi Opera*, pp. 524–8, at p. 527 (recounting a night spent at a monastery in Devon): 'Cum quarta gallicinia | Quasi quarta vigilia | Suscitarent sonantibus | Somniculosos cantibus | Tum binis stantes classibus | Celebramus concentibus | Matutinam melodiam | Ac synaxis psalmodiam.' Translation: Lapidge and Rosier, *Aldhelm: The Poetic Works*, p. 178. The translation of *matutinam melodiam* as 'matins' (see the translators' useful comment on p. 263 n. 11) reflects the ambiguity of whether Aldhelm refers to the Night Office or to Lauds. That this office was sung during the 'fourth watch', however, could signify Lauds, since the Night Office could be thought to comprise three *uigiliae*; cf. Amalarius, *Liber de ordine antiphonarii*, c. 1. 14, ed. Hanssens III, 21.

celebrates with the melody of joyous jubilation this exemplary fact in the solemnity of palms [i.e. Palm Sunday], ringing out with harmonious voice with the double ranks (*binis classibus*) and reverberating 'Osanna' with the twin harmonizers (*geminis concentibus*).[67]

(*De uirginitate* (prose), c. 30)

Æthelwulf quotes Aldhelm in a description of antiphonal singing in his *De abbatibus*, but with sufficient additional detail to show that this was the authentic practice in his monastery too:

> When the revered festivals of God's saints came round, [and when] he [Sigwine] would sing the verses of the psalms among the brethren, who were in two choirs (*classibus geminis*) under the roof of the church (*subter testitudine templi*), they made melody in the sweet-sounding [music] of the antiphon with poured-out song.[68]

All these references to antiphonal singing may indicate the widespread performance of the Office in what was believed to be a Roman style.

Two-choir psalmody does not seem to have been known in Gaul before the Romanizing reforms of the Carolingians; but it does seem to have been part of Roman monastic discipline.[69] The *Regula Magistri* clearly envisages the division of the monks into two choirs on at least some occasions, each led by a dean, with the psalms intoned alternately by members

---

[67] Aldhelm, *De uirginitate* (prose), c. 30, ed. Ehwald, *Aldhelmi Opera*, pp. 226–323, at pp. 268–9: 'Cuius rei regulam nostra quoque mediocritas autentica veterum auctoritate subnixa in sacrosancta palmarum sollemnitate binis classibus canora voce concrepans et geminis concentibus Osanna persultans cum iocundae iubilationis melodia concelebrat.' Translation modified from M. Lapidge and M. Herren, *Aldhelm: The Prose Works* (Cambridge, 1979), p. 90. The translators inadvertently mistook *palmarum* for *psalmorum*, which led to the obscuring of the description of two-choir singing. The two-choir reference in this passage was noted, however, in the subsequent companion volume: Lapidge and Rosier, *Aldhelm: The Poetic Works*, p. 263 n. 11. Aldhelm has in mind the phrase *Benedictus qui uenit in nomine domini* shouted by the Hebrew crowd at the Triumphal Entry (Matt. 21:9).
[68] Æthelwulf, *De abbatibus*, lines 495–8, ed. Campbell, p. 39: 'dum ueneranda dei sanctorum festa redirent | classibus in geminis subter testitudine templi | fratribus inmixtus psalmorum concinat odas, | dulcisona antiphonae modulantur carmine fuse' (my translation). Campbell's translation puts Sigwine 'between two choirs' as if he were singing the psalms by himself while the brethren responded with antiphons.
[69] P. Bernard, 'A-t-on connu la psalmodie alternée à deux chœurs, en Gaule, avant l'époque carolingienne?', *Revue bénédictine* 114 (2004), 291–325, and 115 (2005), 33–60.

of each choir in descending order of seniority.[70] The *Regula S. Benedicti* does not mention that there are two choirs, but a monk is expected to have a usual seat in the oratory corresponding with his rank in the community.[71] The Office in the greater Roman basilicas was also sung by 'two choirs', though in this case each choir was supplied by one of the monasteries attached to the basilica. The Lateran basilica was initially served by two monasteries, an early monastery dedicated to St Pancratius and a second founded by Pope Honorius (625–38). St Pancratius was later refounded by Gregory III (731–41) who ordered that the monks there were to recite the Office in the basilica. The monastery founded by Honorius was refounded by Hadrian I (772–95), who explicitly commanded that the monks of Honorius's monastery were to supply one side of the choir and the monks of St Pancratius the other.[72] Hadrian did likewise with the four monasteries that served St Peter's at the Vatican, assigning two monasteries to each side of the choir.[73] Wilfrid may have seen the two-choir singing of the Roman monks during his several visits to Rome – it may already have been the norm in Canterbury when he was there learning the *Romanum* version of the psalms. And John may have impressed upon his English students the importance of simple two-choir psalmody as a signature of Roman monastic liturgy before moving on to the more demanding oral repertory of antiphons and responsories.

The liturgical decrees of the Council of Clofesho *(747)*

The first clear indication that the Divine Office was expected to be recited according to the Roman pattern in all English churches, at least in the southern province, is found in the canons promulgated by the council convened in 747 by Archbishop Cuthbert (740–60) at the now unknown place called *Clofesho*.[74] *Clofesho* is one of only five Anglo-Saxon synods

---

[70] *Regula Magistri* 22:13–14; cf. 93:64.
[71] *RSB* 43:4; 44:5; 63:4.
[72] Ferrari, *Early Roman Monasteries*, pp. 365–6.
[73] Ferrari, *Early Roman Monasteries*, p. 368.
[74] The canons survive in a single eighth-century manuscript badly damaged in the Cotton Library fire of 1731, now split into two fragmentary parts: BL Cotton Otho A. i. 1, and Oxford, Bodleian Library, Arch Selden B. 26, fol. 34 (see *CLA* II, 2nd edn, nos. 188 and 299, where the manuscript is identified as 'insular, s. viii[2]'). On the manuscript and its date, see S. Keynes, 'The reconstruction of a burnt Cottonian manuscript: The case of Cotton Ms. Otho A. I', *British Library Journal* 22 (1996), 113–60 (on the script see pp. 117, 139–40).

known to have promulgated a set of canons. The *Clofesho* canons, the only ones to give special attention to the liturgy, attest 'a concerted programme of secular and ecclesiastical reform, orchestrated by Cuthberht, Archbishop of Canterbury, and Æthelbald, King of the Mercians, both of whom were acting in response to appeals made from the continent by Boniface, Archbishop of Mainz'.[75] Two canons are directly relevant to the Divine Office:

> It is defined in the thirteenth decree, that the holy feasts of the Lord's dispensation in the flesh [i.e. the feasts of the Temporale][76] be celebrated in one and the same way in all the things that rightly pertain to them: that is, in the office of baptism, in the celebration of Masses, and in the manner of singing, they should be celebrated according to the written exemplar that we have [received] from the Roman Church. And moreover, that the feast days of the saints throughout the whole circle of the year [i.e. the Sanctorale] be venerated on one and the same day, according to the martyrology of the same Roman Church, with the psalmody and chant appropriate to them.[77]
>
> In the fifteenth heading, [the bishops] determined that the seven canonical hours of prayer of the day and night must be observed with diligent care, together with the psalmody and chant

---

The standard edition of the canons remains that of Haddan and Stubbs, *Councils* III, 360–76. A translation originally published in 1720, from the earlier edition of Spelman (with the translator's own editorial emendations), is available in J. Johnson, *A Collection of the Laws and Canons of the Church of England: From its First Foundation to the Conquest, and from the Conquest to the Reign of King Henry VIII*, new edn ed. J. Baron, 2 vols., Library of Anglo-Catholic Theology (Oxford, 1850–1) I, 242–63. This translation has been consulted but not reproduced here.

[75] Keynes, 'The reconstruction of a burnt Cottonian manuscript', p. 135. The *Clofesho* canons were to influence all subsequent early Anglo-Saxon ecclesiastical legislation: Cubitt, *Anglo-Saxon Church Councils*, pp. 62–3 and 99–101. Cubitt devotes a complete chapter to *Clofesho*'s liturgical provisions (pp. 125–52).

[76] The feasts celebrating events in the life of Christ from Advent to Pentecost. Here, *dispensatio* is probably used in the sense of the Greek *oikonomia*: the divine plan, or divine economy (cf. Eph. 3:9 in the original Greek and in the Latin Vulgate).

[77] Ed. Haddan and Stubbs, *Councils* III, 367: 'Tertio decimo definitur decreto: Ut uno eodemque modo Dominicae dispensationis in carne sacrosanctae festivitates, in omnibus ad eas rite competentibus rebus, id est, in Baptismi officio, in Missarum celebratione, in cantilenae modo celebrantur, juxta exemplar videlicet quod scriptum de Romana habemus Ecclesia. Itemque per gyrum totius anni natalitia sanctorum uno eodemque die, juxta martyrologium ejusdem Romanae Ecclesiae, cum sua sibi convenienti psalmodio seu cantilena venerentur.'

appropriate to each of them; and that the same equality of monastic psalmody must be followed everywhere. No one should presume to sing or read anything that common use does not admit. Rather, they may sing and read only what derives from the authority of the holy scriptures and what the custom of the Roman Church permits; so that, unanimous, they may praise God with one mouth. And they also agreed this: that ecclesiastics [i.e. secular clergy] and monastics should remember to implore the clemency of the divine compassion, not only for themselves, but for kings and for the safety of the whole Christian people, during the appropriate hours of prayer.[78]

Canon 13 has mainly to do with the ecclesiastical calendar, requiring all churches to keep major feasts on the dates given in the Roman martyrology and to celebrate them with chants and psalms according to a Roman 'exemplar'. This exemplar should probably not be interpreted as a single book or set of books introduced to England shortly before 747. The *Clofesho* canons seem to be 'consolidating Romanization and not introducing it'.[79] Archbishop Ecgberht of York (732–66) believed that York's liturgical books descended from originals brought from Rome by Augustine of Canterbury, having compared his own books with others in Rome itself:

> The same blessed Gregory established, through his aforementioned legate [i.e. Augustine], in his antiphoner and sacramentary (*missale*),[80] that this fast should be celebrated in the week after Pentecost by the English Church. Not only our antiphoners testify

---

[78] Ed. Haddan and Stubbs, *Councils* III, 367: 'Quinto decimo definierunt capitulo: Ut septem canonicae orationum diei et noctis horae diligenti cura cum psalmodia et cantilena sibimet convenienti observantur, et ut eandem monasterialis psalmodiae parilitatem ubique sectentur, nihilque quod communis usus non admittit, praesumant cantare aut legere, sed tantum quod ex sacrarum Scripturarum auctoritate discendit, et quod Romanae Ecclesiae consuetudo permittit, cantent vel legant; quatenus unanimes, uno ore laudent Deum. Sed et hoc quoque condixerunt, ut non solum pro se ecclesiastici sive monasteriales, sed etiam pro Regibus, et totius populi Christiani incolumitate Divinae pietatis clementiam exorare, per competentes orationum reminiscant horas.'

[79] Cubitt, *Anglo-Saxon Church Councils*, p. 148; cf. Brooks, *The Early History*, p. 93.

[80] Despite the survival of a number of late eighth-century fragments from 'missals' properly so called, it seems likely that Ecgberht has in mind the sacramentary. Anglo-Saxon writers use the Latin *missale* and the Old English *mæssboc* to denote both kinds of book. See Gneuss, 'Liturgical books in Anglo-Saxon England', pp. 99–100. Continental writers also use the words interchangeably; see E. Palazzo, *A History of Liturgical Books from the Beginning to the Thirteenth Century*, tr. M. Beaumont (Collegeville, MN, 1998), pp. 29–31.

to this, but also the antiphoners that we inspected at the thresholds of the apostles Peter and Paul, together with their Mass-books.[81]

Prior to this passage, Ecgberht had justified an earlier fast in the first week of Lent by invoking only English liturgical books (albeit attributed to Gregory).[82] In justifying only the post-Pentecost fast with reference to books he inspected in Rome, Ecgberht tacitly recognizes differences between English antiphoners and sacramentaries (probably of the 'Gelasian' type) and those that he saw in Rome in the first half of the eighth century.[83] *Clofesho*'s canon 18 also refers to a Roman exemplar as the authority for the Ember fasts of 'the fourth, seventh, and tenth month'.[84] In many cases, what was regarded as 'Roman' liturgy will have been received in England through Continental intermediaries, with Continental adaptation.[85] The Council of *Clofesho* itself seems to have been convened at the prompting of Boniface, who wrote to Archbishop Cuthbert informing him of the resolutions of his own synods in Francia.[86]

Canon 15 flags two traits as characteristic of the Roman Office: the number of hours celebrated each day (seven), and an 'equality of monastic

---

'Antiphoner' may refer to a book containing only chants of the Mass, or of both Mass and Office.

[81] Ecgberht of York, *Dialogus ecclesiasticae institutionis*, Responsio XVI, ed. Haddan and Stubbs, *Councils* III, 403–13, at p. 412: 'Hoc autem jejunium idem beatus Gregorius, per praefatum legatum, in Antiphonario suo et Missali, in plena epdomada post Pentecosten Anglorum aecclesiae celebrandum destinavit. Quod non solum nostra testantur Antiphonaria, sed et ipsa quae cum Missalibus suis conspeximus apud apostolorum Petri et Pauli limina.'

[82] Ecgberht, *Dialogus*, Responsio XVI, 'De Primo Jejunio', ed. Haddan and Stubbs, *Councils* III, 411.

[83] D. Bullough, 'Roman books and Carolingian *renovatio*', in his *Carolingian Renewal: Sources and Heritage* (Manchester, 1991), pp. 1–33, at p. 6; originally published in *Studies in Church History* 14 (Oxford, 1977), pp. 23–50. Bullough also argued that the *Dialogus* could be more plausibly assigned to Ecgberht's successor, Ælberht, since Ecgberht 'is not known ever to have journeyed to Rome', apparently overlooking Bede's *Epistola Ecgberhti*, which reports that Ecgberht did indeed go to Rome as a younger man, and was there ordained a deacon. See Alcuin's *Versus de patribus*, ed. Godman, p. 99 n. 1268.

[84] Ed. Haddan and Stubbs, *Councils* III, 368; on the fasts themselves, see p. 376 n. i. For the slightly differing Continental practice, see Vogel, *Medieval Liturgy*, pp. 312–13.

[85] As J. M. Wallace-Hadrill noted of the major episcopal sees of southern Gaul, 'Their sources of supply were various and near. Rome for all her riches was not near' ('Rome and the early English Church: Some questions of transmission', in *La Chiese nei regni dell'Europa occidentale e i loro rapporti con Roma sino all'800*, 2 vols., Settimane di studio del Centro italiano di studi sull'alto medioevo 7 (Spoleto, 1960) II, 519–48, at p. 534). See also E. Ó Carragáin, *Ritual and the Rood: Liturgical Images and the Old English Poems of the 'Dream of the Rood' Tradition* (London, 2005), p. 223.

[86] Cubitt, *Anglo-Saxon Church Councils*, pp. 102–10.

psalmody'. As has already been noticed, this canon applies to both monks and secular clerics, who are to be 'unanimous' and to 'praise God with one mouth'. In referring to an 'equality of monastic psalmody', the author of this canon, presumably Cuthbert himself, probably alludes to the requirement in the *Regula S. Benedicti* that the whole psalter be sung every week, which is fulfilled in the Roman *cursus*.[87] *Clofesho*'s canon 27 also alludes to the *Regula S. Benedicti* in calling psalmody an *opus diuinum*, a synonym in the Rule for the *Opus Dei*, the Divine Office. The whole canon is an extended gloss on St Benedict's admonition that mind and voice must agree in prayer.[88] The Rule emerges in the *Clofesho* canons as a valuable guide to liturgical devotion and intercession. But the Rule's teachings apply in this respect equally to monks and secular clerics, and they in no way alter the expectation that the 'custom of the Roman Church' will be followed by both groups.

Evidence for the Roman Office horarium *in Anglo-Saxon sources*

Clofesho's canon 15 refers to 'seven canonical hours of prayers of the day and night'. As was shown in Chapter 2, a sevenfold *horarium* is particularly associated with the Roman Office. Aldhelm refers to a sevenfold Office:

> Indeed the diurnal and nocturnal intervals of the hours – in which we perform without ceasing the offices of prayers as if it were a revenue owed to the state or a payment to the treasury – are turned round when the sevenfold pause of the synaxis has been repeated. It is concerning this that I reckon the psalmist-seer to have sung,

---

[87] *RSB* 18:24–5; on the wider monastic tradition of a minimum '*pensum*' of psalmody, see Vogüé, *La Règle de Saint Benoît* V, 545–54.

[88] Ed. Haddan and Stubbs, *Councils* III, 372–4, at p. 372: 'Psalmodia (inquiunt) opus Divinum, spiritu et mente agentibus, magnum est ac multiplex animarum medicamentum suarum.' ('Psalmody, the [bishops] say, is a divine work, and for those who perform it in spirit and in mind, it is a great and manifold remedy of their souls.') Cf. *RSB* 19:1–2, 7: 'Vbique credimus diuinam esse praesentiam et oculos Domini in omni loco speculari bonos et malos, maxime tamen hoc sine aliqua dubitatione credamus cum ad opus diuinum adsistimus. ... et sic stemus ad psallendum ut mens nostra concorde uoci nostrae.' (We believe that the divine presence is everywhere and that in every place the eyes of the Lord are watching the good and the wicked. But beyond the least doubt we believe this to be especially true when we celebrate the divine office. ... let us stand to sing the psalms in such a way that our minds are in harmony with our voices.')

Seven times a day have I praised you.[89]

A letter of Ælfwald, king of East Anglia, written between 747 and 749, likewise promises that 'the memory of your name must be celebrated in the sevenfold synaxis of our monasteries, for the perfect are often signified by the number seven'.[90] References to a sevenfold Office in which the Roman *cursus* is explicitly intended also appear in tenth-century Anglo-Saxon sources: the *Regularis concordia* (*c*.970)[91] and the pastoral letters of Ælfric of Eynsham (*c*.955–1020?), who clearly sees the Night Office and Lauds as a single office.[92] The Roman rationale for the Office *ho*-

---

[89] Aldhelm, *De metris et enigmatibus ac pedum regulis*, ed. Ehwald, *Aldhelmi Opera*, pp. 59–204, at p. 71: 'siquidem diurna et nocturna horarum intervalla, quibus indesinenter, quasi quoddam rei publicae vectigal et fiscale tributum, orationum officia persolvimus, septena sinaxeos intercapedine revoluta rotantur; unde reor psalmigraphum vatem cecinisse: *Septies in die laudem dixi tibi.*'

[90] Ælfwald, *Epistola Bonifatio* (747×749), ed. M. Tangl, *Die Briefe Bonifatius und Lullus*, MGH Epp. selectae 1 (Berlin, 1916), no. 81 (pp. 181–2), at p. 181: 'Memoria nominis uestri in septenis monasteriorum nostrorum synaxis perpetua lege censeri debet, quia in septenario numero perfecti sepe designantur.' This passage is noticed in Foot, *Monastic Life*, p. 197.

[91] *Regularis concordia*, § 50, ed. Symons p. 49 (CCM § 78, p. 123): 'In die sancte Paschae septem canonicae horae a monachis in ecclesia Dei more canonicorum ... celebrandae sunt.' ('On Easter Day, the seven canonical hours are to be celebrated by the monks in the Church of God after the manner of canons.') On this exception to the usual practice assumed in the *Concordia*, see p. 182 below.

[92] *Die Hirtenbriefe Aelfrics in altenglischer und lateinischer Fassung*, ed. B. Fehr (Hamburg, 1914), repr. with a supplement to the introduction by P. Clemoes, Bibliothek der angelsächsischen Prosa 9 (Darmstadt, 1966), p. 43 (*Brief 2*, §§ 62–5): 'Dico uobis nunc apertius clericis, quia hii sancti patres septem sinaxes canendas constituerunt, quas omni die singulis horis canere debetis. Quarum prima est nocturnalis [siue matutinalis, *add.* MS C] sinaxis, secunda prima hora die, tertia ipsa hora est quam terciam uocamus, quarta uero sexta hora est, sexta autem sinaxis uespera hora est, septimam namque sinaxim completorium uocitamus. Has ergo septem sinaxes omni die debetis sollicite reddere deo pro uobis et pro omni populo Christiano, sicut psalmista testatur dicens: Septies in die laudem dixi tibi super iudicia iustitię tuę.' ('Now I say to you clergy more clearly that these holy fathers established seven synaxes to be sung, each hour of which you must sing every day. The first of these is the nocturnal synaxis; the second is the first hour of the day [i.e. Prime]; the third is that hour that we call Terce; the fourth is the sixth hour [Sext]; the fifth is the ninth hour [None]; the sixth synaxis is the evening hour [Vespers]; and the seventh synaxis we are wont to call Compline. Therefore these seven synaxes you must render carefully unto God every day, for yourselves and for the whole Christian people, as the psalmist gives witness, saying: 'Seven times a day have I praised you because of the justice of your judgements.') This passage was subsequently adopted into the second Old English pastoral letter (*Brief II*, § 72, ed. Fehr, pp. 98–101, readings of MS *O*), and into Recension B of Archbishop Wulfstan's canon law collection, § 29, ed. and tr. J. E. Cross and A. Hamer, *Wulfstan's Canon Law Collection* (Cambridge, 1999), pp. 123–4. The influence of Ælfric's letters on the whole collection is discussed at pp. 17–22.

rarium given by the *Regularis concordia* and by Ælfric probably derives from pre-tenth-century English tradition, since it is not found in any of the Continental sources cited in the writings of the tenth-century reformers.

Apart from these references to a sevenfold Office, it is difficult to establish that all the hours of the Roman *cursus* were observed in any one Anglo-Saxon minster. All the hours except Compline are attested at Wearmouth and Jarrow.[93] The only unambiguous reference to Compline in early Anglo-Saxon literature is found in Stephen of Ripon's Life of Wilfrid.[94] Compline may also be described in a passage in Æthelwulf's *De abbatibus*:

> This house once in the time of dark night, the brothers, following their usual custom, were at pains to enter after their hymns, to complete their solemnities of spirit (*complent sollempnia mentis*). They desired to hurry thence to their beds.[95]

The 'house' in question is the original church built by the monastery's founder, Eanmund, as opposed to a more recent church built by Abbot Sigbald. The phrase *complent sollempnia mentis* could be a poetic description of Compline (*completorium*); following these 'solemnities', the monks go to bed. If the custom of Æthelwulf's house was to recite Compline in a building other than the main monastery church, this would partly agree with *Ordo Romanus XVIII*, which says that Compline should be sung in the dormitory immediately before the community retires. It is equally possible, however, that Compline is indicated by the 'hymns' preceding the *sollempnia mentis*, the latter being a period for quiet reflection before retiring.

Æthelwulf's *De abbatibus* contains three further descriptions of the Office whose details are remarkably consistent with the Roman monastic

---

[93] The episode of the plague at Jarrow cited above mentions Lauds and Vespers and refers collectively to the lesser daytime hours. Bede sees Old Testament precedent for Prime, Terce, Sext, and None, as well as the custom of reading long passages of scripture during the Night Office, in his *Expositio in Ezram et Neemiam*, III (at 2 Esd. 9:3), ed. D. Hurst, *Bedae Venerabilis Opera exegetica*, IIA, CCSL 119A (Turnhout, 1969), p. 372.

[94] Stephen of Ripon, *Vita S. Wilfridi*, c. 68, ed. and tr. Colgrave, *The Life of Bishop Wilfrid*, pp. 148–9. Foot's suggestion that Wilfrid's use of the *Regula S. Benedicti* explains the practice of Compline at Ripon (*Monastic Life*, p. 200) ignores the existence of Compline from an early stage in the Roman Office.

[95] Æthelwulf, *De abbatibus*, lines 659–62, ed. and tr. Campbell, pp. 51–2: '... hanc dudum nigre sub tempore noctis | moribus ex solitis post ymnos uisere certant | fratres, atque sue complent sollempnia mentis. | ocius inde suos cupiunt adcurre lectos'.

custom of the 'second sleep' after the nocturnal hours. The first describes the devotion of the community's blacksmith:

> While the brothers sang the nocturnal hymns in sacred concert, and departed to return to their retirement, the brother we have mentioned [Cwicwine] kept to the confines of the church, and did not refrain from pressing the floor with his knees, as he earnestly commended himself to God [to journey] to the stars. The brothers, when the light of the sun came, would again wish to commend themselves to God with many prayers. The monk loved to join their holy troops and to say the psalms, and he would commend himself and all of them to the Lord. Then, when the matin psalms (*matutini psalmi*) had been duly completed, forthwith the hammer rang on the anvil as the metal ...[96]

Here, a nocturnal office of psalmody is followed by a return to sleep, piously foregone by Cwicwine. The brothers then rise to recite the *matutini psalmi*, probably to be identified with Prime, since they are immediately followed by a period of manual labour.[97] Two further passages suggest that Æthelwulf's monastery used the same timetable for the Night Office as the *Regula Magistri*:

> It was the hour of the night when the cock announces the approach of dawn, and after I had relaxed my chill limbs in rest after the singing of hymns, a lurking dream came and stole before my eyes.[98]

---

[96] Æthelwulf, *De abbatibus*, lines 293–303, ed. and tr. Campbell, pp. 47–8: 'nocturnos fratres sacris concentibus ymnos | dum caelebrant, rursusque suas uisitare quietes | incipiunt, frater memoratus septa sacelli | incoluitque suis non parcit tundere membris | marmora, seque deo diligenter mandat ad astra | at rursus fratres, ueniunt cum lumina Phoebi, | se precibus cupiunt domino mandare profusis. | coetibus hic sanctis coniunctus dicere psalmos | dulce habuit, sese domino commendat et omnes. | hic matutinis completis quam bene psalmis, | continuo insonuit percussis cudo metallis'.

[97] See *Regula Magistri* 33:17, and *RSB* 48:3. A similar case of voluntary wakefulness is found in Bede's account of Adomnan's solitary vigils at Coldingham while the other monks slept (Bede, *Historia ecclesiastica*, IV. 25, ed. Plummer I, 264–5), which should not be interpreted (as in Foot, 'Anglo-Saxon minsters', p. 201 n. 28) as proof that Coldingham lacked a Night Office. Prof. Foot omits this reference from her *Monastic Life*, and has perhaps changed her mind, though one would have expected Adomnan to be mentioned in her discussion of supererogatory vigils (p. 199 n. 59).

[98] Æthelwulf, *De abbatibus*, lines 692–4, ed. and tr. Campbell, pp. 53–4: 'tempore erat noctis, lucem cum predicat ales, | algida post ymnos laxassem membra quieti, | furtiuus adueniens somnus subrepsit ocellis.'

Æthelwulf has here returned to bed following the conclusion of the nighttime 'hymns', just at cockcrow. This is the time when, in the winter *horarium* of the *Regula Magistri*, the Night Office must be concluded (which explains his frigid limbs). In the following passage, however, the Night Office is only begun at cockcrow, suggesting the *Regula Magistri*'s summer timetable:

> Later, when the cock was announcing the time from red throat, arising again he observed the hour with the customary hymns.[99]

The Night Office *horarium* known to Æthelwulf may derive from the Roman monastic tradition that informed the *Regula Magistri* and *Ordo Romanus XVIII*. It could not, in any case, have been learned from the *Regula S. Benedicti*. Æthelwulf's monastery seems to have been founded with the assistance of Lindisfarne, which had accepted Roman customs in the time of St Cuthbert.[100] A Roman monastic tradition could also have been obtained from York, where Æthelwulf may have studied.[101]

The history of St Augustine's monastery in Canterbury by Thomas of Elmham, written in the fifteenth century, may preserve evidence of the use of the full round of daily offices in Canterbury in the earliest years of its history. Describing an ancient psalter kept on the high altar and believed to have been brought to England by Augustine ('Psalterium Augustini quod sibi misit idem Gregorius'), Thomas lists a collection of fifteen Latin hymns found in an appendix to the psalms, the first nine of which are rubricated for the daily hours:[102]

Primus hymnus pro medio noctis est iste:	Mediae noctis tempus est
secundus ad gallicantum:	Aeterne rerum conditor
ad matutinas:	Splendor paternae gloriae
ad primam:	Venite fratres ocius
ad tertiam:	Iam surgit hora tertia

---

[99] Æthelwulf, *De abbatibus*, lines 560–1, ed. and tr. Campbell, pp. 43–4: 'hinc iterum surgens, horam dum predicat ales | gutture de rubro, solitis complebat in hymnis'.
[100] Lapidge, 'Aediluulf and the School of York', p. 382.
[101] Lapidge, 'Aediluulf and the School of York', pp. 387–93.
[102] Thomas of Elmham, *Historia monasterii S. Augustini Cantuariensis*, II. 6, ed. C. Hardwick, Rolls Series 8 (London, 1858), p. 97. Thomas gives the history of the monastery to 1418. I reproduce the list with the orthography given in H. Gneuss, 'Zur Geschichte des Ms. Vespasian A. I', *Anglia* 75 (1957), 125–33, at p. 126; repr. as ch. VII in his *Books and Libraries in Early England*, Variorum Collected Studies 558 (Aldershot, 1996).

ad sextam:	Bis ternas horas explicans
ad nonam:	Ter hora trina uoluitur
ad vesperas:	Deus creator omnium
ad completorium:	Te deprecamur domine

The *Psalterium Augustini*, now lost, may have been one of the exemplars of the eighth-century 'Vespasian Psalter', whose other liturgical features are discussed at length below.[103]

The Office sung in the greater Roman basilicas did not make use of hymns until the twelfth century, although liturgical books from these basilicas acknowledge the use of hymns elsewhere in Rome.[104] The *Regula S. Benedicti* makes use of hymns in all the offices, calling them *ambrosiana*, perhaps an indication that they were borrowed from a tradition other than Rome's.[105] The hymns mentioned in the *Psalterium Augustini* are from the primitive collection known as the 'Old Hymnal', a small collection of around fifteen hymns (precisely those listed by Thomas of Elmham) that began to circulate in 'the fifth century at the very latest'.[106] Helmut Gneuss has suggested that 'the Old Hymnal was introduced [to England] very early, at the time of St Augustine of Canterbury, and it is possible, though not certain, that it did not come directly from Rome but from the church of Gaul.'[107] If Augustine was not the agent of transmission, Benedict Biscop could have learned the Old Hymnal during his monastic novitiate at Lérins, prior to his tenure as abbot of SS. Peter and Paul in Canterbury.[108]

---

[103] The Vespasian Psalter includes three of these hymns in its own abbreviated appendix of non-psalmic liturgical texts.

[104] See Bäumer, *Histoire du bréviaire* I, 368; Batiffol, *History of the Roman Breviary*, pp. 139–40; Callewaert, *De breviarii Romani liturgia*, p. 109. Among the medieval witnesses to the absence of hymns from the Roman Office is Pseudo-Amalarius (tenuously associated with Adhemar of Chabannes, d.1034), *De Regula sancti Benedicti praecipui abbas*, § 76, ed. Hanssens III, 292: 'Ut enim romana consuetudo sine himnis officia canit horarum.' The Roman Office known to Hildemar of Corbie in the ninth century seems not to have included them either (see p. 70 above), nor are they mentioned by Amalarius of Metz.

[105] *RSB* 9:4.

[106] H. Gneuss, 'Latin hymns in medieval England: Future research', in B. Rowland (ed.), *Chaucer and Middle English Studies in Honour of Rossell Hope Robbins* (London, 1974), pp. 407–24, at p. 408; repr. as ch. XI in Gneuss, *Books and Libraries*.

[107] Gneuss, 'Latin hymns', p. 409; cf. his *Hymnar und Hymnen im englischen Mittelalter: Studien zur Überlieferung, Glossierung und Übersetzung lateinischer Hymnen in England* (Tübingen, 1968), pp. 33–8.

[108] H. Gneuss, 'Anglo-Saxon libraries from the Conversion to the Benedictine Reform', in *Angli e sassoni al di qua e al di là del mare*, Settimane di studio del Centro italiano di studi

No matter how the Old Hymnal reached Canterbury, the rubrics to the hymns in the *Psalterium Augustini* suggest that the full Roman Office *horarium* was in use there from an early date. Helmut Gneuss ingeniously suggests that the provision of two hymns for the Night Office pointed to the Office liturgy of Lérins where a hymn was used in each of the two nocturns of the the Night Office in the winter.[109] But the rubrication of one hymn *pro medio noctis* and the other *ad gallicantum* (themes also reflected in the texts of the hymns themselves) points instead to the winter and summer schedules of early Roman monastic tradition. The use of the Old Hymnal nevertheless illustrates how technically 'non-Roman' material could be incorporated into an otherwise faithful performance of the Roman Office. It is possible that the *Regula S. Benedicti* would have been seen to provide sufficient authority for their incorporation – though it must be stressed that the use of the Old Hymnal, though it seems to be attested in the Rule, should not be seen as proof that the Benedictine *cursus* was used in England, as some commentators have argued.[110]

The evidence adduced so far points to the use of the sevenfold Roman Office *horarium* at Aldhelm's Malmesbury *c.*700, Wearmouth and Jarrow during Bede's lifetime, East Anglia under Ælfwald in the mid-eighth century, and the unknown house (possibly Crayke) described by Æthelwulf in the first quarter of the ninth century. If the testimony of Thomas of Elmham may be trusted, the full Roman *horarium* was also observed from a very early date at St Augustine's, Canterbury. Considered collectively, this evidence lends some support to the view that the Romanizing liturgical prescriptions put forward at the Council of *Clofesho* in 747 should be viewed as a consolidation and strengthening of a form of the Office liturgy first introduced by Roman missionaries and gradually accepted as normative throughout the English Church.

---

sull'alto medioevo 32 (Spoleto, 1986), pp. 643–88, at p. 659 n. 50; repr. as ch. II in Gneuss, *Books and Libraries*. The Old Hymnal was certainly known at Wearmouth and Jarrow; Bede's *De arte metrica* is one of the chief witnesses to the Old Hymnal's contents (Gneuss, *Hymnar und Hymnen*, pp. 13–25).

[109] See I. B. Milfull, *The Hymns of the Anglo-Saxon Church: A Study and Edition of the 'Durham Hymnal'*, Cambridge Studies in Anglo-Saxon England 17 (Cambridge, 1996), p. 5. The Office of Lérins is purportedly transmitted in the *Regula monachorum* of Aurelian of Arles (*c.*547). See Taft, *The Liturgy of the Hours in East and West*, pp. 103–4.

[110] C. Hohler, 'Theodore and the liturgy', in M. Lapidge (ed.), *Archbishop Theodore: Commemorative Studies on his Life and Influence*, Cambridge Studies in Anglo-Saxon England 11 (Cambridge, 1995), pp. 222–35, at p. 222.

Evidence for the Roman division of the psalter

As was seen in Chapter 2, the Roman Office is distinctive not just for its *horarium*, but for its unique distribution of the 150 psalms over the course of the week. This division of the psalter seems to have been altered in significant ways several times between the sixth and ninth centuries; but at each stage of its development, the distribution of psalms was unmistakeably 'Roman'. Strong evidence for the use of the Roman division of the psalter in England is found in three surviving manuscript psalters copied in England in the eighth century. These psalters are decorated in such a way that significant psalms within the Roman division receive special importance. As shall be demonstrated below, the decorations further point to an interim stage in the development of the Roman distribution, perhaps to be placed in the sixth century.

The manuscripts in question are the 'Vespasian Psalter', BL Cotton Vespasian A. I (St Augustine's, Canterbury, s. viii$^{2/4}$),[111] the 'Salaberga Psalter', Berlin, Staatsbibliothek Preussischer Kulturbesitz, Hamilton 553 (Northumbria, prob. Lindisfarne, s. viii^1),[112] and the 'Blickling Psalter', New York, Pierpont Morgan Library, M. 776 (Southern England?, s. viii med.).[113] Irish missionaries working in England used the *Gallicanum* from the first.[114] All three contain the version of the Latin psalms known since the ninth century as the *Psalterium Romanum*, a distinct textual tradition within the larger group of Latin biblical versions known as the *Vetus*

---

[111] Gneuss, *Handlist*, no. 381; *CLA* II, no. 193; Gamber, *CLLA*, no. 1612; Ker, *Catalogue*, no. 203. *The Vespasian Psalter: British Museum, Cotton Vespasian A.I*, facsimile ed. D. H. Wright, EEMF 14 (Copenhagen, 1967). *The Vespasian Psalter* (text), ed. S. M. Kuhn (Ann Arbor, MI, 1965). Students of Old English psalter glosses refer to it as 'MS A'. It is collated under siglum 'A' in *Le Psautier romain et les autres psautiers latins*, ed. R. Weber, Collectanea biblica latina 10 (Rome, 1953).

[112] Gneuss, *Handlist*, no. 790; *CLA* VIII, no. 1048; Gamber, *CLLA*. Collated under siglum 'H' in Weber's *Le Psautier romain*.

[113] Also known as the 'Morgan' or 'Lothian' Psalter. Gneuss, *Handlist*, no. 862; Ker, *Catalogue*, no. 287. Variously localized; southern England, s. viii, suggested by Lowe, *CLA* XI, no. 1661. Students of Old English psalter glosses call this 'MS M'. Collated by Weber under siglum 'N'. It has several lacunae, but agrees with the Roman divisions in all the expected places.

[114] A good text of the *Gallicanum* is preserved in the 'Cathach of St Columba', Dublin, Royal Irish Academy, *s.n.*, copied around the same time that St Aidan embarked on his mission of conversion in Northumbria in 635; *CLA* II, no. 266; cf. Bede, *Historia ecclesiastica*, III. 5, ed. Plummer I, 135–7 (see Plummer's notes II, 136). See also *The Vespasian Psalter*, ed. Wright, p. 45.

Latina.[115] This was the preferred version of the Latin psalter in England until the eleventh century, when contacts with Continental monasticism brought into favour the Vulgate text known as the *Psalterium Gallicanum*.[116] The Vespasian, Salaberga, and Blickling Psalters have been described as 'textually related',[117] which is true to the extent that they are included among the five oldest complete copies taken as the best textual witnesses of the *Romanum*.[118] But they do not appear to derive from a common exemplar, nor have they ever been arranged in a stemma.[119] Art-historical evidence suggests that the Vespasian Psalter was compiled in imitation of at least three different exemplars, at least one of them Italian (perhaps Thomas of Elmham's *Psalterium Augustini*).[120] The differences in wording between the *Romanum* and the *Gallicanum* are small but pervasive.[121] Bishop Wilfrid learned the *Gallicanum* by heart as a boy on Lindisfarne; he later had to unlearn the version preferred by his Irish superiors to learn the *Romanum* at Canterbury prior to his first pilgrimage to Rome in the company of Benedict Biscop.[122] This would have been

---

[115] For the various versions of the Latin psalter, see M. Gretsch, 'The Roman psalter, its Old English glosses and the English Benedictine Reform', in H. Gittos and M. B. Bedingfield (eds.), *The Liturgy of the Late Anglo-Saxon Church*, HBS Subsidia 5 (London, 2005), pp. 13–28, at pp. 15–18. See also *eadem*, *The Intellectual Foundations of the English Benedictine Reform*, Cambridge Studies in Anglo-Saxon England 25 (Cambridge, 1999), pp. 21–5. The *Romanum* is sometimes identified with a lost 'first revision' of the psalter made 'hastily' (*cursim*) by St Jerome: *Praefatio in libro psalmorum*, ed. R. Weber, et al., *Biblia sacra iuxta vulgata versionem*, 4th edn, ed. R. Gryson, et al. (Stuttgart, 1994), p. 767. This view is oft repeated despite challenges by D. de Bruyne, 'Le Problème du psautier romain', *Revue bénédictine* 42 (1930), 101–26, and A. Allgeier, 'Die erste Psalmenübersetzung des hl. Hieronymus und das Psalterium Romanum', *Biblica* 12 (1931), 447–82. The extensive literature on the Latin texts of the psalter is listed in Gretsch, *Intellectual Foundations*, pp. 23–4 n. 46.

[116] A revision made by St Jerome (389×392) of a *Vetus Latina* version of the psalms, based on comparison with the Greek Septuagint and Origen's Hexapla. A further Latin version of the psalter by Jerome, made from the original Hebrew (*Psalterium Hebraicum* or *iuxta Hebraeos*), was commonly copied in early medieval bibles but never used liturgically.

[117] Cubitt, *Anglo-Saxon Church Councils*, p. 141.

[118] The *famille ancienne* in Weber's critical edition (*Le Psautier romain*, p. ix). The other two are The 'Stuttgart Uncial Psalter', Stuttgart, Württembergische Landesbibliothek, Bibl. fol. 12a–c (English foundation on the Continent, s. viii); *CLA* IX, no. 1353; Gamber, *CLLA*, no. 1610; and the 'Montpellier Psalter', Montpellier, Faculté de Médecine H. 409 (Notre-Dame de Soissons, s. viii ex.); *CLA* VI, no. 795.

[119] *The Vespasian Psalter*, ed. Wright, p. 46.

[120] Lowe, *CLA* II, no. 193, regarding the David miniature on fol. 30v: 'manifestly taken from an older Italian model'.

[121] For examples, see Gretsch, 'The Roman psalter', p. 18.

[122] Stephen of Ripon, *Vita S. Wilfridi*, cc. 2–3, ed. Colgrave, *The Life of Bishop Wilfrid*,

essential if he was to participate in the Divine Office in Canterbury and later in Rome.[123] Stephen of Ripon's account of Wilfrid's death gives the words of the psalm being sung at the moment of death as *Emitte spiritum tuum*, the *Romanum* reading of Psalm 103:30 (the *Gallicanum* would have read *emittes*).[124]

The *Romanum* version of the psalter was the version on which Roman cantors based their musical compositions for the proper chants of the Mass and Office, whose texts were retained unchanged even after the *Gallicanum* superseded the *Romanum* as the preferred version of the psalter for liturgical use. The use of the *Romanum* version of the psalms in the Vespasian, Salaberga, and Blickling Psalters should therefore be seen against a Roman liturgical background.[125] This connection is strengthened by the decoration of these three manuscripts. The psalms as transmitted in the Hebrew bible were grouped into five 'books' in imitation of the Pentateuch, each book ending with a doxology.[126] Christian exegetes were more likely to see the psalter as divided into 'Three Fifties', and medieval illuminators frequently marked these 'scholarly' divisions with special decoration at Psalms 1, 51, and 101.[127] In some manuscripts, the scholarly threefold division is replaced, or supplemented, by a liturgical division. Psalters decorated according to the secular (Roman) *cursus*

---

pp. 6–9 (notes p. 152).

[123] É. Ó Carragáin, *The City of Rome and the World of Bede*, Jarrow Lecture (Jarrow, 1994), p. 6.

[124] Stephen of Ripon, *Vita S. Wilfridi*, c. 65, ed. and tr. B. Colgrave, *The Life of Bishop Wilfrid by Eddius Stephanus* (Cambridge, 1927), pp. 140–1.

[125] There are other eighth-century English manuscript witnesses to the *Romanum*: Cambridge, University Library, Ff. 5. 27, fol. i (Wearmouth-Jarrow, s. vii/viii), fragment of a *Psalterium Romanum* (Gneuss, *Handlist*, no. 9; *CLA* Supplement, no. 1682); Basel, Universitätsbibliothek, N. I. 2, fol. 1 (English, s. viii), fragment of a *Psalterium Romanum* (Gneuss, *Handlist*, no. 788; *CLA* VII, no. 850); Rome, Biblioteca Apostolica Vaticana, Pal. lat. 68, fols. 1–46 (Northumbria, s. viii), a 'Catena on the Psalms' (Gneuss, *Handlist*, no. 909; *CLA* I, no. 78).

[126] See *The New Oxford Annotated Bible with the Apocryphal/Deuterocanonical Books (New Revised Standard Version)*, ed. B. M. Metzger and R. E. Murphy (New York, 1994), p. 709 OT, note to Ps. 41:13; the doxologies, eventually read as part of the texts of the preceding psalms, are found at Pss. 40:14 (Hebrew numbering 41:13); 71:18–19 (72:18–19); 88:53 (89:52); 105:48 (106:48); and 150:6.

[127] This division is sometimes thought to have originated in the Irish ascetical practice of reciting the entire psalter in three sections of fifty psalms each (on the Irish 'Office of the Three Fifties', see Jeffery, 'Eastern and Western elements', pp. 102–8), but this threefold division is first mentioned by Cassiodorus in the sixth century, and seems to derive from scholarly, not liturgical, influences: Cassiodorus, *Expositio psalmorum*, praefatio, lines 32–8, ed. Adriaen I, 3–4; and see Gretsch, *Intellectual Foundations*, pp. 266–7.

usually have special initials or display lines to mark the first psalm sung every day at the Night Office (Psalms 1, 26, 38, 52, 68, 80, and 97) and also the first psalm of Vespers on Sunday (Psalm 109). Psalters decorated according to the monastic (Benedictine) *cursus* are usually decorated according to the same principle: the first psalm sung at the Night Office each day is marked (Psalms 20, 32, 45, 59, 73, 85, and 101). Sometimes the first psalm of the second nocturn is also marked (Psalms 26, 38, 52, 68, 79, 95, and 105), as may be the first psalm of Vespers for every day of the week (Psalms 109, 113, 129, 134, 138, 141, and 144).[128]

As may be seen in Table 2.1,[129] the decorations of the Vespasian Psalter clearly follow the Roman division, not the Benedictine. For the sake of comparison, the Benedictine decorations of the 'Bosworth Psalter', BL Add. 37517 (Canterbury, s. x^2), perhaps the oldest witness to the use of the Benedictine *cursus* in England, are shown in Table 2.2.[130] The Salaberga and Blickling Psalters have the same divisions as the Vespasian Psalter. Their geographical distribution – Vespasian at Canterbury, Salaberga in Northumbria (perhaps Lindisfarne), and Blickling probably somewhere in southern England – suggests that the Roman *cursus* was known in various places, lending plausibility to the requirement of the 747 Council of *Clofesho* that the same monastic psalmody was to be followed 'everywhere'.

The liturgical divisions found in the Vespasian and Salaberga Psalters differ in one important respect from the expected Roman pattern. In both psalters, Psalm 17 (*Diligam te domine*) receives special decoration. The Blickling Psalter has a lacuna at this point, so Ps. 17 may have been specially marked in it as well. In the Vespasian Psalter, the display line at Psalm 17 is given a medium level of decoration, found elsewhere in the manuscript only at the beginning of Psalm 118 (*Beati inmaculati*). The

---

[128] The various liturgical divisions of the psalter are discussed in K. Wildhagen, 'Studien zum *Psalterium Romanum* in England und seinen Glossierungen', in F. Holthausen and H. Spies (eds.), *Festschrift für Lorenz Morsbach*, Studien zur englischen Philologie 50 (Halle, 1913), pp. 418–72, at pp. 423–5; *The Salisbury Psalter*, ed. C. Sisam and K. Sisam, EETS 242 (London, 1949), p. 4 and n. 1. Hughes, *Medieval Manuscripts for Mass and Office*, pp. 225–9, presents a thorough treatment of later medieval choir psalters and their divisions. The Anglo-Saxon sources are considered in P. Pulsiano, 'Psalters', in Pfaff, *The Liturgical Books*, pp. 61–85, at pp. 72–3.

[129] See p. 16 above.

[130] See p. 18 above. Not every psalm of significance in the monastic *cursus* is marked in this example; the actual implementation of the liturgical system of decoration could be somewhat haphazard (Pulsiano, 'Psalters', p. 73). The Bosworth Psalter also marks, with even more impressive decoration, the threefold scholarly division of Psalms 1, 51, and 101.

twenty-two sections of Psalm 118 were distributed daily across Prime, Terce, Sext, and None in the Roman *cursus*, which explains why it received special decoration in the Vespasian Psalter. But as a number of scholars have observed, and as may be seen in Table 2.1, Psalm 17 has no obviously prominent place in the secular *cursus*, falling at the end of the second nocturn on Sundays.[131] David Wright supposed that Psalm 17 must have had a special role in the English form of the Office 'not known from other evidence'.[132] Catherine Cubitt was careful to note, however, that this emphasis on Psalm 17, along with certain other oddities in English liturgical sources of the eighth century, could equally 'stem from ancient or otherwise unknown Roman traditions'.[133] As was shown in Chapter 2,[134] the development of the *cursus* of psalmody in the Roman Office seems to have included a stage in which the psalms were divided between just two nocturns, with the second likely beginning with Psalm 17. No liturgical books preserving this early (and till now hypothetical) form have ever been identified. But it seems logical to conclude that this decoration indicates the subdivision of the psalmody of the Sunday Night Office into two nocturns, which would explain why Psalm 17 receives only a medium level of decoration in the Vespasian Psalter.

That the Vespasian Psalter was based on an earlier form of the Roman *cursus* than that familiar from other medieval Office books is also indicated by the biblical canticles appended to the text of the psalms.[135] Like most stand-alone psalter manuscripts intended for liturgical use, both the Vespasian and Salaberga Psalters have an appendix of Old and New Testament canticles (the Blickling Psalter has no such appendix). The content of the canticles section in most early psalters is fixed and stable for the first nine canticles, following exactly the pattern found in the Vespasian Psalter: the six variable Old Testament canticles sung on weekdays at Lauds, the *Benedicite* sung on Sundays, the gospel canticle of Lauds (*Benedictus*), and the gospel canticle of Vespers (*Magnificat*). The Salaberga Psalter places the *Benedicite* first in its series of canticles, not in the more usual seventh position. (This is perhaps further evidence of the mutual independence of these manuscripts.) The Salaberga Psalter breaks off

---

[131] Wildhagen, 'Studien zum Psalterium Romanum', p. 423; *The Vespasian Psalter*, ed. Wright, p. 47; Cubitt, *Anglo-Saxon Church Councils*, p. 141.
[132] *The Vespasian Psalter*, ed. Wright, p. 47.
[133] Cubitt, *Anglo-Saxon Church Councils*, p. 147 n. 105.
[134] See the section 'The Roman Office and its development', beginning on p. 30 above.
[135] See Pulsiano, 'Psalters', pp. 80–4.

after the variable Lauds canticles. The Vespasian Psalter continues with the invariable gospel canticles of Lauds (*Benedictus*) and Vespers (*Magnificat*). In most early psalters, the 'first series' of nine stable canticles is usually followed by a 'second series', unstable in selection and ordering of texts. The second series might include the *Nunc dimittis*, the *Te deum*, the *Gloria in excelsis*, and one or more creeds.[136] The fixed form of the 'first series' therefore lacks the invariable gospel canticle of Compline, the *Nunc dimittis* (or *Nunc dimitte* in the *Romanum* version). As David Wright has observed, the irregularity of the selection and ordering of the texts in the 'second series' found in psalter manuscripts 'seems to confirm that the early Roman usage included only the nine canticles found in the Vespasian Psalter, and so did not provide for Compline. That conclusion in turn suggests that the canticles in the Vespasian Psalter were copied from a relatively early Roman manuscript, probably the same one which served as the exemplar for the [text of the psalms themselves]'.[137] The omission of the *Nunc dimittis* from the canticles of the Vespasian Psalter therefore points to a stage in the development of the Roman *cursus*, already described in Chapter 2, when the *Nunc dimittis* was not yet sung at Compline. The liturgical divisions and sets of canticles in these manuscript psalters are therefore indicative of a form of the Roman *cursus* that may have been current in the lifetime of Augustine of Canterbury.

The three manuscript psalters described above provide the strongest concrete evidence for the use of the Roman *cursus* in early Anglo-Saxon England. Several references in literary sources to specific psalms and canticles being sung on particular days have also been linked to different *cursus* of the Office, all of them first noticed by Charles Plummer. The interest of these references to historians has been their use in clarifying the dates of events recorded by Bede. Unfortunately, two of these should probably be discounted since they do not describe the liturgy of the daily Office, but rather special vigils of psalmody at the deathbeds of Benedict Biscop and Bishop Wilfrid.[138] The one secure report of a psalm being

---

[136] Pulsiano, 'Psalters', p. 81. The identification of two different 'series' of canticles was made by Mearns, *The Canticles of the Christian Church*.

[137] *The Vespasian Psalter*, ed. Wright, pp. 52–3.

[138] Bede says that Benedict Biscop died as the monks of Wearmouth were chanting Psalm 82 (*Deus quis similis erit tibi*) on 12 January, without stating the year (Bede, *Historia abbatum*, § 14, ed. Plummer I, 378). Plummer observed that is assigned to Thursdays at the Night Office in the Benedictine *cursus* (it is sung on Fridays in the Roman), which might, he thought, tip the weight of evidence towards 691 (II, 364). But Bede says explicitly that as soon as it became clear that Biscop was soon to die the brethren gathered and began to sing

sung at a specific place in the ferial Office is found in Bede's account of the death of St Cuthbert, based on the testimony of an eye-witness:

> I immediately went out and announced his death to the brethren who had passed the night in watching and prayers, and were then by chance, according to the order of nocturnal praise, singing the fifty-ninth psalm, which begins 'O God, thou hast cast us off and broken us down; thou hast been angry and hast had compassion on us.' Without delay one of them ran out and lit two torches: and holding one in each hand, he went on to some higher ground to show the brethren who were in the Lindisfarne monastery that his holy soul had gone to be with the Lord: for this was the sign they had agreed upon amongst themselves to notify his most holy death. When the brother had seen it, who had been keeping watch and awaiting the hour of this event far away in the watch-tower of the island of Lindisfarne opposite, he quickly ran to the church where the whole assembly of the brethren were gathered together celebrating the solemnity of nocturnal psalmody; and it happened that they also, when he entered, were singing the above-mentioned psalm.[139]

---

the psalter in order (*psalterium ex ordine decantantes*), a common practice before specific death liturgies came into wider use (Bede, *Historia abbatum*, § 14, ed. Plummer I, 378). See the more precise death liturgies in D. Sicard, *La Liturgie de la mort dans l'église latine des origines à la réforme carolingienne*, Liturgiewissenschaftliche Quellen und Forschungen 63 (Münster, 1978), pp. 43–52. A second doubtful example, already alluded to above, is in Stephen of Ripon's account of Bishop Wilfrid's death, describing how his monks at Oundle gathered to 'sing psalms together day and night' (*illi vero in choro die noctuque indesinenter psalmos canentes*). According to Stephen, Wilfrid died on a Thursday (the year was 709); but his feast day was later observed on 12 October, a Saturday in 709 (*A Handbook of Dates for Students of British History*, ed. C. R. Cheney, new edn rev. M. Jones, Royal Historical Society Guides and Handbooks 4 (Cambridge, 2000), p. 175). Borrowing from Charles Plummer's notes on this event, Colgrave observed that Psalm 103 'occurs in the ordinary course of the Psalms for Saturday mattins in both the Roman and Benedictine breviaries' (*The Life of Bishop Wilfrid*, p. 186; cf. Plummer II, 328, commenting on Bede, *Historia ecclesiastica*, V. 19, ed. Plummer I, 330). But the brethren were singing the psalms *indesinenter*, which is not suggestive of the daily Office.

[139] Bede, *Vita prosaica S. Cuthberti*, c. 40, ed. and tr. Colgrave, *Two Lives of St Cuthbert*, pp. 142–307, at pp. 284–7: 'At ego statim egressus nuntiaui obitum eius fratribus, qui et ipsi noctem uigilando atque orando transegerant, et tunc forte sub ordine nocturnae laudis dicebant psalmum quinquagesimum nonum cuius initium est, *Deus reppulisti nos et destruxisti nos, iratus es, et misertus es nobis*. Nec mora currens unus ex eis accendit duas candelas, et utraque tenens manu ascendit eminentiorem locum ad ostendendum fratribus qui in Lindisfarnensi monasterio manebant, quia sancta illa anima iam migrasset ad Dominum. Tale

Although the brethren had 'passed the night in watching and prayers', Bede is careful to say that Psalm 59 was sung 'according to the order of nocturnal praise' (*sub ordine nocturnae laudis*). It was part of the appointed psalmody of that night. The miracle was not that the same psalm was being sung both by the monks on Lindisfarne and by those attending Cuthbert at his hermitage on Farne, but that the saint's death coincided with the singing on both islands of a psalm warning of impending tribulation, which, says Bede without elaboration, followed swiftly. Bede records elsewhere that Cuthbert died on 20 March 687, a Wednesday.[140] As Charles Plummer correctly noted, Psalm 59 'forms part of the office for Matins [i.e. the Night Office] on Wednesday in both the Roman and Benedictine breviaries'.[141] If he may be taken as reliable, Bede's eyewitness (Herefrith)[142] provides valuable evidence that in 687 the monks of Lindisfarne were using either a Roman or a Benedictine distribution of psalms. Psalm 59 occurs on Wednesday both in the medieval secular Office and in the reconstructed sixth-century Roman Office. Allowance must be made for a backward interpolation of later Lindisfarne customs, since Bede recorded the story only some time before 705.[143] Cuthbert had at

---

namque inter se signum sanctissimi eius obitus condixerant. Quod cum uideret frater qui in specula Lindisfarnensis insulae longe de contra euentus eiusdem peruigil expectauerat horam, cucurrit citius ad aecclesiam ubi collectus omnis fratrum coetus nocturnae psalmodiae solennis celebrabat. Contigitque ut ipsi quoque intrante illo praefatum canerent psalmum, quod superna dispensatione procuratum rerum exitus ostendit.' Translation of liturgical terms modified slightly from Colgrave's version.

[140] Bede, *Historia ecclesiastica*, IV. 27, ed. Plummer I, 275; *A Handbook of Dates*, ed. Cheney and Jones, p. 188.

[141] Plummer II, 270. Bertram Colgrave, paraphrasing Plummer, caused some confusion about this passage when he wrote that Psalm 59 'forms part of the office for mattins or lauds on Wednesday in both the Roman and Benedictine breviaries' (*Two Lives of St Cuthbert*, p. 357), translating *sub ordine nocturnae laudis* as 'according to the order of lauds'. Sarah Foot, relying on Colgrave's note, has in turn argued that to link this reference to Psalm 59 with either the Roman or the Benedictine *cursus* 'confuses the issue', since the office in question clearly took place in the middle of the night and not at dawn, when Lauds would be expected to be sung (*Monastic Life*, p. 200 and n. 69). There is no question that Bede is here describing the Night Office, not Lauds. In choosing his words, Bede may have had in mind the *Regula S. Benedicti*, which in one place refers to the Night Office specifically as *nocturna laus* (*RSB* 10, title: 'Qualiter aestatis tempore agatur nocturna laus').

[142] Bede, *Vita prosaica S. Cuthberti*, c. 37, ed. and tr. Colgrave, *Two Lives of St Cuthbert*, pp. 272–3.

[143] Psalm 59 is also mentioned in in connection with Cuthbert's death in Bede's *Vita metrica S. Cuthberti*, c. 37 (lines 786–812), ed. W. Jaager, *Bedas metrische Vita sancti Cuthberti*, Palaestra 198 (Leipzig, 1935), pp. 118–20, composed before 705. The *Vita prosaica* dates from around 720 (see Plummer I, pp. cxlvi and cxlviii).

one time rejected the Roman calculation of the date of Easter, along with 'other canonical rites according to the custom of the Roman and apostolic Church' (*ceterosque ritus canonicos iuxta Romanae et apostolicae ecclesiae consuetudinem recipere*),[144] choosing to leave Ripon when Wilfrid gained control of it. But he accepted the ruling in favour of Rome at the Synod of Whitby in 664, and, as has been seen, subsequently imposed a new rule of life at Lindisfarne.[145] Bede seems to assume that Cuthbert introduced a Roman tradition of monasticism to Lindisfarne, which the monks there at first vehemently resisted in favour of their *prisca consuetudo*.[146] Singers from Lindisfarne may have been among those who came from far afield to hear the teaching of John the Archcantor at Wearmouth between 678 and 680.

Bede mentions several canticles of the Office elsewhere in his writings: the *Magnificat* he places daily at Vespers;[147] the canticle of Habakkuk, *Domine audiui* (Hab. 3:1–19), was sung at Lauds on Fridays;[148] the canticle of Moses in Deuteronomy, *Audite caeli* (Deut. 32:1–43), was sung at Lauds on Saturdays.[149] The placement of all these canticles in the weekly *cursus* agrees with both the Roman and the Benedictine arrangements. That Bede has the Roman *cursus* in mind is probably indicated in his commentary on the canticle of Habakkuk, in which he says that the canticle is repeated every Friday in 'the custom of the holy and universal and apostolic Church' (*consuetudine sanctae et universalis et apostolicae Ecclesiae*). Quoting Wilfrid, Bede elsewhere equates the teachings of the *uniuersalis ecclesia* with those of the *sedes apostolica* (Rome).[150] If the teachings of John the Archcantor were still being followed at Wearmouth and Jarrow later in Bede's life, it is probably safe to assume that the distribution of psalms and canticles throughout the week followed the pattern used in St Peter's in Rome.

---

[144] Bede, *Historia ecclesiastica*, V. 19, ed. Plummer I, 325 (and see II, 193). Cf. Bede, *Vita prosaica S. Cuthberti*, c. 8, ed. and tr. Colgrave, *Two Lives of St Cuthbert*, pp. 180–1.

[145] See Plummer's reconstruction of the chronology of events from various sources under his note on 'Eata', *Venerabilis Bedae Opera historica* II, 192–3; cf. Colgrave, *Two Lives of St Cuthbert*, pp. 6–8.

[146] Bede, *Vita prosaica S. Cuthberti*, c. 16, ed. and tr. Colgrave, *Two Lives of St Cuthbert*, pp. 210–11.

[147] Bede, *Homeliarum euangelii libri II*, I. 4, ed. Hurst, pp. 21–31, at p. 30.

[148] Bede, *In canticum Abacuc*, praefatio, ed. J. E. Hudson, in *Bedae Venerabilis Opera exegetica*, IIB, CCSL 119B (Turnhout, 1973), pp. 381–409, at p. 381.

[149] Bede, *In Lucae evangelium expositio*, at Luke 4:16, ed. D. Hurst *Bedae Venerabilis Opera exegetica*, III, CCSL 120 (Turnhout, 1960), pp. 5–425, at p. 102.

[150] Bede, *Historia ecclesiastica*, III. 25, ed. Plummer I, 188.

Having adduced what evidence there is for the use in early Anglo-Saxon England of an archaic form of the Roman Office not otherwise directly attested, we must admit that the argument for this position risks becoming circular. It is perhaps too convenient that the reconstruction in Chapter 2 of the early development of the Roman Office anticipates evidence in the Vespasian Psalter for two nocturns in the Sunday Night Office (dividing at Ps. 17) and no *Nunc dimittis* at Compline. The evidence is open to other interpretations, such as one recently suggested by Richard Pfaff:

> James Mearns, in his old but still standard work on canticles in general, expressed puzzlement as to why the *Nunc dimittis* was not included [in the Vespasian Psalter]. The answer is clear and instructive: that since the canticle has never been part of the monastic form of compline, its absence here shows that the Canterbury monks' office c. 725 is the monastic, not the secular, one. That so apparently obvious a point is worth making is an indication of how rudimentary our knowledge still is.[151]

It will be clear from what has gone before that Pfaff's central contention cannot be correct. It is anachronistic to speak of a 'secular' *cursus* in the early eighth century, and in any case the Vespasian Psalter is decorated according to the Roman, not the Benedictine, divisions.[152] But this error points to an intriguing possibility: might the monks of Canterbury have altered the Roman *cursus* to make it agree more nearly with the requirements of the *Regula S. Benedicti*? To remove the *Nunc dimittis* from Compline would be the simplest step in that process. Squeezing the twenty-three psalms of the Sunday Night Office into two nocturns would leave room in the third for three 'monastic canticles', and the resulting distribution would perfectly satisfy the Rule's permissive prescriptions in this regard (though there are no 'monastic canticles' provided in the psalter itself). And as has already been suggested, the presence of hymns in the Vespasian Psalter could be seen as an answer to Benedict's requirement that *ambrosiana* be sung in the Office.

As has been seen, the Rule was studied and glossed at Canterbury

---

[151] R. W. Pfaff, *The Liturgy in Medieval England: A History* (Cambridge, 2009), p. 53 and n. 67.

[152] This is an unfortunate oversight on Pfaff's part given that he edited the volume containing Pulsiano's account of the surviving Anglo-Saxon psalters, including their liturgical divisions.

under Hadrian and Theodore. Moreover, although there is no evidence that they used the Benedictine *cursus* of psalmody, there is evidence that early Anglo-Saxon monks studied the Rule's liturgical prescriptions. When Ceolfrith ordered a reduction in the singing of antiphons after the plague at Jarrow, he acted in accordance with the Rule's provisions for small communities.[153] Bede, in his commentary on Nehemiah 9:3, which describes how the Israelites listened to the reading of the Law four times in the day and four times in the night, compares this practice to the daily Office *horarium* and makes a verbal allusion to the Rule's requirement that the short lesson (*capitulum*) at Lauds be recited by heart (*ex corde*):[154]

> For who would not be amazed that such a great people had such extraordinary concern for devotion that four times a day – that is, at the first hour of the morning, the third, the sixth and the ninth, when time was to be made for prayer and psalmody – they gave themselves over to listening to the divine law in order to renew their mind in God and come back purer and more devout for imploring his mercy; but also four times a night they would shake off their sleepiness and get up in order to confess their sins and to beg pardon. From this example, I think, a most beautiful custom has developed in the Church, namely that through each hour of daily psalmody (*per singulas diurnae psalmodiae horas*) a passage from the Old or New Testament is recited by heart (*ex corde*) for all to hear, and thus strengthened by the words of the apostles or the prophets, they bend their knees to perseverance in prayer, but also at night (*horis nocturnis*), when people cease from the labours of doing good works, they turn willing ears to listen to divine readings.[155]

---

[153] See above, p. 93 n. 53.

[154] *RSB* 12:4; cf. 13:11 'memoriter'.

[155] Bede, *In Ezram et Neemiam libri III*, ed. D. Hurst, *Bedae Venerabilis Opera exegetica*, IIA, CCSL 119A (Turnhout, 1969), pp. 235–392, at p. 372: 'Quis enim non miretur tantum populum tam eximiam habuisse curam pietatis ut quater in die, hoc est primo mane tertia hora sexta et nona quibus orationi siue psalmodiae uacandum erat, auditui se legis diuinae contraderent quo innouata in Deum mente purior ac deuotior ad deprecandum eius misericordiam rediret sed et in nocte quater excusso torpore somni ad confitenda peccata sua et postulandam ueniam exsurgerent. Quo exemplo reor in ecclesia morem inoleuisse pulcherrimam ut per singulas diurnae psalmodiae horas lectio una de ueteri siue nouo testamento cunctis audientibus ex corde dicatur et sic apostolicis siue propheticis confirmati uerbis ad instantiam orationis genua flectant sed et horis nocturnis cum a laboribus cessatur

Bede's reading of the biblical passage is obviously informed by his experience of the daily Office, and his reference to the recitation of lessons *ex corde* is almost certainly an allusion to the Rule.[156]

But even this evidence for attention to the Rule's directions regarding the manner in which the Office is to be performed does not imply that the Office itself conformed to the prescriptions of the Rule. If anything, the passage from Bede just quoted seems to imply the opposite. Bede mentions the recitation of lessons *ex corde* only during the daytime offices (*per singulas diurnae psalmodiae horas*). At night, Bede envisages lengthier 'divine readings' (*lectiones diuinae*). The Rule, on the other hand, requires a short lesson also to be recited by heart every night in the second nocturn of the Night Office. Furthermore, as in his description of the canticles at Lauds, Bede claims to be describing the custom of 'the Church'.

In another scenario, the Vespasian Psalter would transmit the liturgical arrangements of a Roman monastery's attempt to align its liturgical practices more closely with the Office laid down in the *Regula S. Benedicti*. As Constant Mews has recently argued, the Rule may have been more influential in seventh-century Rome than has previously been allowed.[157] It is certainly important to bear in mind that Rome was not a liturgical monolith at any time during the early Middle Ages.

The main objection to this speculation, apart from the evidence marshalled in Chapter 2, is that the fundamental similarities between the Roman and Benedictine *cursus* arise precisely because Benedict drew on contemporary Roman customs. When evidence of authentic early Roman liturgical practices has survived, despite the pervasive and suffocating influence of the late medieval curial breviary, it has often revealed that what previously seemed an original development in the Benedictine liturgical code is in fact a faithful witness to an archaic Roman custom.[158] It therefore seems more likely that the Vespasian Psalter and its relatives reflect something of the Roman *cursus* as it may have been known to Benedict, rather than the influence of the Benedictine *cursus* on Rome.

---

operum liberas auditui lectionum diuinarum aures accommodent.' Translation: S. DeGregorio, *Bede: On Ezra and Nehemiah*, Translated Texts for Historians 47 (Liverpool, 2006), pp. 200–1.
[156] S. DeGregorio, 'Bede, the monk, as exegete: Evidence from the commentary on Ezra-Nehemiah', *Revue bénédictine* 115 (2005), 343–69, at 357–9.
[157] C. Mews, 'Gregory the Great, the Rule of Benedict and Roman liturgy: The evolution of a legend', *Journal of Medieval History* 37 (2011), 125–44, at pp. 138–40.
[158] Batiffol, *History of of the Roman Breviary*, p. 74 and n. 4.

The Ushaw lectionary fragment

Apart from the early psalters with liturgical divisions, only one fragment has ever been identified that may have belonged to a book used in the actual performance of the early Anglo-Saxon Office liturgy. Within the binding of an early printed book in the library of Ushaw College, near Durham, Ian Doyle discovered part of a single bifolium written in insular half-uncial script of a style comparable to that seen in Lindisfarne manuscripts of the eighth century.[159] Only the bottom portion of the bifolium survives. On the recto and verso sides of the first leaf are written passages from Isaiah (41:28–9; 42:3–4, 7; and 51:9–10) apparently arranged as liturgical readings. The first two portions may be part of a single reading. The third portion begins with large initial, apparently the beginning of a separate reading. The second leaf has passages from two sermons of St Augustine: *Sermones* 194 and 369.[160]

Isaiah is the biblical book *par excellence* for Advent and Christmas, and both sermons are for Christmas Day. Doyle therefore suggests that these readings were intended to be used together in the Night Office of Christmas Day. Based on the layout of the text, Doyle proposes several possible arrangements of readings, including a pattern of three readings per nocturn, with room for hypothetical responsory chants between the readings.[161] Doyle suggests that the readings from Isaiah would have been used in the first nocturn, the sermons in the second, perhaps because in later medieval secular and monastic breviaries the first nocturn has

---

[159] The manuscript is now catalogued as Ushaw, St Cuthbert's College 44, but it is shelved in a guardbook next to the printed book from which it was removed, at XVIII. B. 1. 2(6). It is no. 757 in Gneuss's *Handlist*. See A. I. Doyle, 'A fragment of an eighth-century Northumbrian Office book', in M. Korhammer (ed.), *Words, Texts and Manuscripts: Studies in Anglo-Saxon Culture Presented to Helmut Gneuss on the Occasion of his Sixty-fifth Birthday* (Cambridge, 1992), pp. 11–27.

[160] *Sermo* 194, *PL* XXXVIII, 1015–17; Doyle notes that the authenticity of the attribution to Augustine was questioned, the true author suggested as the Frankish abbot and exegete Ambrose Autpert (d.784) in E. Dekkers, *Clavis patrum Latinorum*, 2nd edn, CCSL *extra seriem* (Turnhout, 1961), p. 61. The third edition of *CPL* (Steenbrugge, 1995) lists the sermon among Augustine's genuine works, with the exception of an interpolated passage printed in the notes in *PL*. See J. Machielsen, *Clavis patristica pseudepigraphorum medii aevi* IA, CCSL *extra seriem* (Turnhout, 1990), pp. 90–1 (no. 581). If Ambrose Autpert were the author of *Sermo* 194, the Ushaw fragment could probably not be dated earlier than the closing years of the eighth century; and if the fragment really was copied in Northern England, as seems probable, then Autpert's works would have to have been available there during his lifetime or shortly after his death. *Sermo* 369, *PL* XXXVIII, 1655–7.

[161] Doyle, 'A fragment', pp. 16–17.

scriptural readings, the second nocturn patristic or hagiographical readings, and the third nocturn one or more homilies on the Gospel pericope of the Mass for the day.[162]

As Doyle points out, the readings from Isaiah do not correspond to any surviving scheme of lections for Christmas, including those of the Roman Office recorded in *Ordo Romanus XIIIA* (usage of the Lateran Basilica, s. viii[1]) and early Office lectionaries:[163]

	Ushaw	Roman
I.	?	9:1 ff.
II.	[...] 41:28–42:7 [...]	40:1 ff.
III.	51:9 ff.	52:1 ff.

Doyle suggests that the Ushaw readings might have been borrowed from another tradition or might have been compiled according to a purely local custom, while the sermons may derive from an authentic Roman collection.

It is nevertheless possible that the biblical readings in the Ushaw fragment were part of the Roman tradition as it was known to the copyist of this lectionary. The last reading from Isaiah in the fragment begins 'Consurge, consurge induere fortitudinem brachium Domini' (Isa. 51:9), which is almost identical to the third Roman reading, 'Consurge, consurge induere fortitudine tua Sion' (Isa. 52:1). *Ordo Romanus XIIIA* gives only

---

[162] Doyle, 'A fragment', p. 13. Harper, *The Forms and Orders of Western Liturgy*, p. 81. The basic difference between sermons and homilies is that a sermon (*sermo*) expounds the significance and meaning of a feast day or season, without being limited to a specific scriptural text; a homily (*homelia*) is an exposition and interpretation of a Gospel reading (Martimort, *Les Lectures liturgiques et leurs livres*, pp. 80–1). The two non-biblical texts preserved in the Ushaw fragment are *sermones* in this technical sense, and so would appear in the second nocturn of a 'standard' festal Night Office in later medieval books. Compare the Night Office of Christmas in the pre-Vatican II Roman breviary, where the lessons of the first nocturn are from Isaiah, those of the second from a *sermo* of Leo the Great on the significance of Christmas, and the those of the third from three different 'homilies' by Gregory I, Ambrose (in fact from his commentary on Luke), and Augustine: see *The Liber Usualis with Introduction and Rubrics in English*, ed. the Benedictines of Solesmes (Tournai, 1963), pp. 375–7, 381–4, 389–91.

[163] *Ordo Romanus XIIIA*, § 13, ed. Andrieu II, 485–6. The same readings are indicated in the homiliary of Alan of Farfa, from which, in conjunction with several other medieval lectionaries, certain aspects of the lectionary of St Peter's in Rome may be reconstructed (Martimort, *Les Lectures liturgiques*, pp. 83–6). The same readings remained in continual use during subsequent centuries, and were incorporated in the Tridentine breviary (*Breviarium Romanum: Editio princeps*, pp. 183–7). *Ordo Romanus XIV*, recording the practice of St Peter's at the Vatican, gives only the titles of the books to be read on various occasions, and so is of no help here (ed. Andrieu III, 39–41).

the cue 'Consurge, consurge, induere fortitudine' which could mislead someone without direct experience of the Roman liturgy.[164] As for the other portions of Isaiah, it is not impossible that they were part of a very long lesson that began at 40:1 (*Consolamini consolamini*), since according to *Ordo Romanus XIIIA* each lesson ended only at the discretion of the prior. It is also possible, however, that the Ushaw fragment might originally have given an edited selection of verses from Isaiah 40:1 onwards, a practice not uncommon in the scriptural readings of later breviaries. One of the sermons in the fragment seems to have been edited in this way.[165]

The Ushaw fragment might instead represent a form of the Christmas Night Office pre-dating the form represented in *Ordo Romanus XIIIA* and in Frankish books from the ninth century onwards, which was in fact the product of a combination of two separate vigil offices that were sung on Christmas Eve in Rome: one celebrated by the pope in the Basilica of St Mary Major, and a second celebrated by the clergy in St Peter's. This is witnessed by Amalarius of Metz,[166] and perhaps in an even more ancient state in *Ordo Romanus XII* (s. viii$^{4/4}$):

> This is how the vigils of the Lord's Nativity are performed at St Mary's. At the beginning, the invitatory is not said, but [the antiphon] *Dominus dixit ad me* is begun immediately, with the rest as it is written down. The responsories are: ℟. *Ecce iam veniet hora*; ℟. *Hodie nobis caelorum*; ℟. *Beata Dei genitrix*; ℟. *Hic qui advenit*; ℟. *O regem caeli*; ℟. *Quem vidistis pastores*; ℟. *Haec est dies*; ℟. *Continet in gremio*. At Lauds, it is as in the *capitulare*. Then, at midnight, after Mass is ended, Nocturns follows. At the beginning, [the versicle] *Domine labia mea aperies*. [The

---

[164] *Ordo Romanus XIIIA*, § 13, ed. Andrieu II, 485–6: 'In vigilia natalis domini legunt primum de Esaia lectiones tres, id est, prima lectio sic continet in capite: *Primo tempore adleviata est terra Zabulon*. Secunda lectio sic continet in capite: *Consolamini, consolamini*. Tertia lectio sic continet in capite: *Consurge, consurge, induere fortitudine*. Et istae tres lectiones non terminantur, sed sicut voluerit prior cui proprium est. Deinde leguntur sermones vel omelias catholicorum patrum ad ipsum diem pertinentes, id est Agustini, Gregorii, Hieronimi, Ambrosi vel ceterorum.' ('In the vigil of the Lord's Nativity, they first read three lessons from Isaiah, that is, the first lesson has as its first line: *Primo tempore adleviata est terra Zabulon*. The second lesson has as its first line: *Consolamini, consolamini*. The third lesson has as its first line: *Consurge, consurge, induere fortitudine*. And these three lessons are not ended until the prior wishes, for this is his prerogative. Then are read sermons or homilies of the Catholic Fathers appropriate to the selfsame day, that is of Augustine, of Gregory, of Jerome, of Ambrose, or of others.')

[165] Doyle, 'A fragment', pp. 14–15.

[166] Reported by Amalarius, *Liber de ordine antiphonarii*, c. 15, ed. Hanssens III, 140.

invitatory antiphon] with the *Venite* is *Christus natus est nobis.* Then the twelve psalms of the weekday, nine lessons, and eight responsories of the Lord's Nativity.[167]

The Franks conflated the two vigils into a single Night Office.[168] The double vigil survived in Rome at least into the twelfth century, when it was described in an *Ordo officiorum* of the Lateran Basilica, including the following scheme of readings:[169]

Vigil I

III lectiones de Isaia *Primo tempore* [9:1 ff.], *Consolamini* [40:1 ff.], *Consurge consurge* [52:1 ff.].

Tres de sermonibus sanctorum patrum.

Tres de omeliis trium euangeliorum, prima Gregorii [on Luke 2:1 ff.], secunda Ambrosii [on Luke 2:15 ff.], tertia Augustini [on John 1:1 ff.].

Vigil II

Sex lectiones de sermonibus sanctorum patrum legantur, III de omelia Origenis.

It is striking that the patristic readings of the second nocturns in both vigils are still left unspecified.[170] The second vigil has no biblical lessons at all. Amalarius and *Ordo Romanus XII* say nothing about the readings of the Christmas double vigil. It is not at all clear that codified schemes of specific Night Office readings for feasts days even existed in Rome in the

---

[167] *Ordo Romanus XII*, § 4, ed. Andrieu II, 460–1: 'Item in natale domini, ad vigilias, sicut agitur ad sanctam Mariam. In primo non dicitur invitatorium, sed statim incipitur *Dominus dixit ad me*, et reliqua, sicut scriptae sunt. Reponsoria: ℟. *Ecce iam veniet hora*; ℟. *Hodie nobis caelorum*; ℟. *Beata Dei genitrix*; ℟. *Hic qui advenit*; ℟. *O regem caeli*; ℟. *Quem vidistis pastores*; ℟. *Haec est dies*; ℟. *Continet in gremio*. In matutinis sicut in capitulare. Item in media nocte, post finitam missam, ad nocturnos. In primo *Domine labia mea aperies*. In *Venite*, *Christus natus est nobis*. Psalmos cottidianos XII, lectiones VIIII, responsoria VIII de natale domini.'

[168] As Raymond Le Roux has shown, the chants for the two separate vigils were later distributed between a single Night Office of Christmas and the Night Office for the Octave of Christmas (the feast of the Circumcision): 'Aux origines de l'office festif', pp. 67–9.

[169] Bernhardus cardinalis, *Ordo officiorum ecclesiae Lateranensis*, §§ 25 and 27, ed. L. Fischer, Historische Forschungen und Quellen 2–3 (Munich, 1916), pp. 10–11.

[170] For any given Sunday or feast, Bernhardus almost invariably specifies a particular homily or set of homilies for the third nocturn, giving the name of the author and the first words of the homily itself or of the Gospel pericope on which it is based.

eighth century.[171] There is therefore no way to judge whether the Ushaw fragment does or does not conform to 'Roman' practice as it may have been known in eighth-century Northumbria.

The flexibility of the early medieval Office with regard to the lections of the Night Office makes the Ushaw fragment all the more remarkable as a book type. In *Ordo Romanus XIIIA*, even where a specific cue for a lesson is given, its duration is still within the discretion of the prior. In the Ushaw fragment, the exact content and length of the biblical lections seems to have been pre-determined, perhaps with editorial abridgements.[172] Even straightforward Office lectionaries giving specific readings for the major feasts of the Temporale and Sanctorale, let alone for ferial days, are extremely rare for this early period, since the liturgy seems not yet to have required them. It is hard to think where the community that used the Ushaw lectionary would have found a model for this kind of book.

Among the most pressing reasons for making such a book would be a small community's lack of copies of the works of the various 'Catholic Fathers' that were read, in addition to the scriptures, during the Night Office throughout the year.[173] Among the writings of the Fathers that would be difficult to obtain, Bede specifically mentions the works of St Augustine. Unlike the homiliary of Paul the Deacon, compiled at Charlemagne's request to replace inaccurate or corrupt texts,[174] a book like the Ushaw lectionary might been designed to meet economic and practical necessities.

---

[171] *Ordo Romanus XIIIA* gives incipits of readings only for Maundy Thursday and Good Friday (both apparently Frankish interpolations), Christmas (repeated on the octave), Epiphany (repeated on the octave), and St Peter. The number of specifically indicated proper biblical lessons was considerably augmented in *Ordo Romanus XIIIB*, dating from around the turn of the ninth century (ed. Andrieu II, 499–506). Such augmentation would be essential for communities farther afield seeking to imitate Rome.

[172] Doyle's suggestion that each lesson may have been followed by a responsory chant text is tantalizing but highly improbable. The earliest examples of 'breviaries', in which readings, prayers, and chants are arranged in their liturgical order within a single volume, post-date this fragment by as much as a century. And even the earliest breviary fragments may simply be survivals from *libelli* used in votive offices, like the Office of the Dead and the annual Dedication festival of a church. See Gamber, *CLLA*, nos. 1680–94.

[173] On the reading of the Fathers in the Divine Office, A. Martimort, *Les Lectures liturgiques et leurs livres*, pp. 71–94; and J. D. Billett, '*Sermones ad diem pertinentes*: Sermons and homilies in the liturgy of the Divine Office', in M. Diesenberger, Y. Hen, and M. Pollheimer (eds.), '*Sermo doctorum*': *Compilers, Preachers, and their Audiences in the Early Medieval West*, SERMO 9 (Turnhout, 2013), pp. 339–73.

[174] Charlemagne, *Epistola generalis*, ed. Boretius.

Chant texts in Alcuin's De laude Dei

Alcuin's devotional *florilegium De laude Dei*, apparently compiled before 786, includes a section called *De antiphonario*, in which some ninety-three chant texts provide the only surviving witness to the ancient antiphoner of York, and indeed to any English antiphoner.[175] This selection 'carries back the history of some "chants" a full century and provides a documentation, albeit highly selective, for the liturgy of a northern European church which is without parallel in the pre-Carolingian period',[176] and provides valuable evidence for the observance of the complete cycle of the daily Office by the secular clergy of the cathedral at York.[177] That the repertory represented in the *De laude Dei* may have been known more widely in England is suggested by the seventh 'Old English Advent Lyric' (in the poem dubbed *Christ I* by modern critics), which is based on a 'Great O' Advent antiphon *O Ioseph quomodo credidisti*, found uniquely in the *De laude Dei* but evidently known to the poet from a different source.[178] Susan Rankin argues persuasively that Alcuin had to

---

[175] Two manuscripts are known to transmit the *De laude Dei*: El Escorial, Real biblioteca, B. IV. 17, fols. 93–108 (s. ix), and Bamberg, Staatsbibliothek, Msc. Patr. 17/B. II. 10, fols. 133–62 (s. xi in.). The chant texts have been edited, from the Bamberg manuscript, in R. Constantinescu, 'Alcuin et les "libelli precum" de l'époque carolingienne', *Revue d'histoire et de la spiritualité* 50 (1974), 17–56, at pp. 38–50. R.-J. Hesbert published an account of a fragment of a palimpsest antiphoner from early England: 'Un curieux antiphonaire palimpseste de l'Office: Rouen, A. 292', *Revue bénédictine* 64 (1954), 28–45. It has since been argued to be of French origin and not a palimpsest at all: K. D. Hartzell, 'An English antiphoner of the ninth century?', *Revue bénédictine* 90 (1980), 234–48.

[176] D. A. Bullough, 'Alcuin and the Kingdom of Heaven: Liturgy, theology, and the Carolingian age', in his *Carolingian Renewal*, pp. 161–240, at p. 164; originally published in U.-R. Blumenthal (ed.), *Carolingian Essays: Andrew W. Mellon Lectures in Early Christian Studies* (Washington, DC, 1983), pp. 1–69.

[177] Bullough, 'Alcuin and the Kingdom of Heaven', p. 164. The only other evidence for the Office at York is found in the anonymous *Vita Alcuini*, composed between 823 and 829 probably at Ferrières, where Alcuin had been lay abbot. It describes Alcuin's boyhood attendance at the daily hours, mentioning his rare appearances at the Night Office (*Vita Alcuini*, § 2, ed. W. Arndt, in *Vitae aliaeque historiae minores*, MGH SS 15.1 (Hanover, 1887), pp. 184–97, at p. 185). Lauds (*matutinale officium*), Terce, Sext, None, and Vespers are also mentioned at various points, though not all specifically in passages describing Alcuin's life at York. One such passage does, however, make clear reference to Compline, and Alcuin's ascetic private prayers offered daily before this hour (§ 5, ed. Arndt, p. 187).

[178] *Christ I* is preserved in the 'Exeter Book': Exeter, Cathedral Library, 3501, fols. 8–14 (s. x^2), given to Exeter Cathedral by Bishop Leofric (1050–72); *The Exeter Book of Old English Poetry*, facsimile and commentary ed. R. W. Chambers, M. Förster, and R. Flower (London, 1933). *O Ioseph* is one of ten 'Great O' antiphons listed by Alcuin, ed. Constan-

hand a copy of York's antiphoner when making this selection, since the texts, which follow the order of the liturgical year, begin with Advent, as in the earliest antiphoners (sacramentaries begin with Christmas).[179]

The first editor of the chants in the *De antiphonario*, Radu Constantinescu, made a beguiling case for John the Archcantor as the compiler of the antiphoner that was Alcuin's source.[180] Alcuin writes of the tenure of Bishop Bosa (678–86 and 691–705) in terms compatible with the introduction of a new musical-liturgical practice at York during or after John's sojourn at Wearmouth,[181] though he also credits Archbishop Ecgberht (732–66) with training liturgical singers.[182] The anonymous *Vita Alcuini* says that Alcuin learned to recite the psalter from memory under Ecgberht's instruction.[183] But as Susan Rankin has shown in her detailed study of the chants in the *De laude Dei* for Advent, Christmas, and Epiphany, the York antiphoner seems to have had an eclectic mix of chants from non-Roman as well as Roman traditions, with parallels in the strictly 'Roman' chants mentioned in the writings of Amalarius of Metz, in the Romano-Frankish 'Gregorian' repertory (including the well-known list of Advent chant incipits in Lucca, Biblioteca Capitolare, 490, fols. 30r–31r, copied *c.*796),[184] in the one surviving Mozarabic antiphoner,[185] in the Milanese repertory,[186] and in two bifolia from what appears to be an antiphoner, copied in a ninth-century Irish hand, for the

---

tinescu, 'Alcuin et les "libelli precum" ', p. 41 (no. 27), also transcribed in Rankin, 'The liturgical background', p. 340. The poet of the lyrics knew texts absent from the *De laude Dei*, and used a source textually distinct from Alcuin's *florilegium* (Rankin, 'The liturgical background', p. 333).

[179] S. Rankin, 'Beyond the boundaries of Roman-Frankish chant: Alcuin's *De laude Dei* and other early medieval sources of Office chants', in M. Cuthbert, S. Gallagher, and C. Wolff (eds.), *City, Chant, and the Topography of Early Music: Essays in Honor of Thomas Forrest Kelly* (Cambridge, MA, 2013), pp. 229–62, at pp. 232–3.

[180] Constantinescu, 'Alcuin et les "libelli precum" ', pp. 54–5.

[181] See Alcuin, *Versus de patribus*, lines 857–70 (quoted above, p. 88), where the main emphasis is obviously liturgical.

[182] Alcuin, *Versus de patribus*, lines 1271–2, ed. and tr. Godman, pp. 100–1: 'Davidisque alios fecit concinnere canna, | qui Domino resonent modulatis vocibus hymnos.' ('Others he taught to sing with David's pipe and resound hymns to God in well-trained voices.')

[183] *Vita Alcuini*, § 4, ed. Arndt, p. 186.

[184] Edited with a facsimile in J. Froger, 'Le fragment de Lucques (fin du VIIIe siècle)', *Etudes grégoriennes* 18 (1979), 145–55.

[185] León, Archivo de la Catedral, 8 (s. x), ed. L. Brou and J. Vives, *Antifonario visigotico mozarabe de la Catedral de León*, 2 vols. (Barcelona, 1953–9).

[186] BL Add. 34209 (s. xii); facsimile and edition: *Antiphonarium ambrosianum du Musée britannique (XII siècle): Codex Additional 34209*, 2 vols., Paléographie musicale 5–6 (Solesmes, 1896–1900).

Hiberno-Gallican liturgy of a Continental church, containing chants for Advent, Christmas, Epiphany, Purification, and Lent (BnF n. a. lat. 1628, fols. 1–4).[187] In the absence of early antiphoners from Rome itself, the Romano-Frankish 'Gregorian' repertory is the only substantial body of chant that can claim to represent Roman practice. According to Rankin's analysis, only about half of the chants in the *De laude Dei* agree with the Gregorian. This is the same degree of relatedness shown between the Romano-Frankish repertory and BnF n. a. lat. 1628. The York antiphoner known to Alcuin could therefore have been, in a sense, 'Gallican'. But the *De laude Dei*'s agreements with the Gregorian corpus are more frequent in the chants for Christmas and Epiphany than in those for Advent. The liturgy of Advent developed rather late compared to other seasons, and Rankin makes the provocative suggestion that the York antiphoner may have descended in part from Roman books in which the chants for Advent had not reached their eventual stable form.

Some of the non-Gregorian chants in the *De laude Dei*, far from being 'Gallican', may well have had an exclusively Roman pedigree. The responsory *Credimus saluatorem* occurs in the *De laude Dei*,[188] and in BnF n. a. lat. 1628,[189] and is used as an introit in the Milanese liturgy of the Mass.[190] It is not mentioned by Amalarius, and it is completely absent from the Gregorian repertory.[191] The same text also appears in a source brought to light by Peter Jeffery.[192] Sankt Paul im Lavanttal (Kärnten, Austria), Stiftsbibliothek, 2/1, fol. 1v, is written in an Insular minuscule hand of the eighth century. The fragment contains what is apparently a previously unknown *Ordo Romanus* for the readings at the Night Office during the course of the year, with more specific directions given for the

---

[187] The text is edited in G. Morin, 'Fragments inédits et jusqu'à présent uniques d'antiphonaire gallican', *Revue bénédictine* 52 (1905), 329–56. Peter Jeffery has suggested that the fragment shows signs of an interaction with the Roman Office ('Eastern and Western elements', pp. 130–2).

[188] Constantinescu, 'Alcuin et les "libelli precum"', p. 39, no. 8.

[189] Morin, 'Fragments inédits', p. 343 lines 30–4.

[190] *Ingressa* for Dominica VI de Aduentu: *Missale Ambrosianum duplex (Proprium de Tempore): Editiones Puteobonellianae et typica (1751–1902)*, ed. A. M. Ceriani, A. Ratti, and M. Magistretti, Monumenta sacra et profana 4 (Milan, 1913), p. 29.

[191] Not merely from the twelve sources edited in the first four volumes of R.-J. Hesbert's *Corpus antiphonalium officii*, but also from the 800 Advent *ordines* tabulated in the fifth and sixth volumes.

[192] Prof. Jeffery presented his findings in papers read at the 2003 meeting of the American Musicological Society in Houston, TX, and at the 2006 International Medieval Congress in Leeds, where I had the pleasure of presenting a paper alongside him.

chants and readings of the *Triduum sacrum*, which, Jeffery argues from significant textual parallels, is a predecessor to *Ordines Romani XXXA* and *XXXB* (Jeffery dubs it '*Ordo Romanus XXX*'). This *Ordo* is followed by three complete chant texts apparently unrelated to the preceding material, the third being *Credimus saluatorem*:[193]

> Credimus saluatorem nostrum uenturum esse cum gloria et uos estote parati suscipere regnum Dei.[194]
>
> (We believe that our saviour shall come in glory; be you also ready to receive the kingdom of God.)

The chant expresses the familiar Advent theme of readiness for the Second Coming. Apart from scriptural quotations and allusions,[195] the opening of the chant is obviously based on the Nicene Creed in its original conciliar form (*credimus* instead of *credo*).[196] *Credimus saluatorem* is absent from the Gregorian corpus, but like other material in the Sankt Paul fragment it may be a genuine Roman composition.

A specific seventh-century Roman context can be established for the non-Gregorian *De laude Dei* chant *Laudate caeli*:

> Laudate celi et exultet terra · quia homoocυων patri · ante secula natus · Idem ipse ad nos · ex uirginali utero · homo natus aduenit · Ex nostra natura passibilis et in sua · miraculis · coruscabat · et refulsit deus.[197]

---

[193] The first and third chants are *Laudate caeli* and *Credimus saluatorem*, discussed at length below. The second is is *Coeperunt eum omnes turbae*, familiar from the Palm Sunday Office in the Gregorian repertory. See Hesbert, *CAO* III, no. 1840.

[194] The text is identical in the Bamberg and Escorial manuscripts of the *De laude Dei*. In BnF n. a. lat. 1628 (fol. 2v), the same text (but with *parati* spelt *parete*) is preceded by a verse: *Vox clamantis in diserto parate uiam domini rectas facite semitas dei nostri* (Morin, 'Fragments inédits', p. 343).

[195] Luke 12:40 or Matt. 14:44 (*et uos estote parati*). *Suscipere regnum dei* is also reminiscent of Mark 10:15 (*receperit regnum Dei*), though this is from a rather different context.

[196] The summaries of belief promulgated (in Greek) by the great Ecumenical Councils were always phrased in the plural, and this is how they appear in the the Latin translations made by Hilary of Poitiers (d. *c*.368), *Liber de synodis*, c. 84, *PL* X, 536; and Dionysius Exiguus (d. *ante* 544), *Codex canonum ecclesiasticarum*, *PL* LXVII, 186 and 227. The Creed was not recited liturgically in the West before the reforms of the Carolingians, and not in Rome before 1014: Cross and Livingstone, *The Oxford Dictionary of the Christian Church*, under 'creed'; and W. Smith and S. Cheetham (eds.), *A Dictionary of Christian Antiquities*, 2 vols. (London, 1875–80) I, 492, §§ 15–16. See also p. 56 n. 147 above.

[197] This is the text of the Escorial manuscript. The Bamberg manuscript gives a shortened text: 'Ex nostra natura passibilis et in sua miraculis choruscabat et refulsit Deus' (Constan-

(Praise, o heavens, and let the earth rejoice, for he that is consubstantial with the Father, born before the ages, the selfsame comes to us, born as a man from a virgin womb. Through our nature he was able to suffer; and in his own [nature], God gleamed and shone forth with miracles.)

The same text, with only slight variation, is found in the Sankt Paul fragment:

> Laudate caeli et exultet terra quia homousion patris ante saecula natus hodie idem ipse ad nos ex uirginali utero humanitatis uenit ex nostra natura passibilis et in sua miraculis coruscabat et refulsit deus alleluia.

> (Praise, o heavens, and let the earth rejoice, for he that is consubstantial with the Father, born before the ages, the selfsame comes to us today out of a virgin womb of human nature. Through our nature he was able to suffer; and in his own [nature], God gleamed and shone forth with miracles. Alleluia.)

The chant opens with words from Isaiah 49:13, followed by a set of statements about the two natures of Christ: one mortal, derived from his Virgin Mother, in which he was capable of suffering; the other immortal, 'consubstantial' with the Father, emphasized by the grecism *hom(o)ousion* (with Greek characters in the Escorial manuscript of the *De laude Dei*).[198] The contrast between Christ's mortal and divine natures is very strongly connected with the language of the canons of the Lateran Council of 649, summoned by Pope Martin I to address the Monothelite heresy, the denial by some of the Eastern bishops that Christ had two wills, one human, one divine.[199] The main purpose of John the Archcantor's journey to England was not to teach chant and psalmody, but to ensure the correct belief of the English Church on the question of Monothelitism, and to seek the support of the English bishops in the pope's stand against Constantinople. The resulting synod, held in 679 at *Haethfeld*, was asked to affirm the canons of the Lateran Council. These treated under several headings

---

tinescu, 'Alcuin et les "libelli precum" ', p. 42, no. 32). I gratefully acknowledge Michael Reeve's correction of my translation on a couple of important points.

[198] This is the equivalent of the *consubstantialem patri* of the Nicene Creed, with the Greek added parenthetically in the translations of Hilary of Poitiers and of Dionysius Exiguus. A connection with the Creed in this chant makes the allusion in *Credimus saluator* all the more apparent.

[199] Constantinescu, 'Alcuin et les "libelli precum" ', pp. 52–4.

Christ's two natures as well as his two wills, which united him with divine intention but left him with free choice.[200] *Laudate caeli* may well have been composed as a musical expression of this orthodoxy, finding its way into York's antiphoner through the Council of *Haethfeld* or John the Archcantor's teaching in the north.[201] This might also have happened at the synod convened by papal legates in 786, at which Alcuin was present, which stressed the importance of defending the orthodox faith, to the point of death if necessary.[202] The existence of the Sankt Paul fragment, in an Insular hand though not necessarily copied in England, shows that chants like *Credimus saluatorem* and *Laudate caeli* could circulate as independent compositions, though personal contact would be necessary for their melodies to be transmitted with their texts. The teaching of new, supplementary music seems to be implied in Bede's report of the singing master Maban, retained by Bishop Acca at Hexham for twelve years, who taught the Hexham cantors 'such music as they did not know, while the music which they once knew and which had begun to deteriorate by long use or by negligence was restored to its original form'.[203] Benedict Biscop and Wilfrid may themselves have learned new pieces on their several visits to Rome.

As Susan Rankin points out, textual agreements between 'Roman' and 'non-Roman' sources of chant need not depend on the transmission of fixed compositions, but could instead be explained 'if there was shared understanding about the themes relevant to the liturgical season and which passages of scripture were suitable for use in singing, but no strong central control of textual expression'. Prior to the firmer codification and propagation of the Gregorian repertory, texts in various local traditions 'were made and remade', only becoming fixed some time between Alcuin's *De laude Dei* (before 786) and the late ninth century'.[204] When a community lost its living teacher, who may have left only a list of chant incipits (as in

---

[200] The Council of *Haethfeld* was convened by Archbishop Theodore, with John the Archcantor. Its existence is known only from Bede, *Historia ecclesiastica*, IV. 17–18, ed. Plummer I, 238–42. See Cubitt, *Anglo-Saxon Church Councils*, pp. 252–8. For a useful view of the Anglo-Saxon reaction to Monothelitism, see Ó Carragáin, *The City of Rome and the World of Bede*, pp. 16–18, and *idem*, *Ritual and the Rood*, pp. 81–3 and 225–8.
[201] Ambrose may have provided for the use of chant as theological propaganda, having composed new chants to strengthen his flock in face of Arianism. See J. Hourlier, 'Notes sur l'antiphonie', in W. Arlt et al. (eds.), *Gattungen der Musik in Einzeldarstellungen: Gedenkschrift Leo Schrade* (Bern and Munich, 1973), pp. 116–43, at pp. 121–2.
[202] The canons are printed in Haddan and Stubbs, *Councils* III, 448–50.
[203] Bede, *Historia ecclesiastica*, V. 20, ed. Plummer I, 331; tr. Colgrave, p. 275.
[204] Rankin, 'Beyond the boundaries,' p. 249.

Lucca, Biblioteca Capitolare, 490) as the enduring record of his teaching, the subsequent development of the text might depart from its original.

Conclusions

Of the non-Roman traditions of the Office that must have been known in England, at least prior to the Council of Whitby, not a trace remains. We have no idea, for instance, how the Office was sung at the Irish foundation of Lindisfarne during Wilfrid's boyhood. Only the Roman Office seems to have left its mark in the surviving evidence, which suggests that the liturgical decrees of *Clofesho* in 747 were realistic. That is to say, it was realistic to expect that a minster governed by a nobleman and furnished with a scriptorium capable of producing high-status liturgical psalters, or at least Latin histories of its saints, would be able to follow a Roman *horarium* and distribution of the psalms in its performance of the Office. Of the many lesser communities of whose practices we are basically ignorant, it may well be that they too eventually adopted a Roman observance, their resources perhaps supplemented with dedicated Office books like the Ushaw lectionary fragment. Beyond the essential Roman structure of the Office, however, when it comes to the more specific contents of individual hours of the Office as they were observed on particular days, the readings and chants (we can say nothing at all about the prayers of the Office), it becomes extremely difficult to speak definitively of 'Roman' and 'non-Roman' elements. Rome's own Office liturgy was never static, and 'imitating Rome' could often mean learning from Continental churches how to apply Roman liturgical ideas to humbler settings and differing local needs.[205] The basic Roman pattern will have been enriched through various kinds of exchange, with Rome and other sources, as well as through local innovation, while retaining its structural integrity.

---

[205] Ó Carragáin, *Ritual and the Rood*, p. 223.

4

The Divine Office in England from the First Viking Age to the Abbacy of Dunstan at Glastonbury, c.835–c.940

The ninth century has been seen as a period of anxiety and decline for the English Church.[1] Threatened by domestic political strife and harassed by pagan invaders, so the traditional narrative goes, monasteries lost all semblance of the true monastic life and the clergy descended into poverty and ignorance. 'Learning had declined so thoroughly in England,' lamented King Alfred (871–99), 'that there were very few men on this side of the Humber who could understand their divine services in English, or even translate a single letter from Latin into English: and I suppose that there were not many beyond the Humber either.'[2] When the ninth-century decline is considered from a liturgical perspective, however, there is reason to think, despite a lack of conclusive evidence, that the tradition of the Divine Office established in England in the seventh and eighth centuries survived between 835, when the Anglo-Saxon Chronicle first mentions a Viking invasion in the south, and the beginning of Alfred's educational and religious reforms.

---

[1] See P. Wormald, 'The ninth century', in J. Campbell (ed.), *The Anglo-Saxons* (London, 1982), pp. 132–57 (notes pp. 253–4).
[2] Text: *King Alfred's West-Saxon Version of Gregory's Pastoral Care*, ed. H. Sweet, 2 vols., EETS 45, 50 (London, 1871–2), I, 3: 'Swæ clæne hio wæs oðfeallenu ón Angelcynne ðæt swiðe feawa wæron behionan Humbre ðe hiora ðeninga cuðen understondan ón Englisc, oððe furðum án ærendgewrit óf Lædene ón Englisc areccean; & ic wene ðæt[te] noht monige begiondan Humbre næren.' Translation: S. Keynes and M. Lapidge, *Alfred the Great: Asser's 'Life of King Alfred' and Other Contemporary Sources* (London, 1983), p. 125.

The ninth-century decline and its liturgical implications

The poor state of the English Church in the ninth century has been associated with three detrimental conditions: the ever-worsening attacks of Viking raiders, the decline of Latin learning, and the 'secularization' of minsters.[3] The Vikings have usually shouldered most of the blame. Clauses in ninth-century charters guaranteeing the validity of transactions only 'as long as the Christian faith (or baptism) should last in Britain' show how seriously the Viking threat was taken.[4] But while a Viking raid could be extremely destructive, as at *Medeshamstede* (Peterborough) in 879, when they 'burnt and destroyed it, killed the abbot and monks and all they found there, and brought it to pass that it became nought that had been very mighty',[5] it did not always spell the end of the human community. Lindisfarne recovered from a major attack in 793, and the community of St Cuthbert only departed the island in 875, 'making a series of planned moves between estates which they already owned', eventually settling at Chester-le-Street in 883.[6] The female community of St Mildrith likewise maintained its identity in a new home.[7] Some minster communities took care to secure estates to which they might relocate in the event of attack.[8] Horningsea in Cambridgeshire not only survived the devastation of East Anglia, but had 'a substantial community of clerks' (*non parva congregatio clericorum*) and received donations of land from pagans who turned to Christianity.[9] Viking attacks could even prompt the foundation of new minsters, like the 'chapel of rude construction' that according to Abbo of Fleury's *Passio S. Eadmundi* was built over the tomb of King Eadmund after his martyrdom at the hands of Ivarr 'the Boneless' in 860.[10] It is

---

[3] See Blair, *The Church in Anglo-Saxon Society*, pp. 339–49, assessing the impact of the ninth-century decline. Useful unpublished material may still be sought in Sarah Foot's doctoral dissertation, 'Anglo-Saxon minsters A.D. 597–*ca* 900: The religious life in England before the Benedictine reform', University of Cambridge, 1989, pp. 333–53.

[4] N. Brooks, 'England in the ninth century: The crucible of defeat', *Transactions of the Royal Historical Society*, 5th ser., 29 (1979), 1–20, at p. 13.

[5] Anglo-Saxon Chronicle (MS 'E'), *s.a.* 870, tr. Whitelock, *EHD* I, 192 n. 6 (no. 1).

[6] Blair, *The Church in Anglo-Saxon Society*, p. 312.

[7] S. Foot, *Veiled Women*, I: *The Disappearance of Nuns from Anglo-Saxon England* (Aldershot, 2000), p. 76.

[8] S. Foot, 'Violence against Christians? The Vikings and the Church in ninth-century England', *Medieval History* 1.3 (1991), pp. 3–16, at p. 14.

[9] *Liber Eliensis*, § 32, ed. E. O. Blake, Camden 3rd ser. 92 (London, 1962), pp. 105–6.

[10] Abbo, *Passio S. Eadmundi*, § 13, ed. M. Winterbottom, *Three Lives of English Saints*, Toronto Medieval Latin Texts 1 (Toronto, 1972), pp. 67–83, at p. 82: 'aedificata uili opere

possible that a liturgical life was maintained at this shrine – as it certainly was later on in the grand church at *Bedrici-curtis* – with Viking toleration: memorial coins of St Eadmund were minted in the Danelaw in the 890s.[11]

Manuscript survivals show that Viking armies did not always destroy libraries. York's library seems to have escaped unscathed, and 'if the Danes did not destroy books and libraries in York, there is perhaps no need to suppose that they did so elsewhere'.[12] A large proportion of the manuscripts that survived the ninth century are biblical or liturgical, to which might be added a number of manuscripts containing patristic commentaries that may have been read in the Night Office. While these may have been saved primarily because of their value or appearance,[13] their preservation at least meant that they were available for liturgical use. As for manuscript production, only three complete manuscripts apparently written in England survive from the middle of the ninth century, none itself strictly liturgical. But the Durham *Liber uitae*, BL Cotton Domitian vii (Lindisfarne or Wearmouth-Jarrow?, c.840), is connected with liturgical commemoration of the living and the dead. The texts collected in Oxford, Bodleian Library, Digby 63 (844 [or 867] × 892) include computus material, a kalendar, and writings on the dating of Easter. Oxford, Bodleian Library, Bodley 426 (Wessex, 838×847) contains the commentary on the Book of Job by Philippus Presbyter, which could possibly have been a source of readings in the Night Office.[14] Such manuscript production as could be undertaken amid threats of Viking attack seems to have had liturgical relevance.

The decline of Latinity in England seems to have been independent of the Viking problem. The Preface to the Old English version of Gregory's

---

desuper basilica'. Translation: F. Hervey, *Corolla Sancti Eadmundi: The Garland of Saint Edmund King and Martyr* (London, 1907), pp. 6–59, at p. 43 (here c. 14).

[11] See Blair, *The Church in Anglo-Saxon Society*, p. 317 and n. 146.

[12] M. Lapidge, 'Latin learning in ninth-century England', in his *Anglo-Latin Literature, 600–899* (London, 1996), pp. 409–39, at p. 432.

[13] Lapidge, 'Latin learning', p. 414: 'at the first sign of danger they were carried to a safe place'.

[14] On the use of patristic writings and scripture commentaries in the Night Office, see p. 125 n. 173 above. In the extant reading schemes for the Roman Night Office, the book of Job was read either in September (Lateran Basilica: *Ordo Romanus XIIIA*, § 9, ed. Andrieu II, 484) or January (Vatican Basilica: *Ordo Romanus XIV*, § 8, ed. Andrieu III, 40). A letter of Gregory I reveals that his own *Moralia in Iob* was being read during vigils at Ravenna, though he felt that the work was too difficult for non-specialist hearers: *S. Gregorii Magni Registrum epistularum*, XII. 6, ed. D. Norberg, 2 vols, CCSL 140, 140A (Turnhout, 1982) II, 974–7, at pp. 975–6.

Cura pastoralis reveals that Alfred, born in 848, remembered that Latin learning was non-existent well before the arrival of the first 'great army' in 865:

> When I reflected on all this, I recollected how – before everything was ransacked and burned – the churches throughout England stood filled with treasures and books. Similarly, there was a great multitude of those serving God. And they derived very little benefit from those books, because they could understand nothing of them, since they were not written in their own language.[15]

Surviving ninth-century charters confirm the poor state of Latinity in England, displaying 'at best mere competence (and not without flaws)' and 'at worst ... mere gibberish'.[16]

But Michael Lapidge's criteria for affirming continuity of Latin learning – namely, 'evidence of skilled original composition in Latin, or, at least, of scholarly activity of some sort' – are too ambitious a standard against which to measure competence in performing the Latin liturgy.[17] Complaints about the clergy's ignorance of Latin are a commonplace from the writings of Archbishop Theodore and Bede down through the Middle Ages.[18] Even at Wearmouth and Jarrow it was expected that readings from a Latin text as fundamental as the *Regula S. Benedicti* would need

---

[15] *King Alfred's Pastoral Care*, ed. Sweet, p. 5: 'Ða ic ða ðis eall gemunde ða gemunde ic eac hu ic geseah, ærðæmðe hit eall forhergod wære & boca gefyldæ ond eac micel men[i]geo Godes ðiowa & ða swiðe lytle fiorme ðara boca wiston, forðæmðe hie hiora nan wuht óngiotan ne meahton forðæmðe hie næron ón hiora agen geðiode awritene.' Translation: Keynes and Lapidge, *Alfred the Great*, p. 125. On the chronology, see H. Gneuss, 'King Alfred and the history of Anglo-Saxon libraries', in P. R. Brown, G. R. Crampton, and F. C. Robinson (eds.), *Modes of Interpretation in Old English Literature: Essays in Honour of Stanley B. Greenfield* (Toronto, 1986), pp. 29–49, at p. 31 (repr. as ch. III in his *Books and Libraries*).

[16] Lapidge, 'Latin learning', p. 436.

[17] Lapidge, 'Latin learning', p. 433.

[18] See Foot, 'Anglo-Saxon minsters', pp. 327–9; and, in more general terms, her *Monastic Life*, pp. 345–6. The thirteenth-century Oxford Franciscan Roger Bacon murmured that 'boys gabble through the psalter which they have learnt, and ... clerks and country priests recite the Church services, of which they know little or nothing, like brute beasts' (cited in G. G. Coulton, *Studies in Medieval Thought* (London, 1940), p. 77). Ordinary clergy were seldom ever expected to do more than pronounce the words of the liturgy correctly, as in the *Cura clericalis* (London: Thomas Petyt, 1542), A.i.: 'Ideo dicuntur ethimologice sacerdotes quasi missarum celebratores. Quare tantum de scientia habere debent quam sciant recte et distincte legere et ea que in misse officio continentur ad minus grammaticaliter intellegere, congrue pronunciare, et accentuare et debite pronunciare.' ('"Priests" are so called, etymologically, because they are celebrants of Masses. They need only so

simultaneous translation and explanation in English if all were to understand.[19] The prelates assembled at *Clofesho* in 747 decreed that 'even though someone may not understand the Latin words while he is singing the psalms, he nevertheless ought humbly to engage and direct the intentions of his heart to those things that at the present time are to be asked of God for men', going on to explain that it is the divine inspiration of the words that makes the psalms effective, so long as the singer has the proper inward disposition.[20] An understanding of Latin vocabulary and grammar was by no means essential to the competent performance of the liturgy,[21] and the basic vocabulary of the psalter will have been familiar to most clerics. The interlinear Old English gloss of the Vespasian Psalter, written in a mid-ninth-century script,[22] is not itself evidence that the glossator was able to translate the text of the psalms himself.[23] But it shows that translations were still available from which the meaning of the Latin text could be learned: according to Alfred, many could still read English.[24] The poor state of Latin learning in ninth-century England does not automatically imply discontinuity in the performance of the Divine

---

much knowledge as is necessary for them to be able to read correctly and distinctly, and at least as much grammatical understanding of what is contained in the Mass as will suffice for him to pronounce it properly and with correct accentuation.') See E. Duffy, *The Stripping of the Altars: Traditional Religion in England c. 1400–c. 1580* (New Haven, CT, 1992), p. 57.

[19] As is clear from Alcuin's *Epistola 19*, cited above, p. 82.

[20] Ed. Haddan and Stubbs, *Councils* III, 372–3 (c. 27): 'unde quamvis psallendo Latina quis nesciat verba, suas tamen cordis intentiones, ad ea quae in praesenti poscenda sunt a Deo, suppliciter referre, ac pro viribus detinere debet.'

[21] Even in the court chapel of Charlemagne, according to Notker Balbulus, liturgical readers did not necessarily understand Latin (*Gesta Karoli magni imperatoris*, I. 7, ed. H. F. Haefele, *Notker der Stammler: Taten Kaiser Karls des Grossen*, MGH SRG 12 (Berlin, 1959), p. 10): 'Sed cuncti omnia, quę legenda erant, ita sibi nota facere curarunt, ut, quando inopinato legere iuberentur, inreprehensibiles apud eum invenirentur. ... et hoc modo factum est, ut, etsiamsi non intellegerent, omnes in eius palatio lectores optimi fuissent.' ('They all took such care to acquaint themselves with what was to be recited that, when they were called upon to read unexpectedly, they performed so well that the Emperor never had occasion to reproach them. ... One result of this was that all those in the p[a]lace became excellent readers, even if they did not understand what they read.') Translation: L. Thorpe, *Two Lives of Charlemagne* (London, 1969), pp. 100–1.

[22] This was the opinion of Neil Ker, *Catalogue*, no. 203.

[23] Lapidge ('Latin learning', pp. 436–7) notes that certain errors prove the gloss to have been copied from an older manuscript, now lost.

[24] *King Alfred's Pastoral Care*, ed. Sweet, p. 7: 'Ða ic ða gemunde hu sio lar Lædengeðiodes ær ðissum afeallan wæs giond Angelcynn, & ðeah monige cuðon Englisc gewrit arædan....' ('When I recalled how knowledge of Latin had previously decayed throughout England, and yet many could still read things written in English ...') Translation: Keynes and Lapidge, *Alfred the Great*, p. 126.

Office.

The most significant change in the ninth-century English Church, in the eyes of contemporary and modern commentators, was the 'secularization' of minsters.[25] In the seventh and eighth centuries, minsters had housed both enclosed contemplatives and clerics involved in pastoral care. From the later ninth century onwards, however, they typically adopted the form of 'the "secular" community of men in priest's orders: living at a central site, associated in the service of one central church ... but not necessarily holding assets in common, sleeping in a dormitory, or bound to any strict liturgical round'.[26] The clearest picture of this clericalization of a minster community emerges in the charters of Christ Church, Canterbury, where the cathedral personnel seem to have been almost exclusively secular from the time of Wulfred (805–32).[27] Because of their sacramental functions, 'priests were essential as monks and nuns were not, and it is reasonable to suppose that diligent bishops encouraged them when they could'; and with many minsters falling into the control of kings and ealdormen greedy for their revenues,[28] 'such priests were probably of humbler status, or at any rate less luxurious in their expectations, than the noble monks and nuns of a century earlier, and were correspondingly cheaper to support'.[29] Diminished resources could impair the maintenance of the Divine Office.[30] But in any moderately sized community, the majority of the members will not have been fully ordained as presbyters,

---

[25] Asser (*De rebus gestis Ælfredi*, c. 93, ed. W. H. Stevenson, *Asser's Life of King Alfred, together with the Annals of Saint Neot's, erroneously ascribed to Asser*, re-issued with an introduction by D. Whitelock (Oxford, 1959), p. 81) complained that existing minsters in Alfred's reign did not 'maintain the rule of monastic life in any consistent way' (*nullo tamen regulam illius vitae ordinabiliter tenente*); translation: Keynes and Lapidge, *Alfred the Great*, p. 103. So also Knowles (*The Monastic Order*, pp. 554 and 695) saw true monasticism as extinct in England by *c.*900.

[26] Blair, *The Church in Anglo-Saxon Society*, p. 342. The clergy of pre-reform Abingdon seem to have had separate dwellings: A. Thacker, 'Æthelwold and Abingdon', in Yorke, *Bishop Æthelwold*, pp. 43–64, at pp. 47–8.

[27] Brooks, *The Early History*, pp. 160–4.

[28] A useful summary of the situation may be found in Blair, *The Church in Anglo-Saxon Society*, pp. 323–9. King Alfred, for example, made a present of two minsters to his adviser and biographer, Asser, who promptly went to inspect them as sole proprietor (Asser, *De rebus gestis Ælfredi*, c. 81, ed. Stevenson, pp. 67–8; tr. Keynes and Lapidge, *Alfred the Great*, p. 97). See Blair, *The Church in Anglo-Saxon Society*, pp. 324–5.

[29] Blair, *The Church in Anglo-Saxon Society*, p. 125.

[30] Such was the excuse offered by a number of Frankish monasteries to Benedict of Aniane for failing to sing the Office: Robertson, *The Service-Books of the Royal Abbey of Saint-Denis*, p. 35.

but rather in lesser clerical grades (mere *preostas*, rather than *mæssepreostas*).³¹ Horningsea, for example, seems to have been led by a single priest-abbot, the rest of the inmates being in lesser orders.³² The main liturgical function of the remainder of the non-priests in this community will have been to sing the Divine Office. In some cases, a shift to clerical personnel should probably be interpreted not as an indication that the liturgical life of a minster suffered, but that the liturgy was taken out of the hands of contemplatives and 'professionalized' in the service of wealthy donors.³³

Whatever their other effects, the attacks of the Vikings, the decline in Latin learning, and the clericalization of minsters that characterized the ninth century need not have been fatal to the tradition of the Divine Office in England.

Evidence for liturgical continuity through the ninth century

A number of sources from the Viking period refer to an ongoing tradition of the Divine Office in at least a few places. A grant of one Oswulf to the community at Lyminge (Kent) in 798, couched in terms that recognize the Viking threat, seems to suppose that special prayers could be incorporated within an existing round of daily liturgical services, apparently including the Office (*in psalmodiis*):

> [The grant is made] with this condition added, that, beginning twelve months after our death, every year the day shall be celebrated by the community at Lyminge with a fast and with divine prayers in [their] psalmodies and celebrations of Masses, so long

---

[31] See J. Barrow, 'Grades of ordination and clerical careers, *c.* 900–*c.* 1200', in C. Matthews (ed.), *Anglo-Norman Studies 30: Proceedings of the Battle Conference 2007* (Woodbridge, 2008), pp. 41–61, at p. 46. For the terminological distinction I am indebted to Julia Barrow.

[32] A kinsman of the priest-abbot Herewulf had to be ordained priest to serve as his deputy, and later assumed sole leadership of the community (*Liber Eliensis*, § 32, ed. Blake, p. 106). Other houses, including St Augustine's, Canterbury, were likewise governed by priest-abbots (Brooks, *The Early History*, p. 163).

[33] The twenty-seventh decree of the Council of *Clofesho* indicates that wealthy laymen could be very interested in paying for intercessory psalmody, not always with the purest motives (ed. Haddan and Stubbs, *Councils* III, 373–4). The Roman basilican monasteries were gradually converted into communities of secular canons precisely because their chief function became more and more the professional performance of the Office. See Ferrari, *Early Roman Monasteries*, p. 368.

as the Catholic faith shall abide among the English people.[34]

When Ealdorman Ælfred redeemed the 'Golden Gospels' (Stockholm, Kungliga biblioteket, A. 135) from a Danish army, he inscribed the book to 'the religious community which daily raises praise to God in Christ Church'.[35] In an 848 charter Berhtwulf, king of the Mercians, required of the church of Breedon-on-the-Hill in Leicestershire 'that the memory of Berhtwulf and of the prince Humberht, and of all the nobles of the Mercian people, be mentioned in their holy prayers in the days and in the nights'.[36] The reference to diurnal and nocturnal prayers almost certainly means the Divine Office. A charter of Ealdorman Æthelred and Æthelflæd (884×901) conferring rights on the cathedral church in Worcester lists all eight daily offices (in Old English), suggesting that the Office was fully observed by the secular community there.[37] While such clear references to the daily communal Office are relatively rare, many charters mention extra psalmody to be performed on behalf of benefactors.[38]

Occasionally, direct continuity between the ninth and tenth centuries can be established, as in a mid-ninth-century will of a certain Ealhburg granting rents to St Augustine's, Canterbury, on the condition that Psalm 19, *Exaudiat te dominus*, be recited daily for the benefit of the donor.[39] This corresponds precisely to the *Regularis concordia*'s prescription that

---

[34] BCS 289 (S 153): 'hac vero condicione interposita ut unicuique anno post .XII. mensibus migrationis nostrae tempus ab illa familia aet limingge caelebratur quamdiu fides catholica in gente Anglorum perseveret . cum jejunio divinisque orationibus in psalmodiis et missarum celebrationibus.'

[35] BCS 634: '⁊ ðæm godcundan geferscipe to brúcen[ne] ðe ín Cristes circan ðæghpæmlice Godes lof ræraδ'; tr. Whitelock, *EHD* I, 539 (no. 98).

[36] S 197 (BCS 454): 'Et ut memoria regis Beorhtuulfi ac Humberhti principis et omnium optimatum gentis Merciorum in eorum sacris orationibus diebus ac noctibus memoretur.' The text of this charter is also found, with substantial alteration, in S 193 (BCS 434), where it is made to support Worcester's claim to ownership of Bredon, Worcestershire: J. Barrow, 'The chronology of forgery production at Worcester from *c*. 1000 to the early twelfth century', in J. S. Barrow and N. P. Brooks (eds.), *St Wulfstan and his World*, Studies in Early Medieval Britain 4 (Aldershot, 2005), pp. 105–22, at p. 108.

[37] S 223, ed. and tr. as no. 12 in *Select English Historical Documents of the Ninth and Tenth Centuries*, ed. F. E. Harmer (Cambridge, 1914), text pp. 22–5, tr. pp. 54–5, notes pp. 106–7 (this passage pp. 23 and 55). Also tr. Whitelock, *EHD* I, 540–1 (no. 99), though the use here of the term 'matins' to translate *uhtsong* (the Night Office) is unhelpfully ambiguous.

[38] For example S 304 (BCS 468), Æthelwulf, king of the West Saxons, to 'the English Church' for fifty psalms each Saturday; and S 215 (BCS 540), Ceolwulf II, king of the Mercians, to Worcester, for daily 'commemoration and the Lord's prayer'.

[39] BCS 501 (undated, but *c*.831–3): 'tha hiwan asingan ælce dæge . fter hyra ferse thane sealm for hia . "Exaudiat te dominus".'

Psalm 19 be sung every day after the Night Office 'for the King, Queen and benefactors (*familiares*)', and seems to confirm the opinion of the *Concordia*'s editor, Thomas Symons, that the special prayers for the king and other benefactors were derived from long-standing English traditions, not a Continental monastic model.[40]

Continuity is also evident in the 'Junius Psalter', Oxford, Bodleian Library, Junius 27, probably copied at Winchester in the 920s.[41] Despite its somewhat mutilated state, with some initials cut out and some leaves missing from the beginning and end of the manuscript, it is clear that, in addition to a threefold 'scholarly division', marking Psalms 1, 51, and 101, the Junius Psalter was decorated according to the eight liturgical divisions of the Roman *cursus*, including the unusual decoration of Psalm 17 found in the eighth-century Vespasian and Salaberga Psalters, which, as has been argued above, were made for an archaic form of the Roman Office that had only two nocturns in the Night Office on Sundays.[42] It has been suggested that the Junius Psalter was made from a Canterbury exemplar, perhaps the Vespasian Psalter itself, based on its kalendar and its 'A-type' Old English gloss,[43] which might mean that Psalm 17 was decorated in imitation of the exemplar, not contemporary liturgical practice

---

[40] *Regularis concordia*, § 18, ed. Symons p. 13 (CCM § 19, p. 83): 'Peractis Nocturnis dicant duos psalmos, *Domine ne in furore tuo* (i) et *Exaudiat te Dominus*, unum uidelicet pro rege specialiter, alterum uero pro rege et regina ac familiaribus.' On the *Concordia*'s use of *familiares* to mean 'benefactors', see *Regularis concordia*, ed. Symons, p. 12 n. 1. On the *Concordia*'s preservation of native English traditions, see T. Symons, 'Sources of the Regularis Concordia', *Downside Review* old ser. 59, new ser. 40 (1941), 14–36, 143–70, and 264–89, at pp. 146–9; and *Regularis concordia*, ed. Symons, p. lxvi.

[41] Bodleian Summary Catalogue, no. 5139; Ker, *Catalogue*, no. 335; Gneuss, *Handlist*, no. 641. The text (which is of the *Romanum* type) and its Old English gloss are ed. E. Brenner, *Der altenglische Junius-Psalter: Die Interlinear-Glosse der Handschrift Junius 27 der Bodleianer zu Oxford*, Anglistiche Forschungen 23 (Heidelberg, 1908). The date and localization are based on art-historical, palaeographical, and liturgical evidence (from its kalendar): F. Wormald, 'The "Winchester School" before St. Æthelwold', in P. Clemoes and K. Hughes (eds.), *England Before the Conquest: Studies in Primary Sources Presented to Dorothy Whitelock* (Cambridge, 1971), pp. 305–12, at p. 305. Wormald refers to E. Bishop, *Liturgica historica* (Oxford, 1918), pp. 254–5. For the association with Winchester on palaeographical grounds, see H. Gneuss, *Lehnbildung und Lehnbedeutungen im Altenglischen* (Berlin, 1955), p. 43; *The Salisbury Psalter*, ed. Sisam and Sisam, p. 48; and T. A. M. Bishop, 'An early example of the Square minuscule', *Transactions of the Cambridge Bibliographical Society* 4 (1964–8), 246–52, at p. 247.

[42] See the section 'Evidence for the Roman division of the psalter', beginning on p. 109 above.

[43] D. N. Dumville, *Liturgy and the Ecclesiastical History of Late Anglo-Saxon England* (Woodbridge, 1992), chapter 1 (pp. 1–38): 'The kalendar of the Junius Psalter'.

at Winchester. But the Vespasian and Junius glosses are far from identical, the Junius gloss incorporating West Saxon phonological and dialectical variants.[44] And while the scribes of the manuscript followed Insular models, they also imitated Continental practices in their preparation of the parchment for writing and followed a Continental rationale for grades of script. The illuminations show an awareness and adaptation of Continental motifs.[45] The scheme of liturgical divisions in the Junius Psalter cannot have been made in direct imitation of the Vespasian Psalter since the latter does not include the threefold scholarly division at Psalms 1, 51, and 101, and the Junius Psalter omits decoration of Psalm 26, which receives the highest grade of decoration in the Vespasian Psalter. It is quite probable, therefore, that the archaic Roman divisions in the Junius Psalter were included as a conscious artistic reflection of a living liturgical practice. If the English tradition of the Roman Office was to survive anywhere, it had the best chance at Winchester. The south-western heartlands of the West Saxon kings suffered minimally from Viking attacks, and were virtually impregnable under Alfred's burghal system.[46]

King Alfred may have complained that there were very few men south of the Humber who could understand the Latin of their divine services; but points of evidence like these corroborate what Alfred himself implied, namely that these services continued to be performed, understood or not.

Restoration and innovation under Alfred and his heirs

Having secured peace within his borders, from about 885 onwards King Alfred was able to take positive steps to improve the state of education and religion. One aspect of Alfred's reforms was the inception of a royal programme of monastic foundation: a monastery at Athelney and

---

[44] Gretsch, *Intellectual Foundations*, pp. 315–25.
[45] M. B. Parkes, 'The palaeography of the Parker manuscript of the *Chronicle*, laws and Sedulius, and historiography at Winchester in the late ninth and tenth centuries', *Anglo-Saxon England* 5 (1976), 149–71, at pp. 161–2.
[46] See the paths of Viking activity before and after Alfred's defeat of Guthrum plotted in Wormald, 'The ninth century', p. 151 (after D. Hill, *An Atlas of Anglo-Saxon England*, 2nd edn (Oxford, 1984)). Worcester likewise escaped relatively unscathed, which may have something to do with the relative prominence of references to 'psalmody' in Worcester charters compared with those from other areas. On both, see Blair, *The Church in Anglo-Saxon Society*, p. 300 (Winchester) and pp. 296 (Fig. 35) and 306 (Worcester).

a nunnery at Shaftesbury.[47] His eldest daughter, Æthelflæd (d.918), is credited with founding the minster of St Oswald in Gloucester, as well as a number of other houses.[48] Edward the Elder (899–924) realized his father's plan for the New Minster, Winchester,[49] and, with his mother, probably founded several houses of nuns (Winchester's Nunnaminster, Romsey, and Wilton).[50] Æthelstan (924–39) is reported to have founded (or re-founded) Milton Abbas (Dorset) and Muchelney Abbey (Somerset).[51] An interest in monastic life continued into the reign of Eadmund (939–46), who after his famous narrow escape at Cheddar Gorge gave the abbacy of Glastonbury to Dunstan.[52]

David Dumville has proposed that these instances of monastic foundation and assistance of monasteries should be viewed as part of a royal policy devised by Alfred and faithfully implemented by his heirs.[53] Alfred's translation projects may have been designed to foster fresh interest in monasticism among the nobility, with the ultimate goal of training up qualified candidates for the episcopacy.[54] It may be no accident that monastic bishops re-appear in England in the 920s and 930s, some of whom may have fostered monastic interests (Theodred of London, Æthelhelm of Canterbury), while others certainly did so (Koenwald of Worcester, Ælfeah of Winchester, Oda of Ramsbury).[55] In Dumville's interpretation, Edgar's support of the Benedictine reform movement in

---

[47] For which see Asser, *De rebus gestis Ælfredi*, cc. 92–8, ed. Stevenson, pp. 79–85; tr. Keynes and Lapidge, *Alfred the Great*, pp. 102–5.
[48] William of Malmesbury, *Gesta pontificum Anglorum*, ed. N. E. S. A. Hamilton, Rolls Series 52 (London, 1870), p. 293.
[49] On the complex evidence for the New Minster's foundation, see P. Grierson, 'Grimbald of St. Bertin's', *English Historical Review* new ser. 55, old ser. 220 (1940), 529–61, at pp. 553–7. The definitive pre-Conquest history of the house is *The Liber Vitae of the New Minster and Hyde Abbey, Winchester: British Library Stowe 944*, ed. S. Keynes, EEMF 26 (Copenhagen, 1996), pp. 16–41.
[50] Foot, *Veiled Women*, pp. 152–3, 221–31, and 243–52.
[51] Known chiefly from William of Malmesbury, *De gestis pontificum Anglorum*, II. 85 (Milton) and II. 93 (Muchelney), ed. Hamilton, pp. 186, 199–200.
[52] B., *Vita S. Dunstani*, § 14, ed. and tr. M. Winterbottom and M. Lapidge, *The Early Lives of St Dunstan*, Oxford Medieval Texts (Oxford, 2012), pp. 1–109, at pp. 48–51.
[53] D. N. Dumville, *Wessex and England from Alfred to Edgar: Six Essays on Political, Cultural, and Ecclesiastical Revival*, Studies in Anglo-Saxon History 3 (Woodbridge, 1992), pp. 185–205.
[54] Dumville, *Wessex and England*, pp. 199–200. Asser complained of the nobility's indifference to the monastic vocation (*De rebus gestis Ælfredi*, c. 93, ed. Stevenson, p. 93; tr. Keynes and Lapidge, p. 103).
[55] Dumville, *Wessex and England*, pp. 193 and 203.

the second half of the tenth century was the natural conclusion of Alfred's initial policy. And it is certainly striking that Æthelwold's zeal for monasticism should have arisen from his reading of Bede's *Historia ecclesiastica*, translated at Alfred's instigation.[56]

While Alfred continued to support the more usual clerical ministers,[57] and while the major foundations of his successors were more likely clerical than 'strictly monastic',[58] Alfred's foundations at Athelney and Shaftesbury are nowadays viewed as 'monastic in a strict sense'.[59] This definition works to the extent that Alfred aspired to a return to the enclosed contemplative life with communal living and no private ownership of property.[60] In asking what form of the Divine Office was used at Athelney and Shaftesbury, however, it is important not to confuse strict monasticism with the reformed Benedictine monasticism promoted on the Continent in the ninth century.[61] Alfred's chief Continental advisers, Grimbald of Saint-Bertin and John 'the Old Saxon', are both described as 'priest and monk' (*sacerdos et monachus*),[62] but this does not mean that they were reformed Benedictines.[63] Grimbald's original monastery, Saint-Bertin, was only reformed as a Benedictine house under Gerard of Brogne in 944, which prompted a large group of the house's inmates to flee across the Channel in search of refuge with King Eadmund, who gave them the vacant minster of Bath.[64] Too little of John's background

---

[56] Foot, *Monastic Life*, pp. 18–19.
[57] The 'neighbouring monasteries' (*finitima monasteria*) that received one eighth of Alfred's annual income: Asser, *De rebus gestis Ælfredi*, c. 102, ed. Stevenson, p. 89; tr. Keynes and Lapidge, *Alfred the Great*, p. 107.
[58] Blair, *The Church in Anglo-Saxon Society*, p. 348.
[59] Blair, *The Church in Anglo-Saxon Society*, p. 347.
[60] Blair, *The Church in Anglo-Saxon Society*, p. 343.
[61] David Dumville seems to use 'monastic' and 'Benedictine' as synonyms: *Wessex and England*, pp. 185–205. John Blair contrasts 'secular' with 'strict monastic' in describing tenth-century minsters, revealing only occasionally that for him 'strict monastic' means 'Benedictine': *The Church in Anglo-Saxon Society*, pp. 346–9.
[62] Asser, *De rebus gestis Ælfredi*, c. 78, ed. Stevenson, p. 63; tr. Keynes and Lapidge, p. 93.
[63] As Mechthild Gretsch assumes, 'Cambridge, Corpus Christi College 57: A witness to the early stages of the Benedictine reform in England?', *Anglo-Saxon England* 32 (2003), 111–46, at p. 138.
[64] A. Dierkens, *Abbayes et chapitres entre Sambre et Meuse (VIIe–XIe siècles): Contribution à l'histoire religieuse des campagnes du Haut Moyen Âge*, Beihefte der Francia 14 (Sigmaringen, 1985), pp. 238–9; Folcuin, *Gesta abbati S. Bertini Sithiensium*, c. 107, ed. O. Holder Egger, MGH SS 13 (Hanover, 1881), pp. 607–35, at p. 628. Folcuin mistakenly has the refugees arriving at the court of Æthelstan, who had died five years earlier. See also Knowles, *The Monastic Order*, p. 33 and n. 1.

is known to form a judgement.⁶⁵ However 'strict' the monasticism may have been at Athelney and Shaftesbury, there is no evidence that the Office was sung there according to the Benedictine *cursus*.

Instead, where novelties were introduced into the Office liturgy sung in Alfred's court chapel – and Asser reports that Alfred was a keen student of the daily hours, occasionally participating 'in certain psalms and prayers in the day-time and night-time offices'⁶⁶ – these were probably in response to Continental developments in the performance of the Roman Office (the secular *cursus*). Evidence of contact with Continental Office liturgy is furnished by the manuscript variously known as the Durham Collectar or the Durham Ritual (Durham, Cathedral Library, A. IV. 19), copied in southern England some time between 890 and 930 from a Continental exemplar.⁶⁷ Alicia Corrêa has suggested that this exemplar was brought to England by Grimbald.⁶⁸ A collectar contains the prayers offered by the officiant during the Divine Office, as well as the short readings (*capitula*) recited at the day hours.⁶⁹ The contents of a collectar do not generally reveal whether the secular or the monastic *cursus* is intended, but the texts in the Durham Collectar are suited to the needs of a secular community.⁷⁰ Another English manuscript of the same period

---

⁶⁵ Though a stronger argument could be made if Mabillon's hunch that he was from Corvey in Saxony could stand. See J. Mabillon, *Annales ordinis S. Benedicti occidentalium monachorum patriarchae*, 6 vols. (Paris, 1703–39) II, 435; III, 223, 226.

⁶⁶ Asser, *De rebus gestis Ælfredi*, c. 24, ed. Stevenson, p. 21; and quoted passage, c. 76, ed. Stevenson, p. 59. Translation: Lapidge and Keynes, *Alfred the Great*, p. 91.

⁶⁷ The Durham Collectar has been edited several times: *Rituale ecclesiae Dunelmensis: The Durham Ritual*, ed. U. Lindelöf, with an introduction by A. H. Thompson, Surtees Society 160 (London, 1927); this is a revision of an earlier edition by J. Stevenson, *Rituale ecclesiae Dunelmensis*, Surtees Society 10 (London, 1841), preserving the same pagination; the more recent edition by Alicia Corrêa (*The Durham Collectar*) includes only the original layer of the manuscript, and none of the later additions. There is also a published facsimile, *The Durham Ritual: A Southern English Collectar of the Tenth Century with Northumbrian Additions*, ed. T. J. Brown, with contributions from F. Wormald, A. S. C. Ross, and E. G. Stanley, EEMF 16 (Copenhagen, 1969). The date range is Brown's, who favoured the latter end (pp. 37–9). Corrêa suggests that the earlier years of the range would also be plausible (p. 81 n. 16).

⁶⁸ *The Durham Collectar*, ed. Corrêa, pp. 121–2.

⁶⁹ *The Durham Collectar*, ed. Corrêa, pp. 3–4; A. Corrêa, 'Daily office books: Collectars and breviaries', in Pfaff, *The Liturgical Books*, pp. 45–60. See also Gneuss, 'Liturgical books in Anglo-Saxon England', pp. 112–13. The collectar is sometimes called a book for the day hours. This is misleading, since the Night Office has no collect and no short lesson, and so makes no use of the two main contents of a collectar. In other words, there could be no such thing as a 'nocturnal collectar'. See *The Durham Collectar*, ed. Corrêa, p. 124 n. 23.

⁷⁰ The inclusion of rites for baptism and marriage points to a pastoral context (*The Durham*

derived from Continental exemplars, the pontifical sacramentary known as the 'Leofric Missal' (Oxford, Bodleian Library, Bodley 579), probably made for Alfred's archbishop, Plegmund, gives in its original layer a set of nine blessings to precede the nine lessons of the Night Office on Christmas Day, indicating the secular *cursus*.[71]

Asser calls Grimbald *cantator optimus*.[72] If Grimbald was involved in teaching liturgical music, he may have introduced books of Office chant containing the Romano-Frankish repertory known as 'Gregorian', adapted and codified under the Carolingians.[73] As has already been seen, this repertory differs in significant ways from the English repertory of Office chants represented in Alcuin's *De laude Dei*.[74] The Gregorian repertory also had a distinctive musical dialect, its origins hotly debated by musicologists, which was first notated on the Continent late in the ninth century.[75] All surviving notated English chant books, the earliest dating from the tenth century, contain this Gregorian musical dialect. English awareness of Gregorian chant may date to the time of Alcuin: according to the anonymous *Vita Alcuini*, a companion of Alcuin's youth, Sigulf, was sent to Metz, the seat of Carolingian musical reform, to be

---

Collectar, ed. Corrêa, pp. 220–34). See Corrêa's remarks on p. 79 n. 11, although the absence of St Benedict's feast on 21 March is not in itself evidence of a non-monastic origin: Froger, 'Le Lieu de destination', p. 346.

[71] *The Leofric Missal*, ed. N. Orchard, 2 vols., HBS 113–14 (London, 2002) I, 30–1, and II, 16–17.

[72] *De rebus gestis Ælfredi*, c. 78, ed. Stevenson, p. 63.

[73] See the discussion of the work of Helisachar at p. 62 above; and also Huglo, 'Les remaniements de l'antiphonaire grégorien'. The two earliest complete examples of 'Gregorian' antiphoners, are BnF lat. 17436 ('Antiphoner of Charles the Bald', prov. Compiègne, 860×880), ed. in Hesbert, *CAO* I (MS *C*); and Albi, Bibliothèque municipale Rochegude, 44 (written at Albi for an unknown church, *c*.890), ed. J. A. Emerson and L. Collamore, *Albi, Bibliothèque Municipale Rochegude, Manuscript 44: A Complete Ninth-Century Gradual and Antiphoner from Southern France* (Ottawa, 2002). Neither manuscript has musical notation, though on the early leaves of Albi 44 space is left in the text for notated melismas.

[74] See pp. 126–132 above.

[75] An indication of the current controversy may be found in the diametrically opposed positions of Helmut Hucke, 'Toward a new historical view of Gregorian chant', *Journal of the American Musicological Society* 33 (1980), 437–67, and Kenneth Levy, 'Gregorian chant and the Romans', *Journal of the American Musicological Society* 56 (2003), 5–41. On the fundamental difficulty of determining the character of 'Roman' chant prior to the Carolingian reforms, see also H. Hucke and J. Dyer, 'Old Roman chant', in S. Sadie and J. Tyrrell (eds.), *The New Grove Dictionary of Music and Musicians*, 2nd edn (London, 2001) XVIII, 381–5. A helpful summary of the historical background is given in Hiley, *Western Plainchant*, pp. 514–23.

instructed in chant (and not, as Wilhelm Levison noted, to Canterbury).[76] It is impossible to say if English clerics continued to go to Metz to be trained in singing between Alcuin's time and the beginning of the tenth century. The ninth century probably afforded few opportunities for English minsters to establish *scholae cantorum*, the well-funded, stable institutions on which the faithful oral transmission of the Gregorian repertory depended. The restoration of peace under Alfred, along with the Continental contacts that he nurtured, may have been more conducive to the establishment of a new musical tradition. The earliest examples of musical notation in English manuscripts are in the style known as

---

[76] *Vita Alcuini*, c. 8, ed. Arndt, p. 189: 'Quo in tempore sociatur illi vir Deo amabilis, animi carnisque nobilitate insignis, Sigulfus presbiter, custos Eboricae civitatis ecclesiae, perpetuo ut illi iam haereret, qui suo cum avunculo Autberto presbitero puer partes has petierat, Romamque ecclesiasticum ordinem discendum ab eo ductus fuerat, necnon Mettis civitatem causa cantus directus.' ('At that time the priest Sigulf, a man beloved of God, notable for his nobility of soul and body, keeper of the church of the city of York, joined him [Alcuin] and clung to him perpetually. This boy, together with his uncle, the priest Autbert, was making for the same regions: and he was led by him [Autbert] to Rome that he might learn ecclesiastical matters, and was likewise directed to the city of Metz to learn chant.') Levison, *England and the Continent*, p. 99. Metz was officially sanctioned by Charlemagne as the authoritative source of 'Roman' chant, to be imitated throughout his kingdom: see the *Capitulare missorum in Theodonis villa datum primum, Mere ecclesiasticum 805*, ed. A. Boretius, MGH Cap. 1 (Hanover, 1883), pp. 121–2, canon 2, 'De cantu'; and also the letter of Leidrad, archbishop of Lyons, cited above, p. 56. English awareness of Carolingian liturgical reforms may also be indicated by references to a new sacramentary, perhaps to be identified with the *Hadrianum* version of the Gregorian sacramentary first popularized under Charlemagne as a replacement for the 'Gelasian' sacramentary (on these sacramentaries, see Vogel, *Medieval Liturgy*, pp. 73 and 117 n. 175 (Gelasian) and pp. 80–2 (Gregorian)). See Alcuin's reply to the 801 letter of Eanbald II, archbishop of York, requesting information about the new ordering of the 'missal': 'Surely you have plenty of missals following the Roman rite? You also have enough of the larger missals of the old rite. What need is there for new when the old are adequate?' (Alcuin, *Epistola 226*, ed. E. Dümmler, p. 370; tr. S. Allott, *Alcuin of York: His Life and Letters* (York, 1974), pp. 27–8.) The 'Old English Martyrology', a work of the ninth century, likewise mentions an 'old massbook' and a 'new massbook', possibly referring to the Gelasian and Gregorian sacramentaries (Gneuss, 'Anglo-Saxon libraries', p. 663). See also *Das altenglische Martyrologium*, ed. G. Kotzor, 2 vols., Bayerische Akademie der Wissenschaften, philosophische-historische Klasse, Abhandlungen, neue Folge 88 (Munich, 1981) I, 258–66; J. E. Cross, 'On the library of the Old English Martyrologist', in Lapidge and Gneuss, *Learning and Literature*, pp. 227–49, at p. 234; and Lapidge, 'Latin learning', pp. 437–8. The Gelasian type seems to have predominated in early Anglo-Saxon England, the Gregorian in later centuries: H. T. Bannister, 'Liturgical fragments, A: Anglo-Saxon sacramentaries', *Journal of Theological Studies* 9 (1908), 398–427; R. W. Pfaff, 'Massbooks' in *idem* (ed.), *The Liturgical Books*, pp. 7–34, at pp. 10–11.

'Breton'.[77] The Viking occupation of Brittany in 910 sent many Breton clerics into exile in England up to the 930s.[78]

Conclusions

The ninth-century decline in the English Church did not spell the end of the Divine Office. Despite the stress caused by poor standards of education, the secularization of minsters, and the attacks of the Vikings, it would appear that a number of minsters, especially in the West Saxon heartlands, will have been able to maintain their liturgical traditions. Significant change to the inherited English tradition of the Roman Office may have come first through the reforms of King Alfred and the programme of monastic foundation apparently pursued by his successors. It is impossible to know exactly what texts and music were sung in the Office by Alfred's 'learned men'.[79] But it seems likely that the clerics of the court chapel and perhaps of the minsters founded or supported by Alfred and his successors will have performed the Office – according to the secular *cursus* – in a way resembling contemporary Continental practice. On the eve of the tenth-century Benedictine reform, the Divine Office was probably celebrated in England with highly variable mixtures of traditional and Continental elements, but within the stable framework of the Roman *cursus*, either in its archaic seventh-century form or the form then current on the Continent, which differed significantly only in the structure of the Sunday Night Office.

---

[77] S. Rankin, 'Neumatic notations in Anglo-Saxon England', in M. Huglo (ed.), *Musicologie médiévale: Notations et séquences*, Actes de la Table Ronde du CNRS à l'Institut de recherche et d'histoire des textes, 6–7 septembre 1982 (Paris, 1987), pp. 129–44, 262–3, and Plates XIV–XXI, at p. 131.
[78] Dumville, *Wessex and England*, pp. 200–1.
[79] Lapidge and Keynes, *Alfred the Great*, p. 26.

5

The Divine Office and the Tenth-Century English Benedictine Reform

The history of the Divine Office in England from the Augustinian mission to the first decades of the tenth century, which has been reconstructed in the preceding chapters, may be briefly summarized as follows. A Roman form of the Office was introduced to England in the early seventh century, perhaps by the Roman missionaries, and by the middle of the eighth it had effectively supplanted the forms of the Office derived from British, Irish, or Gallican traditions that must previously have had some currency in England but which have left no trace and whose forms cannot be reconstructed with any certainty. This seventh-century Roman Office was enriched with material from various traditions while maintaining its structural integrity. Outside England, the Roman Office was subjected to various modifications, both in Rome itself, where the Office continued to evolve, and in Frankish Gaul, where the Roman Office was adapted and standardized in distinctive ways. The little evidence that survives suggests that some English churches kept pace with these developments while others conservatively maintained the earlier tradition. Either approach could legitimately be claimed as 'Roman'. There is no evidence that separate forms of the Office were used by secular and monastic churches – and these labels are in any case problematic when speaking of the early centuries. In particular, there is no evidence that the form of the Office described in the *Regula S. Benedicti* was used anywhere in England, despite the importance of the Rule in English monastic life.

The prevailing practice began to change dramatically in the middle of the tenth century. The English Benedictine reform movement has been so intensely studied that no lengthy account of its history is necessary here.[1] It began, according to the traditional interpretation, with King Eadmund's

---

[1] Three older narrative accounts of the reform remain very useful: Knowles, *The Monastic Order*, pp. 31–56; F. M. Stenton, *Anglo-Saxon England*, 3rd edn (London, 1971),

installation of St Dunstan as abbot of Glastonbury (940×946). Dunstan's first biographer, the clerk known only as 'B.', reports that Dunstan began immediately to implement the teachings of the *Regula S. Benedicti*.[2] By 963, Dunstan, his early disciple Æthelwold, and his later protegé Oswald occupied between them, through the patronage of King Edgar, the sees of Canterbury, Winchester, and Worcester (Oswald adding York in 972). The 'turning point' of the reform has usually been taken to be Æthelwold's expulsion of the secular clerks from the Old and the New Minsters in Winchester in 964.[3] Their replacement with Benedictine monks from Æthelwold's first monastery at Abingdon gave England its first monastic cathedral.[4] According to Oswald's disciple and biographer Byrhtferth of Ramsey, writing 997×1002, at its apex the movement could boast over forty (*plus quam quadraginta*) reformed or newly founded Benedictine monasteries,[5] though evidence is only available for just over half that number during Edgar's reign. And in addition to the *Regula S. Benedicti*, all of them recognized, at least in theory, the authority of a mutually agreed monastic customary, the *Regularis concordia*, adopted at the undated Council of Winchester, *c*.970.

Most of the surviving literary accounts of England's ecclesiastical history during the second half of the tenth century were written by the apologists of the reform. (A notable exception, Dunstan's biographer B., was

---

pp. 433–69; and the introduction by T. Symons to his edition of the *Regularis concordia* (London, 1953), pp. ix–xxviii. A brief summary presented with scholarly detachment may be found in D. H. Farmer, 'The progress of the monastic revival', in D. Parsons (ed.), *Tenth-Century Studies: Essays in Commemoration of the Millennium of the Council of Winchester and 'Regularis Concordia'* (London, 1975), pp. 10–19. The careers of the three main leaders of the movement are explored in the introductory chapters to the volumes compiled on the millennial anniversaries of their deaths: Yorke, *Bishop Æthelwold*; N. Ramsay, M. Sparks, and T. Tatton-Brown (eds.), *St Dunstan: His Life, Times and Cult* (Woodbridge, 1992); and N. Brooks and C. Cubitt (eds.), *St Oswald of Worcester: Life and Influence* (London, 1996). The contributions in these volumes are helpfully digested in C. Cubitt, 'Review article: The tenth-century Benedictine Reform in England', *Early Medieval Europe* 6 (1997), 77–94. To them may now be added the admirable concise critical synthesis by Blair, *The Church in Anglo-Saxon Society*, pp. 346–54.

[2] B., *Vita S. Dunstani*, § 15. 1, ed. and tr. Winterbottom and Lapidge, *Early Lives*, pp. 50–1.
[3] Farmer, 'The progress of the monastic revival', p. 12.
[4] Wulfstan, *Vita S. Æthelwoldi*, cc. 16–20, ed. and tr. M. Lapidge and M. Winterbottom, *Wulfstan of Winchester: The Life of St Æthelwold* (Oxford, 1991), pp. 29–37; *Anglo-Saxon Chronicle* 'A', *s.a.* 964, ed. Plummer, *Two of the Saxon Chronicles Parallel* I, 116. See Farmer, 'The progress of the monastic revival', p. 12.
[5] Byrhtferth of Ramsey, *Vita S. Oswaldi*, III. 11, ed. M. Lapidge, *Byrhtferth of Ramsey: The Lives of St Oswald and St Ecgwine*, Oxford Medieval Texts (Oxford, 2009) pp. 1–203, at pp. 76–7.

a secular cleric writing in hope of preferment.[6]) Whereas the first modern historical accounts of the reform movement took the statements of contemporary writers more or less at face value, more recent scholarship has questioned the reform's extent, character, and significance within the wider context of the tenth-century English Church. The reformed monasteries made up only an influential minority – about ten per cent – of England's several hundred minsters.[7] And if the lay nobility recognized any substantial difference between reformed and unreformed communities, this made no discernible difference in their donations, which were more often governed by familial connections or political expediency.[8] What Byrhtferth portrayed as anti-monastic sentiment by one section of the nobility following the death of Edgar is better seen as part of a dispute over the royal succession, in which reformed and unreformed houses alike were used or abused to serve the ends of the rival parties.[9]

Just as the reformed monasteries are now seen as part of a wider network of English minsters, so the leaders of the Benedictine movement have emerged as men of their time: not just as extremely wealthy and well-connected men of high birth, but also as skilled political operatives capable of a certain amount of ruthlessness in the advancement of their goals. As John Nightingale has noted, 'reform was a potent weapon with which to wrest or secure control of an abbey and its landholdings from rivals'.[10] There is some evidence to suggest that Æthelwold's unprecedented eviction of the Winchester clerks should be seen as part of a rivalry of this kind.[11] Dunstan's elevation to Canterbury, which required the uncanonical deposition of the incumbent, Byrhthelm, has been called 'a disgrace' and 'a shameless *putsch*'.[12] Oswald's habit of lending Worcester land to his kinsmen throws the monks' supposed disdain of 'overlordship

---

[6] M. Lapidge, 'B. and the *Vita S. Dunstani*', in Ramsay et al., *St Dunstan*, pp. 247–59, at p. 259.
[7] Blair, *The Church in Anglo-Saxon Society*, p. 351.
[8] J. M. Pope, 'Monks and nobles in the Anglo-Saxon monastic reform', *Anglo-Norman Studies* 17 (1994), 165–80, at pp. 165 and 177.
[9] Byrhtferth, *Vita S. Oswaldi*, IV. 11, ed. and tr. Lapidge, pp. 122–3. D. J. V. Fisher, 'The anti-monastic reaction in the reign of Edward the Martyr', *Cambridge Historical Journal* 10 (1952), 254–70; Pope, 'Monks and nobles', p. 179.
[10] 'Oswald, Fleury and continental reform', in Brooks and Cubitt, *St Oswald*, pp. 23–45, at p. 33.
[11] P. Wormald, 'The strange affair of the Selsey bishopric, 953–963', in R. Gameson and H. Leyser (eds.), *Belief and Culture in the Middle Ages: Studies Presented to Henry Mayr-Harting* (Oxford, 2001), pp. 128–41, at p. 140.
[12] Brooks, *The Early History*, p. 243; Wormald, 'The strange affair', p. 128.

of secular persons' (*saecularium prioratus*) into a more realistic light.[13]

In addition to all this, it has become less and less clear that Dunstan and his circle can be credited with instigating an entirely original and clearly defined movement. As David Dumville has reasonably argued, much that has been attributed to the Benedictine reformers can be traced back to the ecclesiastical programme of King Alfred, which was carried forward by his successors.[14] Reformed monks may have enjoyed King Edgar's special favour at the expense of their unreformed counterparts to an extent not previously seen under any other king. But King Eadred (946–55) seems to have supported the nascent Benedictines; and if the old order found succour in the pro-Winchester policies of Edgar's brother and rival Eadwig (955–9) – and even he offered some support to Æthelwold's Abingdon[15] – this merely shows how Edgar's exclusive support for the Benedictines was as much about securing his political interests as about reforming the English Church.[16] Traits often linked with 'reformed monastic culture', such as Caroline minuscule and the *Gallicanum* version of the Latin psalter, are not to be linked exclusively to the reformers. Caroline minuscule seems to have been known in England as early as c.900, and the reformed Benedictines continued to prefer the traditional *Romanum* text of the psalter throughout the tenth century.[17]

Nevertheless, the distinctiveness and originality of the tenth-century Benedictine reform, and the spread of its ideology, can be clearly discerned in at least one of its achievements: the establishment of the Benedictine form of the Divine Office in reformed monasteries. As a uniform observance of the Rule's liturgical code had been the hallmark of the Frankish monastic reforms of the ninth century, so it was in the English reforms of the tenth. Unlike earlier periods, the later tenth century can boast a handful of fragmentary examples of English Benedictine Office books. It is to the analysis of these fragments – with an eye to determining

---

[13] Pope, 'Monks and nobles', p. 175. On *saecularium prioratus*, see *Regularis concordia*, § 10, ed. Symons p. 7 (CCM § 10, pp. 75–6), and E. John, 'The king and the monks in the tenth-century reformation', in his *Orbis Britanniae*, Studies in Early English History 4 (Leicester, 1966), pp. 154–80, at p. 156.
[14] See above, p. 143.
[15] Thacker, 'Æthelwold and Abingdon', p. 52.
[16] *The Liber Vitae of the New Minster*, ed. Keynes, pp. 23–5; John, 'The king and the monks', pp. 178–9.
[17] On Caroline minuscule, see p. 306 below. On the versions of the psalter, see above, p. 110 n. 115; and on the adoption of the *Gallicanum* in the tenth and eleventh centuries, see below, p. 191.

the Continental traditions that lie behind them and the different ways in which a reformed monastery might establish a strict Benedictine Office observance – that subsequent chapters of this study are devoted. The present chapter sets out a chronological framework for the adoption of the Benedictine *cursus* in England against which the surviving fragments may be assessed. Four main periods may be discerned: (a) an early phase of reform at Glastonbury, during which texts of the ninth-century Frankish monastic reforms were studied by the new English Benedictines; (b) a period of exposure to Continental customs, including Dunstan's exile to Ghent, Oswald's sojourn at Fleury, and Æthelwold's procurement of teachers from Corbie; (c) the expansion and self-promotion in the movement in the 960s; and (d) the consolidation of the movement, represented by the promulgation of the *Regularis concordia*. A final section examines a variety of sources supplying approximately datable evidence for the use of the Benedictine *cursus* at specific monasteries and cathedral priories.

Glastonbury and the Aachen texts (940×946–957)

'Sit in this seat, high and powerful, as the loyal abbot of this church. Whatever your own resources lack to increase divine worship and fulfil the holy rule, *I* shall make up with a king's bounty.' So after that Dunstan, servant of God, took up his office, to rule at the king's command. And this is how, following the principles of St Benedict, which bring salvation, he shone forth as the premier abbot of the English people.[18]

So B. relates Dunstan's instalment as abbot of Glastonbury at the hand of King Eadmund. Of monastic life at Glastonbury when Dunstan was first abbot there (940×946–956) little can be known apart from what B. reports. Although he is uninformed about Dunstan's later career as Archbishop of Canterbury – B. seems to have accompanied Dunstan on his

---

[18] B. *Vita S. Dunstani*, §§ 14. 6–15. 1, ed. and tr. Winterbottom and Lapidge, *Early Lives*, pp. 50–51: ' "Esto sedis istius princeps potensque insessor, et presentis aecclesiae fidelissimus abbas; et quicquid tibi ad diuini cultus augmentum uel ad sacrae regulae supplementum de propria adminiculatione defuerit, ego illud regia largitate deuote subplebo." Igitur post haec seruus Dei Dunstanus iam dictam dignitatem iussu regis regendi gratia suscepit, et hoc predicto modo saluberrimam sancti Benedicti sequens institutionem primum abbas Anglicae nationis enituit.'

journey to Rome to receive the pallium in 960, perhaps remaining on the Continent afterwards[19] – he has detailed knowledge of Dunstan's time at Glastonbury; and since he was not himself a monk, there is no reason to assume that he exaggerates when he says that the *Regula S. Benedicti* was followed there.[20] And as Thomas Symons observed, a single textual parallel with the Rule in B.'s *Vita*, where he records Dunstan's transfer of the abbey's secular concerns to his brother Wulfric lest he or any other monk should have to 'roam outside', suggests that the Rule was followed closely.[21] This does not mean, however, that the Office liturgy of Glastonbury suddenly became Benedictine. Even if this were desired at the outset, it would be a massive project. And it is not at all obvious that Dunstan would have had any immediate plans to alter the (probably) Roman *cursus* already in use. The Roman Office had, after all, been sung for centuries in monasteries where the *Regula S. Benedicti* was venerated and studied. The adoption of the Benedictine *cursus* in Frankish monasteries in the ninth century had been an occasion for some controversy, and the process was by no means complete there in the tenth century. Even if he were aware that monasteries on the Continent were using the Benedictine *cursus*, Dunstan would have to be persuaded that this was appropriate for his monastery too. As Patrick Wormald might protest, the adoption of the Benedictine *cursus* cannot be passed off automatically as a 'manifestation of the *Zeitgeist*'.[22]

So where did the English Benedictines get the idea to use the Benedictine *cursus*? They read about it. In particular, they read about it in texts produced and promoted by the Frankish monastic reformers of the ninth century. Reflection on these texts led the English Benedictines to see the use of the Benedictine *cursus* as an essential aspect of the monastic virtue of obedience, to the Rule and to St Benedict himself.

Glastonbury under Dunstan was a place of study. As B. puts it, Dunstan 'began to nourish with the food of God's word the company that had gathered and been entrusted to him, and to water them with the fountain of heaven, the honeyed teaching of holy scripture'.[23] Among the pupils who

---

[19] Lapidge, 'B. and the *Vita S. Dunstani*', pp. 248–9 and 259.
[20] N. Brooks, 'The career of St Dunstan', in Ramsay et al., *St Dunstan*, pp. 1–23, at p. 12.
[21] *Regularis concordia*, ed. Symons, p. xvi and n. 2. B., *Vita S. Dunstani*, § 18. 1, ed. and tr. Winterbottom and Lapidge, *Early Lives*, pp. 58–9: 'ne uel ipse uel quispiam ex monastica professione foris uagaretur' ('that neither he nor any professed monk should have to go out'). Cf. *RSB* 66:7: 'ut non sit necessitas monachis uagandis foris'.
[22] Wormald, 'Æthelwold and his Continental counterparts', p. 14.
[23] B., *Vita S. Dunstani*, § 15. 2, ed. and tr. Winterbottom and Lapidge, *Early Lives*, pp. 52–3:

sought Dunstan's instruction was Æthelwold, who, Wulfstan reports, excelled in grammar, poetry, and the study of the best Catholic authors.[24] In addition to these subjects, the inmates of Glastonbury will also, of course, have studied the *Regula S. Benedicti* and texts related to it. That a number of the texts promoted by Benedict of Aniane were studied at Glastonbury has been proposed afresh by Mechthild Gretsch in an important study of Cambridge, Corpus Christi College 57 (Abingdon or perhaps Christ Church, Canterbury, s. x/xi).[25] This manuscript served as Abingdon's chapterhouse copy of the *Regula S. Benedicti* from at least the mid-eleventh century.[26] Appended to the text of the Rule is a set of texts linked with the reforms of Benedict of Aniane: (a) 'Pseudo-Fulgentius', a brief hortatory text advocating strict adherence to the *Regula S. Benedicti*;[27] (b) *Memoriale qualiter*, an eighth-century Benedictine customary popularized by Benedict of Aniane;[28] (c) *De festiuitatibus anni*, a directory of feast days to be observed throughout the Carolingian empire;[29] (d) *Collectio capitularis* (818×819), also known as the *Regula S. Benedicti Anianensis*, a widely circulated digest of the Aachen reform legislation;[30] (e) *Martyrologium* of Usuard of Saint-Germain-des-Prés;[31] (f) *Diadema monachorum* of Smaragdus of Saint-Mihiel (ends incompletely).[32]

Through a careful analysis of textual variants and peculiarities of layout in Corpus 57 and several other late Anglo-Saxon manuscripts containing these texts, with reference to the most closely related Continental recensions, Gretsch has been able to suggest, with great caution, that Corpus 57 had as its exemplar the original chapterhouse book of Glastonbury Abbey during the abbacy of St Dunstan. Even if this highly tentative suggestion cannot be definitively relied upon, Gretsch has shown beyond

---

'adgregatum coenobium sibique commissum diuini uerbi coepit fomento nutrire et fonte superno, sacrae scilicet scripturae mellifluo documento, potare'.

[24] Wulfstan, *Vita S. Æthelwoldi*, c. 9, ed. and tr. Lapidge and Winterbottom, pp. 14–15.
[25] Gretsch, 'Cambridge, Corpus Christi College 57'.
[26] The text of the Rule in Corpus 57 is ed. J. Chamberlin, *The Rule of St Benedict: The Abingdon Copy*, Toronto Medieval Latin Texts 13 (Toronto, 1982).
[27] The text is ed. in H. Sauer, 'Die Ermahnung des Pseudo-Fulgentius zur Benediktregel und ihre altenglische Glossierung', *Anglia* 102 (1984), 412–25.
[28] Ed. C. Morgand, in *Initia consuetudinis Benedictinae*, ed. Hallinger, CCM 1, pp. 230–61.
[29] Ed. from English MSS in J. E. Cross, '*De festivitatibus anni* and Ansegisus, *Capitularum collectio* (827) in Anglo-Saxon manuscripts', *Liverpool Classical Monthly* 17.8 (1992), 119–21.
[30] Ed. J. Semmler, in *Initia consuetudinis Benedictinae*, ed. Hallinger, CCM 1, pp. 515–36.
[31] Ed. J. Dubois, *Le Martyrologe d'Usuard: Texte et commentaire* (Brussels, 1965).
[32] *PL* CII, 593–690.

reasonable doubt that a 'dossier' of texts connected with the ninth-century Frankish reforms was available and studied at Glastonbury between Dunstan's appointment and Æthelwold's departure c.954. This dossier included two further texts not found in Corpus 57: (g) the *Expositio in Regulam S. Benedicti* of Smaragdus, of which a mid-tenth-century copy survives with annotations in Dunstan's hand (Cambridge, University Library, Ee. 2. 4), and to which Æthelwold referred in his Old English translation of the Rule (which he completed, Gretsch has argued, in the early Glastonbury period, not 964×975 as usually stated);[33] and (h) the *Institutio sanctimonialium*, rules for female canonesses, promulgated by the Synod of Aachen in 816, which was another source used in Æthelwold's translation of the Rule.[34] It seems likely, though it cannot be proved, that this text would have circulated together with the *Institutio canonicorum* (for the male secular clergy) promulgated at the same synod, the two of them making up a 'secular dossier'.[35]

The availability of the Aachen decrees for seculars suggests that these texts arrived during a period 'with less exclusively monastic preoccupations'.[36] Gretsch suggests that the Aachen texts may have been among the books brought to the court of Alfred in the 880s by Grimbald of Saint-Bertin or John the Old Saxon.[37] This suggestion is based in large measure on Gretsch's assumption that Grimbald and John were 'Benedictine monks', which, as has been seen, is highly unlikely in Grimbald's case and unprovable in John's.[38] The period between c.910 and c.930, when England played host to displaced Breton clerics, seems more probable: the monks of Brittany had embraced Benedict of Aniane's reforms more readily than those of most other regions.[39] Whenever these texts arrived,

---

[33] *Smaragdi abbatis Expositio in Regulam S. Benedicti*, ed. Spannagel and Engelbert; several leaves originally from CUL Ee. 2. 4, which includes annotations in 'Hand D', are now Oxford, Bodleian Library, lat. theol. c. 3, fols. 1, 1*, and 2 (the whole MS: Glastonbury?, s. x med.). On this and other examples of Dunstan's hand, see M. Budny, ' "St Dunstan's Classbook" and its frontispiece: Dunstan's portrait and autograph', in Ramsay et al., *St Dunstan*, pp. 103–42, at p. 137 and Plate 8a. On an early date for Æthelwold's translation of the Rule, see Gretsch, *Intellectual Foundations*, pp. 233–60.
[34] Ed. Werminghoff, *Concilia aevi Karolini* I, 422–56. On Æthelwold's use of this text, see Gretsch, *Intellectual Foundations*, pp. 255–9.
[35] For this text, see p. 65 and n. 176 above.
[36] Gretsch, *Intellectual Foundations*, p. 138.
[37] Gretsch, 'Cambridge, Corpus Christi College 57', pp. 138–9.
[38] See p. 144 above.
[39] J. H. M. Smith, 'Culte impérial et politique frontalière dans la vallée de la Vilaine: Le témoignage des diplômes carolingiens dans le cartulaire de Redon', in M. Simon (ed.),

they seem to have been available to the group of disciples that gathered around Dunstan at Glastonbury.

The ninth-century texts studied at Glastonbury, while rich in information about the ideals and practicalities of a reformed monastic life, have relatively little to say about the form and content of the Divine Office. 'Pseudo-Fulgentius' merely exhorts monks to keep the whole of the Rule faithfully, and it could be argued that this could be done – and had been done – without the use of the Benedictine *cursus*. The *Memoriale qualiter* has much to say about the timing of the offices during the day, the deportment of the monks as they perform them, and how they are to arrive and depart. But it never says explicitly that the Office of the Rule is to be used,[40] which is unsurprising given that eighth-century Frankish monks seem to have used the Roman *cursus*, even in conjunction with the *Regula S. Benedicti*. The *Collectio capitularis* reproduces, without elaboration, the 816 synodal decree ordering monks to celebrate the Office 'according to what is contained in the Rule of St Benedict'.[41] This decree was, as has been seen, open to varied interpretations; and whether a small group of English monks would consider an old Frankish imperial capitulary to be binding on them is hard to say.

The decisive text may have been the *Expositio in Regulam* of Smaragdus. As was seen in Chapter 2, Smaragdus acknowledges that St Benedict gave permission to change the form of the Office, specifically the distribution of psalms (*RSB* 18:22), but he nevertheless advises monks to put their trust in the Rule and to follow it to the letter, confident that this will lead to salvation.[42] In CUL Ee. 2. 4 (fol. 119r), at the point where Smaragdus speaks of Benedict's leaving the distribution of psalms 'to the judgement of a discerning person' (*iudicantis ... arbitrium*), over the word *arbitrium*, in the hand believed to be Dunstan's, is the gloss *in suo arbitrio (sic)*, 'in his/their own judgement'. This is probably an allusion to the fifth chapter of the *Regula S. Benedicti*, which describes renunciation of the personal

---

Landévennec et le monachisme breton dans le haut Moyen Âge (Landévennec, 1986), pp. 126–39; and eadem, *Province and Empire: Brittany and the Carolingian Church* (Cambridge, 1992), p. 72.

[40] The closest it comes is in § 9 (p. 239): 'Cum ad opus diuinum horis canonicis auditum fuerit signum, sicut continetur in regula, reliquentes statim quicquid in manubus est...'; this 'as is contained in the Rule' invokes *RSB* 43:1, which does not refer to the form of the Office, but rather requires monks, on hearing the bell for the Divine Office, to drop whatever is in their hands and go immediately.

[41] *Collectio capitularis*, c. 3, ed. Morgand, p. 517. Cf. p. 64 above.

[42] See p. 68 above.

will as the fundamental principle of communal monastic life:

> They no longer live by their own judgment (*non suo arbitrio uiuentes*), giving in to their whims and appetites; rather they walk according to another's decisions and directions (*alieno iudicio et imperio*), choosing to live in monasteries and to have an abbot over them.[43]

The glossator has noticed that St Benedict seems to contradict himself here by leaving room for personal judgement. What monk, the gloss seems to ask, would ever presume to indulge his own 'whim and appetite', especially over the judgement of Benedict himself? On this view, it would seem, St Benedict was not to be understood literally to be giving permission to depart from his instructions. Hildemar of Corbie similarly dismissed the Rule's permission to alter the distribution of the psalms by noting that Benedict was merely speaking 'in the manner of holy doctors' (*more sanctorum doctorum locutus est*), who were too humble to claim that their definitive pronouncements were above challenge.[44] The glossator's interpretation of the passage would appear to be an original contribution, since the glosses in CUL Ee. 2. 4 seem to derive from independent study of Smaragdus's *Expositio* and not from any other known source.[45]

This view of the authority of the Benedictine distribution of the psalms finds expression in an alteration to the text of the Rule in Corpus 57. Where St Benedict had required only that any newly devised distribution of the psalms be taken up 'from the beginning' (*a caput* in the *textus purus*; *a capite* in the *textus receptus* used by the reformed Benedictines) every Sunday, Corpus 57 has 'from the twentieth psalm' (*a uigesimo psalmo*).[46] The Benedictine *cursus* places Psalm 20 at the beginning of the Night Office on Sunday (*RSB* 18:6). The alteration in Corpus 57

---

[43] *RSB* 5:12: 'ut non suo arbitrio uiuentes uel desideriis suis et uoluptatibus oboedientes, sed ambulantes alieno iudicio et imperio, in coenobiis degentes abbatem sibi praeesse desiderant'.

[44] Hildemar, *Expositio Regulae*, c. 18, ed. Mittermüller, p. 311: 'For the holy doctors have settled a given matter more deeply, such that it could not be better settled. Nevertheless, by reason of humility, after their explanation they say, "If someone else shall judge better, let him do so," as did the blessed Gregory in his *Moralia in Iob*.' ('Sancti enim doctores definiunt causam profundius, quae melius non potest definiri, et tamen post definitionem causa humilitatis dicunt: si alius judicaverit melius, faciat, veluti B. Gregorius in libris moralium facit.') Hildemar goes on to quote *Moralia in Iob*, XXX. 27 (§ 81), ed. Adriaen III, 1546–7.

[45] See *Smaragdi abbatis Expositio*, ed. Spannagel and Engelbert, p. liii.

[46] *RSB* 18:23, ed. Chamberlin, *The Rule*, p. 39, and see the list of variants on p. 78.

effectively neutralizes St Benedict's permission to use a different distribution of psalms. Moreover, if *a capite* were construed to mean 'from the first psalm', this alteration would specifically rule out the use of the Roman distribution of psalms, in which the Sunday Night Office begins with Psalm 1.[47] To judge from the critical apparatus in the (admittedly unreliable) edition of Rudolph Hanslik, this reading is unique to Corpus 57.[48] Mechthild Gretsch's observation of a connection between Psalm 20, with its reference to God setting a 'crown of fine gold' upon the head of the righteous ruler, and the depiction of a crowned St Benedict in the Benedictional of Æthelwold might have something to say about Corpus 57's insistence on the primacy of this psalm.[49] No such importance is accorded to it in the original version of the Rule: St Benedict makes it clear that this aspect of his distribution is a numerical accident.

These two points of evidence suggest that the English reformers' early study of the Rule and the Aachen texts led them to aspire to total obedience to St Benedict's teachings, and that this would extend to the performance of the Office. The theme of obedience receives special emphasis in one of eight unusual interpolations in the text of the Rule in Corpus 57.[50] The eighth interpolation, shared only with one other English copy of the Rule, BL Cotton Tiberius A. iii (Christ Church, Canterbury, s. xi med.), is found at *RSB* 7:55 (quoted on p. 26 above), the 'eighth step of humility'. It takes the form of three scriptural citations justifying St Benedict's command that the monk should not do anything that is not endorsed by the common rule of the monastery or the example of the seniors.[51] Most of the other

---

[47] See p. 58 above.
[48] *Benedicti Regula*, ed. R. Hanslik, 2nd edn, Corpus scriptorum ecclesiasticorum Latinorum 75 (Vienna, 1976).
[49] Gretsch, *Intellectual Foundations*, pp. 297–304, with specific reference to the *cursus* at pp. 303–4. She does not note in her argument the alteration of the text of the Rule in Corpus 57.
[50] All but one of these interpolations supply prayers and versicles and responses to accompany actions that seem to require such things to be recited but for which the original text of the Rule makes no provision. See Gretsch, 'Corpus 57', pp. 129–32.
[51] Ps. 118:107; Matt. 11:29b; and 1 Pet. 5:6–9; ed. Chamberlin, *The Rule*, p. 31: 'Octauus humilitatis gradus est si nihil agat monachus nisi quod communis monasterii regula uel maiorum cohortantur exempla, sicut scriptum est, "Humiliatus sum usquequaque, Domine, uiuifica me secundum uerbum tuum." Et Dominus dixit, "Discite a me quia mitis sum et humilis corde, et inuenietis requiem animabus uestris"; et Apostolus Petrus, "Humiliamini sub potenti manu Dei ut uos exaltet in tempore uisitationis, omnem sollicitudinem uestram proicientes in eum quoniam ipsi cura est de uobis. Sobrii estote et uigilate quia aduersarius uester diabolus tamquam leo rugiens circuit quaerens quem deuoret. Cui resistite fortes in fide scientes eandem passionem ei quae in mundo est uestrae fraternitatis fieri."'

'steps' have such citations in the original text of the Rule, and Gretsch remarks that all three passages are an appropriate expansion of the Rule's text, since each has to do with humility.[52] It could be argued that the interpolation is even more appropriate, and sophisticated, than this, since each biblical interpolation is preceded, in its original scriptural context, by a passage of direct relevance to the theme of obedience, each with a plausible parallel in the Rule. These may be compared directly as follows, with the interpolation (a) followed by the passage that precedes it in its scriptural context (b) and then the passage of the Rule that expresses the same sentiment (c):

Interp. 1   Humiliatus sum usquequaque, Domine, uiuifica me secundum uerbum tuum. (Ps. 118:107)
Context   iuraui et statui *custodire iudicia* iustitiae tuae (Ps. 118:106)
Parallel   promiserit se omnia *custodire* et cuncta sibi *imperata* seruare (*RSB* 58:14)

Interp. 2   Discite a me quia mitis sum et humilis corde, et inuenietis requiem animabus uestris. (Matt. 11:29b)
Context   tollite *iugum* meum super uos (Matt. 11:29a)
Parallel   non liceat ... nec collum excutere de sub *iugo* regulae (*RSB* 58:16)

Interp. 3   Humiliamini sub potenti manu Dei ... quae in mundo est uestrae fraternitatis fieri. (1 Pet. 5:6–9)
Context   similiter adulescentes subditi estote *senioribus* (1 Pet. 5:5a)
Parallel   Octauus humilitatis gradus est si nihil agat monachus, nisi quod communis monasterii regula vel *maiorum* cohortantur exempla. (*RSB* 7:55 itself)

The first two interpolations point to the part of the Rule concerned with the admission of new monks, who are solemnly warned that once they promise to live under the Rule they may never again depart from it. The third points directly to the original text in the Rule where the interpolations occur (*RSB* 7:55). All of them reveal the interpolator's desire to emphasize, through a subtle use of intertextuality, the importance of obedience to the 'common rule of the monastery'.

This concern could well have been inspired by study of the texts appended to the Rule in Corpus 57 and other pre-Conquest English copies.

---

[52] Gretsch, 'Cambridge Corpus Christi College 57', p. 129.

The Aachen texts take obedience to such great lengths that all personal initiative is excluded, as in the following passage from the *Memoriale qualiter*:

> Let no one presume to perform any work, even if it seems good to him, without the permission or blessing of the prior.[53]

This goes well beyond the spirit of *RSB* 7:55. The *Memoriale qualiter* was an important source text in Æthelwold's drafting of the *Regularis concordia*,[54] and it was obviously the main influence on the *Concordia*'s specific teachings on obedience:

> Let no one presume to do anything whatsoever, however small, of his own, and as if it were a personal choice; neither let him leave the church during the celebration of the appointed hours nor the cloister, as the Rule enjoins, nor, puffed up by overweening pride, let him dare to do the least thing without the permission of the prior ... lest by careless neglect of the smallest precept of the Rule he become guilty, as the apostle says, of all the commandments: which God forbid.[55]

This kind of obedience underpins two miracles in Wulfstan's *Vita S. Æthelwoldi*: the brother who obeys Æthelwold's command to plunge his hand into boiling water, withdrawing it unharmed, and the brother who falls from a great height but survives uninjured because he was employed in carrying out Æthelwold's instructions.[56]

The Rule compares its twelve steps of humility to Jacob's vision of a ladder between heaven and earth: by progressively humbling himself

---

[53] *Memoriale qualiter*, c. 4, ed. Morgand, p. 247: 'Nullus opus, etiam sibi bonum uideatur, sine permissione uel benedictione prioris agere praesumat.'

[54] See the notes throughout the first chapter of the *Concordia* in both its editions: §§ 14–27, ed. Symons pp. 11–24 (CCM §§ 15–38, pp. 80–94). In Symons's 1953 edition, the *Memoriale qualiter* is designated in the notes by the letters 'OQ'.

[55] *Regularis concordia*, § 64, ed. Symons p. 63 (CCM § 97, p. 140): 'Nullus quippiam quamvis parum sua ac quasi propria adinuentione agere praesumat; nec ecclesia, horas celebrando constitutas, nec claustro uti regula praecipit egredi, nec parum quid sine prioris licentia superbiae tumore inflatus audeat. ... ne regulae praeceptorum minima praetereat, ac sic, dicente apostolo, omnium mandatorum quod abisit reus existat.' This text also incorporates words from *RSB* 67:16–18. Compare a similar passage in *Regularis concordia*, § 6, ed. Symons p. 4 (CCM § 6, p. 73), which uses language reminiscent of the Corpus 57 interpolations, especially the 'yoke of the Rule', which also appears in § 8, ed. Symons p. 5 (CCM § 8, p. 74), in the context of a quotation of the eighth step of humility.

[56] The cauldron: Wulfstan, *Vita S. Æthelwoldi*, c. 14, ed. and tr. Lapidge and Winterbottom, pp. 26–9; the fall: c. 34, (pp. 52–3).

on earth, the monk ascends to heaven (*RSB* 7:5–9). The originator of the interpolation at *RSB* 7:55 in Corpus 57 and Tiberius A. iii sought to emphasize the importance of the eighth rung of this ladder, obedience to the 'common rule of the monastery'. In the *Regularis concordia*, this obedience excludes all personal initiative on the part of a monk. Within this interpretation, Smaragdus's recommendation to follow the Benedictine *cursus* with trusting obedience will have been taken very seriously.

What should be clear is that this reading of the Rule and of the Aachen texts was in no way an unthinking duplication of a Continental example. The text of the Rule itself in Corpus 57, like all surviving tenth- and eleventh-century English copies of the Rule, may be set firmly within the *textus receptus* tradition introduced to England from the Continent some time before the Benedictine reform. But it nevertheless contains a disproportionate number of variants introduced from the old *interpolatus* tradition whose earliest witness is English (Oxford, Bodleian Library, Hatton 48). Some of the *interpolatus* readings in Corpus 57 are not found in Hatton 48, so it remains a possibility that the recension of the Rule in Corpus 57 derives directly from a lost Continental exemplar. But Corpus 57 is more closely related to Hatton 48 than any surviving English copy, which suggests that it was produced within the English textual tradition of the Rule. It is probable that the unique conflation of readings in Corpus 57 was the product a careful study and collation of both the *receptus* and the *interpolatus* traditions, perhaps with reference to a now lost English copy of the *interpolatus* text that differed somewhat from Hatton 48.[57] This is yet one more example of how, to use Christopher Jones's phrase, England's 'reception of Carolingian sources was productive rather than merely passive'.[58] Even an enthusiast for Continental monasticism like Æthelwold could consider, as is revealed in his 'Old English Account of King Edgar's establishment of monasteries', that the English Benedictine movement was less an innovation than a return to England's glorious monastic past.[59] This should warn us that an English version of

---

[57] Gretsch, 'Cambridge Corpus Christi College 57', pp. 127–8 and 142.
[58] C. A. Jones, 'The book of the liturgy in Anglo-Saxon England', *Speculum* 73 (1998), 659–702, at p. 681.
[59] The 'Old English account' is ed. and tr. by Whitelock in *Councils and Synods with Other Documents Relating to the English Church*, I: *A.D. 871–1204*, ed. D. Whitelock, M. Brett and C. N. L. Brooke, 2 vols. (Oxford, 1980) I, 142–54. See Wormald, 'Æthelwold and his Continental counterparts', pp. 40–1; Thacker, 'Æthelwold and Abingdon', p. 55; A. Gransden, 'Traditionalism and continuity during the last century of Anglo-Saxon monasticism', *Journal of Ecclesiastical History* 40 (1989), 159–207, at pp. 162–3; and Foot, *Monastic*

the Benedictine *cursus* would not necessarily duplicate an existing Continental model. We should instead expect a combination of old and new material, Insular and Continental.

It is impossible to say for sure whether the Benedictine Office was actually implemented at Glastonbury in the early years of the reform. No Glastonbury Office books survive, and the narrative sources are silent on the subject. Two facts militate against assuming that the Benedictine Office was used. First, it is hard to know what models would be available from which to produce the required books. It is far from certain, as was mentioned in Chapter 2, that 'Benedictine' chant books were widely available on the Continent in the middle of the tenth century. While it is true that the the Aachen legislation of 816 seems to assume that no special measures were needed for monks to begin reciting the Benedictine Office right away, for any monastery (Continental or English) to produce Benedictine books on its own initiative would at least require expertise that may not have been immediately to hand. In Glastonbury's case, there would have been no other English monastery in which the Benedictine Office was used to which Dunstan could have turned for advice and support. Second, and more important, the Glastonbury community seems to have persisted as a mix of secular clerics and vowed monks throughout this early period, as is shown from certain episodes in B.'s Life and from Æthelwold's having taken three Glastonbury *clerici* with him when he departed to become abbot of Abingdon.[60] Dunstan himself had taken the tonsure at Glastonbury as a young man, spending the first part of his ecclesiastical career as a 'secular cleric'.[61] While Dunstan and his fledgling monks at Glastonbury may have been coming to the conclusion that true obedience to the Rule meant singing the Office according to the Benedictine *cursus*, they will nevertheless have been equally aware from their study of the Aachen texts that this would be completely inappropriate for secular clerics, who had their own form of the Office, the Roman *cursus*. The Roman *cursus* is assumed in the *Institutio canonicorum* and it is minutely described and allegorized in the works of Amalarius of Metz, which had been available and studied in England since the early years of the tenth century.[62] Short of excluding the seculars from the choral recitation of the Office, Dunstan may have had little choice but to have

---

Life, pp. 13–19.
[60] See Brooks, 'The career of St Dunstan', p. 13.
[61] B., *Vita S. Dunstani*, § 5. 1, ed. and tr. Winterbottom and Lapidge, *Early Lives*, pp. 16–17.
[62] Jones, 'The book of the liturgy', p. 676.

his monks continue to follow the Roman *cursus*, which at least had the authority of tradition. Were he to misunderstand the Aachen texts completely and try to force the seculars to follow the Benedictine *cursus*, it may have been difficult to secure their cooperation. When the tide turned against Dunstan at court after he dragged Eadwig from the arms of Æthelgifu and her daughter and back to his coronation banquet, his own pupils at Glastonbury turned him out.[63] If men such as these were to refuse to comply with a revised liturgy, there is probably little that Dunstan could have done to compel their obedience.

If it proved impossible to institute the Office of the Rule at Glastonbury, it would only have been a matter of time before the situation became untenable for monks now persuaded that their calling was to total obedience of the Rule. This may have been a factor in Æthelwold's desire to go abroad 'to know the scriptures more thoroughly and to receive a more perfect grounding in a monk's religious life'.[64] He was dissuaded from this course by King Eadred's offer to give him the minster of Abingdon *c*.954, which with his abbot's blessing he accepted. And although Æthelwold was followed to Abingdon by a number of *clerici*, we are informed by his biographer that in a short time he was abbot over a *grex monachorum*.[65] This was to be no mixed community, and a reform of the community's liturgy was on Æthelwold's agenda.

Continental contacts (c.950–963)

Whereas the first decade of reformed English monasticism at Glastonbury, to the extent that Glastonbury was 'reformed' at all, was founded mainly on the study of Frankish monastic texts in the light of earlier English traditions, the next decade was to permit direct experience of reformed monastic life in Continental houses. Table 5.2 presents a basic chronology of these contacts within the context of the reformers' activities in England. Of the ways in which this Continental exposure affected the Office liturgy of English monasteries, relatively little can be said from the narrative sources alone.

---

[63] B., *Vita S. Dunstani*, §§ 21–22, ed. and tr. Winterbottom and Lapidge, *Early Lives*, pp. 66–71; see Brooks, 'The career of St Dunstan', pp. 14–15.
[64] Wulfstan, *Vita S. Æthelwoldi*, c. 10, ed. and tr. Lapidge and Winterbottom, pp. 18–19: 'cupiens ampliori scripturarum scientia doceri et monastica religione perfectius informari.'
[65] Wulfstan, *Vita S. Æthelwoldi*, c. 11, ed. and tr. Lapidge and Winterbottom, pp. 20–1.

Table 5.2 Chronology of Continental contacts during the first twenty years of the English Benedictine reform

	940×946	Dunstan appointed abbot of Glastonbury
*	c.950	Oswald takes the habit at Fleury, where he remains and commits the chant to memory
	c.954	Æthelwold is given Abingdon
*	c.954×963?	Æthelwold brings chant teachers from Corbie
*	956–7	Dunstan in exile at Ghent
	957	Dunstan returns, becomes bishop first of Worcester then also of London
	958	Oswald returns to England on the death of his uncle, Archbishop Oda
*	958–9?	Oscytel of York goes to Rome to receive the pallium, accompanied by Oswald and Germanus (the latter remaining at Fleury on the return)
	957×960	Oswald and Dunstan meet
	959	Dunstan is Archbishop of Canterbury
	961	Oswald is Bishop of Worcester
*	c.960×963	Æthelwold sends Osgar to Fleury
	962	Oswald founds Westbury-on-Trym
	963	Æthelwold is bishop of Winchester
*	964	Germanus recalled from Fleury to train monks at Oswald's Westbury
	964	Æthelwold expels the clerks from the Winchester minsters; Osgar is abbot of Abingdon

* denotes a moment of direct Continental contact

Oswald, who had had no part in Dunstan's work at Glastonbury, was the first to venture abroad. Having been disappointed by life as the head of an unknown unreformed house in Winchester, purchased with money from his uncle, Archbishop Oda, he took the monastic habit at Fleury c.950.[66] According to Byrhtferth, Oswald took special care to study and memorize the liturgy used there:

According to the custom of monastic law, he began to memorize

---

[66] Byrhtferth, *Vita S. Oswaldi*, II. 1–10, ed. and tr. Lapidge, pp. 32–52.

and duly to master the monastic offices, desiring – with the Lord's merciful support – to teach those things which he had learned from strangers abroad to his own people at home.[67]

Memory was essential to the performance of the liturgy, including the Office. This was especially true of liturgical music: neumatic musical notation, which was probably known at Fleury at this time, assumed on the part of the singer an existing familiarity with the melody. Oswald, Byrhtferth affirms from personal experience (*ut autumo*), was a skilled singer, endowed with a fine, high voice.[68] That Oswald already had a plan to teach the Fleury liturgy to 'his own countrymen' (*in patria suis*) may be an invention of hindsight on Byrhtferth's part: Oswald would not found his first monastery, Westbury-on-Trym, until after he was appointed bishop of Worcester. But Oswald later invited his friend Germanus, who had spent 'many months' (*plurimis mensibus*) at Fleury, and who studiously committed its monastic customs to memory, to teach his fledgling community, thus continuing a Fleury connection.[69] What effect, if any, this connection had on the liturgy of Oswald's network of houses has proved virtually impossible to gauge, since the later liturgical manuscripts of Worcester, Ramsey, and Winchcombe reveal a variety of influences, none of them certainly Fleury.[70]

Dunstan's time abroad at Ghent was never part of a plan to bring a Continental monastic observance back to England. But he did participate in the singing of the Office there, as we learn from one of Dunstan's visions recounted by B., in which Dunstan is encouraged by the singing of the Magnificat antiphon *Quare detraxistis sermonibus ueritatis* at Vespers.[71] Like Oswald, Dunstan enjoyed a reputation as a skilled musician, and miracles associated with Dunstan often had a musical element, including episodes in which he taught new music to his monks.[72] Attempts

---

[67] Byrhtferth, *Vita S. Oswaldi*, ed. and tr. Lapidge, pp. 54–5: 'Coepit more sancte monastice legis memoriter agnoscere et ecclesiastica digniter officia retinere, desiderans (Domino clementer annuente) in patria docere suis quae extra proprium solum didicit ab extraneis.'

[68] Byrhtferth, *Vita S. Oswaldi*, ed. and tr. Lapidge, pp. 50–1: 'tria in uno dono Dei habebat dona, ut autumo: uocis pulchritudinem et pulchritudinis suauitatem et altitudinem cum uocis modulatione.'

[69] Byrhtferth, *Vita S. Oswaldi*, III. 7, ed. and tr. Lapidge, pp. 66–7. Lapidge notes (p. 67 n. 66) that Germanus must have been at Fleury for several years, at least 958–61.

[70] A. Corrêa, 'The liturgical manuscripts of Oswald's houses', in Brooks and Cubitt, *St Oswald*, pp. 285–324.

[71] B., *Vita S. Dunstani*, § 23. 3, ed. and tr. Winterbottom and Lapidge, *Early Lives*, pp. 74–5.

[72] See B. Ó Cuív, 'St Gregory and St Dunstan in a Middle-Irish poem on the origins of

have been made to trace certain chant texts in surviving English Office books to Dunstan's sojourn at Ghent.[73] But there is no indication that Dunstan ever promoted a systematic imitation of a Continental liturgical model.

Æthelwold was the only leader of the English Benedictines never to spend time in a Continental monastery, which may explain, as Patrick Wormald suggested, why his approach to monastic reform, in particular his monasticization of the cathedral chapter at the Old Minster, differed so drastically from Continental norms.[74] Unlike Dunstan and Oswald, Æthelwold receives no praise from his biographers for special musical gifts. As Smaragdus remarked, it was not necessary that an abbot qualified to exercise a ministry of governance should also possess the skills of a cantor.[75] But what his monks could not learn from his own example they could learn from the teachers that he obtained for them, as in this well-known passage from the *Historia ecclesiae Abbendonensis* (*ante* 1117):

> The holy father considered that his monks could not imitate the custom of the religious life of anyone better than the monastery of Fleury, adorned with the relics of St Benedict, and sent one of his monks, Osgar, there to be instructed. He returned with other fellow soldiers and kindly imparted by teaching what he had learnt. Moreover, to follow the stricter way of life, very many men of God, from diverse parts of England and instructed in different manners of reading and singing, heard of the holiness of Æthelwold, came to him, and were received. Wishing them to sing praise to God in church with a harmonious voice, he summoned from the monastery of Corbie (situated in France and with a very high reputation for ecclesiastical discipline at that time) highly skilled men whom his own monks might imitate in reading and chanting.[76]

---

liturgical chant', in Ramsey et al., *St Dunstan*, pp. 273–97, at pp. 284–5.
[73] D. Chadd, 'Liturgical books: Catalogues, editions and inventories', in D. Hiley (ed.), *Die Erschließung der Quellen des mittelalterlichen Gesangs*, Wolfenbütteler Mittelalter-Studien 18 (Wiesbaden, 2004), pp. 43–74, at pp. 57–9.
[74] Wormald, 'Æthelwold and his Continental counterparts', p. 38.
[75] Smaragdus, *Expositio in Regulam*, c. 11, ed. Spannagel and Engelbert, pp. 199–200; tr. Barry, pp. 319–20.
[76] *Historia ecclesie Abbendonensis*, § 31, ed. and tr. J. Hudson, *The History of the Church of Abingdon*, 2 vols., Oxford Medieval Texts (Oxford, 2002–7) I, 54–7: 'Religionis morem sanctus pater nequaquam ab aliis melius ratus suos exequi quam a Floriaco monasterio, sancti Benedicti reliquiis decorato, de suis monachis unum Osgarum illuc instrui derexit. Isque reuersus ceteris commilitonibus, que didicerat edocendo benigne impertiit. Vt [Ad?]

Osgar's mission to Fleury is recorded in similar terms by Wulfstan.[77] The arrival of singing experts from Corbie is not related in any of the earlier sources, but something of the sort certainly took place. Many surviving Anglo-Saxon musical-liturgical books – specifically those in which a 'Winchester' influence has been discerned – are textually, melodically, and notationally related to liturgical books from Corbie.[78] Æthelwold's desire that his monks should imitate Corbie in their liturgy seems to have been very successfully realized.

This passage highlights two important points about Continental influence on the English Benedictine movement. First, the organization of monastic customs and the performance of the liturgy were treated as distinct components of a monastery's life. Just because Æthelwold had decided that the Fleury customary was the best example for the monks of Abingdon to imitate, it did not follow that the specific contents of the Fleury liturgy would be used as well. Second, the use of Fleury and Corbie as models for imitation was based on Æthelwold's personal selective judgement. As John Nightingale has argued, Fleury was attractive for having Benedict's bones as much as anything else.[79] And as was seen in the previous section, the English Benedictines were chiefly interested in Benedict and his authority as expressed in the Rule. Not every abbot would necessarily be of Æthelwold's opinion. As Thomas Symons noted, B. puts Dunstan in exile at Ghent looking back nostalgically on the 'excellence of the life at Glastonbury', rather than appreciating the supposedly superior observance of a reformed Continental house.[80] We should

---

districtioris autem uite tramitem, cum e diuersis Anglie partibus uiri Dei, audita Æthelwoldi sanctitate, plurimi differenti more legendi canendique instituti, ad eum conuenirent atque reciperentur; uolens eos in ecclesia consona Deo uoce iubilare, ex Corbiensi cenobio (quod in Francia situm est, ecclesiastica ea tempestate disciplina opinatissimo) uiros accersiit sollertissimos quos in legendo psallendoque sui imitarentur.' In addition to Hudson's introduction, a brief notice of the *Historia*'s contents and date may be sought in Thacker, 'Æthelwold and Abingdon', p. 44.

[77] Wulfstan, *Vita S. Æthelwoldi*, c. 14, ed. and tr. Lapidge and Winterbottom, pp. 26–7.

[78] On texts, see Chadd, 'Liturgical books', *passim*; on melodies, D. Hiley, 'Thurstan of Caen and plainchant at Glastonbury: Musicological reflections on the Norman Conquest', *Proceedings of the British Academy* 72 (1987 for 1986), 57–91, at p. 67 n. 1 and p. 69, and Examples 3–6; on notation, Rankin, 'Neumatic notations in Anglo-Saxon England', pp. 131–2; and *eadem*, *The Winchester Troper: Facsimile Edition and Introduction*, Early English Church Music 50 (London, 2007), pp. 22–3.

[79] Nightingale, 'Oswald, Fleury, and Continental reform'.

[80] *Regularis concordia*, ed. Symons p. xvi n. 4; cf. B., *Vita S. Dunstani*, § 23. 3, ed. and tr. Winterbottom and Lapidge, *Early Lives*, pp. 72–3: 'quoties constitutus in exilio meminit quantam religionis celsitudinem in monasterio dereliquit' ('whenever, now an exile, he

therefore not expect that the uptake of Continental liturgical material – which is not to be confused with aspects of the monastic customary – will have been uniform across all the houses founded or reformed by the different English Benedictine leaders.

Furthermore, it goes without saying that the contacts between the English Church and the Continent were far more numerous and varied than the crude chronology in Table 5.2 would suggest. Contact with Fleury, for example, was established at the latest by Archbishop Oda, who made his own monastic profession there well before Oswald's tenure.[81] Koenwald of Worcester's tour of German monasteries will suffice as a single example of the many other points of contact that existed, with reformed and unreformed houses alike.[82] To turn up an otherwise unattested channel of Continental influence on the Office liturgy of the English Benedictines would not be in the least surprising.

Finally, the report in the *Historia ecclesie Abbendonensis* of men 'instructed in different manners of reading and singing' recalls the continued existence in the tenth century, already investigated in Chapter 4, of a 'native' English musical-liturgical tradition. The passage gives no hint that Æthelwold was 'dismayed' by the variety inherent in this tradition, as one influential commentator suggested.[83]

The movement spreads (963–c.970)

After Edgar's accession to the throne, and the appointment of Dunstan, Æthelwold, and Oswald to the episcopate, the Benedictine movement was able to spread, with new houses founded and old ones reformed.[84] No evidence survives from this period of expansion of how the Divine Office was performed in any of the newly Benedictine monasteries. The Benedictine *cursus* would, of course, have been the ideal; but, if the progress made on the Continent after the ninth-century reforms is a reliable indicator, its adoption was probably a very slow process. Nevertheless, a number of texts that were produced in this period, or that refer back to it, mention the

---

recalled the grand religious life he had left behind in his monastery').
[81] Byrhtferth, *Vita S. Oswaldi*, II. 4, ed. and tr. Lapidge, pp. 38–9.
[82] See S. Keynes, 'King Athelstan's books', in Lapidge and Gneuss, *Learning and Literature*, pp. 143–201, at pp. 198–201.
[83] Knowles, *The Monastic Order*, p. 522.
[84] See Knowles's reconstructon of the spread of the reform in *The Monastic Order*, Figure I (p. 721).

Office. These references may be grouped into two categories: attestations of the importance of the Divine Office to the reform leaders themselves; and polemical attacks on the secular clergy in which the Divine Office is mentioned within the context of the monks' superior powers of intercession.

The Office seems to have continued pre-eminent in the monastic lives of the reform leaders themselves, even after their elevation. B. says that when Dunstan was on his way to Rome to receive the pallium, he frustrated his steward not only by giving away their provisions but also by reciting Vespers at the appointed time wherever they happened to be.[85] The difficulty that the monk-bishops may have faced in reconciling their episcopal responsibilities with the liturgical side of a monastic vocation is brought out poignantly in an anecdote about Dunstan in Byrhtferth's *Vita S. Oswaldi*. It is based on the account in B.'s *Vita S. Dunstani* of a miracle that occurred as Dunstan pursued his habit of visiting the holy places of Canterbury during the night, singing psalms as he went. In the B. version, one night, while praying in St Augustine's, Dunstan has a miraculous vision of a choir of holy virgins singing a hymn of Sedulius.[86] How reliable a tradition this is, given B.'s lack of direct information about Dunstan's life as archbishop, is open to question.[87] In Byrhtferth's adaptation, Dunstan's nightly circuit involves going to the monastery of St Augustine with the specific purpose of reciting the Office:

> When Dunstan came to this aforementioned place, he used to chant the night offices in the company of a young boy, in the manner of St Benedict; it was his custom to go to St Augustine's monastery and there to remain a long while in prayer.[88]

According to Byrhtferth, the miracle occurred on one such night after Dunstan returned to Christ Church, where he beheld a vision of a choir, this time of the souls of those buried in the church, singing Sedulius. As Michael Lapidge has observed, Byrhtferth's description of Dunstan's habit as 'in the manner of St Benedict' (*more pii Benedicti*) may refer to the biography of Benedict in Gregory's *Dialogi*, where Benedict is said to

---

[85] B., *Vita S. Dunstani*, § 27. 3, ed. and tr. Winterbottom and Lapidge, *Early Lives*, pp. 82–3.
[86] B., *Vita S. Dunstani*, § 36, ed. and tr. Winterbottom and Lapidge, *Early Lives*, pp. 100–1.
[87] Lapidge, 'B. and the *Vita S. Dunstani*', p. 249.
[88] Byrhtferth, *Vita S. Oswaldi*, V. 7, ed. and tr. Lapidge, pp. 162–3: 'Cumque ad locum ueniret predictum, nocturnis psallebat horis cum quodam puerulo more pii Benedicti; ⟨solebat⟩ ire ad coenobium sancti Augustini atque ibidem orationibus diutius persistere.'

have 'spent a long time in prayer' one night on a mountain in the company of a young boy.[89] The presence of the small boy (*puerulus*) in the singing of the Night Office, however, is also reminiscent of the anonymous *Vita Ceolfrithi*, which tells of how after a plague at Jarrow had carried off all those who were able to sing or to read in the liturgy, Abbot Ceolfrith maintained the solemn performance of the daily Office with the help of the *puerulus* traditionally believed to be none other than Bede.[90] If Byrthferth had this story in mind too – which is far from certain, since he does not quote from the *Vita Ceolfrithi* elsewhere – it would be possible that *more pii Benedicti* could also be construed to apply to the pattern of psalmody that Dunstan followed in his nocturnal prayers, i.e. the Benedictine *cursus*. It seems likely that a Benedictine propagandist like Byrhtferth will hardly have imagined Dunstan using any other *cursus* of psalmody. Byrhtferth's reliability as a historian is minimal, especially when he quotes from pre-existing narratives for his own purposes.[91] Historical or not, however, this episode could reveal that Byrhtferth assumed that Dunstan could not have sung the Office following the Benedictine *cursus* as part of the formal communal liturgy of either Christ Church or St Augustine's.

Æthelwold's devotion to the Divine Office is not mentioned by his biographers. The existence of the text *De horis peculiaribus*, however, which describes a set of private devotional offices (for the Virgin, SS. Peter and Paul, and All Saints) that Æthelwold composed and commended to the monks at the Old Minster, shows him to have been working creatively with the Office liturgy.[92] The *De horis peculiaribus* does not itself give the texts of any of these offices. Michael Lapidge has, however, identified likely candidates for the Office of the Virgin (BL Cotton Titus D. xxvii, fols. 81v–85r; New Minster, Winchester, 1030s) and an Office of All Saints (BL Cotton Tiberius A. iii, fol. 57; Christ Church, Canterbury, s. xi med., from a Winchester exemplar).[93] The *Regularis concordia* requires, but does not describe, an Office of All Saints after Lauds and Vespers.[94] The text in Tiberius A. iii is likely to be the one envisaged

---

[89] Gregory, *Dialogi*, II. 5. 2, ed. Vogüé, p. 154; tr. White, p. 174.
[90] See p. 93 above.
[91] Lapidge, 'Byrhtferth and Oswald', in Brooks and Cubitt, *St Oswald*, pp. 64–83, at p. 70 and *passim*.
[92] The text is ed. and tr. Lapidge and Winterbottom, in *Wulfstan of Winchester: The Life of St Æthelwold*, pp. lxviii–lxix.
[93] Both are ed. and tr. Lapidge and Winterbottom, *Wulfstan of Winchester: The Life of St Æthelwold*, pp. lxx–lxxiv and lxxv–lxxvii.
[94] *Regularis concordia*, § 19, ed. Symons p. 15 (CCM § 21, p. 84) for Lauds only, and

in the *Concordia*. But the *De horis peculiaribus* makes clear that these offices were for Æthelwold's own monks rather than for universal use, which suggests that they were devised in the 960s, before the promulgation of the *Regularis concordia*. As Lapidge has suggested, these 'peculiar hours' demonstrate how liturgical observances clarified monastic allegiances within the reform movement: 'it was the expectation and performance of these additional devotions which distinguished Æthelwold's monks from all others'.[95] For present purposes, it is interesting to note that both the Office of the Virgin and the Office of All Saints have only four psalms at Vespers and a brief responsory at both Vespers and Lauds; that is, both have been composed according to the pattern of the Benedictine *cursus*. In this respect, they differ from the other extra devotional Office prescribed in the *Concordia*, the Office of the Dead. This appears always to have been sung according to a secular pattern, with five psalms and no brief responsory at Lauds or Vespers.[96] The Office of the Dead envisaged in the *Concordia*, secular in form, had been learned from the practices of reformed monks on the Continent. That Æthelwold's own contributions, in the Office of All Saints and of the Virgin, followed the Benedictine *cursus* may indicate that English reformed monks were even more zealous than their Continental counterparts in their adherence to the Rule's liturgical code.[97]

A second category of references to the Divine Office in the 'expansion period' of the 960s is found in attacks on the 'old order' of secular clerks. This is most direct in an undated charter of Edgar in favour of the Old Minster (964×975), which says that the cathedral clerks had been so pre-

---

§ 56, ed. Symons p. 55 (CCM § 85, p. 132) for both Lauds and Vespers; see also Symons's comments on p. xxxii (1953 edn).

[95] Lapidge, 'Æthelwold as scholar and teacher', in Yorke, *Bishop Æthelwold*, pp. 89–117, at p. 105.

[96] T. Symons, 'Monastic observance in the tenth century, I: The Offices of All Saints and of the Dead', *Downside Review* 50, new ser. 31 (1932), 449–64, and 51, new ser. 32 (1933), 137–52, at p. 450.

[97] There is some indication that the Office of All Saints may have followed the Benedictine pattern in some later Continental monastic customaries (Symons, 'Monastic observance', p. 450 n. 2). The Office of the Virgin, however, appears to be Æthelwold's own creation. English Benedictine creativity in the Office of the Dead may be represented in a set of fourteen abecedarian rhyming 'antiphons', with neumes, in Oxford, Bodleian Library, Bodley 572, fols. 47r–48v (these texts copied at Winchester?, *c*.1000). Some of the pieces are shared with the 'Red Book of Darley', Cambridge, Corpus Christi College 422, pp. 480–90 (Winchester for Sherborne?, *c*.1061). The eighth chant in Bodley 572 (which also occurs in Corpus 422) refers to Benedict as the father of monks.

occupied with sins of the worst kind (especially keeping wives) that they had neglected to keep the Divine Office in the church.[98] David Knowles probably had this text in mind when he argued that 'one of the chief motives for the expulsion of the secular clerks from the Old and New Minsters was that the offices might be more worthily accomplished.'[99]

Reform propagandists on the Continent had often felt it necessary 'to paint as black a picture of the unreformed as possible in order to cover up the shaky legal grounds on which the external parties had intervened.'[100] The same principle operated in England. So far as the Winchester clerks' liturgical observance is concerned, there is no evidence that these attacks were justified. Wulfstan's *Vita S. Æthelwoldi* has the Abingdon monks arriving at the Old Minster to expel the clerks only to find them celebrating Mass. Moreover, the clerks are interrupted while singing the communion antiphon proper to the day of their expulsion, the Saturday after Ash Wednesday: *Seruite domino in timore*.[101] As Michael Lapidge has perceptively shown, *timor Dei* is one of the hallmarks of Benedictine monasticism, so the text of this chant may be too convenient to Wulfstan's purposes to be taken as historically reliable.[102] But Wulfstan was in any case untroubled at having to depict the clerks as competent liturgical performers.

None of these texts mention the form of the Office to be used. Another passage from Edgar's 'Confirmation' for the Old Minster could be read to mean that Edgar specifically desired that the monks should use the Benedictine *cursus* in the Office:

[The minster] should remain always as he established it with monks with the help of Almighty God when he drove out from there the proud priests because of their evil deeds and lodged monks therein so that they might [perform] God's service according to the teaching of Saint Benedict and might daily call on God for the salvation of all Christian people.[103]

---

[98] 'Confirmation by King Edgar of the endowment and privileges of the Old Minster' (964×975), § 14 (S 818), ed. and tr. A. R. Rumble, *Property and Piety in Early Medieval Winchester*, Winchester Studies 4.3 (Oxford, 2002), pp. 98–135, at p. 131.
[99] Knowles, *The Monastic Order*, p. 60.
[100] Nightingale, 'Oswald, Fleury and Continental reform', p. 40.
[101] Wulfstan, *Vita S. Æthelwoldi*, c. 17, ed. and tr. Lapidge and Winterbottom, pp. 30–3. Cf. *Antiphonale missarum sextuplex*, ed. R.-J. Hesbert (Brussels, 1935), § 39.
[102] M. Lapidge, 'Byrhtferth and Oswald', pp. 81–2.
[103] An Old English section of the 'Confirmation' (S 817(4)), ed. and tr. Rumble, *Piety and*

'God's service' (*Godes þeopdom*) can refer in Old English to the liturgy, which in this case would be 'the liturgy according to the teaching of St Benedict'. The context, however, deals more generally with the monastic life, which if kept well will aid the monks' intercessory prayers mentioned immediately afterwards. The monks, as has already been seen, will have thought it entirely fitting that secular clerks should use the secular (Roman) *cursus* appropriate to them. There was therefore no polemical advantage in claiming to use a supposedly superior form of the Office. The monks' advantage lay, rather, in their supposedly superior morality.

'King Edgar's Privilege for the New Minster, Winchester', recorded in an extraordinary deluxe tenth-century libellus, commemorates the establishment of monks in the New Minster after the eviction of the clerks in 964.[104] Æthelwold's long and self-effacing subscription suggests him as the author.[105] The words he puts in Edgar's mouth explain that the New Minster clerks were expelled because they were unprofitable in their intercessions for king and people:

> *By what manner, [after] expelling the clerks, he installed the monks.*
>
> Fearing lest I should incur eternal misery if I, on the acquisition of power, should not do what He wishes who Himself administers everything in Heaven and [who] has become known on earth as a Righteous Judge from his warning punishments, I, the vicar of Christ, have expelled the crowds of depraved canons from the various monasteries of our kingdom. Because they had been no benefit to me with their intercessory prayers, but rather, as the blessed Gregory said, they had 'provoked the vengeance of the Just Judge', they who were contaminated with diverse blemishes of vices were not performing the things which God wished in His commandments, and were rebelliously doing all things which God did not

---

Property, p. 113: 'spa spa he hit mid Godes ælmihtiges fultume gesette. þa þa he hit þa modigan preostas for heora mandædon þanan ut adrefde . 7 þerinne munecas gelogode þæt hi Godes þeopdom æfter sancte Benedictes tæcinge . 7 dæghpamlice to Gode cleopodon for ealles Cristenes folces alidsednesse.'

[104] BL Cotton Vespasian A. VIII, fols. 1–33. The text is edited and discussed in *Charters of the New Minster, Winchester*, ed. S. Miller, Anglo-Saxon Charters 9 (Oxford, 2001), pp. 95–111 (no. 23), and in *Councils and Synods* I, 119–33 (no. 31). The script is consistent with Winchester, and there is nothing in the hand or diplomatic to contradict the given date of 966 (*Charters of the New Minster*, ed. Miller, p. 109.)

[105] *Councils and Synods* I, 119.

wish, I, a keen investigator, turning my attention to these matters, have joyously installed, in the monasteries within our jurisdiction, monks pleasing to the Lord, who might intercede unhesitatingly for us.[106]

The remainder of the charter, which blends aspects of a customary with the immunities and anathemas common to diplomatic texts, was intended to be read to the New Minster monks throughout the year (though the portion following the heading of this prescription is on a missing leaf or leaves).[107] The impression given is therefore of a contract: the king guarantees the monastery's privileges, and for their part the monks must strive to live worthily, lest their intercessions, like those of the clerks before them, become 'unprofitable'.

Byrhtferth artfully articulates a similar kind of contract in his account of a great Easter council supposedly convened to sanction the expulsion of clerks from unnamed monasteries, presumably from Winchester and, since it was Oswald's idea, apparently also from Worcester, though this is not made explicit. Byrhtferth may be conflating the events of 964 with the c.970 Council of Winchester. The story turns on the celebration of Vespers by the assembled monks and nuns of the nation. It is so worthily performed that Edgar decides to install monks in the minsters throughout his kingdom:

> Now this King Edgar, mighty in arms, exulting in sceptres and diadems and regally protecting the laws of the kingdom with militant authority, had trampled under his feet all the proud necks of his enemies. It was not only the chieftains and rulers of this island who feared him, but also the kings of many foreign peoples: hearing of his great wisdom they were struck with fear and terror. He was militant like that 'excellent psalmist' the son of Jesse [*scil.*

---

[106] S 745; ed. Miller, *Charters of the New Minster*, pp. 98–9 (no. 23, § 7): '*Qua ratione clericos eliminans monachos collocauit*. VII. Timens ne eternam incurrem miseriam si adepta potestate non facerem quod ipse qui operatur omnia quae in celo uult et in terra suis exemplis iustus examinator innotuit. uitiosorum cuneos canonicorum. e diuersis nostri regiminis coenobiis Christi uicarius eliminaui. Quod nullus mihi intercessionibus prodesse poterant. sed potius ut beatus ait Gregorius iusti uindictam iudicis prouocarent qui uariis uitiorum neuis contaminati. non agentes quę Deus iubendo uolebat. omnia quę nolebat rebelles faciebant auidus inquisitor aduertens. gratos Domino monachorum cuneos qui pro nobis incunctanter intercederunt. nostri iuris monasteriis deuotus hilariter collocaui.' Translation: Rumble, *Property and Piety*, p. 87.
[107] *Charters of the New Minster*, ed. Miller, p. 107.

David], wise like Solomon, just like St Paul, merciful like Moses, daring like Joshua, 'terrible like the battle-line of camps drawn up', gentle and kindly to everyone but especially to monks, whom he honoured as brothers and loved like dear sons. He held clerics in contempt; he honoured men of our order, as I have said, once the trifles (*neniae*) of the clerics had been cast out of the monasteries. Even 'the comic writer Turpilius' – if he had been present – would not, 'in treating the vicissitudes of letters', have been able to record Edgar's excellent accomplishments and to elucidate all of them as they happened. It is appropriate for me, however, to record some notice of this very mighty, very benevolent king – indeed he is *our* king! – who built so many monasteries, provided them with an establishment of monks, admonishing on his own behalf the pastors whom he placed in charge of them that they in turn exhort their spiritual charges to live righteously and blamelessly in order to be pleasing to Christ and His saints. 'While I am alive', he said, 'neither cruel tyrant nor rapacious wolf will be able to harm you; but I fear that, after the dissolution of my mortal frame, not only bears but even lions will come who will disperse wickedly those whom my munificence had assembled kindly.'

One particular day, when he was standing royally with his attendants in a lofty place and the sacristan of that place rang the bell to the Almighty, all the bishops with their clergy immediately rose up, as did all the abbots with their monks and all the abbesses with their nuns, and they hastened on foot and in an orderly manner to Vespers, which they were obliged to chant harmoniously in the presence of the celestial King and the earthly one. And King Edgar, surveying this large number of excellent fathers and venerable mothers with all their sons and daughters, is said to have shouted out to the Lord and to have said to Him from the very depths of his heart: 'I give thanks to You, Jesus Christ, Great King, You Who rule those whom You love and Who placed me over Your people: may perpetual praise and inexhaustible glory be Yours, Who have granted it to me to assemble so many serving-men and serving-women, who can render Your praise with due honour.' This king, who took such delight in their divine services, ordered more than forty monasteries to be established with monks, loving in every respect Christ the Lord and His most worthy soldier St Benedict, whose reputation he knew through the report of the holy bishop Oswald. For this same king had been instructed in the knowledge of the True King by Æthelwold, the holy bishop of the town of Winchester. Æthelwold urged the king above all to expel the clerics from the monasteries and to bestow them on our order, being his principal adviser. I shall leave Æthelwold's saintly accomplishments, which have been recorded clearly enough, to his own followers; let me continue what I have started.

And when the Lord's armies had solemnly enacted the Easter services with the earthly king, he discharged everyone to return home. Having been given this permission, they all set off, praying for the king's good fortune and asking the Lord to preserve him and give him strength and increase his blessings on earth and not 'deliver him into the hands of his enemies'.[108]

---

[108] Byrhtferth, *Vita S. Oswaldi*, III. 10–12, ed. and tr. Lapidge, pp. 74–9: 'Rex autem armipotens Eadgar, sceptris et diadematibus pollens et iura regni bellica potestate regaliter protegens, cuncta inimicorum superba colla pedibus suis strauit. Quem pertimuerunt non solum insularum principes et tiranni, sed etiam reges plurimarum gentium; ipsius audientes prudentiam, timore atque terrore perculsi sunt. Erat bellicosus ut "egregius saltes" filius Iesse, sapiens ut ⟨Salomon⟩, iustus ut Paulus, misericors ⟨ut⟩ Moyses, audax ut Iosue, "terribilis ut castrorum acies ordinata", mitis et bonus omnibus, maxime monachis, quos honorabat ut fratres, diligebat ut karissimos filios. Clericos perosos habuit; nostri habitus uiros (sicut diximus) honorauit, abiectis ex cenobiis clericorum neniis. "Turpilius comicus, tractans de uicissitudine literarum", si adesset, non quiuisset egregia ipsius gesta reuoluere et cuncta ut sunt patrata enucliari. Nos uero tam potentis, tam benigni imperatoris – quin immo magis nostri regis! – mentionem conuenit facere, qui quot cenobia construxit, tot cum monachis instituit, ammonens per se pastores quos ipsis preposuit ut suos admonerent filios, ut rite et inreprehensibiliter uiuerent quatinus Christo placerent et sanctis eius. "Me", inquit, "uiuente, non dirus tyrannus neque mordax lupus uobis noceri poterit; sed timeo post obitum mee resolutionis, ut non ursi sed etiam leones adueniunt qui dispergunt male quos mea munificentia congregauerat bene."

'Quadam die, dum regali more in edito cum suis staret loco et edituus templi ipsius cloccam personaret altissimo, mox surrexerunt omnes episcopi cum clericis suis, et cuncti abbates cum monachis suis, atque omnes abbatisse cum monialibus suis, et properabant pedetemptim et ordinate ad uespertinam horam, quam ante conspectum celestis regis et terreni debebant modulanter concinere. At ille tot patres egregios et uenerandas matres cum filiis et filiabus suis circumspiciens, exclammasse fertur ad Dominum atque ex intimo cordis affectu dixisse ad eum: "Gratias tibi ago, Iesu Christe, rex magne, qui regis quos diligis et me constituisti super populum tuum: tibi sit perpes laus et gloria indeficiens, qui michi concessisti tot famulos famulasque congregari, qui tuas laudes possunt debitis honoribus persoluere." Delectatus uero rex in eorum sacris officiis, plus quam quadraginta iussit monasteria constitui cum monachis, diligens per omnia Christum Dominum eiusque famam per pii Osuualdi episcopi narrationem agnouit. Instructus ⟨namque erat⟩ idem rex ad cognitionem ueri regis ab Æþeluuoldo sanctissimo episcopo Wintoniensis ciuitatis. Iste enimuero ipsum regem ad hoc maxime prouocauit, ut clericos a monasteriis expulit et ut nostris ordinibus contulit,

The story is framed by a nice conceit of military imagery. At first, Edgar is called 'mighty in arms', a king who strews his way with the necks of his enemies. This warlike king addresses the monks in the words of a protector: 'While I am alive, neither cruel tyrant nor rapacious wolf will be able to harm you.' At the end of the story, however, the monks and nuns are called 'the armies of the Lord', and it is they who are able to offer to the King protection and deliverance from his enemies. The chiastic structure of the narrative turns around a central event: the singing of Vespers by all the assembled monks and nuns. Upon hearing the singing, Edgar renders thanks to God that there are now servants 'who can render Your praise with due honour'. Byrhtferth immediately adds that the king 'took ... delight in their divine services' and was prompted to establish monks in more than forty monasteries, out of love for Christ 'and His most worthy soldier (*militem*) St Benedict'. The military imagery may have been inspired by the *Regula S. Benedicti* itself:

> This message of mine is for you, then, if you are ready to give up your own will, once and for all, and armed with the strong and noble weapons of obedience to do battle for the true King, Christ the Lord.[109]

The monks, through demonstrating their skill and worthiness in the performance of the Divine Office, persuade Edgar that they, like him, are powerful warriors, the *exercitus Domini*. The clerks, of course, are found unworthy, and summarily expelled. Their intercession cannot have been helped by the 'puerile ditties' (*neniae*) that, according to Byrhtferth, characterized their liturgy – unless he is referring instead to carousing with secular music. The whole text is a piece of brilliantly crafted propaganda designed to persuade the reader that monks make powerful allies.[110]

Edgar's prediction of trouble after his death came true in the so-called 'anti-monastic reaction'. The monks' powers of intercession are recalled

---

quia eius erat eximius consiliarius. Relinquam ergo sua beata gesta suis, que satis lucide descripta sunt; nos uero cepta persequamur.

'Cumque pascalia festa celebriter exercitus Domini cum terreno rege egissent, dimisit unumquemque redire in locum suum. Qui omnes licentia accepta reuersi sunt, prospera postulantes regi et Dominum rogantes ut "eum conseruaret et uiuificaret, ac beatum faceret in terra, et ut non traderet eum in manus inimicorum suorum".'

[109] *RSB*, prologue 3: 'Ad te ergo nunc mihi sermo dirigitur, quisquis abrenuntians propriis uoluntatibus, Domino Christo uero regi militaturus, oboedientiae fortissima atque praeclara arma sumis.'

[110] Cf. Pope, 'Monks and nobles', p. 170.

in a speech attributed by Byrhtferth to Ælfwold, brother of Ramsey Abbey's co-founder, Ealdorman Æthelwine, opposing the confiscation of monastic property by lay nobles:

> 'How then', said Ælfwold, 'can we preserve our possessions without His mighty protection? On behalf of Him Who caused me to be reborn let me not allow that such men be driven from our lands, since it is only through their prayers that we can be snatched away from our enemies.'[111]

The 960s yield mixed evidence for the Divine Office in England. The reformed Benedictine commitment to the Office as the highest monastic duty is evident, both in accounts of the reform leaders' personal lives and in the movement's self-promoting propaganda. But the evidence says little about the content of the Office. Æthelwold's monks may have been singing something like a full Benedictine *cursus*. If Dunstan was keeping the Benedictine *cursus* too, we are asked to believe that he was doing so alone.

Regularis concordia *(c.970)*

The first clear evidence for the use of the Benedictine *cursus* in England is found in the *Regularis concordia*. The name of this customary reveals the influence of the Frankish monastic reforms of the ninth century. It is obviously derived from Benedict of Aniane's *Concordia regularum*, in which excerpts from the many early monastic rules of East and West preserved in his monumental *Codex regularum* are grouped under the chapters of the *Regula S. Benedicti* to facilitate study of the monastic tradition, to illustrate its unity, and in particular to demonstrate that the *Regula S. Benedicti* is an authoritative digest of that tradition.[112] But in *Regularis concordia*, the *Regula S. Benedicti* is already assumed to be the only monastic rule followed in England, hence it is is not an agreement 'of the rules'

---

[111] Byrhtferth, *Vita S. Oswaldi*, ed. and tr. Lapidge, pp. 128–9: ' "Quomodo", inquit, "nostra custodire possumus sine illius magno presidio? Per illum qui me renasci fecit non sustineam ut eicientur tales uiri a finibus nostris, per quorum preces possimus eripi ab inimicis nostris." '

[112] *Codex regularum*, PL CIII, 393–702; *Concordia regularum*, PL CIII, 713–1380. Smaragdus's *Expositio in Regulam* quotes the *Concordia regularum* extensively, and it may have been through Smaragdus that the English Benedictines were most familiar with its contents.

(*regularum*), but a 'monastic' (*regularis*) agreement. The Frankish debates of the ninth century are taken as read. There is only the statement that the Rule has been 'accepted with the greatest goodwill', implying a period prior to the Council of Winchester during which the Rule was promoted as the ideal standard of monastic life, before which, according to Æthelwold's 'Old English account', Glastonbury alone kept the 'right rule' (*rihtum regule*).[113] Although it is devoted in large measure to liturgical customs, the *Concordia* says little about specific texts to be recited in the Office. It rarely mentions proper chants. In its description of First Vespers of Christmas, it says that 'the psalms shall be sung with proper antiphons suitable to the fullness of time' (*congrue de ipsa completione temporis*).[114] As Thomas Symons noted, this wording is suggestive of the antiphons *Completi sunt dies* and *Ecce completa sunt*, found at this point in the Worcester Antiphoner.[115] But this text is an interpretation of the liturgy's meaning rather than a clear direction to sing particular texts.[116] At Second Vespers of Christmas, 'the antiphons *Tecum principium* and the rest shall be said', the one example in the *Concordia* of the requirement to sing a specific Office antiphon.[117] But it is obvious that the remaining three antiphons of Vespers are familiar enough, and the context of the passage is an explanation of when proper and ferial antiphons are to be used during the Octave of Christmas.[118] The versicle at Lauds on Easter Day is given as *Surrexit Dominus de sepulchro*.[119] The *Concordia* therefore assumes on the part of its readers the existence of a complete Office liturgy and access to appropriate liturgical books, the character and contents of which cannot be ascertained from the *Concordia* itself, and which may have differed in their contents significantly from house to house.

The *Concordia* likewise omits any explicit command about the form of the Office that is to be used. Individual hours are, as a rule, mentioned

---

[113] *Regularis concordia*, § 4, ed. Symons p. 2 (CCM § 4, p. 70): 'Regulari itaque sancti patris Benedicti norma honestissime suscepta.' Æthelwold, 'Old English account', ed. Whitelock, *Councils and Synods* I, 148.

[114] *Regularis concordia*, § 31, ed. Symons p. 28 (CCM § 46, p. 98).

[115] *Regularis concordia*, ed. Symons p. 28 n. 3.

[116] On the liturgy as a subject for commentary and interpretation, see Jones, 'The book of the liturgy'.

[117] *Regularis concordia*, § 31, ed. Symons p. 29 (CCM § 48, p. 99).

[118] A similar explanatory passage is given for the period between the Octave of Christmas and Epiphany: *Regularis concordia*, § 33, ed. Symons p. 30 (CCM §§ 51–3, p. 100).

[119] *Regularis concordia*, § 52, ed. Symons p. 51 (CCM § 79, p. 127). I have not listed references to proper psalms and to familiar items like the *Haec dies* used in place of the short responsory during the Easter season.

only by name in the midst of detailed descriptions of other practices. So, for example, after describing the extra devotion of the *Trina oratio*, accompanied by the ringing of bells, that precedes the Night Office, the *Concordia* continues, 'Nocturns [i.e. the Night Office] shall be begun. After Nocturns they shall say two psalms ...'.[120] No information is given about how the Night Office itself is to be observed.

The Office intended in the *Concordia* nevertheless clearly follows the Benedictine *cursus*, with the daily hours called *horae regulares*,[121] as opposed to *horae canonicae*, which in the *Concordia* means the secular *cursus*.[122] This terminology departs from the Rule itself, where *horae canonicae* is used in the more traditional sense of 'canonical hours', i.e. the customary, authoritatively sanctioned times of prayer.[123] The distinction is made in the *Concordia* because the secular *cursus* is commended as an appropriate private devotion outside the monastic choir, for example in the interval given to manual labour after daily Chapter: 'The brethren shall then perform the work laid upon them, reciting as they do so the Office of Canons (*cum decantatione canonici cursus*) and the Psalter until the sound of the bell for vesting. At this they shall come from their work and hasten to the *Opus Dei*.'[124] The *Opus Dei* is the genuine communal Office of the Rule (in this case, Sext), as opposed to the private devotions that accompany work outside the oratory. A number of Æthelwold's monks had previously been clerks, and Æthelwold himself probably sang the secular *cursus* at Glastonbury. It would be easy enough for such men to murmur the psalms to themselves according to the secular *cursus* in the midst of their labours. With this in mind, it is perhaps significant that a later English monastic customary, Ælfric's 'Letter to the Monks of Eynsham', which draws heavily on the *Regularis concordia*, never suggests the Office

---

[120] *Regularis concordia*, §§ 17–18, ed. Symons p. 13 (CCM §§ 18–19, pp. 82–3): '... incipiant Nocturnam. Peractis Nocturnis dicant duos psalmos ...'

[121] E.g. *Regularis concordia*, § 11, ed. Symons p. 7 (CCM § 11, p. 76): 'ut horas regulares ... compleant'.

[122] E.g. *Regularis concordia*, § 20, ed. Symons p. 16 (CCM § 23, p. 86): 'horas canonicas ... psallendo'.

[123] *RSB* 37:3, 67:3. The *Regularis concordia* slips into this more traditional usage once (§ 27, ed. Symons p. 23 (CCM § 37, p. 93)): 'Finito Completorio, ut in ultima hora canonica ...'.

[124] *Regularis concordia*, § 25, ed. Symons p. 21 (CCM § 32, p. 91): 'Tunc cum decantatione canonici cursus et psalterii operentur quod eius iniungitur usque dum audiunt signum ad induendum. Quod cum audierint disiungant se singuli ab operibus suis festinantes ad Opus Dei.' The little hours of the secular *cursus* had also been used as an extra devotion in Benedict of Aniane's own monastery of Inde (see p. 75 above).

of Canons as a suitable private devotion for monks. By 1005 (the approximate date of the text's composition) there may have been fewer monastic novices who had previous direct experience of the secular *cursus*.[125]

That the *Regularis concordia* envisages the use of the Benedictine *cursus* is most obvious in its provisions for certain days of the year when the secular *cursus* is to be used in its place: the *Triduum sacrum* of Maundy Thursday, Good Friday and Holy Saturday; and the week from Easter Day until First Vespers of Low Sunday. On the feast of Pentecost, the Night Office alone is to be performed according to the secular *cursus*. The other hours on the feast day itself and during the following week are to follow the 'monastic order' (*regularis ordo*), 'chanted according to the Rule' (*normaliter psallantur*).[126] At every stage, the *Concordia* provides careful explanations of how the secular *cursus* differs from the Benedictine, noting the different number of psalms, antiphons, and responsories, and the presence or absence of a short responsory in the day hours. The most complete description is given for Easter Day, when the whole of the Office is to follow the secular pattern (*more canonicorum*).[127] These detailed notices of changes from the normal routine reveal that the Benedictine *cursus* was the expected pattern for the daily Office in houses subscribing to the *Concordia*.

In requiring the use of the secular *cursus* on certain days, the *Regularis concordia* was within the mainstream of tenth- and eleventh-century Continental monastic tradition. The *Concordia* is unusual, however, in referring to 'the antiphoner' as the authority for these departures. So on Maundy Thursday, 'the night Office shall be performed according as is set down in the antiphoner'.[128] On Easter Day, 'the seven canonical hours are to be celebrated by monks in the Church of God after the manner of Canons, out of regard for the authority of the blessed Gregory, Pope of the Apostolic See, as set forth in his antiphoner'.[129] In the *Concordia*,

---

[125] *Ælfric's Letter to the Monks of Eynsham*, ed. and tr. C. A. Jones, Cambridge Studies in Anglo-Saxon England 24 (Cambridge, 1998). The directions for private recitation of the Office of Canons would have been expected in c. 2 (p. 110).

[126] *Regularis concordia*, § 59, ed. Symons p. 58 (CCM § 89, p. 135).

[127] *Regularis concordia*, §§ 50–3, ed. Symons pp. 49–52 (CCM §§ 78–80, pp. 123–9).

[128] *Regularis concordia*, § 37, ed. Symons p. 36 (CCM § 61, p. 108): 'nocturnale officium agatur secundum quod in antiphonario habetur'. (Here and in the next quotation, Symons's translation uses the spelling 'Antiphonar'.)

[129] *Regularis concordia*, § 50, ed. Symons p. 49 (CCM § 78, p. 123): 'septem canonicae horae a monachis in ecclesia Dei more canonicorum, propter auctoritatem beati Gregorii papae sedis apostolicae quam ipse Antiphonario dictauit, celebrandae sunt.'

the Office contained in 'the antiphoner' is never the same as the Office described in the *Regula S. Benedicti*. After Easter, 'the monastic order (*ordo regularis*) is fully begun with Vespers of the Octave of Easter'.[130] There is no indication that the contents of 'the antiphoner' at First Vespers of the Octave of Easter will have conformed to the *ordo regularis*. The contrast between antiphoner and Rule is clearest in the Concordia's description of Pentecost: 'On that Sunday the night Office shall be carried out with three psalms and the like number of lessons and responds, as laid down in the antiphoner. At the other hours of this day and of the week following the monastic order (*ordo regularis*) shall be kept.'[131] It is possible that the *Concordia* assumes the availability of a monastic antiphoner of the kind familiar from the eleventh century onwards, in which the chants are arranged for the Benedictine *cursus* except on those days when the secular *cursus* was followed. But the opposition in the *Concordia* between 'the antiphoner' and the Office of the Rule could also imply that the compiler of the *Concordia* (Æthelwold) did not expect that a reformed English monastery would necessarily possess an antiphoner organized according to the Benedictine *cursus*. It may simply have been expected that the precentor would choose appropriate chants for the monastic Office from the repertory contained in a secular antiphoner.

None of the customaries or capitularies associated with the Continental reform tradition ever refer to the antiphoner as an authority when recommending the substitution of the secular *cursus* for the Office of the Rule.[132] The *Concordia*'s reference to Gregory the Great as the author of the antiphoner could derive from an early English tradition, first attested by Bishop Ecgberht.[133] But Æthelwold may have encountered this tradi-

---

[130] *Regularis concordia*, § 54, ed. Symons p. 53 (CCM § 81, p. 129): 'Vespera uero octauarum Paschae ordo iam regularis pleniter inchoetur'. Symons translates this passage as 'The full regular order shall begin with Vespers of the Octave of Easter'.

[131] *Regularis concordia*, § 59, ed. Symons p. 58 (CCM § 89, p. 135): 'Illa dominica nocte tribus psalmis totidemque lectionibus cum responsoriis agitur Nocturna laus, uti in Antiphonario titulatur; ceteris uero horis diei et hebdomadae sequentis, regularis ordo teneatur.' Symons translates *ordo regularis* as 'the regular order'.

[132] *Regularis concordia*, CCM edn, p. 123 nn. 5–6. The only parallel case I have been able to discover is in *Ordo Romanus L*, compiled between 950 and 962 at St Alban's, Mainz (c. 25. 2, ed. Andrieu V, 41–414, at p. 186): 'cantor incipit in psalmis antiphonam *Zelus domus tuae*, et reliqua, sicut in antiphonario continentur.' (On the date and origin of the *ordo*, see Andrieu V, 72, and also Vogel, *Medieval Liturgy*, pp. 233–4.) But this excerpt refers only to the antiphons that are to be sung, and not to a departure from the Benedictine pattern of the Office.

[133] See p. 100 above. On the origin of the Gregory tradition, see A. Thacker, 'Memorializing

tion more directly in Frankish sources: the Carolingians were interested in Gregory as a liturgical authority and the prefaces to Frankish books of Mass chants attribute their compilation to Gregory.[134] Either way, the *Concordia*'s invocation of Gregory's authority is designed to show that the established Continental practice is accepted not only because of the example of the great houses of Fleury and Ghent, whence representatives had been invited to attend the Council of Winchester, but because the secular *cursus* carried the authority of Rome and of Gregory the Great (just as the monastic *cursus* carried the authority of the Rule and of St Benedict's personal holiness).[135] Indeed, the *Regularis concordia* even justifies the participation of monks from Fleury and Ghent by referring to Gregory's advice to Augustine of Canterbury that any liturgical customs learned in Gaul that were likely to help the advancement of Christianity in England should be adopted.[136] The *Concordia* presents the adoption of Continental monastic customs as acceptable only because this kind of eclecticism had the approval of the Apostle to the English. Its unique use of 'Gregory's antiphoner' to establish the appropriateness of the secular *cursus* for monastic use on certain days could therefore be seen as a way of 'naturalizing' a foreign tradition – even if the attribution of the antiphoner to Gregory was based on Frankish tradition. This should also remind us that

---

Gregory the Great: The origin and transmission of a papal cult in the seventh and early eighth centuries', *Early Medieval Europe* 7 (1998), 59–84.

[134] On the various sources attributing liturgical activity to Gregory the Great, see Hiley, *Western Plainchant*, pp. 503–13. On Charlemagne's request for a copy of the 'Gregorian' sacramentary, see Hen, *The Royal Patronage of Liturgy*, pp. 74–6. See also L. Treitler, 'Homer and Gregory: The transmission of epic poetry and plainchant', in his *With Voice and Pen: Coming to Know Medieval Song and How it was Made* (Oxford, 2003), pp. 131–85, at pp. 153–9 (originally published in *Musical Quarterly* 60 (1974), 333–72). Interestingly, though, Gregory is never invoked as an authority in the Aachen monastic reform legislation. Indeed, the commentary on the Rule by Hildemar of Corbie invokes Gregory's *Responsiones* to Augustine of Canterbury to justify his opposition to the Aachen texts' requirement that monks use the secular *cursus* during Holy Week. Whereas, according to Hildemar, Frankish bishops were urging liturgical unity with Rome during the festivals of Holy Week, Gregory had taught that liturgical diversity did no harm to the Catholic faith (*Expositio Regulae*, c. 14, ed. Mittermüller, p. 302): 'sicut S. Gregorius dicit, nihil nocet in fide catholica et in bonis moribus consuetudines diversae.' There is no hint of this ninth-century Frankish controversy in the *Concordia*.

[135] Ælfric of Eynsham was later to credit the 325 Council of Nicaea with the authorship of the secular *cursus*. See his Old English pastoral letter for Bishop Wulfsige III of Sherborne (993×c.995), § 12, ed. and tr. Whitelock in *Councils and Synods* I, 191–226, at p. 198, and his first Old English pastoral letter for Wulfstan 'the Homilist' of Worcester and York (c.1006), §§ 69–74, ed. and tr. Whitelock, *Councils and Synods* I, 255–302, at pp. 276–7.

[136] *Regularis concordia*, § 5, ed. Symons p. 3 (CCM § 5, pp. 71–2).

the reformed monks will have held the secular *cursus* in high regard, with many of them having received their liturgical formation in unreformed minsters.

The *Concordia* also reveals that the reformed monks were not entirely reliant on Continental practices (regardless of the rationalization used to justify them) for examples of how to interpret the Rule's liturgical code. In prescribing that 'throughout the summer, except on feast days, there shall be at Nocturns one lesson only, said by heart, and a short responsory, as laid down in the Rule', the *Concordia* agrees precisely with the Rule's shortened scheme for ferial days in summer (*RSB* 10:2).[137] The common Continental practice, however, was to ignore St Benedict's concession and to maintain the winter burden of three biblical lessons and three great responsories throughout the summer.[138] (This custom was also later taken up, ignoring the *Concordia*, in Ælfric's 'Letter to the Monks of Eynsham'.[139]) This instance of independence shows that Æthelwold and his colleagues would not adopt a new tradition merely to 'keep up with Continental developments'. The *Concordia* underpins a strict, narrow interpretation of the text of the Rule. The refusal to alter the summer Night Office – even in a way that could be argued to show more devotion – is reminiscent of the exhortation in the 'Pseudo-Fulgentius' text (found appended to English copies of the Rule) neither to add to the Rule nor to take away from it, since it is entirely sufficient in itself.[140]

To summarize, the *Regularis concordia* implies the existence of a fully implemented Benedictine *cursus*. Indeed, it takes care to explain any and every departure from the expected pattern of the monastic Office. But it is not clear that a book of Office chants adapted to the Benedictine *cursus* was assumed to be available. This may require us to imagine the use of a secular antiphoner as a resource from which chants were taken in the course of the Benedictine Office. While certain Continental monastic customs are endorsed in the *Concordia*, this is done within a consciously English tradition, in which Continental innovations and departures from

---

[137] *Regularis concordia*, § 54, ed. Symons p. 53 (CCM § 81, p. 129): 'una tantum lectio memoriter ac breue responsorium, exceptis festiuis diebus, ad Nocturnam uti regula praecepit tota aestate dicantur'. Fry et al. translate *breue responsorium* as 'short respond'.

[138] See Theodemar's *Epistola ad Karolum regem*, quoted above, p. 59 n. 156. Hildemar, *Expositio Regulae*, c. 10, ed. Mittermüller, pp. 283–5 (explaining St Benedict's scheme as concession to monks engaged in heavy agricultural labour).

[139] *Ælfric's Letter to the Monks of Eynsham*, § 80, ed. and tr. Jones, pp. 148–9 (and see the editor's commentary on p. 227).

[140] Sauer, 'Die Ermahnung des Pseudo-Fulgentius', p. 423.

the Rule (as in the use of the secular *cursus*) are justified by reference to the authority of Gregory the Great as expressed in the *Responsiones* to Augustine and in 'his antiphoner'. This fits well with the now prevailing interpretation of Æthelwold's reform aspirations as an attempt to restore England's imagined monastic past.[141] Despite its manifestly Continental derivation, the *Regularis concordia* nevertheless consciously positions itself within English monastic tradition, at least as interpreted by Æthelwold.

Evidence for Benedictinization

The *Regularis concordia* provides the first secure indication that there was an expectation in at least some houses (Æthelwold's) that the full Benedictine *cursus* would be sung daily. Such an achievement would probably signal the completion of 'reform' in any institution. So, for instance, Donald Bullough judged that the question of when 'the monastic way of life' could truly be said to have been established at Oswald's new cathedral in Worcester (St Mary's) could be answered when it could be shown that at least part of the cathedral's community consisted of 'professed monks, celebrating the office in the forms ("Use") appropriate to their order'.[142] Despite the absence of the sources needed to answer this question for most monasteries, it is still the right question to ask, and it is seldom asked. With the case reasonably secure for Æthelwold's first foundations, some attention may be directed at what can be known of those associated with Oswald and Dunstan.

We know nothing about the Office at Oswald's first foundation, Westbury-on-Trym, beyond what can be gleaned from a single passage in Byrhtferth's *Vita S. Oswaldi*:

> Oswald housed them in a certain parish of his diocese which is called Westbury, where they assiduously performed the divine services and Offices (*diuina orgia et munia*) in the way that the monastic rule prescribes, desiring with all their heart to receive the reward of the eternal coin.[143]

---

[141] See the works by Patrick Wormald, Antonia Gransden, and Sarah Foot referred to in n. 59 above.

[142] D. Bullough, 'St Oswald: Monk, bishop and archbishop', in Brooks and Cubitt, *St Oswald*, pp. 1–22, at p. 19.

[143] Byrhtferth, *Vita S. Oswaldi*, III. 8, ed. and tr. Lapidge, pp. 68–71: 'Collegit eosdem in

The words *diuina orgia et munia*, which Lapidge plausibly translates as 'divine services and Offices', probably imply no more in this context than the twofold monastic duty of liturgical prayer and manual labour, as was earlier seen in a similar passage in the *Vita S. Bonifatii*.[144] Manual labour is certainly suggested by the passage's reference to the *denarius* in the parable of the workers in the vineyard. The *cursus* followed in the Office at Westbury was not necessarily that of the Rule.

Turning to Oswald's cathedral at Worcester, the evidence for its eventual conversion into a fully monastic priory has yielded extremely varied interpretations: some post-Conquest sources say that Oswald expelled the clerks, others say that he won Worcester to Benedictine monasticism with 'holy guile'.[145] Eric John has argued that Oswald proceeded in Worcester much as Æthelwold had done in Winchester.[146] Byrhtferth's *Vita S. Oswaldi* reports that Oswald found in his cathedral *diacones et struciones* ('deacons and evil creatures' in John's translation), whom Oswald replaced with monks (*monachi*).[147] John further suggests that certain portions of the twelfth-century forged charter *Altitonantis*, which speaks of King Edgar's having permitted Oswald to expel the clerks from Worcester, derive from authentic tenth-century documents.[148] By contrast, Julia Barrow has pointed to Eadmer's claim that Oswald was unable to force the clerks' hand in Worcester and instead allowed the secular clerks to remain in the original cathedral, St Peter's, opting to construct a new cathedral, St Mary's, intended as a monastic priory. Benedictine monks were evidently introduced into St Mary's at some point during the period 966–77.[149] Looking at the witness lists of Worcester charters, P. H.

---

quadam parochia sui episcopatus que Westbirig dicitur; quo assidue diuina patrauere orgia et munia sicut demonstrat regularis norma, desiderantes pleno corde percipere aeterni denarii palmam.'

[144] See p. 85 above.

[145] E. John, 'The church of Worcester and St Oswald', in Gameson and Leyser, *Belief and Culture*, pp. 142–57, at p. 142; J. Barrow, 'Worcester', in M. Lapidge (ed.), *The Blackwell Encyclopaedia of Anglo-Saxon England* (Oxford, 1999), pp. 488–90.

[146] John, 'The church of Worcester', reinforcing the position first argued in his 'St. Oswald and the tenth century reformation', *Journal of Ecclesiastical History* 9 (1958), 159–71 (as also 'The king and the monks', pp. 162–3).

[147] This is the reading in the edition by J. Raine, *The Historians of the Church of York and its Archbishops*, 3 vols., Rolls Series 71 (London, 1879–94) I, 399–475, at p. 462; John, 'The church at Worcester', p. 146 and n. 15.

[148] John, 'The church of Worcester', p. 147.

[149] J. Barrow, 'The community of Worcester, 961–c. 1100', in Brooks and Cubitt, *St Oswald*, pp. 84–99, at p. 98.

Sawyer argued that the cathedral community became progressively more monastic through a process of 'natural wastage',[150] a process that may not have been completed until the episcopate of Wulfstan II (1062–95), who pulled down St Peter's in 1084 to make way for new buildings.[151]

Both positions are open to critique. As its most recent editor has pointed out, the unique manuscript of Byrhtferth's *Vita S. Oswaldi* should almost certainly be emended to read *dracones et struciones*, 'dragons and ostriches' (Isa. 43:20):[152]

> What shall I report or say concerning the place in which his episcopal see was situated? Did he not make monks to serve God in that place, where once dwelled 'dragons and ostriches'?[153]

Such an emendation lends support to Barrow's suggestion that this passage describes, not Worcester, but Ripon, and that the episcopal see in question is not Oswald's but Wilfrid's – Wilfrid's relics having been mentioned in the previous sentence.[154] It is true, as John protests, that Ripon was not Wilfrid's episcopal see; but Byrhtferth could have been influenced by Bede's reference to Eadhæd's appointment *c*.679 as *praesul* of Ripon (which the Old English translation of the *Historia ecclesiastica* translates as *biscop*), and Wilfrid's biographer Stephen notes that Wilfrid opposed an attempt to create a bishopric at Ripon during his lifetime.[155] We are therefore safest in seeing this passage as a reference to Oswald's restoration of Ripon, where formerly dwelt only 'dragons and ostriches', and not to an ejection of clerks from Worcester.

On the other hand, the witness lists of Worcester leases issued during

---

[150] P. H. Sawyer, 'Charters of the reform movement: The Worcester archive', in Parsons, *Tenth-Century Studies*, pp. 84–93, at p. 89.

[151] Barrow, 'The community of Worcester', pp. 98–9.

[152] Lapidge earlier considered the possiblity that *struciones* (normally spelled *struthiones* and normally meaning 'ostrich') was here being used to refer to 'some ecclesiastical order': 'The hermeneutic style in tenth-century Anglo-Latin literature', in his *Anglo-Latin Literature, 900–1066*, pp. 105–49, at p. 132 (originally published in *Anglo-Saxon England* 4 (1975), 67–111). One is at a loss to see how John determined that this word meant 'evil creatures'.

[153] Byrhtferth, *Vita S. Oswaldi*, V. 9, ed. and tr. Lapidge, pp. 172–3: 'De loco in quo eius pontificalis cathedra posita est, quid referam quidue dicam? nonne in eo – quo quondam mansitabant "dracones et struciones" – fecit Deo seruire monachos?'

[154] Barrow, 'The community of Worcester', p. 96.

[155] John, 'The church of Worcester', p. 146 n. 15; Bede, *Historia ecclesiastica*, III. 28, ed. Plummer I, 195, and see Plummer's notes II, 224–5; Stephen of Ripon, *Vita S. Wilfridi*, c. 45, ed. and tr. Colgrave, pp. 92–3.

Oswald's pontificate do not necessarily indicate a policy of 'natural wastage'. There are some instances where witnesses who are normally known by their minor clerical grades are instead styled *monachus*, revealing that they were in fact professed monks. It may well be that the composition of the cathedral community was substantially similar to Æthelwold's Winchester, whether or not there was a forcible expulsion or conversion of secular clerks.[156]

No 'Worcester books of a specifically monastic character' have survived from before c. 1000 to settle the matter of Worcester's monastic conversion.[157] Marginal additions to the 'Royal Prayer Book', BL Royal 2. A. XX, made perhaps at Worcester in the second half of the tenth century include several Mass orations mentioning St Benedict, but these cannot be taken to show that the Benedictine *cursus* was followed in the Office at Worcester; they may reflect no more than the private piety of a member of the community.[158] Among the additions are several collects appropriate to different hours in the Divine Office: one for Prime (no. 26), one or possibly two for Terce (nos. 25, 27), one possibly for None (no. 14), one for Vespers (no. 28), one for Compline (no. 22), and two found assigned to various hours in other sources (nos. 15, 34).[159] The oldest surviving sacramentaries all include lists of collects from which selections can be made at Lauds and Vespers, and the earliest collectars (books making specific provision for the collects of the Office) tend to draw on prayers already available in sacramentaries.[160] The collector(s) of the prayers in Royal 2. A. XX seem to have been more specifically interested in prayers for daily use at the lesser daytime hours. Only one of the prayers that may have been intended for use in the Office mentions St Benedict (no. 25), and it is in any case more likely for use in the Mass. The same text is assigned, however, to the hour of Terce on the feast of St Lawrence (with Lawrence's

---

[156] *The Liber Vitae of the New Minster*, ed. Keynes, pp. 64–5.

[157] Bullough, 'St Oswald: Monk, bishop and archbishop', p. 19.

[158] Dumville, *Liturgy and the Ecclesiastical History*, p. 102 n. 33. The texts were first printed in Corrêa, 'The liturgical manuscripts', pp. 311–18. They have now been painstakingly edited in J. P. Crowley, 'Latin prayers added into the margins of the prayerbook British Library, Royal 2.A.XX at the beginnings of the monastic reform in Worcester', *Sacris erudiri* 45 (2006), 223–303.

[159] Crowley, 'Latin prayers', p. 246; numbers are those assigned to the prayers in his edition.

[160] P. Salmon, *L'Office divin au Moyen Age: Histoire de la formation du bréviaire du IXe au XVIe siècle*, Lex orandi 43 (Paris, 1967), pp. 23–6. See, for example, *Le Sacramentaire grégorien: Ses principales formes d'après les plus anciens manuscrits*, ed. J. Deshusses, 2nd and 3rd edns, 3 vols., Spicilegium Friburgense 16, 24, 28 (Freiburg, Switzerland, 1988–92) I, 328–34 (nos. 935–79); cf. *The Leofric Missal*, ed. Orchard I, 457–60, nos. 2610–2652.

name replacing Benedict's) in the eleventh-century Exeter Office book known as the 'Leofric Collectar', BL Harley 2961 (Exeter, 1050×1072), which may draw on a Worcester source.[161]

Ultimately the main interest of these additions is not so much what they say about Worcester's Office liturgy as what they may reveal about the kinds of sources that were available to a reform-minded monk or cleric in England in the tenth century. The one Office chant among the additions, the All Saints antiphon *Saluator mundi salua nos omnes* (no. 9), is intriguing.[162] This antiphon is found in all six of the early monastic antiphoners edited in R.-J. Hesbert's *Corpus antiphonalium officii*, but in only two of Hesbert's six secular antiphoners.[163] In the oldest of Hesbert's monastic antiphoners, the late tenth-century 'Hartker' antiphoner, St Gall, Stiftsbibliothek, 390 and 391, this chant is found in a 'supplement' copied by a different but nearly contemporary hand, perhaps at the beginning of the eleventh century.[164] This invites speculation that *Saluator mundi* is a 'monastic' chant that circulated among reformed Benedictine monasteries, perhaps in a libellus containing other materials useful for establishing a fully Benedictine observance (as seems to be the case with the ninth-century Prüm *Chorbuch*, Trier, Stadtbibliothek, 1245/597).[165] Might the marginal additions in Royal 2. A. XX be drawn from a 'liturgical dossier' comparable to the dossier of ninth-century Frankish monastic texts that, as has already been seen, lies behind the Abingdon copy of the *Regula S. Benedicti*, Cambridge, Corpus Christi College 57? Whatever its source, the antiphon *Saluator mundi*, calling as it does on Christ and on the intercessions of the Virgin and of apostles, martyrs, confessors, and holy virgins to deliver from evil and to secure good, was probably included in Royal 2. A. XX as eminently suitable for private prayer.

Perhaps the best evidence for the adoption of the Benedictine *cursus* in one of Oswald's houses survives in the 'Ramsey Psalter', BL Harley 2904 (Winchester or Ramsey?). A Ramsey origin of this manuscript, on

---

[161] Crowley, 'Latin prayers', pp. 280–81; J. D. Billett, 'The Divine Office and the secular clergy in later Anglo-Saxon England', in D. Rollason, C. Leyser, and H. Williams (eds.), *England and the Continent in the Tenth Century: Studies in Honour of Wilhelm Levison (1876–1947)*, Studies in the Early Middle Ages 37 (Turnhout, 2010), pp. 429–71, at pp. 436–9.

[162] Crowley, 'Latin prayers', pp. 263–4.

[163] Hesbert, *CAO* III, 450, no. 4689.

[164] *L'Antiphonaire de Hartker*, ed. Froger, p. 189; the 'supplement' is discussed on p. 30*. On this antiphoner, see p. 73 above.

[165] See p. 72 above.

palaeographical and art-historical grounds, is gaining greater acceptance. Whatever its origin, it is very likely that it was prepared for Oswald's personal use.[166] The manuscript contains a good deal of liturgical material. Significant for the present question is the division of longer psalms in agreement with the Rule.[167] It is also worth noting that the text of the Ramsey Psalter is of the *Gallicanum* type. Only one other complete *Gallicanum* psalter copied in England survives from the tenth century, the 'Salisbury Psalter', Salisbury, Cathedral Library, 150 (Southwest England, Shaftesbury?, 969×978).[168] As Mechthild Gretsch has shown, even though we may assume that the replacement of the *Romanum* in England with the *Gallicanum* text must have been 'well advanced' by the 970s, the familiar *Romanum* text of the psalter continued to be preferred even by Bishop Æthelwold.[169] If the Ramsey Psalter was in fact prepared for Bishop Oswald, the use of the *Gallicanum* version may reflect his long sojourn at Fleury, where, as has been seen, he applied himself to the memorization of the liturgy.

Similar problems surround the monasticization of Christ Church, Canterbury, and here the surviving manuscripts are of some assistance. Christ Church was apparently secular at Dunstan's enthronement, and there is no record of his having replaced the clerks with monks.[170] But the community seems to have been fully monastic, and celebrating the Office according to the Benedictine *cursus*, by the 1020s. The 'Eadui Psalter', BL Arundel 155 (1012×1023), copied by the famous Christ Church scribe Eadwig Basan (using the *Romanum* text), is decorated according to the Benedictine divisions. When and how this change happened is hard to say. A forged charter dated 1006, but created by Eadwig Basan perhaps in the second quarter of the eleventh century, reports that Archbishop Ælfric (995–1005) expelled the secular clerks from Christ

---

[166] The origin of the manuscript is uncertain (Bullough, 'St Oswald', p. 21; R. Gameson, 'Book production and decoration at Worcester in the tenth and eleventh centuries', in Brooks and Cubitt, *St Oswald*, pp. 194–243, at pp. 201–4); but it is in any case very likely Oswald's personal book (Gameson, 'Book production', p. 201).
[167] Corrêa, pp. 292–6, esp. p. 292.
[168] See the list of English psalters in Pulsiano, 'Psalters', pp. 62–7. The 'Harley Psalter', BL Harley 603 (Christ Church, Canterbury, s. x/xi or s. xi^1), uses the *Gallicanum* text for Pss. 100–105:25. Two tenth-century English fragments also contain the *Gallicanum* text: Worcester, Cathedral Library, F. 173, fol. 1 (s. x^2), and Leuven, Katholieke Universiteit, Centrale Bibliotheek, *s.n.* (s. x med.). The *Gallicanum* version was, however, known in England from a much earlier stage, at least through imported Irish and Continental manuscripts.
[169] Gretsch, 'The Roman psalter', p. 26. See also her *Intellectual Foundations*, pp. 287–96.
[170] Brooks, *The Early History*, p. 252.

Church with both royal and papal approval. This version of the story was taken up in Osbern's *Vita S. Ælphegi* and in an interpolation in the Canterbury (F) text of the Anglo-Saxon Chronicle, both of which belong to the end of the eleventh century.[171] Nicholas Brooks has suggested that the forgery was crafted as the monastic community's response to the appointment of King Cnut's priest Ælfwine to Canterbury in 1032, supplying a 'foundation charter' to defend both the cathedral priory's landed wealth and, at least in principle, its right to elect the archbishop from among its members, in accordance with the *Regula S. Benedicti* and the *Regularis concordia*.[172] Later accounts by John of Worcester and Gervase of Canterbury credit Archbishop Sigeric (990–4) with the expulsion of the secular community.[173] There is no independent corroboration for any of these suspect accounts. Brooks proposes that the monasticization of Christ Church may instead have been a 'gradual evolution', presided over by a succession of five reformed monk-archbishops, in which only new members of the community were required to take monastic vows.[174] This would be consistent with Dunstan's earlier policy at Glastonbury, where clerks had been tolerated alongside monks.[175]

At what point in this process would the Christ Church community have adopted the Benedictine *cursus*? An attribution of the 'Bosworth Psalter', BL Add. 37517 (s. x^2), to Christ Church would suggest that liturgical reform preceded complete constitutional reform.[176] The Bosworth Psalter is the earliest English example of a psalter decorated with the Benedictine divisions (see Table 2.2) and was obviously intended for use in a

---

[171] BL Cotton Claudius A. iii, fols. 2–6, ed. J. M. Kemble, *Codex diplomaticus aevi Saxonici*, 6 vols. (London, 1839–48), no. 715. Osbern of Canterbury, *Vita S. Elphegi*, ed. H. Wharton, *Anglia sacra*, 2 vols. (London, 1691) II, 135–6. *Anglo-Saxon Chronicle* (F), *s.a.* 995, ed. Plummer, *Two of the Saxon Chronicles Parallel* I, 128–31.
[172] Brooks, *The Early History*, p. 258.
[173] John ('Florence') of Worcester, *Chronicon ex chronicis*, *s.a.* 990, ed. R. R. Darlington and P. McGurk, tr. J. Bray and P. McGurk, *The Chronicle of John of Worcester*, II: *The Annals from 450 to 1066*, Oxford Medieval Texts (Oxford, 1995), pp. 436–9. Gervase of Canterbury, *Acta pontificum Cantuariensis ecclesiae*, ed. W. Stubbs, *The Historical Works of Gervase of Canterbury*, 2 vols., Rolls Series 73 (London, 1879–80) II, 357. William of Malmesbury rejected the suggestion that Ælfric had installed monks in Canterbury, asserting that there had been monks in Christ Church continuously since the early seventh century: *Gesta pontificum Anglorum*, I. 20. 1, ed. and tr. M. Winterbottom, Introduction and Commentary by R. M. Thomson, *The History of the English Bishops*, 2 vols., Oxford Medieval Texts (Oxford, 2007) I, 42–3; and see commentary II, 341.
[174] Brooks, *The Early History*, p. 256.
[175] Brooks, *The Early History*, p. 252.
[176] Brooks, *The Early History*, pp. 252–3 and 256.

community of monks or nuns that kept the Benedictine *cursus*. Attempts to localize the manuscript have focused on its kalendar, which, since it includes Dunstan's feast day, must have been copied after 988. Michael Korhammer's arguments for placing the kalendar at Christ Church have enjoyed wide acceptance.[177] The Christ Church attribution has, however, been overturned by Nicholas Orchard, who has shown convincingly that the kalendar must have been produced at St Augustine's, Canterbury.[178] But as H. M. Bannister observed long since, the kalendar is a later addition to the psalter, and it is impossible to say that the psalter 'was made for one who publicly said the Benedictine office at Canterbury'.[179] Anglo-Saxon Square minuscule script, in which the Bosworth Psalter was written, is notoriously difficult to date and localize. While some palaeographers have been content with a Christ Church origin, Westminster has also been suggested on the strength of similarities with the hands in several Westminster charters.[180] Orchard favours an origin outside Canterbury, proposing an attractive scenario in which the manuscript would have been given to St Augustine's by a Benedictine monk who had arrived in Canterbury to join the *familia* of Christ Church, where, in Orchard's view, a psalter decorated for the Benedictine *cursus* would at this earlier date (998×1012) have served no practical purpose.[181]

The most striking evidence for the transition from the secular to the monastic *cursus* is found in two pontificals of probable Christ Church origin. The 'Pontifical of St Dunstan', BnF lat. 943 (960×973?), probably Dunstan's own book, contains the Office for the Dedication of a Church, arranged for the secular *cursus* with nine lessons (fols. 33r–37v).[182] The 'Anderson Pontifical', BL Add. 57337, also apparently copied at Christ Church, c.1000, gives the Dedication Office in the arrangement of the

---

[177] P. M. Korhammer, 'The origin of the Bosworth Psalter', *Anglo-Saxon England* (1973), 173–87.

[178] N. A. Orchard, 'The Bosworth Psalter and the St Augustine's Missal', in R. Eales and R. Sharpe (eds.), *Canterbury and the Norman Conquest: Churches, Saints and Scholars* (London, 1995), pp. 87–94.

[179] H. M. Bannister, in a review of F. Gasquet and E. Bishop, *The Bosworth Psalter* (London, 1908), *English Historical Review* 25 (1910), 148–51, at p. 150.

[180] Korhammer, 'The origin of the Bosworth Psalter', pp. 182–7; see also J. Rosenthal, 'The Pontifical of St Dunstan', in Ramsay et al., *St Dunstan*, pp. 143–63, at pp. 145–6.

[181] *The Leofric Missal*, ed. Orchard I, 178.

[182] J. Rosenthal, 'The Pontifical of St Dunstan', in Ramsay et al., *St Dunstan*, pp. 143–163, at p. 150. On the date, origin, and ownership of the manuscript, see J. L. Nelson and R. W. Pfaff, 'Pontificals and benedictionals', in Pfaff, *The Liturgical Books*, pp. 87–98, at pp. 89–90, and the literature cited there.

monastic *cursus*, with twelve lessons.[183] The textual relatedness of the benedictional component of the Anderson Pontifical to the 'Benedictional of St Æthelwold' (BL Add. 49598) suggests the influence of Winchester, which would accord with the affiliations of later Office books from Christ Church.[184] Either Ælfric (995–1005), who had been a monk at Abingdon, or Ælfeah (1006–12), who had earlier succeeded Æthelwold as Bishop of Winchester, could be seen as the instigator of liturgical change.[185] Later Christ Church tradition points to Ælfric as the scourge of the clerks. But Ælfeah's liturgical activity may be suggested by Adelard's *Lectiones in depositione S. Dunstani*, which is dedicated to him. Adelard arranged the Life so that it could be read in the twelve lessons required by a Benedictine festal Night Office. His preface also mentions that the lessons have been devised so that 'the responsories may accord with the lections and the lections with their responsories', but no responsories are included in any manuscript of the *Lectiones*.[186]

---

[183] Rosenthal, 'The Pontifical of St Dunstan', p. 150; Nelson and Pfaff, 'Pontificals and benedictionals', pp. 91–2. Ker, *Catalogue*, p. 575 (Supplement), no. 416. Compare the Dedication Office, also in monastic form, in *Pontificale Lanaletense (Bibliothèque de la ville de Rouen A. 27. CAT. 368): A Pontifical Formerly in Use at St. German's, Cornwall*, ed. G. H. Doble, HBS 74 (London, 1937), pp. 28–37.

[184] See p. 333 n. 86 below.

[185] Brooks, *The Early History*, p. 279.

[186] Adelard, *Lectiones in depositione S. Dunstani*, dedicatory epistle, ed. and tr. Winterbottom and Lapidge, *Early Lives*, pp. 111–45, at pp. 112–13: 'Scias autem in opere isto hystoriam uitae eius non contineri, sed ex eadem uita quasi breuem sermonis uersiculum, ita compactum et ita distinctum ut et in conuentu piorum auditorum totus quasi hystorialiter recenseatur, et uice sermonis inter sacras uigilias in lectiones ter quaternas distinguatur, ea uidelicet ratione ut ab exordio usque ad sanctum consummationem uitae, eodem fere sensu eisdemque miraculis, et responsoria lectionibus suis et lectiones respondeant responsoriis suis.' ('But you should realize that in this work is contained no history of Dunstan's life, but rather a brief extract from that life, so put together and marked out in sections that it can be rehearsed as a whole in a meeting of devout listeners, just like a history, but can also be divided, like a sermon, into twelve lessons at the sacred vigils [i.e. Matins], in such a manner that from the beginning to the holy end of his life, with no change of sense or of miracles, the responsories may accord with the lections and the lections with their responsories.') Adelard been asked to turn the B. life into verse, but declined. For the responsories of the feast of Dunstan's Deposition (19 May), see *Le Codex F. 160 de la bibliothèque de la cathédrale de Worcester*, p. 312.

Conclusions

One of the hallmarks of reformed monasticism in tenth-century England was the conviction that true obedience to the *Regula S. Benedicti* entailed the use of the Benedictine *cursus* in the Divine Office. This conviction was inspired not primarily by an awareness of contemporary developments in monastic liturgy on the Continent, but by close study on the part of Dunstan and his disciples of the Rule itself and of the ninth-century monastic reform texts promoted in Francia in the ninth century. The *Regularis concordia* is a witness, for example, to Æthelwold's preference to adhere to the Rule strictly as he understood it rather than to follow prevailing Continental customs. And in the *Concordia*, departures from the Benedictine *cursus* are justified by reference, not to Continental practices (which these departures clearly imitate), but to the authority of Gregory the Great.

The practical implementation of this ideal, however, may have varied considerably from place to place. The Ramsey Psalter, with its *Gallicanum* text and division of longer psalms in agreement with Benedictine norms, could indicate that Oswald sought to recreate at Westbury, Worcester, and Ramsey the liturgy that he had committed to memory at Fleury, though no other evidence is available to corroborate that suspicion. A full Benedictine Office is assumed in the *Regularis concordia*, which suggests that it was firmly established by the Council of Winchester (*c.*970) at least in houses under Æthelwold's influence. His policy of expelling the incumbent secular clergy from minsters under his control will have freed his monks from the need to respect long-standing local liturgical traditions, and this would also apply to those fenland houses that he founded outright or re-founded after a period of dereliction (Peterborough, Ely, Thorney, and possibly Crowland and St Neots).[187] By *c.*1005, Æthelwold's erstwhile disciple Ælfric wrote that the monks of Eynsham had been observing at least one aspect of the liturgy described in the *Letter to the Monks of Eynsham* 'for years now' (*iam praeteritis annis tenuimus*), which suggests that the Benedictine *cursus* was well established among the houses of 'Æthelwold's connexion'.[188]

The situation was probably quite different in houses with a long-standing, but unreformed, monastic tradition. Inmates would have to be

---

[187] Knowles, *The Monastic Order*, pp. 50–1.
[188] *Ælfric's Letter to the Monks of Eynsham*, c. 80, ed. and tr. Jones, pp. 148–9. Thacker, 'Æthelwold and Abingdon', pp. 59 and 63.

persuaded to abandon traditions and habits hallowed and ingrained over years of continual repetition. The houses founded in Wessex the first half of the tenth century (like Athelney and Muchelney), and perhaps also Glastonbury, might fall into this category, as might Westminster and St Augustine's, Canterbury. These are all houses associated with Dunstan, who, it would appear, was more tolerant of secular clerks than Æthelwold. Dunstan's annotations to the *Expositio in Regulam* of Smaragdus attest to his own belief that the Benedictine *cursus* was the ideal standard of monastic Office liturgy. Whether it was imposed during his lifetime on the houses under his influence is harder to say.

These conclusions, drawn largely from narrative and non-liturgical manuscript evidence, set up several questions to ask of the surviving Office books of the tenth century. Do they show any signs that the Benedictine *cursus* had been only recently introduced? Are different approaches to establishing a Benedictine Office liturgy discernible, perhaps linked to the different leaders of the reform movement? And can an earlier English tradition be seen to have been adapted for use in a new Benedictine liturgical framework?

Part II

Manuscript Evidence for English Office Chant in the Tenth Century

6

A Methodology for the Study of Anglo-Saxon Chant Books for the Office

Despite its place at the centre of the Divine Office, the particular arrangement of the *cursus* of psalmody and readings used in a given church or monastery, once identified, is of limited use and interest. It will be either 'secular' or 'monastic', except in those rare sources that witness the more fluid situation that prevailed before the spread of the Carolingian two-Office ideal. It is very surprising ever to find an Office book whose disposition of psalms does not correspond to one of the two expected patterns. More often than not, the psalms to be sung at each hour are not even recorded, being too familiar to need explanation. Great variation between different Office manuscripts is found, however, in the chants that accompany the psalms and readings: the antiphons and responsories. Manuscripts of chants for the Mass can display a relatively high degree of uniformity in selection of chant texts without necessarily being closely related. But it is rare to find two Office books in close agreement with each other unless they are from the same locality or they are derived from exemplars circulating in a 'reform' movement.[1] This comparable variety makes it possible to compare Office books based on the repertory of chants that they contain and to draw certain conclusions about their relatedness to each other and about the historical circumstances that brought them to their surviving forms.

A methodology based on this premise has been employed in Chapters 7 to 9 of the present study, which are devoted to the analysis of tenth-century English witnesses to the chant of the Divine Office. Because a number of the conclusions drawn from the manuscript evidence have been reached with this methodology, it is important to give a full explanation of it here, particularly since some specialists have criticized similar method-

---

[1] See Hesbert, *CAO* I, pp. xi–xii.

ologies as unsafe, especially the theories presented by R.-J. Hesbert in the final two volumes of his *Corpus antiphonalium officii*.² At the risk of causing some confusion, the word *ordo* has been used as a shorthand term to refer to the selection and ordering of chants in a given manuscript's formulary for a particular liturgical occasion (as in 'the Night Office *ordo* for St Lawrence in Rawl. D. 894' or 'Palm Sunday *ordines* in English Office books'). This usage follows the example of the late David Chadd, whose contribution to the study of English Office books is explained below.

The moyen court *of Gabriel Beyssac and its development by Victor Leroquais*

The principles underlying the methodology used in the present study were first explained in print by Victor Leroquais in 1934 in the introduction to his huge descriptive catalogue of manuscript breviaries in French libraries. Leroquais likened the process of localizing a manuscript of unknown origin to a legal interrogation,³ since a breviary only rarely announces its origin or use in a title or colophon. Of the 914 manuscripts described in his catalogue, only 272 could be identified so easily. For the rest, Leroquais sought evidence for each manuscript's origin in ten places: (1) the kalendar; (2) the psalter (identifying either the secular or monastic *cursus*); (3) litanies; (4) suffrages; (5) rubrics; (6) responsories assigned to the Night Office on the four Sundays in Advent; (7) Night Office responsories of the Triduum; (8) saints named in the Sanctorale; (9) the Little Office of the Virgin; and (10) the Office of the Dead.⁴

It is immediately clear that most of these points of interest have to do with identifying saints associated with particular churches (kalendar,

---

² See the section 'Hesbert's *Corpus antiphonalium officii*', beginning on p. 203 below.

³ V. Leroquais, *Les Bréviaires manuscrits des bibliothèques publiques de France*, 6 vols. (Paris, 1934) I, p. lxii: 'An examining magistrate in front of an indicted man: such is, or very nearly so, the attitude of a researcher with regard to a manuscript. The same questions present themselves and follow each other, precise, prying, unrelenting: "Who are you? Where do you come from? How old are you? Through whose hands have you passed before coming to us?" And the interrogator continues, close, systematic, inquiring after details, throwing light on darkened points, recording the responses obtained, approaching the subject from many angles, until the accused, in this case the manuscript breviary, has given away all his secrets.' Leroquais's introduction, especially its third section, 'Comment identifier un bréviaire manuscrit?', should be commended as essential reading to any serious student of the Office.

⁴ Leroquais, *Les Bréviaires manuscrits* I, p. lxiii.

litanies, suffrages, Sanctorale; rubrics may mention the dedications of altars visited during processions). The localization of manuscripts based on references to unusual local saints, especially in kalendars, is familiar to most medievalists, even those without interests or specialities relating directly to the liturgy. But when information about unusual saints' feasts was entirely absent, a situation that Leroquais faced frequently enough in his investigations, he turned to the texts of the chants found in the main body of the book, especially the responsories of the Night Office. Leroquais made special use of the four Sundays of Advent and the last three days of Holy Week; but he observed that other parts of a breviary could be equally useful, such as the responsories of Sundays in Lent or those following Pentecost.[5]

The utility of this method lay in the inherent variety of the responsories assigned to Sundays and feast days in different breviary manuscripts, a variety not so much of texts used, since many were found to be shared between many manuscripts, but rather a variety of the orders in which the texts appear in a given source, the combination of selection and order referred to here as *ordo*. Leroquais observed two important facts about the various *ordines*. First, they were unique to particular churches. Second, once established in a given church, they remained unchanged over long periods of time:

> On the one hand, these lists of responsories vary from church to church and abbey to abbey: those of Lyons differ from those of Paris, and those of Cluny do not at all resemble those of Monte Cassino. On the other hand, these same series are constant in the breviaries of the same church or the same abbey: they are found to be identical in Cluniac breviaries from the eleventh to the sixteenth century and even in the first printed breviaries; it is the same with those of Paris or of Cambrai. In this way each of these lists becomes a distinctive trait, a characteristic mark for each church or abbey. There are, of course, some variants here and there: it would not do to ask for an absolute unity; but the rule explained above bears itself out, and is based on many observations.[6]

This method had been pioneered by another Benedictine, Gabriel Beyssac. From the 1920s to the 1950s, Beyssac compiled a huge collection of notes on liturgical books, identifying commonly occurring chants

---

[5] Leroquais, *Les Bréviaires manuscrits* I, p. lxxxi.
[6] Leroquais, *Les Bréviaires manuscrits* I, p. lxxviii.

by number so that their arrangement could be compared at a glance. Beyssac described his method as a *moyen court* ('short way') that would allow the identification of the origin of an Office book 'with the minimum of labour and cerebral effort'. When presented with an unlocalized Office book, he would take note of chant incipits from six different places in the book: the Annunciation (the complete Office); the Assumption (invitatory and responsories); the Triduum of Maundy Thursday, Good Friday and Holy Saturday (responsories only); All Saints (invitatory and responsories); the feast for the Dedication of a Church (invitatory and responsories); and the Office of the Dead (complete).[7] These he would compare with his own notes taken from hundreds of other manuscripts of known origin.[8] Following Beyssac's example, Leroquais too compiled an impressive collection of notes on the selection and ordering of chants in Office books.[9] He gave the following succinct explanation of the rationale behind his own approach:

> If each list of responsories bears the mark of a particular church, it becomes a very efficient means to discover the origin of a breviary. It will suffice to collect these different lists, to arrange them in alphabetical order, and so to make up a repertory. Each time a manuscript of uncertain attribution presents itself, it will require no more than to compare its list of responsories with those of the repertory to know to which church it ought to be attributed.[10]

---

[7] Beyssac's *moyen court* is explained in H. Möller, 'Research on the antiphoner: Problems and perspectives', *Journal of the Plainsong and Mediæval Music Society* 10 (1987), 1–14, at p. 8. The quotation is from Beyssac's 'Note sur le Graduel-Sacramentaire de St. Pierre–St. Denys de Bantz, du XIIe siècle', *Revue bénédictine* 31 (1921), 190–200, at p. 190; the translation is Möller's, p. 13 n. 51.

[8] The *cahiers* containing Beyssac's notes, totalling 1200 numbered sheets (one for each manuscript he encountered), were never published; but they have been preserved in the monastery of Foyer Saint-Benoît à Port-Valais, Le Bouveret, Switzerland, where he spent the last years of his life. See E. Drigsdahl, '*Hore Beate Marie Virginis*: Reference to secondary sources', Center for Håndskriftstudier i Danmark <http://www.chd.dk/use/secsour.html> last visited 5 April 2013.

[9] Unpublished, these are now BnF n. a. lat. 3162–3167. Beyssac and Leroquais's notes on the responsories of the Office of the Dead have been collated in K. Ottosen, *The Responsories and Versicles of the Latin Office of the Dead* (Aarhus, 1993). In addition to using these methods to further their own research, both Beyssac and Leroquais were not infrequently consulted about the identities of breviaries and antiphoners sold at auction. Their notes often preserve the only information available to scholarship about a number of manuscripts that subsequently disappeared into private collections.

[10] Leroquais, *Les Bréviaires manuscrits* I, p. lxxx.

Beyssac and Leroquais's discovery that variations in *ordo* were not random but rather directly linked to the places of origin (or the monastic affiliations, as with, for example, Cistercian books) of antiphoners and breviaries was revolutionary at a time when even basic information, such as whether a manuscript followed the secular or the monastic *cursus*, was incorrect or unrecorded in existing catalogues. Comparing series of responsories to ascertain the origin of unlocalized manuscripts has remained a favourite tool of students of the liturgy,[11] and also of art historians working with books of hours, which usually draw their *ordines* for the Office of the Dead from the breviary of the cathedral of the diocese in which they were copied or for which they were destined. But this method, in this its simplest form, leaves important questions unanswered. When and how did the different *ordines* peculiar to individual churches arise? Is it really safe to assume that the *ordo* found in a breviary of the fifteenth century is probably identical to what would be found in an antiphoner of the same church copied in the eleventh century? To this second question, Leroquais could only point to his 'many observations' of breviaries from the same church or monastery copied centuries apart that used exactly the same *ordines*, or nearly so. As for the origin of the 'astonishing and prodigious diversity' of *ordines* in the manuscript corpus, Leroquais asked the question only to leave it unresolved.[12] He did note, however, that Amalarius of Metz, writing in the first half of the ninth century, referred (with some surprise) to a number of repertorial differences between the antiphoners he inspected, differences Leroquais suspected would only have multiplied in subsequent centuries. He did consider the possibility, however, that if enough manuscripts were collated they could be grouped into 'families' and arranged in some sort of stemma, perhaps even permitting the reconstruction of 'the antiphoner of St Gregory'.[13] Such a task was outside the remit of his catalogue, which dealt almost exclusively with late medieval breviaries.

Hesbert's Corpus antiphonalium officii

The possibility held out by Leroquais of reconstructing an 'Urtext' of the Office antiphoner through the collation of lists of responsories was taken

---

[11] See the demonstration in Hiley, *Western Plainchant*, pp. 336–8.
[12] Leroquais, *Les Bréviaires manuscrits* I, p. lxxxi.
[13] Leroquais, *Les Bréviaires manuscrits* I, p. lxxix.

up with enthusiasm by a third Benedictine scholar, René-Jean Hesbert. In the years following the publication of his parallel edition of six early manuscripts of the Gradual of the Mass,[14] Hesbert began to investigate whether an 'original' form of the antiphoner could be restored using the genealogical principles of textual criticism first developed by editors of classical texts and the Bible.[15] The details of the genesis and evolution of this project, along with scholarly assessments of Hesbert's methods in their early stages, have been carefully assembled by Hartmut Möller.[16] It need only be observed here that Hesbert sought to restore 'the most ancient, most authentic and also the purest stage of the Roman tradition'.[17] The fruits of his years of labour appeared between 1963 and 1979 in the six volumes of *Corpus antiphonalium officii* (*CAO*). The first two volumes present, in parallel columns, the incipits of every chant in each of twelve manuscripts: six antiphoners following the secular *cursus*, and six following the monastic. The manuscripts were selected as the oldest copies surviving in a relatively complete state, without any claim that they were somehow representative of the whole tradition. The third and fourth volumes of *CAO* present a version of the complete text of each chant, listing the variants found in each manuscript. These first four volumes were, in Hesbert's view, purely a preliminary exercise, though they proved immediately useful in their own right as a learned contribution to discussions during the Second Vatican Council about how the Roman Catholic breviary might be reformed. The major work relating to the 'archetype' of the Office antiphoner was left to volumes five and six. In these, Hesbert collected responsory *ordines* for the four Sundays of Advent and the Advent Ember Days from 800 antiphoners and breviaries. He then subjected this information to a series of statistical analyses with a threefold aim: first, to identify the 'archetypal' form of each *ordo*; second, to determine which of the 800 manuscripts were the best witnesses to the 'archetype'; and third, to determine which manuscripts transmitted most faithfully the texts of the chants themselves. Hesbert identified seventeen manuscripts

---

[14] *Antiphonale missarum sextuplex* (1935).
[15] The best introduction to the various theories and principles of textual criticism current in the nineteenth and twentieth centuries is B. M. Metzger, *The Text of the New Testament: Its Transmission, Corruption, and Restoration*, 3rd edn (New York, 1992).
[16] Möller, 'Research on the antiphoner', pp. 1–2.
[17] R.-J. Hesbert, 'Les séries de répons des dimanches de l'avent', *Questions liturgiques et paroissiales* 39 (1958), 299–326, at p. 318; quotation tr. Möller, 'Research on the antiphoner', p. 1. In this article, Hesbert set out the results of a trial study of twenty-five manuscripts.

as closest to the archetypal *ordo*, proposing them as the basis for a reconstruction of the 'original' Roman antiphoner, a project he left for others to complete.[18]

Hesbert's achievement in *CAO* can scarcely be denied. The sheer mass of material assembled has laid the foundations for all subsequent work on the history of the chants of the Office. His analytical methods, however, and in particular the assumptions on which they were founded, have been strongly criticized.[19] The rejection of certain aspects of Hesbert's work has put in jeopardy the legitimate and substantial benefits that are to be had from analysing manuscripts in the light of their liturgical *ordines*. It is important, therefore, to see where Hesbert's method falls down and what aspects of this tool for the study of the Office may be safely retained. Detailed descriptions and criticisms of each stage of Hesbert's analysis are already available in the reviews by Jacques Froger.[20] It will suffice here to address the fundamental issues.

Leaving to one side for the moment the questionable merits of searching for an 'archetype' of the Office antiphoner in the first place, there are problems with Hesbert's conception of what this archetype would look like and his method of finding it. The archetype of the Roman antiphoner, Hesbert believed, provided nine responsories for each Sunday and major feast day. These responsories were arranged in a deliberate order. Over time, however, through the accidents of copying and the addition of later compositions, the original *ordines* were corrupted and distorted. Every surviving manuscript was related through its ancestors to the original form, but some preserved the likeness of the original better than others. To restore the original form, it was only necessary to observe which readings enjoyed the support of the majority of the sources. These 'readings', however, would not have to do with textual variants, as in a literary text, but with the chants included in each manuscript and the numerical position of each chant within a given *ordo*. In order to take into account both selection and position, Hesbert viewed every *ordo* as a succession of pairs. In an *ordo* of nine responsories, there were nine pairs. Representing the responsories with the letters *a* to *i*, the pairs would be as follows:

---

[18] Hesbert, *CAO* VI, 384.
[19] A full list of substantial reviews is given in Möller, 'Research on the antiphoner', p. 11 n. 14.
[20] J. Froger, 'La méthode de Dom Hesbert dans le volume V du *Corpus antiphonalium officii*', *Études grégoriennes* 18 (1979), 97–143; *idem*, 'La méthode de Dom Hesbert dans le volume VI du *Corpus antiphonalium officii*', *Études grégoriennes* 19 (1980), 185–96.

a-b b-c c-d d-e e-f f-g g-h h-i i-End

Representing each *ordo* in this way meant that a large amount of information could be encoded in a single step: which chants the *ordo* contained, what preceded each chant, and what followed it. (In Hesbert's system, the final chant in each *ordo* is paired with the 'invisible chant' *Fin* to show that the list ends there.) With each *ordo* encoded this way, all that was necessary was to run the data through a computer (a mainframe system reading punched cards) to discover which pairs occurred most frequently, having first taken into account the skewing effect of manuscripts with identical *ordines*. The resulting pairs were then stitched together: if, for example, *b-c* and *c-d* both occurred in the majority list, it was obvious that they should be joined at their common element to produce the segment *b-c-d*. In this way, an 'archetype' *ordo* was produced for each Sunday in Advent.

The problem arose, however, that this 'majority method' did not produce the expected result. An *ordo* of nine responsories did emerge rather easily for the first Sunday in Advent; but the subsequent Sundays were less cooperative. As Jacques Froger revealed through his own calculations, the second Sunday had a majority series of only eight responsories. The third and fourth had ten.[21] Hesbert himself never admitted this plainly, adopting instead a series of complex arguments to force his data into his preconceived ideas about a 'normal *cursus Romanus* series of nine responsories'.[22] The secular *cursus* did, in its final stage of development, make use of nine responsories on Sundays. It is by no means certain, however, that any Roman 'archetype' received and propagated by the Frankish Church conformed to this pattern. In early Roman practice, the final lesson of the Night Office was followed directly by the *Te deum*, meaning that only eight responsories were sung on any one Sunday.[23] Indeed, as has been shown elsewhere in this study, the number of nocturns in the Night Office seems to have evolved over time. An original Roman 'core' of the Office antiphoner may have supplied as few as five responsories, if not as few as two.

By contrast, the earliest complete antiphoners tend to supply many more than the requisite complement of nine responsories for the secular *cursus* or twelve for the monastic. The presence of these 'supernumerary' chants cannot be attributed to one specific reason. They seem

---

[21] Froger, 'La méthode ... volume V', p. 110.
[22] Hesbert, *CAO* V, 159; tr. Möller, 'Research on the antiphoner', p. 6.
[23] Le Roux, 'Les repons "De Psalmis" ', p. 49.

chiefly to have been used as substitutes for some of the Sunday responsories that would otherwise be recycled during the subsequent weekdays. Some, however, may have been included for use on Sunday *ad libitum*. Still others may never have been sung, being copied only out of a preservationist tendency on the part of the scribe. In some sources, the supernumerary responsories may be distributed randomly within each *ordo*, not just appended to the end, often making it impossible to tell which responsories originally belonged to the core Sunday set and which were for use on ferial days.[24] It was only in breviaries, which developed relatively late, that the number of responsories listed was fixed at nine, one for each reading. That an 'archetypal' series of nine responsories was wrung from Hesbert's data may be less a fact of history and more a product of his own preconceptions and the late date of most of his sources. As Froger pointed out, the late date of Hesbert's sources also brings into question the actual chants included in Hesbert's 'archetype':

> Indeed, if one applies the majority criterion to all forms of the Antiphoner from the end of the eighth century up to the beginning of the seventeenth, without taking into account the dates of the documents, one risks reconstituting for the four Sundays *listes-types* that are not exactly those of the archetype, but rather those that were more widely in use in more recent times when the greater part of the documents originated.[25]

Having established what he believed to be the 'archetypal' form of the Advent responsory *ordines*, Hesbert set about determining which of the 800 manuscripts surveyed in his study were most closely related to the archetype. Whatever may be thought of the 'archetype' as Hesbert reconstructed it, his method of quantifying the relationship between the surviving manuscripts and the hypothetical archetype is interesting, because it reveals his thinking about how all antiphoners and breviaries may be compared with each other. Hesbert devised a means of calculating what he called the 'distance coefficient' (*coéfficient d'écart*) between any two manuscripts. The distance coefficient is a fraction in which the total number of points of agreement between any two *ordines* is divided by the total number of comparable elements (points of agreement plus points of disagreement). This may be illustrated by adapting an example cited by

---

[24] Froger, 'La méthode ... volume V', pp. 99–100.
[25] Froger, 'La méthode ... volume V', p. 111.

Froger.[26] Taking again the imaginary series of nine responsories labelled *a* to *i*, it may be compared to a second imaginary series:

I: *a b c d e f g h i* End
II: *a b c d x e f g i h y* End

In the second *ordo*, there are two additional responsories (*x* and *y*) and responsories *h* and *i* are inverted compared to their order in the first *ordo*. Hesbert reckoned agreements in terms of pairs. The following pairs are shared between these two *ordines*: *a-b b-c c-d e-f f-g*. This makes five points of agreement. Hesbert reckoned as points of disagreement only those situations in which a chant was present in both *ordines* but not in the same pairing. So here, responsory *d* is present in both lists, but the pairings are different. In the first, the pair is *d-e*; in the second, *d-x*. Other contrasting pairings are *g-h* and *g-i*; *h-i* and *h-y*; *i-End* and *i-h*. Because responsory *y* is found only in the second *ordo*, Hesbert's calculation rules it out of consideration as not susceptible to comparison. That is to say, the pair *y-End* in the second series has no comparable pair beginning with *y* in the first. This leaves four discordant pairings. To achieve the distance coefficient, the number of agreements is divided by the number of agreements plus the number of disagreements. In this case, 4 is divided by $4 + 5$. The distance coefficient is 44% (4/9).

As Hartmut Möller has observed, Hesbert introduced his formula for the distance coefficient 'without reflection or discussion about the method'.[27] As Möller goes on to note, there are many other formulas that might have been considered, none of which is completely satisfactory. The difficulty of quantifying the relationship between two *ordines* can be illustrated by the following example. We imagine a responsory series of ten chants, denoted by the letters *a* to *j*. One of these (let us assume it is the last) is a supernumerary responsory to be sung on a ferial day. The other nine are to be sung on the Sunday itself:

a b c d e f g h i j

But this series could be written in another way. The supernumerary responsory might instead be copied directly after the chant it is meant to replace (let us suppose it replaces chant *a*) during the following week:

a j b c d e f g h i

---

[26] Froger, 'La méthode ... volume V', p. 112.
[27] Möller, 'Research on the antiphoner', p. 7.

These two *ordines* should be considered as identical for practical purposes. But the transposition of responsory *j* introduces three points of disagreement in Hesbert's distance coefficient: *a-j* in place of *a-b*, *i-End* in place of *i-j*, and *j-b* in place of *j-End*. There are seven concordant pairs (*b-c*, *c-d*, *d-e*, *e-f*, *f-g*, *g-h*, and *h-i*). This gives a distance coefficient of 33% (3/10). Now let us imagine another series that differs from the first in just one element:

a b x d e f g h i j

According to Hesbert's system, there is only one point of disagreement here, the pair *b-x*. The pairs *c-d* and *x-d* he discounts as not comparable, and he removes this instance from the total number of elements (the denominator of the coefficient). There remain the concordant pairs *a-b*, *d-e*, *e-f*, *f-g*, *g-h*, *h-i*, *i-j*, and *j-End*, eight in all. The distance coefficient between these pairs Hesbert would reckon as 12.5% (1/8). It is obviously nonsensical that an *ordo* that actually differs in its selection of chants should seem more closely related than an *ordo* that preserves all the same chants only slightly rearranged. Simple inspection tells us that one series differs from the other in having chant *x* rather than chant *c*. But that both use chant *j* could also indicate relatedness through another route. It is impossible to be absolutely sure without reference to the origin and provenance of the book in which the *ordo* is found and to the varying layers of intervention that may be discerned, of which Hesbert's formula takes no notice.

It would be a discredit to Hesbert's great contribution to the study of the Office not to mention some of his less controversial, and therefore enduringly valuable, conclusions. His examination of 800 Office books confirmed impressively that the phenomenon of a direct link between liturgical *ordo* and particular churches first observed by Beyssac and Leroquais is real, and for the most part generally reliable, if approached purely from the perspective of identifying local traditions, not a phantom 'archetype'. The numerical lists of responsories in *CAO* have been made available in a form more useful for this kind of investigative work.[28]

Hesbert's truly crucial discovery, however, was that all *ordines* in monastic antiphoners and breviaries originally arose as expansions of

---

[28] K. Ottosen, *L'Antiphonaire latin au Moyen Âge: Réorganisation des séries de répons de l'Avent classés par R.-J. Hesbert*, Rerum ecclesiasticarum documenta, *extra seriem* (Rome, 1986).

Table 6.1 Two different 'Benedictinizations' of the same secular responsory series for the second Sunday in Lent

Hartker		Muchelney		Hyde Abbey	
1.	Tolle arma	1.	=	1.	=
2.	Ecce odor	2.	=	2.	=
3.	Det tibi	3.	=	3.	=
				4.	*Dum iret*
4.	Dum exiret	4.	=	5.	=
		5.	*Surgens mane*	6.	*Uere dominus*
5.	Si dominus	6.	=	7.	=
6.	Erit mihi	7.	=	8.	=
7.	Orauit iacob	8.	=	9.	=
				10.	*Minor sum*
8.	Dixit angelus	9.	=	11.	=
9.	Uidi dominum	10.	=	12.	=
		11.	*Dum iret*		
		12.	*Minor sum*		

Hartker: St Gall, Stiftsbibliothek, 390
Muchelney: BL Add. 43405
Hyde Abbey: Bodleian, Rawl. liturg. e.1*

secular *ordines*.[29] Certain responsories in the Advent repertory occur predominantly in monastic books. In the majority of cases, a monastic *ordo* will have three 'monastic' responsories and nine 'normal' responsories. When the three monastic chants are removed, the remaining *ordo* of nine responsories almost invariably corresponds to an already existing *ordo* from a secular antiphoner or breviary. It is very often the case that a monastic *ordo* will be based on the secular *ordo* used in the local cathedral, though some monasteries derived their *ordines* from exemplars farther afield. Table 6.1 shows how one secular series in widespread use was expanded to produce two different monastic *ordines*.[30]

The dependence of monastic *ordines* on secular *ordines* is further

---

[29] This subject is treated *passim* in *CAO* V–VI; see also Palazzo, *A History of Liturgical Books*, p. 135.
[30] This example is drawn from J. D. Billett, 'The Muchelney Breviary and Anglo-Saxon monastic liturgy in the eleventh century', Unpublished M.Phil. dissertation, University of Cambridge, 2003, p. 34.

proof – though Hesbert did not explore this corollary – of the original universality of the Roman Office in Carolingian monasticism. There was nothing like a 'Benedictine archetype' (originating, as might have been thought, at Monte Cassino) from which monastic antiphoners descended independently. Benedictine antiphoners were adapted from secular antiphoners that had themselves already evolved to make use of varied repertories of chants and *ordines*. The monastic augmentation of secular *ordines* simply yielded a further degree of variability.

A more flexible approach to analysing Office *ordines*

Hesbert's attempt to sweep aside the details of context, history and, above all, human agency, was characteristic of a whole movement in the humanities, starting around the turn of the twentieth century, that placed confidence in the reliability of statistics, and eventually computers, over mere human observation. But, to quote a contemporary critic of this thinking, 'the methodical elimination of the element of human intelligence can hardly be the ideal of science'.[31] The great weakness of Hesbert's formula is that it assumes that all changes in a church's Office *ordines* over time are to be counted as 'errors' in the otherwise faithful transmission of a deliberately composed 'archetype'. These changes may better be considered as rational (or indeed capricious) human interventions, not in an 'archetype', but in a repertory probably assembled gradually from many different *libelli* that may themselves have enjoyed independent circulation and supplementation before they were ever gathered into a single book, the 'antiphoner'.[32] As soon as any local tradition is examined closely, it can emerge that it has been susceptible to many outside influences and just as many internal revisions. P. M. Gy was unable, for instance, to identify an 'archetypal' form behind the early breviaries of St Gall, though the earliest manuscripts did share a 'common repertory' of chants, variously arranged by successive copyists.[33]

---

[31] George Foot Moore, in his preface to H. St. J. Thackeray, *Josephus: The Man and the Historian* (New York, 1929), p. v; quoted in Metzger, *The Text of the New Testament*, p. 169.
[32] Möller, 'Research on the antiphoner', p. 14 n. 75, citing a work I have not been able to examine: R. Stephan, 'Antiphonarstudien I: Quellen und Studien zur Geschichte des Gesanges im Stundengebet vor der Jahrtausendwende, I: Die Gesänge des Sanctorale', Unpublished *Habilitationschrift*, Göttingen, 1962, pp. 107–15.
[33] P.-M. Gy, 'Les premiers bréviaires de Saint-Gall (deuxième quart du XIe s.)', in W. Düring (ed.), *Liturgie: Gestalt und Vollzug: Festschrift für Joseph Pascher zum 70.*

Gy's observations demonstrate concretely what should be intuitively obvious. Any reviser of a church's Office *ordines* could choose to rearrange and reassign chants already present in the community's existing repertory of antiphons and responsories. Something comparable to this kind of revision is apparent in the famous tenth-century antiphoner of Mont-Renaud, in whose margins Roman numerals have been added to change the order in which many of the responsory *ordines* are to be performed (though in this case the reviser was also reducing the number of responsories in each *ordo* to the nine required for the secular *cursus*, the manuscript having been prepared originally for a monastic church).[34] The introduction of new chants, however, would represent a different kind of revision. This would require either the work of a skilled liturgical composer with the authority to make such a change (a reforming abbot or a liturgically minded bishop), or, as is to be expected in the larger number of cases, a borrowing from the repertory of a church whose liturgical innovations were becoming known beyond its walls through various kinds of contact. Networks of contact between churches and monasteries are likely to be revealed by the presence of chants that are peculiar to a certain group. Distinctive chants could certainly find their way into the repertories of various churches through irregular, chance exchanges. But significant alterations to the Office *ordines* of a church – those changes involving more than the addition of a single chant to what might already be a substantial list of supernumerary responsories for use *ad libitum* – arose through upheavals of greater moment.

The most commonly raised objection to the use of responsory *ordines* as a tool for localizing manuscripts, an objection raised with apprehension by historians in particular, is that manuscripts of relatively late date should not be relied upon as faithful witnesses to the liturgical practices of earlier centuries in the communities where they were copied and used. The point is demonstrated vividly by the three St Gall breviaries studied by Gy, all of which were copied during the second quarter of the eleventh century, and which differ from each other to a surprising extent. Not all monasteries, however, were as liturgically volatile as St Gall seems to have been. Where

Geburtstag (Munich, 1963), pp. 104–13.
[34] See the Introduction to the facsmile edition: *Antiphonaire du Mont-Renaud*, pp. 25–6. For a useful recent account of creative interventions in the liturgical books of Winchester, see S. Rankin, 'Making the liturgy: Winchester scribes and their books', in Gittos and Bedingfield, *The Liturgy*, pp. 29–52, at pp. 32–4. Pure re-arrangement with Roman numerals may be seen in the ninth-century *Chorbuch* in Trier, Stadtbibliothek, 1245/597 (for which see p. 72 above).

the tradition cannot be ascertained as fixed from an early stage, observed changes can often be attributed to known historical events.

The most important work in recent years on the historical background of the surviving witnesses to the monastic Office in England was conducted by David Chadd, whose untimely death in 2006 left incomplete a major study of all the surviving complete copies of English Benedictine breviaries and antiphoners.[35] This book, which may yet appear in some form, was founded on the years of careful study that also gave birth to the 'Cursus Project', which made available on the Internet transcriptions of significant portions of the manuscripts in question. The site has since gone offline.[36] The methodology used here in Chapters 8 and 9 was developed partly as a result of a number of conversations with Professor Chadd and also through examination of draft copies of material from his book, which with characteristic generosity he freely shared with me once he learned of my own research. Chadd gave a brief exposition of his methods in a paper read at the 39th Symposium of the Herzog August Bibliothek, Wolfenbüttel, in 1996.[37]

Chadd's Wolfenbüttel paper identifies Corbie, Dijon, and Bec as the chief sources of the liturgical material found in English antiphoners and breviaries. These identifications are not new in themselves. They were announced with a note of triumph by Hesbert himself in a short study of English Office books based on the material collected in *CAO*.[38] Similar conclusions were reached by David Hiley in a subsequent study of liturgical and musical variants preserved in English and Continental missals and graduals, as well as antiphoners.[39] These connections, Hiley remarked, would cause no surprise:

> (i) It was from Corbie, according to the Abingdon Chronicle, that Ethelwold summoned monks in the tenth century to help improve the performance of the liturgy in England; (ii) it was from St-Bénigne at Dijon that Duke Richard summoned Abbot William in

---

[35] Its provisional title was given on the author's webside as *Insular Monastic Office Antiphoners: A Study of the Sources*, in preparation for the Boydell Press.
[36] 'CURSUS: An Online Resource for Medieval Liturgical Texts', hosted by the University of East Anglia <http://www.cursus.uea.ac.uk/> last visited 26 July 2008; the site has been offline since 2011/2012.
[37] Chadd, 'Liturgical books'.
[38] Hesbert, 'Les antiphonaires monastiques insulaires'. The English material surveyed in Le Roux's 'Les repons "De Psalmis"' tells a similar story.
[39] Hiley, 'Thurstan of Caen'.

1001 to revive the church in his duchy; and (iii) it was ultimately from Bec that England acquired two archbishops of Canterbury, Lanfranc and Anselm, as well as many other important churchmen.[40]

The historical context of the development of *ordines* in English Office books should therefore be seen, at least in crude outline, as twofold: the Benedictine reform in the tenth century, and the Norman Conquest in the eleventh. As Chadd points out, however, the evidence on which to assess how English Office books were affected by these events, and the contacts they brought about, is restricted to the Office books themselves, which are mostly of late date:

> It will be evident from my table of sources that almost all of them date from a period after – sometimes considerably after – the period *ca.* 950–1100 about which I am asking the questions. Working with later sources is endemic to this kind of study (in the sense that, if one leaves them out of the count, there is simply nothing to say) and the technique must be to use them with the 'due precaution' which Christopher Hohler urged about employing the incunable mass-books of Reims in the context of a tenth-century argument. Like the site of an archaeological dig, a liturgical book is apt to throw up not only signs of simply-layered superimposition and straightforward wholesale substitution, but also innumerable indications of what might be called (to keep the analogy with archaeology) 'successive occupation'.[41]

Christopher Hohler's approach to identifying material that may have belonged to early (that is, pre-Carolingian) recensions of the sacramentary as used in England, alluded to in the passage from Chadd's paper just quoted, raises issues of direct relevance to Office books:

> There are three points which I should like to emphasise in conclusion. The first is that the fact that a liturgical book is 'late' does not mean that it can be disregarded for early liturgical history, and particularly not if it comes from an important centre from which the evidence of earlier books is inadequate. ... The second point is that all these early books are complicated, indeed Dom Deshusses's admirable dictum that each successive copy of

---

[40] Hiley, 'Thurstan of Caen', pp. 61–2.
[41] Chadd, 'Liturgical books', p. 53.

a liturgical manuscript was 'une petite édition critique' is liable, though I should hesitate slightly about the word *critique*, to be true down to the thirteenth century. This means that, if one is to understand them historically one has got to compare them with a fair number of related books; and not least of the problems, since the body of surviving medieval liturgical texts is so gigantic, is finding the books with which comparisons are most likely to be instructive and fruitful. My last point ... is that the tenth- and eleventh-century English books do not present a clear picture of continental usages being adopted, but rather stages in the adjustment, by fairly stupid men most of the time, of some pre-existing body of texts and usages of Italian origin current in England to what, by the tenth century, was fashionable in Northern Europe.[42]

As will be clear from earlier chapters of this book, identifying items in English Office books derived from Italian precursors introduced through the Augustinian mission would be even more delicate an endeavour than what Hohler had in mind with sacramentaries. This detail aside, we should accept as valid his arguments that later books must be accepted as a class of evidence; that appropriate books for comparison must be chosen; and that the liturgical forms found in these later books are probably the result of an adaptation of pre-existing texts rather than of a direct substitution. Where David Chadd succeeded so greatly was is in his identification of useful points of comparison and in his keen discernment of instances of straightforward adoption of outside material on the one hand, and of adaptation of existing material on the other. As an example of his apt comparisons, his extensive knowledge of the Office liturgies of the houses connected with William of Dijon, which might by anyone else be simply grouped under the heading 'Dijon', allowed him to judge whether the Winchcombe breviary was more similar in its *ordines* to Mont Saint-Michel or to Jumièges.[43] As for adoption versus adaptation, he perceived that the *ordo* of responsories to be sung with the *historia de Noe* from Genesis in the Winchcombe breviary was based on a core from a Bec *ordo* subsequently revised to imitate, in certain respects, an *ordo* devised by William of Dijon, and then subjected to a further revision affecting only its final responsory, the result being an *ordo* unique to

---

[42] C. Hohler, 'Some service books of the later Saxon Church', in Parsons, *Tenth-Century Studies*, pp. 60–83, at pp. 80–1.
[43] Chadd, 'Liturgical books', p. 58 n. 42.

Winchcombe.[44]

Chadd's success was possible largely because he rejected statistical approaches in favour of tracing the presence or absence of individual chants of apparent significance:

> In all this, what I am trying to point to is the problem of identifying that which is significant and getting to some sense of what significance actually is. It has been traditional to study the arrangement of responds (and antiphons) as a series, and to place weight upon their juxtaposition. This approach, which taken to the extreme can make this whole phenomenon of liturgical *historiae* into some kind of rather arid statistical playground, begs the question of the significance of such phenomena as the transposition of constituents. In the case of *de Noe*, for instance, I simply do not know what to make out of the fact that nos. 17 and 18 [*Per memetipsum* and *Ponam arcum meum*] sometimes occur in one order and sometimes the other, and I suspect that it signifies nothing very fundamental.[45]

Rather than relying purely on tabulating the occurrence of successive pairs, as Hesbert had done, Chadd proceeded by a more cautious method of inspection, observing that certain chants were present in some groups of manuscripts and not in others. Moreover, three or more chants might appear in various combinations, two present and one absent, allowing a group of ordines to be classified along the lines of $+a, +b, -c$.[46] He acknowledged that this approach could be, from a certain point of view, as arbitrary as Hesbert's *coéfficient d'écart*, since it was necessarily based on a human understanding of the relationship between the sources:

> My employment [of characteristic chants as classificatory criteria] has no significance at the moment save in that they seem to be one way in which one can understand and categorise the fundamental differences between families which can be otherwise observed through their identity. My selection of them is however a function of that observation, and I have no means of knowing as things

---

[44] Chadd, 'Liturgical books', pp. 53–4.
[45] Chadd, 'Liturgical books', p. 56. The problem of transposition of elements in Hesbert's distance formula has been addressed above, p. 208.
[46] As in his analytical tables showing the *ordines* of the *historia de Iacob*, 'Liturgical books', p. 65 (Table 8.4).

stand whether these are truly 'significant' criteria, or more important than others one might adopt.[47]

Given this proviso, Chadd's approach to the analysis of Office *ordines* might fairly be judged 'the worst one, except for all the others that have been tried from time to time'.

Adaptation to the analysis of early fragments

David Chadd never applied his methods to fragments of Anglo-Saxon Office books. Nor did Hesbert to any comparable source except the scrappy eighth-century list of Advent Office chant incipits in Lucca, Biblioteca Capitolare, 490, whose contents he misrepresented in *CAO* to bolster his case for an archetype.[48] The advantage of working with a pre-Conquest English fragment is obvious: it needs none of the deciphering necessary for a later medieval book that has been altered, even if only slightly, over time. It is a direct witness to the liturgical practices of a real community during the period of greatest liturgical interest in the history of the Office in England. Such a fragment is only useful, however, if it can be situated within the context of all the other surviving evidence for the Office in England in the tenth and eleventh centuries. This evidence is bound up in antiphoners and breviaries, both English and Continental, copied between the twelfth and fifteenth centuries, since it is rare indeed for two fragments to contain directly comparable material.

Furthermore, a fragment presents dangers not encountered with complete books. As László Dobszay has persuasively pointed out, one of the great weaknesses of the kinds of *sondage* used by Leroquais and Beyssac to localize antiphoners and breviaries was that only a handful of indices were used to assess the book in question. That strong agreement may be found between an unlocalized book and a book of known origin on one, two, or even three Sundays or feast days does not mean that agreement will prevail throughout.[49] Likewise, genuine agreements may be concealed by the kinds of rearrangements mentioned above in the discussion of Hesbert's statistical methods. It is therefore unsafe to make a case

---

[47] Chadd, 'Liturgical books', p. 56.
[48] On this manuscript, see p. 127 above. Other, innocent, errors in *CAO* have been listed in Ottosen, *L'Antiphonaire latin*, pp. 23–5.
[49] L. Dobszay, 'Reading an Office book', in Fassler and Baltzer, *The Divine Office in the Latin Middle Ages*, pp. 48–73, at p. 48.

for the localization of a fragment purely on the basis of liturgical *ordo*, although correspondence in *ordo* may do much to strengthen a case built on palaeographical and codicological considerations.

The procedure followed in Chapters 8 and 9 (Chapter 7 requiring a slightly different approach) may be summarized as follows. First, a liturgical occasion found in the fragment is selected as offering the best material for comparison with other sources (usually a complete *ordo* of responsories, sometimes needing partial reconstruction). Chants for this occasion are then extracted from a pool of complete sources. The sources selected are mainly those used by Chadd, with several others. Some of Chadd's sources have had to be excluded because it was impossible to obtain microfilms and impractical to visit the actual archives. The manuscripts are cited with abbreviated *sigla* usually indicating their place of origin (listed on pp. xix–xxii above). Some sources are necessarily excluded from particular comparisons, such as the Gloucester Diurnal and the Wulfstan Portiforium, which contain chants for the day hours only. The selected sources include most of the surviving complete late medieval English Benedictine antiphoners and breviaries. To these are added manuscripts representing the various Continental traditions identified by Chadd and others as significant for English monastic Office liturgy: the uses of Corbie, Bec, and Dijon. Also included are books from Cluny, Ghent, Fleury, and Saint-Vaast in Arras, as well as the six monastic antiphoners edited in *CAO*. Nine antiphoners following the secular *cursus* have also been included: the six secular antiphoners in *CAO*, the ninth-century Albi antiphoner, the antiphoner of Notre-Dame in Paris, and the antiphoner of Cambrai. These are useful for identifying the secular *ordines* that were in many cases adapted in the monastic books.

The chants occurring on the selected liturgical occasion in each source are collected and presented in tabular form. In this first arrangement, the chants are simply listed alphabetically in incipit and assigned numbers according to their alphabetical order. Each column in the table shows the chants present in an individual source, with a number showing the position of the chant in that source's *ordo* (the selection of responsory verses is marked with a cross or, if there is more than one verse, with two or more letters). This arrangement makes it possible to see at a glance which sources contain a particular chant. The columns are arranged so that the *ordo* of the fragment appears first, followed by the English monastic sources. These are followed by the Continental monastic sources. The secular *ordines* appear last. This first arrangement reveals which chants are unique to particular sources, and therefore not helpful for comparison.

Chants appearing universally are also identified.

This information forms the basis for a careful analysis of the various *ordines* to identify chants whose presence or absence is characteristic of particular groups of sources. This allows the presentation of the data in a second arrangement, in which the *ordo* in each source is represented by a horizontal row of numerals. These rows are grouped according to the presence or absence of significant chants, with each group labelled with numerals representing these chants (e.g. $-12,+4$).[50] It then becomes possible to see similarities between the fragment and potentially related groups, and to consider the implications of that similarity in the light of what else can be determined about the fragment's history through is codicological setting, script, and other evidence.

The number of sources to which this methodology might be applied is surprisingly large.[51] The remaining chapters of this book are concerned only with the three sources securely datable to the tenth century, though some of the later fragments are drawn upon for purposes of comparison. This methodology shows the importance of situating tenth- and eleventh-century Anglo-Saxon Office books in their wider European context. This is no less crucial for interpreting evidence for the Office in earlier centuries, when manuscript survivals are not so plentiful.

---

[50] See the account of David Chadd's approach on p. 216 above.
[51] Space prohibits a complete list of fragments and marginal survivals here, for which the index to Gneuss's *Handlist* and Hartzell's *Catalogue* should be consulted.

7

Two Witnesses to the Chant of the Secular Office in England in the Tenth Century

Durham, Cathedral Library, A. IV. 19, and Cambridge, Corpus Christi College 41

It has been argued in the first part of this book that the Benedictine reformers of the tenth century were probably familiar with an existing liturgical tradition of the Divine Office sung by both 'monks' and secular clerics in cathedrals and minster churches. A lack of Office chant books surviving from earlier than the end of the tenth century – and the earliest are mere fragments – makes it very difficult to determine the actual content of this tradition, or the Continental traditions that may have influenced it. Important sources of this kind of information are, however, preserved in two manuscripts in which lists of Office chants were copied as additions to the original contents. These are the 'Durham Collectar' and the Parker Old English Bede. The similarity of their contents makes it appropriate that they should be evaluated side by side.

Codicological setting and liturgical contents

The place of origin of the original layer of the Durham Collectar (Durham, Cathedral Library, A. IV. 19, s. ix/x) is unknown.[1] By *c*.970 at the latest, the manuscript was owned by the community of St Cuthbert at Chester-le-Street, where the original text received a vernacular gloss. Around the same time, three new quires were added, and these received, apparently within a short time, several liturgical and educational texts, including some of the earliest evidence for the chants of the Divine Office in

---

[1] See the discussion of this manuscript above, p. 145.

any English manuscript. These additions have never been the subject of a close investigation, and were not included in the most recent edition of the text.[2] The date of the additions is roughly fixed by a set of Mass prayers for St Cuthbert copied by Aldred, prior of the community and the famous glossator of the Lindisfarne Gospels.[3] According to a colophon following these prayers, Aldred copied them in 970 while travelling in Wessex as a member of the retinue of Bishop Ælfsige (968–90).[4]

Several sets of additions relate to the performance of the Office. These include a set of benedictions to be read before lessons in the Night Office. As was first noticed by Suitbert Bäumer, these benedictions tend to be grouped in threes and nines, which is indicative of the secular *cursus*.[5] This arrangement for the secular *cursus* throws some doubt on a story told of the Chester-le-Street community's descendants by Symeon of Durham, according to which Bishop Walcher (1071–80) had to instruct his clerks 'to observe the day-time and night-time offices according to the customs of clerks, for previously they had rather imitated the customs of monks in these offices, as they had always learned them from the traditions of their forefathers (as mentioned earlier) who had been cared for and educated among monks'.[6] If we are to understand Symeon to mean that the clerks were following the Benedictine *cursus*, then we must probably conclude that this is an invention on his part, in line with his general aim of emphasizing the monastic past of Durham's cathedral community.[7]

Also included are several lists of Office chant incipits for the period from August to September when the biblical books of Kings, Wisdom, and Job are read at the Night Office (fol. 76[69], too illegible to be

---

[2] Though they did receive very helpful discussion in *The Durham Collectar*, ed. Corrêa, pp. 76–80.
[3] *The Durham Collectar*, ed. Corrêa, p. 76 n. 2.
[4] The colophon is on fol. 84rb; the colophon and the prayers are ed. Lindelöf, *Rituale*, p. 185; and see Thomson's comments on pp. xiv–xix. The colophon is also discussed in *The Durham Collectar*, ed. Corrêa, pp. 78–9.
[5] *Rituale*, ed. Lindelöf, pp. 127–9. Bäumer, *Histoire du bréviaire* I, 372.
[6] Symeon of Durham, *Libellus de exordio atque procursus istius hoc est Dunhelmensis ecclesie (Tract on the Origins and Progress of this Church of Durham)*, III. 18, ed. and tr. D. Rollason, Oxford Medieval Texts (Oxford, 2000), pp. 194–7: 'Qui cum clericos ibidem inueniret, clericorum morem in diurnis et nocturnis officiis eos seruare docuit, nam antea magis consuetudines monachorum in his imitati fuerant, sicut a progenitoribus suis (ut supradictum est) qui inter monachos nutriti et educati extiterant, hereditaria semper traditione didicerant.' See also J. Barrow, 'English cathedral communities and reform in the late tenth and eleventh centuries', in D. Rollason, M. Harvey, and M. Prestwich (eds.), *Anglo-Norman Durham, 1093–1193* (Woodbridge, 1994), pp. 25–39, at p. 33.
[7] Barrow, 'English cathedral communities', pp. 25–6.

transcribed),[8] and the period from September to November when Tobit, Judith, Maccabees, and the Minor Prophets are read (fols. 64v–65r).[9] Added elsewhere in the extra leaves, in a different but contemporary hand, is an incomplete list of antiphon and responsory incipits for the four Sundays of Advent (fol. 84v).[10] The scribal hands responsible for these chants have already received the expert attention of Julian Brown.[11] Both scribes wrote in a Caroline minuscule of the kind associated with Winchester, with periodic lapses into insular letter-forms. This suggests both that they were trained in the old ways of writing and that they had contact with 'reformed' scriptoria, or at least that they learned to imitate the script found in manuscripts produced in such places.

Cambridge, Corpus Christi College 41 has as its main text the Old English version of Bede's *Historia ecclesiastica*, copied in the first half of the eleventh century at an unidentified southern English scriptorium.[12] Its margins are crammed with additional texts, mostly liturgical, written by a single hand dated by Neil Ker to the first half or the middle of the eleventh century, apparently before the book came into the possession of Bishop Leofric, who donated it to Exeter.[13] The marginal additions of Corpus

---

[8] On the contents of fol. 76[69], see *The Durham Ritual*, ed. Brown, p. 49. The page is nearly impossible to read and is not printed in Lindelöf's edition. (The numbering of the folio is that of the facsimile, which takes into account the transposition of one quire when the manuscript was rebound: the first number is the 'correct' one for the manuscript's original state.)

[9] The contents of fols. 64v–65r are ed. Lindelöf, *Rituale*, pp. 132–5. On the annual cycle of scriptural readings at the Night Office current in later Anglo-Saxon England, see Gatch, 'The Office in late Anglo-Saxon monasticism', pp. 352–6.

[10] *Rituale*, ed. Lindelöf, pp. 185–7.

[11] Both fol. 76[69] and fols. 64v–65r were copied by Brown's 'Scribe F' (*The Durham Ritual*, pp. 33–4 and 48). Fol. 84v is the work of Brown's 'Scribe E' (pp. 33 and 50).

[12] The manuscript is no. 32 in M. Budny, *Insular, Anglo-Saxon, and Early Anglo-Norman Manuscript Art at Corpus Christi College, Cambridge: An Illustrated Catalogue*, 2 vols. (Kalamazoo, MI, 1997) I, 501–24, and II, Plates 396–444 (for origin and provenance, see I, 507–9).

[13] Ker, *Catalogue*, p. 45. A list of the additions is given in M. R. James, *A Descriptive Catalogue of the Manuscripts in the Library of Corpus Christi College, Cambridge*, 2 vols. (Cambridge, 1912) I, 82–5 (to avoid confusion, it should be noticed that James uses the term 'office' to refer to material for use at the Mass; chants for the Divine Office are described instead as 'antiphons' or 'responses'). See also now Hartzell, *Catalogue*, pp. 18–22 (no. 20). Some of the contents are printed and discussed in R. J. S. Grant, *Cambridge, Corpus Christi College 41: The Loricas and the Missal*, Costerus: Essays in English and American Language and Literature, new ser. 17 (Amsterdam, 1979), and in S. L. Keefer, 'Margin as archive: The liturgical marginalia of a manuscript of the Old English Bede', *Traditio* 51 (1996), 147–77. But the best analysis of the additions remains the concise and

41 include incipits of Office chants for various occasions: Advent (pages 61–70), Christmas (pages 70–71 and 75), the feasts of St Stephen and St John (page 75), the period from September to November when Job, Judith, and the Minor Prophets are read (pages 475–7), the feast of St Martin (page 478), and (in a very tiny script filling all the available space on page 482) Pentecost, the feasts of John the Baptist, of SS. John and Paul, and of SS. Peter and Paul, and the Commemoration of St Paul. The script of the additions is an idiosyncratic Caroline minuscule in which Insular **g** and horned **e** appear, with Insular **f** written in the Caroline position with its descender on the baseline. Mildred Budny suggests this points to copying by a provincially-trained scribe.[14] The same scribe added neumes of the type usually called 'Breton' to the verse of the Tobit responsory *Peto Domine* on page 475, one of only a handful of texts given in full. The neumes trace the recognizable outline of the first mode verse tone that would be expected for this chant.[15] The presence of Breton neumes, found mainly in manuscripts from Canterbury, may indicate that the scribe operated well outside the influence of Winchester.[16]

Interpretation of the liturgical additions to Durham A. IV. 19 and Corpus 41 has centred around their characters as 'book types'. Noting the varied material added to the Durham Collectar, Alicia Corrêa suggests that it may be best understood as a commonplace book to which reference could be made for later copying.[17] Sarah Larratt Keefer judges the marginal additions to Corpus 41 to be 'disparate texts brought together on whatever vellum was best available, and awaiting the next stage of reorganization and recopying into a volume where they would form at least part of the main liturgical text'.[18] This is sensible to a point. But Keefer sees Corpus 41 as an interim stage in the production of a composite liturgical book (she gives as an example the pontifical, without implying, one hopes, that Corpus 41 was a bishop's book). Budny likewise judges Corpus 41 to

---

devastating review of Grant's book by Christopher Hohler in *Medium aevum* 49 (1980), 275–8.

[14] Budny, *Insular, Anglo-Saxon, and Early Anglo-Norman Manuscript Art* I, 508.

[15] Cf. P. Ferretti, *Esthétique grégorienne, ou Traité des formes musicales du chant grégorien* (Solesmes, 1938), p. 248, and *Le Codex F. 160 de la bibliothèque de la cathédrale de Worcester*, p. 176 line 7.

[16] There are West Saxon exceptions, notably the 'Pontifical of St Dunstan' (BnF lat. 943), originally from Canterbury, which contains Breton neumes among additions in Anglo-Caroline script made at Sherborne. See M. Huglo, 'La domaine de la notation bretonne', *Acta musicologica* 35 (1963), 54–84, at pp. 70–71.

[17] *The Durham Collectar*, ed. Corrêa, p. 78.

[18] Keefer, 'Margin as archive', p. 151.

be 'a liturgical compendium, in an early stage in the development of a portable service-book or portiforium'.[19] Such an interpretation might be applicable to the additions to Durham A. IV. 19, which are mostly for the Divine Office. It is entirely inappropriate, however, for Corpus 41, which includes material that would probably never be united between the covers of a single liturgical book: texts for Mass, Office, and pastoral rituals, along with several Old English homilies.[20]

The most satisfying explanation of the marginalia in Corpus 41 has been offered by Christopher Hohler, who, based on the unique wording of one of the Mass collects among the additions, suggests that its owner, and the scribe of the additions, was a 'priest in charge of a small minster':

> As four verses of St Sechnall's Hymn are among the things he entered, it would be natural to suppose that he lived somewhere near the obvious centre of the cultus of St Patrick in England (namely Glastonbury), and that he was being told to bring his liturgical books up to date by a reforming bishop of Wells, probably, then, Dudoc (1033–61), less probably Giso (1061–1088). ... His books, considering what he adds and what they therefore must have lacked, would seem to be a missal roughly like the *Manuscript Irish Missal* in Corpus Christi College Oxford [MS 282] ... and an office-book-cum-manual roughly like the *Durham Ritual* ... His missal lacked, as the Irish one does, the masses for weekdays, and for several Sundays, in Lent. These were copied in the margins of his Bede (which, I take it, he used for this purpose because he had not foreseen when he came into the cathedral that he would be called on to do all this writing and had brought no clean parchment) from at least two models (probably I take it, because the copying took him some time and he was liable to find

---

[19] Budny, *Insular, Anglo-Saxon, and Early Anglo-Norman Manuscript Art* I, 506.

[20] The 'Red Book of Darley', Cambridge, Corpus Christi College 422 (Sherborne or New Minster, Winchester?, *c*.1061), is an obvious exception. On its origin and varied contents, including items of a pastoral nature, see Corrêa, 'Daily Office books', p. 56; S. Keynes, 'Wulfsige, monk of Glastonbury, abbot of Westminster (*c* 990–3), and bishop of Sherborne (*c* 993–1002)', in K. Barker, D. A. Hinton, and A. Hunt (eds.), *St Wulfsige and Sherborne: Essays to Celebrate the Millennium of the Benedictine Abbey 998–1998*, Bournemouth University School of Conservation Sciences Occasional Paper 8 (Oxford, 2005), pp. 53–94, at pp. 75–6; and H. Gittos, 'Is there any evidence for the liturgy of parish churches in late Anglo-Saxon England? The Red Book of Darley and the status of Old English', in F. Tinti (ed.), *Pastoral Care in Late Anglo-Saxon England*, Anglo-Saxon Studies 6 (Woodbridge, 2005), pp. 63–82.

someone else was using the model he used last) ... Besides the additions to his missal he entered a lot of office chants. These are for the secular office with nine lessons at Sunday matins, not the Benedictine twelve. They are mostly standard 'histories', and there are very similar entries in the *Durham Ritual*.[21]

While Hohler did not claim to have found a definitive solution, his suggestion that the marginal material was entered to supplement existing liturgical books that lacked texts – or the right kinds of texts – for these occasions is, as his comparison with Oxford, Corpus Christi College 282 shows, very plausible. The implication for the Office chants in Corpus 41 is that this priest's antiphoner lacked chants for the occasions listed above. If this is the case, it is significant that both Durham A. IV. 19 and Corpus 41 supply antiphons and responsories for Advent and for the books read throughout the summer. Amalarius of Metz reports that in ninth-century Rome the summer lessons had no proper responsories; instead, responsories from the psalms were used.[22] Advent was among the last liturgical seasons to achieve an enduring form.[23] It was probably observed in England in Alcuin's lifetime, for instance, as a season of six Sundays, not the four found in Continental books after *c*.800.[24] So far as the repertory of Advent Office chants in eighth-century England can be known at all – the main witness is the selection of chant texts from the York antiphoner included by Alcuin in his *De laude Dei* (*ante* 786) – it seems to have borne only an imperfect likeness to the 'Gregorian' repertory in surviving Continental books (though this characterization would admittedly appear to apply to the whole of the York repertory as transmitted by Alcuin).[25]

The contents of Durham A. IV. 19 and Corpus 41 may therefore imply the existence in England in the later tenth and early eleventh centuries of antiphoners containing what could have been a ninth-century (or earlier) 'pre-Gregorian' Roman repertory of Office chants. The 'supplementary'

---

[21] Hohler, Review of Grant, *Corpus*, pp. 275–6, referring to *The Manuscript Irish Missal belonging to the President and Fellows of Corpus Christi College, Oxford*, ed. F. E. Warren (London, 1879). Digital images of this manuscript are now available through 'Early Manuscripts at Oxford University' <http://image.ox.ac.uk/> last visited 5 April 2013.
[22] Amalarius, *Liber de ordine antiphonarii*, prologus §§ 4–5 and cc. 71. 1–76. 1, ed. Hanssens III, 13–14 and 100–5. See Le Roux, 'Les répons "De Psalmis" ', p. 40.
[23] On the early medieval development of Advent, see M. E. Fassler, 'Sermons, sacramentaries, and early sources for the Office in the Latin West: The example of Advent', in Fassler and Baltzer, *The Divine Office in the Latin Middle Ages*, pp. 15–47.
[24] Bullough, *Alcuin*, p. 194.
[25] See p. 127 above.

chants preserved in the two manuscripts, moreover, conform exactly to what would be expected in a ninth-century Frankish 'Gregorian' antiphoner, based on the testimony of Amalarius. For example, Amalarius remarks that only six responsories are provided for the readings from the book of Tobit, the rest to be borrowed from those taken from Job.[26] Table 7.1 gives the responsories for Tobit as found in Durham A. IV. 19 and Corpus 41.[27] Each list gives six responsories and verses. These are identical, with two exceptions. The verse in the first responsory in the Durham Collectar is *Qui regis Israel intende*, against *Omnia iudicia tua* in Corpus 41. Corpus 41 provides a full text for its verse, complete with neumes, which may signal a conscious departure from a more familiar verse, probably that recorded in Durham A. IV. 19.[28] The refrain of the last responsory in Durham A. IV. 19, *Tempus est ut reuertar*, is given as *Te in omnem* in Corpus 41. Both have the same verse (*Benedicite*). The Corpus 41 version is probably a copying error: its incipit does not occur in *CAO* or in the CANTUS Database, and the Durham version follows a familiar pattern in having as its refrain the verse of the preceding responsory. Both lists, in any case, match the expectation for six responsories established by Amalarius, and both are within the 'Gregorian' tradition represented by the manuscripts edited in *CAO*.

We have in Durham A. IV. 19 and Corpus 41, therefore, evidence that just may indicate the existence of an early, 'pre-Gregorian' Roman Office antiphoner, now lost, known in England at a relatively late date, and for the availability of a Frankish Office antiphoner that may have been used to supplement it. It would be very desirable to ascertain the Continental tradition that lies behind all the Office chants added to Durham A. IV. 19 and Corpus 41. The presence in both sources of responsories for the four Sundays of Advent makes it possible to compare at least this portion of

---

[26] *Liber de ordine antiphonarii*, c. 73. 1–2, ed. Hanssens III, 102.
[27] Corpus 41, p. 475; *Rituale*, ed. Lindelöf, p. 132.
[28] This was, incidentally, the only change necessary to make the Tobit *ordo* in Durham A. IV. 19 conform to the Corbie *ordo* as witnessed by the Saint-Denis and Mont-Renaud antiphoners (*D, CAO* II, § 134; *MoR*, fol. 126r), though *MoR* muddies the waters in having the verse altered by a second hand to the Durham verse *Qui regis*! The sixth responsory in *MoR*, *Tempus est*, has the variant verse *Confitemini ei coram omnibus*, which the second hand has corrected to the Saint-Denis (and Durham/Corpus) verse *Benedicite*. The Corpus 41 repertory is preserved in the Worcester Antiphoner (*Wor*, p. 176). A rather different set of verses, akin to those in the antiphoner of Silos (*S*) and the southern Italian antiphoner *L*, is given in the thirteenth-century Muchelney Breviary (*Mch*, fol. 243r): ℟. *Omni tempore* ℣. *Inquire ut facias*; ℟. *Memor esto fili* ℣. *In mente habeto*; ℟. *Benedicite deum celi* ℣. *Ipsum benedicite et cantate*.

Table 7.1 Responsories for the Book of Tobit in Durham, Cathedral Library, A. IV. 19 and Cambridge, Corpus Christi College 41

Durham A. IV. 19	Corpus 41
1. ℟. Peto domine ut de uincula ℣. Qui regis israel intende	1. ℟. Peto Domine ℣. Omnia iudicia tua …[a]
2. ℟. Omni tempore benedic deus ℣. Memor esto filii quoniam pa[uperem]	2. ℟. Omni tempore ℣. Memor esto filii
3. ℟. Memor esto filii quoniam ℣. Fiducia magna est	3. ℟. Memor esto filii ℣. Fiducia magna
4. ℟. Sufficiebat nobis ℣. Heu me fili mi ut qui	4. ℟. Sufficiebat nobis ℣. Heu me fili mi
5. ℟. Benedicite deum caeli ℣. Te[m]pus est ut reuer[tar]	5. ℟. Benedicite deum ℣. Tempus est
6. ℟. Tempus est ut reuer[tar] ℣. Benedicite deum caeli	6. ℟. Te in omnem ℣. Benedicite

[a] The text of the verse is given in full, with Breton neumes.

their combined repertory with the eight hundred Advent *ordines* collected by Hesbert in his *Corpus antiphonalium officii*.

Liturgical ordo *and Continental affiliation*

The responsories for the four Sundays of Advent in Durham A. IV. 19 and Corpus 41 are printed in Table 7.2. (This and other tables relevant to this analysis are printed together at the end of this chapter, beginning on page 235.) Each Sunday has nine responsories (Durham A. IV. 19 is incomplete on the fourth Sunday). This is the pattern of the secular *cursus*, which, as has been argued in Part I of this book, was used by both monks and secular clerics in England even in the early years of the Benedictine reform. The numbers and letters printed to the right of each list in Table 7.2 give Hesbert's shorthand siglum for each responsory refrain (a number) and its verse (a letter). Using the data collected by Hesbert, it is possible to set the lists in Durham A. IV. 19 and Corpus 41 within their wider European context. As has already been seen in Chapter 6, Hesbert's working methods impose certain limitations. In its current form,

Hesbert's *Corpus* is suited only to the identification of sources in which the same chants occur in the same arrangement. It would be preferable to know all the sources that contain the same repertory of chants as Durham A. IV. 19 and Corpus 41, irrespective of arrangement. Bearing this in mind, some preliminary conclusions may nevertheless be drawn.

Durham A. IV. 19 shares its series of responsories – up to the point where it breaks off – with twenty-seven of Hesbert's eight hundred *CAO* sources (listed in Table 7.3). The list in Corpus 41 does not exactly match any known source. This belies its substantial agreement with Durham A. IV. 19. The two lists in Table 7.2 differ in only two places: the ninth responsory of Advent I (Durham A. IV. 19: *Laetentur caeli* ℣. *Ecce dominator*, *CAO* 19A; Corpus 41: *Alieni non* ℣. *Veniam dicit*, *CAO* 62A), and the ninth responsory of Advent III (Durham A. IV. 19: *Docebit nos* ℣. *Ex Sion*, *CAO* 70B; Corpus 41: *Ecce radix* ℣. *A solis*, *CAO* 39F). Otherwise, the same responsories appear in the same positions, and with identical verses. This raises the possibility that both are related, though not necessarily directly, to a common source.

Tables 7.5–7.8 display, using Hesbert's shorthand, the responsories and verses for the four Sundays of Advent as they are found in Durham A. IV. 19, in Corpus 41, and in each manuscript in Table 7.3. A key for interpreting the tables is given in Table 7.4, though it is sufficient for the present discussion simply to note those points where the *CAO* manuscripts differ from Durham A. IV. 19 and Corpus 41.[29] For Advent III, several sources in Table 7.7 (nos. 177, 180, 186, 206, 471, and 496) include Corpus 41's ninth responsory, 39 (*Ecce radix*), as a supernumerary alternative to the Durham A. IV. 19 responsory, 70 (*Docebit nos*). The Advent III chants in Durham A. IV. 19 and Corpus 41 could conceivably have been drawn from a single original series with several supernumerary chants, differing in their ninth responsories only because of different decisions about which nine chants were to be used.[30]

It is unlikely that the appearance of responsory 62 (*Alieni non*) in Corpus 41 as the ninth responsory of Advent I can be explained in the same way. Perusal of Hesbert's data suggests that this is essentially a 'western' chant in what is otherwise (as shall be seen) an 'eastern' Frankish *ordo*. It may have been introduced to the Corpus 41 repertory through some

---

[29] The key is drawn from *CAO* V, 32–3, and VI, 7–55.
[30] On the tricky problems in discerning actual liturgical practice from scribal tendencies towards archiving, see Dobszay, 'Reading an Office book', p. 53.

secondary channel of influence.[31] But it does nevertheless appear as one of the three extra 'monastic' chants (making up the monastic complement of twelve responsories) in a breviary from the Benedictine monastery of St Maximin in Trier, where it is paired with responsory 18 (*Obsecro Domine*), as in Corpus 41.[32] It is not impossible that it was native to a now unknown eastern Frankish responsory series.

Examination of the responsory verses (represented by letters in Hesbert's shorthand) permits further refinement. The rows in Tables 7.5–7.8 are distributed based on the number of times each source gives the same verse assignment as Durham A. IV. 19 and Corpus 41. None of Hesbert's *CAO* sources are identical to Durham A. IV. 19 or Corpus 41 in their verse assignments, but several have 35 out of 38 possible matches (the combined repertory of the Durham and Corpus lists). The number of verse matches often correlates with the place of origin of a manuscript, most strikingly with the five books from Aosta, counted as having 12.5 matches to take into account their consistent use of two variable verses with responsory 11, *Aspiciens a longe*. (*Aspiciens* is always found with two invariable verses, *Quique terriginae* and *Qui regis*, followed by at least one variable verse. The order of verses in Corpus 41 is unorthodox.[33]) The major centres with verse assignments most closely related to Durham A. IV. 19 and Corpus 41 are Trier, Mainz, and Würzburg. Indeed, the verse assignments in Durham A. IV. 19 and Corpus 41 agree almost perfectly with Hesbert's reconstruction of the typical 'Germanic' (as opposed to 'Latin') set of responsory verses.[34] Hesbert based his reconstruction of this *liste-type* on the evidence of mainly later medieval antiphoners and breviaries. But the same list is embedded in a ninth-century manuscript containing material for the choral celebration of the Office according to the Benedictine *cursus* of which Hesbert, if he was aware of it, made no use.[35] Like the manuscript of St Maximin's in Trier

---

[31] Compare occurrences of responsory 62 in Hesbert's Germanic 'deuxième groupe' (*CAO* VI, 122) with those in his Latin 'premier groupe' (VI, 131).

[32] Karlsruhe, Badische Landesbibliothek, Aug. CCLXVI (s. xiv). See *CAO* V, 39 (no. 638).

[33] Hesbert, *CAO* VI, 2.

[34] *CAO* VI, 141. The verses would seem to rule out an otherwise possible connection with Metz, whose Office books (along with the Cistercian books derived from them) transmit between them the whole repertory of Advent responsories found in Durham A. IV. 19 and Corpus 41 (including the pairings 19–62 and 39–70), but with different verse assignments (*CAO*, nos. 321, 600, 667, 714, and 716).

[35] See the review of vol. 5 of *CAO* by Michel Huglo in *Revue de musicologie* 63 (1977), 164–8.

referred to above, the early Prüm *Chorbuch* contained in Trier, Stadbibliothek, 1245/597 includes within its monastic sets of twelve responsories for each Sunday in Advent (fol. 107) all the responsories attested by Durham A. IV. 19 and Corpus 41:[36]

Advent I:	11B	12B	13A	14B	15B	62A	16B	61A	17B	18A	60A	19A
Advent II:	21A	22B	23A	24B	25B	77A	26B	27B	73A	28B	92A	29A
Advent III:	31B	32B	33B	34B	35B	38B	36A	37B	81A	94A	39B	70B
Advent IV:	41B	42A	43A	44A	45B	46B	47B	48A	49A	71D	93A	91A

Durham A. IV. 19 and Corpus 41 depart from Hesbert's Germanic *liste-type* at two points. In the first, an intriguing link is observed with the thirteenth- or fourteenth-century breviary of the Augustinian canons of Sankt Florian, near Linz in Austria (no. 496), which not only includes the extra responsory 39, but also, like Corpus 41, assigns to it verse 'F' (*A solis ortu*).[37] This verse assignment is found in only one other *CAO* source, Copenhagen, Kongelige Bibliothek, Ny kgl. S. 137 4° (no. 206 in Table 7.3), localized by Hesbert to 'Bavaria'.[38] (It was included in Table 7.3 for this reason, despite several departures from the arrangement in Durham A. IV. 19. The obvious relationship between the Sankt Florian and Copenhagen Advent *ordines* underscores the limitations of a purely mechanistic approach.) The Sankt Florian book would be an even closer match but for its unique verse in responsory 38.[39] The appearance of 39F in the Sankt Florian breviary could indicate that the repertory behind Corpus 41 (and perhaps Durham A. IV. 19) should be localized somewhere east of the Rhine.

In a second departure from the expected Germanic set of responsory verses, responsory 37 (*Descendet dominus*) appears in both Durham A. IV. 19 and Corpus 41 with the verse *Ex Sion* (Hesbert's verse 'E'). This verse occurs in only one manuscript in Hesbert's *Corpus*: the thirteenth-century breviary of Muchelney Abbey (*Mch*). This would appear to be

---

[36] See p. 72 above. A later hand has marked each series with Roman numerals to put the responsories into a different order.

[37] Sankt Florian, Chorherren-Stiftsbibliothek, XI. 384. Hesbert dates this manuscript to the twelfth century and calls it an antiphoner. But see its entry, with digital images, in 'OLIVER', The Hill Museum and Manuscript Library Manuscript Database <http://www.hmml.org/research2010/research10.htm> last visited 5 April 2013.

[38] *CAO* V, 7, no. 206. E. Jørgensen, *Catalogus codicum Latinorum medii aevi Bibliothecae regiae Hafniensis* (Copenhagen, 1926), p. 214, dates this manuscript to the fourteenth century and describes it as 'Codex mutilus. *Breviarium. Prov. Germania.*'

[39] Verse 'D', *Deus a Libano* (*CAO* VI, 30).

an insular variant in an otherwise eastern Frankish responsory series, though it is again possible that verse E was originally found in a Frankish model no longer extant. Although the Muchelney Advent responsory series seems to be the product of considerable editorial rearrangement, its monastic set of twelve responsories nevertheless embraces all the responsories preserved in Durham A. IV. 19 and Corpus 41, including the responsory pairings 19–62 and 39–70:

Advent I:	11–	12A	13A	14A	17A	15B	18A	16A	19A	62A	60A	63A
Advent II:	21A	22A	24A	25B	26A	27A	28B	29A	64B	80C	72–	81A
Advent III:	31B	32B	33A	34B	35B	38B	36A	37E	39A	70A	73A	92A
Advent IV:	41A	42A	43A	44A	45B	46B	47A	48A	49A	25B	93A	91A

The verse assignments in *Mch* are eclectic; but Hesbert noted that the proportion of 'Germanic' verses (over half) was unusually large for an English monastic breviary.[40] The repertory represented in Durham A. IV. 19 and Corpus 41 may therefore have had an important influence on the the monastic Office liturgy sung at Muchelney.

Date of transmission and place of reception

How and when did this eastern Frankish repertory of Advent responsories reach England, and to what English church would it first have been transmitted? In the earliest scenario that can be conceived (if only to be dismissed), this repertory would in fact be English in origin, and its presence in eastern Frankish sources would be explained by the missionary activities of Boniface. One of the dioceses that he founded, Passau, embraced Sankt Florian and perhaps the Bavarian church that produced the related manuscript Copenhagen Ny kgl. S. 137 4°. As has already been noted, however, what can be known about the English repertory of Office chants in Boniface's time tends not to support such a hypothesis.[41]

At the latest end of the possible chronological range (established by the date of the Chester-le-Street additions, *c*.970), an example of cultural contact between England and Trier is found in the well-known Benna, a

---

[40] Hesbert, 'Les antiphonaires monastiques insulaires', pp. 363–6 and 370–1.

[41] See pp. 126–132 above. This is not to deny that Boniface may have introduced other English liturgical texts at his Continental foundations; cf. C. Hohler (with A. Hughes), 'The Durham services in honour of St. Cuthbert', in C. F. Battiscombe (ed.), *The Relics of Saint Cuthbert* (Oxford, 1956), pp. 155–91, at p. 158.

canon of St Paulinus in Trier. Summoned to be tutor to King Edgar's daughter Edith (*ante* 975), he later decorated her church at Wilton (*c*.984) and, on a return visit to Trier, secured for Wilton a relic of the Holy Nails.[42] The Trier monastery of Mettlach had an Anglo-Saxon abbot, Leofsige, in the later tenth century.[43]

A date of transmission somewhere between these extremes seems most probable. Christopher Hohler's suggestion of Wells as the home of the exemplars behind the additions to Corpus 41 would put this Office repertory in the southwest of England, which would fit well if transmission were imagined to have occurred in Alfred's reign or, indeed, in Æthelstan's – Æthelstan's sister Edith (d.946) married Emperor Otto I, and diplomatic, ecclesiastical, and artistic contacts between England and Ottonian Germany (including gifts of manuscripts) may be traced thereafter into the eleventh century.[44] As for Durham A. IV. 19, Chester-le-Street's links with Wessex in the tenth century are well known, and it is possible that the lists of Office chants in Durham A. IV. 19 were copied on the same journey through Wessex during which Aldred copied the prayers for St Cuthbert. The Cuthbert prayers may have been copied at the same centre that produced Cambridge, Corpus Christi College 183, the famous copy of the Life and rhymed Office of Cuthbert, commissioned by Æthelstan, 934×939. The prayers copied by Aldred use the versions found in Corpus 183.[45] Simon Keynes has suggested Glastonbury and Wells

---

[42] According to the Life of Edith by Goscelin of Saint-Bertin (*c*.1080): A. Wilmart, 'La légende de Ste Edith en prose et vers par le moine Goscelin', *Analecta Bollandiana* 56 (1938), 5–101 and 265–307, at pp. 73 and 86–7. For brief notice and further references, see M. Hare, 'Abbot Leofsige of Mettlach: An English monk in Flanders and Upper Lotharingia in the late tenth century', *Anglo-Saxon England* 33 (2004), 109–44 and Plates I and II, at pp. 140–1 and n. 174.

[43] Hare, 'Abbot Leofsige'.

[44] R. Deshman, '*Christus rex et magi reges*: Kingship and Christology in Ottonian and Anglo-Saxon art', *Frühmittelalterliche Studien* 10 (1976), 367–405, at pp. 390–404.

[45] The conventional belief that this manuscript was commissioned as a gift for Chester-le-Street has been challenged by David Rollason, 'St Cuthbert and Wessex: The evidence of Cambridge, Corpus Christi College Ms 183', in G. Bonner, D. Rollason, and C. Stancliffe (eds.), *St. Cuthbert, his Cult and his Community to AD 1200* (Woodbridge, 1989), pp. 413–24. The office was apparently composed for the court chapel (Hohler, 'The Durham services', p. 159). The books given by Æthelstan to Chester-le-Street were nevertheless liturgical in emphasis: 'a missal, two gospel-books ornamented with gold and silver, and a Life of St Cuthbert written in verse and prose' (*Historia de S. Cuthberto*, § 26, ed. T. Arnold, *Symeonis monachi Opera omnia*, 2 vols., Rolls Series 75 (London, 1882–5) I, 211: 'et unum missalem, et duos Evangeliorum textus, auro et argento ornatos, et unam sancti Cuthberti vitam, metrice et prosaice scriptam'). The rhymed Office in honour of St Cuthbert in Corpus

(but not Winchester) as possible origins of Corpus 183.[46] Liturgical books with Trier connections were apparently available in England in the latter years of Alfred's reign. The original layer of the Leofric Missal includes the names of three saintly archbishops of Trier 'high up in the litany, among the Fathers,' in one of its litanies.[47] The introduction of the repertory of Office chants preserved in Durham A. IV. 19 and Corpus 41 could be attributed to one of Alfred's Continental advisers. Asser's description of Grimbald of Saint-Bertin as *cantator optimus* could, as David Knowles thought, imply a musical-liturgical dimension to Alfred's educational and ecclesiastical reforms.[48] The link between Corpus 41 and later manuscripts from Sankt Florian and Bavaria could point instead to John the Old Saxon, whose sobriquet suggests an origin east of the Rhine.[49] Nothing so specific implicates Æthelstan's clergy; but his circle was certainly in touch with Continental liturgical developments.[50] If Muchelney Abbey was, as William of Malmesbury testifies, founded by Æthelstan, then the presence of elements of this Germanic Office chant repertory in its later books may be the result of the promotion of this repertory among the houses established in the royal monastic programme carried forward in Wessex by Alfred and his successors.

Conclusions

The date of this repertory's transmission must remain for now a matter for speculation. But the chant lists in Durham A. IV. 19 and Corpus

---

183 (fols. 92v–95v) is ed. (from a later manuscript, with collation tables) by Hohler, 'The Durham services', pp. 169–77 and 188–9.

[46] Keynes, 'King Athelstan's books', pp. 184–5, observing that 'it is especially interesting to find that when the king wished to commission a manuscript he turned not to Winchester but to a house in the south-western heartland of his kingdom' (p. 185).

[47] Hohler, 'Some service books', p. 78. The names in the litany are in *The Leofric Missal*, ed. Orchard II, 390 (no. 2300, Maximinus and Paulinus) and p. 391 (Modestus). See also Orchard's discussion of the litany at I, 66.

[48] See above, p. 146.

[49] M. Lapidge, 'John the Old Saxon (*fl. c.*885–904)', in H. C. G. Matthew and Brian Harrison (eds.), *Oxford Dictionary of National Biography*, 60 vols and Index of Contributors (Oxford, 2004) XXX, 204.

[50] The Cuthbert rhymed office in Corpus 183 is itself a witness to this kind of contact, being the earliest English example of a rhymed office, and indeed 'one of the earliest four or five known of its kind' (Hohler, 'The Durham services', p. 156). Christopher Hohler judged it to be probably the work of 'a clerk from the Low Countries' (p. 157); see also Rollason, 'St Cuthbert and Wessex', p. 417.

41 nevertheless imply the availability in England in the tenth century of Office chant books containing the 'Gregorian' repertory first codified in Frankish Gaul under the Carolingians, with the chants ordered for the stable medieval form of the Roman Office eventually called the 'secular' *cursus*. This tradition of Office chant was introduced through a channel apparently outside those usually associated with the tenth-century English Benedictine reform, and perhaps before Dunstan's appointment as abbot of Glastonbury. The predominance of 'German' verses in the Advent responsories of the later Muchelney breviary could indicate that this existing (secular) Office tradition was not wholly replaced, but adapted for use in a reformed Benedictine context. It was perhaps this secular tradition that gave the future leaders of the Benedictine reform their first liturgical formation at Glastonbury, even if Æthelwold would later reject it in favour of a different Continental model from Corbie.

Table 7.2 Responsories for the four Sundays of Advent added to Durham, Cathedral Library, A. IV. 19 and Cambridge, Corpus Christi College 41

ADVENT I

Durham A. IV. 19		Corpus 41	
1. Aspiciens a longe	11B	1. Aspiciens	11B
℣. Quique terriginae	n.a.	℣. Quique	n.a.
℣. Qui regis Israel	n.a.	℣. Tollite	(B)
℣. Tollite portas	(B)	℣. Qui regis Israel	n.a.
2. Aspiciebam	12B	2. Aspiciebam	12B
℣. Ecce dominator		℣. Ecce dominator	
3. Missus est Gabriel	13A	3. Missus est Gabriel	13A
℣. Aue Maria		℣. Aue Maria	
4. Aue Maria	14B	4. Aue Maria	14B
℣. Tollite portas		℣. Tollite	
5. Saluatorem	15B	5. Saluatorem	15B
℣. Preo[c]cupemus		℣. Preo[c]cupemus	
6. Audite uerbum	16B	6. Audite uerbum	16B
℣. A solis ortu		℣. A solis ortu	
7. Ecce uirgo con[cipiet]	17B	7. Ecce uirgo	17B
℣. Tollite		℣. Tollite	
8. Obsecro Domine	18A	8. Obsecro Domine	18A
℣. A solis ortu		℣. A solis ortu	
9. Laetentur caeli	19A	9. Alieni non	62A
℣. Ecce dominator		℣. Veniam dicit	

Continued on next page

Table 7.2 (continued)

ADVENT II

Durham A. IV. 19		Corpus 41	
1. Hierusalem cito ℣. Israhel si me audieris	21A	1. Hierusalem cito ℣. Israel si me	21A
2. Ecce Dominus ueniet et omnes sancti ℣. A solis ortu	22B	2. Ecce Dominus ℣. A solis ortu	22B
3. Ierusalem surge ℣. Leua in circuitu	23A	3. Hierusalem ℣. Leua in circu[itu] oculos	23A
4. Ciuitas Ierusalem ℣. Ecce dominator	24B	4. Ciuitas Hierusalem ℣. Ecce dominator	24B
5. Ecce ueniet Dominus ℣. Ecce dominator	25B	5. Ecce ueniet [Dominus] protec[tor] ℣. Ecce domi[nator]	25B
6. Sicut mater ℣. Deus a Libano	26B	6. Sicut mater ℣. Deus a Libano	26B
7. Ierusalem plantabis ℣. Deus a Libano	27B	7. Hierusalem plan[tabis] ℣. Deus a Libano	27B
8. Egredietur Dominus ℣. Deus a Libano	28B	8. Egredietur Dominus de Samaria ℣. Deus a Liba[no]	28B
9. Rex noster adueni ℣. Ecce agnus dei	29A	9. Rex noster ℣. Ecce agnus dei	29A

Continued on next page

Table 7.2 (continued)

ADVENT III

Durham A. IV. 19		Corpus 41	
1. Ecce apparebit	31B	1. Ecce a[p]parebit	31B
℣. Ecce dominator		℣. Ecce dominator	
2. Betle[e]m ciuitas	32B	2. Beth[le]em ciuitas	32B
℣. Deus a Libano		℣. Deus a Libano	
3. Qui uenturus est	33B	3. Qui uenturus	33B
℣. Ex [S]ion species		℣. Ex [S]ion	
4. Suscipe uerbum	34B	4. Suscipe uerbum	34B
℣. Aue Maria		℣. Aue Maria	
5. Egipte noli	35B	5. Egiptae noli	35B
℣. Ecce dominator		℣. Ecce dominator	
6. Prope est	36A	6. Prope est	36A
℣. Qui uenturus est		℣. Qui uenturus	
7. Descendet Dominus	37E	7. Descendit Dominus	37E
℣. Ex [S]ion		℣. Ex [S]ion species	
8. Ueni Domine et noli	38B	8. Ueni Domine	38B
℣. A solis ortu		℣. A solis	
9. Docebit nos	70B	9. Ecce radix	39F
℣. Ex [S]ion		℣. A solis	

Continued on next page

Table 7.2 (continued)

ADVENT IV

Durham A. IV. 19		Corpus 41	
1. Canite tuba in Sion ℣. A solis ortu	41B	1. Canite tuba ℣. A solis	41B
2. Octaua decima ℣. Ego sum Dominus	42A	2. Octaua decima ℣. Ego sum Dominus Deus	42A
3. Non auferetur ℣. Pulchriores sunt	43A	3. Non auferetur ℣. Pulchriores	43A
4. Me oportet ℣. Hoc est testimonium	44A	4. Me oportet ℣. Hoc est testimonium	44A
5. Ecce iam uenit (no verse)	45	5. Ecce iam ueniet ℣. Prope est ut	45B
6.		6. Uirgo Israel ℣. A solis ortu	46B
7.		7. Iuraui dicit Dominus ℣. A solis ortu	47B
8.		8. Non discedimus ℣. Domine Deus uirtutum	48A
9.		9. Intuemini ℣. Et dominator	49A

Table 7.3 Sources in *CAO* with Advent responsory lists identical to that in Durham, Cathedral Library, A. IV. 19

CAO siglum	Shelfmark (Origin, Date) **matching verses**
109	Aosta, Biblioteca Capitolare della Cattedrale, *s.n.* (Aosta, s. xiii) **12.5 matches**
110	Aosta, Biblioteca Capitolare della Cattedrale, *s.n.* (Aosta, s. xiv) **12.5 matches**
111	Aosta, Collegio Sant'Orso, *s.n.* (Aosta, St Jacquême, s. xiii) **9/18 matches** *This source is defective at the first and fourth Sundays of Advent.*
113	Aosta, Biblioteca del Seminario maggiore, *s.n.* (Augustinian, s. xiii) **15 matches**
114	Aosta, Biblioteca del Seminario maggiore, *s.n.* (Aosta, s. xiv) **12.5 matches**
177	Karlsruhe, Badische Landesbibliothek, Schwarzach 17 (Germany, s. xiv) **33 matches**
180	Kassel, Landesbibliothek, Theol. fol. 121 (Fritzlar, St Peter, s. xiv) **33 matches**
186	Kassel, Landesbibliothek, Theol. fol. 161 (Fritzlar, St Peter, s. xiv) **34 matches**
199	Koblenz, Staatsarchiv, 109 (Trier, s. xiv med.) **35 matches**
206	Copenhagen, Kongelige Bibliotek, Ny kgl. S. 137 4° (Bavaria, s. xiv) **34 matches** *This source inverts the order of responsories 25 and 26 on Advent II; but on Advent III it shares with Corpus 41 the responsory and verse '39F', found elsewhere only in Hesbert's no. 496 (see below).*
251	Le Grand-Saint-Bernard Hospice *s.n.* (Grand-Saint-Bernard, s. xiv) **17 matches**
255	Hanover, Landesbibliothek, I. 101 b (Unlocalized, s. xv ex.) **32 matches**
355	Oxford, Bodleian Library, Lat. lit. e 5 (Geneva, s. xv) **26 matches**

Continued on next page

Table 7.3 (continued)

CAO siglum	Shelfmark (Origin, Date) **matching verses**
356	Oxford, Bodleian Library, Laud. misc. 284 (Würzburg, s. xii–xiii) **34 matches**
358	Oxford, Bodleian Library, Laud. misc. 382 (Germany, s. xv) **31 matches**
407	BnF lat. 1062 (Mainz, s. xv) **34 matches**
432	BnF lat. 16307 (Geneva, s. xiii)[2] **28 matches**
471	Raigern, Klásterní Knihovna benediktin, S F/K 1 α 1 (Trebič, 1395) **33 matches**
474	Rome, Biblioteca Angelica, 440 (Grand-Saint-Bernard, s. xiv) **11 matches**
475	Rome, Biblioteca Apostolica Vaticana, lat. 4751 (Krakow, s. xv) **22 matches**
496	Sankt Florian, Chorherren-Stiftsbibliothek, XI. 384 (Sankt Florian, s. xiv) **35 matches**
537	Toledo, Biblioteca capitular, 37.2 (Aosta, 1433) **12.5 matches**
547	Trier, Bistumsarchiv, 523 (Trier, s. xiv) **34 matches**
549	Trier, Dombibliothek, 180 F (Trier?, s. xiv) **34 matches**
553	Trier, Stadtbibliothek, 427 (Trier, s. xiv[2]) **35 matches**
580	Vercelli, Biblioteca Capitolare, CCX (Aosta, s. xiv) **12.5 matches**
596	Würzburg, Universitätsbibliothek, Mp th. f. 168 (Würzburg, St Kylian, c.1304) **no verses** *This source gives refrains only, no verses.*
395	BnF lat. 781 (Limoges?, s. xii) **7 matches**

Table 7.4 Key to Hesbert's shorthand for *CAO* Advent responsories and verses included in Tables 7.5–7.8

01	Sanctificamini filii
	A Ecce Dominus veniet
01	Sanctificamini hodie
	A Hodie scietis
02	Constantes estote
	A Uos qui in puluere
11	Aspiciens a longe
	A Excita **B** Tollite
12	Aspiciebam
	A Potestas **B** Ecce dominator
13	Missus est
	A Aue Maria
14	Aue Maria
	A Quomodo **B** Tollite
15	Saluatorem
	A Sobrie **B** Praeoccupemus
16	Audite uerbum
	A Annuntiate et auditum **B** A solis ortu
17	Ecce uirgo
	A Super solium **B** Tollite
	C Factus est
18	Obsecro
	A A solis ortu **B** Qui regis
19	Laetentur caeli
	A Ecce dominator **B** Orietur
21	Ierusalem cito
	A Israel **B** Ego enim
22	Ecce dominus ueniet et omnes ... et erit
	A Ecce cum uirtute **B** A solis ortu
23	Ierusalem surge
	A Leua in circuitu
24	Ciuitas Ierusalem
	A Ecce in fortitudine **B** Ecce dominator dominus

Continued on next page

Table 7.4 (continued)

25	Ecce ueniet dominus protector	
	A Et dominabitur **B** Ecce dominator	
26	Sicut mater	
	A Dabo in Sion **B** Deus a Libano	
27	Ierusalem plantabis	
	A Exulta satis **B** Deus a Libano	
	C Et tu exultabis	
28	Egredietur dominus de Samaria	
	A Et praeparabitur **B** Deus a Libano	
29	Rex noster	
	A Ecce agnus dei **B** Super ipsum	
31	Ecce apparebit	
	A Apparebit **B** Ecce dominator	
	C Dominus sicut fortis	
32	Bethleem	
	A Loquetur **B** Deus a Libano	
	D De Sion	
33	Qui uenturus est	
	A Deponet **B** Ex Sion	
	C Et auferet	
34	Sucipe uerbum	
	A Paries **B** Aue Maria	
35	Aegypte	
	A Ecce ueniet dominus **B** Ecce dominator	
36	Prope est	
	A Qui uenturus	
37	Descendet	
	A Et adorabunt **B** A solis ortu	
	C Et dominabitur **E** Ex Sion	
38	Ueni domine	
	A Excita **B** A solis ortu	
	D Deus a Libano	
39	Ecce radix Iesse ascendet	
	A Dabit ei **B** Deus a Libano	
	F A solis ortu	

Continued on next page

Table 7.4 (continued)

41 Canite tuba
A Annuntiate in finibus **B** A solis ortu
C Annutiate et auditum **D** Congregate
42 Uigesima quarta (Octaua decima) die
A Ego sum
43 Non auferetur
A Pulchriores sunt
44 Me oportet
A Hoc est testimonium
45 Ecce iam ueniet
A Propter nimiam **B** Prope est
46 Uirgo Israel
A In caritate **B** A solis ortu
C Reuertetur
47 Iuraui
A Iuxta est **B** A solis ortu
C Assument montes **E** In caritate
48 Non discedimus
A Domine deus **B** Memento nostri
C Ostende nobis
49 Intuemini
A Et dominabitur **B** Praecursor
59 Radix Iesse qui exurget
B Ex Sion
62 Alieni non transibunt
A Ego ueniam
70 Docebit nos
A Uenite ascendamus **B** Ex Sion
C Domus Iacob
81 Egredietur uirga
B Ex Sion **C** Rorate
91 Nascetur
A Ecce aduenit **B** In ipso
93 Annuntiatum est
A Aue Maria

Table 7.5 Responsories and verses of Advent I in sources related to Durham A. IV. 19 and Corpus 41

Durham A. IV. 19
    11B   12B   13A   14B   15B   16B   17B   18A   19A
Corpus 41
    11B   12B   13A   14B   15B   16B   17B   18A   62A
496 Sankt Florian (35 matches)
    11B   12B   13A   14B   15B   16B   17B   18A   19A
199 Trier (35 matches)
    11B   12B   13A   14B   15B   16B   17B   18A   19A
553 Trier (35 matches)
    11B   12B   13A   14B   15B   16B   17B   18A   19A
547 Trier (34 matches)
    11B   12B   13A   14A   15B   16B   17B   18A   19A
549 Trier? (34 matches)
    11B   12B   13A   14A   15B   16B   17B   18A   19A
206 Bavaria (34 matches)
    11B   12B   13A   14B   15B   16B   17B   18A   19A
180 Fritzlar, St Peter (34 matches)
    11A   12B   13A   14B   15B   16B   17B   18A   19A
186 Fritzlar, St Peter (34 matches)
    11A   12B   13A   14B   15B   16B   17B   18A   19A
407 Mainz (34 matches)
    11A   12B   13A   14B   15B   16B   17B   18A   19A
356 Würzburg (34 matches)
    11B   12B   13A   14B   15B   16B   17B   18A   19A
596 Würzburg, St Kylian (no verses)
    11–   12–   13–   14–   15–   16–   17–   18–   19–
177 Germany (33 matches)
    11A   12B   13A   14B   15B   16B   17B   18A   19A
471 Trebič (33 matches)
    11A   12B   13A   14B   15B   16B   17B   18A   19A
255 Unlocalized (32 matches)
    11A   12B   13A   14B   15B   16B   17B   18A   19A

Continued on next page

Table 7.5 (continued)

358 Germany (31 matches)
   11A   12B   13A   14B   15B   16B   17B   18A   19A
432 Geneva (28 matches)
   11A   12A   13A   14B   15B   16A   17B   18A   19A
355 Geneva (26 matches)
   11A   12A   13A   14A   15B   16A   17B   18A   19A
475 Krakow (22 matches)
   11B   12A   13A   14A   15A   16B   17B   18A   19A
111 Aosta, St Jacquème (9/18, defective here)
   00   00   00   00   00   00   00   00   00
251 Grand-Saint-Bernard (17 matches)
   11B   12A   13A   14A   15A   16A   17C   18A   19A
113 Augustinian (15 matches)
   11A   12B   13A   14A   15A   16B   17A   18B   19B
109 Aosta (12.5 matches)
   11AB 12A   13A   14A   15A   16A   17C   18A   19B
110 Aosta (12.5 matches)
   11AB 12A   13A   14A   15A   16A   17C   18A   19B
114 Aosta (12.5 matches)
   11AB 12A   13A   14A   15A   16A   17C   18A   19B
537 Aosta (12.5 matches)
   11AB 12A   13A   14A   15A   16A   17C   18A   19B
580 Aosta (12.5 matches)
   11AB 12A   13A   14A   15A   16A   17C   18A   19B
474 Grand-Saint-Bernard (11 matches)
   11A   12A   13A   14A   15A   16A   17A   18A   19B
395 Limoges? (7 matches)
   11A   12A   13B   14A   15A   16A   17A   18A   19B

Table 7.6   Responsories and verses of Advent II in sources related to Durham A. IV. 19 and Corpus 41

Durham A. IV. 19
    21A 22B 23A 24B 25B 26B 27B 28B 29A
Corpus 41
    21A 22B 23A 24B 25B 26B 27B 28B 29A
496 Sankt Florian (35 matches)
    21A 22B 23A 24B 25B 26B 27B 28B 29A
199 Trier (35 matches)
    21A 22B 23A 24B 25B 26B 27B 28B 29A
553 Trier (35 matches)
    21A 22B 23A 24B 25B 26B 27B 28B 29A
547 Trier (34 matches)
    21A 22B 23A 24B 25B 26B 27B 28B 29A
549 Trier? (34 matches)
    21A 22B 23A 24B 25B 26B 27B 28B 29A
206 Bavaria (34 matches)
    21A 22A 23A 24B ⟦26B 25B⟧ 27B 28B 29A
180 Fritzlar, St Peter (34 matches)
    21A 22B 23A 24B 25B 26B 27B 28B 29A
186 Fritzlar, St Peter (34 matches)
    21A 22B 23A 24B 25B 26B 27B 28B 29A
407 Mainz (34 matches)
    21A 22B 23A 24B 25B 26B 27B 28B 29A
356 Würzburg (34 matches)
    21A 22B 23A 24B 25B 26B 27B 28B 29A
596 Würzburg, St Kylian (no verses)
    21– 22– 23– 24– 25– 26– 27– 28– 29–
177 Germany (33 matches)
    21A 22B 23A 24B 25A 26B 27B 28B 29A
471 Trebič (33 matches)
    21A 22B 23A 24B 25B 26B 27B 28B 29A
255 Unlocalized (32 matches)
    21A 22B 23A 24B 25B 26B 27B 28B 29A

Continued on next page

Table 7.6 (continued)

- **358 Germany (31 matches)**
  21A 22B 23A 24B 25B 26B 27B 28B 29A
- **432 Geneva (28 matches)**
  21A 22B 23A 24B 25B 26B 27B 28B 29A
- **355 Geneva (26 matches)**
  21A 22B 23A 24B 25B 26B 27B 28B 29A
- **475 Krakow (22 matches)**
  21A 22A 23A 24B 25A 26A 27A 28B 29A
- **111 Aosta, St Jacquème (9/18 matches)**
  21A 22B 23A 24B 25A 26B 27A 28A 29A
- **251 Grand-Saint-Bernard (17 matches)**
  21A 22B 23A 24A 25B 26B 27C 28A 29A
- **113 Augustinian (15 matches)**
  21A 22A 23A 24A 25A 26B 27A 28A 29A
- **109 Aosta (12.5 matches)**
  21A 22A 23A 24A 25A 26A 27A 28A 29A
- **110 Aosta (12.5 matches)**
  21A 22A 23A 24A 25A 26A 27A 28A 29A
- **114 Aosta (12.5 matches)**
  21A 22A 23A 24A 25A 26A 27A 28A 29A
- **537 Aosta (12.5 matches)**
  21A 22A 23A 24A 25A 26A 27A 28A 29A
- **580 Aosta (12.5 matches)**
  21A 22A 23A 24A 25A 26A 27A 28A 29A
- **474 Grand-Saint-Bernard (11 matches)**
  21A 22A 23A 24A 25A 26A 27A 28A 29A
- **395 Limoges? (7 matches)**
  21A 22B 23A 24A 25A 26A 27A 28A 29B

Table 7.7   Responsories and verses of Advent III in sources related to Durham A. IV. 19 and Corpus 41

Durham A. IV. 19
  31B 32B 33B 34B 35B 36A |37E| 38B 70B
Corpus 41
  31B 32B 33B 34B 35B 36A |37E| 38B |39F|
496 Sankt Florian (35 matches)
  31B 32B 33B 34B 35B 36A 37B 38D 70B |39F|
199 Trier (35 matches)
  31B 32B 33B 34B 35B 36A 37B 38B 70B
553 Trier (35 matches)
  31B 32B 33B 34B 35B 36A 37B 38B 70B
547 Trier (34 matches)
  31B 32B 33B 34B 35B 36A 37B 38B 70B
549 Trier? (34 matches)
  31B 32B 33B 34B 35B 36A 37B 38B 70B
206 Bavaria (34 matches)
  31B 32B 33B 34B 35B 36A 37B   70B |39F|
180 Fritzlar, St Peter (34 matches)
  31B 32B 33B 34B 35B 36A 37B 38B 70B 39B
186 Fritzlar, St Peter (34 matches)
  31B 32B 33B 34B 35B 36A 37B 38B 70B 39B 81B
407 Mainz (34 matches)
  31B 32B 33B 34B 35B 36A 37B 38B 70B
356 Würzburg (34 matches)
  31B 32B 33B 34B 35B 36A 37B 38B 70B
596 Würzburg, St Kylian (no verses)
  31– 32– 33– 34– 36– 36– 37– 38– 70–
177 Germany (33 matches)
  31B 32B 33B 34B 35B 36A 37B 38B 70B 39A
471 Trebič (33 matches)
  31B 32B 33B 34B 35B 36A 37A 38A 70B 39B
255 Unlocalized (32 matches)
  31B 32B 33B 34B 35B 36A 37B 38A 70B

Continued on next page

Table 7.7 (continued)

358 Germany (31 matches)
　　31B 32B 33B 34B 35B 36A 37B 38B 70B
432 Geneva (28 matches)
　　31B 32D 33B 34B 35B 36A 37C 38B 70B
355 Geneva (26 matches)
　　31B 32D 33B 34B 35B 36A 37C 38B 70B
475 Krakow (22 matches)
　　31A 32A 33A 34A 35B 36A 37A 38B 70A
111 Aosta, St Jacquème (9/18 matches)
　　31B 32A 33A 34A 35B 36A 37A 38A 70A
251 Grand-Saint-Bernard (17 matches)
　　31C 32A 33A 34A 35A 36A 37C 38B 70C
113 Augustinian (15 matches)
　　31A 32A 33B 34A 35A 36A 37A 38A 70A
109 Aosta (12.5 matches)
　　31C 32D 33C 34A 35A 36A 37C 38B 70C
110 Aosta (12.5 matches)
　　31C 32D 33C 34A 35A 36A 37C 38B 70C
114 Aosta (12.5 matches)
　　31C 32D 33C 34A 35A 36A 37C 38B 70C
537 Aosta (12.5 matches)
　　31C 32D 33C 34A 35A 36A 37C 38B 70C
580 Aosta (12.5 matches)
　　31C 32D 33C 34A 35A 36A 37C 38B 70C
474 Grand-Saint-Bernard (11 matches)
　　31A 32A 33A 34A 35A 36A 37A 38A 70A
395 Limoges? (7 matches)
　　31A 32A 33A 34A 35A 36A 37A 38A 70A

Table 7.8 Responsories and verses of Advent IV in sources related to Durham A. IV. 19 and Corpus 41

Durham A. IV. 19
41B 42A 43A 44A 45–
Corpus 41
41B 42A 43A 44A 45B   46B 47B 48A   49A
496 Sankt Florian (35 matches)
41B 42A 43A 44A 45B   46B 47B 48A   49A
199 Trier (35 matches)
41B 42A 43A 44A 45B   46B 47B 48A   49A
553 Trier (35 matches)
41B 42A 43A 44A 45B   46B 47B 48A   49A
547 Trier (34 matches)
41B 42A 43A 44A 45B   46B 47B 48A   49A
549 Trier? (34 matches)
41B 42A 43A 44A 45B   46B 47B 48A   49A
206 Bavaria (34 matches)
41B 42A 43A 44A 45B   46B 47B 48A   49A
180 Fritzlar, St Peter (34 matches)
41B 42A 43A 44A 45B   46B 47B 48A   49A
186 Fritzlar, St Peter (34 matches)
41B 42A 43A 44A 45B   46B 47B 48A   49A
407 Mainz (34 matches)
41B 42A 43A 44A 45B   46B 47B 48A   49A
356 Würzburg (34 matches)
41B 42A 43A 44A 45B 91A 46B 47B   49A
596 Würzburg, St Kylian (no verses)
41– 42– 43– 44– 45– 91– 46– 47– 48–
177 Germany (33 matches)
41B 42A 43A 44A 45B   46B 47B 48A   49A
471 Trebič (33 matches)
41B 42A 43A 44A 45B   46B 47B 48A   49A 91A
255 Unlocalized (32 matches)
41B 42A 43A 44A 45B   46B 47B 49A   93A

Continued on next page

Table 7.8 (continued)

358 Germany (31 matches)
41B 42A 43A 44A 45B   46B   01A[51] 02A 01A
432 Geneva (28 matches)
41D 42A 43A 44A 45B   46C 47C 48A   49A 91A
59B 81C 93–
355 Geneva (26 matches)
41D 42A 43A 44A 45B   46C 47C 48C   49A 91A
59B 81C 93A
475 Krakow (22 matches)
41C 42A 43A 44A 45B   46B 47B 48A   49A
111 Aosta, St Jacquème (9/18 matches, defective here)
00 00 00 00 00   00 00 00   00
251 Grand-Saint-Bernard (17 matches)
41D 42A 43A 44A 45B   46C 47C 48A   49B
113 Augustinian (15 matches)
41A 42A 43A 44A 45B   46C 47E 48A   49A
109 Aosta (12.5 matches)
41D 42A 43A 44A 45B   46C 47C 48A   49B
110 Aosta (12.5 matches)
41D 42A 43A 44A 45B   46C 47C 48A   49B
114 Aosta (12.5 matches)
41D 42A 43A 44A 45B   46C 47C 48A   49B
537 Aosta (12.5 matches)
41D 42A 43A 44A 45B   46C 47C 48A   49B
580 Aosta (12.5 matches)
41D 42A 43A 44A 45B   46C 47C 48A   49B
474 Grand-Saint-Bernard (11 matches)
41A 42A 43A 44A 45A   46A 47A 48A   49A
395 Limoges? (7 matches)
41A 42A 43A 44B 45A   46A 47A 48B   91B

---

[51] Hesbert grouped a number of rare responsories under the generic sigla '01' and '02'. For these chants in the 'German' MS (Hesbert's no. 358), see *CAO* VI, 7 n. 7, and p. 11 n. 45.

8

A Fragment of a Tenth-Century English Benedictine 'Breviary'

London, British Library, Royal 17. C. XVII, fols. 2–3 and 163–6

The five parchment end-leaves of Royal 17. C. XVII in the British Library (fols. 2–3 and 163–6) are all that remains of what was apparently once a complete liturgical book containing biblical readings, prayers, and chants for the eight daily services of the Divine Office as it was sung in an Anglo-Saxon church. It has received very little attention from scholars. Appearing as number 498 in Helmut Gneuss's *Handlist*, it is described as a fragmentary breviary dating from the end of the tenth century or the first half of the eleventh.[1] The British Library's catalogue entry for Royal 17. C. XVII offers slightly more information:

> The vellum end-leaves (their true order is ff. 163, one missing, 164–166, 2, 3), in an English hand of the 10th cent., are portions of a lectionary in *Latin* for the greater hours, with collects and antiphons, containing the days from Monday in Passion Week till Easter Eve. There is nothing to indicate provenance.[2]

It is easy to see why this source has not been the subject of deeper investigation. Apart from several simple initials, it lacks any decoration. Its chants are not provided with musical notation. The text is so badly worn as to be illegible in places, and whole lines have been trimmed off. On first inspection, the fragment thus presents little interest to the art historian or the musicologist, and the palaeographer faces obstacles from

---

[1] Gneuss, *Handlist*, no. 498.
[2] G. F. Warner and J. P. Gilson, *Catalogue of Western Manuscripts in the Old Royal and King's Collections in the British Museum*, 4 vols. (London, 1921) II, 245.

the outset. Even the persistent reader is likely to be disappointed. The readings, prayers and chants gathered in this fragment are those traditionally assigned to Holy Week; they are to be found in Western liturgical manuscripts of every locale and almost every period in the Middle Ages. The fragment honours no unusual local saint (indeed, no saint at all), has no unique entries in a kalendar, has no unusual chant texts, and can tell us nothing of their melodies. It is, on the whole, unpromising. Nevertheless, close examination of its contents reveals important information about the sources available to some English monasteries as they adopted the Benedictine form of the Office in the second half of the tenth century.

Materials and preparation

The main contents of Royal 17. C. XVII are copied on paper and date from the fifteenth century: a manual of Latin vocabulary and grammar, a collection of poems in a northern-English dialect, and several other prose additions, from prayers to recipes. Parchment end-leaves are bound at the front (fols. 2 and 3) and back (fols. 163–6) of the book. These contain liturgical material and have no obvious connection with the manuscript's main contents. As the British Library catalogue entry correctly notes, the original order of the leaves was 163, [a missing leaf], 164–6, 2, 3. There would be room on a single leaf for the texts that would be expected between fols. 163 and 164.

The leaves containing liturgical material (hereafter referred to as *Roy*) were severely trimmed to match the size of the main contents of Royal 17. C. XVII. Their shape is not perfectly rectangular: the maximum height for each leaf is about 207 mm, but they can be as short as 202 mm. The maximum width of each leaf is about 137 mm, but this is hard to measure for fols. 163–6. These have undergone a modern restoration to fill in their deficient edges with thin paper. Their inner margins have likewise been strengthened.

The binding is very tight, and subsequent restoration work has rendered it impossible to see how these leaves might have lined up in quires. One can imagine various solutions; either fols. 2 and 3 were part of the quire next to that containing fols. 163–6, or they were all part of a single quire. The latter scenario seems more probable, because it suggests a quire of eight continuous leaves:

[x] – 163 – [y] – 164 – 165 – 166 – 2 – 3

The original bifolia seem to have been cut along their folds, making it easier for the leaf between fols. 163 and 164 to be lost (although it may already have been gone by the time the breviary was dismembered). The alternative view – that fols. 2 and 3 are from a separate quire – would require the second quire to be a single bifolium; otherwise, the text would not continue directly from fol. 2v to fol. 3r. The first solution would not rule out the presence of one or two more bifolia in the original quire. Quires of ten leaves are less common than gatherings of eight or twelve, but they are not abnormal.[3]

The Continental arrangement of leaves within the gatherings has been followed. Hair side faces hair side, and flesh faces flesh (HFFH). The writing surface was ruled with a dry point. No prickings survived when the margins were trimmed. The absence of prickings from the inner margins shows that the gatherings were not pricked and ruled in the old Insular fashion, in which both margins were pricked after the quire had been folded.[4] The influence of Continental habits in the preparation of manuscripts and in their script is to be detected in English manuscripts throughout the tenth century. From the middle of the tenth century onwards, however, the retention of the Insular 'HFHF' pattern in an English manuscript is best interpreted as a sign of conservatism.[5] The furrows and ridges of the ruling are more pronounced on some leaves than on others, but it is not clear if several leaves were ruled at once.

The writing surface was ruled for thirty long lines, spaced about 7 mm apart. The distance from the baseline of the first written line to the baseline of the last written line is 195 mm. Double vertical bounding lines, 6 mm apart, appear at the left and the right of each page. These were ruled slightly crookedly, so that they do not make a perfect perpendicular with the horizontal rules. The distance between the innermost bounding lines leaves a writing space of 110 mm. The scribe always started writing at the innermost bounding line at the left margin, but felt free to stray into the bounding lines at the right margin when this was necessary. The upper, lower, and outer margins have been trimmed very closely. The top line of text is partly missing on fols. 163–6. The inner margins, however, seem

---

[3] Especially in small books, such as the 'Winchester Troper', Cambridge, Corpus Christi College 473 (Old Minster, Winchester, s. xi^1), which has alternating quires of eight and ten leaves (*The Winchester Troper*, facsimile ed. Rankin, p. 3).

[4] Lowe, *CLA* II, p. x; B. Bischoff, *Latin Palaeography: Antiquity and the Middle Ages*, tr. D. Ó Cróinín and D. Ganz (Cambridge, 1990), p. 22 and n. 16.

[5] D. N. Dumville, 'English square minuscule script: The mid-century phases', *Anglo-Saxon England* 23 (1994), 133–64, at p. 141.

always to have been quite narrow, and the trimmed margins may not have been especially large. Economy of parchment may have been a concern. This was a small volume, possibly for the use of one person. If the original book contained most of the Office texts required for the whole ecclesiastical year, it would have been thick but not too heavy to be held easily in the hands.

Script and decoration

The text of *Roy* is written throughout in Square minuscule, the work of a single scribe. As in many liturgical books, the texts of chants are distinguished from the texts of readings and prayers by the use of a smaller size of script. The office of St Cuthbert included in Cambridge, Corpus Christi College 183, dating from the 930s, is an excellent early English example of this kind of layout, which can be seen in earlier centuries on the Continent. In later years, the extra space above chants written with small letters would be filled with musical notation. Originally, though, this layout seems to have been designed to clarify the kinds of texts on the page. 'It may be that small text was originally used to indicate those text passages that the priest should not read, since they would be sung by the cantor.'[6] The use of small text for the chants here may indicate that this was a book for the officiant at the Office and not for the choirmaster.

No musical notation was ever intended: abbreviations are used freely in the chants, and no horizontal space has been left after syllables to which long musical melismas might be attached.[7] There are no extra spaces or examples of cramped writing to suggest that the two sizes of text were added in separate stages. The scribe simply changed to a quill with a smaller nib when he arrived at a chant text. Punctuation, using the familiar system of *positurae*, is used carefully and extensively in the texts of the fragment intended for reading (the readings and prayers), but not at all in the chant texts.[8] At a time when singers performed from memory, a book of this kind would be of greater practical use during the Office in the

---

[6] S. Rankin, 'An early eleventh-century missal fragment copied by Eadwig Basan: Bodleian Library, MS. Lat. liturg. D. 3, fols. 4–5', *Bodleian Library Record* 18 (2004), 220–52, at p. 242 n. 43.

[7] See S. Rankin, 'Music books', in R. Gameson (ed.), *The Cambridge History of the Book in Britain*, I: *c.600–1100* (Cambridge, 2011), pp. 482–506, at pp. 486–7.

[8] M. B. Parkes, *Pause and Effect: An Introduction to the History of Punctuation in the West* (Aldershot, 1992), pp. 35–40, 76–80, 104–5, 191–7. See also P. Clemoes, *Liturgi-*

hands of those reading the lessons and intoning the collects. The layout and punctuation of the manuscript would be suited to this purpose.

The main scribe's black ink has generally survived in a legible state, though it can become illegible at the edges of the page. The rubricator seems to have used two varieties of red ink. One, a metallic red, has since oxidized. Letters written with this ink are either sharp and black or obscured by the spread of the oxidized stain. The other ink seems to have been of a vegetable base. This has been largely rubbed away. Some of its faintest traces are more visible under ultra-violet light. The main scribe left space for rubrics, but he and the rubricator seem to have had different ideas about the project. When a reading or prayer began on a new line, the rubricator preferred to write large initials in the margin, ignoring the indentation left for him by the text scribe. The text scribe often failed to leave sufficient space for the rubricator to add the conventional A͞., R͞., and V͞. symbols before antiphons, responsories, and versicles. Sometimes these are added in a very small space; sometimes they are omitted. The rubricator adopted a higher grade of script (uncial, with occasional *capitalis* letter-forms) for his contribution.

Analysing Anglo-Saxon Square minuscule hands is made difficult by the comparative scarcity of dated examples and the great variety of scribal styles that the term embraces. The general traits of the script were first described by N. R. Ker and T. A. M. Bishop. The only attempt at a detailed and systematic treatment of the script is contained in two articles by David Dumville.[9] These two papers examine the early years of Square minuscule and its development during the middle of the tenth century. Professor Dumville has indicated that he will treat later Square minuscule hands in a third instalment.[10] A brief summary of the basic features of Square minuscule and of Dumville's approach to dating it will be useful before describing the script of *Roy* in more detail.

Square minuscule grew out of Insular minuscule. Its name derives from its appearance, and especially from the characteristic way in which

---

cal *Influence on Punctuation in Late Old English and Early Middle English Manuscripts* (Cambridge, 1952), repr. Old English Newsletter, Subsidia 4 (Binghamton, NY, 1980).
[9] D. N. Dumville, 'English Square minuscule script: The background and earliest phases', *Anglo-Saxon England* 16 (1987), 147–79; idem, 'Mid-century phases', *Anglo-Saxon England* 23 (1994), 133–64. My personal knowledge of Square minuscule owes much to lectures given by Dr Tessa Webber in the Cambridge History Faculty in 2002–3.
[10] In the meantime, he directs us to his 'Beowulf come lately: Some notes on the palaeography of the Nowell Codex', *Archiv für das Studium der neuern Sprachen und Literaturen* 225 (1988), 49–63. See also Chapter 3 in his *Wessex and England*.

many Square minuscule scribes wrote the letter **a**: with a single compartment and a thin, almost horizontal top (though this form is not universally used). Certain other letter-forms distinguish it from the Half-uncial script of earlier centuries, and from Caroline minuscule, which was introduced into England during the tenth century:

- **d** single stroke; ascender slopes to the left (as in uncial)
- **e** shaft has a distinct approach stroke, with a pronounced 'shoulder'.
- **f** stem is a descender, the second horizontal stroke sits on the rule.
- **g** has a flat top; the tail may be closed or open.
- **r** stem is a descender (length varies); its shoulder stroke comes down to the rule and curves back up slightly.
- **s** stem is a descender and is easily confused with **r**. Round-**s** and long-**s** with its stem sitting on the rule are also seen.

These forms are common to Insular minuscule throughout its history. Square minuscule is distinctive for its proportions and ornamentation. Letters have a breadth comparable to the height of the minim. Ascenders tend to be quite short; it is often correctly noted that Square minuscule tends towards a two-line script, with no true ascenders above the x-height.[11] Minims and the tops of ascenders are often ornamented with the wedges inherited from earlier Insular script styles. Square minuscule further distinguishes itself from earlier styles of Insular minuscule by its avoidance of ligatures. Only in a tall form of **e** does the tongue form a coupling stroke with a following letter, and in these cases the **e** will usually have a distinctive bulbous top stroke. In its simplicity and clarity, Square minuscule shares the ethos of Caroline minuscule.

David Dumville proposes a classification of the surviving specimens – a classification not universally accepted – according to no fewer than six phases. Phase I (910s–920s) is a precursor to a 'Canonical' form, Phase II (930s). Phase II was the point of departure for several subsequent phases. In the first, Phase III, Dumville sees a 'decorative style' practised between 940 and 959. Phase IV, of only limited lifespan, lost much of its square appearance under the influence of Caroline minuscule (from which Phase III scribes borrowed letter-forms according to their preference). Phase V

---

[11] Dumville, 'English Square minuscule script: The background and earliest phases', p. 151.

arose in the 960s as a 'universal development' from Phase II.[12] A further phase, Phase VI, descended from Phase III, and existed alongside Phase V.[13] The most recent Anglo-Saxon royal diploma to have been written in Square minuscule dates to 987;[14] but other examples of Square minuscule may be datable to the first dozen or so years of the eleventh century. Dumville includes the second hand of the Nowell Codex (BL Cotton Vitellius A. xv, second manuscript) in this latest period.[15]

The identification of the features of one of Dumville's six phases in a specimen of Square minuscule ought, in theory, to allow it to be dated with relative precision. This is possible, Dumville argues, because of the influence on scribal habits exerted by the royal chancery, whose practices changed in line with political developments.[16] These stylistic developments were not, Dumville contends, solely to do with scribes' preferences:

> In as much as Square minuscule has not previously received palaeographical description, there has been a tendency to treat stylistic phases as representing instead the work of individual scribes.[17]

Turning to the hand of *Roy*, however (see Illustration 8.1 on page 259), it is very difficult to make this example of Square minuscule script conform to one of Dumville's six phases. The script is Square minuscule, rather than the later Insular minuscule used in vernacular texts. Its broad proportions and short ascenders cannot be reconciled with the lateral compression and long ascenders seen in eleventh-century hands, foreshadowed in the second hand of the Nowell Codex.[18] The wedges on the tops of ascenders and some minims are also quite pronounced. Based on these characteristics, one might happily associate it with Dumville's 'Canonical' Phase II, and date the script as far back as the reign of Æthelstan (927×939).

Other features, however, might suggest a later date. The definitive 'square **a**', with a horizontal connecting top stroke, is not used in *Roy*. The

---

[12] Dumville, 'Mid-century phases', p. 155.
[13] Dumville, 'Mid-century phases', p. 156.
[14] S 864.
[15] This is the 'Beowulf' manuscript; see *The Nowell Codex: British Museum, Cotton Vitellius A.XV, second ms*, facsimile ed. K. Malone, EEMF 12 (Copenhagen, 1963). Dumville, 'Beowulf come lately', pp. 53–4, 57.
[16] Dumville, 'Mid-century phases', pp. 156–64.
[17] Dumville, 'Mid-century phases', p. 149.
[18] Dumville, 'Beowulf come lately', p. 53.

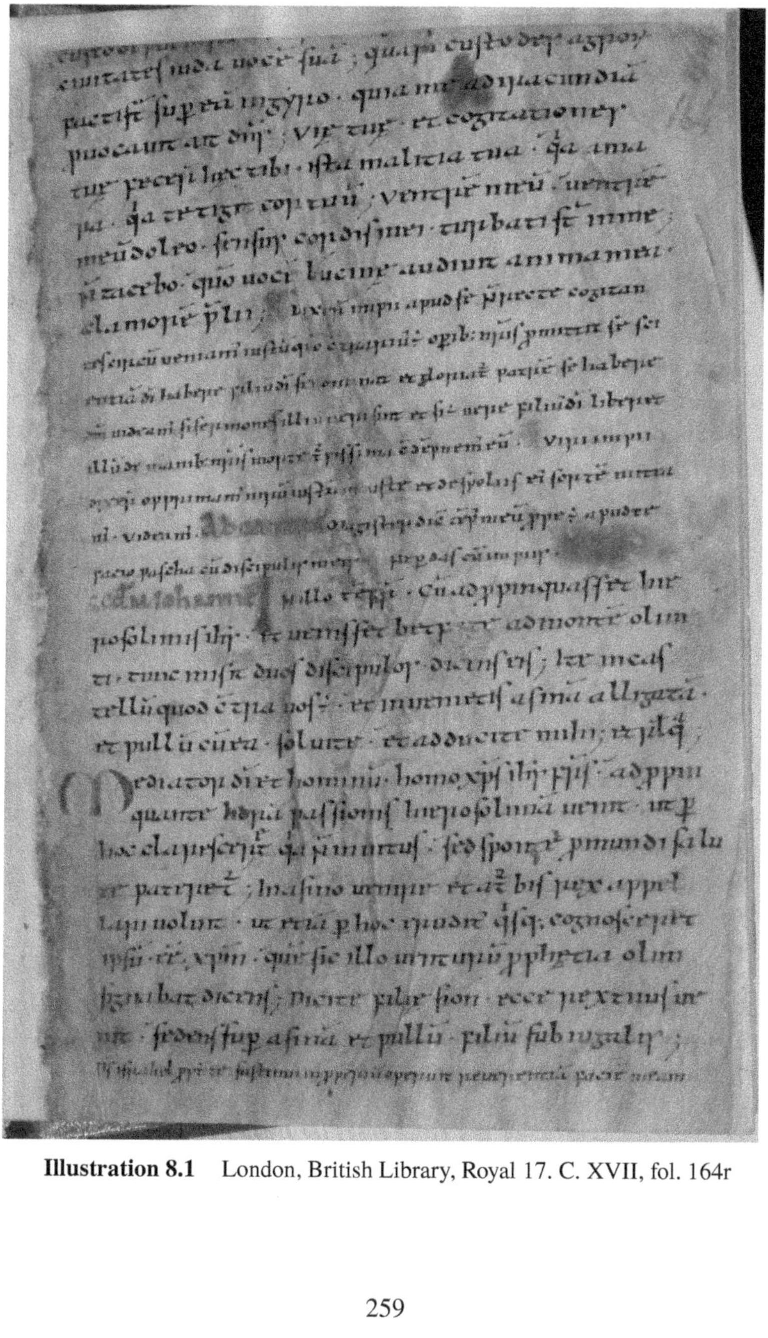

Illustration 8.1 London, British Library, Royal 17. C. XVII, fol. 164r

scribe formed **a** with a single compartment in which the left stroke meets the right stroke in a point at the top of the letter. This is not anomalous for Square minuscule manuscripts; a similar avoidance of flat-topped **a** is found, for example, on fol. 28r of the Parker Chronicle, where the annals for the years 955–967 are recorded.[19] Certain older specimens of Square minuscule feature a form of **p** in which the bottom of the bow does not touch the vertical stroke, but **p** is invariably closed in *Roy*.

The most perplexing trait of this hand is its use (or rather non-use) of a tall form of **e** when the tongue is made a coupling stroke with a succeeding letter. This use of tall **e** is typical of Square minuscule specimens (and earlier Insular scripts), and the resulting letter-form usually has a bulbous top stroke that often curves over the following letter. This variety of **e** is found through the whole gamut of Square minuscule manuscripts. In *Roy*, however, it is completely absent. Our scribe certainly allows the tongue of **e** to elide with the onset of some following letters, especially **r** and **a**. For **e+t**, he will even allow the top stroke of **e** to rise slightly higher than normal. Nowhere, however, do we see the altered form of **e** that is so prominent in other Square minuscule hands. Tall **e** is only ever found as a *littera notabilior* at the beginning of a sentence. In these cases, however, the scribe has assiduously avoided the creation of a coupling stroke with any following letter. While some elision can be observed occasionally, it is usually disrupted by the application of more pressure with the pen, marking clearly the dividing point between the two letters.

The reserve displayed by the scribe in use of **e** in ligature does not extend to other ligature forms. The fragment contains several examples of **c+t**. Long-**s+t** is heavily used. These ligature forms, which are most 'at home' in Caroline minuscule, go hand in hand with the scribe's dominant choice of an almost Caroline long-**s** that rises above most ascenders, preferring this to the less frequently used Insular **s**. The two forms sometimes appear side by side. Noting these Caroline features, we might invoke Phase IV. Dumville notes, however, that Phase IV is especially characterized by a lateral compression of the letter-forms to the point that the script can hardly be called 'square'.[20] The hand of *Roy*, although it is rather more 'round' than other, more angular hands typical of the script, firmly retains square proportions, and therefore cannot be labelled as Phase IV. Judgement must be reserved about later phases pending the

---

[19] *The Parker Chronicle and Laws: Corpus Christi College, Cambridge, ms. 173: A Facsimile*, ed. R. Flower and H. Smith, EETS 208 (Oxford, 1941).
[20] Dumville, 'Mid-century phases', pp. 153–4 and 160.

promised third instalment of Dumville's analysis; but the diplomas so far cited by Dumville as examples of Phases V and VI likewise bear little resemblance to the script of *Roy*.[21]

David Ganz has recently proposed that Dumville's close reading of stylistic variants in Square minuscule manuscripts has led to an overly ambitious division of the sources into chronological developmental phases.[22] Stylistic variants, Ganz suggests, could have as much to do with the class and quality of the manuscript being written as with the exemplars available to scribes. Generational shifts in scribal preferences, involving stylistic overlap over long periods, would make it unsafe to insist on clear chronological boundaries for different styles.[23]

Palaeographical analysis alone, therefore, cannot supply a precise dating of *Roy*. There is no reason to suspect that it dates from later than *c.*1000, because it does not show any of the signs of evolution towards late Insular minuscule. The use of Square minuscule in a Benedictine Office book is somewhat surprising in the light of the Benedictine reformers' preference for Caroline minuscule, and this might suggest a copying date early in the reform period. But the influence of Caroline minuscule might account for the scribe's avoidance of the distinctive **e** letter-form with coupling strokes, contrary to usual Square minuscule practice. The 'Pontifical of St Dunstan' (BnF lat. 943), apparently copied for St Dunstan around the time of King Edgar's coronation in 973 or within the following decade,[24] shows that England's highest ranking prelate, himself a monk and an accomplished practitioner of Caroline minuscule, saw nothing amiss in commissioning a deluxe liturgical book copied entirely in Square minuscule. *Roy* was not part of a high-grade manuscript; it was prepared with practical, not display, purposes in mind. It is all the more plausible, therefore, that the fragment might have been prepared by a conservative scribe in a scriptorium that also produced Caroline manuscripts. Palaeographical considerations present no obstacle to dating the fragment to the last quarter of the tenth century, which, as shall be seen, is the date that best explains certain of its liturgical characteristics.[25]

---

[21] Dumville, 'Mid-century phases', pp. 155–6 nn. 122–3. Phase V: S 697, S 736, S 1211; Phase VI: S 1215, S 1326.
[22] D. Ganz, 'Square Minuscule', in Gameson, *Book in Britain*, pp. 188–96, at p. 190.
[23] Ganz, 'Square Minuscule', pp. 190–91.
[24] Rosenthal, 'The Pontifical of St Dunstan'.
[25] The provisionality of my conclusion about the *Roy*'s date is demonstrated by the conflicting judgements of two palaeographers whose opinion I sought about the hand: one suggested

Liturgical contents and book type

Roy contains chants, readings, and prayers for the Divine Office during the two weeks before Easter. It begins incompletely with material for Monday in the fifth week of Lent. The missing leaf between fols. 163 and 164 would have covered the Friday and Saturday before Palm Sunday. The fragment ends incompletely with the first nocturn of the Night Office on Good Friday. There is very little in the way of rubrication to assist the reader to navigate the text. It is quite clear, however, that the texts in the fragment are consistent with the Office liturgy as it would have been sung in a reformed Benedictine monastery. Enough of the Palm Sunday Night Office is preserved to show that the third nocturn has four lessons (not three as in the secular Office), each followed by a responsory. The third nocturn is provided with a single antiphon under the rubric *ad cantica* (*Magister dicit tempus meum*; see no. 20 in the transcription in Appendix B).[26] As prescribed in the *Regularis concordia*, the texts in the fragment for Maundy Thursday and Good Friday are arranged for the secular *cursus*, not the Benedictine.[27] The Night Office for Maundy Thursday (page 368) has nine lessons. In the third nocturn, instead of a single antiphon *ad cantica*, there are three antiphons, each followed by a psalm cue (page 370). Vespers on Maundy Thursday has the five psalm antiphons of the secular Office, rather than the Benedictine four (see page 372).[28] The use of the secular Office for certain days in *Roy* conforms exactly to what would be expected in tenth-century reformed English Benedictine practice.

The antiphons and responsories in *Roy* are examined minutely in the section on 'Liturgical *ordo*' below (beginning on page 267). The fragment's other texts, though not susceptible to the same level of analysis, are worthy of comment. Several short cues after antiphons indicating what psalm is to be sung show that *Roy* assumes the use of the *Romanum* text of the psalter.[29] For example, the psalm after the third antiphon at the

---

that if I were to tell him, from other evidence, that it had been copied in the reign of Æthelstan he would not be able to contradict me; the other judged it 'not really square at all' and suggested that it had more in common with the hands found in eleventh-century copies of vernacular texts.

[26] On the Benedictine third nocturn, see p. 20 above.
[27] See the section '*Regularis concordia* (*c*.970)', beginning on p. 179 above.
[28] Benedictine: see *RSB* 17:7. Secular: see Amalarius of Metz, *Liber officialis*, IV. 7. 6, ed. Hanssens II, 432.
[29] See p. 110 and n. 115 above.

Night Office on Maundy Thursday, Psalm 70, is given as 'Deus in te speraui'. The *Gallicanum* version reads 'In te Domine speraui' (see no. 96, page 368). The use of the *Romanum* text in *Roy* confirms the expectation that the *Romanum* text continued to be used in reformed English Benedictine houses during the tenth century, even, as shall shortly be shown, when Continental liturgical models were largely followed in other respects.

The biblical readings in *Roy* are mostly drawn from the Prophet Jeremiah, including the Lamentations of Jeremiah during Holy Week. This is a standard assignment for this period of the ecclesiastical calendar. It would be desirable to know if the biblical text could be traced to any known textual tradition. The text of the Old Testament known in Anglo-Saxon England cannot be linked to one particular influence.[30] The 'only comprehensive evidence of a Vulgate Old Testament copied and used during, or immediately following' the Benedictine reform is BL Royal 1. E. VII–VIII. Unfortunately, the text of this witness was not incorporated into the apparatus of the major critical edition of the Vulgate Old Testament.[31]

Any attempt to trace the stemma to which the biblical texts in *Roy* belong would probably be misplaced. Once scriptural texts enter liturgical books, future copies are made from those liturgical books, not from bibles, setting up a separate stream of textual transmission. Liturgical versions of biblical readings take great liberties with the text, substituting proper names for pronouns, omitting unnecessary words and phrases, and even inserting brief explanatory sentences to set the scene.[32] *Roy* behaves in this way, even transposing two verses in one instance.

In Benedictine Office books, the first reading of the third nocturn is always preceded by the first few phrases from the Gospel pericope of the day, to introduce the theme of the homily from which the four readings are drawn. The full text of the Gospel (never included in breviaries) is then read at the conclusion of the Night Office (after the *Te deum*).[33] The Gospel pericope provided for Palm Sunday in *Roy* begins with Matthew 21:1–2. The rubricator, however, has labelled it *secundum Iohannem*. The Matthew passage is found in a number of sources, and is the text

---

[30] R. Marsden, *The Text of the Old Testament in Anglo-Saxon England*, Cambridge Studies in Anglo-Saxon England 15 (Cambridge, 1995), p. 447.
[31] Marsden, *The Text of the Old Testament*, p. 337. The major critical edition of the Vulgate Old Testament is *Biblia sacra iuxta latinam vulgatam versionem ad codicem fidem*, ed. the Monks of the Pontifical Abbey of St Jerome in the City (Rome, 1926–94).
[32] Rankin, 'An early eleventh-century missal fragment', pp. 236–7.
[33] See Table 2.3 on p. 21 above.

assumed in Bede's Homiliary and in the Homiliary of Paul the Deacon.[34] The *Regularis concordia*, however, prescribes John 12:12–19 to be read at the door of the church before the blessing of palms for the Palm Sunday procession (the Gospel at Mass itself being one of the Passions).[35] The rubricator's error could, therefore, indicate that the fragment was copied after the promulgation of the *Regularis concordia*: the rubricator might have been influenced by the prescriptions of the *Concordia* without checking to see which pericope the main scribe had actually copied.

The four homiletic readings in the third nocturn on Palm Sunday are drawn from the third sermon in Bede's second book of homilies.[36] This is one of two Palm Sunday sermons recommended in the homiliary of Paul the Deacon.[37] It is found in no other homiliary but this (and, of course, Bede's own). This is the standard text for Palm Sunday in English Benedictine breviaries of the later Middle Ages. Whether Paul's homiliary was introduced to England through the Benedictine reform, or whether it had been known for some time already, is an interesting question. Gneuss's *Handlist* records sixteen manuscripts of the homiliary in England before 1100, but the earliest of these dates to the first half of the eleventh century. Paul's homiliary was the basic source for the Old English homilies of Ælfric of Eynsham (*c*.955–1020?).[38]

The text of the homily has been subjected to even more radical editing than the biblical texts. Far from simply adapting the continuous text to suit a four-lesson format, the original editor of the text as it is found in the breviary fragment removed whole chunks of the text, weaving what is almost a new narrative. In later breviaries, patristic readings, like biblical lessons, are frequently found in a very altered state. Moreover, as David Chadd remarked, the assignment of readings to particular days within surviving breviaries is highly variable ('the lessons and homilies cause their

---

[34] U. Lenker, *Die westsächsische Evangelienversion und die Perikopenordnungen im angelsächsischen England*, Texte und Untersuchungen zur englischen Philologie 20 (Munich, 1997), p. 316.

[35] *Regularis concordia*, § 36, ed. Symons p. 35 (CCM § 60, p. 106); Lenker, *Die westsächsiche Evangelienversion*, p. 316.

[36] Bede, *Homeliarum evangelii libri II*, II. 3, ed. Hurst, pp. 200–6.

[37] Gregoire, *Les Homéliaires du Moyen Âge*, no. 97, p. 91. On Paul the Deacon's homiliary, see p. 54 n. 144 above. Joyce Hill, in her *Bede and the Benedictine Reform*, Jarrow Lecture (Jarrow, 1998), traces the influence of Bede on later homiliaries, especially those of Paul the Deacon and Smaragdus, both of which were influential in the Benedictine reform movement.

[38] C. L. Smetana, 'Aelfric and the early medieval homiliary', *Traditio* 15 (1959), 163–204; J. E. Cross, 'Ælfric and the mediaeval homiliary – objection and contribution', *Scripta minora Regiae societatis humaniorum litterarum Lundensis* 1961–1962:4 (1963), 3–34.

own kind of nightmare').[39]

Four collects are recorded in the fragment (nos. 46, 93, 131, and 140 in Appendix B). The third of these, *Deus qui per crucem* (for Good Friday), appears to be unique among catalogued sacramentaries, missals, and collectars. It is absent from the indices of Dom Deshusses's editions, and from the indices of the various volumes published by the Henry Bradshaw Society. It is further absent from the index volume of the *Corpus orationum*.[40] It is somewhat unusual in addressing Christ as *Deus*:

> Deus qui per crucem et passionem tuam redemisti mundum, libera nos ab omni peccato.

> (O God, who through your cross and passion have redeemed the world, free us from every sin.)

A similar text is found in a blessing for the Exaltation of the Holy Cross (14 September) in the 'Canterbury Benedictional', BL Harley 2892 (Christ Church, Canterbury, *c*.1030):

> Deus qui per crucem passionis suae mundum voluit redimere, eiusdem sanctae crucis munimine, mala omnia a vobis dignetur expellere.[41]

> (May God, who through the cross of his passion desired to redeem the world, by the defence of the same cross deign to drive away every evil from you.)

Texts addressing Christ directly as 'God' first emerged in the East in opposition to Arianism and adoptionism, later spreading to Spain and then to Ireland and England. Similar texts may be found in the ninth-century 'Book of Cerne', Cambridge, University Library, Ll. 1. 10 (Mercia, *c*.820 ×840). It was long thought that this idea was introduced to the Frankish liturgy by Alcuin, whose writings often refer to Christ as 'God' or 'creator', though Benedict of Aniane, of Visigothic birth and familiar with the Spanish liturgy, is an equally likely intermediary.[42] Although this collect

---

[39] Chadd, 'Liturgical books', p. 50.
[40] *Corpus orationum* XI, ed. E. Moeller, I. M. Clément, and B. Coppieters't Wallant, CCSL 160J (Turnhout, 1999).
[41] Ed. E. Moeller, *Corpus benedictionum pontificalium*, 4 vols., CCSL 162, 162A–C (Turnhout, 1971–9) II, 431 (no. 1057).
[42] L. van Tongen, *Exaltation of the Cross: Toward the Origins of the Feast of the Cross and the Meaning of the Cross in Early Medieval Liturgy*, Liturgia condenda 11 (Leuven, 2000), pp. 265–7.

may not have originated in England, its apparent uniqueness may indicate that it is a survival of the pre-reform English liturgy, perhaps dating back to the period of Alcuin's *De laude Dei*.

The readings, prayers, and chants are arranged, for the most part, in their liturgical order. This is most obvious in the Palm Sunday material. Each reading at the Night Office is followed directly by its responsory. The third nocturn (the only one whose beginning survives) begins with its appointed antiphon. Lauds is provided with the requisite five psalm antiphons. These are followed by a selection of antiphons to be sung with the Benedictus. In the middle of this selection are cues for two versicles and responses, and a cue for a great responsory presumably taking the place of the short responsory that would be expected on an ordinary Sunday. Following the Benedictus antiphons there is a short reading (*capitulum*) and a collect. The collect is in the right position, at the end of Lauds. The correct liturgical order for the other texts would have been *capitulum*, (short) responsory, (hymn), versicle and response, Benedictus antiphon, collect (see *RSB* 12). Less 'proper' material was required for ferial days: three Night Office lessons (sometimes followed by responsory cue) and the antiphons to be sung with the Benedictus at Lauds and the Magnificat at Vespers. The other texts would be either common (recited throughout the year) or seasonal (recited throughout Lent).

If *Roy* is to be classed in a known book-type, the arrangement of the texts in liturgical order gives it the character of a breviary, and it may legitimately be described in this way. As such, it is not only the earliest example of an English breviary of the Benedictine reform period, but it is one of the earliest examples of a breviary from anywhere in early medieval Europe. While composite Mass books (missals) survive from as early as the eighth century, breviaries do not become common until the twelfth century.[43] As has just been noted, however, the arrangement in *Roy* is not strictly what would be expected in a later breviary. Moreover, it is less prescriptive than a later breviary would be: rather than assigning particular antiphons to the Benedictus and Magnificat, the fragment contains lists from which selections may be made. As shall shortly be seen,

---

[43] The disparity is adequately illustrated in Gamber, *CLLA*: breviaries II, 606–14 and Suppl. pp. 164–6 (nos. 1680–98); missals II, 527–47 and Suppl. pp. 135–44 (nos. 1401–99*, including nos. 1440–2*, which are combined missal-breviaries). Some quasi-missals and quasi-breviaries, combining Mass and Office antiphoners with sacramentaries or lectionaries, are recorded at II, 521–6 and Suppl. pp. 133–4 (nos. 1380–99*). Gamber's terminology may not be strictly appropriate in all cases.

this is characteristic not of breviaries but of early Office antiphoners. The appearance of the *capitulum* out of its liturgical place at the end of Lauds with the collect could indicate that both *capitulum* and collect were copied from another kind of Office book, the collectar. The fragment gives the overall impression of an antiphoner into which Night Office readings have been inserted in the appropriate places, and to which material from a collectar (or even a sacramentary) has been added without concern for rearrangement into strict liturgical order. A similar approach seems to lie behind the somewhat later 'Muchelney Breviary' fragment, but here the *capitula* are found in their correct position.[44] In its original complete state, the manuscript of which *Roy* was a part may have included, like the eleventh-century Portiforium of St Wulfstan (*Wul*), a separate psalter (probably arranged in numerical, not liturgical, order) and a separate hymnal. If standard ferial antiphons and other common texts were included elsewhere (either at the beginning or, as is often seen in later books, after the Octave of Epiphany), the volume would have contained everything necessary for the recitation of the Office throughout the year.

Liturgical ordo

Enough chants are contained in *Roy* to permit two separate repertorial analyses of liturgical *ordines* using the methods described in Chapter 6, first with responsories for the Night Office on Palm Sunday, and then with antiphons for the Benedictus and Magnificat at Lauds and Vespers during the first part of Holy Week. These two analyses are followed by a brief consideration of the responsories given in the secular *ordo* for Maundy Thursday.

Analysis I: Palm Sunday Night Office responsories

There was originally another leaf between fols. 163 and 164 of *Roy*. It contained chants and readings for the Friday and Saturday in the fifth week of Lent, as well as the beginning of the Night Office for Palm Sunday. Of the Night Office, only the five final readings remain, together with the following five responsories:

---

[44] See the transcription in Billett, 'The Muchelney Breviary', pp. 63–4.

Table 8.1 Responsories assigned to Monday, Tuesday, and Wednesday in Holy Week in Royal 17. C. XVII

Mon	Tue	Wed
1 In die qua*	Saluum me fac*	Synagoge populorum*
2 Fratres mei*	Noli esse mihi*	Insurrexerunt in me*
3 Attende domine*	Dominus mecum est*	Contumelias et...

An asterisk (*) signifies that only the first few words of the chant are given.

8. *Dixerunt impii apud se*
9. *Deus Israel propter te*
10. *Synagoge populorum*
11. *Insurrexerunt in me*
12. *Viri impii dixerunt*

On their own, these are insufficient to make a comparison of responsory series with other manuscripts. But the responsories used on Monday, Tuesday, and Wednesday in Holy Week seem to have been drawn from the Palm Sunday series, making a partial reconstruction of the Sunday series possible. Table 8.1 lists the responsories assigned to the weekdays after Palm Sunday up to Wednesday (Maundy Thursday has its own special series). With one exception, *Contumelias*, all the responsories for the weekdays following Palm Sunday are given in incipit; these cues point back to chants that were probably given in full on the missing leaf of the fragment devoted to Palm Sunday.

The three responsories assigned to Monday appear as the first three responsories of Palm Sunday in a number of the antiphoners edited in Hesbert's *Corpus antiphonalium officii* (*CAO*). By the same reasoning, it appears that the responsories assigned to Tuesday are the next three in the Sunday series. Wednesday begins as if using the last three chants of the Sunday series, but the last chant, *Viri impii dixerunt*, is replaced with a new responsory, *Contumelias*, of which the complete text is given. If Maundy Thursday did not have its own proper series of responsories, Thursday would have used the seventh, eighth and ninth responsories from Sunday. The special arrangement used for Holy Week creates a problem, because what would have been the seventh responsory in the Sunday series was not named in the Wednesday list. Allowing for this gap, the original twelve-responsory *ordo* for Palm Sunday in *Roy* may be reconstructed as follows: a. *In die qua*; b. *Fratres mei*; c. *Attende domine*; d. *Saluum me fac*; e. *Noli esse mihi*; f. *Dominus mecum est*; g. *[Unknown]*; h. *Dixerunt impii*; i. *Deus Israel*; j. *Insurrexerunt in me*; k. *Viri impii dixerunt*. This reconstructed *ordo* may now be compared with a pool of sources relevant to surviving English Benedictine Office books.

Tables 8.2 (beginning on page 286) and 8.3 (beginning on page 292) list the responsories (and verses) assigned to Palm Sunday in thirty-eight Office books of varying origin and date. Table 8.2 lists the responsories in alphabetical order, assigning each a number and noting the sigla of the sources in which each text appears. In Table 8.3, each source's siglum is followed by a numerical series indicating the responsories in the order in which they are found in that source (the numbers are those assigned in Table 8.2). The sources in Table 8.3 are arranged in groups whose rationale will be explained presently. First it is necessary to give an overview of the sources and the total repertory that they transmit.

Of the sources consulted, twelve, including *Roy*, are English Benedictine books. Seventeen are Continental Benedictine books, including the six monastic antiphoners edited in *CAO*. A further nine sources follow the secular *cursus*, the six secular *CAO* antiphoners and *Cbr*, *A44*, and *Par*. Taken together, the thirty-eight sources contain a combined repertory of thirty responsories, which are deployed in highly variable configurations in the sources. Nine are *unica*: *1. Animae impiorum fremebant* (in *C* only); *2. Animam meam dilectam* (*D*); *9. De ore leonis* (*L*); *14. Erue a framea* (*L*); *15. Expandi manus meas* (*A44*); *21. Ne perdas cum impiis* (*L*); *25. Principes persecuti sunt* (*L*); *27. Sicut agnus* (*C*); and *30. Usquequo exaltabitur*. A further responsory, *24. Pacifice loquebantur*, is found in only two sources (*R* and *L*). Most of these *unica* are supernumerary responsories in the sources in which they appear. They may be significant in families of manuscripts not apparent in this sample, but they had no influence on the English sources. Several responsories are found universally, or nearly so. *17. In die qua* is the first responsory in every series. *16. Fratres mei* is the second responsory in all but two sources (the idiosyncratic *Flr* and *Nor*). *3. Attende domine* is found almost universally in the third position; it is the second responsory in *Flr* and *Nor* (which both lack *16. Fratres mei* usually found here), and the fourth in *V*. These three might belong to some 'original' (even 'Roman'?) layer.

The case of *26. Saluum me fac*, found in all but three of the sources in Table 8.2, is slightly more complicated. It is found in the six secular manuscripts edited in *CAO* (*C*, *G*, *B*, *E*, *M*, and *V*), but it is absent from two other secular series, *Cbr* and *Par*. It is a supernumerary responsory in the secular series of the ninth-century antiphoner *A44*, and so should probably be considered 'foreign' in this series as well. It becomes clear, therefore, that the presence of 26. *Saluum me fac* in any one monastic series could have arisen either because it was originally found in the secular series on which that monastic series was based, or because it was among the three 'monastic additions' needed to bring a secular series of nine reponsories up to the full monastic complement of twelve. For example, the series in *Vst* is based on the secular series of *Cbr* and 'monasticized' by the addition of 29. *Uiri impii*, 7. *Contumelias et terrores*, and 26. *Saluum me fac*. The same secular series underlies the monastic series of *L*. In this very unusual series six responsories have been added, but not 26. *Saluum me fac*. Which twelve responsories were actually sung during the Night Office out of the fifteen provided in *L* is impossible to say. The two approaches may be simply illustrated as follows (with responsories unique to *L* given in bold; *24* is found elsewhere only in *R*):

```
Cbr  17 16 3 6              22 13 11    19              18
Vst  17 16 3 6              22 13 11 29 19 7 26         18
L    17 16 3 6 14 9 21 22 13 11         19 7 24 25 18
```

By contrast, 26. *Saluum me fac* is native to the secular series of *G* (identical to that in *B*). The same series clearly underlies the monastic *ordo* of *Mch*. But in *Mch*, the creation of the monastic series has involved not only the addition of three responsories (6. *Conclusit uias meas*, 11. *Dixerunt impii*, and 4. *Circumdederunt me*), but the transposition of 19. *Insurrexerunt in me* from final position to the end of the first nocturn:

```
Mch  17 16 3 19 26 22 13 6 18 23    11 4
G       17 16 3    26 22 13    23 18 19
```

The inverted order of 23. *Opprobrium factus sum* and 18. *Ingrediente domino* in *Mch*, which would have heavily skewed a calculation of the *coéfficient d'écart* between these two sources using Hesbert's methods, is probably insignificant. The monastic sources play various games of this kind, making it difficult to group them into families with reference only to conjoint responsory pairs.

Similarly difficult is 18. *Ingrediente domino*, which is found in all but three sources (*Hyd*, *Par*, *B*). It is found in seven of the nine secular *ordines*, so its appearance in all but one of the monastic *ordines* could be quite natural. But in the monastic sources it is frequently found as part of a special sub-*ordo* that requires special explanation. Of the twenty-nine monastic sources given in Table 8.2, thirteen (eight of them English) end with the same four responsories: *12. Dominus iesus, 5. Cogitauerunt autem principes, 8. Cum audisset turba,* and *18. Ingrediente domino.* As has already been noted, this last is widely used among the sources. It could possibly have been the seventh responsory in *Roy.* It is found in various positions among the different sources; but when these three other responsories are present (12, 5, and 8), it always takes final position in the third nocturn. This little set of responsories is remarkable for several reasons. Of all thirty responsories in Table 8.2, only these four draw their texts from the New Testament. All the others are from the psalms and the prophetic books (especially Jeremiah), with texts obviously chosen to foreshadow the approaching Passion of Jesus, rather than to celebrate his Triumphal Entry into Jerusalem. The first three of the set are not found in *CAO*, nor are they found in the earliest sources in the table. The sources always assign the same verses to each responsory. *18. Ingrediente domino* is found with three different verses in the various sources; but in the presence of 12, 5, and 8, it always uses the same verse (*18B. Cum audisset populus*). The impression is of a carefully composed set of responsories, an impression strengthened by an examination of the texts.

The texts of the four responsories, together with the verse texts, form a tightly constructed narrative excerpted mainly from the Gospel of John. Approaching Jerusalem, Jesus reaches Bethany, the place where he had earlier raised Lazarus from the dead:

> Dominus iesus ante sex dies paschae uenit bethaniam ubi fuerat lazarus mortuus quem suscitauit iesus.
> ℣. Conuenerunt autem ibi multi iudaeorum ut lazarum uiderent. Quem ...
>
> *Six days before the Passover, the Lord Jesus came to Bethany, where Lazarus had been dead, whom Jesus raised.* (John 12:1)
> ℣. *Many of the Jews gathered there that they might see Lazarus, whom* ... (John 12:9)

Cogitauerunt autem principes sacerdotum ut et lazarum interficerent propter quem multi ueniebant et credebant in iesum.
℣. Testimonium ergo perhibebat turba quae erat cum eo quando lazarum uocauit de monumento et suscitauit eum a mortuis. Propter quem ...

The chief priests thought to kill Lazarus also, by reason of whom many were coming to Jesus and believing in him. (John 12:10–11)
℣. *The crowd therefore gave testimony who had been with him when he called Lazarus out of the tomb and raised him from the dead, by reason of whom* ... (John 12:17)

Cum audisset turba quia uenit iesus hierosolymam cum ramis palmarum processerunt ei obuiam.
℣. Et cum appropinquasset ad descensum montis oliueti omnes turbae gaudentes et deum uoce magna collaudantes. Cum ramis palmarum ...

When the crowd heard that Jesus was coming to Jerusalem, with palm branches they went forth to meet him. (John 12:12–13)
℣. *And when he was coming near the descent of the Mount of Olives, all the crowds, rejoicing and praising God with a great voice, with palm branches* ... (Luke 19:37)

Ingrediente domino in sanctam ciuitatem Hebraeorum pueri resurrectionem uitae pronuntiantes cum ramis palmarum hosanna clamabant in excelsis.
℣. Cum audisset populus quia iesus uenit hierosolymam exierunt ei obuiam. Cum ramis ...

When the Lord was entering the holy city, the children of the Hebrews, telling out the resurrection unto life, with palm branches were crying 'Hosanna in excelsis'. (Free composition based on John 12; but cf. John 5:29)
℣. *When the people heard that Jesus was coming to Jerusalem, they went out to meet him, with palm branches* ... (John 12:12–13)

The narrative makes a direct causal link between the raising of Lazarus and the enthusiasm of the crowds greeting Jesus on his arrival at Jerusalem. The Lazarus story is unique to the Gospel of John. And even in John this link is not explicit. Neither is Lazarus mentioned in Bede's homily on Palm Sunday, *Mediator dei et hominum*, which is assigned to the third nocturn in every source in Table 8.2 that specifies readings (i.e. not antiphoners and not all customaries). Bede's homily does, however, build up the same kind of dramatic tension found in this responsory series that so often accompanies it, making extensive use of repetition, especially of the phrase *ante quinque dies*.

The key to understanding how this set of texts was conceived seems to lie in the last responsory, *18. Ingrediente domino*. It is almost certainly older than the other three. As Thomas Symons observed, it is 'found in all forms of the Palm Sunday rites'.[45] Its proper place is in the Palm Sunday procession, sung either at the entry into the church before Mass (as in the *Regularis concordia*),[46] or at the entry into the gates of the city, as in the much larger procession envisaged in Lanfranc's *Decreta*.[47] When used in procession, the verse is often *Ex ore infantium et lactantium* ('Out of the mouth of babes and sucklings'), evidently taking up the idea of the 'children of the Hebrews' (*pueri Hebraeorum*) in the refrain.[48] The boys of the monastery were very important in the Palm Sunday procession, with widespread tradition assigning to them the verses of *Gloria, laus et honor* (familiar even today as the hymn 'All glory, laud and honour').[49] Having begun as a processional antiphon, *18. Ingrediente domino* seems to have migrated to the responsories of the Night Office somewhat later. This explains its absence from the Night Office series of *Hyd*, *Par*, and *B* (and possibly *Roy*), and also its use as a supernumerary responsory in *H*, *L*, *A44*, and *V*. These series, in which the main Palm Sunday responsories have texts relating to the Passion drawn from the psalms and the prophets, probably represent an earlier state of the material.

Despite its great thematic difference from the other Palm Sunday Night Office responsories, *18. Ingrediente domino* seems to have been accepted by itself as a natural addition to the core psalmic and prophetic responsories in a number of series: *Mch*, *Yor-M*, *Cor1*, *Cor2*, *Gnt*, *MoR*, *D*, and *F* (monastic); and *C*, *G*, *E*, and *M* (secular). At some point, however, this responsory served as a point of departure for the creation of a set of texts based on the Gospel narrative. The text of *18. Ingrediente domino* is a very free composition based on John 12. But the words 'resurrection unto life' (*resurrectio uitae*) come from an entirely different context, a

---

[45] *Regularis concordia*, ed. Symons p. 35 n. 7.
[46] *Regularis concordia*, § 36, ed. Symons p. 35 (CCM § 60, p. 106).
[47] Lanfranc, *Decreta monachis Cantuariensibus transmissa*, c. 25, ed. D. Knowles and C. N. L. Brooke, *The Monastic Constitutions of Lanfranc* (Oxford, 2002), pp. 38–9.
[48] As in the thirteenth-century *Consuetudines Floriacences* (*Flr*), c. 117, ed. Davril, p. 63 line 15 and p. 64 line 28.
[49] As in the *Regularis concordia*, § 36, ed. Symons p. 35 (CCM § 60, p. 107): 'As soon as the Mother church is reached the procession shall wait while the children, who shall have gone on before, sing *Gloria laus* with its verses, to which all shall respond *Gloria laus*, as the custom is.' Cf. Lanfranc's *Decreta*, c. 25 (ed. and tr. Knowles and Brooke, pp. 38–9), where the verses are given explicitly.

saying of Jesus in John 5:29, in which the resurrection unto life, which awaits those who have done good deeds, is contrasted with a 'resurrection unto judgement' awaiting those who have done evil. In the context of the Palm Sunday procession, *resurrectio uitae* may originally have served as a kind of synonym for the 'good news' or 'new birth' preached by Jesus and his disciples. But in its later position in the Night Office, alongside Bede's sermon about the days leading up to the crucifixion (*ante quinque dies*), *resurrectio uitae* took on a different meaning, bringing to mind the excitement in Bethany six days before the Passover. No longer were the people rejoicing over the 'good news'. They announced instead the coming of a prophet able to raise the dead to life (*resurrectionem uitae pronuntiantes*). And this gives rise to three complementary texts that concisely explain the situation and the consequent anxiety of the chief priests to eliminate this threat.[50]

Based solely on the admittedly limited sample of sources assembled in Table 8.2, it would seem that the three extra responsories, and their fixed arrangement with *18. Ingrediente domino*, emerged either at Bec or in one of the houses reformed by William of Dijon. The Bec customary used elsewhere in this study gives no information about the responsories of the Night Office on Palm Sunday,[51] but the antiphoner of the Priory of Notre-Dame de Bonne-Nouvelle in Rouen (*BnR*) derived its liturgy directly from Bec. The work of William is reflected in the ordinal of the abbey of Fécamp (*Féc*) and in the Troarn breviary (*Tro*). In favour of a Bec origin is the presence of *12. Dominus iesus* among the processional responsories in the Bec customary.[52] In favour of William is that reformer's penchant for carefully constructed *ordines* of Night Office responsories. David Chadd observed in responsory *ordines* from Fécamp a distinctive 'narrative pace', as in the following example referring to the Fécamp *ordo* for the *Historia de Noe*:

> I am certainly struck by the number of occasions where *ordines* apparently originating in William's work seem to involve the adoption of a 'prefatory gesture' of this sort. It seems to me highly characteristic that this rather leisurely approach to the telling of

---

[50] The anxiety of the priests was already recognized in another chant found universally in the Palm Sunday procession, *Collegerunt* (variously labelled as either an antiphon or a responsory). But its text makes no reference to Lazarus. See *Graduale triplex* (Solesmes, 1979), p. 135.
[51] *Consuetudines Beccenses*, ed. M. P. Dickson, CCM 4 (Siegburg, 1967), p. 224.
[52] *Consuetudines Beccenses*, c. 67, ed. Dickson, p. 36.

the story should be employed even where we are dealing with a compressed *historia*.[53]

It is tempting to think that William saw that *18. Ingrediente domino*, and indeed the whole story of Palm Sunday, required a rather substantial 'prefatory gesture', taking into account the sixth day before the Passover, not just the five days covered in Bede's sermon.[54] It is worth observing that this set seems not to have originated at Cluny, since it is absent from those sources known to have been influenced by Cluny *ordines* (*Cor2*, *Gnt*, and *F*).

The composition of the three new responsories (12, 5, and 8) may have coincided with the provision of three readings from John 12 (beginning *Ante sex dies paschae*) for the Night Office on Monday following Palm Sunday. The monastic *cursus* calls for only three responsories, and the 'new' texts are all drawn from John 12. Several sources in addition to *Féc* and *Bec* do repeat these responsories on Monday (for example *Ely* and *Wor*, though the latter, as an antiphoner, does not indicate the readings). In the Bec customary, which gives no information about the Night Office on Palm Sunday itself, these new responsories for the Monday Night Office are given in a different order (5, 12, 8).[55] The provision in *Hyd* is very interesting: the Sunday *ordo* rejects all the (apparently) later additions, including *18. Ingrediente domino*; but on Monday three readings from John 12 are given with all four responsories of the new set, the last reading having two responsories (8 and 18).[56] This suggests that if the readings from John 12 for Monday in Holy Week were devised before the responsories, perhaps inspiring them, the responsories were still in a fixed group of four by the time the readings and the chants came into wide circulation.

The foregoing discussion might seem to have little relevance to the case of *Roy*. It does not include responsories 12, 5, and 8. The gap in its reconstructed Palm Sunday *ordo* might have been filled by *18. Ingrediente*

---

[53] Chadd, 'Liturgical books', p. 55 n. 34.

[54] *Mediator dei et hominum* is explicitly assigned to the third nocturn in *Féc* (ed. Chadd I, 211).

[55] *Consuetudines Beccenses*, c. 70, ed. Dickson, p. 37. This passage also provides some useful information about how responsories for Sunday were distributed on ferial days throughout the week: 'Feria secunda post Palmas ad Matutinas dicuntur haec tria responsoria *Cogitaverunt*, *Dominus Ihesus*, *Cum audisset*. Si ista feria secunda impedita fuerit festivitate Annuntiationis, quia alia festivitas in hac hebdomada non fit, tunc illa tria responsoria omnes remanent. In feria tertia incipitur historia *In die qua invocavi* et sic prosequantur.'

[56] See *The Monastic Breviary of Hyde Abbey*, ed. Tolhurst I, fol. 92r.

domino, but not necessarily. This responsory does appear in incipit later in *Roy*, assigned to Lauds on Palm Sunday (see no. 42 in the transcription, page 362). It is not unusual for a great responsory to be used in place of a brief responsory at one of the day hours on a major feast. That its full text is not given could indicate that it had already appeared earlier in the missing material; but it is equally possible that this incipit simply refers to a text familiar from the Palm Sunday procession and that the gap in the Night Office *ordo* was filled by some other responsory. But even if none of this material found a home in the *Roy* order, understanding its development is crucial to discerning the extent to which *Roy* is related to other sources.

However the new set of four chants originated, it proved very popular. But it did not circulate within a unified *ordo* of twelve responsories. The four responsories were adopted separately, apparently on their own merits, into the traditions of individual monasteries. Each time this happened, four responsories were displaced from the original *ordo*. These were not necessarily the last four responsories; and even in sources that may have had identical *ordines* to begin with, the responsories omitted seem to have varied. The resulting *ordines*, even if closely related, look very different from each other, especially in the second nocturn. This is a vivid example of what David Chadd called, using his archaeological metaphor, 'successive occupation'.[57] So the 12–5–8–18 set can distort the true relatedness of certain *ordines* from the same tradition. But it is also found in *ordines* of several different traditions, making it very difficult to arrange the various *ordines* in 'family groups'.

Table 8.3 presents an analytical grouping of the material in Table 8.2 based on apparently significant repertorial differences. Of the thirty responsories found in these sources, eighteen must be disregarded for analytical purposes as unique, universal, or misleading. This leaves just twelve responsories as potentially significant, and they are found in many different and complicated configurations. Nevertheless, the thirty-eight *ordines* may be divided into two basic groups: those that include the responsory *23. Opprobrium factus sum* (Group B in Table 8.3), and those that do not (Group A). To these must be added a third group that cuts across the basic two (Group C), namely those *ordines* with the special final nocturn *12–5–8–18*. This very simple classification can be further refined by the identification of distinctive chants within each basic group.

---

[57] See p. 214 above.

Roy falls into Group A, the group lacking *23. Opprobrium factus sum.* It is just possible that this was its missing seventh responsory, but *Roy* shows strong affinity with other *ordines* in the −23 group. Both *MoR* and *D* include all of *Roy*'s eleven extant Palm Sunday responsories. Several other manuscripts in the sample (*H, F, A44, C,* and *V*) also have all eleven of these chants, but these are all large series of fifteen or sixteen chants. The next closest relatives to *Roy* are *Cor1* and *Hyd,* each with ten of the eleven responsories in *Roy.* Part of the extra difference between *Hyd* and *Roy* seems to come from *Hyd*'s use of *7. Contumelias* on Palm Sunday itself, whereas *Roy* uses it on a ferial day. All of these seem to be based on the secular *ordo* in *Par,* augmented with the monastic set of *26. Saluum me fac, 10. Deus Israel,* and *28. Synagoge populorum.* Three of these *ordines* (*D, MoR, Cor1*) have, however, been altered by the insertion of *18. Ingrediente domino* from the Palm Sunday processional liturgy, displacing from the original secular responsories either *19. Insurrexerunt in me* or *29. Uiri impii.* The one chant found consistently in these *ordines* absent in *Roy* is *6. Conclusit uias.* This could be the missing seventh responsory, or it could have been replaced there by *18. Ingrediente.*

A subset of the −23 group comprises the two monastic *ordines* of *Vst* and *L,* both of which, as has already been seen, are expansions of the secular *ordo* in *Cbr.* This subset is distinguished from that containing *Roy* by the absence of *10. Deus Israel.* The secular *ordines Par* and *Cbr* are further distinguished by the presence or absence of *29. Uiri impii,* a fact obscured by the occasional substitution of this chant with *18. Ingrediente* in some of the *ordines* based on *Par.* Two further secular *ordines* in this group, *E* and *M,* appear to be unrelated to the monastic sources under consideration.

It seems very likely that each of these sources originally had an *ordo* imitating the Mont-Renaud/Corbie group, perhaps already including *18. Ingrediente domino.* When the extra chants of the special third nocturn were adopted, presumably under the influence of Norman sources (Bec or Dijon), three or four chants had to be discarded; the rest of the original *ordo* was retained. The choice of which chants to discard varied between *Wor, Pet, Ely* and *Evm* (it is possible that *Cdm* is derived from *Wor,* via Evesham and Durham).[58]

---

[58] Coldingham was a daughter priory of Durham, which itself was re-founded as a Benedictine house shortly after the Conquest by reformed monks from the Severn valley (Knowles, *The Monastic Order,* pp. 159–71). Through their quick support of the Conqueror, Worcester and Evesham, 'together with a few neighbours and dependencies, stood for a long time

To this sub-group should be added, for special reasons, *Yor-M*. On its face, it is out of place here, because its *ordo* lacks the special *12–5–8–18* third nocturn and includes *23. Opprobrium factus sum*. It is unique in this sample, however, in having *5. Cogitauerunt* without its usual companions:

Yor-M 17 16 3 22   26 13 **23** 18   19 10 28 **5**

If the two chants shown in bold type were removed, the *ordo* would be similar in other respects to the Mont-Renaud/Corbie group. It seems likely that St Mary's, York, or another English source on which it was dependent liturgically, originally had a Palm Sunday *ordo* of the Mont-Renaud/Corbie type. This *ordo* was subsequently modified under the influence of a probable Bec source (+*23*), but with the adoption of only one of the special third nocturn responsories (significantly, in final position).

The analysis of the Palm Sunday responsory *ordo* in *Roy* reveals a strong affinity with a group of sources related to Mont-Renaud/Corbie, including *Hyd*. Sifting out later interpolations adds to this group a significant number of other English sources (*Cdm*, *Ely*, *Evm*, *Pet*, *Wor*, *Yor-M*). Of the remaining English sources, *Alb* has adopted a Bec *ordo*, and *Cht* and *Wcb* take their *ordines* from houses influenced by William of Dijon. *Mch*, as might be expected based on past investigations, is independent, though it may have an indirect affiliation with *Flr* or *Nor*. The connection between the majority of the English sources and Mont-Renaud/Corbie may be further explored through the examination of antiphons used at the Benedictus and Magnificat during Holy Week.

Analysis II: Holy Week Benedictus and Magnificat antiphons

In most breviaries and antiphoners, proper antiphons are assigned to the Benedictus and Magnificat for every day in Holy Week. Table 8.4 shows the Benedictus and Magnificat antiphons used at Lauds and Vespers on Palm Sunday and on Monday, Tuesday, Wednesday, and Thursday in Holy Week, the days with complete provision in *Roy*. To the thirty-eight sources considered in the analysis of the Palm Sunday Night Office responsories may be added two further English books that contain chants only for the day hours: the 'Portiforium of St Wulfstan' (*Wul*) and the 'Gloucester Diurnal' (*Glo*). These forty sources between them transmit seventy antiphons. This number is inflated somewhat by the presence of twenty-nine

outside the stream of Norman monastic influence' (p. 159).

unica, fifteen of which are found in a single manuscript, the Compiègne antiphoner (*C*). Even discounting the *unica*, however, the sources display considerable variety in repertory and ordering. The earlier sources in particular tend to give lists of *antiphonae in euangelio* from which antiphons for the Benedictus and Magnificat might be selected, presumably at the discretion of the cantor. Antiphons not used at Lauds or Vespers might be used as the single psalm antiphons at the little hours, and this is where many are found in later, more prescriptive antiphoners and breviaries (not shown in Table 8.4).

The great variety of antiphon *ordines* stands in the way of any attempt at a systematic classification based on the presence or absence of significant chants. No special authority is claimed for the groupings given in Table 8.4. The Holy Week antiphon *ordines* nevertheless qualify and refine some of the relationships identified through the Palm Sunday responsory *ordines*. *Mch*, linked by its responsories to *G*, is here apparently identical to *Yor-M*, whose responsories were those of the Corbie/Mont-Renaud group, modified under the influence of Bec or William of Dijon. It is hard to know what to make of the appearance of *29. Infirmata est* as the Magnificat antiphon for Monday in *Mch*, and perhaps originally in the same place in *Yor-M*, where no Magnificat antiphon is prescribed. This chant appears elsewhere only in *H*, *C*, and *E*, whose contents defy classification within this sample. Behind its very long lists of supernumerary antiphons, *E* seems somehow to be related to the Northern French sources. Its use of both *54. Recordare mei* and *29. Infirmata est* in its provisions for Monday might have something to say about the appearance of the latter chant in *Mch*. *OuR*, whose responsory *ordo* was independent, relies for its antiphons on an *ordo* apparently devised by William of Dijon. These examples may serve as a useful reminder that agreement between sources in one aspect of liturgical *ordo* does not guarantee agreement in other respects, even (as here on Palm Sunday) on the same day in the liturgical calendar.

Roy shows a strong affiliation with a handful of sources from the group dubbed 'Corbie/Mont-Renaud' in the analysis of responsory *ordines*. This affiliation is illustrated in greater detail in Table 8.5, which gives in parallel the antiphons assigned to each day in *MoR*, *Cor1*, *D*, *Wul*, and *Wor*. There is a certain amount of variation between these sources. The greatest is in the antiphons for Palm Sunday, where chants normally sung in the Palm Sunday procession (*50. Pueri Hebreorum tollentes* and

51. Pueri Hebreorum uestimenta)[59] have, as in other *ordines* in Table 8.4 (e.g. *A44*), found their way into the lists of antiphons *in euangelio* (*MoR*) or, as in *D* and *Cor1* (and prescriptively in *Wor*), into lists of antiphons *pro horis*, that is, antiphons for the little hours. *Roy* lacks *10. Ceperunt omnes*, found in *MoR*, *D*, and *Wul* as a Magnificat antiphon on Palm Sunday. *Roy* further lacks *01. Accepto pane*, found as a final alternative Magnificat antiphon in *MoR* and *Cor1* on Maundy Thursday. *69. Uide domine* is unique to *MoR* in the whole sample of forty sources (Monday *in euangelio*).

These differing chants are additions, not substitutions, to a common repertory shared with *Roy*. Even with these small differences, the agreement between the six sources is remarkable, all the more so in the face of the tremendous variety recorded in Table 8.4. The strongest point of agreement is found on Tuesday in Holy Week, for which the same four antiphons *in euangelio* appear in each source and in exactly the same order (except in *Wor*, which is more prescriptive and gives only two antiphons, but in an order consistent with the others). The use of *54. Recordare mei* in second position on Monday is characteristic of this group. The same three chants are found in two different configurations on Wednesday. *Roy* follows the same order found in *Cor1* and *Wul*. The use of *08. Cena facta* at Vespers on Maundy Thursday in *Roy*, *MoR*, *Cor1*, and *Wor* is highly distinctive. This chant is found elsewhere in the sample only in the Compiègne and Ivrea antiphoners (*C* and *E*).[60]

The correspondence between these sources, particularly their identical provision for Tuesday in Holy Week, raises the possibility that all of them descend from a common ancestor. It is further possible that most of the English sources represented in the sample, omitting those aligned with Bec and William of Dijon (*Alb*, *Cht*, *Evm*, *Wcb*), belong to the same tradition. The antiphon *ordines* in *Pet*, *Hyd*, *Ely*, and *Cdm* all differ from each other in certain respects, but they could have arisen from the same repertory and basic distribution of chants found in *Roy*, except for *10. Ceperunt omnes turbe*, which is found in *D* and *MoR*, and in *Par*, which, as in their responsory *ordines*, may underlie both. Some caution is necessary,

---

[59] Cf. *L'Antiphonaire de Hartker*, p. 174, where these appear in a list headed *Ad processionem*.

[60] *Cena facta* is recorded in only four other manuscripts in the CANTUS Database, and in these it is always for use *ad mandatum* (during the ceremonial footwashing on Maundy Thursday), and not at Vespers: Berlin, Staatsbibliothek, Preußischer Kulturbesitz, Mus. 40047, fol. 63v; Graz, Universitätsbibliothek, 29 (*olim* 38/8 f.), fol. 158v; Karlsruhe, Badische Landesbibliothek, Musikabteilung, Aug. LX; Stuttgart, Württembergische Landesbibliothek, HB. I. 55, fol. 76r.

however, because the normally distinct Cambrai/Saint-Vaast sources are in this case very similar in their antiphon *ordines* to the Corbie/Mont-Renaud group, being distinguished only by their different treatment of Monday and (in the case of *Vst*) Tuesday. Otherwise, they form with Corbie/Mont-Renaud a 'Northern French' bloc.

Among the Continental sources, *Roy*'s closest relative is *Cor1*, which includes in its Palm Sunday Magnificat list *42. Omnes collaudant*, found elsewhere in this position only in the exhaustive collection preserved in *C* (Table 8.4 necessarily excludes potential matches at the little hours). Like *Roy*, *Cor1* lacks *10. Ceperunt omnes turbe*. Among the English sources, *Wul* has the distinctive Tuesday list, though it uses *10. Ceperunt omnes turbe* as the Magnificat antiphon on Palm Sunday. Given that *Wul* is a Worcester book, it is interesting that *Wor* diverges from it in certain respects, but remains strongly linked to *Roy*. It assigns *42. Omnes collaudant* to None on Sunday. Most important, it prescribes *08. Cena facta* for the Magnificat on Maundy Thursday. The absence of this last chant from *Wul* could indicate that *Wor* is related (perhaps indirectly) to liturgical material that was available at Worcester when *Wul* was copied (*c.*1060) but that was not incorporated into *Wul*.

The Maundy Thursday responsories

As was noted earlier, *Roy* gives a secular series of responsories for Maundy Thursday. This is to be expected in a monastic Office book of this period. Although this series is not useful as a primary point of analysis, since a larger number of secular sources would have to be added to the comparison pool, some confirmation of the results already obtained may be sought in the large study of responsories for the Triduum and Easter undertaken by Raymond Le Roux.[61] Le Roux's very large sample of sources includes several Insular books considered in the present study: *Hyd* (his 'HyA'), *Pet*, *Wcb* (his 'Win'), *Wor* and *Yor-M* (his 'MaY'). Absent are *Alb*, *Cdm*, *Cht*, *Ely*, *Mch*, and of course the two diurnals *Glo* and *Wul*. Le Roux shows the *Wcb ordo* to be identical to those of Office books influenced by William of Dijon (*Féc*, etc., Le Roux's Group 17). *Hyd* is unique among all Le Roux's sources, with three *unica* in its third nocturn. The Maundy Thursday series in *Roy* is identical to that found

---

[61] R. Le Roux, 'Les répons du Triduo Sacro et de pâques', *Études grégoriennes* 18 (1979), 157–76, at pp. 168–9.

in *Pet, Wor* and *Yor-M*. These belong to a large group of manuscripts (Le Roux's Group 22) that includes *Cor1* and *D*. *MoR* is excluded from Le Roux's general classification because it has an extra responsory in its second nocturn; but it otherwise agrees with Group 22. Also in this group are manuscripts of the secular use of York and the breviary of St Peter's Abbey, Abbotsbury (Dorset), copied *c*.1400. This last was inaccessible in a private collection until 2003, when it was acquired by Lambeth Palace Library. When subjected to further study, it may prove very valuable in clarifying the sources of English Benedictine Office liturgy.

Somewhat surprisingly, the majority of the sources in Le Roux's Group 22 are not from northern France but from Germanic centres, notably Mainz and Trier. The abbey of St Maximin in Trier, following its rebuilding in 934, was highly influential in the dissemination of the monastic reforms begun at Gorze throughout the rest of Germany.[62] Further study will be necessary to examine whether any further connection may exist between the monastic Office books of Corbie and Saint-Denis and those of the loosely affiliated houses of the Gorze reform.

Conclusions

Considered together, the palaeographical and liturgical evidence available in the surviving leaves of *Roy* offers very valuable information about the state of English monastic Office liturgy in the later tenth century, but little about the origins of the fragment itself. The strong liturgical connection between *Roy* and two Worcester sources (*Wul* and *Wor*) could indicate that the fragment originated at Worcester. The humble status of the manuscript is out of character with the high-status manuscripts normally associated with Worcester,[63] and its script has no connection to any known Worcester scribe. This is not to say that a Square minuscule manuscript would be out of place in the scriptorium of a reformed Benedictine monastery. Depending on the nature of the book, it was possible for practitioners of Square and Anglo-Caroline minuscules to collaborate, each 'forming letters as seemed fitting in a particular place at a particular

---

[62] V. Ortenberg, *The English Church and the Continent in the Tenth and Eleventh Centuries: Cultural, Spiritual, and Artistic Exchanges* (Oxford, 1992), p. 45.

[63] Gameson, 'Book production'.

time'.⁶⁴

Nevertheless, given the comparative harmony between *Roy* and the later medieval Office books of houses historically affiliated with the 'Æthelwold connexion' (*Ely, Hyd, Pet*), it is just as likely that *Roy* was the product of Abingdon, one of the Winchester minsters, or some other house influenced by Æthelwold. The Portiforium of St Wulfstan (*Wul*) itself has long been thought to have been copied from an Old Minster, Winchester, exemplar.⁶⁵ Bishop Oswald may have chosen early in favour of unity with Winchester in matters of liturgy, as he may also have done in script: Oswald may himself have written the earliest dated example of 'Style I' Anglo-Caroline minuscule in the attestation section of a 961 charter of King Edgar in favour of Abingdon.⁶⁶ If the use of Winchester Office liturgy at Worcester did not begin with Oswald, then it is significant that his successor as bishop, Ealdwulf (992–1002), was formerly abbot of Peterborough. Whether the next bishop, Wulfstan 'the homilist' (1002–16), had been a monk in an Æthelwoldian house is unknown; but he wrote extensively about the liturgy, and could plausibly have reformed Worcester's Office liturgy along Winchester lines.⁶⁷ If the rubricator's error in attributing the gospel pericope on Palm Sunday to St John was through the influence of the *Regularis concordia*, then it must further be acknowledged that *Roy* might have been copied at a house initially outside the 'Æthelwold connexion' that subsequently adopted the *Concordia*, at

---

⁶⁴ Ganz, 'Square Minuscule', p. 191, citing the evidence of BL Royal 13. A. XV (Felix, *Vita S. Guthlaci*, s. x med.), in which both Square minuscule and Anglo-Caroline minuscule hands appear. On the varied attributions of Royal 13. A. XV to Worcester and Ramsey, see Gameson, 'Book production', p. 198 n. 15 and p. 243, suggesting Ramsey as a possibility, based on the similarity of the Caroline hand to BL Harley 2908 (the 'Psalter of St Oswald'), which seems to have been executed at either Ramsey or Winchester. Gneuss, *Handlist*, no. 483: 'prob. Worcester'.

⁶⁵ Hohler, 'Some service books', p. 73.

⁶⁶ BL Cotton Aug. ii. 39; S 690; partial facsimile and discussion in T. A. M. Bishop, *English Caroline Minuscule* (Oxford, 1971), p. 9 (no. 11), Plate IX; complete facsimile: *Facsimiles of Ancient Charters in the British Museum*, ed. E. A. Bond, 4 vols. (London, 1873–8) III, no. 23. The attribution of the hand is based on Oswald's attestation of the charter, which reads, 'I ... fashioned this testament with my own hand' (*hoc eulogium propria manu depinxi*). Spelling and grammatical errors in the list of attestations cause Michael Lapidge to doubt Oswald to have been the actual scribe ('Æthelwold as scholar and teacher', pp. 92–3). David Dumville observes, however, that it is somewhat odd that there should be a new hand using a new script for the attestations, and wonders if the second scribe was Oswald himself after all: *English Caroline Script and Monastic History: Studies in Benedictinism, A.D. 950–1030* (Woodbridge, 1993), pp. 52–3.

⁶⁷ Corrêa, 'The liturgical manuscripts', p. 286 n. 2.

least nominally, as its customary.

The breviary fragment in Royal 17. C. XVII cannot be specifically localized on palaeographical or liturgical grounds. It is nevertheless of crucial importance as an early example of the use of apparently unaltered Continental monastic Office formularies in a reformed English monastery. The analyses presented in this chapter reveal the close agreement of *Roy* with what has been referred to, in imitation of Chadd, as a 'Corbie/Mont-Renaud group' of sources. While a case could also be made for a link with Saint-Denis in Paris (based on similarities with *D*),[68] the case for Corbie is somewhat stronger, since we have the testimony of the Abingdon Chronicle that Æthelwold brought singers from Corbie to establish agreement among his Abingdon monks in their liturgical reading and singing.[69] Corbie has also been suggested as a point of imitation for the Caroline minuscule script of Æthelwold's houses.[70]

It seems very likely, therefore, that *Roy* was copied in part from an exemplar derived from the Corbie liturgical tradition, probably first introduced to England during Æthelwold's abbacy at Abingdon (959–964) or some time afterwards, and presumably disseminated to his other monastic

---

[68] See Robertson, *The Service-Books of the Royal Abbey of Saint-Denis*, pp. 425–34. David Hiley points out that, although it has been customary in published studies to identify Corbie as the main Continental influence discernible in Anglo-Saxon liturgical books, 'the uses of Corbie and Saint-Denis ... are practically indistinguishable according to the rough tests so far developed' (*Western Plainchant*, p. 582 with other studies cited). Cf. Robertson, *The Service-Books of the Royal Abbey of Saint-Denis*, pp. 103–4. The complicated relationship between Corbie and Saint-Denis is in some ways illustrated by the complex history of the 'Sacramentary of Ratoldus' (BnF lat. 12052), which was commissioned by a monk of Corbie, perhaps copied at Saint-Vaast, based on a Saint-Denis sacramentary but incorporating a pontifical perhaps brought from Canterbury. See the substantial analytical introduction by Nicholas Orchard in his recent edition of the manuscript, *The Sacramentary of Ratoldus*, HBS 116 (London, 2005). There are limited examples of English links with Saint-Denis. In 984, St Edith of Wilton asked Archbishop Dunstan to consecrate her rebuilt abbey in honour of St Denis: see Wilmart, 'La Légende de Ste Édith', pp. 86–7. Edward the Confessor adopted St Denis as a patron saint, and may have built Westminster Abbey as a royal necropolis in imitation of Saint-Denis, and gave the church of Deerhurst to Saint-Denis *c*.1059 (Ortenberg, *The English Church and the Continent*, pp. 86 and 247 and p. 235). Cambridge, Pembroke College 23–24 (Saint-Denis, s. xi med.), a selection from the homiliary of Paul the Deacon, was owned by Bury St Edmunds by *c*.1100; it was presumably brought to England by Abbot Baldwin during Edward's reign: Antonia Gransden, 'Some manuscripts in Cambridge from Bury St Edmunds Abbey: Exhibition catalogue', in A. Gransden (ed.), *Bury St Edmunds: Medieval Art, Architecture, Archaeology and Economy*, The British Archaeological Association Conference Transactions 20 (Leeds, 1998), pp. 228–85, at p. 254.
[69] See p. 167 above.
[70] See p. 305 n. 12 below.

foundations. A related exemplar seems to have been available at Worcester in the middle of the eleventh century. This Corbie exemplar was evidently not a complete breviary. It seems more likely to have been an antiphoner that was enriched by individual houses from other sources – in the case of *Roy*, by the addition of readings and collects. The strange collect *Deus qui per crucem*, which may be a survival of a much earlier English liturgical tradition, militates against any assumption that *Roy* represents the wholesale adoption of a Continental Office liturgy by an English house. The Corbie antiphoner obviously commended itself to this particular community, but other sources were used for this compilation. The use of the Square minuscule script and the *Romanum* text of the psalter are further indications of retained English traditions. Other monasteries may have been far more conservative in retaining, so far as possible, existing English antiphoners as the basis for establishing a strictly Benedictine Office liturgy. The next chapter will examine a manuscript fragment in which the process of adapting an existing English Office liturgy for the Benedictine pattern appears to be in its first stages.

Table 8.2 Responsories for Palm Sunday (arrangement 1)

The following table lists the responsories, with their verses, provided for the Night Office of Palm Sunday in 38 sources. Each verse is followed by the sigla of all the sources that include that pairing of responsory and verse in their Palm Sunday *ordines*.

Each siglum is followed by a number showing where the responsory occurs in that source (e.g. *Mch* 3 means the third responsory in the Palm Sunday *ordo* of *Mch*). If a source does not indicate a verse, its siglum is given under the heading 'No verse'. An asterisk indicates that only the first few words of the responsory are given in a source.

Sigla are printed in the following order:

    English monastic:
        Roy Alb Cdm Cht Ely Evm Hyd Mch Pet Wcb Wor Yor-M
    Continental monastic:
        BnR Cor1 Cor2 Féc Flr Gnt MoR Nor OuR Tro Vst H R D F S L
    Continental secular:
        Cbr A44 Par C G B E M V

1 Animae impiorum fremebant
    Verse Contumelias et terrores
        C 13

2 Animam meam dilectam
    Verse Insurrexerunt in me absque
        D 15

3 Attende domine ad me
    Verse A Homo pacis meae in quo sperabam
    Ely 3 *Hyd* 9 *Mch* 3 *Pet* 3 *Cor1* 3 *Gnt* 3 *MoR* 3 *Nor* 2 *H* 3
    R 3 *D* 3 *Par* 3 *C* 3 *G* 3 *B* 3 *E* 3 *M* 3 *V* 3
    Verse B Recordare quod steterim
    Alb 3 *Cdm* 3 *Cht* 3 *Evm* 3 *Wcb* 3 *Wor* 3 *BnR* 3 *Cor2* 3 *Féc* 3
    OuR 3 *Tro* 3 *Vst* 3 *F* 3 *S* 3 *L* 3 *Cbr* 3 *A44* 3
    No verse *Roy* 3* *Yor-M* 3* *Flr* 2*

Continued on next page

Table 8.2 (continued)

4 **Circumdederunt me uiri**
   Verse Quoniam tribulator proxima
      Mch 12 *Nor* 8 *E* 9 *M* 11 *V* 9
   No verse *Flr* 8*

5 **Cogitauerunt autem principes sacerdotum**
   Verse Testimonium ergo perhibebat turba
      Alb 10 *Cdm* 10 *Cht* 10 *Ely* 10 *Evm* 10 *Pet* 10 *Wcb* 10
      Wor 10 *BnR* 10 *Féc* 10 *Nor* 10 *OuR* 10 *Tro* 10
   No verse *Yor-M* 12*

6 **Conclusit uias meas**
   Verse A Factus sum in derisum
      Cht 7 *Ely* 4 *Hyd* 12 *Wcb* 7 *Cor1* 5 *Cor2* 4 *Féc* 7 *Gnt* 4
      MoR 4 *OuR* 5 *Tro* 7 *Vst* 4 *D* 4 *F* 4 *S* 4 *L* 4 *Cbr* 4 *A44* 4
      Par 4 *M* 9
   Verse B Omnes inimici mei aduersum me
      Mch 8 *Nor* 3 *H* 4 *C* 4 *V* 3
   No verse *Flr* 3*

7 **Contumelias et terrores passus sum**
   Verse A Omnes inimici mei aduersum me
      Roy ferial *Cor2* 8 *Gnt* 8 *H* 15 *D* 14 *F* 7 *C* 14 *V* 13
   Verse B Omnes inimici mei audierunt
      L 12
   Verse C Iudica domine ... meae defensor
      Hyd 4 *Wcb* 5 *Féc* 5 *Tro* 5 *Vst* 10 *A44* 10

8 **Cum audisset turba quia uenit iesus**
   Verse Et cum appropinquasset ad decensum
      Alb 11 *Cdm* 11 *Cht* 11 *Ely* 11 *Evm* 11 *Pet* 11 *Wcb* 11
      Wor 11 *BnR* 11 *Féc* 11 *Nor* 11 *OuR* 11 *Tro* 11

9 **De ore leonis libera me**
   Verse Erue a framea deus animam
      L 6

10 **Deus israel propter te sustinui**
   Verse A Deus deus meus respice in me
      H 9 *R* 10 *C* 16 *V* 15

Continued on next page

Table 8.2 (continued)

Verse B Improperia improperantium
   Roy 9 *Cht* 6 *Evm* 6 *Hyd* 3 *Pet* 7 *Wcb* 6 *Cor1* 10 *Féc* 6
   MoR 10 *Tro* 6 *D* 10 *F* 16 *A44* 12
Verse C Intende animae meae (?)
   Nor 7
No verse *Yor-M* 10* *Flr* 7*

11 **Dixerunt impii apud se**
   Verse A Tamquam nugaces aestimati sumus
      Cht 5 *OuR* 7 *Vst* 7 *F* 14 *S* 8 *Cbr* 7 *A44* 7
   Verse B Uiri impii dixerunt opprimamus
      Roy 8 *Ely* 8 *Hyd* 6 *Mch* 11 *Cor1* 8 *MoR* 8 *H* 12 *D* 8 *Par* 7
      C 9 *M* 10 *V* 8
   Verse C Haec cogitauerunt et errauerunt
      L 10

12 **Dominus iesus ante sex dies paschae**
   Verse Conuenerunt autem ibi multa
      Alb 9 *Cdm* 9 *Cht* 9 *Ely* 9 *Evm* 9 *Pet* 9 *Wcb* 9 *Wor* 9 *BnR* 9
      Féc 9 *Nor* 9 *OuR* 9 *Tro* 9

13 **Dominus mecum est tamquam bellator**
   Verse A Et uim faciebant
      Alb 6 *Cdm* 6 *Ely* 7 *Mch* 7 *Pet* 6 *Wor* 6 *BnR* 6 *Cor1* 7
      Cor2 10 *MoR* 7 *Nor* 6 *OuR* 6 *H* 7 *R* 8 *D* 7 *S* 11 *Par* 6 *C* 8
      G 6 *B* 6 *E* 7 *M* 7 *V* 7
   Verse B Tu autem domine sabaoth
      Evm 7 *Hyd* 7 *F* 13
   Verse C Uidisti domine iniquitates
      Vst 6 *L* 9 *Cbr* 6 *A44* 6
   No verse *Roy* 6* *Yor-M* 6* *Flr* 6*

14 **Erue a framea deus animam meam**
   Verse De ore leonis libera me
      L 5

15 **Expandi manus meas**
   Verse Qui dicunt recede
      A44 15

Continued on next page

Table 8.2 (continued)

16 **Fratres mei elongauerunt a me**
    Verse A Amici mei aduersum me
        Mch 2 *H* 2 *R* 2 *B* 2 *E* 2 *M* 2
    Verse B Amici mei et proximi mei
        Alb 2 *Cdm* 2 *Ely* 2 *Pet* 2 *Wor* 2 *BnR* 2 *Cor1* 2 *Gnt* 2 *MoR* 2
        OuR 2 *D* 2 *Par* 2 *C* 2 *G* 2 *V* 2
    Verse C Derelinquerunt me proximi
        Cht 2 *Evm* 2 *Hyd* 2 *Wcb* 2 *Cor2* 2 *Féc* 2 *Tro* 2 *Vst* 2 *F* 2 *S* 2
        L 2 *Cbr* 2 *A44* 2
    No verse *Roy* 2* *Yor-M* 2*

17 **In die qua inuocaui te**
    Verse A Audisti opprobria eorum domine
        Cor2 1
    Verse B Deus deus meus respice in me
        E 1
    Verse C Deus meus eripe me de manu
        Nor 1 *H* 1 *R* 1 *C* 1 *G* 1 *M* 1 *V* 1
    Verse D In die tribulationis meae
        Alb 1 *Cdm* 1 *Cht* 1 *Ely* 1 *Evm* 1 *Hyd* 1 *Mch* 1 *Pet* 1 *Wcb* 1
        BnR 1 *Cor1* 1 *Féc* 1 *Gnt* 1 *MoR* 1 *OuR* 1 *Tro* 1 *Vst* 1 *D* 1
        F 1 *S* 1 *L* 1 *Cbr* 1 *A44* 1 *Par* 1 *B* 1
    No verse *Roy* 1* *Yor-M* 1* *Flr* 1*

18 **Ingrediente domino in sanctam ciuitatem**
    Verse A Cumque audissent quia iesus
        MoR 9B *Vst* 12 *H* 11 *R* 12 *S* 12 *L* 15 *Cbr* 9 *A44* 16 *G* 8 *E* 6
    Verse B Cum[que] audisset populus
        Alb 12 *Cdm* 12 *Cht* 12 *Ely* 12 *Evm* 12 *Mch* 9 *Pet* 12 *Wcb* 12
        Wor 12 *BnR* 12 *Cor2* 7 *Féc* 12 *Gnt* 7 *Nor* 12 *OuR* 12 *Tro* 12
        F 8 *M* 6
    Verse C Ex ore infantium deus et lactantium
        Cor1 9 *MoR* 9A *D* 9 *C* 7 *V* 10
    No verse *Roy* [7] *Yor-M* 8* *Flr* 12*

Continued on next page

Table 8.2 (continued)

19 **Insurrexerunt in me uiri iniqui**
   Verse A Et dederunt in escam meam fel
   Roy 11 *Cdm* 8 *Cht* 8 *Evm* 8 *Hyd* 8 *Mch* 4 *Wcb* 8 *Wor* 8
   Cor2 12 *Féc* 8 *Gnt* 12 *MoR* 12 *OuR* 8 *Tro* 8 *H* 13 *D* 12 *F* 12
   S 10 CaoL 11 *Par* 9A *C* 12 CaoG 9 CaoB 9 *E* 8 CaoM 8
   CaoV 14
   Verse B Effuderunt furorem suum in me
   Vst 9 *Cbr* 8 *A44* 9 *Par* 9B
   No verse *Yor-M* 9* *Flr* 9*

20 **Ne auertas faciem tuam a puero tuo**
   Verse Intende animae meae
   Cor2 9 *Gnt* 9 *F* 9

21 **Ne perdas cum impiis deus animam**
   Verse Ne tradideris me in animas
   L 7

22 **Noli esse mihi domine alienus**
   Verse Confundantur omnes inimici mei
   Alb 5 *Cdm* 5 *Ely* 6 *Evm* 5 *Hyd* 11 *Mch* 6 *Pet* 5 *Wor* 5 *BnR* 5
   Cor1 6 *Cor2* 6 *Gnt* 6 *MoR* 6 *Nor* 5 *Vst* 5 *H* 6 *R* 6 *D* 6 *F* 6
   S 6 *L* 8 *Cbr* 5 *A44* 5 *Par* 5 *C* 6 *G* 5 *B* 5 *E* 5 *M* 5 *V* 6
   No verse *Roy* 5* *Yor-M* 4* *Flr* 5*

23 **Opprobrium factus sum nimis inimicis**
   Verse A Insurrexerunt in me
   Gnt 10 *B* 7
   Verse B Locuti sunt aduersum me
   Alb 8 *BnR* 8 *S* 7 *A44* 13
   Verse C Persequar inimicos meos
   Mch 10 *H* 8 *R* 9 *F* 10 *C* 11 *G* 7 *V* 12
   No verse *Yor-M* 7* *Flr* 10*

24 **Pacifice loquebantur mihi inimici mei**
   Verse A Ego autem dum mihi molesti
   L 13
   Verse B Omnes inimici mei aduersum me
   R 7

Continued on next page

Table 8.2 (continued)

25 **Principes persecuti sunt me gratis**
   Verse Quasi qui inuenit spolia
   L 14

26 **Saluum me fac deus**
   Verse Intende animae meae
   Alb 4 *Cdm* 4 *Cht* 4 *Ely* 5 *Evm* 4 *Hyd* 10 *Mch* 5 *Pet* 4 *Wcb* 4
   Wor 4 *BnR* 4 *Cor1* 4 *Cor2* 5 *Féc* 4 *Gnt* 5 *MoR* 5 *Nor* 4
   OuR 4 *Tro* 4 *Vst* 11 *H* 5 *R* 5 *D* 5 *F* 5 *S* 5 *A44* 11 *C* 5 *G* 4
   CaoB 4 *E* 4 *M* 4 *V* 5
   No verse *Roy* 4* *Yor-M* 5* *Flr* 4*

27 **Sicut agnus ductus sum**
   Verse Omnes inimici mei aduersum me
   C 15

28 **Synagoge populorum circumdederunt**
   Verse A Iudica me domine secundum iustitiam
   Roy 10 *Pet* 8 *Cor1* 11 *Cor2* 11 *Gnt* 11 *MoR* 11 *D* 11 *F* 11
   A44 14
   Verse B Tu autem domine susceptor
   Alb 7 *Cdm* 7 *Wor* 7 *BnR* 7 *H* 10 *R* 11 *C* 17 *B* 8 *V* 16
   No verse *Yor-M* 11* *Flr* 11*

29 **Uiri impii dixerunt opprimamus**
   Verse A Dixerunt impii apud se
   Roy 12 *Cor1* 12 *MoR* 13 *H* 14 *D* 13 *Par* 8 *C* 10 *V* 11
   Verse B Haec cogitauerunt
   Hyd 7 *Vst* 8 *F* 15 *S* 9 *A44* 8

30 **Usquequo exaltabitur inimicus meus**
   Verse Qui tribulant me exultabunt
   R 4

Table 8.3 Responsories for Palm Sunday (arrangement 2)

Numerals denote the texts in Table 8.2.

Group A: *Ordines that omit responsory 23*

−23, +10 Corbie/Mont-Renaud

Roy	17	16	3	26	22	13	[ ]	11	10	28	19	29	(7)		
D	17	16	3	6	26	22	13	11	18	10	28	19	29	7	2
MoR	17	16	3	6	26	22	13	11	18	10	28	19			
Cor1	17	16	3	26	6	22	13	11	18	10	28	29			
Hyd	17	16	10	7	13	11	29	19	3	26	22	6			

−23, −10 monastic ordines

Vst	17	16	3	6	22	13	11	29	19	7	26	18			
L	17	16	3	6	14	9	21	22	13	11	19	7	13	25	18

−23 secular ordines

Par	17	16	3		6	22	13	11	29	19
Cbr	17	16	3		6	22	13	11	19	18
E	17	16	3		26	22	18	13	19	4
M	17	16	3		26	22	18	13	19	6	11	4

Continued on next page

Table 8.3 (continued)

Group B: *Ordines that include responsory 23*

+23, −29 monastic ordines

Mch	17	16	3	19	26	22	13	6	18	23	11	4
Flr	17	3	6	26	22	13	10	4	19	23	28	18
R	17	16	3	30	26	22	24	13	23	19	28	18

+23, −29 secular ordines

B	17	16	3		26	22	13	23	28	19
G	17	16	3		26	22	13	23	18	19

+23, +29 monastic ordines

S	17	16	3	6	26	22	23	11	29	19	13	18

+23, +29 secular ordines

A44	17	16	3		6	22	13		11	29	19	7	26	10	23	28	15	18
H	17	16	3		6	26	22		13	23	10	28	18	11	19	29	7
C	17	16	3		6	26	22		18	13	11	29	23	19	1	7	27	10	28
V	17	16	6		3	26	22		13	11	4	18	29	23	7	19	10	28

+23, +20 Cluny influence

Cor2	17	16	3	6	26	22	18	7	20	13	28	19
Gnt	17	16	3	6	26	22	18	7	20	23	28	19
F	17	16	3	6	26	22	7	18	20	23	28	19	13	11	29	10

Continued on next page

Table 8.3 (continued)

Group C: Special third nocturn

+22, −23 Modified Corbie/Mont-Renaud

Cdm	17	16	3	26	22	13	28	19	12	5	8	18
Wor	17	16	3	26	22	13	28	19	12	5	8	18
Pet	17	16	3	26	22	13	10	28	12	5	8	18
Ely	17	16	3	6	26	22	13	11	12	5	8	18
Evn	17	16	3	26	22	10	13	19	12	5	8	18
Yor-M	17	16	3	22	26	13	23	18	19	10	28	5

+22, +23 Bec

| BnR | 17 | 16 | 3 | 26 | 22 | 13 | 28 | 23 | 12 | 5 | 8 | 18 |
| Alb | 17 | 16 | 3 | 26 | 22 | 13 | 28 | 23 | 12 | 5 | 8 | 18 |

−22, −23 William of Dijon

Féc	17	16	3	26	7	10	6	19	12	5	8	18
Tro	17	16	3	26	7	10	6	19	12	5	8	18
Wcb	17	16	3	26	7	10	6	19	12	5	8	18
Cht	17	16	3	26	11	10	6	19	12	5	8	18

Independent Norman

| Nor | 17 | 3 | 6 | 26 | 22 | 13 | 10 | 4 | 12 | 5 | 8 | 18 |
| OuR | 17 | 16 | 3 | 26 | 6 | 13 | 11 | 19 | 12 | 5 | 8 | 18 |

Table 8.4 Antiphons for the Benedictus and Magnificat during Holy Week

B = Benedictus; M = Magnificat. Bold figures signify *unica*. Asterisks denote incipits. Alternatives are separated by slashes (/). An undifferentiated list of chants *in euangelio* is enclosed in parentheses. A dash indicates that no chant is provided in that position. The key to the texts follows on page 298.

	Palm Sunday		Monday		Tuesday		Wednesday		Maundy Thursday	
	B	M	B	M	B	M	B	M	B	M
Northern French (and English under Northern French influence)										
Roy	(67/43/42/41)		(38/54)		(37/52/48/14)		(62/63/16)		(66/08/09)	
D	67/41/50/51/43	10	(38/54)		(37/52/48/14)		(62/16/63)		66/01	09
MoR	67	41/50/51/43/10	(38/54/**69**)		(37/52/48/14)		62	16/63	66	09/08/01
Cor1	67	42/41/51/43	(38/54)		(37/52/48/14)		(62/63/16)		66	08/01
Wul	—	10	38	54	37	52/48/14	62	63/16	—	09
Wor	67	41	38	54	37	14	62	16	66	08
Pet	67	10	38	54	37	48	62	63	66	09
Hyd	67	10	38	51	37	48	07	16	66	09
Ely	67	10	38	48	62	49	07	16	66	09
Cdm	67	41	38	48	37	54	62	16	66	09
Par	67	10	38	54	37	48	62	16	66	09
Cbr	67	41	54	38	37	48	62	63	66	09
Mch	67	41	38	29	37	48	62	16	66	09
Yor-M	67*	41*	38*	—	37*	48*	62*	16*	66*	09*
Vst	67	41	48	38	14	37	63	16	66	09

Continued on next page

Table 8.4 (continued)

	Palm Sunday B	M	Monday B	M	Tuesday B	M	Wednesday B	M	Maundy Thursday B	M
Cluny										
Cor2	67	10	38	41	62	16	05	63	66	09
Gnt	67	10	38	41	62	16	05	63	66	09
F	67/50/51/**53**/35	41/10	(38/54/64/31/52/45)	(38/54/64/31/52/45)	(62/48/40/39/46/16)	(62/48/40/39/46/16)	(05/03/**17**/44/14/63)	(05/03/**17**/44/14/63)	66/01/60/06/**55**/	09
S	67	41/10	38	52	62	16	05	23	66	09
Bec										
BnR	67	58	38	48	37	39	14	16	66	09
Alb	67	58	38	48	37	39	14	16	66	09
William of Dijon										
Féc	41	58	61	35	06	63	16	45	66	09
Tro	41	58	61	35	06	63	16	45	66	09
OuR	67	58	61	35	06	63	16	45	66	09
Evm	41	58	61	35	06	63	16	45	66	09
Cht	41	58	61	**02**	06	63	16	45	66	09
Wcb	41	58	61	35	06	63	16	45	66	09
Glo	—	58	61	35	06	63	16	45	—	09

Continued on next page

BL ROYAL 17. C. XVII

Table 8.4 (continued)

	Palm Sunday		Monday		Tuesday		Wednesday		Maundy Thursday	
	B	M	B	M	B	M	B	M	B	M
Unclassified										
H	67	58/64/34/31	38/54	29	(37/52/39/48)		(63/05/14)		66/03	09/01/60
R	67	58	38	63	37	48	16	23	66	09
L	67	61*/10/41	07	**11**	49*	58	63	05	66	09
G	(67/50/51/64/31)		(**15**/14)		(16/06)		(07/62/63)		66	09
B	67	**70**/58	(38/31/63)		(37/16)		(62/**30**/23)		66	09
E	(67/**36**/43/50/51/64/31/03/05/**57**)		(38/54/29)		(06/37/48/52/39)		(62/07*/19*/16/14/63/60)		66/03*/60*	09/01/08
M	(67/50/51/41)		(07*/38)		(49*/37/48)		(62/63)		66	09
V	(58/25/67/50/51)		(38/54)		(37/52/48)		(62/63/24)		66	09
A44	(43/50/67/51)		(**33**/38/54)		(06/40/14/58)		(07/19/46/**26**/16)		66	09/01
Nor	**18**	10	38	48	37	45	63	24	66	09
Flr	43*	67*	54*	45*	37*	63*	16*	24*	66*	09*
C	Sun: (67/43/41/25/51/50/64/31/34/42/10/**56**) Tue: (49*/37/52/48/58/40/**12**) Thu B: 66/**28**/03/44									
	Mon: (07/38/54/29/06) Wed: (62/14/**21**/63/16/05/**04**/**65**) Thu M: 09/01/**22**/60/08/**32**/20/59/27/**47**/**68**/**13**									

Key to texts on next page

Key to texts in Table 8.4

01 Accepto pane Iudas
02 Adiuua nos deus
03 Ait Pilatus
04 Amen dico uobis
05 Ancilla dixit Petro
06 Ante diem festum
07 Appropinquabat autem dies
08 Cena facta dixit Iesus
09 Cenantibus autem accepit
10 Ceperunt omnes turbe
11 Clarifica me
12 Collegerunt pontifices
13 Congregauit nos Christus
14 Consilium fecerunt inimici
15 Consilium fecerunt ut Iesum
16 Cotidie apud uos
17 Cum accepisset
18 Dederunt in escam
19 Desiderio desideraui
20 Diligamus nos inuicem
21 Dominus mecum est
22 Ecce dico uobis
23 Factus Iesus in agonia
24 Filie Ierusalem
25 Hodie namque
26 Iesus factus in agonia
27 In diebus illis
28 In humilitate
29 Infirmata est
30 Ingressus Pilatus
31 Inuocabo nomen tuum
32 Mandatum nouum
33 Maria ergo unxit
34 Missus sum
35 Mittens hec mulier
36 Multa turba
37 Nemo tollit a me
38 Non haberes in me
39 Non sis mihi
40 Nunc clarificatus est
41 Occurrunt turbe
42 Omnes collaudant
43 Osanna filio Dauid
44 Petrus autem sequaebatur
45 Pilatus dicebat ego nullam
46 Positis autem genibus
47 Postquam surrexit
48 Potestatem habeo ponendi
49 Principes sacerdotum
50 Pueri Hebr. tollentes
51 Pueri Hebr. uestimenta
52 Quia ego tecum sum
53 Quid molesti estis
54 Recordare mei domine
55 Repleuit et inebriauit
56 Rex Israel
57 Rogaui patrem
58 Scriptum est percutiam
59 Si ego dominus
60 Si male locutus
61 Sinite mulierem
62 Symon dormis non potuisti
63 Tanto tempore uobiscum
64 Tibi reuelaui
65 Tradetur enim gentibus
66 Traditor autem
67 Turba multa que conuenerat
68 Ubi fratres in unum
69 Uide domine et considera
70 Usquequo exaltabitur

Table 8.5 Holy Week antiphon *ordines* related to Royal 17. C. XVII

B = Antiphon for the Benedictus; *M* = Antiphon for the Magnificat; *E* = *Antiphona in euangelio* (for either Benedictus or Magnificat); *H* = *Antiphona pro horis* (the single antiphons at P[rime], T[erce], S[ext], and N[one], given as a set under this rubric). When more than one antiphon is given in one category, each is numbered in the order found in the manuscript.

	Roy		MoR		D
Palm Sunday					
E1	Turba multa	*B*	Turbe multa	*B*	Turba multa
E2	Osanna filio	*M1*	Occurrunt turbe	*H1*	Occurrunt turbe
E3	Omnes conlaud.	*M2*	Pueri Hebr. toll.	*H2*	Pueri Hebr. toll.
E4	Occurrunt turbe	*M3*	Pueri Hebr. uest.	*H3*	Pueri Hebr. uest.
		M4	Osanna filio	*H4*	Osanna filio
		M5	Coeperunt omnes	*M*	Ceperunt omnes
Monday					
E1	Non haberes	*E1*	Non haberes	*E1*	Non haberes
E2	Recordare mei	*E2*	Recordare mei	*E2*	Recordare mei
		E3	Uide domine		
Tuesday					
E1	Nemo tollet	*E1*	Nemo tollit	*E1*	Nemo tollit
E2	Quia ego tecum	*E2*	Quia ego tecum	*E2*	Quia ego tecum
E3	Potestatem habeo	*E3*	Potestatem habeo	*E3*	Potestatem habeo
E4	Consilium fecerunt	*E4*	Consilium fecerunt	*E4*	Consilium fecerunt
Wednesday					
B	Simon dormis	*B*	Symon dormis	*E1*	Symon dormis
M1	Tanto tempore	*M1*	Cotidie apud uos	*E2*	Cotidie apud uos
M2	Cotidie apud uos	*M2*	Tanto tempore	*E3*	Tanto tempore
Maundy Thursday					
B	Traditor autem	*B*	Traditor autem	*B*	Traditor autem
M1	Cena facta	*M1*	Cenantibus autem	*M*	Cenantibus autem
M2	Cenantibus autem	*M2*	Cena facta		
		M3	Accepto pane		

Rows continue across next page

Table 8.5 (continued)

	Cor1		*Wul*		*Wor*
Palm Sunday					
B	Turba multa	B	—	B	Turba multa
H1	Omnes collaudant	P	—	P	Pueri Hebr. uest.
H2	Occurrunt turbę	T	Occurrunt turbe	T	Pueri Hebr. toll.
H3	Pueri Hebr. uest.	S	Osanna filio Dau.*	S	Osanna filio Dau.*
H4	Osanna filio	N	Omnes conlaud.*	N	Omnes collaud.
		M	Ceperunt omnes	M	Occurrunt turbe
Monday					
E1	Non haberes	B	Non haberes	B	Non haberes
E2	Recordare mei	M	Recordare mei	M	Recordare mei
Tuesday					
E1	Nemo tollit	B	Nemo tollat	B	Nemo tollit
E2	Quia ego tecum	M1	Quia ego tecum		
E3	Potestatem habeo	M2	Potestatem habeo		
E4	Consilium fecerunt	M3	Consilium fecerunt	M	Consilium fecerunt
Wednesday					
E1	Symon dormis	B	Symon dormis	B	Symon dormis
E2	Tanto tempore	M1	Tanto tempore		
E3	Cotidie apud uos	M2	Cotidie apud uos	M	Cotidie apud uos
Maundy Thursday					
B	Traditor autem	B	—	B	Traditor autem
M1	Cena facta	M	Cenantibus autem	M	Cena facta
M2	Accepto pane				

9

A Fragment of a Tenth-Century English Benedictine Chant Book

Oxford, Bodleian Library, Rawl. D. 894, fols. 62–3

Rawlinson D. 894 in the Bodleian Library (Summary Catalogue 13660) is a guardbook containing, in the main, fragments from liturgical and musical manuscripts of varying date. Folios 62 and 63 are the two leaves of a small bifolium. The first extended notice of this fragment was given in S. J. P. Van Dijk's handlist of liturgical manuscripts in the Bodleian:

> FRANCE 10th (?) century
>
> From the sanctorale: portions of the Commemoration of St Paul (30 June), the night office of St Lawrence (10 Aug.) and a part of the office of the Assumption (15 Aug.). Several texts in full, some music.
>
> Parchm., 2 consecutive fol., 155×108 mm., lower margins and 1 or 2 lines of text cut; 23 or 24 lines and 2 col. orig. about 140×80 mm. Some fine adiastematic, non-rhythmical neums for the resp. Meruit esse hostia levita Laurentius and Beatus fuit [*sic*] Laurentius qui post. Perhaps from a kind of primitive breviary.[1]

The fragment was included in Helmut Gneuss's 'Preliminary list of manuscripts written or owned in England up to 1100'[2] on the advice of Neil Ker, who said of these leaves, 'Bodleian, Rawlinson D. 894, no. 43 I thought at some time probably English, s. x/xi.'[3] It was retained as

---

[1] S. J. P. Van Dijk, 'Handlist of the Latin Liturgical Manuscripts in the Bodleian Library, Oxford', 7 vols. in 8, Unpublished typescript held in Duke Humfrey's Library, Oxford, 1957–60, VI, 368. Van Dijk misread the beginning of the responsory *Beatus uir*.
[2] *Anglo-Saxon England* 9 (1981), 1–60.
[3] Private correspondence with Gneuss dated 19 December 1979. I am grateful to Prof. Gneuss for relating this to me in a letter of 1 May 2006, in which, and in a subsequent letter,

number 663 in Gneuss's 2000 *Handlist*, where it is described as 'Responsoriale (f[ragment]) : s. x/xi'. K. D. Hartzell calls the fragment a 'directory of an antiphoner – a list by incipit of antiphons, their psalms, and responsories', noting that it is arranged for the monastic *cursus*. He notes that the same scribe copied a noted 'versary' (cantatorium?), which survives as a single strip from the bottom of a bifolium, now privately owned by Mr R. A. Linenthal, and assigns both fragments, apparently on palaeographical grounds, to Christ Church, Canterbury.[4]

This chapter comprises a fresh evaluation of Rawl. D. 894, fols. 62–3, affirming on palaeographical evidence, in agreement with Ker's suspicion, that they were copied in England during the tenth century, and, *pace* Hartzell, almost certainly at St Augustine's, Canterbury. Consideration is also given to their liturgical contents and their implications for Benedictine Office liturgy in England during and following the reform period of the tenth century.

Materials and preparation

In its current state, fol. 62 has a maximum height of 158 mm and a maximum width of 108 mm. The bifolium was trimmed at some point after it was copied; the bottom of each page probably had a further two lines of writing. The absence of prickings in the outer margins suggests that the sides were also trimmed. Even with its trimmed parchment restored, however, the book to which *Rwl* belonged would still have been very small, perhaps not more than 195 mm in height.

The bifolium is folded with the hair side out, which is rubbed and soiled. The flesh side is still pale and relatively clean. Both leaves have been punctured straight through in four places next to the fold, which suggests that the bifolium survived as a pair of endleaves before being excised and pasted into the guardbook where it now resides. Before the leaves were trimmed, the text was continuous from the bottom of fol. 62v to the

---

he offered much helpful information and comment.

[4] Hartzell, *Catalogue*, pp. 494–5 (no. 286), quotation from p. 494. The 'versary' is described on pp. 340–1 (no. 199). Both sides of the 'Linenthal leaf' are reproduced in E. Hornby, 'Interactions between Brittany and Christ Church, Canterbury in the tenth century: The Linenthal leaf', in E. Hornby and D. Maw (eds.), *Essays on the History of English Music in Honour of John Caldwell: Sources, Style, Performance, Historiography* (Woodbridge, 2010), pp. 47–65, at p. 49. Hornby follows Hartzell in assigning both the Linenthal leaf and Rawl. D. 894 to Christ Church.

top of 63r. The bifolium therefore either stood alone or was the inner sheet of a quire. Quires in most Anglo-Saxon manuscripts are arranged so that, when folded, the hair side of the outer sheet faces outward. Most Anglo-Saxon quires comprised four sheets, for a total of eight leaves.[5] If *Rwl* did not originally stand alone, and if its quire comprised the usual four sheets (or any even number), and if the outer sheet were folded with its hair side facing out as normal, then for *Rwl* to have its flesh side forming the inner opening would require the 'Insular' arrangement of leaves (HFHF) rather than the 'Continental' (HFFH). This arrangement began to disappear in the tenth century, but persisted in certain scriptoria until the beginning of the eleventh.[6] Several ways of making up quires may be seen in surviving Anglo-Saxon manuscripts, and at least one example has quires folded with all the flesh sides facing out, contrary to the usual practice.[7] That *Rwl* was quired in the old HFHF manner is statistically probable, but not certain.

Only some of the ruling is now visible. Ruling seems to have been done on the hair side, and the faint impressions may be the result of several sheets having been ruled simultaneously. Later Anglo-Saxon scribal practice was to rule sheets individually, but before the beginning of the eleventh century it was common for two or more sheets to be ruled simultaneously.[8] Each leaf is ruled with twenty-two long lines (probably twenty-four before trimming), at roughly 9 mm intervals, leaving a top margin of 19 mm above the writing block. A double bounding line is just barely discernible about 10 mm from the inner margin of fol. 62v. No corresponding bounding line is visible in the outer margins. There may be a double bounding line at the left side of fol. 63r, though this is obscured by a ridge at the point where the back of the leaf is fixed to the guardbook. Certain portions of the text are arranged as if they were written in columns, but these are merely short chant cues that are still to be read from left to right across the whole width of the page. Folio 62r seems to have been ruled with two vertical lines, 8 mm apart at roughly the centre of the page, to assist with the layout of these pseudo-columns. (Fol. 63v,

---

[5] Ker, *Catalogue*, p. xxiii; see p. xxiv for exceptions.
[6] Ker, *Catalogue*, p. xxv.
[7] Ker, *Catalogue*, p. xxv. The manuscript in question is Ker's no. 133, BL Add. 47967; this is the Old English Orosius, Gneuss, *Handlist*, no. 300: 's. x^1 or $x^{2/4}$, Winchester?'. A few Continental manuscripts are also arranged with at least the outer sheet of each quire folded with the flesh side out.
[8] Ker, *Catalogue*, p. xxiv.

which has the same amount of text in columnar layout, has no such ruling now visible.) There is no pricking in the inner margins, which indicates that the sheets were ruled before folding. Prickings in the inner margins became unusual in English manuscripts copied after $c.900$.[9]

Script and decoration

The decoration of *Rwl* is of the most basic kind. The few rubrics are written in *capitalis* (but with minuscule **h**), using a mixed metallic and non-metallic red pigment, now mostly oxidized. These rubrics are confined to the names of feast days, liturgical subdivisions (nocturns), and labels of chant types (R̃., Ã., etc.). *Litterae notabiliores* mark the beginning of each chant text or verse. A large initial is placed at the beginning of the first responsory of each feast day (fol. 62r line 22: 'Quo'; fol. 63v line 22: 'Vidi'), written in the same black-brown ink as the main text.

Rwl was copied by a single mediocre English hand writing in Caroline minuscule of the kind labelled 'Style II' by T. A. M. Bishop. A brief general account of Style II Anglo-Caroline minuscule is necessary in order to set out the extent to which the hand of *Rwl* can be localized and dated.[10]

Tenth-century specimens of Anglo-Caroline minuscule may be classed into two fundamentally different styles.[11] 'Style I' Anglo-

---

[9] Bishop, *English Caroline Minuscule*, p. xii. Two early tenth-century exceptions are noted in Parkes, 'The palaeography of the Parker manuscript', p. 158.

[10] For what follows, see now also the summary in R. Rushforth, 'English Caroline Minuscule', in Gameson, *Book in Britain*, pp. 197–210.

[11] This was first noticed by Ker and elaborated by Bishop in the course of a series of studies published between 1957 and 1971. Bishop's final synthesis was published in his *English Caroline Minuscule*, with Styles I and II described on pp. xxi–xxiii. The limits imposed by his publishers prevented this book from superseding his earlier articles in *Transactions of the Cambridge Bibliographical Society*: 'Notes on Cambridge manuscripts, Part IV: MSS. connected with St Augustine's, Canterbury', *Transactions* 2/iv (1957), 323–36 and Plates XIII–XIV; 'Part V: MSS. connected with St Augustine's, Canterbury, continued', *Transactions* 3/i (1959), 93–5; 'Part VI: MSS. connected with St Augustine's, Canterbury, continued', *Transactions* 3/v (1963), 412–13; 'Part VII: The early minuscule of Christ Church, Canterbury', *Transactions* 3/v (1963), 413–23 and Plates XIII–XIV. These articles are referred to below as 'Notes IV', etc. Supplements and corrections to these articles were given in an Appendix to *English Caroline Minuscule*, pp. xxv–xxvi. Bishop's other writings on Anglo-Caroline minuscule are listed in the bibliography on p. xxvii. Bishop acknowledged Neil Ker as the first to observe the two different styles in 'Notes IV', p. 332 n. 1. Style I and Style II are given their first contrasting descriptions and manuscript attributions on pp. 333–4 of that article.

Caroline minuscule, which was favoured by Bishop Æthelwold and his reformed monastic circle, is round, large (even monumental), and generally free from Insular letter-forms.[12] 'Style II', by contrast, is 'small and elegant'[13] and 'preserves whatever of the English element would not be objectionable or unintelligible to a Continental reader'.[14] The earliest examples of this script have been attributed to Dunstan.[15] All safely localized specimens of Style II originated in the scriptoria of St Augustine's and Christ Church, Canterbury,[16] and behind the Canterbury hands Bishop saw the influence of an unidentified Continental model other than the models of Style I.[17] According to Bishop, Anglo-Saxon Square minuscule continued to be used at St Augustine's as the new Caroline script was introduced in the second half of the tenth century. At Christ Church, however, 'scribes seem to have abandoned the insular script all at once', learning the new script from St Augustine's hardly much earlier 'than the last decade of the tenth century'.[18]

---

[12] Bishop saw in ninth-century manuscripts of Fleury and Corbie the probable point of imitation for Style I; see his *English Caroline Minuscule*, p. xi n. 1: 'All [Continental palaeographers] emphasize the influence of the Fleury scriptorium in the origins of English Caroline.' Bishop was careful also to stress 'the influence of Corbie liturgy and liturgica on the script of Abingdon and Winchester', citing O. Homburger, 'Eine spätkarolingische Schule von Corbie', *Forschungen zur Kunstgeschichte und christilichen Archäologie* 3 (1957), 412–26 and figs. 168–84, at p. 426 and fig. 184. See Bishop, *English Caroline Minuscule*, p. 12 (no. 14), Plate XII, a mid-ninth-century Corbie sacramentary, which Bishop links to the script of Abingdon, seen in no. 15, Plate XIII. Bishop's own exhaustive work on the script of Corbie, the subject of his 1974–5 Lyell Lectures at Oxford University, has never been published. Bernhard Bischoff saw also the influence of Saint-Amand; see his *Latin Palaeography*, p. 124. Style I may also have been favoured by St Oswald; see p. 283 above.
[13] Bishop, 'Notes VI', p. 418.
[14] *Aethici Istrici Cosmographia Vergilio Salisburgensi rectius adscripta: Codex Leidensis Scaligeranus 69*, facsimile ed. [T. A.] M. Bishop, Umbrae codicum occidentalium 10 (Amsterdam, 1966), p. ix.
[15] The 'Hand D' that appears in additions and corrections to several tenth-century books, including 'St Dunstan's Classbook' (Oxford, Bodleian Library, Auct. F. 4. 32), thought to contain Dunstan's portrait. See M. Budny, ' "St Dunstan's Classbook" and its frontispiece', pp. 136–41. It is not certain whether Dunstan adopted the Continental minuscule during his time as a monk and abbot of Glastonbury or after his departure into exile in Ghent in 956. See Brooks, 'The career of St Dunstan', pp. 14–18.
[16] Dumville, *English Caroline Script*, p. 3.
[17] 'Notes IV', p. 334: 'Perhaps it would be safer to take ... some ... recurrent features of the Caroline of this series [from St Augustine's] ... as deriving from the style of a particular and perhaps rather backward continental scriptorium. Wherever this was (I don't think it was Fleury), the generally excellent script of this series need not be supposed to derive from any first-rate model.'
[18] Bishop, 'Notes VII', pp. 419 and 418.

Against Bishop's chronology, David Dumville points out that the 'Leofric Missal' (Oxford, Bodleian Library, Bodley 579) received a number of additions written in Caroline minuscule during the tenth century while the book was apparently at Christ Church, Canterbury,[19] which would put the introduction of the Continental script at Christ Church nearly half a century earlier.[20] And now that the original layer of the Leofric Missal is also considered to have been copied in England, even if by a Continental scribe, the history of Caroline minuscule writing in England may have to be pushed back to the turn of the tenth century.[21] None of the scribes of the tenth-century Anglo-Caroline additions to the manuscript ('Leofric B') can be linked to the products of either Canterbury scriptorium,[22] though certain hands do retain some Square minuscule letterforms along with the spiky aspect of the earliest examples of Style II at St Augustine's.[23]

Bishop saw Style II being taken up at St Augustine's some time after the production of a group of Square minuscule manuscripts that he dated on stylistic grounds between c.940 and c.970.[24] Dumville has argued, based on his disputed system of classification, that these Square minuscule manuscripts should be dated much earlier, implying an earlier introduction of Caroline minuscule at St Augustine's.[25] It has already been noted that Dumville's classification of Square minuscule according

---

[19] Dumville, *English Caroline Script*, pp. 94–9.

[20] Dumville, *English Caroline Script*, p. 96.

[21] See the discussion of 'Leofric A' in *The Leofric Missal*, ed. Orchard I, 23–131, and the concluding remarks on p. 131. Christopher Hohler suggested this possibility with forceful language in his 'Some service books', p. 78. The original hand of the Leofric Missal had previously been described as 'a regional type of Continental Carolingian minuscule (profoundly influenced by Insular features)' (Dumville, *Liturgy and the Ecclesiastical History*, p. 42). Certain passages of 'Leofric A' are indeed strikingly Insular in aspect (e.g. fol. 15r). The manuscript has been completely digitized in colour and made available to the public online through 'Early Manuscripts at Oxford University' <http://image.ox.ac.uk> last visited 10 November 2013. A complete palaeographical study of Bodley 579 has been promised by Richard Gameson (*The Leofric Missal*, ed. Orchard I, 13).

[22] *The Leofric Missal*, ed. Orchard I, 151 and 157.

[23] Compare, for example, fol. 254r with the two hands of Oxford, Bodleian Library, Auct. D. Inf. 2. 9 reproduced in Bishop, 'Notes IV', Plate XIII.

[24] Based on alleged similarities in these manuscripts to the hands of royal diplomas copied between these dates (Bishop, 'Notes IV', p. 325).

[25] The manuscripts of this group do not share stylistic links with Dumville's 'Phase III' Square minuscule of the period 939–59, or indeed of the subsequent period, which saw 'an abrupt change of style' (*English Caroline Script*, p. 88). Dumville considers that Cambridge, Trinity College 241 (a copy of Amalarius's *Liber officialis*) may be 'attributed with confidence to the 930s' (*English Caroline Script*, pp. 88–9). Bishop, by contrast, placed this

to chronologically narrow stylistic phases has not won universal acceptance.[26] Dumville's palaeographical argument for an early adoption of Caroline minuscule in Canterbury seems to be informed, to a certain degree, by the questionable belief that both Canterbury houses received Benedictine monasticism in Dunstan's pontificate at the latest.

Localization of Style II manuscripts is a less controversial matter. Bishop's attributions of Style II Canterbury manuscripts to either St Augustine's or Christ Church, based as it is on relationships between recognizable scribal hands, are little disturbed by Dumville's proposed chronological revision. Dumville too is satisfied that the Canterbury scriptoria practised two 'distinctive house-variants' of Style II,[27] though he would see in the script of Christ Church a separate indebtedness to manuscripts of the Style I tradition.[28] It is a simpler matter, therefore, to determine the scriptorium in which *Rwl* was copied, even if the date cannot be ascertained with confidence.

Turning to the script of *Rwl* itself (see Illustration 9.1 on page 308, reproducing fol. 63r), it is immediately clear that it does not belong to the Style I group associated with Æthelwold. The hand in *Rwl* is smaller than would be expected in a Style I manuscript (it is even rather small for Style II). The size of the script, adopted for a page of unusually small dimensions, goes some way to hiding the scribe's inadequacies. This scribe struggled or neglected to produce letter-forms of consistent size and aspect. The characteristic features of the hand may be summarized as follows:

> **a** is Insular, a single compartment with no protruding headstroke. Rather than the prominent nearly horizontal top stroke seen in some Square minuscule hands, the first stroke descends sharply down and left.
>
> **b** and other ascenders (**d, l**) are all Caroline, but often have a slight wedge at the top of the ascender. In the absence of a wedge, the ascender sometimes leans backwards to the left, in marked contrast to the rest of the letter-forms, which tend to slope significantly to the right.

---

manuscript chronologically in the middle of his first St Augustine's group on codicological grounds, noting that the parchment is arranged entirely in the Continental manner (Bishop, 'Notes IV', p. 324).

[26] See Chapter 8, p. 261.
[27] *English Caroline Script*, pp. 3–4.
[28] *English Caroline Script*, pp. 102–8.

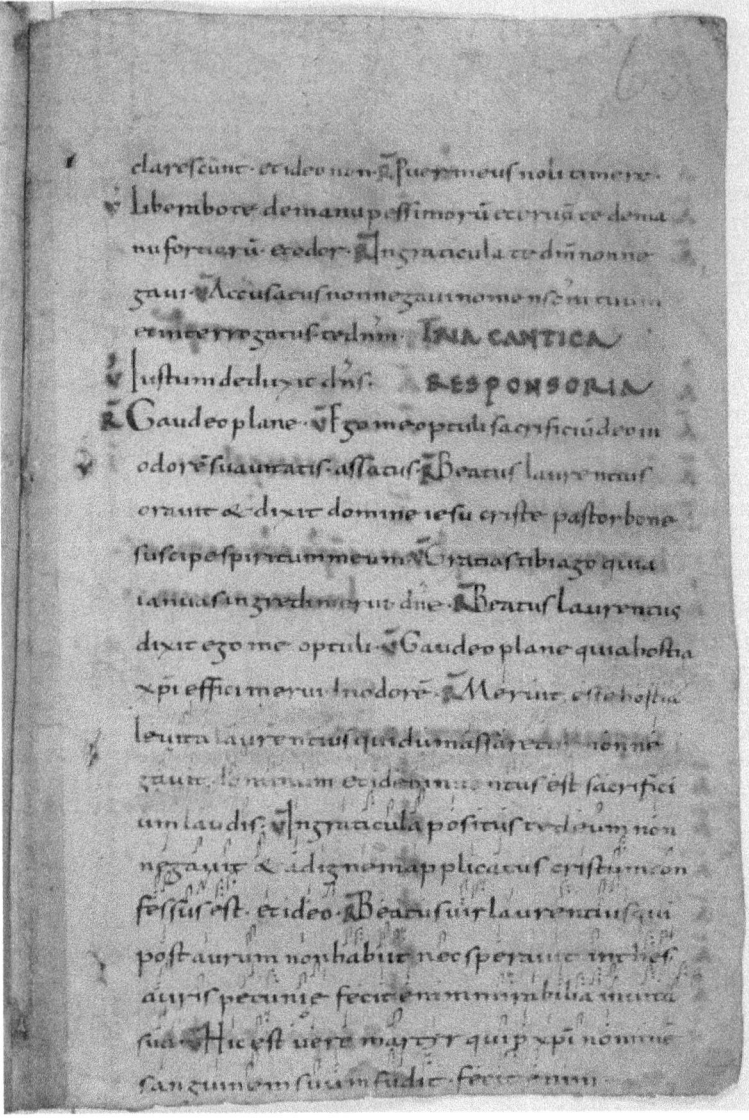

Illustration 9.1 Oxford, Bodleian Library, Rawl. D. 894, fol. 63r

e is Caroline in form, though it is sometimes tall when followed by, for example, **a** or **t**.

g is flat topped with an open tail. This form is not in itself Insular, and is probably derived from the Continental model imitated by the scribe. The top of a genuine Insular **g** is quite straight, whereas this scribe draws the top as a gentle wave. The tail of **g** is formed with a smooth continuous stroke, like a stylized round-**s**.

h takes the Caroline form, with its limb curving clockwise, not turned out to the right at the baseline as in Square minuscule.

p is usually begun with a wedge. Together with **q**, its descender is drawn to a sharp point.

r is Caroline in form, but its stem is often a slight descender. The scribe strove to draw the descender to a sharp point, but was inconsistent. The descending stem and the connecting stroke to shoulder stroke are significantly separated from each other at the top, giving a triangular appearance. The whole form slopes to the right.

s is Caroline in form, but also a slight descender, frequently but not always drawn to a sharp point, as also **f**. The scribe was very inconsistent in forming **s**. Its stem sometimes begins with a spur-like approach stroke, sometimes with a thickened blob, and other times it is perfectly smooth, with no discernible approach stroke. On two occasions (fol. 63r line 11 and fol. 63v line 4), a trailing round **s** is used at a line end (in the first instance creating the misspelling 'laurentus' for 'laurentius').

x has a prominent second stroke usually drawn back sharply below the previous letter. The first stroke often cuts down to the right at a shallow, almost horizontal angle.

y occurs seven times in the bifolium (thanks to a hymn, two martyrs, one tyrant, and St Hippolytus), each time in the 'rounded' rather than the 'straight-limbed' form, and always dotted.[29]

Ligatures are limited to **a+e**, **c+t**, and **s+t**. This last tends to be horizontally compressed and slants to the right.

The same letter-forms occur in the 'Linenthal leaf', which was indeed

---

[29] See Ker, *Catalogue*, p. xxxi.

written by a very similar, perhaps identical, hand. The only additional letter-form to note in the Linenthal leaf is a 2-shaped **r** (fol. 2v, line 2).

The features listed above are consistent with Style II Caroline minuscule, which is found only in manuscripts associated with the two Canterbury houses. Ligatures provide a useful tool for discriminating between the house styles of Christ Church and St Augustine's, apart from Bishop's observation that early examples from Christ Church are 'more constrained and sedate' and later in aspect than those from St Augustine's.[30] Christ Church hands are more likely to use the **r+a** ligature and less likely to use **c+t** and **r+t** than hands attributed to St Augustine's. Within its four leaves, *Rwl* presents twenty-six opportunities for the use of an **r+a** ligature, but it is never used. Six opportunities arise to use **c+t**. In three cases, no ligature is used. In two additional cases, the word is broken across two lines between **c** and **t**, so a ligature might have been used otherwise. In the final case, **c+t** is used (fol. 63v line 17: 'Eructauit'). Eight opportunities to use **r+t** produced no ligatures. These results, from an admittedly limited sample, point to St Augustine's.

Bishop further observed that Christ Church scribes made comparatively greater use of the vertical mark of abbreviation than St Augustine's scribes. The scribe of *Rwl* seems to have devised his own system for marks of abbreviation: a horizontal stroke indicates the omission of a single letter; a vertical mark denotes a contraction in which several letters are missing (as in the various *nomina sacra*). Where he has broken his own rule, it is always in favour of a horizontal stroke where a vertical would have been expected (as on fol. 63r line 13: 'christi'). Here too St Augustine's may be indicated, though given the scribe's rule for abbreviation marks, the predominance of horizontal abbreviation marks in this small fragment may have arisen from the accidents of the text's contents and not from a house style.

It has not been possible to examine every hand identified in Bishop's study of surviving St Augustine's and Christ Church manuscripts. A large number of these hands are represented, however, in two manuscripts. Oxford, Bodleian Library, Auct. D. Inf. 2. 9 (Part I, Cassian) was copied at St Augustine's in the second half of the tenth century. Although it does not represent an impressive calligraphic performance, it contains all the hands by which the Style II St Augustine's manuscripts are interconnected, with

---

[30] 'Notes VII', p. 418. Bernhard Bischoff described the Christ Church style as 'a finer script' (*Latin Palaeography*, p. 124).

ten main scribes and a few other hands that contributed minor additions.[31] Cambridge, Trinity College B. 4. 27 (141) (Isidore, Gregory, Augustine), is attributed to Christ Church, written by twenty scribes working in close collaboration, though perhaps not in a continuous writing campaign.[32] An inspection of these two manuscripts reveals a marked affinity of aspect between *Rwl* and the various St Augustine's hands, though this is somewhat more pronounced in some hands than others.[33] Shared traits are also visible in published reproductions of other St Augustine's manuscripts.[34] Especially similar is the original hand of Oxford, Bodleian Library, Auct. F. 1. 15 (Part I, Boethius).[35] This last is the work of a scribe far more competent than the scribe who copied *Rwl*, but it displays a related script. The crucial letter-forms shared by these hands are the 3-shaped **g**, the round form of **y**, and an **e**-caudata formed with a long stroke pulled back diagonally. All St Augustine's hands habitually make **r** and **s** slight descenders. The top points of **r** are usually usually separated, creating a triangular shape. All descenders receive a refined treatment, usually being pulled down to a sharp point. The scribe of *Rwl* was often lazy and inconsistent in producing this effect, but he was certainly capable of it.[36] Even the feet of some minims are sharpened, especially the first stroke of **m**.

The hand of *Rwl* is very similar to Bishop's 'tenth hand' in Auct. D. Inf. 2. 9. This scribe has not been identified in any other manuscript.[37] Bishop describes this hand as 'incompetent' and 'remarkably inept'. If *Rwl* is by the same scribe, it is a more mature performance; though this

---

[31] Bishop, 'Notes IV', pp. 327–9 and Plate XIII (showing Bishop's scribes C and E); *English Caroline Minuscule*, p. 5 (no. 7), Plate V (showing the ninth scribe, unidentified in any other manuscript).

[32] Bishop, 'Notes VII', pp. 416–17 and Plate XIV (all three images displaying the work of Bishop's 'scribe iv').

[33] I do not see the resemblance with Bishop's 'scribe viii' noticed by Hartzell in Cambridge, Trinity College O. 2. 31 (1135) (*Catalogue of Manuscripts*, p. 129 (no. 64) and p. 495).

[34] Small examples of Caroline minuscule writing at St Augustine's may be found in E. Temple, *Anglo-Saxon Manuscripts, 900–1066*, Survey of Manuscripts Illuminated in the British Isles 2 (London, 1976): no. 30i (ill. 103), Cambridge, Trinity College O. 1. 18 (1042); no. 30iv (ills. 100 and 106), Oxford, Bodleian Library, Rawl. C. 570; no. 38 (ills. 115, 120, 126, and 127), BL Harley 5431, fols. 6–126v; no. 39 (ills. 131 and 132), London, Lambeth Palace Library, 200 (Part II). Temple's no. 30v (ill. 105), Leiden, Bibliotheek der Rijksuniversiteit, Scaligeranus 69, is available in a complete facsimile: *Aethici Istrici Cosmographia*, ed. Bishop.

[35] Reproduction of fol. 71r in Bishop, *English Caroline Minuscule*, p. 7 (no. 9), Plate VII.

[36] Hartzell goes so far as to call him 'an expert scribe' (*Catalogue*, p. 495).

[37] His work in Auct. D. Inf. 2. 9 is listed in Bishop, 'Notes IV', pp. 328–9.

might require this scribe to have reverted to Insular quiring, whereas the tenth hand of Auct. D. Inf. 2. 9 used the Continental HFFH arrangement (but possibly guided there by Bishop's 'scribe C', suspected by Bishop to be a foreigner). The similarities are most apparent when the scribe of Auct. D. Inf. 2. 9 writes very small, as on the last line of fol. 80r. There is a greater resemblance to *Rwl* in quire XI of Auct. D. Inf. 2. 9 (fols. 80–7), which scribe ten wrote by himself, than in the previous quire, where he was assisted by scribe C. The formation of **g** is identical to that in *Rwl* (especially so on fol. 73v). Also similar is **x**, whose first stroke drops diagonally from left to right at a very shallow angle, with the second stroke pulled sharply down and back below the preceding letter. Of special interest are the backward sloping ascenders found occasionally on **b** and **l** in both *Rwl* and scribe ten's work in Auct. D. Inf. 2. 9. Also shared is a subtle, understated form of the horizontal mark of abbreviation, which, unlike those of scribe ten's colleagues, curves upward only very slightly at the end of the stroke.

It would be premature to assign *Rwl* certainly to scribe ten of Auct. D. Inf. 2. 9 before making a more thorough examination of the other St Augustine's hands not found in this one manuscript. It is nevertheless an attractive thought that a monk whose gifts obviously did not find successful expression in the scriptorium may yet have made a great contribution in the song school. Whatever the quality of his hand, the scribe of *Rwl* seems, as shall shortly emerge, to have been engaged in a project of the greatest importance in the liturgical and musical life of his monastery. The evidence collected above suggests very strongly that this monastery was St Augustine's, Canterbury.

No more specific date for the copying of *Rwl* can be given than the second half of the tenth century. But if, as has been speculated, the original quiring of *Rwl* was Insular (HFHF), *Rwl* may have been copied rather early in the history of Caroline minuscule at St Augustine's. Its place in that history may be illustrated by stylistic similarities with the very accomplished script of Bishop's scribe A.[38] Scribe A, in addition to his work in Auct. D. Inf. 2. 9 and his holograph performance in Auct. F. 1. 15, already mentioned, also wrote most of a copy of the *Regula S. Benedicti* owned by St Augustine's in the later Middle Ages (BL Harl. 5431). Its quires are arranged throughout in the Insular fashion.[39] It may not be a coincidence

---

[38] See Bishop, 'Notes IV', p. 327.
[39] Bishop, 'Notes IV', p. 329.

that a copy of the Rule and a chant book for the Benedictine Office are found written in similar styles at what would appear to be a relatively early stage in the use of Caroline minuscule at St Augustine's.

Delicate Insular neumes were added above two of the texts in *Rwl* by two additional hands, the second less competent than the first.[40] There is no differentiation in the height of the neumes, one neume beginning more or less where the previous one ended. Both neumators make use of liquescent forms.

Liturgical contents and book type

Certain chants in the Rawlinson fragment have been selected for close study and comparison with a good sample of pertinent sources in the section on 'Liturgical *ordo*' below (beginning on page 323). A few remarks may be made first, however, about the liturgical character of the fragment and the type of book that it may represent, mainly by analogy with sources readily available in print or in facsimile. *Rwl* contains three kinds of chant: antiphons, responsories, and versicles. All but a handful of these are given in incipit, with cues not generally exceeding four words. Four feasts of the Sanctorale are represented: the Commemoration of St Paul (30 June), the octave of the SS. Peter and Paul (6 July), St Lawrence (10 August), and the Assumption of the Virgin (15 August). Consulting of any early medieval kalendar will arouse suspicion that *Rwl* might be incomplete in its provision for this part of the ecclesastical year: the pre-1100 English Benedictine kalendars edited by Francis Wormald allow fewer than ten non-festal days between 30 June and 15 August.[41] Of course, not all of these feasts would be expected to have proper chants; but the absence of some of the more important festivals, such as the Translation of St Benedict (11 July) and the feast of St James the Apostle (25 July), requires some explanation, as might the absence of widely culted English saints such as St Oswald, king and martyr (5 August). The kalendar of the Bosworth Psalter (BL Add. 37517, fols. 2–3), which gives the Sanctorale as observed *c.*1000 at

---

[40] Hartzell, *Catalogue*, p. 495. Where Hartzell writes 'the verse of the first respond was notated', he refers to the fourth responsory of the third nocturn for St Lawrence (*Meruit esse hostia*, fol. 63r). The 'second respond' is the fifth responsory (supernumerary) of the same nocturn (*Beatus uir laurentius*, also fol. 63r). Hartzell identifies Breton neumes apparently by the text scribe in the manuscript fragment owned by R. A. Linenthal (no. 199, p. 341).

[41] *English Kalendars Before A.D. 1100*, ed. F. Wormald, HBS 72 (London, 1934).

St Augustine's, Canterbury, is very helpful on this point.⁴² This kalendar marks all days in the year for which the sacramentary (the book of prayers to be recited by the priest at Mass) would contain proper prayers. This is done with either a letter **F** for the most important feasts or a letter **S** for secondary feasts.⁴³ During the period of the Sanctorale contained in *Rwl*, the Bosworth kalendar marks seventeen feasts as secondary (**S**), among them the Translation of St Benedict and the Feast of St Oswald, king and martyr. Only four feasts are given the highest rank (**F**): the Commemoration of St Paul, St James, St Lawrence, and the Assumption. The feast of SS. Peter and Paul (29 June), which occurs outside the period covered in *Rwl*, is also of the highest rank. Its octave is provided with two antiphons in *Rwl*. In the twelve antiphoners edited in Hesbert's *Corpus antiphonalium officii* the feasts marked as secondary in the Bosworth kalendar are rarely provided with proper chants.⁴⁴ The feast of St James, omitted in *Rwl*, is likewise omitted in all twelve of Hesbert's antiphoners; its chants were drawn entirely from the Common of Apostles.⁴⁵ As in *Rwl*, the octave of SS. Peter and Paul is provided with several proper antiphons in three of the *CAO* sources (*B*, *F*, and *L*).⁴⁶ The remaining feasts in *Rwl*, St Lawrence and the Assumption, receive the full provision of proper chants that would be expected in an antiphoner. It would appear, therefore, that the fragment provides chants for every occasion that would be expected in this portion of the Sanctorale.

Still on the subject of the Sanctorale, the Bosworth kalendar is significant in how it names the feasts days celebrated on 29 and 30 June. In most kalendars (and liturgical books), 29 June is *Apostolorum Petri*

---

⁴² The text of the kalendar is ed. Wormald, *English Kalendars*, pp. 57–69. The question of the kalendar's origin has now been definitively settled by Nicholas Orchard ('The Bosworth Psalter'; and see his comments in *The Leofric Missal* I, 178–9). An origin at Christ Church, Canterbury, has been proposed at various times, most systematically by Korhammer, 'The origin of the Bosworth Psalter'.

⁴³ On these letters, see *The Leofric Missal*, ed. Orchard I, 158–9; Korhammer, 'The origin', p. 176; and R. Rushforth, *Saints in English Kalendars Before A.D. 1100*, HBS 117 (Woodbridge, 2008), p. 25. What words the letters stand for is unknown. Some exceptions to the rule are noted in Orchard, 'The Bosworth Psalter', pp. 88–91, and in *The Leofric Missal*, ed. Orchard I, 169–75.

⁴⁴ The Translation of St Benedict (§ 102⁴) is noticed in only one of the six monastic antiphoners, *F* (II, 493–5), and in the oldest of the secular antiphoners, *C* (I, 266–8). See Hesbert's notice at I, p. xix. On its inclusion in *C*, see p. 72 above.

⁴⁵ St James would otherwise be expected in the secular antiphoners at I, 268, and in the monastic at II, 494–7 (between §§ 102⁴ and 102⁵).

⁴⁶ Hesbert, *CAO* I, 266, and II, 493 (§ 102²).

et Pauli, and 30 June is *Sancti Pauli Apostoli* or *Commemoratio sancti Pauli*. The Bosworth kalendar, however, gives 29 June as *Passio sancti Petri principis apostolorum* and 30 June as *Decollatio sancti Pauli*.[47] As Nicholas Orchard has acutely observed, this unique nomenclature emphasizes the original dedication of St Augustine's to Peter and Paul.[48] *Rwl* prefaces the antiphons for the octave day of 29 June with the rubric *Antiphone in octaua apostolorum Petri et Pauli* (see just before no. 5 in the transcription), which might therefore cast doubt on the assignment of the fragment to St Augustine's on palaeographical grounds: if the fragment were really from St Augustine's, the octave day might be expected to mention only Peter. But the Bosworth kalendar gives the day before 29 June as *Uigilia apostolorum* (plural), and the octave day (6 July) as *Octauas apostolorum*. Even at St Augustine's, then, in keeping with universal Western custom, the feast of 29 June was still thought of as celebrating both Peter and Paul. *Rwl* is therefore still compatible with the Bosworth kalendar. The feasts of St Lawrence and the Assumption are likewise 'universal' feasts that spread throughout the West in tandem with the Roman liturgy (Lawrence was one of the three patron saints of Rome, together with Peter and Agnes). It is true that Lawrence was very widely venerated in England in the tenth century, a veneration that may possibly have been intensified through Continental influence after St Lawrence was credited with a decisive military intervention in favour of Otto I in 955. And Archbishop Sigeric (990–4) is known to have visited churches in Rome dedicated to St Lawrence.[49] The appearance of his feast in *Rwl* does not, however, indicate that the fragment comes from a church where Lawrence was especially culted.

Brief notice may be made of the individual chants provided for each feast day. Their function within the liturgy often has to be established through comparison with other sources: apart from indications of feast days and the division of nocturns in the Night Office, rubrication in the fragment is restricted almost entirely to the symbols ℣., ℟., and ℣. The fragment begins incompletely with four antiphons for St Paul (nos. 1–4). The first, *Gratia dei in me*, and the second, *Damasci prepositus*, are typically found as the fourth and fifth psalm antiphons of Lauds for the Commemoration of St Paul.[50] The next two antiphons, *Uos qui reliquistis*

---

[47] Ed. Wormald, *English Kalendars*, p. 63.
[48] Orchard, 'The Bosworth Psalter', pp. 89–90.
[49] Ortenberg, *The English Church and the Continent*, p. 67.
[50] Compare Hesbert, *CAO* I, 264–5 (§ 102b), and II, 490–1 (§ 102c).

and *Ter uirgis*, might be classed as *antiphonae in euangelio*, for use with the Benedictus at Lauds and the Magnificat at Vespers, although they are not rubricated here as such (compare the pair of antiphons *in euangelio* for St Lawrence, nos. 40 and 41).

All four antiphons for St Paul are provided with verses. These confused the rubricator, who sometimes wrote ℟. for ℣. Most of the antiphons provided for St Lawrence in this fragment also have verses. Only a small number of antiphons in the Gregorian repertory are ever provided with verses, usually those connected with feast days of special importance to the city of Rome. Not all sources make use of them. In notated antiphoners, the verse is set to the psalm recitation tone appropriate to the mode of the antiphon, the same tone that would be used for all the verses of the psalm.[51] These verses seem to have been sung after the doxology *Gloria patri* before the final iteration of the antiphon, in a way perhaps comparable to the *uersus ad repetendum* found with Mass introits in some early sources.[52]

Two antiphons are given for the octave of SS. Peter and Paul without an explanation for how they are to be used.[53]

St Lawrence is the only feast for which a complete set of proper chants is preserved in the fragment, and its antiphons and responsories will be examined minutely below. The isolated antiphon *Si quis mihi* (no. 7) with

---

[51] See, for example, the antiphons for the Commemoration of St Paul in *Le Codex F. 160 de la bibliothèque de la cathédrale de Worcester*, pp. 329–30.

[52] Tolhurst, *Introduction to the English Monastic Breviaries*, pp. 181 and 196–7. M. Huglo and J. Halmo, 'Antiphon, § 5(ii): Antiphons with verses', in Sadie and Tyrrell, *The New Grove Dictionary* I, 743–4. Another performance practice is indicated for two Nunc dimittis antiphons identified in Hughes, *Medieval Manuscripts for Mass and Office*, pp. 74 and 366 n. 59. On the *uersus ad repetendum* of the introit, see Hiley, *Western Plainchant*, pp. 109 and 496–8.

[53] Cf. Hesbert's *B, F,* and *L* (*CAO* I, 266, and II, 493, § 102²). The first antiphon, *Isti sunt duae oliuae*, is given as the first (or only?) psalm antiphon of First Vespers of the Octave of SS. Peter and Paul in *Féc* (*The Ordinal of the Abbey of the Holy Trinity, Fécamp (Fécamp, Musée de la Bénédictine, MS 186)*, ed. D. Chadd, 2 vols., HBS 111–12 (Woodbridge, 1999–2002) II, 491), and as one of three antiphons for use on the octave in the antiphoner of Saint-Maur-des-Fossés (*F*), and under the rubric *Ad Vesperos* on the feast day itself in the Saint-Denis Antiphoner (*D*). Neither manuscript clarifies how the antiphon is to be used (*CAO* II, 492–3, § 102d). The second antiphon, *Deus cuius dextera*, does not appear in *CAO*. It does, however, appear in two twelfth-century Italian antiphoners indexed in the 'CANTUS Database' (with the search term 'Deus cujus dextera'), in both cases as the Magnificat antiphon for the octave: Florence, Biblioteca Arcivescovile, *s.n.* (Florence cathedral, s. xii); Florence, Biblioteca Medicea-Laurenziana, Conv. sopp. 560 (Monastery of Vallombrosa, s. xii ex.). The text of the antiphon is apparently drawn from the collect for the Octave of the Apostles. Cf. *Le Sacramentaire grégorien*, ed. Deshusses I, 248 (no. 607).

which the chants for St Lawrence begin in *Rwl* is probably the Magnificat antiphon of First Vespers. Two invitatory antiphons follow (nos. 8 and 9), one proper to the feast and given in full,[54] the other an incipit from the Common of Martyrs. The three nocturns of the Night Office are arranged according to the Benedictine pattern, the first two nocturns having six antiphons (most with verses) and six psalm cues, a versicle, and four responsories. In the responsories, the refrain is always given in incipit, and the verse always in full, followed by a cue for the repetendum of the refrain. The third nocturn begins with the rubric *Tria cantica*. No antiphon is indicated, nor are there cues for the three canticles that would have been sung.[55] The scribe may have expected an antiphon from the Common of Martyrs to be used.[56] It may be, however, that the *Regula S. Benedicti* was strictly followed in its requirement that the canticles, chosen by the abbot, should be sung with the refrain *Alleluia*.[57] In the third nocturn, five responsories are provided (one more than is required in the Benedictine *cursus*), three of them with the full text of the refrain given, as well as the full text of the verse. It is very common to find an extra responsory appended to (or inserted into) one of the nocturns of the Night Office. Trimming has removed about two lines of text from the bottom of folio 63r, where the first four psalm antiphons of Lauds were probably given. The antiphon *Uolo pater* with which fol. 63v begins (no. 38) is usually found as the fifth (and final) antiphon at Lauds.[58] This is followed by a versicle cue and three antiphons *in euangelio*, the last of which is given in full. The provisions for St Lawrence end with a slightly curious set of five antiphons under the rubric *Item aliae antiphonae* followed by two antiphons *in euangelio*. All of these appear to be drawn from Lauds of the Common of One Martyr, although the set of antiphons in *Rwl* does not

---

[54] It is 'proper' only in a limited sense; it could be adapted to the feast of any one martyr by changing the name, which occurs conveniently as the last word of the chant. Nevertheless, it tends to be written out in full with the proper chants of the feast, as in *Cor1* fol. 174v.

[55] To omit cues for the canticles is not, however, unusual. In the six monastic sources edited in *CAO*, only *S* gives a list of canticle cues for St Lawrence, even though the other sources specify specific psalms for the first two nocturns (Hesbert, *CAO* II, 523, § 103b).

[56] Cf. Hesbert, *CAO* II, 680–1 (§ 124b).

[57] *RSB* 11:6 (following the Sunday pattern, as required in the instructions for saints' feasts given in chapter 14). According to Amalarius of Metz, the use of *Alleluia* in the third nocturn was also the Roman custom in the early ninth century: *Liber officialis*, IV. 9. 10, ed. Hanssens II, 444. In most monastic antiphoners and breviaries, the three canticles can be sung with an antiphon with any appropriate text.

[58] Hesbert, *CAO* II, 680–1 (§ 124b).

precisely match any of the sets given in Hesbert's sources.[59] Early chant books intermingle feasts of the Temporale and Sanctorale, and it may be that chants of the Common could be similarly distributed throughout the whole year, instead of being grouped in a separate section as in most surviving antiphoners.[60]

The chants for the Assumption begin in the same way as those for St Lawrence: an antiphon probably for the Magnificat at First Vespers, followed by a single invitatory antiphon, given in full. The first nocturn has six antiphons (without verses), each followed by a psalm cue. The leaf ends partway through the verse of the first responsory.

On the question of *Rwl*'s 'book type', this overview of its contents has shown that the fragment contains the kinds of chant and the feasts that would be expected in an Office antiphoner. Van Dijk's tentative description of *Rwl* as 'a kind of primitive breviary' is not appropriate, since the fragment lacks the prayers and readings that a breviary properly so called would contain. The possibility cannot be excluded that *Rwl* originally belonged to some sort of composite Office book, perhaps with a separate section containing prayers and short readings, the texts found together in a collectar. *Rwl* itself, however, is best considered as a kind of antiphoner. That its chants are mostly given in incipit is not incompatible with such a description. In a study of the earliest Frankish books of Mass chants, Susan Rankin has noted that simple lists of chant incipits, both on their own and as additions to the main material of sacramentaries, figure as a 'book type' of sorts across a wide chronological span, up to the first part of the tenth century.[61] The eighth-century incipits of Advent Office chants in Lucca, Biblioteca Capitolare, 490 furnish the earliest surviving example of a list of Office chants of this kind.[62] In its layout, however, *Rwl* is perhaps nearer in ethos, if not in quality, to the very handsomely presented list of chant incipits that comprises the Gradual of Senlis, Paris, Bibliothèque Sainte-Geneviève, 111 (Senlis, or perhaps Saint-

---

[59] Cf. Hesbert, *CAO* I, 360–1, and II, 680–3 (§ 124b).
[60] In the ninth-century Prüm *Chorbuch*, Trier, Stadtbibliothek, 1245/597, the Common of Confessors is found between the Commemoration of St Paul and the feast of St Lawrence (fol. 121r).
[61] S. Rankin, 'The making of Carolingian Mass chant books', in D. B. Cannata, G. I. Currie, R. C. Mueller, and J. L. Nádas (eds.), *'Quomodo cantabimus canticum?' Studies in Honor of Edward H. Roesner*, Publications of the American Institute of Musicology, Miscellanea 7 (Middleton, WI, 2008), pp. 37–63, at pp. 42–4.
[62] See p. 127 above.

Denis, 877×882).[63] *Rwl* could be seen, in this sense, as a late example of a very old-fashioned kind of chant book. This impression is strengthened by the scribe's use of word spacing to set apart, not individual words, but groups of words, as on the second line of fol. 63r, where the verse of the responsory *Puer meus noli timere* begins 'Liberabote demanupessimorū' (no. 30 in the transcription). As Susan Rankin has pointed out, this is a technique employed in ninth-century Frankish chant books, in particular the Compiègne Gradual-Antiphoner (*C*, 860×877), as one way of achieving the 'visual clarity' that was such an important concern of Frankish scribes of the Carolingian period.[64] The use of this kind of word grouping by the scribe of *Rwl* could indicate old-fashioned scribal habits or an old, perhaps Frankish, exemplar. As the discussion of the fragment's liturgical contents has shown, however, this step towards visual clarity did not remove the need for considerable knowledge and experience on the part of the user of this book. The rubrication is usually insufficient to indicate the precise purpose of any one chant, and an element of executive choice seems to be assumed. Furthermore, the fragment assumes that the complete texts of most of its chants, and all their melodies, are retained in the memory of the singer. This book would have to be studied by a singer in advance of an actual liturgical performance. It could only serve as a prompt to his memory, identifying all the proper chants to be sung that day.

The appearance of some complete texts in *Rwl*, however, raises certain important questions. The verses of responsories, for instance, are always given in full after the incipits of their refrains, which could suggest that *Rwl* was primarily a resource for soloists. The possibility exists, however, that the verses were copied in full to bring the responsorial repertory at St Augustine's into line with the reform of verse texts in Frankish antiphoners undertaken by Helisachar and others in the ninth century.[65] If this is the case, then *Rwl* could be seen as supplementing and correcting a very old antiphoner. Certain other full texts give a similar impression. A proper invitatory for St Lawrence, given in full, is followed by a cue for a generic invitatory from the Common. It might be that a proper invitatory for St Lawrence was previously unknown at St Augustine's. The same might be said for the full text of the invitatory for the Assumption. The list of antiphons from the Common of One Martyr after the proper chants for

---

[63] See Plate VII in Hesbert's *Antiphonale missarum sextuplex*.
[64] Rankin, 'The making'.
[65] See p. 62 above.

St Lawrence is hard to explain. The proper antiphons are given only in incipit, and so do not seem to be supplementing an existing repertory.

The three full responsory refrains found in the third nocturn for St Lawrence are, as further analysis will show, certainly supplementary chants adopted from an outside source. That there are three of them immediately suggests a secular set of nine responsories being expanded to a monastic set of twelve. In the case of *Rwl*, the original secular set seems already to have had a supernumerary tenth responsory. The expansion and reorganization of a secular antiphoner into the monastic pattern is also suggested by the psalm cues given at the Night Office of St Lawrence.

The psalm cues provided for St Lawrence and the Assumption are too short to reveal whether the *Romanum* or the *Gallicanum* version of the Latin psalter was used. But the selection of psalms for the Night Office of St Lawrence is interesting for other reasons. On major feast days, the current psalmody of the normal week is interrupted, and psalms with verses or themes appropriate to the feast are sung instead. These special psalms might be common to feasts of a particular type (e.g. the Common of One Martyr for St Lawrence) or specially selected for the day. Table 9.1 gives the psalms appointed for the Night Office of St Lawrence in *Rwl* and seventeen other Office books, both secular and monastic.

The various sets of psalms for St Lawrence are based on the psalms for the Common of One Martyr. In some sources, psalm cues are given only at those points where the series differs from the Common. In the Hyde Abbey breviary (*Hyd*), only the eighth antiphon of the Night Office is given a psalm cue, implying that all the other antiphons are to take their psalms from the Common:[66]

> Common: 1 2 4 5 8 10 14 20 23 63 64 91
> Lawrence: **16**

In the ordinal of Fécamp, a rubric says explicitly that the psalms for St Lawrence are to be those of the Common, with several exceptions:

> In primo nocturno. A̸. *Quo progrederis*. Et alie antiphone cum uersibus et psalmis de uno martire. [...] In secundo nocturno. A̸. *Strinxerunt corporis*. Ps. *Domine quis habitabit* [Ps. 14].

---

[66] *The Monastic Breviary*, ed. Tolhurst IV, fol. 313v (St Lawrence), and V, fol. 415v (Common of One Martyr). The antiphon *Igne me examinasti*, so appropriate for St Lawrence, is drawn from Psalm 16.

Table 9.1 Psalms assigned to the Night Office of St Lawrence

Monastic (first 2 nocturns)											
Rwl	1	2	3	5	8	10	14	16	20	60	63 64
H	1	2	3	4	5	8	14	16	20	23	33 64
MoR	1	2	4	5	8	10	14	16	20	23	63 64
D, Cor2, Clu	1	2	4	5	8	10	14	16	20	23	63 91
OuR, Wor, F	1	2	4	5	8	10	14	16	23	63	64 91
S	1	2	4	5	8	10	14	20	23	63	64 91
Secular (3 nocturns)											
B, Her, Yor	1	2	3	4	5	8	10	16	20		
C, E, M, Rom	1	2	3	4	5	8	14	16	20		
V	1	2	3	5	8	10	14	16	20		

Sigla not defined on pp. xix–xxii

Her *The Hereford Breviary*, ed. W. H. Frere and L. E. G. Brown [from the Rouen edn of 1505], 3 vols., HBS 26, 40, 46 (London, 1904–15)

Rom *Breviarium Romanum: Editio princeps (1568)*, Edizione anastatica, ed. M. Sodi and A. M. Triacca, Monumenta liturgica Concilii Tridentini 3 (Vatican City, 1999)

Yor *Breviarium ad usum insignis ecclesie Eboracensis*, ed. S. Lawley [from the surviving printed edns of 1493–1533], 2 vols., Surtees Society 71 and 75 (London, 1880–3)

℞. *Igne me examinasti.* Ps. *Exaudi domine iusticiam* [Ps. 16]. Ad alias omnes antiphonas · psalmi de uno martire.[67]

These instructions are somewhat problematic in that Psalm 14 is already assigned to the Common of One Martyr in *Féc*, but the example serves to illustrate the general point:[68]

---

[67] *The Ordinal of the Abbey of the Holy Trinity*, ed. Chadd II, 520.
[68] The psalms of the Common are ed. Chadd II, 643–4. The testimony of other liturgical books from Fécamp complicates the picture. An antiphoner and breviary replace Psalm 60 (*Exaudi deus deprecationem*) in the Common with Psalm 63 (*Exaudi deus orationem meam cum deprecor*). See *The Ordinal of the Abbey of the Holy Trinity*, ed. Chadd II, 644 n. 2. Moreover, both these sources give explicit proper psalms for the Night Office of St Lawrence that differ slightly from those of the Common.

Common: 1 2 4 5 8 10 14 20 60 64 91 96
Lawrence: **14 16**

The sources given in Table 9.1 all give sets of psalms proper to the Night Office of St Lawrence. *Rwl* is unique among them in including Psalm 60, although, as has just been seen, this psalm is found in an otherwise very different set for the Common of One Martyr in the ordinal *Féc*. *Rwl* is also unusual among the monastic sources in including Psalm 3. Hartker's antiphoner (*H*, *c.*1000), peculiar in many respects besides this, is the only other monastic book to include it. Just as monastic responsory sets are often expansions of a secular set of nine chants to the full monastic twelve by the addition of three extra responsories, so festal monastic sets of psalms are expansions from a secular nine to a monastic twelve. The set of psalms in *Rwl* seems to be based on a secular psalm set identical to that in the Verona Antiphoner (*V*), expanded by the addition of Psalms 60, 63, and 64. The psalms in *Rwl* might therefore be a 'home-grown' expansion of a secular psalm set previously available in Canterbury, rather than a copy of a pre-existing monastic exemplar. The Corbie breviary of the turn of the twelfth century (*Cor1*), which as was seen in Chapter 8 preserves a liturgical use that had a significant impact in England through Bishop Æthelwold's activities, gives no proper psalm cues for St Lawrence. The set of psalms given in its Common of One Martyr is identical to the set used by *OuR*, *Wor*, and *F* in Table 9.1. There is no evidence, therefore, that the Corbie liturgy had any impact on this small aspect of the Office as it was celebrated at St Augustine's. The impression is rather of a purely local solution.

In this analysis, the possibility emerges that *Rwl* was prepared as an intentionally transitional document, preparatory to the copying of a complete monastic antiphoner.[69] Chants not previously available are given in full. Others are given in incipit only, but arranged for the Benedictine Office. The extra psalms used for St Lawrence may point to a unique local expansion of an existing secular set. This hypothesis may be further tested by a detailed comparative analysis of its chants for the Night Office of St Lawrence.

---

[69] In this sense, Hartzell's description of the fragment as a 'directory of an antiphoner' is not inappropriate.

Liturgical ordo

The only feast for which a complete set of chants is preserved in *Rwl* is that of St Lawrence. Enough chants are given to support two separate comparative analyses, one of the great responsories and the other of the psalm antiphons of the Night Office. Special notice is due to an eleventh-century fragment of an English monastic antiphoner that also has chants for St Lawrence.

Analysis I: St Lawrence Night Office responsories

Table 9.2 shows the responsories and verses assigned to the feast of St Lawrence in thirty-five sources of varying origin and date. Twenty-seven of these follow the monastic *cursus*. Ten, including *Rwl*, are English Benedictine books. Seventeen are Continental Benedictine books, including the six monastic manuscripts edited in *CAO*. A further eight follow the secular *cursus*: five of the manuscripts edited in *CAO* (*G* has a lacuna here) and *A44*, *Cbr*, and *Par*. The sources contain between them a combined repertory of twenty-three responsories. Some of these responsories must be discounted from a repertorial analysis because they occur too rarely in this sample for their significance to be gauged. There are six *unica*: *1. Beati Laurenti interuentio*, *7. Beatus uir qui inuentus*, *9. Festa dies mundo*, *11. Hic est martyr*, *14. Laurea Laurenti praeclari*, and *19. Protector tuus*. Whatever significance they may have beyond the individual sources in which they occur cannot be assessed within this relatively small sample. *3. Beatus Laurentius dixit disce miser* is found only in three secular manuscripts, and seems not to have had any impact on any of the monastic *ordines* surveyed here. *23. Uir inclitus Laurentius* occurs in two monastic manuscripts (*Vst* and *S*) that, as shall be seen, fall within the same loose grouping; but its appearance in these sources apparently has little to say about the English situation. *8. Concede nobis* is found as the final responsory in several English sources (*Ely*, *Hyd*, *Mch*). The importance of this chant for the post-Conquest history of the English *ordines* is evident from its appearance as a marginal addition in a later Anglo-Saxon fragment, shown in Table 9.2 under the siglum *Brn*: BL Burney 277, fols. 69–72, with Stowe 1061, fol. 125. But it must be considered separately (see p. 331 below). The necessary exclusion of these nine responsories from the account leaves a much more limited selection of just fourteen chants on which to base a repertorial analysis of the sources.

When the lacuna in *Cht* and the uncertainty of two incipits in *Flr* are disregarded, six responsories are seen to be in universal use: *2. Beatus Laurentius clamauit deum meum*, *15. Leuita Laurentius*, *17. Noli me derelinquere*, *20. Puer meus*, *21. Quo progrederis*, and *22. Strinxerunt corporis*. Almost universal is *13. In craticula*; it is absent only in *Gnt*, apparently replaced by *14. Laurea Laurenti praeclari*, unique to *Gnt* in this table.[70] A further responsory, *10. Gaudeo plane*, is found in all but three sources (*H*, *R*, and *B*).

Table 9.3 presents an analytical grouping of the material in Table 9.2. The eight 'universal' responsories just identified are found in three basic secular arrangements, called here Types I, II, and III. Each monastic *ordo* appears to be an expansion of one of these three secular *ordines*. Type I and Type II both make up the secular complement of nine responsories by adding *18. O Hippolyte si credis* to the existing eight universal chants. (*O Hippolyte* is found in most of the secular *ordines*, and so is probably not to be considered a 'monastic' addition.) The difference between them is their arrangement of the same nine chants. Type I typically begins *21–17–18* (with several idiosyncratic variants). Type II begins *15–20–22*. These two types are represented by the two oldest surviving complete Office antiphoners following the secular *cursus*, *A44* (Type I) and *C* (Type II). Both manuscripts date from the later ninth century, which suggests that Type I and Type II should be considered equally early, neither one being a derivative of the other.

A third type appears to lie behind a large group of very uniform monastic *ordines*. Type III, seen in the secular manuscript *Par*, lacks *18. O Hippolyte* and has the characteristic opening *15–21–17*. This group includes a set of nearly identical *ordines* comprising most of the English sources and several Continental ones (*Cor1*, *MoR*, *D*). Assuming that the secular series found in *Par* formed the basic structure for the Type III monastic *ordines* (the possibility cannot yet be excluded out of hand that *Par* was itself influenced by the monastic *ordines*), the additional 'monastic' responsories of this group are different from those of Types I and II. The secular series in *Par* already includes *16. Meruit esse hostia* and *06. Beatus uir Laurentius*, which are used as 'monastic' additions Types I and II. The three supplementary 'monastic' chants in Type III are *05. Beatus Laurentius dixit ego me obtuli*, *10. Gaudeo plane*, and *04. Beatus Laurentius dixit domine*.

Superimposed over all three types are *ordines* from houses associated

---

[70] It is also found in a rhymed Office of St Lawrence printed in *Analecta hymnica* 26, no. 82.

with three different Continental monastic reform movements: Cluny, Bec, and the houses reformed by William of Dijon (here represented by Fécamp). Typical of Cluny and Bec is *12. Hic est uir*. The difference between the two is that Bec adds this responsory to a Type II *ordo* (+*18*); Cluny adds it to a Type III *ordo* (−*18*), rearranged to begin *15–20*. *12. Hic est uir* is also found in *H* and *R*, but not through any obvious Bec or Cluny influence.

Féc does not use *12. Hic est uir*. William of Dijon seems to have accepted a Type I *ordo* identical to the ninth-century series in *A44*. If anything is distinctive about the *ordo* of *Féc* (and presumably also of *Cht*), it is the use of *4. Beatus Laurentius dixit domine* in final position. This responsory occurs twenty-three times in the table (twenty-four if it is one of the indistinguishable incipits in *Flr*), and it is found in *ordines* of each type. Only in *Féc* and *Cht* (which on other liturgical occasions seems to reflect the strong influence of Fécamp-type *ordines*), is it found in final position. Responsories of special significance often seem to be placed as the last responsory of the third nocturn.[71] The last responsory of each nocturn includes the *Gloria patri* (in its short form) in addition to a verse, requiring an extra *repetendum*. The final responsory of the third nocturn is especially prominent because it is followed not by further psalmody or readings, but by the solemn chanting of the *Te deum*, the Gospel of the day, and the Benedictine hymn *Te decet laus*. *04. Beatus Laurentius dixit domine* is also found in final position in *H*, but this manuscript, although arranged for a monastic *cursus* of psalmody, assumes the use of a secular system of nine readings and responsories, so this responsory should probably be considered supernumerary here, as also in *A44*. *04. Beatus Laurentius dixit domine* seems all the more distinctive in *Féc* because it is absent from *ordines* influenced by Cluny and Bec (*Alb*, *Bec*, *BnR*, *Clu*, *Cor2*, *OuR*, and *F*).

A further distinction between the three reformed Continental groups can be made with *06. Beatus uir Laurentius*. This responsory is absent from *ordines* associated with Bec and William of Dijon, but it is present in *Clu* and its derivatives. This is probably because the Cluny series is based on a Type III *ordo*. The monastic Type III *ordines* of the Corbie/Mont-Renaud type (*Brn*, *Cdm*, *Cor1*, *D*, *MoR*, *Pet*, *Ely*, and *Wor*) tend to put *06. Beatus uir Laurentius* in final position, and where it is absent this is probably because of a later substitution (as with *Ely* and *Wor*).

---

[71] See Hughes, *Medieval Manuscripts for Mass and Office*, p. 63.

Cluny and Bec influence is also evident in certain *ordines* that do not necessarily use the chants typical of *Clu* and *Bec*. Both *Gnt* and *Hyd* make use of the Type III (-18) repertory of chants in an arrangement evidently based on *Clu*, but without the distinctive Cluny chant *12. Hic est uir*. Both instead retain *04. Beatus Laurentius dixit domine*, excluded from true Cluny *ordines*. *Alb* appears to be a conflation of the Bec and Cluny patterns, beginning like *Clu*, but ending like *Bec*.

The distinctions within the reformed Continental *ordines* and the distinction between these and the monastic Type III group can be neatly summarized based on the presence or absence of four chants:

	R18	R12	R04	R06
Fécamp (Type I)	+	−	+	−
Bec (Type II)	+	+	−	−
Cluny (Type III)	−	+	−	+
Corbie/Mont-Renaud (Type III)	−	−	+	+

I do not know what to make of the fact that *18* and *06* are mutually exclusive, as are *12* and *04*. It must also be acknowledged that the definition given for Fécamp is sufficient only to differentiate it from other Continental reformed types (Bec and Cluny), and not from Type I *ordines* in general. The *ordo* in *L*, for instance, could be classed as $+18, -12, +4, -16$, but it is patently not related to *Féc*. Furthermore, the sources considered have not yielded an example of a non-Bec Type II monastic *ordo*, except possibly *H* and *R*; these differ from the expected Type II pattern in lacking *10. Gaudeo plane*. *H* is, in any case, not really monastic in its responsory *ordines*.

Two further responsories require comment. *05. Beatus Laurentius dixit ego me obtuli* is found in all the monastic sources save *S* and *L* (it is uncertain whether this is one of the two responsories in *Flr* identified only as *Beatus Laurentius*; there is a lacuna at this point in *Cht*). It is absent from all the secular series, found only as a supernumerary responsory in *C* and *A44*. This is probably best identified as a 'monastic' responsory, one of three necessary to bring a secular series of nine responsories to the full monastic requirement of twelve. Its presence in *A44* and *C* indicates that it was already in circulation in the middle or late ninth century, perhaps composed in the circle of Benedict of Aniane. The same is probably true of *16. Meruit esse hostia*, found in all monastic sources except *Mch*, *H*, and *R* (there is a lacuna in *Cht*); it was almost certainly included in an earlier recension of the *Mch ordo*, replaced after the Conquest by *08. Concede nobis*. It would seem, therefore, that the only real variation in the selection of the three necessary 'monastic' responsories is to be found in the selection of either *4. Beatus Laurentius dixit domine* or *6. Beatus uir Laurentius*. Non-Cluniac Type III *ordines*, which all lack *18. O Hippolyte*, use them both. This requires that one of the 'monastic' set '*04, 05, 06, 16*' was in fact part of the underlying Type III secular series; though there is the intriguing possibility that Type III is based on an original Roman festal *ordo* of only eight responsories that assumed the use of the *Te deum* directly after the ninth lesson. This limited set of possibilities ignores the potential significance of the *unica* found in certain sources.

With this understanding of how the Continental sources behave, several different strands of Continental influence may be discerned in the English sources. Four follow the *ordo* of the Corbie/Mont-Renaud group (*Cor1, MoR, D*) exactly, or nearly so (*Brn, Pet, Ely, Wor*). *Hyd* also seems originally to have followed this pattern. It was probably revised after the Conquest to look like a Cluny *ordo*, but without making use of distinctive Cluny chants. Of these five, three are houses founded or reformed by Æthelwold: Peterborough, Ely, and the New Minster, Winchester (later relocated to Hyde Abbey). As has already been seen,[72] Worcester seems at some early stage to have adopted Winchester models for at least part of its Office liturgy. The eleventh-century fragment *Brn* has not previously been localized.[73] There is little reason to doubt that these *ordines* reflect the liturgical activities of Æthelwold, who used Corbie as a model.[74] The influence of post-Conquest reforms is seen in *Alb*, which imitates both Bec and Cluny. *Cht* seems to follow the use of Fécamp (though its missing leaves preclude any definite conclusions). *Mch* is independent of influence from Æthelwold and the Cluniac sources. It is based on the same Type I secular series found in *A44*. This secular series is almost the same as that of *Cbr*, which differs only by inverting responsories *10* and *13*. The *Vst* series is a monastic expansion of *Cbr*: responsories *05* and *23* were inserted to form the end of the second nocturn, and responsory *16* was placed in penultimate position in the third nocturn. *Mch* simply has a set of monastic responsories added at the end of the secular series. The added chants in *Mch* are *05, 06*, and *08*, though, as has already been suggested, the original last responsory was probably *16*, only replaced by *08. Concede nobis* some time after the Conquest. Responsories *05*,

---

[72] See p. 283 above.
[73] But see the section 'The evidence of Burney 277', beginning on p. 329 below.
[74] See p. 167 above.

06, and *16* probably ought to be considered 'standard' Western monastic additions.

The fragment under consideration, *Rwl*, may now be situated in its wider English and European contexts. The series of responsories in *Rwl* is of Type I. Like *Mch*, it is based on the same secular series as that found in *A44*, and is apparently independent of the Æthelwold group (Corbie/Mont-Renaud). *Rwl* has four additional chants after the secular nine, yielding a supernumerary thirteenth responsory. All four of these additional chants (*04, 05, 16, 06*) are 'standard' extra monastic chants in the repertory assembled in Table 9.2. It is nevertheless possible to be more specific about how the monastic series in *Rwl* was created.

As was already mentioned in under the heading of 'Liturgical contents and book type' (beginning on page 313 above), the scribe of *Rwl* usually copied only the incipit of the refrain of each responsory, always giving the verse in full, followed by a *repetendum* cue. Complete refrain texts are given, however, for three responsories: *04. Beatus Laurentius orauit et dixit domine* (*Rwl*'s text differs from most sources here), *16. Meruit esse hostia*, and *06. Beatus uir Laurentius*. The *Rwl* series can be illustrated as follows, marking with asterisks those responsories whose refrains are given only as incipits, and marking with bold typeface those refrains given in full:

21* 17* 18* 15* 22* 2* 20* 13* 10* **4** 5* **16 6**

It is possible to imagine a number of reasons why these particular responsories might have been written in full. The scribe might, for example, have wanted to correct a textual error that had crept into the performance practice of his monastery. And of course it is possible that the scribe was simply following an eccentric exemplar. But two facts suggest another, more probable interpretation. First, the refrains given in full are always found, at least in the Western monastic traditions examined above, as monastic supplements to existing secular *ordines*. Second, there are three chants treated this way, the same number required to turn a secular responsory series into a monastic one. It would appear, therefore, that the three chants given in full were previously unknown in the liturgical tradition of the house where *Rwl* was written or used, and that they were added to an existing secular *ordo* to create a monastic *ordo* for the feast of St Lawrence. The Type I secular series to which they were added seems already to have had one supernumerary responsory (*05. Beatus Laurentius dixit ego me obtuli*). The presence of a supernumerary responsory is unsurprising, given that only two of the eight secular *ordines* listed in Table 9.2 lack supernumerary chants.

It seems significant that the three additional chants correspond exactly to the final three responsories in the Corbie/Mont-Renaud *ordines* (*16–04–06*). As has already been observed, it is unlikely that these were the 'monastic' additions to the secular *ordo* (found in *Par*) underlying the Corbie/Mont-Renaud monastic group. But if the scribe of *Rwl* had available to him a book of Office chants of the Corbie/Mont-Renaud type, these three chants would have been the only ones not familiar to him. It is very attractive, if necessarily speculative, to imagine that the scribe of *Rwl* was changing the secular responsory series previously used in his community into a monastic series by referring to a monastic antiphoner from one of Æthelwold's reformed houses. If this is what happened, it is interesting to see that the compiler of *Rwl* was not concerned to follow an 'authoritative' Benedictine exemplar procured from the Continent and approved by Æthelwold, but instead took what he needed from it, adding supplementary chants to the existing repertory already in use in his monastery.

The evidence of Burney 277

By a happy coincidence there has survived a fragment from another Anglo-Saxon chant book with responsories for the feast of St Lawrence, preserved in a guardbook, BL Burney 277, fols. 69–72 (cited in the tables above as *Brn*). This fragment is deserving of a full study in its own right. Nevertheless, it is useful for purposes of comparison with Rawl. D. 894, and for understanding the post-Conquest adaptations to which Anglo-Saxon Office *ordines* could be subjected. A brief discussion of it here will suffice for these purposes. A complete transcription of the text of the fragment has been given in Appendix D.

The four leaves preserved in Burney 277 are two disjunct bifolia from what was apparently a complete Office antiphoner, notated throughout in Insular neumes. A large part of folio 69 in the Burney guardbook was cut out, but this piece survives in BL Stowe 1061 (fol. 125), an album of clippings and hand-drawn facsimiles.[75] The collector of the Stowe 1061

---

[75] The leaves in Burney 277 are noted only as 'fragmenta varia' in J. Forshall, *Catalogue of Manuscripts in the British Museum,* new ser. 1.2: *The Burney Manuscripts* ([London], 1840), p. 72. The Burney 277 and Stowe 1061 are connected in Gneuss, *Handlist,* no. 307.2. Hartzell, *Catalogue,* pp. 232–5 (no. 127), gives a detailed description and puts the fragment at Christ Church, Canterbury, s. xi¹.

clipping was interested primarily in its musical notation, writing above it the title 'Musical Notes before the Invention of the Gamut by Guido Aretine'. The correct order of the leaves is 71–72 and 70–69. There was originally intervening material between the two bifolia, which are labelled *Bifolium A* and *Bifolium B* in the transcription in Appendix D.

The original text hand of Burney 277 is an Anglo-Caroline minuscule similar to that used by scribes working at Christ Church, Canterbury, in the first quarter of the eleventh century. It lacks the 'monumental' aspect of the Style I hands associated with Winchester, but it is also rounder and more upright than Style II examples from St Augustine's. It is notable for its use of the **r**+**a** ligature, which is, as has been seen, favoured in Christ Church hands.[76] Other interesting features are a 2-shaped **r** following **o**, **e**-caudata with a tiny loop,[77] and, in particular, a way of writing the *nomen sacrum* (IHU, IHC) sometimes seen as distinctive of the script of the famous Christ Church scribe 'Eadwig Basan', though this fragment is not his work and is of a somewhat earlier aspect.[78] A similar hand, in what might be a somewhat earlier style, is seen in Trinity College B. 4. 27 (141), fols. 16r–20r, copied by T. A. M. Bishop's 'scribe v'.[79] The main difference between 'scribe v' and the Burney hand is the preference of 'scribe v' to write tall **s** as a slight descender. In Burney 277, both **s** and **r** sit squarely on the baseline.

The first bifolium has chants for the Commemoration of St Paul (30 June), the Ordering and Translation of St Martin (4 July), and the Translation of St Benedict (11 July). These last two give the fragment a monastic character, apart from its use of the Benedictine Office. All the chants for Martin and Benedict are given in incipit, whereas the chants for other feasts are given in full. This might indicate the recycling of propers from the main feast days of the two saints. An early eleventh-century kalendar from Christ Church marks the Translation of St Martin as a feast of twelve lessons, and distinguishes the Translation of St Benedict with capital letters.[80] The second bifolium has chants for St Lawrence (10 August) and St Hyppolitus (13 August). Considering only the responsories

[76] As in 'gratiam' (fol. 71r line 8); 'tiranno' (fol. 70r line 6); 'ministrabant', 'cratem' (fol. 70r line 11); 'Liberabo' (fol. 70r line 17); 'gratias' (fol. 70v line 8). There is also an interesting **rr**+**a** in 'enarrant' (fol. 70r line 9).
[77] 'Ceļi', fol. 71r line 9.
[78] Dumville, *English Caroline Script*, p. 130; see fol. 71r line 17.
[79] Bishop, 'Notes VII', pp. 416–17.
[80] BL Arundel 155, fols. 2–7 (Christ Church, Canterbury, 1012–23), ed. Wormald, *English Kalendars*, pp. 170–81, at p. 176.

for St Lawrence, it will be clear from Table 9.3 that *Brn ordo* is identical to that of the Corbie/Mont-Renaud group. This agreement extends to the selection of responsory verses, as may be seen in Table 9.2. Perhaps significantly, *D* differs from *Cor1* and *MoR* in its verse assignment for *06. Beatus ... qui post aurum*. This is one of only a few examples of divergence between these sources, which are, as was seen in Chapter 8, frequently identical. The exemplar of *Brn* may have been related to the same Corbie exemplar from which the breviary fragment in BL Royal 17. C. XVII (*Roy*), discussed in Chapter 8, is probably derived. Compared with each other, *Rwl* and *Brn* illustrate the choices that were available to reformed Anglo-Saxon monks in establishing a strict Benedictine Office liturgy. Whereas the St Lawrence *ordo* in *Rwl* was evidently constructed by combining an already existing secular *ordo* with three supplementary 'monastic' responsories (perhaps derived from a Corbie source), the *ordo* in *Brn* has been taken wholesale from the Corbie model that circulated in houses affiliated with Æthelwold.

Several marginal additions to the Burney fragment illustrate how the *ordines* preserved in the surviving thirteenth- and fourteenth-century English breviaries and antiphoners arose through the modification over time of *ordines* first established in the Anglo-Saxon period, a process that can normally be deduced only through comparative analysis of the later medieval sources. The responsory *Concede nobis domine* (no. 08 in Tables 9.2 and 9.3; no. 58 in the transcription) is added across the lower margins of Burney fol. 70v and Stowe fol. 125v (the inner opening of the second bifolium) in a twelfth-century hand, with heighted neumatic notation. This responsory is found in three other English sources (*Ely*, *Hyd*, and *Mch*), always as the final responsory of the third nocturn. The refrain of the responsory is clearly based on two Mass collects, one for the feast of St Lawrence, and the other for Monday in the first week of Lent:

Responsory

Concede nobis quesumus domine uitiorum flammas extinguere nostrorum qui sancto ac beatissimo tribuisti Laurentio tormentorum incendia superare suorum. ℣. Aspice domine infirmitates nostras et da nobis locum penitentie atque celeri pietate succurre.

(Grant to us we pray, O Lord, that we may extinguish the flames of our vices, just as you conferred on the holy and blessed Lawrence that he might overcome the fires of his torments. ℣. Consider our infirmities, O Lord, and give us a place of penitence, and in your kindness make haste to help us.)

Collect for St Lawrence

Da nobis, quaesumus, omnipotens deus, uitiorum nostrorum flammas extinguere, qui beato laurentio tribuisti, tormentorum suorum incendia superare.[81]

(Give to us we pray, O almighty God, that we may extinguish the flames of our vices, just as you conferred on the blessed Lawrence that he might overcome the fires of his torments.)

Collect for Monday in the First Week of Lent

Vide domine infirmitates nostras et celeri nobis pietate succurre.[82]

(See our infirmities, O Lord, and in your kindness make haste to help us.)

In *Brn*, the responsory is labelled 'XII' and is given a doxology (*Gloria patri*), showing that it was to be used as the final responsory of the third nocturn, which is where it is found in the three later medieval English monastic breviaries. The alteration in *Brn* produces an *ordo* identical to that in the thirteenth-century Ely breviary. *Ely* contains several other chants found as marginal additions in *Brn* (see nos. 1, 2, 9, and 14 in the transcription) that are not found together in other surviving English sources or in electronic liturgical databases. Precedent for the preparation of an Ely liturgical book at Christ Church might be sought in the 'Missal of Robert of Jumièges'. A sacramentary apparently copied from a Peterborough or Ely exemplar (perhaps a conflation of the two), probably not by a scribe of either house, its execution has been placed at Christ Church by David Dumville.[83]

The presence of *Concede nobis* in *Ely* and *Hyd* might be explained by Lanfranc's appointment of Simeon of Saint-Ouen as prior of Winchester and abbot of Ely.[84] But the chant is absent from the Saint-Ouen breviary itself (*OuR*), and this solution does not explain why it is also found in *Mch*. Moreover, the Ely kalendar in the Missal of Robert of Jumièges gives no hint that proper chants were used for the Translation of St Martin.[85]

---

[81] *Le Sacramentaire grégorien*, ed. Deshusses I, 258 (no. 645).

[82] *Liber sacramentorum Augustodunensis*, ed. O. Heiming, CCSL 159B (Turnhout, 1984), no. 1363. Cf. *Le Sacramentaire grégorien*, ed. Deshusses I, 331 (no. 956), which has 'caelebri' for 'celeri'.

[83] Rouen, Bibliothèque municipale 274 (*olim* Y. 6). Dumville, *English Caroline Script*, pp. 118–19.

[84] Knowles, *The Monastic Order*, p. 113.

[85] *The Missal of Robert of Jumièges*, ed. H. A. Wilson, HBS 11 (London, 1896), p. 15.

Depending on their contents, the partial survivals of two late breviaries from Christ Church, which have not formed part of the comparison pool for this study, might bolster the case for a Christ Church provenance for *Brn*.[86] Whatever the origin and provenance of *Brn*, recognizing *Concede nobis* as a post-Conquest innovation strengthens the possibility that *Rwl* and *Mch* originally had identical responsory *ordines* for St Lawrence. The evidence of the antiphons for the Night Office of St Lawrence makes this connection even more likely, and it is to these that we now turn.

Night Office antiphons

In addition to the great responsories for St Lawrence, *Rwl* also has a complete list of cues for psalm antiphons in the first two nocturns. Like the responsories, the antiphons may be used for a supplementary repertorial comparison to confirm and refine the conclusions already reached. Table 9.4 (beginning on page 345) records a repertory of thirty-two Night Office antiphons in twenty-four sources, including *Rwl*. Excluded are the nine secular sources, which all have identical *ordines*, and *Brn*, which lacks Night Office antiphons for St Lawrence.

Although many of the Night Office antiphons have verses in the various sources, there is not enough variety in verse assignments to allow a statistically significant comparison, so the verses are disregarded in Table 9.4. An exception is made for antiphons *04* and *05*, which have the identical antiphon text *Beatus Laurentius dixit* (with occasional textual variants among the sources) and which are distinguishable only by the use of a different verse. Both appear in *Cor1*. The eight secular sources given in Tables 9.2 and 9.3 (*C, B, E, M, V, A44, Cbr, Par*; lacuna in *G*) all use the same set of nine antiphons divided equally over three nocturns: *27–22–23, 04–11–03, 29–16–17*. These antiphons are found universally within the monastic *ordines*, with occasional variations in order. A full monastic Sunday or festal *ordo* requires thirteen antiphons: six for the first nocturn, six for the second, and a single antiphon for the third nocturn. As has already been noted, *Rwl* supplies antiphons for only the first and second nocturns. Outside the 'Cluny' group, there is considerable diversity among the sources in the choice of the *antiphona ad cantica*. This raises the possibility that the use of a proper antiphon in the third nocturn was a

---

[86] Canterbury, Chapter Library, Add. 3 (16 leaves of a breviary of s. xvi); and Add. 6 (the 'Burnt Breviary', fragmented remains of a breviary of s. xiv²). David Chadd's investigations have shown them usually to agree with other English Office books influenced by Corbie.

comparatively late development, at least for the feast of St Lawrence.

It is not necessary to consider every detail of the antiphon *ordines* in Table 9.4. It will suffice to point out some of the connections and distinctions revealed here that were not apparent from the responsories alone. Some of the English monastic books that were strongly aligned with the Corbie/Mont-Renaud group in their responsories are seen here to reflect in varying degrees the influence of Bec, Cluny, and William of Dijon (*Cdm, Ely, Hyd, Wor*). Whereas the responsory *ordines* of *Mch, Vst, Féc*, and *L* were hard to distinguish on purely objective grounds, their antiphon *ordines* are very distinctive.

Most important, the antiphons in *Rwl* are identical to those in *Mch*. Identical in repertory and order, the two *ordines* are distinguished from the rest of the sources in Table 9.4 by their use of *19. Laurentius bonum opus*. This chant is not unique to these sources; it is used as the second antiphon at Lauds in many manuscripts, including five of the *CAO* monastic sources (all except *S*).[87] The use of *19. Laurentius bonum opus* as a Night Office psalm antiphon, however, is very rare. In the CANTUS Database, only one source imitates this practice, the Aquitanian antiphoner Toledo, Biblioteca capitular, 44.1 (Sant Sadurni de Tavèrnoles, *c.*1020–3). The rest of the *ordo* in Toledo 44.1 differs from *Rwl* and *Mch* in significant ways, so it should not be construed as directly related. But whatever sources were consulted in the creation of the unusual *ordo* in *Rwl* and *Mch*, they were obviously different from the Corbie exemplar promoted in Æthelwold's houses. This affirms a special relatedness between *Rwl* and *Mch* that was already suggested by their responsories. This relationship cannot be further explored through comparison of antiphon verses, since *Mch* never gives verses for antiphons. The two sources are further linked, however, by the use of the minority reading *Beatus Laurentius orabat dicens* in antiphon *04*.

Conclusions

Rwl may be localized on palaeographical grounds to St Augustine's, Canterbury. It seems to have been copied relatively early in the history of the Caroline minuscule script as it was practised in the St Augustine's scriptorium. Precisely when in the tenth century this script began to be

---

[87] Hesbert, *CAO* II, 524–5 (§ 103c). The trimming of the foot of fol. 63r makes it impossible to know whether the antiphon was repeated at Lauds in *Rwl*.

used there is uncertain. The fragment looks, on first inspection, like an old-fashioned antiphoner in which chants are given only in incipit. Certain aspects of *Rwl* (its use of incipits, its grouping of words, and the need to replace verse texts) could point to a very old exemplar, perhaps of eighth- or early ninth-century Frankish derivation. The inclusion of a few full texts, however, suggests the expansion of an existing repertory from an outside source. The three responsories for St Lawrence that are copied in full may derive ultimately from a Corbie Office book, probably via the liturgical manuscripts of one of Bishop Æthelwold's reformed houses. These responsories, considered alongside the unusual set of psalms for the Night Office of St Lawrence, give *Rwl* the appearance of a secular antiphoner that has been supplemented and reorganized according to the Benedictine *cursus*. The Continental tradition to which this secular antiphoner belonged has yet to be determined. The omission of an antiphon for the three canticles of the third nocturn could further indicate that this reorganization was carried out with studied deference to the text of the *Regula S. Benedicti* itself, rather than to prevailing Continental reformed monastic practice. *Rwl* should probably be seen as an intermediate step between an old antiphoner of St Augustine's, which must have been arranged for the secular Office, and a planned complete monastic antiphoner, for which *Rwl* would have been a preliminary sketch. Neither the old nor the new antiphoner has survived, but the existence of both seems to be implied by the character of *Rwl*. The compiler of *Rwl* must have had considerable liturgical and musical knowledge, and the authority to devise a new antiphoner for his monastery. This points to the cantor of St Augustine's, if not the abbot himself.

Table 9.2 Responsories for the feast of St Lawrence (arrangement 1)

The following table lists the responsories, with their verses, provided for the Night Office of the feast of St Lawrence in 37 sources. Each verse is followed by the sigla of all the sources that include that pairing of responsory and verse in their Palm Sunday *ordines*.

Each siglum is followed by a number showing where the responsory occurs in that source (e.g. *Mch* 3 means the third responsory in the St Lawrence *ordo* of *Mch*). If a source does not indicate a verse, its siglum is given under the heading 'No verse'. An asterisk indicates that only the first few words of the responsory are given in a source.

Sigla are printed in the following order:

>   English monastic:
>   *Roy Brn Alb Cdm Cht Ely Hyd Mch Pet Wor Yor-M*
>   Continental monastic:
>   *Bec BnR Clu Cor1 Cor2 Féc Flr Gnt MoR OuR Vst H R D F S L*
>   Continental secular:
>   *A44 Cbr Par C G B E M V*

Notes
Cht is missing 9 responsories due to lost leaves.
Flr gives only incipits. Its fourth and sixth responsories are both given as *Beatus Laurentius**, the opening words of ℟.s 2, 3, 4, and 5, and therefore its siglum is followed by a question mark in each of these responsories.
H provides only 11 responsories.

1 Beati Laurentii interuentio
   Verse Floribus roseis
   L 12

2 Beatus Laurentius…deum meum
   Verse Mea nox
   Rwl 6 *Brn* 5 *Alb* 6 *Cdm* 5 *Ely* 5 *Hyd* 5 *Mch* 6 *Pet* 5 *Wor* 5
   BnR 5 *Clu* 8 *Cor1* 5 *Cor2* 8 *Féc* 6 *Gnt* 8 *MoR* 5 *OuR* 5 *Vst* 6
   H 7 *R* 6 *D* 5 *F* 7 *S* 7 *L* 5 *A44* 6 *Cbr* 6 *Par* 5 *C* 6 *B* 6 *E* 6 *M* 6
   V 6
   No verse *Bec* 5* *Flr* ?

Continued on next page

Table 9.2 (continued)

3 **Beatus Laurentius…disce miser**
   Verse A Beatus Laurentius dum
     E 12
   Verse B Ecce miser
     V 12
   Verse C Probasti
     M 10a
   Verse D Carnifices
     M 10b
   No verse *Flr* ?

4 **Beatus Laurentius…domine**
   Verse A Gratias tibi ago
     Rwl 10 *Brn* 11 *Cdm* 11 *Cht* 12 *Ely* 11 *Hyd* 11 *Pet* 11 *Wor* 11
     Cor1 11 *Gnt* 11 *MoR* 11 *H* 11 *R* 10 *D* 11 *B* 7 *V* 9
   Verse B Transiens autem
     Féc 12 *S* 10 *L* 10 *A44* 12
   No verse *Flr* ?

5 **Beatus Laurentius…ego me obtuli**
   Verse A Quoniam ad te
     H 10 *R* 7 *C* 12a
   Verse B Gaudeo plane
     Rwl 11 *Brn* 8 *Alb* 12 *Cdm* 8 *Ely* 8 *Hyd* 8 *Mch* 10 *Pet* 8
     Wor 8 *BnR* 12 *Clu* 6 *Cor1* 8 *Cor2* 6 *Féc* 11 *Gnt* 6 *MoR* 8
     OuR 12 *Vst* 7 *D* 8 *F* 8 *A44* 11
   Verse C Gratias tibi ago
     C 12b
   No verse *Bec* 12* *Flr* ?

6 **Beatus uir Laurentius qui post aurum**
   Verse A Qui potuit transgredi
     Cdm 12 *R* 11 *D* 12 *F* 6 *B* 9
   Verse B Hic est uere martyr
     Rwl 13 *Brn* 12 *Mch* 11 *Pet* 12 *Cor1* 12 *MoR* 12 *Par* 9 *C* 14
   Verse C Potuit enim transgredi
     Clu 7 *Cor2* 7* *Gnt* 7

Continued on next page

Table 9.2 (continued)

7 **Beatus uir qui inuentus**
   Verse Potuit enim transgredi
   E 11

8 **Concede nobis**
   Verse Aspice domine
   Brn 12 *Ely* 12 *Hyd* 12 *Mch* 12
   In *Brn Concede nobis* is added in the margin by a later hand and labelled as the twelfth responsory.

9 **Festa dies mundo**
   Verse Quo uirtute
   Wor 12

10 **Gaudeo plane**
   Verse A Ego me obtuli
   Rwl 9 *Brn* 9 *Alb* 10 *Cdm* 9 *Ely* 9 *Hyd* 9 *Mch* 9 *Pet* 9 *Wor* 9
   BnR 10 *Clu* 9 *Cor1* 9 *Cor2* 9 *Féc* 9 *Gnt* 9 *MoR* 9 *OuR* 10
   Vst 10 *D* 9 *F* 9 *S* 8 *L* 6 *A44* 9 *Cbr* 8
   Verse B Probasti
   C 9 *M* 9 *V* 11
   Verse C Gratias tibi ago
   E 9
   No verse *Bec* 10* *Flr* 11*

11 **Hic est martyr**
   No verse *Flr* 10*

12 **Hic est uir**
   Verse A Iste est
   H 8b *C* 11 *E* 10
   Verse B Armis diuinis
   Alb 8 *BnR* 8 *OuR* 8*
   Verse C Iste sanctus
   Clu 11 *Cor2* 11 *F* 11
   Verse D Probasti
   Bec 8* *H* 8a *R* 9

Continued on next page

Table 9.2 (continued)

13 In craticula
   Verse A Probasti
   Brn 7 *Cdm* 7 *Ely* 7 *Pet* 7 *Wor* 7 *Clu* 12 *Cor1* 7 *Cor2* 12
   MoR 7 *H* 9 *R* 12 *D* 7 *Par* 7 *C* 7 *B* 8 *E* 7 *M* 7 *V* 10
   B Accusatus
   Rwl 8 *Alb* 9 *Hyd* 7 *Mch* 8 *BnR* 5 *Féc* 8 *OuR* 6 *Vst* 12 *F* 12
   S 12 *L* 9 *A44* 8 *Cbr* 9
   No verse *Bec* 6* *Flr* 12*

14 Laurea Laurenti praeclari
   Verse Uictrici tota caeli
   Gnt 12
   Laurea Laurenti praeclari is also found in a rhymed Office printed in *Analecta hymnica* 26, no. 82.

15 Leuita Laurentius
   Verse A Dispersit
   Rwl 4 *Alb* 1 *Cdm* 2 *Ely* 1 *Hyd* 1b (for ferial days) *Mch* 4
   Pet 1 *Wor* 1 *BnR* 1 *Cor1* 1 *Cor2* 1 *Féc* 4 *Gnt* 1 *MoR* 1
   OuR 1 *H* 1 *R* 1 *D* 1 *F* 1? *S* 4 *L* 8 *Cbr* 4 *Par* 1 *C* 1 *B* 1 *E* 1
   M 1 *V* 1
   Verse B Cum apud sedem
   Hyd 1a *Clu* 1 *Vst* 4 *A44* 4
   No verse *Brn* [1] *Bec* 1* *Flr* 4*

16 Meruit esse hostia
   Verse A In craticula
   Rwl 12 *Brn* 10 *Alb* 11 *Cdm* 10 *Ely* 10 *Hyd* 10 *Pet* 10 *Wor* 10
   BnR 11 *Clu* 10 *Cor1* 10 *Cor2* 10 *Gnt* 10 *MoR* 10 *OuR* 11
   D 10 *F* 10 *Par* 8 *C* 10 *V* 8
   Verse B Ecce enim transiuit
   Féc 10 *Vst* 11 *S* 9 *L* 11 *A44* 10
   Verse E Ego me obtuli
   BnR 11 (this verse added in the margin)
   No verse *Bec* 11* *Flr* 9*

Continued on next page

Table 9.2 (continued)

17 Noli me derelinquere
  Verse Nos quasi senes
    Rwl 2 *Brn* 3 *Alb* 4 *Cdm* 3 *Cht* 2 *Ely* 3 *Hyd* 4 *Mch* 2 *Pet* 3
    Wor 3 *BnR* 9 *Clu* 4 *Cor1* 3 *Cor2* 4 *Féc* 2 *Gnt* 4 *MoR* 3
    OuR 9 *Vst* 2 *H* 3 *R* 5 *D* 3 *F* 4 *S* 3 *L* 2 *A44* 2 *Cbr* 2 *Par* 3 *C* 5
    B 5 *E* 5 *M* 5 *V* 5
  No verse *Bec* 9* *Flr* 2*

18 O Hippolyte si credis
  Verse A Si dictis
    Rwl 3 *Alb* 5 *Mch* 3 *BnR* 7 *Féc* 3 *OuR* 7 *Vst* 3 *H* 5 *R* 8 *S* 5
    L 3 *A44* 3 *Cbr* 3
  Verse B Dispersit
    C 8 *E* 8 *M* 8 *V* 7
  No verse *Bec* 7* *Flr* 7*

19 Protector tuus
  Verse Liberasti
    C 13

20 Puer meus
  Verse A Donec ponam
    H 4 *R* 2 *C* 2 *B* 2 *E* 2 *M* 2 *V* 2
  Verse B Liberabo te
    Rwl 7 *Brn* 6 *Alb* 2 *Cdm* 6 *Ely* 6 *Hyd* 2 *Mch* 7 *Pet* 6 *Wor* 6
    BnR 2 *Clu* 2 *Cor1* 6 *Cor2* 2 *Féc* 5 *Gnt* 2 *MoR* 6 *OuR* 2 *Vst* 9
    D 6 *F* 2 *S* 2 *L* 7 *A44* 7 *Cbr* 7 *Par* 6
  No verse *Bec* 2* *Flr* 3*

21 Quo progrederis
  Verse Quid in me
    Rwl 1 *Brn* 2 *Alb* 3 *Cdm* 2 *Cht* 1 *Ely* 2 *Hyd* 3 *Mch* 1 *Pet* 2
    Wor 2 *BnR* 4 *Clu* 3 *Cor1* 2 *Cor2* 3 *Féc* 1 *Gnt* 3 *MoR* 2
    OuR 4 *Vst* 1 *H* 2 *R* 4 *D* 2 *F* 3 *S* 1 *L* 1 *A44* 1 *Cbr* 1 *Par* 2 *C* 4
    B 4 *E* 4 *M* 4 *V* 4
  No verse *Bec* 4* *Flr* 1*

Continued on next page

Table 9.2 (continued)

22 Strinxerunt corporis
  Verse A Carnifices
  Rwl 5 *Brn* 4 *Alb* 7 *Cdm* 4 *Ely* 4 *Hyd* 6 *Mch* 5 *Pet* 4 *Wor* 4
  Clu 5 *Cor1* 4 *Cor2* 5 *Féc* 7 *Gnt* 5 *MoR* 4 *OuR* 3 *Vst* 5 *R* 3
  D 4 *F* 5 *S* 6 *L* 4 *A44* 5 *Cbr* 5 *Par* 4 *C* 3b *B* 3 *E* 3 *M* 3 *V* 3
  Verse B Mea nox
  BnR 3 *H* 6
  Verse C Hic est uir
  C 3a
  No verse *Bec* 3* *Flr* 5*

23 Uir inclitus Laurentius
  Verse A Cuius intercessio
  Vst 8 *S* 11

Table 9.3 Responsories for the feast of St Lawrence (arrangement 2)

Numerals denote the texts in Table 9.2.

Type I +18 ordines

+18 Secular Type I

A44	21	17	18	15	22	02	20	13	10	16	05	04
Cbr	21	17	18	15	22	02	20	10	13			

+18 Monastic Type I

Rwl	21	17	18	15	22	02	20	13	10	04	05	16	06
Mch	21	17	18	15	22	02	20	13	10	05	06	08	
Vst	21	17	18	15	22	02	05	23	20	10	16	13	
L	21	17	18	22	02	10	20	15	13	04	16	01	

+18 Type I modified by William of Dijon

Féc	21	17	18	15	20	02	22	13	10	16	05	04
Cht	21	17	—	—	—	—	—	—	—	—	—	04

+18 Idiosyncratic Type I

Flr	21*	17*	20*	15*	22*	?*	18*	?*	16*	11*	10*	13*	
S	21	20	17	15	18	22	02	10	16	04	23	13	

Continued on next page

Table 9.3 (continued)

Type II +18 ordines

+18 Secular Type II

C	15	20	22	21	17	02	13	18	10	16	12	05	19	06
E	15	20	22	21	17	02	13	18	10	12	07	03		
M	15	20	22	21	17	02	13	18	10	03				
V	15	20	22	21	17	02	18	16	04	13	10	03		

−18 Type III secular ordo

Par	15	21	17	22	02	20	13	16	06

−12,+4 Corbie/Mont-Renaud

Cor1	15	21	17	22	02	20	13	05	10	16	04	06
MoR	15	21	17	22	02	20	13	05	10	16	04	06
D	15	21	17	22	02	20	13	05	10	16	04	06
Cdm	15	21	17	22	02	20	13	05	10	16	04	06
Pet	15	21	17	22	02	20	13	05	10	16	04	06
Ely	15	21	17	22	02	20	13	05	10	16	04	08
Wor	15	21	17	22	02	20	13	05	10	16	04	09
Brn	—	21	17	22	02	20	13	05	10	16	04	06

−12 Type III revised to look like Cluny

Gnt	15	20	21	17	22	05	06	02	10	16	04	14
Hyd	15	20	21	17	02	22	13	05	10	16	04	08

Continued on next page

Table 9.3 (continued)

Bec/Cluny revisions of Type II and Type III

+18,+12,−4 Bec

Bec	15	20	22	21	02	13	18	12	17	10	16	05
BnR	15	20	22	21	02	13	18	12	17	10	16	05
OuR	15	20	22	21	02	13	18	12	17	10	16	05

−18,+12,−4 Cluny

Clu	15	20	21	17	22	05	06	02	10	16	12	13
Cor2	15	20	21	17	22	05	06	02	10	16	12	13
F	15	20	21	17	22	06	02	05	10	16	12	13

+18,+12 Conflation of Bec and Cluny

Alb	15	20	21	17	18	02	22	12	13	10	16	05

−10 Ordines (Variant Types II and III)

H	15	21	17	20	18	22	02		12	13	05	04
R	15	20	22	21	17	02	05	18	12	04	06	13
B	15	20	22		21	17	02		04	13	06	

Table 9.4 Night Office antiphons for the feast of St Lawrence

An asterisk denotes an incipit. Key to texts follows on page 347.

+19 St Augustine's (Glastonbury?)

Rwl	27	22	23	04	11	03	29	16	17	08	25	19
Mch	27	22	23	04	11	03	29	16	17	08	25	19	31

+12, +13 Corbie/Mont-Renaud

Cor1	27	22	23	04	11	05	12	13	06	29	16	17	21*
MoR	27	22	23	04	11	03	29	16	17	12	13	06*	26*
D	27	22	23	04	11	03	29	16	17	12	13	06	26
Pet	27	22	23	04	11	03	29	16	17	12	13	06	24

Influenced by Bec/Cluny (+20) or William of Dijon (+01)

Wor	27	22	23	04	11	03	29	16	17	12	13	25	20
Cdm	27	22	23	04	11	03	29	16	17	12	25	20	31
Hyd	27	22	23	04	11	03	29	16	12	01	17	13	20
Ely	27	22	23	04	11	03	29	16	17	01	12	13	06

+20 Cluny/Bec

+20, +21 Cluny

Clu	27	22	23	04	11	03	29	16	17	20	08	28	21
F	27	22	23	04	11	03	29	16	17	20	08	28	21
Cor2	27	22	23	04*	11*	03	29	16	17	12	20	08	21
R	27	22	23	04	11	03	29	16	17	08	14	25	21

Continued on next page

Table 9.4 (continued)

+20, −21 Bec												
BnR	27	22	23	04	11	03	29	16	17	25	31	20	07
OuR	27	22	23	04	11	03	29	16	17	25	20	07	31
Alb	27	22	23	25	11	03	29	16	17	04	07	31	20
−20,+21 Fleury												
Flr	27*	22*	23*	04*	11*	03*	29*	16*	17*	25*	28*	32*	21*
+01, −12, −13 William of Dijon												
Féc	27	22	23	04	11	03	29	16	10	08	01	17	30
Cht	27	22	23	04	11	03	—	—	—	—	—	—	—
Unclassified												
L	27	22	23	25	11	03	16	29	17	08	12	14	02
H	27	22	23	25	04	11	29	16	03	17	08	17	12
Vst	27	22	23	04	11	03	29	16	15*	18*	09	17	—
S	27	22	23	04	11	03	29	16	17	08	25	26	06

Continued on next page

Key to texts in Table 9.4

01 Accusatus non negaui nomen
02 Beatus Laurentius … deum meum
03 Beatus Laurentius … mea nox
04 Beatus Laurentius dixit
 [or orabat or orabat dicens] domine
 ℣. Quia accusatus
05 Beatus Laurentius dixit
 ℣. Gratias tibi ago
 (04 and 05 are both in Cor1)
06 Beatus Laurentius dum in craticula
07 Beatus Laurentius orabat dicens
08 Beatus Laurentius orauit et dixit
09 Beatus quem elegisti
10 Carnifices uero urgentes
11 Dixit Romanus
12 Gratias ago deo meo
13 Gratias tibi ago domine Iesu Christe
14 Gratias tibi ago domine quia ianuas
15 Hic accipiet
16 Igne me examinasti
17 Interrogatus te dominum
18 Laetabitur iustus
19 Laurentius bonum opus
20 Leuita Laurentius bonum opus
21 Nisi granum frumenti
22 Noli me derelinquere
23 Non ego te desero
24 O bone Laurenti martyr
25 O Hyppolite si credis
26 Qui mihi ministrat me sequatur
27 Quo progrederis
28 Si quis mihi ministrauerit
29 Strinxerunt corporis
30 Transiens autem per ignem
31 Ueni desiderator bone
32 Uolo pater

10

Conclusion: Ways of Making a Benedictine Office

It is now possible to offer some answers to the questions posed at the end of Chapter 5, and to reconstruct the process whereby the ninth-century Frankish concept of a distinctive 'monastic' Office based on the Rule of St Benedict was put into practice in England in the tenth century. The two extant fragments from tenth-century English Benedictine Office books reveal two very different approaches to the creation of a Benedictine Office liturgy. In the breviary fragment in BL Royal 17. C. XVII (*Roy*), an Office antiphoner of Corbie was the source for the texts of the chants and their arrangement. We are probably dealing here with a minster reformed through Æthelwold's influence. Traces of Corbie *ordines* in several later medieval English Benedictine breviaries reveal that Æthelwold's approach was widely imitated. The advantages of adopting wholesale a Continental Benedictine antiphoner will have been obvious to any reforming abbot: not only would appropriate antiphons and responsories be made immediately available, but their arrangement would provide a ready-made framework around which to construct a fully Benedictine Office, with the antiphons automatically requiring the Benedictine distribution of the psalms, and the responsories in the festal and Sunday Night Offices demanding the monastic twelve lessons in place of the secular nine. In *Roy*, the use of the *Romanum* version of the psalms, the deliberately crafted scriptural and patristic lessons at the Night Office, and at least one apparently unique collect all illustrate how an existing Continental Benedictine framework, supplied here by a Corbie antiphoner, could be fleshed out with English content.

In the fragmentary chant book in Oxford, Bodleian Library, Rawl. D. 894, a previously existing antiphoner for the secular *cursus* was reorganized and supplemented with new material to make it suitable for the monastic *cursus*. For the structure of the Office, reference seems to have been made primarily to the *Regula S. Benedicti* itself, if the absence of an antiphon for the canticles in the third nocturn of the feast of St Lawrence is any indication. Although supplementary chants seem to have been taken from a Corbie or Abingdon/Winchester source, the resulting *ordines* are independent of any Continental model. Like the eclectic library of manuscripts copied at St Augustine's in the second half of the tenth century, this approach to the Benedictine Office, on its face so different from Æthelwold's, might have taken its 'first impulse from another, perhaps more humane and certainly more comprehensive mind'.[1] While few would now fully accept the traditional caricatures of 'the vigorous, uncompromising Æthelwold, the gentle Oswald, and the super-gentle Dunstan' on which T. A. M. Bishop's characterization of the St Augustine's scriptorium partly depends,[2] we need not reject the possibility that Rawl. D. 894 was produced at Dunstan's instigation or, as it were, in his image.

Both fragments corroborate the evidence assembled in Part I of this book suggesting that the Benedictine *cursus* was introduced to England much later than has normally been assumed. *Roy* cannot pre-date Æthelwold's invitation of singers from Corbie to Abingdon (954×963?). *Rwl* appears to have been designed to assist the introduction of the Benedictine *cursus* to St Augustine's some time in the second half of the tenth century. Both also reveal a tendency to retain existing liturgical traditions wherever this was practical. Æthelwold's recourse to Corbie, as the *Historia ecclesie Abbendonesis* informs us, arose from the 'different manners of reading and singing' practised by his newly assembled flock at Abingdon.[3] An agreed standard was urgently required, and Corbie had a good reputation. But in a minster like St Augustine's, with an uninterrupted history and an existing liturgical tradition, no such external standard would be necessary. The decision whether to follow a Continental model will have depended on the strength of the existing tradition. It cannot be assumed that Æthelwold will always and everywhere have imposed a Corbie antiphoner: if the clerks of the Old Minster had chosen differently and agreed to take the monastic habit, their Office liturgy might well have survived, remade for Benedictine use.

What we mean by an 'existing tradition', however, must account for the chant repertory preserved in the added leaves of Durham, Cathedral Library, A. IV. 19 and the marginal additions in Cambridge, Corpus Christi College 41. Whereas in a previous study I distinguished only be-

---

[1] Bishop, 'Notes IV', p. 323.
[2] E. John, 'The church of Worcester and St Oswald', p. 143.
[3] See p. 167 above.

tween 'early English tradition' and 'tenth-century Continental monastic imports',[4] I would now argue that at some point before the Benedictine reform, perhaps during Alfred's reign, England received a 'Gregorian' (Romano-Frankish) Office chant repertory distinct from the eclectic pre-Gregorian early English chant repertory attested in Alcuin's *De laude Dei*. The repertory in Durham A. IV. 19 and Corpus 41 seems to have originated in a Lotharingian or Bavarian church. While it cannot be proved that the secular antiphoner behind Rawl. D. 894 contained the same repertory, it is striking that both Rawl. D. 894 (in its chants for St Lawrence) and Durham A. IV. 19 and Corpus 41 (in their Advent responsories) seem to be related in some way to the thirteenth-century breviary of Muchelney Abbey, BL Add. 43405 and 43406 (*Mch*). Laurentia McLachlan and J. B. L. Tolhurst regarded *Mch* as a possible witness to 'the old books of Glastonbury', of which, at least in a later period, Muchelney was a dependency.[5] Like other late medieval English breviaries, *Mch* is inconsistent in its repertorial affiliations, and it sometimes aligns itself with Corbie or Norman *ordines*.[6] But the survival of a breviary fragment of the first half of the eleventh century within a cartulary of Muchelney Abbey (BL Add. 56488, fols. i, 1–5) furnishes proof that at least one of the unusual formularies in *Mch* (Lent II) pre-dates the Conquest.[7] It may be possible to separate the chants in *Mch* into several strands: 'Æthelwoldian', Norman, and perhaps, in the background, a German (or even 'Bavarian') core. For example, Muchelney's verse for the Lent II responsory *Si dominus deus* (℣. *Uere dominus est*), unique among the English sources, is also found in the ninth-century Prüm monastic *Chorbuch*, Trier, Stadtbibliothek, 1245/597 (fol. 114v), whose twelve-responsory Benedictine *ordo* for Lent II seems to have been built on the same nine-responsory secular *ordo* that underlies Lent II in *Mch*.[8]

---

[4] Billett, 'The Muchelney Breviary', pp. 16–36.

[5] *The Ordinal and Customary of the Abbey of Saint Mary, York*, ed. L. McLachlan and J. B. L. Tolhurst, 3 vols., HBS 73, 75, 84 (London, 1936–51) III, p. iv. McLachlan and Tolhurst saw in particular a relationship between *Mch* and the Ordinal of St Mary's, York, Cambridge, St John's College D. 27 (*Yor-M*), which they judged to have a special claim to transmit 'the usages of the Anglo-Saxon monasteries of the tenth century' (III, p. iii). St Mary's, York, was colonized in the eleventh century by monks from Winchcombe and Evesham (see Knowles, *The Monastic Order*, pp. 167–71), and *Yor-M* could therefore be imagined to echo the now obscure pre-Conquest liturgy of these houses (*The Ordinal and Customary*, ed. McLachlan and Tolhurst III, p. ii).

[6] Chadd, 'Liturgical books', pp. 58–9, and throughout the tables in his Appendix.

[7] Billett, 'The Muchelney Breviary'.

[8] I make use here of material kindly shared with me, before his death, by David Chadd,

Further investigation of the connection between *Rwl* and *Mch* may also eventually clarify the chronology of the adoption of the Benedictine *cursus* in monasteries affiliated with Dunstan. *Rwl* seems to have been a local solution devised at the precise moment of transition from the secular to the monastic *cursus* at St Augustine's, so similiarities between *Rwl* and *Mch* could also indicate that Muchelney (and therefore perhaps Glastonbury) received its Benedictine Office liturgy from St Augustine's some time after Dunstan became archbishop. The presence in *Mch* of antiphons that Dunstan may have learned in Ghent lends some support to the assertion, already argued from other evidence, that Glastonbury would not have used the Benedictine *cursus* before Dunstan's Continental exile in 956.[9] Another possibility – at this stage purely speculative, but not without promise – is that the relationship between *Rwl* and *Mch* arises instead from their dependence on the same Germanic secular chant repertory, which, if it was first adopted in Wessex through Alfred's court chapel, could have been introduced to Canterbury by Plegmund. The repertory transmitted by Durham A. IV. 19 and Corpus 41 may have had wider influence in England in the pre-Conquest period than extant post-Conquest antiphoners and breviaries would, on first inspection, lead us to believe.

These larger questions go beyond what the evidence so far examined can tell us, and must be postponed until all the surviving fragments of pre-Conquest English Office books have received close study. It is perhaps enough to say that the tenth-century manuscript sources, considered against the historical background traced in the first part of this book, contribute something to our understanding of the true character and signature traits of the English Benedictine reform movement, a movement whose scope and originality are at the moment the subject of intense critical scrutiny and reassessment. In their reform of the Divine Office, which had been at the heart of the religious life in England from the very beginning, the new Benedictines definitively expressed their radical allegiance to the Rule.

---

who collected Lent II *ordines* from all the later English Benedictine sources. The verse *Uere dominus est* is nevertheless widely attested on the Continent – even in the Saint-Denis and Mont-Renaud books (though in the latter only as an incipit before a fully notated alternative, fol. 76v) – so it need not necessarily have arrived at Muchelney through a specifically Germanic channel.

[9] Proposed with extreme caution and qualification in Chadd, 'Liturgical books', pp. 57–9.

Appendix A

Transcription Conventions

Marks in the text

text   The main text hand in the manuscript, Anglo-Saxon Square minuscule or Anglo-Caroline minuscule, is rendered in roman typeface. The orthography of the scribe is followed. If a scribe uses separate letter-forms for **u** and **v**, the distinction is represented in the transcription.

text   Italic typeface indicates the expansion of an abbreviation or contraction (or, when enclosed in angled brackets, text no longer visible but supplied conjecturally).

TEXT   Text printed in all capital letters indicates a rubric written in red uncial or *capitalis* script. *Litterae notabiliores*, whether decorated or merely set apart from the regular text by size or letter form, are also rendered as single capital letters. U is usually transcribed as **V**.

text   Sans serif type indicates letters or words added by a later hand.

99 (99)   Paragraphs are numbered continuously in the left margin beside the text, and referred to in the notes. Marginal numbers enclosed in parentheses refer to other paragraphs in the text where the same text or chant is given.

⟦   A double left bracket marks the beginning of the recto or verso side of a leaf. The number of the new side is printed in the right margin.

[ ]   Scribal deletions (by erasure, crossing out, or expunction) are enclosed within square brackets. Any letters or words still visible are included within the brackets.

⟨ ⟩ Angled brackets enclose any letter, word or part of a word once written by the scribe but no longer visible or only partially visible through damage, trimming, or being hidden in the gutter of a book. Letters or words no longer decipherable but which can still be guessed at from the context are printed in italic typeface. Undecipherable and unguessable letters are represented by single dots, with one dot for each (conjectural) missing letter.

( ) Letters and words that are not, and never were, present in the manuscript, but which should be supplied to help the sense, or to indicate another plausible transcription, are supplied editorially and enclosed in parentheses. Included in this category are liturgical signposts (A̷., R̷., V̷., days of the week, names of offices, etc.) necessary for the identification of texts. Parentheses are also occasionally used to enclose the form of a word as it was corrected by a contemporary or later hand, and to enclose editorial comments, e.g. (*sic*).

⌐ ¬ Interlinear and marginal additions made either by the scribe or a subsequent corrector are enclosed within caret marks.

A̷. Conventional printed abbreviation for *Antiphona*, found in the manuscripts as ã, or ã̄.

Pl., Ps. Several abbreviations for *Psalmus* commonly occur: P̷L, PS, p̃, etc. These are rendered in the transcriptions as either Pl. or Ps., depending on the letters used in the rubricator's preferred abbreviation.

R̷. Conventional printed abbreviation for *Responsorium*, found in the manuscripts as r̃, or something similar. Indicates a great responsory at the Night Office or a short responsory in the day hours (or, rarely, the choral response in a versicle and response).

V̷. Conventional printed abbreviation for *Versiculum*, found in the manuscripts as ũ or ṽ. Indicates the verse of a responsory (or, sometimes, an antiphon), or a short versicle, usually without the following choral reply. Cues following responsory verses to indicate the *repetendum*, the point from which a responsory is repeated after the verse, are printed as they stand in the sources, without comment.

APPENDIX A: TRANSCRIPTION CONVENTIONS

Symbols used in the notes

* An asterisk following a reference to a published edition indicates that the scribe recorded only the first few words of the text. This could indicate that the text is (or was) available in full earlier in the manuscript, that it was already known from memory, or that the text would be supplied from a different book.

CAO References to chants edited in volumes 3 and 4 of Hesbert, *CAO*. A letter following the four-digit reference number indicates the choice of responsory verse, when two or more options are present. The letter X indicates a verse not found with that responsory in *CAO*.

DC Durham, Cathedral Library, A. IV. 19, ed. A. Corrêa, *The Durham Collectar*, HBS 107 (London, 1992). Citations refer to paragraph numbers in Corrêa's edition.

Ha The *Hadrianum* sacramentary, ed. in vol. 1 of J. Deshusses, *Le Sacramentaire grégorien: Ses principales formes d'après les plus anciens manuscrits*, 2nd and 3rd edns, 3 vols., Spicilegium Friburgense 16, 24, 28 (Freiburg, Switzerland, 1988–92). Citations refer to paragraph numbers in Deshusses's edition.

LM Oxford, Bodleian Library, Bodley 579, ed. N. Orchard, *The Leofric Missal*, 2 vols., HBS 113–14 (London, 2002). Citations refer to paragraph numbers in vol. 2. Unless otherwise indicated, citations refer to the original 'A' layer of the manuscript.

1:1–2 Scriptural references are to the chapter and verse divisions in the following editions: **Old Testament** *Biblia sacra iuxta latinam vulgatam versionem ad codicem fidem*, ed. the Monks of the Pontifical Abbey of St Jerome in the City (Rome, 1926–94); **New Testament** *Novum Testamentum Domini nostri Iesu Christi latine secundum editionem S. Hieronymi*, ed. J. Wordsworth, H. J. White, and H. F. D. Sparks (Oxford, 1889–1954); **Psalms** *Le Psautier romain et les autres anciens psautiers latins*, ed. R. Weber, Collectanea biblica latina 10 (Vatican City, 1953).

355

Appendix B

London, British Library, Royal 17. C. XVII, fols. 2, 3, 163–6 (Text)

(FERIA II POST DOMINICA PASSIONIS)

1 ⟦ cont⟨*endam*⟩ uob*iscum* ait d*omi*nu*s* *et cum filiis* ue*s*tris fol. 163r
dis⟨*ceptabo*⟩ Transite ad insulas cethim ⁒ et in cedar mittite ⁒
et co*n*siderate uehem*enter* · et uidete si factu*m* *est* hui*us*cemodi ·
si mutauit gens deos suos ⁒ et certe ipsi n*on* s*un*t dii ; Populus
uero meus · mutauit gl*ori*am sua*m* in idolu*m* ; obstupescite cęli
sup*er* hoc ⁒ et portę ei*us* desolamini uehem*enter* dic*it* d*omi*nu*s* ;

2 ₳. In die magno festiuitatis stabat ie*sus* et clamabat dicens si quis
sitit ⟨ueen ad⟩¹ ad me et bibat ·

3 ₳. Qui sitit ueniat et bibat et de uentre ei*us* fluent aquę uiue ·

FER*IA* III

4 Duo mala fecit populus meus ⁒ me dereliquérunt fonte*m* aquę
uiuę · et foder*unt* sibi cisternas ; cisternas dissipátas ⁒ quę co*n*-
tinere n*on* ualent aquas ; Nu*m*quid seruus e*st* israhel aut uerna-
culus ? quare ergo fact*us* *est* i*n* pr*ed*am ? Sup*er* eu*m* rugier*unt*
leones ⁒ et dederu*nt* uoce*m* sua*m* ; ⌐ hec dicit ¬²

---
¹The text is damaged and difficult to read. The visible text seems to be a garbling of the expected 'ueniat'.
²The words 'Hec dicit', added by a later hand to this and two other lessons (nos. 6 and 47), remind the reader to use an alternative conclusion to the lesson. Readings from scripture in the Office usually conclude with the versicle *Tu autem domine miserere nobis*, to which the choir responds *Deo gratias*. For readings from the Old Testament, however, the final versicle was sometimes *Haec dicit dominus conuertemini ad me et salui eritis* (Isa. 45:22). The inclusion of these practical notes shows that the fragment was probably used by a reader in the performance of the Office.

---
1. Jer. 2:9–12 **2.** *CAO* 3221 **3.** *CAO* 4497 **4.** Jer. 2:13–15a

APPENDIX B: BL ROYAL 17. C. XVII (TEXT)

5   Hec dic*it* d*omi*nus ; Arguat te malitia tua ׃ et auersio tua íncrepet te ׃ et uide quia malu*m* · et amaru*m* e*st* reliquisse te d*omi*nu*m* d*eu*m tuum ׃ et n*on* esse timore*m* e*ius* apud te ; A seculo c*on*fregisti iugu*m* meu*m* ׃ rupisti uincula mea et dixisti · n*on* seruia*m* ;

6   H*ę*c dic*it* d*omi*nus in om*n*i colle sublími · et sub om*n*i ligno frondóso ׃ tu p*ro*sternabaris méretrix ; Ego aute*m* plantaui te uinea*m* ⟨mea*m*⟩ electa*m* om*n*e seme*n* ueru*m* ; quomodo ergo c*on*uersa es ⟨ma.....adine*m*⟩³ ? Si laueris té nitro ׃ et multiplicáueris tibi herba*m* borith ׃ m⟨a⟩culata es in iniquitate tua cora*m* me dicit d*omi*nus (;) ⌐he¬⁴

7   (A̷.) ⟨Vos ascendite ad die*m* festum ego n*on* ascenda*m* quia te*m*p*us* meu*m* n*on*du*m* ad *ue*n*it*⟩

8   ⟨A̷. Quida*m* aute*m* iudei dicebant qu*ia* bonus *est* · Al*ii* aute*m* dicebant *non* sed s*e*ducit t*ur*bas ·⟩

(FERIA IIII)

9   Hec dic*it* d*omi*nus ; quomodo c*on*funditur ⟨fur quando deprehendit*ur* si⌐c¬ c*on*fusi s*unt* d*omus* israhel ; Ipsi⟩ ⟦ ⟨et reges eoru*m*⟩ · principes et sacerdotes et p*ro*ph*ę*t*ę* eoru*m* ׃ dicentes ligno · pater m*eu*s es tu · et lapidi · tu me genuisti ;   fol. 163v

10 Vertert*unt* ad me ait d*omi*nus tergum et n*on* facie*m* ׃ et in te*m*pore afflictionis su*ę* dicent ׃ surge et libera nos ; Vbi s*unt* dii tui quos fecisti tibi ? Surgant et liberent té · secundu*m* numeru*m* eni*m* ciuitatu*m* tuaru*m* · erant dii tui iuda ;

11 Hec dic*it* d*omi*nus ; Quid uultis mecu*m* iudicio ⌐con¬tendere ? Om*n*es dereliquistis me dic*it* d*omi*nus ; Frustra p*er*cussi filios u*es*tros ׃ disciplina*m* n*on* receper*unt* ; Deuorauit gladius uester p*ro*ph*ę*tas uestros · quasi leo uastatur generatio u*es*t*r*a ;

---

³The partly visible text cannot be reconciled with the biblical 'in prauum uinea aliena'.
⁴See note to no. 4

---

5. Jer. 2:19–20a **6.** Jer. 2:20b–22 **7.** *CAO* 5493 **8.** *CAO* 4534 **9.** Jer. 2:26–27a
10. Jer. 2:27b–28 **11.** Jer. 2:29–31a

12 ℟. Oues mee uocem meam audiunt et ego dominus agnosco eas ·

13 ℟. Multa bona opera operatus sum uobis propter quod opus uultis me occidere ·

(FERIA V)

14 Audite uerbum domini · domus iuda ; Numquid solitudo factus sum israheli · aut terra serotina ? Quare ergo dixit populus meus · recessimus non ueniemus ultra ad te ? Numquid obliuiscitur uirgo ornamenti sui · sponsa fascię pectoralis sui ? Populus uero meus ⁖ oblitus est mei diebus innumeris ;

15 (LECTIO) II. Hęc dicit dominus ; Ecce ego iudicio contendam tecum ⁖ eo quod dixeris · non peccaui ; Quam uilis facta és · iterans uias tuas · et ab ęgypto confundéris ⁖ sicut confusa és ab assur ; Nam et ab ista egredieris · et manus tuę erunt super caput tuum · quoniam obtriuit dominus confidentiam tuam · et nihil habebis prosperum ;

16 ⟨V⟩ulgo dicitur si dimiserit uir uxorem suam ⁖ et recedens ab eo duxerit uirum alterum ⟨ ⁖ ⟩ Numquid reuertetur ad eum ultra ? Numquid non polluta et contaminata erit mulier illa ? tu autem fornicata es cum amatoribus mu⟨lti⟩s · tamen reuertere ad me dicit dominus · et ego suscipi⟨am te ; ⟩

17 ⟨℟. Quid m⟩olesti estis huic mulieri opus enim bonum operata est ⟦ (in me ·)   Missing

(*Lacuna*)

(DOMINICA IN RAMIS PALMARVM)

(IN III NOCTVRNO)

18 ⟦ ⟨custodes uenire *de terra longinqua et dare super*⟩ ciuitates iuda   fol. 164r uocem suam ; Quasi custodes agrorum facti sunt super eam in gyro · quia me ad iracundiam prouocauit ait dominus ; Vię tuę · et

---

12. *CAO* 4203 **13.** *CAO* 3827 **14.** Jer. 2:31a–32 **15.** Jer. 2:35b–37 **16.** Jer. 3:1
17. *CAO* 4527 **18.** Jer. 4:16–19

APPENDIX B: BL ROYAL 17. C. XVII (TEXT)

cogitationes tuę fecer*unt* hęc tibi · ista malitia tua ⁊ q*ui*a amara · q*ui*a tetigit cor tuu*m* ; Ventre*m* meu*m* ⁊ uentre*m* meu*m* doleo · sensus cordis mei · turbati s*unt* in me ; N*on* tacebo ⁊ quo*niam* uoce*m* búcinę audiuit anima mea · clamore*m* pr*e*lii ;

19 ℟. Dixer*unt* impii apud se n*on* recte cogitantes circu*m*ueniam*us* iustu*m* quo*niam* co*n*trariu*s* est op*er*ib*us* no*st*ris p*r*omittit se scientia*m* dei habere filiu*m* dei se ⟨n⟩ominat et gloriat*ur* patre*m* se habere de*u*m uideam*us* si sermones illiu*s* ueri sint et si *est* uere filiu*s* dei liberet illu*m* de manib*us* no*st*ris morte t*ur*pissima co*n*dempnem*us* eu*m* · ℣. Viri impii dixer*unt* opprimam*us* uiru*m* iustu*m* iniuste et de spoliis ei*us* sorte*m* mittam*us* · Videam*us* ·

AD CANTICA

20 (A̷.) Magister dic*it* te*m*p*us* meu*m* pr*o*pe *est* apud te facio pascha cu*m* discipulis meis (·)

21 (℣.) Ne p*er*das cu*m* impiis ·

22 LECTIO SANCTI ⟨EVAN⟩GELII SECVNDVM IOHANNEM[5]
In illo te*m*pore · Cu*m* adpr*o*pinquasset hierosolimis ie*sus* ⁊ et uenisset betfagé ad monte*m* oliueti · tunc misit duos discipulos · dicens eis ; Ite in castellu*m* quod co*n*tra uos *est* ⁊ et inuenietis asina*m* alligata*m* · et pullu*m* cu*m* ea · soluite ⁊ et adducite mihi ; et reliqua ;

23 Mediator dei et hominu*m* · homo chri*stu*s ie*sus* fratres ⁊ adpr*o*pinquante hora passionis hierosolima*m* uenit · ut p*er* hoc clarescer⌐e⌐t q*ui*a n*on* inuitus ⁊ sed sponte p*r*o mundi salute paretur ; In asino uenire et a t*ur*bis rex appellari uoluit · ut etia*m* per hoc erudit*us* q*ui*sq*ue* cognosceret ipsu*m* e*ss*e chri*stu*m ⁊ que*m* sic illo uenturu*m* proph*ę*tia olim signabat dicens ; Dicite filię sión · ecce rex tuus uenit ⁊ sedens sup*er* asina*m* et pullu*m* · filiu*m* subiugalis ;

---

[5]The lesson that follows is from Matthew; but see *Regularis concordia*, § 36, ed. Symons p. 35 (CCM § 60, p. 106), where a passage from John is prescribed.

---

19. *CAO* 6464a **20.** *CAO* 3657 **21.** *CAO* 8146* **22.** Matt. 21:1–2 **23.** Bede, Hom. II.3, CCSL 122, p. 200, lines 1, 3, 4–7; Matt. 2:5 (cf. *PL* XCIV, 121)

24 ℟. De*us* israhel *propter* te sustinui in*pr*operiu*m* operuit reue-
rentia*m* facie*m* mea*m* 〚 ⟨*extraneus factus sum fratribus meis* fol. 164v
et hospes filiis matris mee quo*niam* zelus⟩ dom*us* tue comedit
me · (℣.) In*pr*operia in*pr*operantiu*m* tibi cecider*unt* sup*er* me ·
quo*niam* zelus ·

25 Ante quinq*ue* dies pasch*ę* uenit d*omi*n*us* hierosolima*m* · uoluit ut
p*er* hoc ostenderet se esse agnu*m* inmaculatu*m* ⁓ qui peccata tol-
leret mundi ; Agnus quippe paschalis ⁓ cui*us* immolatione populus isr*a*hel · ab ęgyptior*um* seruitute liberat*us* est ⁓ ante q*u*inq*ue*
dies pasch*ę* · id *est* quarta decima luna ad uesperu*m* · iussus *est*
immolari ⁓ significans eu*m* qui nos suo sanguine rede*m*pturus ·
ante q*u*inq*ue* dies pasch*ę* · id *est* hodierna die · magno *pr*ecedenti-
u*m* sequentiu*m*que populor*um* gaudio deductus · uenit in te*m*plu*m*
dei ⁓ et erat cotidie docens in eo ;

(78) **26** ℟. Sinagoge populor*um* circu*m*dederu*nt* me et n*on* reddidi retri-
buentib*us* m*ihi* mala co*n*summet*ur* d*omi*ne nequitia peccator*um*
et diriges iustu*m* · (℣.)⁶ Iudica me d*omi*ne secundu*m* iustitia*m*
mea*m* et secundu*m* innocentia*m* mea*m* sup*er* me · co*n*summet*ur* ·

27 Ergo d*omi*nus instar agni paschal*is* · ante q*u*inq*ue* dies qua*m* pati
incip*er*et locum passionis adiit · ut se insinuaret esse illu*m* · de
quo *pr*edixi*t* esaias ; Sicut ouis ad occisione*m* ducet*ur* ; Asina
et pullus · quib*us* sedens hierosolima*m* uenit · utriusq*ue* populi ⁓
iudaici scilicet et gentilis · simplicia corda designant q*ui*b*us* ipse *pr*esidens · suo frenans imp*er*io ⁓ ad uisione*m* sup*er*nę pacis
introducit ;

(80) **28** ℟. Insurrexer*unt* in me uiri iniqui absq*ue* misericordia quesier*unt*
me i*nter*ficere et n*on* pepercer*unt* in facie*m* mea*m* spuere et lan-
ceis suis uulnerauer*unt* me et co*n*cussa su*nt* om*n*ia ossa mea ego
aute*m* estimaba*m* me ta*m*quam mortuu*m* sup*er* terra*m* · ℣. Et dederunt in esca*m* mea*m* uel et in siti mea potauerunt me aceto · ego
aute*m* ·

---

⁶(℣.)] The rubricator incorrectly wrote ℟.

---

24. *CAO* 6425B **25.** Bede, Hom. II.3; CCSL 122, pp. 200–1, lines 8–18 (cf.
PL XCIV, 121) **26.** *CAO* 7747B **27.** Bede, Hom. II.3; CCSL 122, p. 201,
lines 24–27, 36–39 (cf. *PL* XCIV, 121) **28.** *CAO* 6973A

APPENDIX B: BL ROYAL 17. C. XVII (TEXT)

29 Ad montem igitur oliueti ueniens dominus ⁚ ad exhibenda sibi duo iumenta discipulos misit ut significaret in utrumque populum · circumcisionis scilicet et preputii · predicatores esse destinandos ; ⌜quoque⌝ Pullus ⦃ ⟨*alligatum fuisse alii euangelistae testantur; Uterque enim populus funibus*⟩ peccatorum erat constructus et sollicitudine diuina opus habebat ; Sedet dominus super asinam et pullum filium subiugalis · quia requiescit in corde humilium et quietorum · e⌜ t⌝ trementium uerba eius ; Uestimenta discipulorum ⁚ opera sunt iustitię · psalmista testante qui ait ; Sacerdotes tui ⁚ induantur iustit(i)am (*sic*) ; fol. 165r

30 ℟. Uiri impii dixerunt opprimamus uirum iustum iniuste et degluttiamus eum tamquam inferi uiuum auferamus memoriam illius de terra et de spoliis eius sortem mittamus inter nos ipsi enim homicide thesaurizauerunt sibi malum insipientes et maligni oderunt sapientiam et regi[7] facti sunt in cogitationibus suis · ℣. Dixerunt impii apud se non recte cogitantes circumueniamus iustum quoniam contrarius est operibus nostris · insipientes ·

⟨IN LAVDIBUS⟩

31 (A̋.) Dominus deus auxiliator meus et ideo non sum confusus ·

32 A̋. Circumdantes circumdederunt me et in nomine domini uindicabor in eis ·

33 A̋. Iudica causam meam defende quia potens es domine ·

34 A̋. Cum angelis et pueris fideles inueniamur triumphatori mortis clamantes osanna in excelsis ·

35 A̋. Confundantur qui me persecuntur et non confundar ego domine deus meus ·

36 ℟. Prin⟨ci⟩pes persecuti sunt me gratis et a uerbis tuis formidauit cor meum letabor ego super eloquia tua · ℣. Quasi inuenit spolia multa · letabor ·

---

[7] Should be *rei*.

---

29. Bede, Hom. II.3; CCSL 122, pp. 202–3, lines 51–52, 56–58, 63, 64–65, 101–103, 109–110 (cf. *PL* XCIV, 122–3)   **30.** *CAO* 7905A   **31.** *CAO* 2405   **32.** *CAO* 1809   **33.** *CAO* 3515   **34.** *CAO* 1974   **35.** *CAO* 1884   **36.** *CAO* 7433

37 ⟨V̊.⟩ Dederunt in escam meam fel ·

IN EVANGELIO

38 ⟨Å.⟩ Turba multa que conuenerat ad diem festum clamabat dominum benedictus qui uenit in nomine domini osanna in excelsis ·

39 Å. Osanna filio dauid benedictus qui uenit in nomine domini rex israhel osanna in excelsis ·

40 (Å.) Omnes conlaudant nomen tuum et dicunt benedictus qui uenit in nomine domini osanna in excelsis ·

41 (V̊.) Benedictus qui uenit in nomine domini ·

42 R̊. ⟨Ingrediente domino⟩

43 (V̊.) Eripe me domine ·

44 Å. Occurrunt turbe cum floribus et palmis ⟨redemtori⟩ obuiam et uictori triumphanti digna dant ⟨obsequie filium dei ore gentes⟩ predicant et in laudem christi uoces sonant per ⟨nubila osanna (·)⟩

CAPITVL⟨VM⟩

45 Circumspexi et non erat ausiliator ⟨∵ quesiui et non erat⟩ qui adiuuaret · et saluabit mihi brachium meum ;

(COLLECTA)

46 Omnipotens sempiterne deus da nobis ita dominice passionis ⟨sacramenta peragere ut indulgentiam percipere mereamur⟩ · per fol. 165v

(FERIA II)

47 ⟨H⟩ęc dicit dominus ; State super uias et uidéte · et interrogate de sémitis antiquis · quę sit uia bona · et ambulate in ea · et inuenietis

---

37. CAO 8006* **38.** CAO 5256 **39.** CAO 3142 **40.** CAO 4117 **41.** CAO 7978* **42.** CAO 6961* **43.** CAO 8054* **44.** CAO 4107 **45.** Isa. 63:5 **46.** Ha 319; DC 156; LM 754 **47.** Jer. 6:16–17

refrigerium animabus uestris ; Et dixerunt ; Non ambulauimus (-⌐b⌐imus) ; Et constitui super uos speculatores · audite uocem tubę ; Et dixerunt ⁊ Non audiemus ; ⟨⌐h...⌐⟩⁸

48 ℟. In die qua ·

49 Ideo audíte gentes et cognóscite · quanta faciam eis ; Ecce ego adducam mala super populum istum · fructum cogitationum eius · quia uerba mea non audierunt ⁊ et legem meam proiecérunt ; ut quid mihi thus de sabá adfertis · et suaue olentem cálamum de terra longinqua ? Holocaustomata uestra non sunt accepta · et uictimę uestrę non placuerunt michi ;

50 ⟨(℟.)⟩ Fratres mei ·

51 Hec dicit dominus ; Ecce ego dabo in populum istum ruinas · et ruent in eis patres et filii ⁊ simul uicinus et proximus peribunt ; Hec dicit dominus ; Ecce populus uenit de terra aquilonis ⁊ et gens magna consurget a finibus terrę ; Sagittam et scutum arripiet · crudelis est et non miserebitur ;

52 ℟. Adtende domine ad me ·

IN LAVDIBUS

53 ℣. Faciem meam non auerti ab increpantibus et conspuentibus in me ·

54 ℣. Framea suscitare aduersus eos qui dispergunt gregem meam ·

55 ℣. Appenderunt merc⟨e⟩dem meam triginta argenteos quos adpretiatus sum ab eis ·

56 ℣. Inundauerunt aquę super caput meum dixi perii inuocaui nomen tuum domine deus ·

57 ℣. Labia insurgentium et cogitationes eorum uide domine ·

---

[8] See note to no. 4.

---

48. *CAO* 6899* **49.** Jer. 6:18–20 **50.** *CAO* 6737* **51.** Jer. 6:21–23a **52.** *CAO* 6137* **53.** *CAO* 2833 **54.** *CAO* 2893 **55.** *CAO* 1463 **56.** *CAO* 3394 **57.** *CAO* 3556

(36, 88) **58** ⟨℞.⟩ Principes persecuti sunt ·

59 ℣. Eripe me de inimicis ·

IN EVANGELIO

60 (A̞.) Non haberes in me potestatem nisi desuper datum tibi fuisset ·

61 A̞. Recordare mei domine et tuere me ab his qui persecuntur me ·

(FERIA III)

62 Hec dicit dominus ; Vox populi qui ueniet ab aquilone · quasi mare sonabit ⸵ et super ęquos ascend⸢e⸣nt · preparati quasi uir ad prelium aduersum te filia sion ; Audiuimus famam eius · dissolute sunt manus nostrę · tribulatio adprehendit nos · dolores ut parturi-⟦ente⟨m⟩ ;   fol. 166r

63 ⟨℞. Saluum me fac⟩

64 ⟨Hec dicit dominus ; Nolite exire ad agros⟩ et in uia ne ambulętis · quoniam gladius et pauor inimici in circuitu uestro ; Filia populi mei accingere cilicio · et conspergere cinere · luctum unigeniti fac tibi planctum amarum · quia repente ueniet uastator super uos ;

65 ℞. Noli esse mihi ·

66 (LECTIO) III. Hec dicit dominus ; probatorem dedi te in populo meo robustum · et scies et probabis uiam eorum ; Omnes isti principes declinantium ambulantes fraudulenter · quasi ęs et ferrum ⸵ uniuersi corrupti sunt ; Defecit sufflatorium · in igne consumptum est plumbum ; frustra conflauit conflator ⸵ malitię enim eorum non sunt consumpte ; Argentum reprobum uocate eos ⸵ quia dominus proiecit illos ;

67 ℞. Dominus mecum est ·

---

58. *CAO* 7433* **59.** *CAO* 8053* **60.** *CAO* 3916 **61.** *CAO* 4577 **62.** Jer. 6:23b–24 **63.** *CAO* 7566* **64.** Jer. 6:25–6 **65.** *CAO* 7219* **66.** Jer. 6:27–30 **67.** *CAO* 6521*

IN LAVDIBUS

68 (℞.) Vide domine et considera quoniam tribulor uelociter exaudi me ·

69 ℞. Discerne causam meam domine ab homine ⟨ini⟩quo et doloso eripe me ·

70 ℞. Dum tribularer clamaui ad dominum de uentre inferi et exaudiuit me ·

71 ℞. Domine uim patior responde pro me quia nescio quid dicam inimicis meis ·

72 ℞. Dixerunt impii opprimamus uirum iustum quoniam contrarius est operibus nostris ·

IN EVANGELIO

73 ℞. Nemo tollet a me animam meam sed ego pono eam et iterum sumo eam ·

74 ℞. Quia ego tecum sum de manu pessimorum liberabo te dicit dominus ·

75 ℞. Potestatem habeo ponendi animam meam et iterum assumendi eam ·

76 ⟨℞.⟩ Consilium fecerunt inimici mei dicentes conteramus eum de terra uiuentium ·

(FERIA IIII)

77 Hęc dicit dominus ; Ergo spelunca latronum ⸫ facta est domus ista in qua inuocatum est nomen meum in oculis uestris ; Ego ego sum · ego uidi dicit dominus · ite ad locum meum in syló · ubi habitauit nomen meum a principio · et uidete quę fecerim ei · propter malitiam populi mei israhel ;

---

68. *CAO* 5379   **69.** *CAO* 2252   **70.** *CAO* 2474   **71.** *CAO* 2359   **72.** *CAO* 2263
73. *CAO* 3874   **74.** *CAO* 4507   **75.** *CAO* 4349   **76.** *CAO* 1895   **77.** Jer. 7:11–12

(26) **78** ℟. Sinagoge populor*um* ·

79 Et nunc quia facis hęc om*n*ia dic*it* d*omi*nu*s* · et locut*us* su*m* ad uos · et n*on* audistis ⁒ uocaui uos · et n*on* respondistis · facia*m* domui huic · in qua uos habetis fiducia*m* · et loco que*m* dedi uob*is* et patrib*us* ue*s*tris · sicut feci syló ; p*r*oicia*m* eni*m* uos om*n*es a fa-⟦⟨*cie mea sicut proieci omnes fratres uestros* uniuersu*m* se- fol. 166v me*n*⟩ ephraým ;

(28) **80** ⟨℟.⟩ Insurrexer*unt* i*n* me ⟨·⟩

81 Tu uero ait d*omi*nu*s* noli orare p*ro* populo hoc · nec adsumas p*ro* eis ⟨lau⟩de*m* et oratione*m* · et n*on* obsistas m*ihi* · qu*ia* n*on* exaudia*m* té ; Nonne uides quid isti faciant i*n* ciuitatib*us* iuda · et i*n* plateis hier*usa*le*m* ? filii collig⟨unt⟩ ligna · et patres succendunt igne*m* · et mulieres conspergunt adipe*m* · ut faciant placentas regi*n*ę cęli · et libent diis alienis · et me ad iracundia*m* p*r*ouocent ; N*on* me i*n* iracundia*m* p*r*ouocant dic*it* d*omi*nu*s* ⁒ sed semet ipsos in c*on*fusione*m* uultus sui ;

82 (℟.) C*on*tumelias et t*e*rrores passus su*m* ab eis q*ui* erant pacifici mei e⟨t⟩ custodientes lat*us* meu*m* dicentes decipiam*us* eu*m* et p*re*ualeam*us* illi sed tu d*omi*ne ⟨mec*um* es⟩ ta*m*qua*m* bellator fortis cadent i*n* obp*ro*briu*m* se*m*pite*r*nu*m* ut uidea*m* uindicta*m* in eis qu*ia* ti*bi* reuelaui causa*m* mea*m* · ℣. Om*n*es inimici mei aduersu*m* me cogitabant mala m*ihi* uerbu*m* iniqu*u*m mandauer*unt* aduersu*m* me dicentes[9] · sed tu d*omi*ne ·

⟨IN LAVDIBUS⟩

83 (A̧.) Libera me de sanguinib*us* de*us* de*us* me*us* et exultabit lingua mea iustitia*m* tua*m* ·

---

[9] The scribe has accidentally copied two different cues for the *repetendum* of the refrain: *dicentes* and *sed tu domine*. *Dicentes* is the most common cue among the *CAO* sources (CGVHR). *Sed tu domine* is found in *D*, and also in *MoR*, which are both closely related to Corbie use. Perhaps the scribe first wrote the cue with which he was familiar and then the cue in his Corbie exemplar.

---

78. *CAO* 7747* **79.** Jer. 7:13–15 **80.** *CAO* 6973* **81.** Jer. 7:16–19 **82.** *CAO* 6335A **83.** *CAO* 3616

84 ⟨A̧.⟩ Contumelias et terrores passus sum ab eis et dominus mecum est tamquam bellator fortis ·

85 A̧. Ipsi uero in uanum quesierunt animam meam introibunt in inferiora terrę ·

86 ⟨A̧.⟩ Omnes inimici mei audierunt malum meum domine letati sunt quoniam tu fecisti ·

87 ⟨A̧.⟩ Alliga domine in uinculis nationes gentium et reges eorum in compedibus ;

88 ⟨Ŗ.⟩ Principes ·

(IN EVANGELIO)

89 (A̧.) Simon dormis non potuistis una hora uigilare mecum ·

IN CENA DOMINI AD VESPERAS

90 A̧. Tanto tempore uobiscum ⟨eram⟩ docens uos in templo et non me tenuistis modo flagellatum ducitis ad crucifigendum ·

91 V̧. Homo pacis mee (in quo) sperabam (·)

IN EVANGELIO

92 A̧. Cotidie apud uos eram in templo docens et non me tenuistis et ecce flagellatum ducitis ad crucifigendum (·)

COLLECTA

93 Deus a quo et iudas proditor reatus sui pęnam et confessionis suę latro premium sumpsit (·) concede nobis tue propitiationis effectum · ut sicut in passione sua iesus christus dominus noster diuersa utrisque intulit stipendia meritorum ⸵ ita nobis ⟦ abla- fol. 2r to uetu⌐ s⌐tatis errore resurrectionis suę gratia largiatur · per dominum · ⌐per⌐

---

84. *CAO* 1913   85. *CAO* 3408   86. *CAO* 4126   87. *CAO* 1355   88. *CAO* 7433*
89. *CAO* 4959   90. *CAO* 5111   91. *CAO* 8090   92. *CAO* 4570   93. *Ha* 328; *LM* 772; *om. DC*

⟨.ACL..⟩ (AD NOCTVRNOS?)

94 (A̵.) Zelus domus tue comedit me et opprobria exprobrantium tibi ciderunt super me · (Pl.) Saluum me fac deus ·

95 A̵. Auertantur retrorsum et erubescant qui cogitant mihi mala · (Pl.) Deus in adiutorium ·

96 (A̵.) Deus meus eripe me de manu peccatoris · (Pl.) Deus in te speraui ·

97 (V̵.) Exurge domine et iudica causam meam ·

98 Quomodo sedet ⌜sola⌝ ciuitas plena populo · facta *est* quasi ⟨u⟩idua domina gentium · princeps prouinciarum facta *est* sub tributo? Plorans plorauit in nocte ⁖ et lacrime eius in maxillis eius · non est qui consoletur eam ex omnibus caris eius · omnes amici eius spreuerunt eam · et facti sunt ei inimici ;

99 R̵. In monte oliueti oraui(t) ad patrem · pater si fieri potest transeat a me calix iste spiritus quidem promptus *est* caro autem infirma fiat uoluntas tua · (V̵.) Veruntamen non sicut ego uolo sed sicut tu uis · fiat ·

100 Migrauit iuda propter afflictionem et multitudinem seruitutis ⁖ habitauit inter gentes · nec inuenit requiem · omnes persecutores eius adprehenderunt eam inter angustias ;

101 (R̵.) ⟨Tristis *est* ani⟩ma mea usque ad mortem sustinete hic et uigilat⟨e⟩ mecum nunc uidebitis ⟨tur⟩bam que circumdant me uos fugam capietis et ego uadam immolari pro uobis · (V̵.) Ecce adpropinquabit hora et filius homi⟨nis t⟩radetur in manus peccatorum · Vos ·

102 ⟨F⟩ilie sion lugent eo quod non sint qui ueniant ad sollempnitatem ; Omnes porte eius destructe sunt ⁖ sacerdotes eius gementes · et ipsa obpressa amaritudine ;

---

94. *CAO* 5516 | Ps. 68   **95.** *CAO* 1547 | Ps. 69   **96.** *CAO* 2174 | Ps. 70   **97.** *CAO* 8071   **98.** Lam. 1:1–2   **99.** *CAO* 6916   **100.** Lam. 1:3   **101.** *CAO* 7780b   **102.** Lam. 1:4

103 (℞.) Ecce uidimus eum non habentem ⟨s⟩peciem neque decorem aspectus eius in eo non est hic peccata nostra portauit et pro nobis dolens ipse autem uulneratus est propter iniquitates nostras cuius liuore sanati sumus · (℣.) ⟨Vere languores nostros ipse tulit et infirmitates nostras ipse portauit · cuius liuore ·⟩

⟨IN II NOCTURNO⟩

104 ℟. Liberauit dominus pauperem a potente et inopem cui non erat adiutor · ⟦ (Pl.) Deus iudicium tuum (·)   fol. 2v

105 ℟. Cogitauerunt impii et locuti sunt nequitiam iniquitatem in excelso locuti sunt (·) ⟨Pl.⟩ Quam bonus deus (·)

106 ℟. Exurge domine et iudica causam tuam ·

107 ℣. Deus meus eripe me de manu peccatoris ·

108 Egressus est a filia sion omnis decor eius ⁖ facti sunt principes eius uelut arietes · non inuenientes pascua · et abierunt absque fortitudine · ante faciem subsequentis ; Facti sunt hostes eius in capite · inimici illius locupletati sunt · quia dominus locutus est super eam · propter iniquitatem eius ; Paruuli eius ducti ⟨sunt⟩ in captiuitatem · a facie tribulantis ;

109 ℟. Vnus ex discipulis meis tradet me hodie ue illi per quem tradar ego melius illi erat si natus non fuisset · ℣. Qui intingit mecum manum in parapside hic me traditurus est in manus peccatorum · melius illi ·

110 LECTIO. Recordata est hierusalem dierum afflictionis et preuaricationis ⁖ omnium desiderabilium suorum · quę habuerat a diebus antiquis · cum caderet populus eius in manu hostili · et non esset auxiliator ; Viderunt eam hostes ⁖ et deriserunt sabbata eius ;

111 (℞.) Eram quasi agnus innocens ductus ⟨sum ad immolan⟩dum et nesciebam consilium fecerunt inimici mei aduersum me dicen⟨t⟩e⟨s u⟩enite mittamus lignum in pane eius et eradamus

---

103. *CAO* 6618   **104.** *CAO* 3624 | Ps. 71   **105.** *CAO* 1844 | Ps. 72   **106.** *CAO* 2823   **107.** *CAO* 8010*   **108.** Lam. 1:6,5   **109.** *CAO* 7809   **110.** Lam. 1:7   **111.** *CAO* 6660

eum de terra uiuentium · (V̄.) Omnes inimici mei aduersum me cogitabant mala mihi uerbum iniqu(u)m mandauerunt aduersum me dicentes · Venit⟨e ·⟩

112 Peccatum peccauit hierusalem ⁓ propterea instabilis facta est; Omnes qui glorificabant eam spreuerunt illam · quoniam uiderunt ignominiam eius · ipsa autem gemens · et conuersa retrorsum ; Sordes eius in pedibus eius ⁓ nec recordata est finis sui · deposita est uehementer · non habens consolatorem ; Vide domine afflictionem meam ⁓ quoniam erectus est inimicus meus ;

113 R̄. Vna hora non potuistis uigilare mecum qui exortabamini mori pro me uel iudam non uidetis quomodo non dormit sed festinat tradere me iudeis · V̄. Dor-[mite iam et requiescite ecce appropinquabit qui me traditurus est · Vel iudam · fol. 3r

⟨IN III NOCTVRNO (?)⟩

114 (Ā.) Dixi iniquis nolite loqui aduersus deum iniquitatem · (Pl.) Confitebimur ·

115 Ā. Terra tremuit et quieuit dum resurgeret in iudicio deus (·) (Pl.) Notus in iudea ·

116 Ā. In die tribulationis mee deum exquisiui manibus meis · (Pl.) Voce ⟨m⟩ea ·

(91) 117 V̄. Homo pacis mee in quo sperabam ·

118 Manum suam misit hostis · ad omnia desiderabilia eius · quia uidit gentes ingressas sanctuarium suum · de quibus preceperas ne intrarent in ęcclesiam tuam ; Omnis po⟨pu⟩lus eius gemens et querens panem ⁓ dederunt pretiosa quęque pro cibo · ad refocillandam animam ; Vide domine et considera · quoniam facta sum uilis ;

119 ⟨R̄.⟩ Seniores populi consilium fecerunt ut iesum dolo tenerent et occiderent cum gladiis et fustibus exierunt tamquam ad latronem ·

---

112. Lam. 1:8–9 113. *CAO* 7807A 114. *CAO* 2265 | Ps. 74 115. *CAO* 5139 | Ps. 75 116. *CAO* 3223 | Ps. 76 117. *CAO* 8090* 118. Lam. 1:10–11 119. *CAO* 7636

℣. Congregauerunt iniquitatem sibi et egrediebantur foras · cum gladiis ·

120 O uos omnes qui transitis per uiam ⁏ adtendite et uidete · si est dolor sicut dolor meus · quoniam uindemiauit me · ut locutus est dominus in die furoris sui ; de excelso misit ignem in ossibus meis · et erudiuit me ; Expandit rete pedibus meis conuertit me retrorsum · posuit desolatam · tota die merore confectam ;

121 ℟. Reuelabunt cęli iniquitatem iudę et terra aduersus eum consurget et manifestum erit peccatum illius in die furoris domini cum eis qui dixerunt domino deo recede a nobis scientiam uiarum tuarum nolumus · ⟨℣.⟩ In die perdition⟨i⟩s seruabitur et ad diem ultionis ducetur · cum eis ·

122 Vigilauit iugum iniquitatum mearum in manu domini · conuolute sunt et inposite collo meo ; Infirmata est uirtus mea ⁏ dedit me in manu de qua non potero exire ; Abstulit omnes magnificos meos dominus · uocauit aduersum me tempus · ut contereret omnes electos meos ; Idcirco ego plorans ⁏ et oculus meus deducens aquam · quia longe factus est a me consolator conuertens animam meam · facti sunt filii mei perditi · quoniam inualuit inimicus meus ;

123 ⟨℟.⟩ O iuda qui dereliquisti consilium pacis et cum iudeis consiliatus es triginta argenteis uendidisti sanguinem iustum et pacem osculo ⟦ ferebas quam in pectore non habebas · ℣. Os tuum abundauit malitia et lingua tua concinnabat dolos · et pacem · fol. 3v

IN LAVDIBUS

124 ℣. Iustificeris domine in sermonibus tuis et uincas cum iudicaris · Pl. Miserere mei deus (·)

125 ℣. Dominus tamquam ouis ad uictimam ductus est et non aperuit os suum · Pl. Domine refugium ·

---

120. Lam. 1:12–13 121. CAO 7543B 122. Lam. 1:14–16 123. CAO 7272
124. CAO 3537 | Ps. 50 125. CAO 2422 | Ps. 89

126 ℟. Contritum est cor meum in medio mei contremuerunt omnia ossa mea · Pl. Deus deus meus ⟨·⟩

127 ℟. Exortatus es in uirtute tua et in refectione sancta tua domine · Pl. Cantemus domino ·

128 ⟨℟.⟩ Oblatus est quia ipse uoluit et peccata nostra ipse portabit · Pl. Laudate dominum de celis ·

129 ℣. Acuerunt linguas suas sicut serpent⟨es⟩ ·

(IN EVANGELIO)

130 ℟. Traditor autem dedit eis signum dicens quem osculatus fuero ipse est tenete eum ·

COLLECTA

131 Deus qui per crucem et passionem tuam redemisti mundum · libera nos ab omni peccato · per

IN CENA DOMINI AD VESPERAS

132 ℟. Calicem salutaris accipiam et nomen domini inuocabo · Pl. Credidi propter ·

133 ℟. Cum his qui oderunt pacem eram pacificus dum loquebar illis inpugnabant me gratis · ⟨Pl.⟩ Ad dominum ·

134 ℟. Ab hominibus iniquis libera me · ⟨Pl.⟩ Eripe me ⟨domine ·⟩

135 ℟. Custodi me a laqueo quem statuerunt mihi et ab scandalis operantium iniquit⟨at⟩em · Pl. Domine clamaui ·

136 ℟. Considerabam ad dexteram et uidebam et non erat qui agnosceret me · Pl. Voce mea ·

137 ℣. Christus factus est pro nobis obediens ·

---

126. *CAO* 1912 | Ps. 21   **127.** *CAO* 2784 | Canticle (Exod. 15:1–19)   **128.** *CAO* 4097 | Pss. 148–50   **129.** *CAO* 7931   **130.** *CAO* 5169   **131.** *om.* Ha, DC, LM   **132.** *CAO* 1754 | Ps. 115   **133.** *CAO* 2008 | Ps. 119   **134.** *CAO* 1199 | Ps. 139   **135.** *CAO* 2082 | Ps. 140   **136.** *CAO* 1891 | Ps. 141   **137.** *CAO* 7983

(IN EVANGELIO)

138 ℟. Cena facta dix*it* ie*sus* discipulis suis amen am*en* dico uob*is* unus u*estru*m me traditurus *est* in (h)ac nocte ·

139 ⟨℟.⟩ Cenantib*us* aute*m* accepit ie*sus* pane*m* benedix*it* ac fregit dedit discipulis suis ·

COLL*EC*TA

140 D*eus* qui peccati ueteris hereditaria*m* morte*m* · *in* qua posteritatis genus om*n*e successerat · chr*ist*i tui d*omi*ni n*ost*ri passione[10] soluisti · da ut c*on*formes eide*m* facti sicut imagine*m* te*rr*eni nature necessitate portauim*us* · ita imagine*m* celestis gr*atie* sa*n*ctificatione portemus chr*ist*i d*omi*ni n*ost*ri · q*ui* ·

⟨*IN* SA*N*CTI FERIA SEXTA IOTH⟩[11]

(AD NOCTVRNOS)

141 (℟.) Adstiter*unt* reges te*rr*e et principes c*on*ruener*unt* in unu*m* aduersus d*omi*nu*m* et aduersus chr*istu*m ei*us* · ⟨Pl.⟩ Quare frem*uerunt* (·)

142 (℟.) Diuiser*unt* sibi uestime*n*ta mea et s⟨u⟩p*er* ueste*m* mea*m* miser*unt* sorte*m* (·) ⟨Pl.⟩ D*eus* d*eus* m*eus* respice ·

143 (℟.) Insurrexer*unt* in me testes iniq*ui* et mentita *est* iniq*ui*tas sibi · [[

End

---

[10] The second **s**, which begins a new line, is insular; the first is a Caroline tall **s**.
[11] *Ioth* may refer to a lesson from the Lamentations for Good Friday. Later Roman usage included Lam. 2:10, 'ɪᴏᴛʜ sederunt in terra', in the Good Friday Night Office lesson. See *LU*, p. 692.

---

138. *CAO* 1780   **139.** *CAO* 1781   **140.** *LM* 783; *om. Ha, DC*   **141.** *CAO* 1506 | Ps. 2   **142.** *CAO* 2260 | Ps. 21   **143.** *CAO* 3358

Appendix C

Oxford, Bodleian Library, Rawl. D. 894, fols. 62–3 (Text)

(IN DECOLLATIONE SANCTI PAVLI)

1 ⁕ ℟. Gratia dei in me · ℣. Gratia dei sum ·   fol. 62r

2 (℟.)[1] Damasci prepositus · ℣. Deus et pater ·

3 ℟. Vos qui reliquistis omnia · (℣.)[2] Cum sederit filius hominis ·

4 (℟.)[3] Ter uirgis cesus sum · (℣.)[4] Nocte ac die ·

ANTIPHONAE IN OCTAVA APOSTOLORVM PETRI ET PAVLI ·

5 ℟. I⟨sti⟩ sunt duae oliuae ·

6 ℟. Deus cuius dextera ·

III · IDVS AGVSTI IN NATALE SANCTI LAVRENTII MARTYRIS ·

7 ⟨℟.⟩ Si quis mihi ministrauerit ·

8 INVITATORIVM Regem sempiternum pronis mentibus adoremus qui martyrem suum digne pro meritis coronauit laurentium ·

---

[1] The scribe wrote ℣.
[2] The scribe wrote ℟.
[3] The scribe wrote ℣.
[4] The scribe wrote ℟.

---

1. *CAO* 2968*   **2.** *CAO* 2096*   **3.** *CAO* 5501*   **4.** *CAO* 5138*   **5.** *CAO* 3438*/3439*   **6.** non-*CAO*   **7.** *CAO* 4910*   **8.** *CAO* 1148

9 ITE*M* Rege*m* martyru*m* ·

IN PRIMA NOCTVRNA ·

10 ℟. Quo progrederis · Pl. Beatus uir · ℣. Beat*us* laurenti*us* dixit ·

11 ℟. Non me derelinquere · Pl. Quare fremuer*unt* · ℣. Quid in me ergo ·

12 ℟. Non ego te desedero (*sic*) · Pl. D*omi*ne quid multiplic*ati* · ℣. Beatus sixtus dixit ·

13 ℟. Beatus laurenti*us* orabat · Pl. Verba mea · ℣. Quia accusatus ·

14 ℟. Dixit romanus · Pl. D*omi*ne d*omi*nus n*os*ter · ℣. Affer⟨e⟩ns aut*em* urceu*m* ·

15 ℟. Beat*us* laurenti*us* dix*it* mea · Pl. In d*omi*no confido · ℣. Quia ipse d*omi*nus nouit ·

16 ℣. Gloria et honore ·

RESPONSORIA

17 ⟨℟. Quo⟩ progrederis sine filio pater · ℣. Quid in me ⟨ergo displicuit paternitati tuae numquid degenerem probasti experire certe utrum idoneum ministrum elegeris cui commisisti dominici corporis⟩[5] ⟦ et sanguinis consecrationem · tu nu*n*qua*m* ·   fol. 62v

18 ℟. Non me derelinquere · ℣. Nos quasi senes leuioris pugnę cursum recipimus te quasi iuuenem magnu*m* gloriosior de tyranno

---

[5]The line beginning *Quo* is partly cut off. The writing area must have continued for several more lines, since fol. 62v begins with the last few words of the responsory verse, *Quid in me*, which must have been written out in full. This verse is subject to great variation in Hesbert's edited sources; its presence in full here may indicate that this *ordo* served to adapt an existing antiphoner to a different textual and liturgical tradition. The missing text is supplied from *CAO* 7502; the surviving text of the verse matches variants in Hesbert's manuscript *M*.

---

9. *CAO* 1136*/1137*   **10.** *CAO* 4556* | Ps. 1   **11.** *CAO* 3892* | Ps. 2   **12.** *CAO* 3908* | Ps. 3   **13.** *CAO* 1640* | Ps. 5   **14.** *CAO* 2308* | Ps. 8   **15.** *CAO* 1641* | Ps. 10   **16.** *CAO* 8081*   **17.** *CAO* 7502*   **18.** *CAO* 7229*

triumphus exspectat post triduum sequeris sacerdote*m* et leuitas ·
non ego ·

19 ℟. O ypolite ⌐si¬ crederis · ℣. Si dictis in quid facta conpenses faciam quę ortaris cui beatus laurentius dixit tu mihi tuu*m* tantummodo prebe assensum · et thesauros ·

20 ℟. Leuita laurentius · ℣. Dispersit dedit pauperibus iustitia eius manet in saeculu*m* saeculi · et thesauros aeccl*es*iae ·

IN SECVNDA NOCTVRNA ·

21 A̷. Strinxerunt · Pl. D*omi*ne quis habitabit · ℣. Carnifices urgentes ·

22 A̷. Igne me examinasti · Pl. Exaudi d*omi*ne iustitia*m* · ℣. Probasti d*omi*ne cor meu*m* ·

23 A̷. Interrogatus te d*omi*ne · Pl. D*omi*ne in uirtute tua · ℣. Gratias tibi ago d*omi*ne ·

24 A̷. Beatus laurenti*us* orabat dicens gratias tibi · Pl. Exaudi d*eus* dep*r*ecatione*m*⁶ ·

25 A̷. O ypolite si credis · Pl. Exaudi d*eus* oratione*m* mea*m* ·

26 A̷. Laurentius bonu*m* opus · Pl. Te decet ymnus d*eus* ·

27 ℣. Posuisti d*omi*ne ·

RESPONSORIA ·

28 ℟. Strinxerunt corporis · ℣. Carnifices uero urg⌐u¬entes ⟨*ministrabant carbones subter cratem ferream · beate ·*⟩⁷

---

⁶This antiphon is not usually found with a verse.
⁷The leaf is cut off under the line beginning *Strinxerunt*. Missing text supplied conjecturally from *CAO* 7711A.

---

19. *CAO* 7271*A   **20.** *CAO* 7089*A   **21.** *CAO* 5035* | Ps. 14   **22.** *CAO* 3167* | Ps. 16   **23.** *CAO* 3381* | Ps. 20   **24.** *CAO* 1643* | Ps. 60   **25.** *CAO* 4032* | Ps. 63   **26.** *CAO* 3597* | Ps. 64   **27.** *CAO* 8170*   **28.** *CAO* 7711*A

29 ⟨℟. *Beatus laurentius clamauit* · ℣. *Mea nox obscurum non habet sed omnia in luce*⟩⁸ 〚 clarescunt · et ideo non ·   fol. 63r

30 ℟. Puer meus non timere · ℣. Liberabo te de manu pessimoru*m* et erua*m* te de manu fortioru*m* · et odor ·

31 ℟. In graticula te de*u*m non negaui · ℣. Accusatus non negaui nomen s*anctu*m tuum et interrogatus · te dominum ·

TRIA CANTICA

32 ℣. Iustum deduxit d*omi*nus ·

RESPONSORIA

33 ℟. Gaudeo plane · ℣. Ego me optuli sacrificiu*m* deo in odorem suauitatis · assatus ·

34 ℟. Beatus⁹ laurentius orauit et dixit domine iesu criste pastor bone suscipe spiritum meum · ℣. Gratias tibi ago quia ianuas ingredi merui · d*omi*ne ·

35 ℟. Beatus laurent(i)us dixit ego me optuli · ℣. Gaudeo plane quia hostia chr*ist*i effici merui · In odore*m* ·

36 ℟. Meruit¹⁰ esse hostia leuita laurentius qui dum assaretur non negauit dominum et ideo inuentus est sacrificium laudis · ℣. In graticula positus te deum non negauit et ad ignem applicatus cristum confessus est · et ideo ·

---

⁸There was another responsory in the missing portion of the leaf. The text at the beginning of fol. 63r is from the responsory *Beatus laurentius clamauit*, supplied here from *CAO* 6213. The respond text was probably an incipit, conjecturally cut off here after *clamauit*. The verse must have been given in full.

⁹This is the first of the responsories to give the respond text in full as well as the verse. It is perhaps significant that the first responsory given in full is the tenth, the first responsory to exceed the number that would have been provided in an antiphoner following the secular *cursus*. There are no abbreviations except for the repetendum cue; might this have been intended for notation?

¹⁰The full text is given without abbreviations, and notation is supplied above in Insular or Northern French neumes (nearly vertical strokes).

---

29. *CAO* 6213   **30**. *CAO* 7449*B   **31**. *CAO* 6896*B   **32**. *CAO* 8115*   **33**. *CAO* 6763*A   **34**. *CAO* 6216*   **35**. *CAO* 6215*B   **36**. *CAO* 7147A

37 ℟. Beatus[11] uir laurentius qui post aurum non habiit nec sperauit in thesauris pecunię fecit enim mirabilia in uita sua · ※. Hic est uere martyr qui pro christi nomine sanguinem suum fudit · fecit enim ·

(Lacuna of approx. 2 lines)[12]

(48) **38** ⟦ A̸. Volo pater ·   fol. 63v

39 ※. Iustus ut palma ·

IN EVANGELIO

40 A̸. In graticula sanctum deum

41 A̸. Beatus laurentius cum in ·

42 A̸. Ueni desiderator bone ueni suscipiant te angeli mei quoniam assatus non negasti me probatus confessus es me

ITEM ALIAE ANTIPHONAE ·

43 A̸. Qui me confessus ·

44 A̸. Qui sequitur me ·

45 A̸. Qu(i) (u)ult uenire ·

46 A̸. Hic est uere martyr ·

47 A̸. Qui odit animam ·

IN EVANGELIO ·

(38) **48** A̸. Uolo pater ·

49 A̸. Iste sanctus pro lege ·

---

[11] The text is given in full and is notated throughout. The only abbreviations are in the verse at *pro christi*.

[12] The next text, *Uolo pater*, appears as the fifth (and final) psalm antiphon for Lauds of St Lawrence in six of the *CAO* manuscripts (*EMVFSL*; see *CAO* I, 279, II, 524–5). The missing lines at the foot of fol. 63r probably contained the cues of the first four antiphons at Lauds.

---

37. *CAO* 6229B **38.** *CAO* 5491* **39.** *CAO* 8117* **40.** *CAO* 3216* **41.** *CAO* 1642* **42.** *CAO* 5319 **43.** *CAO* 4479* **44.** *CAO* 4496* **45.** *CAO* 4506* **46.** *CAO* 3055*/3056* **47.** *CAO* 4488* **48.** *CAO* 5491* **49.** *CAO* 3434*/3435*

INCIPIVNT ANTIPH*ONAE* IN ASSV*MPTIONE* S*ANCT*AE MARIAE ·

50 A̲. Quae est ista quę ascendit ·

51 INVITATORIVM · Uenite adoremus regem regum quia hodie ab aethereis maria uirgo assumpta est in caelos ·

IN PRIMA NOCTVRNA ·

52 A̲. Exaltata est s*anc*ta dei · Pl. D*omi*ne d*ominu*s n*oste*r ·

53 A̲. Paradisi portae · Pl. Caeli enarrant ·

54 A̲. Benedicta tu · Pl. Domini est terr⟨a⟩

55 A̲. Specie tua · Pl. Eructauit ·

56 A̲. Adiuuabit eam · Pl. D*eu*s n*oste*r refugium ·

57 A̲. Pulchra es et decora Pl. Magnus d*ominu*s ·

58 V̲. Diffusa est gratia

RESPONSORIA

59 R̲. ⟨V⟩idi speciosam sicut columba*m* · V̲. Quae est ⟦   End

---

50. *CAO* 4425* **51.** non-*CAO* **52.** *CAO* 2762* | Ps. 8 **53.** *CAO* 4215* | Ps. 18
54. *CAO* 1709* | Ps. 23 **55.** *CAO* 4987* | Ps. 44 **56.** *CAO* 1282* | Ps. 45
57. *CAO* 4418* | Ps. 47 **58.** *CAO* 8014* **59.** *CAO* 7878*A

Appendix D

London, British Library, Burney 277, fols. 69–72, and Stowe 1061, fol. 125 (Text)

(*Bifolium A*)

1 ⟦ gemit tendit crux brachia petri mili⟨ ⟩¹ uictoribus implens · euouae ·²   Burney f⦁

2 AD V*ESPERAS* · Hodie illuxit nobis ·

    (IN COMMEMORATIONE SANCTI PAVLI)

(AD PRIMAS VESPERAS)

3 IN EV*ANGELIO* (A̸.) GLORIOSI PRINCIPES TERRE quomodo in uita sua dilexer*unt* se ita et in morte n*on* sunt separati ·

4 INVITAT*ORIVM* Rege*m* ap*osto*lorum ·

SVPER N*OCTVRNOS* ·

5 A̸. QVI OPERATVS EST PETRO IN APOSTOLATV*M* OPE-RAT*VS* est mihi int*er* gentes et cognouer*unt* grat*ia*m que data est

---

¹The top right corner of the leaf is missing here.

²Bifolium A, like Bifolium B, seems originally to have been ruled for eighteen long lines of text. It has been trimmed severely so that it has lost one line of the original text from the top of each leaf. The first three lines of the remaining portion of fol. 71r, and part of the fourth, have been erased. The text of this antiphon and notation on staves were added in a later hand (s. xii?) over the first two lines of the erasure, leaving one and a half lines of erased text below it. The original text is no longer visible, even under ultraviolet light.

---

2. *CAO* 3102*   **3.** *CAO* 2960   **4.** *CAO* 1125*   **5.** *CAO* 4489 | Ps. 18

APPENDIX D: BL BURNEY 277 and STOWE 1061 (TEXT)

mihi a christo domino · Pl. Cęli enarrant · ℣. Qui me segregauit ex utero matris meę et uocauit per gratiam suam ·

6 ℟. Qui me segregauit ex utero matris meae · Pl. Domini est terra · ℣. Et uocauit per gratiam suam ·

7 ℟. Scio cui credidi et certus sum quia potens est depositum meum seruare in illum diem iustus iudex · Pl. ⌜Beati quorum⌝ ℣. De reliquo reposita est mihi corona iustitie ·

8 ℟. Mihi uiuere christus est et mori lucrum gloriari me oportet in cruce domini mei iesu christi · Pl. ⌜Benedicam⌝ ℣. Per quem mihi

9 (*In the bottom margin: three lines of text in a later hand, with a later neumatic notation, now almost too faint to read. This could possibly be the antiphon* Ne magnitudo reuelationum; *cf. Ely fol. 242b. The hand is probably the same as that of the marginal additions on fol. 70v, no. 58 below.*)

10 ⟨℟. Tu es uas electionis sancte pa⟩-⟦⟨u⟩le³ apostole predicator ueritatis in uniuerso mundo · Pl. C [........] ℣. Per quem omnes gentes cognouerunt gratiam dei · Burney fol. 71v

11 ℟. Magnus sanctus paulus uas electionis uere digne est glorificandus qui et meruit thronum duodecimum possidere · Ps. [.......] ℣. In regeneratione cum sederit filius hominis in sede maiestatis suę ·

12 ℟. Bonum certamen certaui cursum consummaui fidem seruaui · Pl. Exaudi deus [....] · ℣. De cetero reposita est mihi corona iustitie ·

13 ℟. Ter uirgis cesus sum semel lapidatus sum ter naufragium pertuli pro christi nomine · Pl. [......] ℣. Nocte et die in profundum maris fui ·

---

³The top line of the leaf has been trimmed off, and the top left corner of the leaf is missing. Missing text supplied from *CAO* 5211.

---

6. *CAO* 4484 | Ps. 23   7. *CAO* 4831 | Ps. 31   8. *CAO* 3759 | Ps. 33   10. *CAO* 5211   11. *CAO* 3683   12. *CAO* 1743 | Ps. 54, 60, or 63   13. *CAO* 5138

14 ℟. ⌜Dama(s)ci prepositus gentis arethe regis uoluit me conprehendere a fratribus per murum summissus in sporta et sic euasi manus eius in nomine domini · ℣. Deus et pater domini nostra iesu christi scit quia non mencior ·⁴⌝

15 ℟. ⌜Libenter gloriabor in infirmitatibus meis ut inhabitet in me uirtus christi · ℣. Quando enim⁵ infirmor tunc forcior sum et potens⌝

(*There was probably another bifolium inserted between fol. 71 and fol. 72, containing the rest of the Night Office for the Commemoration of St Paul. The next leaf of Bifolium A begins with a blank page (fol. 72r), with show-through from fol. 72v. It seems always to have been blank; there is no sign of erasure.*)

(IN ORDINATIONE ET TRANSLATIONE SANCTI
MARTINI EPISCOPI)

(AD LAVDES MATVTINAS)

16 ⟦ ⟨S............⟩   Burney fol. 72v

17 ⟨℟. Martine misit nos ·⟩

18 ⟨℟. Dum sacramenta ·⟩

19 ⟨℟. Sacerdotes dei⟩

20 ℟. Inposita manu puero ·

(30) **21** (℟.) Iustum deduxit ·

---
⁴This and the following antiphon, *Libenter gloriabor*, are copied in a later hand (s. xiii?) over the last five lines of the original, which have been erased.
⁵This word, which occurs at the beginning of a new line, is preceded in the margin by the abbreviation **PL** in the hand of the s. xi rubricator. The original psalm incipit was erased with the rest of the antiphon replaced by *Libenter gloriabor*, which was written by the same scribe who copied *Damasci prepositus*, above.

---
14. *CAO* 2096   **15.** *CAO* 3614   **16.** Possibly *CAO* 4785: ℟. *Sanctus Martinus*, one of twelve antiphons for St Martin composed by Odo of Cluny (*PL* CXXXIII, 513).   **17.** *CAO* 3710*   **18.** *CAO* 2466*   **19.** *CAO* 4675*   **20.** *CAO* 3201*   **21.** *CAO* 7058*

25) 22 ℣. Ecce sacerdos magn*us* ·

⟨IN EVANGELIO ·⟩

23 ℟. Ora p*ro* nobis ·

AD VESP*ERAS*

24 ⟨℟.⟩ Amauit eu*m* d*ominus* ·

22) 25 ℣. Ecce sacerdos ·

IN EV*A*N*GELIO*

29) 26 ℟. Sacerdos (Sacerdo[*te*]s)⁶ d*e*i martine ·

27 ℟. Tetraditus⁷ ·

28 ℟. O in⟨effabilem⟩ ·

26) 29 ℟. ⟨Sacerdos d*e*i martine ·⟩

⟨IN VIG*ILIA* SA*N*CTI BENEDICTI ABBATIS⟩

⟨AD VESPERAS⟩

21) 30 ⟨℟.⟩ Iustum dedux*it* d*omi*n*u*s ·

31 IN EV*A*N*GELIO* · (℟.) PATER SA*N*CTVS

32 ⟨INVITAT*ORIVM* Confessorum regem ·⟩

33 ITE*M* Rege*m* confessoru*m* ·

34 ℟. Fuit uir uite · Ps. Beatus uir ·

---
⁶Corrected by erasure; cf. no. 19.
⁷Should be *Tetradius*.

---
22. *CAO* 8040*   **23.** *CAO* 4169*   **24.** *CAO* 6080*/6081*   **25.** *CAO* 8040*
26. *CAO* 4670*/4671*   **27.** *CAO* 5141*   **28.** *CAO* 4033*   **29.** *CAO* 4671*/4670*
30. *CAO* 7058*   **31.** *CAO* 4245*   **32.** *CAO* 1056*   **33.** *CAO* 1129*   **34.** *CAO* 2906* | Ps. 1

35 ℟. Nursię prouincia · Ps. Quare ·

36 ℟. Relicta domino[8] · Ps. Cum inuocarem ·

37 ℟. Recessit igitur · Ps. Uerba mea ·

38 ℟. Compassus · Ps. Domine dominus ·

39 ℟. Electus a fratribus Ps. In domino ·

40 ℟. Cumque sibi · Ps. Domine quis habitabit ·

41 ⟨℟. Dum in hac terra · Ps. Domine in uirtute ·⟩

42 ⟨℟. Ab ipso pueritię Ps. Domini est terra⟩

43 ⟨℟. Orabat sanctus benedictus · Ps. Exaudi deus III⟩

44 ⟨℟. Puer quidam par(u)ulus Ps. .....⟩

45 ⟨℟. Tantam gratiam · Ps. Bonum est ·⟩

46 ⟨AD CANTICA ℟. Beatus uir benedictus · Ps. Posui⟩ 〚 end of B fol. 72v

(*Bifolium B*)

(IN FESTO SANCTI LAVRENTII)

(AD NOCTVRNOS)

47 ⟨℟. *Quo progrederis sine filio pater quo sacerdos sancte sine diacono properas tu numquam sine ministro sacrificium offerre consueueras · ℣. Quid in me ergo displicuit paternitati tuae numquid degenerem probasti experire certe utrum idoneum*

---
[8]Should be *domo*.

---
35. *CAO* 3982* | Ps. 2   **36.** *CAO* 4605* | Ps. 4   **37.** *CAO* 4574* | Ps. 5   **38.** *CAO* 1859* | Ps. 8   **39.** *CAO* 2626* | Ps. 10   **40.** *CAO* 2073* | Ps. 14   **41.** *CAO* 2457* | Ps. 20   **42.** *CAO* 1204* | Ps. 23   **43.** *CAO* 4173* | Ps. 63   **44.** *CAO* 4413*   **45.** *CAO* 5105* | Ps. 91   **46.** *CAO* 1673* | Ps. 88:20ff. (cf. *Mch* II, fol. 148r)   **47.** *CAO* 7502

ministrum elegeris cui commisisti dominici⟩[9] 〚 ⌐corporis et sanguinis¬[10] consecrationem · tu nun*quam* Burney fol. 70r

48 ℟. Noli me derelinquere pat*er s*anct*e* quia thesauros tuos iam expendi non ego te desero fili neq*ue* derelinquo · sed maiora tibi debentur p*ro* fide ch*ris*ti certamina · ℣. Nos quasi senes leuioris pugnę cursum s⟨*u*⟩scepimus te quasi iuuene*m* manet gloriosior de tiranno triu*m*phus post triduu*m* me sequeris sacerdote*m* · Sed ma*iora* ·

49 ℟. Strinxerunt corporis membra posita in craticula ⟨su⟩bicientibus prunas exultat leuita ch*ris*ti · beatę laurenti martir ch*ris*ti int*er*cede p*ro* nobis · ℣. Carnifices uero urgen*tes* ministrabant carbones subt*er* crate*m* ferrea*m* · beate ·

50 ℟. Beatus laurentius clamauit et dixit de*u*m meum colo et illi soli seruio et ideo non timeo torme*n*ta tua · ℣. Mea nox obscurum non habet sed om*n*ia in luce clarescunt · Et id*eo* ·

51 ℟. Puer m*eu*s noli timere quia ego su*m* tecum dicit d*omi*n*u*s c*u*m transieris p*er* igne*m* flamina non nocebit te et odor ignis non erit in te · ℣. Liberabo te de manu pessimoru*m* et eruam te de manu fortiu*m* · c*u*m tran*sieris* ·

52 〚 ℟. In craticula te de*u*m non negaui · et ad igne*m* applicat*us* te dom*i*nu*m* ie*su*m ch*ristu*m confessus su*m* · ℣. P*ro*basti domine cor meu*m* et uisitasti nocte · Et ad · Burney fol. 70v

53 ℟. Beatus laurentius dixit ego me obtuli sacrificiu*m* deo in odorem suauitatis · ℣. Gaudeo plane quia hostia ch*ris*ti effici merui · In odor⌐ em¬[11] ·

54 ℟. Gaudeo plane quia hostia ch*ris*ti effic⟨*i*⟩ merui accusatus non negaui int*er*rogatus ch*ristu*m confessus sum assatus gra*tias*

---
[9]Missing text supplied from *CAO* 7502. The extant text has textual variants that match Hesbert's *M*.
[10]Added by a contemporary or slightly later hand over an erasure. The notation above the changed text is also of a different hand. Some sources read only *sanguinis*, rather than *corporis et sanguinis*.
[11]A contemporary correction, perhaps by the neumator.

---
48. *CAO* 7229   **49.** *CAO* 7711A   **50.** *CAO* 6213   **52.** *CAO* 6896A   **53.** *CAO* 6215B   **54.** *CAO* 6763

ago · ℣. Ego me obtuli sacrificium deo in odorem suauitatis · Accusatus ·

55 ℟. Meruit esse hosti⟨a⟩ leuita laurentius qui dum assaretur non negauit dominum et ideo inuentus est sacrificium laudis · ℣. In craticula positus te deum non negauit et ad ignem applicatus christum confessus ⌜est·⌝[12] et ideo ·

56 ℟. Beatus laurentius orauit et dixit domine iesu christe pastor bone suscipe spiritum meum · ℣. Gratias tibi ago domine quia ianuas tuas ingredi merui · Domine ·

57 ℟. B⟨eatus *uir laurentius qui post aurum* non *habiit nec* sperauit in thesauris pecunię ·⟩ ⟦ ⟨*fecit enim mirabilia in uita sua* ℣. hic *est uere martyr* qui *pro* christi *nomine* sanguinem *suum fudit · fecit enim* (?)⟩[13]   Burney f

58 (℟.) XII Concede nobis quesumus domine uitiorum flammas extinguere nostrorum qui sancto ac beatissimo tribuisti laurentio tormentorum incendia supera-⟦ re suorum · (℣.) Aspice domine infirmitates nostras et da nobis locum penitentię atque celeri pietate succurre · Qui sancto (·) Gloria patri et filio et spi[14]   Stowe fol. 125v (bottom margin)

⟦ IN LAVDIBVS ·   Burney f

59 A̧. LAVRENTIVS INGRESSVS EST MARTYR ET CONFESSVS est nomen domini iesu christi ·

60 A̧. Laurentius bonum opus ⟦ operatus est qui per signum crucis cecos illuminauit ·   Stowe fol. 125v

---

[12] The neumator inserted the Insular symbol ÷ and a small medial point.
[13] Bifolium B either stood alone or was the innermost bifolium of a quire. The text on fol. 70v continues at the top of fol. 69r, though the top of the leaf is so damaged that only a few letters may now be discerned. The repetendum given, *fecit enim*, is purely conjectural, based on other sources.
[14] Added in a s. xii hand (apparently identical with that of no. 9 above), with heightened neumatic notation, stretching across the originally empty bottom margins of Burney fol. 70v and Stowe fol. 125v. The text is cut off at the right edge of 125v.

---

55. *CAO* 7147A   56. *CAO* 6216A   57. *CAO* 6229B   59. *CAO* 3598   60. *CAO* 3597

61 ℟. Adhesit anima mea post te quia caro mea igne cremata e*st* p*ro* te d*eu*s meus ·

62 ℟. Misit d*omi*n*u*s ang*e*l*u*m suu*m* et liberauit me de medio ignis et no*n* sum aestuatus ·

63 ℟. Beatus laurentius orabat dicens gra*tia*s tibi ago d*omi*ne quia ianuas tuas ingredi merui ·

64 ℟. [..........][15]

65 ℣. Iustus ut palma ·

66 IN EVA*N*GELIO ℟. In craticula te d*eu*m non negaui et ad ignem applicatus te chr*istu*m co*n*fessus su*m* p*ro*basti cor meu*m* et uisitasti nocte igne me examinasti et n*on* est inuenta in me iniquitas ·

AD VESP*ER*A*S*

67 ℟. Gl*ori*a et honore ·

68 ℣. Posuisti d*omi*ne ·

69 IN EVA*N*GELIO ℟. Ueni desiderator bone ueni suscipiant te ang*e*li mei q*uonia*m assatus non negasti me p*ro*batus co*n*fessus es me ·

IN VIGILIA SA*N*C*T*I YPPOLITI MARTIR(*IS*) AD VES*PE*RAS ·

70 [[℟. Letamini in d*omi*no ·   Burney fol. 69v

71 ℣. Iustoru*m* anime ·

72 IN EVANGELIO · ℟. Gaudent in cęlis anime sa*nct*orum qui chr*ist*i uestigia su*n*t secuti et quia p*ro* eius amore sanguine*m* suu*m* fuder*un*t ideo cum chr*ist*o gaudebunt in aete*r*num ·

---

[15]The erased text is completely invisible even under ultraviolet light. Some neumes are still faintly visible.

---

61. *CAO* 1271   **62.** *CAO* 3784   **63.** *CAO* 1643   **65.** *CAO* 8117*   **66.** *CAO* 3216   **67.** *CAO* 6774*/6775*/6776*   **68.** *CAO* 8170*   **69.** *CAO* 5319   **70.** *CAO* 7065*   **71.** *CAO* 8114*   **72.** *CAO* 2927

73 INVITAT*ORIVM* · [[Regem martyrum dominum ·   Stowe fol. 125

RESPONSOR*IA* ·

74 ℟. BEATISSIMVS CHR*ISTI* MARTYR YPPOLITVS DVM BAPTISMI GRATIAM p*er*cepisset a beato laurentio ponebat manus sup*er* oculos cęcorum et sanabantur · ℣. Caeco (⌜ Cęco⌝) inluminato a s*anc*to laurentio yppolitus credidit et p*er*cipere meruit baptismi sacramentu*m* · ponebat ·

75 ℟. O ypolite si credis in d*omi*nu*m* ie*s*u*m* chr*istu*m et thesauros tibi ostendo et uitam aete*r*nam p*r*omitto · ℣. Si dictis inquit facta co*m*penses facia*m* que (⌜ quę⌝) hortaris · cui beat*us* laurentius dixit tu mihi tuu*m* tantu*m*modo prebe (⌜ prębe⌝) assensum · et thes*auros* ·

76 ℟. Coepit (⌜ Cępit⌝) yppolitus tristis plorare cui beatus laurentius ita dixit noli flere sed magis gaude et post du*m* clamauero audi et [[End

---

73. *CAO* 1137*   **74.** *CAO* 6188   **75.** *CAO* 7271A   **76.** *CAO* 6299

Bibliography

Unpublished Manuscripts

Amiens, Bibliothèque municipale, 115.
Cambridge, Corpus Christi College 41.
Cambridge, Corpus Christi College 391.
Cambridge, Corpus Christi College 422.
Cambridge, Magdalene College F. 4. 10.
Cambridge, University Library, Ee. 2. 4.
Cambridge, University Library, Ii. 4. 20.
London, British Library, Additional 29253.
London, British Library, Additional 37517.
London, British Library, Additional 43405 and 43406.
London, British Library, Additional 56488, fols. i, 1–6.
London, British Library, Burney 277, fols. 69–72.
London, British Library, Harley 4664.
London, British Library, Royal 1. E. VII–VIII.
London, British Library, Royal 17. C. XVII, fols. 2–3 and 163–6.
London, British Library, Stowe 1061, fol. 125.
Oxford, Bodleian Library, Auct. D. Inf. 2. 9.
Oxford, Bodleian Library, Barlow 41.
Oxford, Bodleian Library, Bodley 572.
Oxford, Bodleian Library, Bodley 579.
Oxford, Bodleian Library, Junius 27.
Oxford, Bodleian Library, Lat. liturg. e6, e37, e39, and d42.
Oxford, Bodleian Library, Rawl. D. 894, fols. 62–3.
Oxford, Jesus College 10.
Paris, Bibliothèque nationale de France, lat. 11522.
Paris, Bibliothèque nationale de France, lat. 12601.
Paris, Bibliothèque nationale de France, lat. 13159.
Paris, Bibliothèque nationale de France, lat. 13241 and 13242.
Rouen, Bibliothèque municipale, 252 (*olim* A. 486).
Rouen, Bibliothèque municipale, 254 (*olim* A. 226).
Sankt Paul im Lavanttal (Kärnten, Austria), Stiftsbibliothek, 2/1, fol. 1v.
Trier, Stadtbibliothek, 1245/597.

Facsimiles, Editions, and Translations of Primary Sources

Abbo of Fleury, *Passio S. Eadmundi*, ed. M. Winterbottom, *Three Lives of English Saints*, Toronto Medieval Latin Texts 1 (Toronto, 1972), pp. 67–83. Translation: F. Hervey, *Corolla Sancti Eadmundi: The Garland of Saint Edmund King and Martyr* (London, 1907), pp. 6–59.

Actuum praeliminarium synodi primae Aquisgranensis commentationes sive Statuta Murbacensia, ed. J. Semmler, in *Initia consuetudinis Benedictinae*, ed. Hallinger, CCM 1, pp. 441–50.

Adelard, *Lectiones in depositione S. Dunstani*, ed. and tr. M. Winterbottom and M. Lapidge, *The Early Lives of St Dunstan*, Oxford Medieval Texts (Oxford, 2012), pp. 111–45.

Ælfric's Letter to the Monks of Eynsham, ed. and tr. C. A. Jones, Cambridge Studies in Anglo-Saxon England 24 (Cambridge, 1998).

Ælfwald of East Anglia, *Epistola Bonifatio* (747×749), ed. M. Tangl, *Die Briefe Bonifatius und Lullus*, MGH Epp. selectae 1 (Berlin, 1916), no. 81 (pp. 181–2).

Æthelwulf, *De abbatibus*, ed. and tr. A. Campbell (Oxford, 1967).

Aethici Istrici Cosmographia Vergilio Salisburgensi rectius adscripta: Codex Leidensis Scaligeranus 69, facsimile ed. [T. A.] M. Bishop, Umbrae codicum occidentalium 10 (Amsterdam, 1966).

Agobard of Lyons, *De antiphonario (ad cantores ecclesiae Lugdunensis)*, ed. L. van Acker, *Agobardi Lugdunensis Opera omnia*, CCCM 52 (Turnhout, 1981), pp. 335–51.

Albi, Bibliothèque Municipale Rochegude, Manuscript 44: A Complete Ninth-Century Gradual and Antiphoner from Southern France, ed. J. A. Emerson and L. Collamore (Ottawa, 2002).

Alcuin, *De anima ratione*, PL CI, 639–50.

——, *De laude Dei*, partially ed. Constantinescu, 'Alcuin', pp. 38–50 (see in 'Secondary Literature', below).

——, *Epistolae*, ed. E. Dümmler, *Epistolae Karolini aevi*, II, MGH Epp. 4 (Berlin, 1895). Translation: Allott, *Alcuin of York*.

——, *Expositiones in psalmos poenitentiales, in psalmum 118, et in psalmos graduales*, PL C, 570–639.

——, *Officia per ferias*, PL LI, 509–612.

——, *Versus de patribus regibus et sanctis Euboricensis ecclesiae*, ed. and tr. P. Godman, *Alcuin: The Bishops, Kings, and Saints of York*, Oxford Medieval Texts (Oxford, 1982).

Aldhelmi Opera, ed. R. Ehwald, MGH AA 15 (Berlin, 1919).

Aldhelm, *Carmen ecclesiasticum* III, ed. Ehwald, *Aldhelmi Opera*, pp. 14–18.

——, *Carmen de virginitate*, ed. Ehwald, *Aldhelmi Opera*, pp. 350–471.

——, *Carmen rhythmicum*, ed. Ehwald, *Aldhelmi Opera*, pp. 524–8.

——, *De metris et enigmatibus ac pedum regulis*, ed. Ehwald, *Aldhelmi Opera*, pp. 59–204.

BIBLIOGRAPHY

——, *De uirginitate* (prose), ed. Ehwald, *Aldhelmi Opera*, pp. 226–323.
Allott, S., *Alcuin of York: His Life and Letters* (York, 1974).
Der altenglische Junius-Psalter: Die Interlinear-Glosse der Handschrift Junius 27 der Bodleianer zu Oxford, ed. E. Brenner, Anglistiche Forschungen 23 (Heidelberg, 1908).
Das altenglische Martyrologium, ed. G. Kotzor, 2 vols., Bayerische Akademie der Wissenschaften, philosophische-historische Klasse, Abhandlungen, neue Folge 88 (Munich, 1981).
Amalarii episcopi Opera liturgica omnia, ed. J.-M. Hanssens, 3 vols., Studi e testi 138–40 (Vatican City, 1948–50).
Amalarius of Metz, *Epistola ad Hilduinum*, ed. Hanssens I, 341–63.
——, *Liber de ordine antiphonarii*, ed. Hanssens III, 13–224.
——, *Liber officialis*, ed. Hanssens II.
——, *Prologus antiphonarii a se compositi*, ed. Hanssens I, 361–3.
pseudo-Amalarius [Adhemar of Chabannes?], *De Regula sancti Benedicti praecipui abbas*, ed. Hanssens III, 273–94.
The Anglo-Saxon Chronicle according to the Several Original Authorities, ed. and tr. B. Thorpe, 2 vols., Rolls Series 23 (London, 1861).
The Anglo-Saxon Chronicle: A Collaborative Edition, VIII: *MS F*, ed. P. S. Baker (Cambridge, 2000).
Antifonario visigotico mozarabe de la Catedral de León, ed. L. Brou and J. Vives, 2 vols. (Barcelona, 1953–9).
L'Antiphonaire de Hartker: Manuscrits de Saint-Gall 390–391, facsimile, Paléographie musicale, sér. 2, 1 (Solesmes, 1900; new edn ed. J. Froger, 1970).
Antiphonaire du Mont-Renaud, facsimile ed. the Monks of Solesmes, Paléographie musicale 16 (Solesmes, 1955; 2nd edn 1989).
Antiphonale missarum sextuplex, ed. R.-J. Hesbert (Brussels, 1935).
Antiphonarium ambrosianum du Musée britannique (XII siècle): Codex Additional 34209, 2 vols., Paléographie musicale 5–6 (Solesmes, 1896–1900).
Ardo Smaragdus, *Vita Benedicti abbatis Anianensis et Indensis*, ed. G. Waitz, in *Vitae aliaeque historiae minores*, MGH SS 15.1 (Hanover, 1887), pp. 198–220. Translation: A. Cabaniss, *The Emperor's Monk: Contemporary Life of Benedict of Aniane by Ardo* (Ilfracombe, 1979).
Asser, *De rebus gestis Ælfredi*, ed. W. H. Stevenson, *Asser's Life of King Alfred, together with the Annals of Saint Neot's, erroneously ascribed to Asser*, reissued with an introduction by D. Whitelock (Oxford, 1959).
Augustine of Hippo, *Confessionum libri XIII*, ed. L. Verheijen, CCSL 27 (Turnhout, 1971).
——, *Sermo* 194, *PL* XXXVIII, 1015–17.
——, *Sermo* 369, *PL* XXXVIII, 1655–7.
'B.', *Vita S. Dunstani*, ed. and tr. M. Winterbottom and M. Lapidge, *Early Lives of St Dunstan*, Oxford Medieval Texts (Oxford, 2012), pp. 1–109.
Bede, *Epistola ad Ecgbertum episcopum*, ed. Plummer I, 405–23. Translation:

McClure and Collins, *Bede*, pp. 343–57.

——, *Expositio in Ezram et Neemiam*, ed. D. Hurst, *Bedae Venerabilis Opera exegetica*, IIA, CCSL 119A (Turnhout, 1969).

——, *Historia abbatum*, ed. Plummer I, 364–87. Translation: D. H. Farmer, in Webb and Farmer, *The Age of Bede*, pp. 187–210.

——, *Historia ecclesiastica gentis Anglorum*, ed. Plummer I. Translation: B. Colgrave, in McClure and Collins, *Bede*, pp. 1–295.

——, *Homeliarum evangelii libri II*, ed. D. Hurst, *Bedae Venerabilis Opera homiletica*, CCSL 122 (Turnhout, 1955).

——, *In canticum Abacuc*, ed. J. E. Hudson, in *Bedae Venerabilis Opera exegetica*, IIB, CCSL 119B (Turnhout, 1973), pp. 381–409.

——, *In Ezram et Neemiam libri III*, ed. D. Hurst, in *Bedae Venerabilis Opera exegetica*, IIA, CCSL 119A (Turnhout, 1969), pp. 235–392. Translation: *Bede: On Ezra and Nehemiah*, tr. S. DeGregorio, Translated Texts for Historians 47 (Liverpool, 2006).

——, *In Genesim*, ed. C. W. Jones, *Bedae Venerabilis Opera exegetica*, I, CCSL 118A (Turnhout, 1967).

——, *In Lucae evangelium expositio*, ed. D. Hurst, *Bedae Venerabilis Opera exegetica*, III, CCSL 120 (Turnhout, 1960), pp. 5–425.

——, *Vita metrica S. Cuthberti*, ed. W. Jaager, *Bedas metrische Vita sancti Cuthberti*, Palaestra 198 (Leipzig, 1935).

——, *Vita prosaica S. Cuthberti*, ed. and tr. Colgrave, *Two Lives of St Cuthbert*, pp. 142–307.

Benedict of Aniane, *Codex regularum*, *PL* CIII, 393–702.

——, *Concordia regularum*, *PL* CIII, 713–1380.

Benedicti Regula, ed. R. Hanslik, 2nd edn, Corpus scriptorum ecclesiasticorum Latinorum 75 (Vienna, 1976).

Bernhardus cardinalis, *Ordo officiorum ecclesiae Lateranensis*, ed. L. Fischer, Historische Forschungen und Quellen 2–3 (Munich, 1916).

Biblia sacra iuxta latinam vulgatam versionem ad codicem fidem, ed. the Monks of the Pontifical Abbey of St Jerome in the City (Rome, 1926–94).

Breviarium Romanum: Editio princeps (1568), Edizione anastatica, ed. M. Sodi and A. M. Triacca, Monumenta liturgica Concilii Tridentini 3 (Vatican City, 1999).

Breviarium S. Albani (1532): London, British Library, C.110.a.27.

Byrhtferth of Ramsey, *Vita S. Oswaldi*, ed. and tr. M. Lapidge, *Byrhtferth of Ramsey: The Lives of St Oswald and St Ecgwine*, Oxford Medieval Texts (Oxford, 2009), pp. 1–203.

——, *Vita S. Oswaldi*, ed. J. Raine, *The Historians of the Church of York and its Archbishops*, 3 vols., Rolls Series 71 (London, 1879–94) I, 399–475.

Capitulare missorum in Theodonis villa datum primum, Mere ecclesiasticum 805, ed. A. Boretius, MGH Cap. 1 (Hanover, 1883), pp. 121–2.

*Cartularium Saxonicum: A Collection of Charters relating to Anglo-Saxon His-

tory, ed. W. de G. Birch, 3 vols. and Index (London, 1885–99).
Cassiodorus, *Expositio psalmorum*, ed. M. Adriaen, *Magni Aurelii Cassiodori Expositio psalmorum*, 2 vols., CCSL 97–8 (Turnhout, 1958).
Charlemagne, *Admonitio generalis*, ed. A. Boretius, MGH Cap. 1 (Hanover, 1883), pp. 52–62.
——, *Duplex legationis edictum*, ed. A. Boretius, MGH Cap. 1 (Hanover, 1883), pp. 62–4.
——, *Epistola generalis*, ed. A. Boretius, MGH Cap. 1 (Hanover, 1883), pp. 80–1.
Charters of the New Minster, Winchester, ed. S. Miller, Anglo-Saxon Charters 9 (Oxford, 2001).
Chrodegang of Metz, *Regula canonicorum*, ed. and tr. J. Bertram, in *The Chrodegang Rules*.
The Chrodegang Rules: The Rules for the Common Life of the Secular Clergy from the Eighth and Ninth Centuries, ed. and tr. J. Bertram (Aldershot, 2005).
Chronicon Moissiacense, ed. G. H. Pertz, MGH SS 1 (Hanover, 1826), pp. 282–313.
Codex diplomaticus aevi Saxonici, ed. J. M. Kemble, 6 vols. (London, 1839–48).
Le Codex F. 160 de la bibliothèque de la cathédrale de Worcester : Antiphonaire monastique (XIIIe siècle), ed. the Monks of Solesmes [and Dame Laurentia McLachlan], 2 vols., introduction and facsimile, Paléographie musicale 12 (Tournai, 1922); 2nd edn, single volume, ed. J. Froger (Solesmes, 1997).
Codex iuris canonici, ed. E. Friedburg (Leipzig, 1879).
Collectio capitularis (Regula S. Benedicti Anianensis), ed. J. Semmler, in *Initia consuetudinis Benedictinae*, ed. Hallinger, CCM 1, pp. 515–36.
Columbanus, *Regula monachorum*, ed. and tr. G. S. M. Walker, *Sancti Columbani Opera*, Scriptores Latini Hiberniae 2 (Dublin, 1954; repr. 1970), pp. 122–69.
Concilia aevi Karolini (742–842), ed. A. Werminghoff, 2 vols., MGH Conc. 2.1–2.2 (Hanover, 1906–8).
Consuetudines Beccenses, ed. M. P. Dickson, CCM 4 (Siegburg, 1967).
Consuetudines Floriacenses saeculi tertii decimi, ed. A. Davril, CCM 9 (Siegburg, 1976).
Corpus antiphonalium officii, ed. R.-J. Hesbert, 6 vols., Rerum ecclesiasticarum documenta, Series maior, Fontes, 7–12 (Rome, 1963–79).
Corpus benedictionum pontificalium, ed. E. Moeller, 4 vols., CCSL 162, 162A–C (Turnhout, 1971–9).
Corpus orationum XI, ed. E. Moeller, I. M. Clément, and B. Coppieters't Wallant, CCSL 160J (Turnhout, 1999).
Council of Chelsea (816), ed. Haddan and Stubbs, *Councils* III, 579–85.
Council of *Clofesho* (747), ed. Haddan and Stubbs, *Councils* III, 360–76.
Council of Mainz (813), ed. Werminghoff, *Concilia aevi Karolini* I, 259–73.
Council of Tours (813), ed. Werminghoff, *Concilia aevi Karolini* I, 286–93.
Councils and Ecclesiastical Documents relating to Great Britain and Ireland, ed. A. W. Haddan and W. Stubbs, 3 vols. (Oxford, 1869–71).

Councils and Synods with Other Documents Relating to the English Church, I: *A.D. 871–1204*, ed. D. Whitelock, M. Brett and C. N. L. Brooke, 2 vols. (Oxford, 1980).

Cura clericalis (London: Thomas Petyt, 1542).

Davis, R., *The Lives of the Eighth-Century Popes (Liber Pontificalis): The Ancient Biographies of Nine Popes from AD 715 to AD 817*, Translated Texts for Historians 13 (Liverpool, 1992).

De horis peculiaribus, ed. and tr. M. Lapidge and M. Winterbottom, in their *Wulfstan of Winchester: The Life of St Æthelwold*, Oxford Medieval Texts (Oxford, 1991), pp. lxviii–lxix.

Decrees of the Ecumenical Councils, I: *Nicaea I to Lateran V*, ed. N. P. Tanner (London, 1990).

Dionysius Exiguus, *Codex canonum ecclesiasticarum*, PL LXVII, 27–134.

Diplomata, chartae, epistolae, leges aliaque instrumenta ad res Gallo-Franciscas spectantia, ed. J. M. Pardessus, 2 vols. (Paris, 1843–49).

The Durham Collectar, ed. A. Corrêa, HBS 107 (London, 1992).

The Durham Ritual: A Southern English Collectar of the Tenth Century with Northumbrian Additions, facsimile ed. T. J. Brown, with contributions from F. Wormald, A. S. C. Ross, and E. G. Stanley, EEMF 16 (Copenhagen, 1969).

English Historical Documents, I: *c. 500–1042*, ed. D. Whitelock, 2nd edn (London, 1996).

English Kalendars Before A.D. 1100, ed. F. Wormald, HBS 72 (London, 1934).

Ermoldus Nigellus, *In honorem Hludowici carmen*, ed. and tr. (French) E. Faral, *Ermold le Noir: Poème sur Louis le Pieux et Épitres au Roi Pépin* (Paris, 1964).

The Exeter Book of Old English Poetry, facsimile and commentary ed. R. W. Chambers, M. Förster, and R. Flower (London, 1933).

Facsimiles of Ancient Charters in the British Museum, ed. E. A. Bond, 4 vols. (London, 1873–8).

Ferreolus of Uzès, *Regula ad monachos*, PL LXVI, 959–76.

Folcuin, *Gesta abbati S. Bertini Sithiensium*, ed. O. Holder Egger, MGH SS 13 (Hanover, 1881), pp. 607–35.

pseudo-Fulgentius, see Sauer, 'Die Ermahnung', in 'Secondary Literature'.

Gervase of Canterbury, *Acta pontificum Cantuariensis ecclesiae*, ed. W. Stubbs, *The Historical Works of Gervase of Canterbury*, 2 vols., Rolls Series 73 (London, 1879–80).

Die Gesänge des altrömischen Graduale: Vat. lat. 5139, ed. M. Landwehr-Melnicki, with an introduction by B. Stäblein, Monumenta monodica Medii Ævi 2 (Basel, 1970).

Glossaria Latina, ed. W. M. Lindsay et al., 5 vols. (Paris, 1926–31).

Graduale triplex (Solesmes, 1979).

Gregory I, *Dialogi (Dialogorum libri IV)*, ed. A. de Vogüé, *Grégoire le Grand: Dialogues*, Sources chrétiennes 260 (Paris, 1979). English translation of Book II, C. White, *Early Christian Lives* (London, 1998), pp. 161–204.

Gregory I, *Moralia in Iob*, ed. M. Adriaen, 3 vols., CCSL 143, 143A and 143B (Turnhout, 1979).

S. Gregorii Magni Registrum epistularum, ed. D. Norberg, 2 vols., CCSL 140, 140A (Turnhout, 1982).

Helisachar, *Epistola Nidibrio Narbonensis archiepiscopo*, ed. E. Dümmler (after E. Bishop), *Epistolae Karolini aevi*, III, MGH Epp. 5 (Berlin, 1899), pp. 307–9 (Epistolae variorum, no. 6).

Hilary of Poitiers, *Liber de synodis*, PL X, 471–548.

Hildemar, *Expositio Regulae S. Benedicti*, ed. R. Mittermüller, *Vitae et Regula SS. P. Benedicti una cum expositione Regulae*, III: *Expositio Regulae ab Hildemaro tradita et nunc primum typis mandata* (Regensburg, 1880).

Hildemar [pseudo-Paul Warnefrid], *Expositio Regulae S. Benedicti*, ed. the Monks of Monte Cassino, *Pauli Warnefridi diaconi Casinensis in sanctam Regulam commentarium* (Monte Cassino, 1880).

Die Hirtenbriefe Aelfrics in altenglischer und lateinischer Fassung, ed. B. Fehr (Hamburg, 1914), repr. with a supplement to the introduction by P. Clemoes, Bibliothek der angelsächsischen Prosa 9 (Darmstadt, 1966).

Historia de S. Cuthberto, ed. T. Arnold, *Symeonis monachi Opera omnia*, 2 vols., Rolls Series 75 (London, 1882–5) I, 196–214.

Historia ecclesie Abbendonensis: The History of the Church of Abingdon, ed. and tr. J. Hudson, 2 vols., Oxford Medieval Texts (Oxford, 2002–7).

Hugeburc of Heidenheim, *Hodoeporicon (Vita S. Willibaldi)*, ed. O. Holder-Egger, in *Vitae aliaeque historiae minores*, MGH SS 15.1 (Hanover, 1887), pp. 86–117; tr. Talbot, *The Anglo-Saxon Missionaries*, pp. 153–77.

Initia consuetudinis Benedictinae: Consuetudines saeculi octavi et noni, ed. K. Hallinger, CCM 1 (Siegburg, 1963).

Institutio canonicorum, ed. Werminghoff, *Concilia aevi Karolini* I, 308–421.

Institutio sanctimonialium, ed. Werminghoff, *Concilia aevi Karolini* I, 422–56.

The Irish Liber Hymnorum, ed. J. H. Bernard and R. Atkinson, 2 vols., HBS 13–14 (London, 1989).

Isidore of Seville, *Etymologiae (Etymologiarum siue originum libri XX)*, ed. W. M. Lindsay, 2 vols., Oxford Classical Texts (Oxford, 1911).

Jerome, *Praefatio in libro psalmorum*, ed. R. Weber, et al., *Biblia sacra iuxta vulgata versionem*, 4th edn, ed. R. Gryson, et al. (Stuttgart, 1994), p. 767.

John Cassian, *Institutiones (De institutis coenobiorum)*, ed. and tr. (French) J.-C. Guy, *Jean Cassien: Institutions cénobitiques*, Sources chrétiennes 109 (Paris, 1965).

John of Salerno, *Vita sancti Odonis abbatis Cluniacensis secundi*, PL CXXXIII, 43–86.

John ('Florence') of Worcester, *Chronicon ex chronicis*, ed. R. R. Darlington and P. McGurk, tr. J. Bray and P. McGurk, *The Chronicle of John of Worcester*, II: *The Annals from 450 to 1066*, Oxford Medieval Texts (Oxford, 1995).

Johnson, J., *A Collection of the Laws and Canons of the Church of England: From its First Foundation to the Conquest, and from the Conquest to the Reign of King Henry VIII*, new edn ed. J. Baron, 2 vols., Library of Anglo-Catholic Theology (Oxford, 1850–1).

Keynes, S., and M. Lapidge, *Alfred the Great: Asser's 'Life of King Alfred' and Other Contemporary Sources* (London, 1983).

King Alfred's West-Saxon Version of Gregory's Pastoral Care, ed. H. Sweet, 2 vols., EETS 45, 50 (London, 1871–2).

Lanfranc, *Decreta monachis Cantuariensibus transmissa*, ed. D. Knowles and C. N. L. Brooke, *The Monastic Constitutions of Lanfranc*, Oxford Medieval Texts (Oxford, 2002).

Lapidge, M., and M. Herren, *Aldhelm: The Prose Works* (Cambridge, 1979).

Lapidge, M., and J. L. Rosier, *Aldhelm: The Poetic Works* (Cambridge, 1985).

Legatine Synod (786), ed. Haddan and Stubbs, *Councils* III, 448–50.

Leidrad of Lyons, *Epistola ad Karolum magnum*, ed. E. Dümmler, *Epistolae Karolini aevi*, II, MGH Epp. 5 (Berlin, 1895), pp. 542–4.

The Leofric Missal, ed. N. Orchard, 2 vols., HBS 113–14 (London, 2002).

Liber diurnus, ed. T. Sickel (Vienna, 1889).

Liber Eliensis, ed. E. O. Blake, Camden 3rd ser. 92 (London, 1962).

Liber pontificalis, ed. L. Duchesne, 3 vols., vol. 3 ed. C. Vogel (Paris, 1886–1957).

Liber sacramentorum Augustodunensis, ed. O. Heiming, CCSL 159B (Turnhout, 1984).

Liber sacramentorum Gellonensis, ed. A. Dumas, with introduction and indices by J. Deshusses, 2 vols., CCSL 159 and 159A (Turnhout, 1981).

The Liber Usualis with Introduction and Rubrics in English, ed. the Benedictines of Solesmes (Tournai, 1963).

The Liber Vitae of the New Minster and Hyde Abbey, Winchester: British Library Stowe 944, ed. S. Keynes, EEMF 26 (Copenhagen, 1996).

The Manuscript Irish Missal belonging to the President and Fellows of Corpus Christi College, Oxford, ed. F. E. Warren (London, 1879).

McClure, J., and R. Collins (eds.), *Bede: The Ecclesiastical History of the English People, The Greater Chronicle, Bede's Letter to Egbert*, Oxford World's Classics (Oxford, 1999),

Memoriale qualiter, ed. C. Morgand, in *Initia consuetudinis Benedictinae*, ed. Hallinger, CCM 1, pp. 230–61.

The Missal of Robert of Jumièges, ed. H. A. Wilson, HBS 11 (London, 1896).

Missale Ambrosianum duplex (Proprium de Tempore): Editiones Puteobonellianae et typica (1751–1902), ed. A. M. Ceriani, A. Ratti, and M. Magistretti, Monumenta sacra et profana 4 (Milan, 1913).

The Monastic Breviary of Hyde Abbey, Winchester: MSS. Rawlinson liturg. e. 1*, and Gough liturg. 8, in the Bodleian Library, Oxford, ed. J. B. L. Tolhurst, 6 vols., HBS 69, 70, 71, 76, 78, 80 (London, 1932–42).

Noble, T. F. X., and T. Head (eds.), *Soldiers of Christ: Saints and Saints' Lives from Late Antiquity and the Early Middle Ages* (London, 1995).

Notker Balbulus, *Gesta Karoli magni imperatoris*, ed. H. F. Haefele, *Notker der Stammler: Taten Kaiser Karls des Grossen*, MGH SRG 12 (Berlin, 1959).

Novum Testamentum Domini nostri Iesu Christi latine secundum editionem S. Hieronymi, ed. J. Wordsworth, H. J. White, and H. F. D. Sparks (Oxford, 1889–1954).

The Nowell Codex: British Museum, Cotton Vitellius A.XV, second ms, facsimile ed. K. Malone, EEMF 12 (Copenhagen, 1963).

'An Old English account of King Edgar's establishment of monasteries', ed. and tr. Whitelock, *Councils and Synods* I, 142–54.

The Ordinal and Customary of the Abbey of Saint Mary, York, ed. The Abbess of Stanbrook [L. McLachlan] and J. B. L. Tolhurst, 3 vols., HBS 73, 75, 84 (London, 1936–51).

The Ordinal of the Abbey of the Holy Trinity, Fécamp (Fécamp, Musée de la Bénédictine, MS 186), ed. D. Chadd, 2 vols., HBS 111–12 (Woodbridge, 1999–2002).

Les Ordines Romani du haut Moyen Âge, ed. M. Andrieu, 5 vols., Spicilegium sacrum Lovaniense 11, 23, 24, 28, 29 (Louvain, 1931–61).

Ordo Casinensis II dictus Ordo officii, ed. T. Leccisotti, in *Initia consuetudines Benedictinae*, ed. Hallinger, CCM 1, pp. 113–23.

Osbern of Canterbury, *Vita S. Elphegi*, ed. H. Wharton, *Anglia sacra*, 2 vols. (London, 1691) II, 135–6.

The Parker Chronicle and Laws: Corpus Christi College, Cambridge, ms. 173: A Facsimile, ed. R. Flower and H. Smith, EETS 208 (Oxford, 1941).

Passio S. Eugeniae, in Boninus Mombritius, *Sanctuarium seu Vitae sanctorum*, ed. two anonymous monks of Solesmes, 2 vols. (Paris, 1910) II, 391–7.

Paul Warnefrid ('the Deacon'), *Gesta episcoporum Mettensium*, ed. G. H. Pertz, MGH SS 2 (Hanover, 1829), pp. 260–70.

——, *Homiliarius*, PL XCV, 1159–1566.

Paulinus of Milan, *Vita sancti Ambrosii*, PL XIV, 27–46.

Pontificale Lanaletense (Bibliothèque de la ville de Rouen A. 27. CAT. 368): A Pontifical Formerly in Use at St. German's, Cornwall, ed. G. H. Doble, HBS 74 (London, 1937).

The Portiforium of St Wulstan, ed. A. Hughes, 2 vols., HBS 89–90 (Leighton Buzzard, 1958–60).

Le Psautier romain et les autres anciens psautiers latins, ed. R. Weber, Collectanea biblica latina 10 (Vatican City, 1953).

Ratio de cursus qui fuerunt eius auctores, ed. J. Semmler, in *Initia consuetudinis Benedictinae*, ed. Hallinger, CCM 1, pp. 77–91.

RB 1980: The Rule of St. Benedict in Latin and English with Notes, ed. T. Fry (Collegeville, MN, 1981).

Regula Magistri, ed. and tr. (French) A. de Vogüé, *La Règle du Maître*, 3 vols., Sources chrétiennes 105–7 (Paris, 1964–5).

Regula S. Benedicti, ed. J. Neufville, in A. de Vogüé, *La Règle de Saint Benoît*,

French Translation, Notes, and Commentary, with Latin text and critical apparatus, 7 vols., Sources chrétiennes 181–6, vol. 7 extra seriem (Paris, 1971–7), I–II.

Regularis concordia Anglicae nationis monachorum sanctimonialiumque, ed. and tr. T. Symons, *The Monastic Agreement of the Monks and Nuns of the English Nation*, Nelson's Medieval Classics (Oxford, 1953).

Regularis concordia Anglicae nationis, ed. T. Symons and S. Spath, with M. Wegener and K. Hallinger, in *Consuetudinum saeculi X/XI/XII monumenta non-Cluniacensia*, ed. K. Hallinger, CCM 7.3 (Siegburg, 1984), pp. 61–147.

Rituale ecclesiae Dunelmensis, ed. J. Stevenson, *Rituale ecclesiae Dunelmensis*, Surtees Society 10 (London, 1841).

Rituale ecclesiae Dunelmensis: The Durham Ritual, ed. U. Lindelöf, with an introduction by A. H. Thompson, Surtees Society 160 (London, 1927).

The Rule of St Benedict: The Abingdon Copy, ed. J. Chamberlin, Toronto Medieval Latin Texts 13 (Toronto, 1982).

The Rule of St Benedict: Oxford, Bodleian Library, Hatton 48, facsimile ed. D. H. Farmer, EEMF 15 (Copenhagen, 1968).

The Rule of S. Benet: Latin and Anglo-Saxon Interlinear Version, ed. H. Logeman, EETS 90 (London, 1888).

Le Sacramentaire grégorien: Ses principales formes d'après les plus anciens manuscrits, ed. J. Deshusses, 2nd and 3rd edns, 3 vols., Spicilegium Friburgense 16, 24, 28 (Freiburg, Switzerland, 1988–92).

The Sacramentary of Ratoldus, ed. N. Orchard, HBS 116 (London, 2005).

The Salisbury Psalter, ed. C. Sisam and K. Sisam, EETS 242 (London, 1949).

Select English Historical Documents of the Ninth and Tenth Centuries, ed. F. E. Harmer (Cambridge, 1914).

Smaragdi abbatis Expositio in Regulam S. Benedicti, ed. A. Spannagel and P. Engelbert, CCM 8 (Siegburg, 1974). Translation: D. Barry, *Smaragdus of Saint-Mihiel: Commentary on the Rule of Saint Benedict*, with intr. essays by T. Kardong, J. Leclercq, and D. M. LaCorte, Cistercian Studies 212 (Kalamazoo, MI, 2007).

Smaragdus of Saint-Mihiel, *Diadema monachorum*, PL CII, 593–690.

Statuta Murbacensia, see *Actuum praeliminarium*.

Stephen of Ripon, *Vita S. Wilfridi*, ed. and tr. B. Colgrave, *The Life of Bishop Wilfrid by Eddius Stephanus* (Cambridge, 1927).

Symeon of Durham, *Libellus de exordio atque procursus istius hoc est Dunhelmensis ecclesie (Tract on the Origins and Progress of this Church of Durham)*, ed. and tr. D. Rollason, Oxford Medieval Texts (Oxford, 2000).

Synodi primae Aquisgranensis decreta authentica, ed. J. Semmler, in *Initia consuetudinis Benedictinae*, ed. Hallinger, CCM 1, pp. 457–68.

Talbot, C. H., *The Anglo-Saxon Missionaries in Germany* (London, 1954; repr. 1981), pp. 153–77.

Theodemar, *Epistula ad Theodoricum gloriosum*, ed. J. Winandy and K. Hallinger, in *Initia consuetudines Benedictinae*, ed. Hallinger, CCM 1, pp. 125–36.

——, *Epistola ad Karolum magnum*, ed. E. Dümmler, MGH Epp. 2 (Berlin, 1895), pp. 509–14.

Thomas of Elmham, *Historia monasterii S. Augustini Cantuariensis*, ed. C. Hardwick, Rolls Series 8 (London, 1858).

Thorpe, L., *Two Lives of Charlemagne* (London, 1969).

Two Lives of St Cuthbert, ed. and tr. B. Colgrave (Cambridge, 1940).

Two of the Saxon Chronicles Parallel: A Revised Text, ed. C. Plummer (based on the edition of J. Earle), 2 vols. (Oxford, 1892–9).

Usuard of Saint-Germain-des-Prés, *Martyrologium*, ed. J. Dubois, *Le Martyrologe d'Usuard: Texte et commentaire* (Brussels, 1965).

Venerabilis Baedae Opera historica, ed. C. Plummer, 2 vols. (Oxford, 1896).

The Vespasian Psalter, ed. S. M. Kuhn (Ann Arbor, MI, 1965).

The Vespasian Psalter: British Museum, Cotton Vespasian A.I, facsimile ed. D. H. Wright, EEMF 14 (Copenhagen, 1967).

Vita Alcuini, ed. W. Arndt, MGH SS 15.1 (Hanover, 1887), pp. 184–97.

Vita Ceolfrithi (*Historia abbatum auctore anonymo*), ed. Plummer I, 388–404. Translation: D. H. Farmer, in Webb and Farmer, *The Age of Bede*, pp. 213–29.

Vita S. Cuthberti (anonymous), ed. and tr. Colgrave, *Two Lives of St Cuthbert* (Cambridge, 1940), pp. 60–139.

Walahfrid Strabo, *Libellus de exordiis et incrementis quarundam in observationibus ecclesiasticis rerum*, ed. and tr. A. Harting-Correa (Leiden, 1996).

Webb, J. F., and D. H. Farmer, *The Age of Bede*, rev. edn (London, 1998).

William of Malmesbury, *Gesta pontificum Anglorum (The History of the English Bishops)*, ed. and tr. M. Winterbottom, Introduction and Commentary by R. M. Thomson, 2 vols., Oxford Medieval Texts (Oxford, 2007).

Willibald, *Vita Bonifatii*, ed. W. Levison, *Vitae Bonifatii archiepiscopi Mogutini*, MGH SRG 57 (Hanover, 1905), pp. 1–58. Translation: Talbot, *The Anglo-Saxon Missionaries*, pp. 23–62.

The Winchester Troper: Facsimile Edition and Introduction, by S. Rankin, Early English Church Music 50 (London, 2007).

Wulfstan of Winchester, *Vita S. Æthelwoldi*, ed. and tr. M. Lapidge and M. Winterbottom, *Wulfstan of Winchester: The Life of St Æthelwold*, Oxford Medieval Texts (Oxford, 1991).

Wulfstan's Canon Law Collection, ed. and tr. J. E. Cross and A. Hamer (Cambridge, 1999).

Secondary Literature

Allgeier, A., 'Die erste Psalmenübersetzung des hl. Hieronymus und das Psalterium Romanum', *Biblica* 12 (1931), 447–82.

Angenendt, A., *Monachi peregrini: Studien zur Pirmin und den monastischen*

Vorstellungen des frühen Mittelalters, Münstersche Mittelalterschriften 6 (Munich, 1972).

Arnaldi, F., et al. (eds.), *Novum glossarium mediae Latinitatisis ab anno DCCC usque ad annum MCC* (Heidelberg, 1957–).

Bailey, T., 'Ambrosian psalmody: An introduction', *Rivista internazionale di musica sacra* 1 (1980), 82–99.

Bannister, H. M., 'Liturgical fragments, A: Anglo-Saxon sacramentaries', *Journal of Theological Studies* 9 (1908), 398–427.

Barrow, J., 'English cathedral communities and reform in the late tenth and eleventh centuries', in D. Rollason, M. Harvey, and M. Prestwich (eds.), *Anglo-Norman Durham, 1093–1193* (Woodbridge, 1994), pp. 25–39.

——, 'The community of Worcester, 961–c. 1100', in Brooks and Cubitt, *St Oswald*, pp. 84–99.

——, 'Worcester', in M. Lapidge (ed.), *The Blackwell Encyclopaedia of Anglo-Saxon England* (Oxford, 1999), pp. 488–90.

——, 'The chronology of forgery production at Worcester from c. 1000 to the early twelfth century', in J. S. Barrow and N. P. Brooks (eds.), *St Wulfstan and his World*, Studies in Early Medieval Britain 4 (Aldershot, 2005), pp. 105–22.

——, 'Review article: Chrodegang, his rule and its successors', *Early Medieval Europe* 14 (2006), 201–12.

——, 'Grades of ordination and clerical careers, c. 900–c. 1200', in C. Matthews (ed.), *Anglo-Norman Studies 30: Proceedings of the Battle Conference 2007* (Woodbridge, 2008), pp. 41–61.

Batiffol, P., *History of the Roman Breviary*, tr. A. M. Y. Baylay [from the 3rd French edn] (London, 1912).

Bäumer, S., *Histoire du bréviaire*, tr. R. Biron, 2 vols. (Paris, 1905).

Baumstark, A., *Comparative Liturgy*, tr. F. L. Cross from the 3rd rev. French edn, ed. B. Botte (Westminster, MD, 1958).

Beyssac, G., 'Note sur le Graduel-Sacramentaire de St. Pierre–St. Denys de Bantz, du XIIe siècle', *Revue bénédictine* 31 (1921), 190–200.

Billett, J. D., 'The Divine Office and the secular clergy in later Anglo-Saxon England', in D. Rollason, C. Leyser, and H. Williams (eds.), *England and the Continent in the Tenth Century: Studies in Honour of Wilhelm Levison (1876–1947)*, Studies in the Early Middle Ages 37 (Turnhout, 2010), pp. 429–71.

——, '*Sermones ad diem pertinentes*: Sermons and homilies in the liturgy of the Divine Office', in M. Diesenberger, Y. Hen, and M. Pollheimer (eds.), *'Sermo doctorum': Compilers, Preachers, and their Audiences in the Early Medieval West*, SERMO 9 (Turnhout, 2013), pp. 339–73.

Bischoff, B., *Latin Palaeography: Antiquity and the Middle Ages*, tr. D. Ó Cróinín and D. Ganz (Cambridge, 1990).

Bishop, E., 'A letter of Abbat Helisachar', in his *Liturgica Historica: Papers on the Liturgy and Religious Life of the Western Church* (Oxford, 1918), pp. 333–48.

Bishop, T. A. M., 'Notes on Cambridge manuscripts, Part IV: MSS. connected with St Augustine's, Canterbury', *Transactions of the Cambridge Bibliographical Society* 2/iv (1957), 323–36 and Plates XIII–XIV.

——, 'Notes on Cambridge manuscripts, Part V: MSS. connected with St Augustine's, Canterbury, continued', *Transactions of the Cambridge Bibliographical Society* 3/i (1959), 93–5.

——, 'Notes on Cambridge manuscripts, Part VI: MSS. connected with St Augustine's, Canterbury, continued', *Transactions of the Cambridge Bibliographical Society* 3/v (1963), 412–13.

——, 'Notes on Cambridge manuscripts, Part VII: The early minuscule of Christ Church, Canterbury', *Transactions of the Cambridge Bibliographical Society* 3/v (1963), 413–23 and Plates XIII–XIV.

——, 'An early example of the Square minuscule', *Transactions of the Cambridge Bibliographical Society* 4 (1964–8), 246–52.

——, *English Caroline Minuscule* (Oxford, 1971).

Blair, J., 'Debate: Ecclesiastical organization and pastoral care in Anglo-Saxon England', *Early Medieval Europe* 4 (1995), 192–212.

——, *The Church in Anglo-Saxon Society* (Oxford, 2005).

Bradshaw, P., *Daily Prayer in the Early Church: A Study of the Origin and Early Development of the Divine Office*, Alcuin Club Collections 63 (London, 1981).

Brooks, N., 'England in the ninth century: The crucible of defeat', *Transactions of the Royal Historical Society*, 5th ser., 29 (1979), 1–20.

——, *The Early History of the Church of Canterbury: Christ Church from 597 to 1066* (Leicester, 1984).

——, 'The career of St Dunstan', in Ramsay et al., *St Dunstan*, pp. 1–23.

Brooks, N., and C. Cubitt (eds.), *St Oswald of Worcester: Life and Influence* (London, 1996).

Budny, M., ' "St Dunstan's Classbook" and its frontispiece: Dunstan's portrait and autograph', in Ramsay et al., *St Dunstan*, pp. 103–42.

——, *Insular, Anglo-Saxon, and Early Anglo-Norman Manuscript Art at Corpus Christi College, Cambridge: An Illustrated Catalogue*, 2 vols. (Kalamazoo, MI, 1997).

Bullough, D. A., 'Roman books and Carolingian *renovatio*', in his *Carolingian Renewal*, pp. 1–33; originally published in *Studies in Church History* 14 (Oxford, 1977), pp. 23–50.

——, 'Alcuin and the Kingdom of Heaven: Liturgy, theology, and the Carolingian age', in his *Carolingian Renewal*, pp. 161–240; originally published in U.-R. Blumenthal (ed.), *Carolingian Essays: Andrew W. Mellon Lectures in Early Christian Studies* (Washington, DC, 1983), pp. 1–69.

——, *Carolingian Renewal: Sources and Heritage* (Manchester, 1991).

——, 'St Oswald: Monk, bishop and archbishop', in Brooks and Cubitt, *St Oswald*, pp. 1–22.

——, *Alcuin: Achievement and Reputation* (Leiden, 2004).

Butler, C., 'Was St. Augustine of Canterbury a Benedictine?', *Downside Review*

3 (1882), 45–61 and 223–40.

Callewaert, C., *De breviarii Romani liturgia*, 2nd edn (Bruges, 1939) (=vol. 2 of his *Liturgicae institutiones*).

——, *Sacris erudiri* [collected papers], ed. the Monks of St Peter of Aldeburg (Steenbrugge, 1940).

Cambridge, E., and D. Rollason, 'Debate: The pastoral organization of the Anglo-Saxon Church: A review of the "Minster Hypothesis" ', *Early Medieval Europe* 4 (1995), 87–104.

Chadd, D., 'Liturgical books: Catalogues, editions and inventories', in D. Hiley (ed.), *Die Erschließung der Quellen des mittelalterlichen Gesangs*, Wolfenbütteler Mittelalter-Studien 18 (Wiesbaden, 2004), pp. 43–74.

Clemoes, P., *Liturgical Influence on Punctuation in Late Old English and Early Middle English Manuscripts* (Cambridge, 1952), repr. Old English Newsletter, Subsidia 4 (Binghamton, NY, 1980).

Collamore, L., 'Charting the Divine Office', in Fassler and Baltzer, *The Divine Office in the Latin Middle Ages*, pp. 3–11.

Constantinescu, R., 'Alcuin et les "libelli precum" de l'époque carolingienne', *Revue d'histoire et de la spiritualité* 50 (1974), 17–56.

Corrêa, A., 'Daily Office books: Collectars and breviaries', in Pfaff, *The Liturgical Books*, pp. 45–60.

——, 'The liturgical manuscripts of Oswald's houses', in Brooks and Cubitt, *St Oswald*, pp. 285–324.

Coulton, G. G., *Studies in Medieval Thought* (London, 1940).

Crichton, J. D., 'The Office in the West: The early Middle Ages', in C. Jones, G. Wainwright, E. Yarnold, and P. Bradshaw (eds.), *The Study of Liturgy*, rev. edn (London, 1992), pp. 420–9.

Cross, F. L., and E. A. Livingstone (eds.), *The Oxford Dictionary of the Christian Church*, 3rd edn rev. (Oxford, 2005).

Cross, J. E., 'Ælfric and the mediaeval homiliary – objection and contribution', *Scripta minora Regiae societatis humaniorum litterarum Lundensis* 1961–1962:4 (1963), 3–34.

——, 'On the library of the Old English Martyrologist', in Gneuss and Lapidge, *Learning and Literature*, pp. 227–49.

——, '*De festivitatibus anni* and Ansegisus, *Capitularum collectio* (827) in Anglo-Saxon manuscripts', *Liverpool Classical Monthly* 17.8 (1992), 119–21.

Crowley, J. P., 'Latin prayers added into the margins of the prayerbook British Library, Royal 2.A.XX at the beginnings of the monastic reform in Worcester', *Sacris erudiri* 45 (2006), 223–303.

Cubitt, C., *Anglo-Saxon Church Councils c.650–c.850* (London, 1995).

——, 'Review article: The tenth-century Benedictine Reform in England', *Early Medieval Europe* 6 (1997), 77–94.

Cullin, O., 'De la psalmodie sans refrain à la psalmodie responsoriale: Transformation et conservation dans les répertoires liturgiques latins', *Revue de musi-*

cologie 77 (1991), 5–24.
Deanesly, M., *Augustine of Canterbury* (London, 1964).
de Bruyne, D., 'Le problème du psautier romain', *Revue bénédictine* 42 (1930), 101–26.
DeGregorio, S., 'Bede, the monk, as exegete: Evidence from the commentary on Ezra-Nehemiah', *Revue bénédictine* 115 (2005), 343–69.
de Jong, M., 'Growing up in a Carolingian monastery: Magister Hildemar and his oblates', *Journal of Medieval History* 9 (1983), 99–128.
——, 'Carolingian monasticism: The power of prayer', in R. McKitterick (ed.), *The New Cambridge Medieval History*, II: *c.700–c.900* (Cambridge, 1995), pp. 622–53.
——, *In Samuel's Image: Child Oblation in the Early Medieval West* (Leiden, 1996).
Dekkers, E., *Clavis patrum Latinorum*, 2nd edn, CCSL *extra seriem* (Turnhout, 1961); 3rd edn (Steenbrugge, 1995).
Deshman, R., '*Christus rex et magi reges*: Kingship and Christology in Ottonian and Anglo-Saxon art', *Frühmittelalterlicher Studien* 10 (1976), 367–405.
Dierkens, A., *Abbayes et chapitres entre Sambre et Meuse (VIIe–XIe siècles): Contribution à l'histoire religieuse des campagnes du Haut Moyen Âge*, Beihefte der Francia 14 (Sigmaringen, 1985).
Dobszay, L., 'Reading an Office book', in Fassler and Baltzer, *The Divine Office in the Latin Middle Ages*, pp. 48–73.
Doyle, A. I., 'A fragment of an eighth-century Northumbrian Office book', in M. Korhammer (ed.), *Words, Texts and Manuscripts: Studies in Anglo-Saxon Culture Presented to Helmut Gneuss on the Occasion of his Sixty-fifth Birthday* (Cambridge, 1992), pp. 11–27.
Du Cange (C. du Fresne), *Glossarium mediae et infimae Latinitatis*, new edn by L. Favre, 10 vols. (Niort, 1883–7).
Duffy, E., *The Stripping of the Altars: Traditional Religion in England c. 1400–c. 1580* (New Haven, CT, 1992).
Dumville, D. N., 'English Square minuscule script: The background and earliest phases', *Anglo-Saxon England* 16 (1987), 147–79.
——, 'Beowulf come lately: Some notes on the palaeography of the Nowell Codex', *Archiv für das Studium der neueren Sprachen und Literaturen* 225 (1988), 49–63.
——, *Liturgy and the Ecclesiastical History of Late Anglo-Saxon England* (Woodbridge, 1992).
——, *Wessex and England from Alfred to Edgar: Six Essays on Political, Cultural, and Ecclesiastical Revival*, Studies in Anglo-Saxon History 3 (Woodbridge, 1992).
——, *English Caroline Script and Monastic History: Studies in Benedictinism, A.D. 950–1030* (Woodbridge, 1993).
——, 'English square minuscule script: The mid-century phases', *Anglo-Saxon*

England 23 (1994), 133–64.

Dyer, J., 'Monastic psalmody of the Middle Ages', *Revue bénédictine* 99 (1989), 41–74.

——, 'The singing of psalms in the early-medieval Office', *Speculum* 64 (1989), 535–78.

Farmer, D. H., 'The progress of the monastic revival', in Parsons, *Tenth-Century Studies*, pp. 10–19.

Fassler, M. E., 'Sermons, sacramentaries, and early sources for the Office in the Latin West: The example of Advent', in Fassler and Baltzer, *The Divine Office in the Latin Middle Ages*, pp. 15–47.

Fassler, M. E., and R. A. Baltzer (eds.), *The Divine Office in the Latin Middle Ages: Methodology and Source Studies, Regional Developments, Hagiography* (Oxford, 2000).

Ferrari, G., *Early Roman Monasteries: Notes for the History of the Monasteries and Convents at Rome from the V through the X Century*, Studi di antichità cristiana 23 (Vatican City, 1957).

Ferretti, P., *Esthétique grégorienne, ou Traité des formes musicales du chant grégorien* (Solesmes, 1938).

Fisher, D. J. V., 'The anti-monastic reaction in the reign of Edward the Martyr', *Cambridge Historical Journal* 10 (1952), 254–70.

Foot, S., 'Violence against Christians? The Vikings and the Church in ninth-century England', *Medieval History* 1.3 (1991), pp. 3–16.

——, 'Anglo-Saxon minsters: A review of terminology', in J. Blair and R. Sharpe (eds.), *Pastoral Care before the Parish* (Leicester, 1992), pp. 212–25.

——, *Veiled Women*, II: *Female Religious Communities in England, 871–1066* (Aldershot, 2000).

——, *Monastic Life in Anglo-Saxon England, c. 600–900* (Cambridge, 2006).

Forshall, J., *Catalogue of Manuscripts in the British Museum*, new ser. 1.2: *The Burney Manuscripts* ([London], 1840).

Froger, J., 'La méthode de Dom Hesbert dans le volume V du *Corpus antiphonalium officii*', *Études grégoriennes* 18 (1979), 97–143.

——, 'Le fragment de Lucques (fin du VIIIe siècle)', *Études grégoriennes* 18 (1979), 145–55.

——, 'La méthode de Dom Hesbert dans le volume VI du *Corpus antiphonalium officii*', *Études grégoriennes* 19 (1980), 185–96.

——, 'Le lieu de destination et de provenance du "Compiendiensis"', in J. B. Göschl (ed.), *Ut mens concordet voci: Festschrift Eugène Cardine* (Sankt Ottilien, 1980), pp. 338–53.

Gamber, K., *Codices liturgici Latini antiquiores*, 2nd edn and *Supplementum* (with G. Baroffio), 3 vols., Spicilegii Friburgensis subsidia 1, 1a (Freiburg, Switzerland, 1968–88).

Gameson, R., 'Book production and decoration at Worcester in the tenth and eleventh centuries', in Brooks and Cubitt, *St Oswald*, pp. 194–243.

Gameson, R. (ed.), *The Cambridge History of the Book in Britain*, I: *c.600–1100* (Cambridge, 2011).
Gameson, R., and H. Leyser (eds.), *Belief and Culture in the Middle Ages: Studies Presented to Henry Mayr-Harting* (Oxford, 1992).
Ganz, D., *Corbie and the Carolingian Renaisance*, Beihefte der Francia 20 (Sigmaringen, 1990).
——, 'Square Minuscule', in Gameson, *Book in Britain*, pp. 188–96.
Gatch, M. McC., 'The Office in late Anglo-Saxon monasticism', in Lapidge and Gneuss, *Learning and Literature*, pp. 341–62.
Gittos, H., 'Is there any evidence for the liturgy of parish churches in late Anglo-Saxon England? The Red Book of Darley and the status of Old English', in F. Tinti (ed.), *Pastoral Care in Late Anglo-Saxon England*, Anglo-Saxon Studies 6 (Woodbridge, 2005), pp. 63–82.
Gittos, H., and M. B. Bedingfield (eds.), *The Liturgy of the Late Anglo-Saxon Church*, HBS, Subsidia 5 (London, 2005).
Gneuss, H., *Lehnbildung und Lehnbedeutungen im Altenglischen* (Berlin, 1955).
——, 'Zur Geschichte des Ms. Vespasian A. I', *Anglia* 75 (1957), 125–33; repr. as ch. VII in *idem, Books and Libraries*.
——, *Hymnar und Hymnen im englischen Mittelalter: Studien zur Überlieferung, Glossierung und Übersetzung lateinischer Hymnen in England* (Tübingen, 1968).
——, 'Latin hymns in medieval England: Future research', in B. Rowland (ed.), *Chaucer and Middle English Studies in Honour of Rossell Hope Robbins* (London, 1974), pp. 407–24; repr. as ch. XI in *idem, Books and Libraries*.
——, 'Preliminary list of manuscripts written or owned in England up to 1100', *Anglo-Saxon England* 9 (1981), 1–60.
——, 'Liturgical books in Anglo-Saxon England and their Old English terminology', in Lapidge and Gneuss, *Learning and Literature*, pp. 91–141.
——, 'Anglo-Saxon libraries from the Conversion to the Benedictine Reform', in *Angli e sassoni al di qua e al di là del mare*, Settimane di studio del Centro italiano di studi sull'alto medioevo 32 (Spoleto, 1986), pp. 643–88; repr. as ch. II in *idem, Books and Libraries*.
——, 'King Alfred and the history of Anglo-Saxon libraries', in P. R. Brown, G. R. Crampton, and F. C. Robinson (eds.), *Modes of Interpretation in Old English Literature: Essays in Honour of Stanley B. Greenfield* (Toronto, 1986), pp. 29–49; repr. as ch. III in *idem, Books and Libraries*.
——, *Books and Libraries in Early England*, Variorum Collected Studies 558 (Aldershot, 1996).
——, *Handlist of Anglo-Saxon Manuscripts: A List of Manuscripts and Manuscript Fragments Written or Owned in England up to 1100*, Medieval and Renaissance Studies 241 (Tempe, AZ, 2001).
Godden, M. R., 'Anglo-Saxons on the mind', in Lapidge and Gneuss, *Learning and Literature*, pp. 271–98.

Gransden, A., 'Traditionalism and continuity during the last century of Anglo-Saxon monasticism', *Journal of Ecclesiastical History* 40 (1989), 159–207.

Grant, R. J. S., *Cambridge, Corpus Christi College 41: The Loricas and the Missal*, Costerus: Essays in English and American Language and Literature, new ser. 17 (Amsterdam, 1979).

Gregoire, R., *Les Homéliaires du Moyen Âge: Inventaire et analyse des manuscrits*, Rerum ecclesiasticarum documenta, Series maior, Fontes 4 (Rome, 1966).

——, *Homéliaires liturgiques médiévaux*, Biblioteca degli 'Studi medievali' 12 (Spoleto, 1980).

Gretsch, M., *The Intellectual Foundations of the English Benedictine Reform*, Cambridge Studies in Anglo-Saxon England 25 (Cambridge, 1999).

——, 'Cambridge, Corpus Christi College 57: A witness to the early stages of the Benedictine reform in England?', *Anglo-Saxon England* 32 (2003), 111–46.

——, 'The Roman psalter, its Old English glosses and the English Benedictine Reform', in Gittos and Bedingfield, *The Liturgy*, pp. 13–28.

Grierson, P., 'Grimbald of St. Bertin's', *English Historical Review* new ser. 55, old ser. 220 (1940), 529–61.

Gy, P.-M., 'Les premiers bréviaires de Saint-Gall (deuxième quart du XIe s.)', in W. Düring (ed.), *Liturgie: Gestalt und Vollzug: Festschrift für Joseph Pascher zum 70. Geburtstag* (Munich, 1963), pp. 104–13.

——, 'La Bible dans la liturgie au Moyen Age', in P. Riché and G. Lobrichon (eds.), *Le Moyen Age et la Bible*, Bible dans tous les temps 4 (Paris, 1984), pp. 537–52.

Hafner, P. W., *Der Basiliuskommentar zur Regula S. Benedicti: Ein Beitrag zur Autorenfrage karolingischer Regelkommentare*, Beiträge zur Geschichte des alten Mönchtums und des Benediktinerordens 23 (Münster, 1959).

Hallinger, K., 'Papst Gregor der Grosse und der hl. Benedict', in B. Steidle (ed.), *Commentationes in Regulam S. Benedicti*, Studia Anselmiana 42 (Rome, 1957), pp. 231–319.

A Handbook of Dates for Students of British History, ed. C. R. Cheney, new edn rev. M. Jones, Royal Historical Society Guides and Handbooks 4 (Cambridge, 2000).

Hanssens, J.-M., *Aux Origines de la prière liturgique: Nature et genèse de l'office des matines*, Analecta Gregoriana 57 (Rome, 1952).

Hare, M., 'Abbot Leofsige of Mettlach: An English monk in Flanders and Upper Lotharingia in the late tenth century', *Anglo-Saxon England* 33 (2004), 109–44 and Plates I and II.

Harper, J., *The Forms and Orders of Western Liturgy from the Tenth to the Eighteenth Century: A Historical Introduction and Guide for Students and Musicians* (Oxford, 1991).

Hartzell, K. D., 'An English antiphoner of the ninth century?', *Revue bénédictine* 90 (1980), 234–48.

——, *Catalogue of Manuscripts Written or Owned in England up to 1200 Containing Music* (Woodbridge, 2006).

Haubrichs, W., *Die Kultur der Abtei Prüm zur Karolingerzeit: Studien zur Heimat des althochdeutschen Georgsliedes*, Rheinisches Archiv 105 (Bonn, 1979).

Haugh, R., *Photius and the Carolingians: The Trinitarian Controversy* (Belmont, MA, 1975).

Hausmann, B. A., *Learning the Breviary* (New York, 1932).

Heath, R. G., 'The Western schism of the Franks and the "filioque"', *Journal of Ecclesiastical History* 23 (1972), 97–113.

Heiming, O., 'Zum monastischen Offizium von Kassianus bis Kolumbanus', *Archiv für Liturgiewissenschaft* 7 (1961–2), 89–156.

Hen, Y., *The Royal Patronage of Liturgy in Frankish Gaul to the Death of Charles the Bald (877)*, HBS Subsidia 3 (London, 2001).

——, 'Rome, Anglo-Saxon England and the formation of the Frankish liturgy', *Revue bénédictine* 112 (2002), 301–22.

Hesbert, R.-J., 'Un curieux antiphonaire palimpseste de l'Office: Rouen, A. 292', *Revue bénédictine* 64 (1954), 28–45.

——, 'Les séries de répons des dimanches de l'avent', *Questions liturgiques et paroissiales* 39 (1958), 299–326.

——, 'L'antiphonaire d'Amalaire', *Ephemerides liturgicae* 94 (1980), 176–94.

——, 'Les antiphonaires monastiques insulaires', *Revue bénédictine* 92 (1982), 358–75.

Hiley, D., 'Thurstan of Caen and plainchant at Glastonbury: Musicological reflections on the Norman Conquest', *Proceedings of the British Academy* 72 (1986), 57–90.

——, *Western Plainchant: A Handbook* (Oxford, 1993).

Hill, D., *An Atlas of Anglo-Saxon England*, 2nd edn (Oxford, 1984).

Hill, J., *Bede and the Benedictine Reform*, Jarrow Lecture (Jarrow, 1998).

Hohler, C., 'The Durham services in honour of St. Cuthbert', in C. F. Battiscombe (ed.), *The Relics of St Cuthbert* (Oxford, 1956), pp. 155–91.

——, 'Some service books of the later Saxon Church', in Parsons, *Tenth-Century Studies*, pp. 60–83.

——, Review of Grant, *Cambridge, Corpus Christi College 41*, in *Medium aevum* 49 (1980), 275–8.

——, 'Theodore and the liturgy', in M. Lapidge (ed.), *Archbishop Theodore: Commemorative Studies on his Life and Influence*, Cambridge Studies in Anglo-Saxon England 11 (Cambridge, 1995), pp. 222–35.

Holdsworth, C., 'Saint Boniface the monk', in T. Reuter (ed.), *The Greatest Englishman: Essays on St Boniface and the Church at Crediton* (Exeter, 1980), pp. 47–67.

Homburger, O., 'Eine spätkarolingische Schule von Corbie', *Forschungen zur Kunstgeschichte und christlichen Archäologie* 3 (1957), 412–26 and figs. 168–84.

Hornby, E., 'Interactions between Brittany and Christ Church, Canterbury in the tenth century: The Linenthal leaf', in E. Hornby and D. Maw (eds.), *Essays on the History of English Music in Honour of John Caldwell: Sources, Style, Performance, Historiography* (Woodbridge, 2010), pp. 47–65.

Hourlier, J., 'Notes sur l'antiphonie', in W. Arlt et al. (eds.), *Gattungen der Musik in Einzeldarstellungen: Gedenkschrift Leo Schrade* (Bern and Munich, 1973), pp. 116–43.

Hucke, H., 'Graduale', *Ephemerides liturgicae* 69 (1955), 262–4.

——, 'Toward a new historical view of Gregorian chant', *Journal of the American Musicological Society* 33 (1980), 437–67.

Hucke, H., and J. Dyer, 'Old Roman chant', in Sadie and Tyrrell, *The New Grove Dictionary* XVIII, 381–5.

Hughes, A., *Medieval Manuscripts for Mass and Office: A Guide to their Organization and Terminology* (Toronto, 1982).

Huglo, M., 'La domaine de la notation bretonne', *Acta musicologica* 35 (1963), 54–84.

——, Review of Hesbert, *CAO* V, in *Revue de musicologie* 63 (1977), 164–8.

——, 'Les remaniements de l'antiphonaire grégorien au IXe siècle: Hélisachar, Agobard, Amalaire', in *Culto cristiano, politica imperiale carolinga: 9–12 ottobre 1977*, Convegni dei Centro di studi sulla spiritualità medievali (Università di Perugia) 18 (Todi, 1979), pp. 87–120.

—— (tr. S. Boynton), 'The cantatorium: From Charlemagne to the fourteenth century', in P. Jeffery (ed.), *The Study of Medieval Chant: Paths and Bridges, East and West* (Woodbridge, 2001), pp. 89–101.

Huglo, M., and J. Halmo, 'Antiphon, § 5(ii): Antiphons with verses', in Sadie and Tyrrell, *The New Grove Dictionary* I, 743–4.

James, M. R., *A Descriptive Catalogue of the Manuscripts in the Library of Corpus Christi College, Cambridge*, 2 vols. (Cambridge, 1912).

Jeffery, P., 'Eastern and Western elements in the Irish monastic prayer of the Hours', in Fassler and Baltzer, *The Divine Office in the Latin Middle Ages*, pp. 99–143.

John, E., 'St. Oswald and the tenth century reformation', *Journal of Ecclesiastical History* 9 (1958), 159–71.

——, 'The king and the monks in the tenth-century reformation', in his *Orbis Britanniae*, Studies in Early English History 4 (Leicester, 1966), pp. 154–80.

——, 'The church of Worcester and St Oswald', in Gameson and Leyser, *Belief and Culture*, pp. 142–57.

Jones, C. A., 'The book of the liturgy in Anglo-Saxon England', *Speculum* 73 (1998), 659–702.

——, *A Lost Work by Amalarius of Metz: Interpolations in Salisbury, Cathedral Library MS 154*, HBS Subsidia 2 (Woodbridge, 2001).

Jørgensen, E., *Catalogus codicum Latinorum medii aevi Bibliothecae regiae Hafniensis* (Copenhagen, 1926).

Jullien, M.-H., and J. Perelman (eds.), *Clavis scriptorum Latinorum medii aevi: Auctores Galliae, 735–937*, II: *Alcuinus*, CCCM *extra seriem* (Turnhout, 1999).

Keefer, S. L., 'Margin as archive: The liturgical marginalia of a manuscript of the Old English Bede', *Traditio* 51 (1996), 147–77.

Ker, N. R., *A Catalogue of Manuscripts Containing Anglo-Saxon* (Oxford, 1957; re-issued with supplement originally printed in *Anglo-Saxon England* 5 (1977), 121–31, 1990).

Kéry, L., *Canonical Collections of the Early Middle Ages (ca. 400–1140): A Bibliographical Guide to the Manuscripts and Literature*, History of Medieval Canon Law (Washington, DC, 1999).

Keynes, S., 'King Athelstan's books', in Gneuss and Lapidge, *Learning and Literature*, pp. 143–201.

———, 'The reconstruction of a burnt Cottonian manuscript: The case of Cotton Ms. Otho A. I', *British Library Journal* 22 (1996), 113–60.

Knowles, D., *The Monastic Order in England: A History of its Development from the Times of St Dunstan to the Fourth Lateran Council, 940–1216*, 2nd edn (Cambridge, 1963).

Korhammer, P. M., 'The origin of the Bosworth Psalter', *Anglo-Saxon England* (1973), 173–87.

Langefeld, B., '*Regula canonicorum* or *Regula monasterialis uitae*? The Rule of Chrodegang and Archbishop Wulfred's reforms at Canterbury', *Anglo-Saxon England* 25 (1996), 21–36.

Lapidge, M., 'The School of Theodore and Hadrian', in idem, *Anglo-Latin Literature, 600–899*, pp. 141–68, at pp. 151 and 156 (originally published in *Anglo-Saxon England* 15 (1986), 45–72).

———, 'Æthelwold as scholar and teacher', in Yorke, *Bishop Æthelwold*, pp. 89–117.

———, 'Aediluulf and the School of York', in idem, *Anglo-Latin Literature, 600–899*, pp. 381–98 (originally published in A. Lehner and W. Berschin (eds.), *Lateinische Kultur im VIII. Jahrhundert: Traube-Gedenkschrift* (St Ottilien, 1990), pp. 161–78).

———, 'B. and the *Vita S. Dunstani*', in Ramsay et al., *St Dunstan*, pp. 247–259.

———, 'The hermeneutic style in tenth-century Anglo-Latin literature', in his *Anglo-Latin Literature, 900–1066*, pp. 105–49 (originally published in *Anglo-Saxon England* 4 (1975), 67–111).

———, *Anglo-Latin Literature, 900–1066* (London, 1993).

———, 'Byrhtferth and Oswald', in Brooks and Cubitt, *St Oswald*, pp. 64–83.

———, 'Latin learning in ninth-century England', in his *Anglo-Latin Literature, 600–899*, pp. 409–39.

———, *Anglo-Latin Literature, 600–899* (London, 1996).

———, 'John the Old Saxon (*fl. c.*885-904)', in H. C. Matthew and Brian Harrison (eds.), *Oxford Dictionary of National Biography*, 60 vols and Index of Contributors (Oxford, 2004) XXX, 204.

Lapidge, M., and H. Gneuss (eds.), *Learning and Literature in Anglo-Saxon England: Studies presented to Peter Clemoes on the occasion of his Sixty-fifth Birthday* (Cambridge, 1985).

Le Roux, R., 'Aux origines de l'office festif: Les antiennes et les psaumes aux matines de noël et de la circoncision', *Études grégoriennes* 4 (1961), 65–170.

——, 'Les repons "De Psalmis" pour les matines de l'épiphanie à la septuagésime selon les cursus romain et monastique', *Études grégoriennes* 6 (1963), 39–148.

——, 'Les répons du Triduo Sacro et de pâques', *Études grégoriennes* 18 (1979), 157–76.

Lenker, U., *Die westsächsische Evangelienversion und die Perikopenordnungen im angelsächsischen England*, Texte und Untersuchungen zur englischen Philologie 20 (Munich, 1997).

Leroquais, V., *Les Bréviaires manuscrits des bibliothèques publiques de France*, 6 vols. (Paris, 1934).

Levison, W., *England and the Continent in the Eighth Century* (Oxford, 1946).

Levy, K., 'Abbot Helisachar's antiphoner', in his *Gregorian Chant and the Carolingians* (Princeton, 1998), pp. 179–86 (originally published in the *Journal of the American Musicological Society* 48 (1995), 171–2 and 177–84).

——, 'Gregorian chant and the Romans', *Journal of the American Musicological Society* 56 (2003), 5–41.

Lowe, E. A., *Codices Latini antiquiores: A Palaeographical Guide to Latin Manuscripts Prior to the Ninth Century*, 12 vols. (Oxford, 1934–71).

——, *English Uncial* (Oxford, 1960).

Maasen, F., *Geschichte der Quellen und der Literatur des canonischen Rechts im Abendlande*, I: *Die Rechtssammlungen bis zur Mitte des 9. Jahrhunderts* (Graz, 1870).

Mabillon, J., *Annales ordinis S. Benedicti occidentalium monachorum patriarchae*, 6 vols. (Paris, 1703–39).

Machielsen, J., *Clavis patristica pseudepigraphorum medii aevi*, IA, CCSL *extra seriem* (Turnhout, 1990).

Maiani, B., 'Readings and responsories: The eighth-century Night Office lectionary and the *Responsoria prolixa*', *Journal of Musicology* 16 (1998), 254–82.

Marsden, R., *The Text of the Old Testament in Anglo-Saxon England*, Cambridge Studies in Anglo-Saxon England 15 (Cambridge, 1995).

Martimort, A.-G., *Les 'Ordines', les ordinaires et les cérémoniaux*, Typologie des sources du Moyen Âge occidental 56 (Turnhout, 1991).

——, *Les Lectures liturgiques et leurs livres*, Typologie des sources du Moyen Âge occidental 64 (Turnhout, 1992).

Masai, F., 'Observations sur le Psautier dit de Charlemagne (Paris lat. 13159)', *Scriptorium* 6 (1952), 299–303.

McKinnon, J., 'The emergence of Gregorian chant in the Carolingian era', in *idem* (ed.), *Antiquity and the Middle Ages: From Ancient Greece to the 15th Century*, Man and Music 1 (Basingstoke, 1990), pp. 88–119.

——, *The Advent Project: The Later-Seventh-Century Creation of the Roman Mass Proper* (Berkeley, CA, 2000).

McKitterick, R., *The Frankish Kingdoms under the Carolingians, 751–987* (Harlow, 1983).

——, 'Knowledge of canon law in the Frankish kingdoms before 789: The manuscript evidence', *Journal of Theological Studies* 36 (1985), 97–117.

——, 'Royal patronage of culture in the Frankish kingdoms under the Carolingians: Motives and consequences', in *Committenti e produzione artistico-letteraria nell'alto medioevo occidentale*, 2 vols., Settimane di studio del centro italiano di studi sull'alto medioevo 39 (Spoleto, 1992) I, 93–135.

Mearns, J., *The Canticles of the Christian Church, Eastern and Western, in Early and Medieval Times* (Cambridge, 1914).

Metzger, B. M., *The Text of the New Testament: Its Transmission, Corruption, and Restoration*, 3rd edn (New York, 1992).

Mews, C., 'Gregory the Great, the Rule of Benedict and Roman liturgy: The evolution of a legend', *Journal of Medieval History* 37 (2011), 125–44.

Meyvaert, P., 'Towards a history of the textual transmission of the *Regula S. Benedicti*', *Scriptorium* 17 (1963), 83–110.

——, 'Diversity within unity: A Gregorian theme', *Heythrop Journal* 4 (1963), 141–62; repr. as ch. VI in his *Benedict, Gregory, Bede and Others* (London, 1977).

Milfull, I. B., *The Hymns of the Anglo-Saxon Church: A Study and Edition of the 'Durham Hymnal'*, Cambridge Studies in Anglo-Saxon England 17 (Cambridge, 1996).

Möller, H., 'Research on the antiphoner: Problems and perspectives', *Journal of the Plainsong and Mediæval Music Society* 10 (1987), 1–14.

Moore, G. F., Preface to H. St. J. Thackeray, *Josephus: The Man and the Historian* (New York, 1929).

Morin, G., 'Fragments inédits et jusqu'à présent uniques d'antiphonaire gallican', *Revue bénédictine* 52 (1905), 329–56.

Neufville, J., 'L'authenticité de l'"Epistula ad regem Carolum de monasterio sancti Benedicti directa et a Paulo dictata"', *Studia monastica* 13 (1971), 295–309.

The New Oxford Annotated Bible with the Apocryphal/Deuterocanonical Books (New Revised Standard Version), ed. B. M. Metzger and R. E. Murphy (New York, 1994).

Nightingale, J., 'Oswald, Fleury and continental reform', in Brooks and Cubitt, *St Oswald*, pp. 23–45.

Nowacki, E., 'The performance of Office antiphons in twelfth-century Rome', in *Cantus planus: Papers Read at the Third Meeting* (Budapest, 1990), pp. 79–91.

Ó Carragáin, É., *The City of Rome and the World of Bede*, Jarrow Lecture (Jarrow, 1994).

Ó Carragáin, É., *Ritual and the Rood: Liturgical Images and the Old English Poems of the 'Dream of the Rood' Tradition* (London, 2005).

Ó Cuív, B., 'St Gregory and St Dunstan in a Middle-Irish poem on the origins of liturgical chant', in Ramsey et al., *St Dunstan*, pp. 273–97.

Orchard, N. A., 'The Bosworth Psalter and the St Augustine's Missal', in R. Eales and R. Sharpe, *Canterbury and the Norman Conquest: Churches, Saints and Scholars* (London, 1995), pp. 87–94.

Ortenberg, V., *The English Church and the Continent in the Tenth and Eleventh Centuries: Cultural, Spiritual, and Artistic Exchanges* (Oxford, 1992).

Ottosen, K., *L'Antiphonaire latin au Moyen Âge: Réorganisation des séries de répons de l'Avent classés par R.-J. Hesbert*, Rerum ecclesiasticarum documenta, extra seriem (Rome, 1986).

——, *The Responsories and Versicles of the Latin Office of the Dead* (Aarhus, 1993).

Oury, G., 'Psalmum dicere cum alleluia', *Ephemerides liturgicae* 79 (1965), 97–108.

Palazzo, E., *A History of Liturgical Books from the Beginning to the Thirteenth Century*, tr. M. Beaumont (Collegeville, MN, 1998).

Parkes, M. B., 'The palaeography of the Parker manuscript of the *Chronicle*, laws and Sedulius, and historiography at Winchester in the late ninth and tenth centuries', *Anglo-Saxon England* 5 (1976), 149–71.

——, *English Cursive Bookhands 1250–1500* (Oxford, 1969; rev. repr. London, 1979).

——, *Pause and Effect: An Introduction to the History of Punctuation in the West* (Aldershot, 1992).

——, *Their Hands Before Our Eyes: A Closer Look at Scribes* (Aldershot, 2008).

Parsons, D. (ed.), *Tenth-Century Studies: Essays in Commemoration of the Millennium of the Council of Winchester and 'Regularis concordia'* (London, 1975).

Pascher, J., *Das Stundengebet der römischen Kirche* (Munich, 1954).

——, 'Das Psalterium der Apostelmatutin', *Münchener theologische Zeitschrift* 8 (1957), 1–12.

——, 'Sinneinheiten in der Verteilung der Psalmen des Breviers: Ein weihnachtlicher und ein österlicher Typus', *Münchener theologische Zeitschrift* 8 (1957), 190–205.

——, 'Der Psalter für Laudes und Vesper im alten römischen Stundengebet', *Münchener theologische Zeitschrift* 8 (1957), 255–67.

——, 'Zur Frühgeschichte des römischen Wochenpsalteriums', *Ephemerides liturgicae* 79 (1965), 55–8.

——, 'De psalmodia vesperarum', *Ephemerides liturgicae* 79 (1965), 317–26.

——, *Die Methode der Psalmensauswahl im römischen Stundengebet* (Munich, 1967).

Pfaff, R. W., 'The "sample week" in the medieval Latin Divine Office', in R. N. Swanson (ed.), *Continuity and Change in Christian Worship*, Studies in Church History 25 (Woodbridge, 1999), pp. 78–88.

——, 'Massbooks' in *idem*, *The Liturgical Books*, pp. 7–34.

——, *The Liturgy in Medieval England: A History* (Cambridge, 2009).
Pfaff, R. W. (ed.), *The Liturgical Books of Anglo-Saxon England*, Old English Newsletter, Subsidia 23 (Kalamazoo, MI, 1995).
Pope, J. M., 'Monks and nobles in the Anglo-Saxon monastic reform', *Anglo-Norman Studies* 17 (1994), 165–80.
Pulsiano, P., 'Psalters', in Pfaff, *The Liturgical Books*, pp. 61–85.
Ramsay, N., M. Sparks, and T. Tatton-Brown (eds.), *St Dunstan: His Life, Times and Cult* (Woodbridge, 1992).
Rankin, S., 'The liturgical background of the Old English Advent lyrics: A reappraisal', in Gneuss and Lapidge, *Learning and Literature*, pp. 317–40.
——, 'Neumatic notations in Anglo-Saxon England', in M. Huglo (ed.), *Musicologie médiévale: Notations et séquences*, Actes de la Table Ronde du CNRS à l'Institut de recherche et d'histoire des textes, 6–7 septembre 1982 (Paris, 1987), pp. 129–44, 262–3, and Plates XIV–XXI.
——, 'An early eleventh-century missal fragment copied by Eadwig Basan: Bodleian Library, MS. Lat. liturg. D. 3, fols. 4–5', *Bodleian Library Record* 18 (2004), 220–52.
——, 'Making the liturgy: Winchester scribes and their books', in Gittos and Bedingfield, *The Liturgy*, pp. 29–52
——, 'The making of Carolingian Mass chant books', in D. B. Cannata, G. I. Currie, R. C. Mueller, and J. L. Nádas (eds.), *'Quomodo cantabimus canticum?' Studies in Honor of Edward H. Roesner*, Publications of the American Institute of Musicology, Miscellanea 7 (Middleton, WI, 2008), pp. 37–63.
——, 'Music Books', in Gameson, *The Cambridge History*.
——, 'Beyond the boundaries of Roman-Frankish chant: Alcuin's *De laude Dei* and other early medieval sources of Office chants', in M. Cuthbert, S. Gallagher, and C. Wolff (eds.), *City, Chant, and the Topography of Early Music: Essays in Honor of Thomas Forrest Kelly* (Cambridge, MA, 2013), pp. 229–62.
Righetti, M., *Manuale di storia liturgica*, 4 vols., vols. 1–3 3rd edn, vol. 4 2nd edn (1959–69).
Robertson, A. W., *The Service-Books of the Royal Abbey of Saint-Denis: Images of Ritual and Music in the Middle Ages* (Oxford, 1991).
Rollason, D., 'St Cuthbert and Wessex: The evidence of Cambridge, Corpus Christi College Ms 183', in G. Bonner, D. Rollason, and C. Stancliffe (eds.), *St. Cuthbert, his Cult and his Community to AD 1200* (Woodbridge, 1989), pp. 413–24.
Rosenthal, J., 'The Pontifical of St Dunstan', in Ramsay et al., *St Dunstan*, pp. 143–163.
Rumble, A. R., *Property and Piety in Early Medieval Winchester*, Winchester Studies 4.3 (Oxford, 2002).
Rushforth, R., *Saints in English Kalendars Before A.D. 1100*, HBS 117 (Woodbridge, 2008).
——, 'English Caroline Minuscule', in Gameson, *Book in Britain*, pp. 197–210.

Sadie, S., and J. Tyrrell (eds.), *The New Grove Dictionary of Music and Musicians*, 2nd edn (London, 2001).
Salmon, P., *The Breviary through the Centuries*, tr. Sister David Mary [from *L'Office divin: Histoire de la formation du bréviaire*, Lex orandi 27 (Paris, 1959)] (Collegeville, MN, 1962).
——, *L'Office divin au Moyen Age: Histoire de la formation du bréviaire du IXe au XVIe siècle*, Lex orandi 43 (Paris, 1967).
Sauer, H., 'Die Ermahnung des Pseudo-Fulgentius zur Benediktregel und ihre altenglische Glossierung', *Anglia* 102 (1984), 412–25.
Sawyer, P. H., *Anglo-Saxon Charters: An Annotated List and Bibliography*, Royal Historical Society Guides and Handbooks 8 (London, 1968).
——, 'Charters of the reform movement: The Worcester archive', in Parsons, *Tenth-Century Studies*, pp. 84–93.
Schneider, H., *Die altlateinischen biblischen Cantica*, Texte und Arbeiten 29–30 (Beuron, 1938).
Schroll, M. A., *Benedictine Monasticism as Reflected in the Warnefrid–Hildemar Commentaries on the Rule*, (Columbia University) Studies in History, Economics, and Public Law 478 (New York, 1941).
Semmler, J., 'Reichsidee und kirchliche Gesetzgebung bei Ludwig dem Frommen', *Zeitschrift für Kirchengeschichte* 71, 4th ser. 9 (1960), 37–65.
——, 'Pippin III. und die fränkischen Klöster', *Francia* 3 (1975), 88–146.
——, 'Benedictus II: Una regula – una consuetudo', in W. Lourdaux and D. Verhelst (eds.), *Benedictine Culture 750–1050*, Mediaevalia Lovaniensia, ser. 1, 11 (Leuven, 1983), pp. 1–49.
Sicard, D., *La Liturgie de la mort dans l'église latine des origines à la réforme carolingienne*, Liturgiewissenschaftliche Quellen und Forschungen 63 (Münster, 1978).
Siffrin, P., 'Der Collectar der Abtei Prüm im neunten Jahrhundert (Trier, Stadtbibliothek 1245/597, Bl. 129^v–138^v)', in *Miscellanea liturgica in honorem L. Cuniberti Mohlberg*, 2 vols., Bibliotheca 'Ephemerides liturgicae' 22–3 (Rome, 1948–9) II, 223–44.
Silva-Tarouca, C., 'Giovanni "Archicantor" di S. Pietro a Roma e l'"Ordo Romanus" da lui composto (anno 680)', *Memorie*, I.1, Atti della Pontificia Accademia di Archeologia, Serie 3 (Rome, 1923), pp. 159–219.
Sims-Williams, P., *Religion and Literature in Western England, 600–800*, Cambridge Studies in Anglo-Saxon England 3 (Cambridge, 1990).
Smetana, C. L., 'Aelfric and the early medieval homiliary', *Traditio* 15 (1959), 163–204.
——, 'Paul the Deacon's patristic anthology', in P. E. Szarmach (ed.), *The Old English Homily and its Backgrounds* (Albany, NY, 1978), pp. 75–97.
Smith, J. H. M., 'Culte impérial et politique frontalière dans la vallée de la Vilaine: Le témoignage des diplômes carolingiens dans le cartulaire de Redon', in M. Simon (ed.), *Landévennec et le monachisme breton dans le haut Moyen Âge*

(Landévennec, 1986), pp. 126–39.

——, *Province and Empire: Brittany and the Carolingian Church* (Cambridge, 1992).

Smith, W., and S. Cheetham (eds.), *A Dictionary of Christian Antiquities*, 2 vols. (London, 1875–80).

Stenton, F. M., *Anglo-Saxon England*, 3rd edn (London, 1971).

Stevenson, J. B., 'Hiberno-Latin hymns: Learning and literature', in P. Ní Chatháin and M. Richter (eds.), *Irland und Europa im früheren Mittelalter: Bildung und Literatur / Ireland and Europe in the Early Middle Ages: Learning and Literature* (Stuttgart, 1996), pp. 99–135.

Symons, T., 'Monastic observance in the tenth century, I: The Offices of All Saints and of the Dead', *Downside Review* 50, new ser. 31 (1932), 449–64; and 51, new ser. 32 (1933), 137–52.

——, 'Sources of the Regularis Concordia', *Downside Review* 59, new ser. 40 (1941), 14–36, 143–70, 264–89.

Taft, R., *The Liturgy of the Hours in East and West: The Origins of the Divine Office and its Meaning for Today*, 2nd rev. edn (Collegeville, MN, 1993).

Temple, E., *Anglo-Saxon Manuscripts, 900–1066*, Survey of Manuscripts Illuminated in the British Isles 2 (London, 1976).

Thacker, A., 'Æthelwold and Abingdon', in Yorke, *Bishop Æthelwold*, pp. 43–64.

——, 'Memorializing Gregory the Great: The origin and transmission of a papal cult in the seventh and early eighth centuries', *Early Medieval Europe* 7 (1998), 59–84.

Tolhurst, J. B. L., *Introduction to the English Monastic Breviaries*, HBS 80 (London, 1942) (=vol. 6 of his edn of *The Monastic Breviary of Hyde Abbey*).

Traube, L., *Textgeschichte der Regula S. Benedicti*, 2nd edn, ed. H. Plenkers (Munich, 1910).

Treitler, L., 'Homer and Gregory: The transmission of epic poetry and plainchant', in his *With Voice and Pen: Coming to Know Medieval Song and How it was Made* (Oxford, 2003), pp. 131–85 (originally published in *Musical Quarterly* 60 (1974), 333–72).

Van Der Walt, A. G. P., 'Reflections on the Benedictine Rule in Bede's homiliary', *Journal of Ecclesiastical History* 37 (1986), 367–76.

Van Dijk, S. J. P., 'Handlist of the Latin Liturgical Manuscripts in the Bodleian Library, Oxford', 7 vols. in 8, Unpublished typescript held in Duke Humfrey's Library, Oxford, 1957–60.

Van Dijk, S. J. P, and J. H. Walker, *The Origins of the Modern Roman Liturgy: The Liturgy of the Papal Court and the Franciscan Order in the Thirteenth Century* (Westminster, MD, 1960).

Van Tongen, L., *Exaltation of the Cross: Toward the Origins of the Feast of the Cross and the Meaning of the Cross in Early Medieval Liturgy*, Liturgia condenda 11 (Leuven, 2000).

Vogel, C., 'Saint Chrodegang et les débuts de la romanisation du culte en pays franc', in *Saint Chrodegang: Communications présentées au colloque tenu à Metz à l'occasion du douzième centenaire de sa mort* (Metz, 1967), pp. 91–109.

——, *Medieval Liturgy: An Introduction to the Sources*, rev. and tr. W. Storey and N. Rasmussen (Portland, OR, 1986).

Vogüé, A. de, 'Sub regula uel abbate: A study of the theological significance of the ancient monastic rules', in M. B. Pennington (ed.), *Rule and Life: An Interdisciplinary Symposium*, Cistercian Studies 12 (Spencer, MA, 1971), pp. 21–64.

Vogüé, *La Règle de Saint Benoît*, see *Regula S. Benedicti* in 'Printed Primary Sources'.

Wallace-Hadrill, J. M., 'Rome and the early English Church: Some questions of transmission', in *La Chiese nei regni dell'Europa occidentale e i loro rapporti con Roma sino all'800*, 2 vols., Settimane di studio del Centro italiano di studi sull'alto medioevo 7 (Spoleto, 1960) II, 519–48.

——, *Bede's Ecclesiastical History of the English People: A Historical Commentary*, with additions by P. Wormald and T. Charles-Edwards, Oxford Medieval Texts (Oxford, 1993).

Warner, G. F., and J. P. Gilson, *Catalogue of Western Manuscripts in the Old Royal and King's Collections in the British Museum*, 4 vols. (London, 1921).

Wildhagen, K., 'Studien zum *Psalterium Romanum* in England und seinen Glossierungen', in F. Holthausen and H. Spies (eds.), *Festschrift für Lorenz Morsbach*, Studien zur englischen Philologie 50 (Halle, 1913), pp. 418–72.

Wilmart, A., 'La légende de Ste Edith en prose et vers par le moine Goscelin', *Analecta Bollandiana* 56 (1938), 5–101 and 265–307.

Wollasch, J., 'Benedictus abbas romensis: Das römische Element in der frühen benediktinischen Tradition', in N. Kamp and J. Wollasch (eds.), *Tradition als historische Kraft: interdisziplinäre Forschungen zur Geschichte des früheren Mittelalters* (Berlin, 1982), pp. 119–37.

Wormald, F., 'The "Winchester School" before St. Æthelwold', in P. Clemoes and K. Hughes (eds.), *England Before the Conquest: Studies in Primary Sources Presented to Dorothy Whitelock* (Cambridge, 1971), pp. 305–12.

Wormald, P., 'Bede and Benedict Biscop', in G. Bonner (ed.), *Famulus Christi: Essays in Commemoration of the Thirteenth Centenary of the Birth of the Venerable Bede* (London, 1976), pp. 141–69.

——, 'The ninth century', in J. Campbell (ed.), *The Anglo-Saxons* (London, 1982), pp. 132–57 (notes pp. 253–4).

——, 'Æthelwold and his Continental counterparts', in Yorke, *Bishop Æthelwold*, pp. 13–42.

——, 'The strange affair of the Selsey bishopric, 953–963', in Gameson and Leyser, *Belief and Culture*, pp. 128–41.

Yorke, B. (ed.), *Bishop Æthelwold: His Career and Influence* (Woodbridge, 1988).

Zelzer, K., 'Überlegungen zu einer Gesamtedition des frühnachkarolingischen Kommentars zur Regula S. Benedicti aus der Tradition des Hildemar von Corbie', *Revue Bénédictine* 91 (1981), 373–82.

Unpublished Dissertations

Billett, J. D., 'The Muchelney Breviary and Anglo-Saxon monastic liturgy in the eleventh century', Unpublished M.Phil. dissertation, University of Cambridge, 2003.

Foot, S. R. I., 'Anglo-Saxon minsters A.D. 597–*ca* 900: The religious life in England before the Benedictine Reform', Ph.D. dissertation, University of Cambridge, 1989.

Stephan, R., 'Antiphonarstudien I: Quellen und Studien zur Geschichte des Gesanges im Stundengebet vor der Jahrtausendwende, I: Die Gesänge des Sanctorale', Unpublished *Habilitationschrift*, Göttingen, 1962.

Websites

'CANTUS: A Database for Latin Ecclesiastical Chant', now hosted by the University of Waterloo <http://cantusdatabase.org/> last visited 5 April 2013.

Chadd, D., 'CURSUS: An Online Resource for Medieval Liturgical Texts', hosted by the University of East Anglia <http://www.cursus.uea.ac.uk/> last visited 26 July 2008; offline as of 2011/2012.

Drigsdahl, E., '*Hore Beate Marie Virginis*: Reference to secondary sources', hosted by the Center for Håndskriftstudier i Danmark <http://www.chd.dk/use/secsour.html> last visited 5 April 2013.

'Early Manuscripts at Oxford University' <http://image.ox.ac.uk/> last visited 5 April 2013.

'Gallica: Bibliothèque numerique', Bibliothèque nationale de France <http://gallica.bnf.fr> last visited 15 April 2013.

'OLIVER', The Hill Museum and Manuscript Library Manuscript Database <http://www.hmml.org/research2010/research10.htm> last visited 5 April 2013.

Index of Manuscripts

Albi, Bibliothèque municipale
Rochegude, 44: 146 n. 73, 218, 269,
270, 273, 277, 280, 286–91, 293,
297, 323, 324, 325, 326, 327, 328,
333, 336–41, 342
Amiens, Bibliothèque municipale,
115: 273, 275, 286–91, 293, 296,
321, 325, 336–41, 344, 345
Aosta, Biblioteca del Seminario
maggiore, *s.n.* (s. xiii): 239, 245,
247, 249, 251
Aosta, Biblioteca del Seminario
maggiore, *s.n.* (s. xiv): 239, 245,
247, 249, 251
Aosta, Biblioteca capitolare della
Cattedrale, *s.n.* (s. xiii): 239, 245,
247, 249, 251
Aosta, Biblioteca capitolare della
Cattedrale, *s.n.* (s. xiv): 239, 245,
247, 249, 251
Aosta, Collegio Sant'Orso, *s.n.*: 239,
245, 247, 249, 251
Arras, Bibliothèque municipale, 465
(*olim* 893): 270, 277, 281, 286–91,
292, 295, 323, 327, 334, 336–41,
342, 346
Bamberg, Staatsbibliothek, Lit. 23:
269, 270, 273, 286–91, 293, 297,
314, 316 n. 53, 321, 324, 333,
336–41, 344
Bamberg, Staatsbibliothek, Msc. Patr.
17/B. II. 10: 126 n. 175, 129 n. 194,
129 n. 197
Basel, Universitätsbibliothek, N. I. 2:
111 n. 125
Benevento, Archivio capitolare, 21:
226 n. 28, 269, 270, 273, 277,
286–91, 292, 297, 314, 316 n. 53,
326, 334, 336–41, 342, 346
Berlin, Staatsbibliothek Preussischer
Kulturbesitz, Hamilton 553
(Salaberga Psalter): 109–13, 141
Berlin, Staatsbibliothek Preussischer
Kulturbesitz, Mus. 40047: 280 n. 60
Cambrai, Bibliothèque municipale, 38
(*olim* 40): 218, 269, 270, 277,
286–90, 292, 295, 323, 327, 333,
336, 338–41, 342
Cambridge, Corpus Christi College 41
(Parker Old English Bede): 220–51,
349–51
Cambridge, Corpus Christi College 57:
155–6, 158–60, 161 n. 55, 162, 190
Cambridge, Corpus Christi College
173 (Parker Chronicle): 260
Cambridge, Corpus Christi College
183: 232–3, 255
Cambridge, Corpus Christi College
391 (Portiforium of St Wulfstan):
218, 267, 278, 279–80, 281, 282,
283, 295, 300
Cambridge, Corpus Christi College
422 (Red Book of Darley): 172
n. 97, 224 n. 20
Cambridge, Corpus Christi College
473 (Winchester Troper): 254 n. 3
Cambridge, Magdalene College F. 4.
10: 277, 278, 280, 281–2, 283,

INDEX OF MANUSCRIPTS

286–91, 294, 295, 325, 327, 336–41, 343, 345
Cambridge, Pembroke College 23–24: 284 n. 68
Cambridge, St John's College D. 27: 273, 278, 279, 281–2, 286, 288–91, 294, 295, 336, 350 n. 5
Cambridge, Trinity College 241: 306 n. 25
Cambridge, Trinity College B. 4. 27: 311, 330
Cambridge, Trinity College O. 1. 18: 311 n. 34
Cambridge, Trinity College O. 2. 31: 311 n. 33
Cambridge, University Library, Ee. 2. 4: 156, 157–8
Cambridge, University Library, Ff. 5. 27: 111 n. 125
Cambridge, University Library, Ii. 4. 20: 275, 277, 278, 280, 281, 283, 286–91, 294, 295, 323, 325, 327, 331, 332, 334, 336–41, 343, 345, 381
Cambridge, University Library, Ll. 1. 10 (Book of Cerne): 265
Canterbury, Chapter Library, Add. 3: 333 n. 86
Canterbury, Chapter Library, Add. 6 (Burnt Breviary): 333 n. 86
Cologne, Dombibliothek, 213: 79 n. 2
Copenhagen, Kongelige Bibliotek, Ny kgl. S. 137 4°: 230, 231, 239, 244, 246, 248, 250
Dublin, Royal Irish Academy, *s.n.* (Cathach of St Columba): 109 n. 114
Durham, Cathedral Library, A. IV. 19 (Durham Collectar, Durham Ritual): 4 n. 3, 145, 220–51, 349–51, 355
Durham, Cathedral Library, B. III. 11: 269, 270, 273, 279, 286, 288–91, 293, 297, 323, 333, 336

El Escorial, Real biblioteca, B. IV. 17: 126 n. 175, 129 n. 194, 129 n. 197, 130
Exeter, Cathedral Library, 3501: 126 n. 178
Fécamp, Musée de la Bénédictine 186: 274, 275, 281, 286–91, 294, 296, 316 n. 53, 321–2, 325, 326, 334, 336–41, 342, 346
Florence, Biblioteca Arcivescovile, *s.n.*: 316 n. 53
Florence, Biblioteca Medicea-Laurenziana, Conv. sopp. 560: 316 n. 53
Graz, Universitätsbibliothek, 29 (*olim* 38/8 f.): 280 n. 60
Hanover, Landesbibliothek, I. 101 b: 239, 244, 246, 248, 250
Ivrea, Biblioteca capitolare, CVI (Ivrea Antiphoner, Codex Eporediensis): 41, 48, 269, 273, 277, 279, 280, 286–91, 292, 297, 321, 333, 336–41, 343
Karlsruhe, Badische Landesbibliothek, Aug. perg. XIX: 55 n. 144
Karlsruhe, Badische Landesbibliothek, Aug. perg. XXIX: 55 n. 144
Karlsruhe, Badische Landesbibliothek, Aug. perg. CCLXVI: 229 n. 32
Karlsruhe, Badische Landesbibliothek, Musikabteilung, Aug. LX: 280 n. 60
Karlsruhe, Badische Landesbibliothek, Schwarzach 17: 239, 244, 246, 248, 250
Kassel, Landesbibliothek, Theol. fol. 121: 239, 244, 246, 248, 250
Kassel, Landesbibliothek, Theol. fol. 161: 239, 244, 246, 248, 250
Koblenz, Staatsarchiv, 109: 239, 244, 246, 248, 250
Le Grand-Saint-Bernard Hospice, *s.n.*: 239, 245, 247, 249, 251
Leiden, Bibliotheek der

INDEX OF MANUSCRIPTS

Rijksuniversiteit, Scaligeranus 69: 311 n. 34
León, Archivo de la Catedral, 8: 127
Leuven, Katholieke Universiteit, Centrale Bibliotheek, *s.n.*: 191 n. 168
London, British Library, Additional 29253: 273, 275, 286-287, 289–91, 293, 296, 324, 326, 336–41, 343
London, British Library, Additional 30850: 226 n. 28, 286–91, 293, 296, 317 n. 55, 321, 323, 326, 334, 336–41, 342, 346
London, British Library, Additional 34209: 127 n. 186
London, British Library, Additional 37517 (Bosworth Psalter): 19, 112, 192–93, 313–15
London, British Library, Additional 43405–43406 (Muchelney Breviary): 210, 226 n. 28, 230–31, 234, 267, 270, 273, 278, 279, 281, 286–91, 293, 295, 323, 326, 327, 328, 331, 332–3, 334, 336–41, 342, 345, 350–51
London, British Library, Additional 47967: 303 n. 7
London, British Library, Additional 49598 (Benedictional of St Æthelwold): 159, 194
London, British Library, Additional 56488: 350
London, British Library, Additional 57337 (Anderson Pontifical): 193–4
London, British Library, Arundel 155 (Eadui Psalter): 191, 330 n. 80
London, British Library, Burney 277: 323, 325, 327, 329–33, 336–41, 343, 380–8
London, British Library, Cotton Aug. ii. 39: 283 n. 66
London, British Library, Cotton Claudius A. iii (Anglo-Saxon Chronicle, F-text): 192 n. 171
London, British Library, Cotton Domitian vii: 135
London, British Library, Cotton Nero A. ii: 26 n. 25
London, British Library, Cotton Otto A. i. 1: 98 n. 74
London, British Library, Cotton Tiberius A. iii: 159, 162, 171
London, British Library, Cotton Titus D. xxvii: 171
London, British Library, Cotton Vespasian A. I (Vespasian Psalter): 17, 107, 109–14, 118, 120, 137, 141–2
London, British Library, Cotton Vespasian A. VIII: 174 n. 104
London, British Library, Cotton Vitellius A. xv (Nowell Codex): 258
London, British Library, Harley 603 (Harley Psalter): 191 n. 168
London, British Library, Harley 2892 (Canterbury Benedictional): 265
London, British Library, Harley 2904 (Ramsey Psalter): 190–1, 195
London, British Library, Harley 2908 (Psalter of St Oswald): 283 n. 64
London, British Library, Harley 2961 (Leofric Collectar): 190
London, British Library, Harley 4664: 277, 278, 280, 281, 286–91, 294, 295, 325, 334, 336–41, 343, 345
London, British Library, Harley 5431: 311 n. 34, 312
London, British Library, Royal 1. E. VII–VIII: 263
London, British Library, Royal 2. A. XX (Royal Prayer Book): 189, 190
London, British Library, Royal 13. A. XV: 283 n.64
London, British Library, Royal 17. C. XVII: 252–300, 331, 336, 348, 349, 356–73

INDEX OF MANUSCRIPTS

London, British Library, Stowe 1061: 323, 325, 327, 329, 331–3, 336–41, 343, 380–8
London, Lambeth Palace Library, 200: 311 n. 34
London, Lambeth Palace Library, 1212: 90 n. 39
Lucca, Biblioteca capitolare, 490: 127, 132, 217, 318
Montpellier, Faculté de Médecine, H. 409 (Montpellier Psalter): 110 n. 118
Monza, Basilica S. Giovanni C. 12/75: 269, 273, 277, 286–91, 292, 297, 321, 333, 336–41, 343, 375 n. 5, 385 n. 9
New York, Pierpont Morgan Library, M. 776 (Blickling Psalter, Morgan Psalter, Lothian Psalter): 109–13
Orléans, Bibliothèque municipale, 129 (*olim* 107): 269, 273 n. 48, 278, 286–91, 293, 297, 323, 325, 326, 336–41, 342, 346
Oxford, Bodleian Library, Arch Selden B. 26: 98 n. 74
Oxford, Bodleian Library, Auct. D. Inf. 2. 9.: 306 n. 23, 310–12
Oxford, Bodleian Library, Auct. F. 1. 15.: 311, 312
Oxford, Bodleian Library, Auct. F. 4. 32. (St Dunstan's Classbook): 305 n. 15
Oxford, Bodleian Library, Barlow 41: 277, 278, 280, 286–91, 294, 296
Oxford, Bodleian Library, Bodley 426: 135
Oxford, Bodleian Library, Bodley 572: 172 n. 97
Oxford, Bodleian Library, Bodley 579 (Leofric Missal): 146, 233, 306, 355
Oxford, Bodleian Library, Digby 63: 135
Oxford, Bodleian Library, Hatton 48: 81 n. 10, 81 n. 11, 162
Oxford, Bodleian Library, Junius 27 (Junius Psalter): 141–2
Oxford, Bodleian Library, Lat. liturg. d. 3: 255 n. 6
Oxford, Bodleian Library, Lat. liturg. e. 5: 239, 245, 247, 249, 251
Oxford, Bodleian Library, Lat. liturg. e. 6, e. 37, e. 39, and d. 42: 278, 280, 281, 286–91, 294, 296, 323, 325, 326, 327, 336–7, 340, 342, 346
Oxford, Bodleian Library, Lat. theol. c. 3: 156 n. 33
Oxford, Bodleian Library, Laud. misc. 284: 240, 244, 246, 248, 250
Oxford, Bodleian Library, Laud. misc. 382: 240, 245, 247, 249, 251
Oxford, Bodleian Library, Rawl. C. 570: 311 n. 34
Oxford, Bodleian Library, Rawl. D. 894: 200, 301–47, 348–51, 374–9
Oxford, Bodleian Library, Rawl. liturg. e.1*: 210, 270, 273, 275, 277, 278, 280, 281, 283, 286–91, 292, 295, 320, 323, 326, 327, 331, 332, 334, 336–41, 343, 345
Oxford, Corpus Christi College 282: 224–5
Oxford, Jesus College 10 (Gloucester Diurnal): 218, 278, 281, 296
Paris, Bibliothèque nationale de France, lat. 781: 240, 245, 247, 249, 251
Paris, Bibliothèque nationale de France, lat. 943 (Pontifical of St Dunstan): 193, 223 n. 16, 261
Paris, Bibliothèque nationale de France, lat. 1062: 240, 244, 246, 248, 250
Paris, Bibliothèque nationale de France, lat. 1208 (Bec Customary): 274, 275, 325–6, 336–41, 344
Paris, Bibliothèque nationale de

France, lat. 1276: 269, 278, 286–91, 294, 297
Paris, Bibliothèque nationale de France, lat. 11522: 273, 277, 279–80, 281, 282, 286–91, 292, 295, 300, 317 n. 54, 322, 324, 325, 327, 331, 333, 336–41, 343, 345, 347
Paris, Bibliothèque nationale de France, lat. 12052 (Sacramentary of Ratoldus): 284, n. 68
Paris, Bibliothèque nationale de France, lat. 12584: 273, 275, 277, 286–91, 293, 296, 314, 316 n. 53, 321, 322, 325, 336–41, 344, 345
Paris, Bibliothèque nationale de France, lat. 12601: 321, 325–6, 336–41, 344, 345
Paris, Bibliothèque nationale de France, lat. 13159: 63–4
Paris, Bibliothèque nationale de France, lat. 13241 and 13242: 274, 286–91, 294, 296
Paris, Bibliothèque nationale de France, lat. 15181 and 15182: 218, 269, 270, 273, 277, 280, 286–91, 292, 295, 323, 324, 329, 333, 336–7, 339–41, 343
Paris, Bibliothèque nationale de France, lat. 16307: 240, 245, 247, 249, 251
Paris, Bibliothèque nationale de France, lat. 17296: 226 n. 28, 269, 273, 277, 279–80, 282, 284, 286–91, 292, 295, 299, 316 n. 53, 321, 324, 325, 327, 331, 336–41, 343, 345, 366 n. 9
Paris, Bibliothèque nationale de France, lat. 17436 (Antiphoner of Charles the Bald, Compiègne Antiphoner): 72, 146 n. 73, 269, 273, 277, 279, 280, 281, 286–91, 293, 297, 314 n. 44, 319, 321, 324, 326, 333, 336–41, 343
Paris, Bibliothèque nationale de France, n. a. lat. 1628: 128, 129 n. 194
Paris, Bibliothèque nationale de France, n. a. lat. 3162–3167: 202 n. 9
Paris, Bibliothèque Sainte-Geneviève, 111 (Gradual of Senlis): 318
Raigern, Klásterní Knihovna benediktin, S F/K 1 α 1: 240, 244, 246, 248, 250
Rome, Biblioteca Angelica, 440: 240, 245, 247, 249, 251
Rome, Biblioteca Apostolica Vaticana, lat. 4751: 240, 245, 247, 249, 251
Rome, Biblioteca Apostolica Vaticana, Pal. lat. 68: 111 n. 125
Rouen, Bibliothèque municipale, 244 (olim A. 261): 274, 275, 281, 286–91, 294, 296, 316 n. 53, 321–2, 325, 326, 334, 336–41, 342, 346
Rouen, Bibliothèque municipale, 245 (olim A. 190): 274, 275, 281, 286–91, 294, 296, 316 n. 53, 321–2, 325, 326, 334, 336–41, 342, 346
Rouen, Bibliothèque municipale, 252 (olim A. 486): 279, 286–91, 294, 296, 321, 322, 325, 332, 336–41, 344, 346
Rouen, Bibliothèque municipale, 254 (olim A. 226): 274, 286–91, 294, 296, 325, 336–41, 344, 346
Rouen, Bibliothèque municipale, 274 (olim Y. 6) (Missal of Robert of Jumièges): 332
Salisbury, Cathedral Library, 150 (Salisbury Psalter): 191
Salisbury, Cathedral Library, 154: 57
Sankt Florian, Chorherren-Stiftsbibliothek, XI. 384: 230, 240, 244, 246, 248, 250
Sankt Paul im Lavanttal (Kärnten,

Austria), Stiftsbibliothek, 2/1 (Sankt Paul fragment): 128–31
St Gall, Stiftsbibliothek, 349: 50 n. 129
St Gall, Stiftsbibliothek, 390–391 (Hartker Antiphoner): 73, 190, 210, 273, 277, 279, 286–91, 293, 297, 321, 322, 324, 325, 326, 336–41, 344, 346
St Gall, Stiftsbibliothek, 914: 58, 81 n. 11
Stockholm, Kungliga biblioteket, A. 135 (Golden Gospels): 140
Stuttgart, Württembergische Landesbibliothek, Bibl. fol. 12a–c (Stuttgart Uncial Psalter): 110 n. 118
Stuttgart, Württembergische Landesbibliothek, HB. 1. 55: 280 n. 60
Toledo, Biblioteca capitular, 37.2: 240, 245, 247, 249, 251
Toledo, Biblioteca capitular, 44.1: 334
Trier, Bistumsarchiv, 523: 240, 244, 246, 248, 250
Trier, Dombibliothek, 180 F: 240, 244, 246, 248, 250
Trier, Stadtbibliothek, 427: 240, 244, 246, 248, 250
Trier, Stadtbibliothek, 1245/597: 72–3, 190, 212 n. 34, 230, 318 n. 60, 350
Ushaw, St Cuthbert's College 44: 121 n. 159
Ushaw, St Cuthbert's College XVIII. B. 1. 2(6) (Ushaw Lectionary): 121–5, 132
Valenciennes, Bibliothèque municipale, 116: 278, 280, 281, 286–91, 294, 296
Vercelli, Biblioteca Capitolare, CCX: 240, 245, 247, 249, 251
Verona, Biblioteca Capitolare, XCVIII: 269, 273, 277, 286–91, 293, 297, 321, 322, 333, 336–41, 343
Worcester, Cathedral Library, F. 160 (Worcester Antiphoner): 6, 7, 180, 226 n. 28, 275, 277, 278, 279–80, 281–2, 286–91, 294, 295, 300, 321, 322, 325, 327, 334, 336–41, 343, 345
Worcester, Cathedral Library, F. 173: 191 n. 168
Würzburg, Universitätsbibliothek, Mp th. f. 168: 240, 244, 246, 248, 250
Zurich, Zentralbibliothek, Rheinau 28: 269, 270, 286–91, 293, 297, 324, 325, 326, 336–41, 344, 345

Manuscripts in private collections

'Antiphoner of Mont-Renaud': 73, 212, 226 n. 28, 273, 277, 279–80, 282, 286–91, 292, 295, 299, 321, 324, 325, 327, 331, 336–41, 343, 345, 366 n. 9
'Linenthal leaf': 302, 309–10, 313 n. 40

Index of Liturgical Forms

This index lists in alphabetical order the incipits of all chants, prayers, and other liturgical items (excepting psalms, canticles, and readings) that are transcribed in the appendices or mentioned in the main text. The liturgical genre of each text is indicated in square brackets after the incipit as follows:

A̸.	antiphona	Invit.	antiphona ad invitatorium
Or.	oratio, collecta	R̸.	responsorium
Grad.	graduale	V̸.	versus
Hym.	hymnus	V̸.(R̸.)	versiculus et responsorium

Verses of responsories (and of antiphons when these occur) are printed twice: once under the refrains to which they belong, and again in alphabetical order, followed by the incipits of their refrains. Paragraph numbers of texts transcribed in the appendices are given in parentheses and boldface type: (**B119**) means 'Appendix B, number 119'. Whereas the main text usually reproduces the orthography of manuscripts and editions, spellings in the index have necessarily been standardized. Diphthongs (*ae*, *oe*, *ę*) are replaced by *e*; *j* and *v* are replaced by *i* and *u*; in compound words, prepositions are assimilated to the following consonant (*adpropinquabant* becomes *appropinquabant*; *adstiterunt* becomes *astiterunt*). Otherwise, spelling follows the preferences of *CAO* (*craticula*, not *graticula*; *Hippolytus*, not *Yppolitus*). Textual variants are occasionally noted in square brackets.

A solis ortu [V̸. cf. Audite uerbum (R̸.)] 230, 235, 241, 244–5

A solis ortu [V̸. cf. Canite tuba in Sion (R̸.)] 230, 238, 243, 250–1

A solis ortu [V̸. cf. Descendet dominus (R̸.)] 230, 242, 248–9

A solis ortu [V̸. cf. Ecce dominus ueniet et omnes sancti (R̸.)] 230, 236, 246–7

A solis ortu [V̸. cf. Ecce radix Iesse ascendet (R̸.)] 237, 230, 239, 242, 248

A solis ortu [V̸. cf. Iuraui dicit dominus (R̸.)] 230, 238, 243, 250–1

A solis ortu [V̸. cf. Obsecro domine (R̸.)] 230, 231, 235, 241, 244–5

A solis ortu [V̸. cf. Ueni domine et noli (R̸.)] 230, 231, 237, 242, 248–9

A solis ortu [V̸. cf. Uirgo Israel (R̸.)] 230, 231, 238, 243, 250–1

Ab hominibus iniquis libera me [A̸.] 327 (**B134**)

Ab ipso pueritie [A̸.] 384 (**D42**)

Accepto pane Iudas [A̸.] 280, 295–8, 299–300

Accusatus [V̸. cf. In craticula te deum non negaui (R̸.)] 339, 377 (**C31**)

INDEX OF LITURGICAL FORMS

Accusatus non negaui nomen [℣.] 345–7
Acuerunt linguas suas sicut serpentes [℣.(℟.)] 372 (**B129**)
Adhesit anima mea post te [℣.] 387 (**D61**)
Adiuua nos deus [℣.] 296, 298
Adiuuabit eam [℣.] 379 (**C56**)
Afferens autem urceum [℣. cf. Dixit Romanus (℣.)] 375 (**C14**)
Ait Pilatus [℣.] 296–7, 298
Alieni non [℟.] 228, 230, 231, 235, 243, 244
℣. Ueniam dicit 230, 231, 235, 243, 244
Alliga domine in uinculis nationes gentium [℣.] 367 (**B87**)
Amauit eum dominus [℟.] 383 (**D24**)
Amen dico uobis [℣.] 297, 298
Amici mei aduersum me [℣. cf. Fratres mei elongauerunt a me (℟.)] 289
Amici mei et proximi mei [℣. cf. Fratres mei elongauerunt a me (℟.)] 289
Ancilla dixit Petro [℣.] 296–7, 298
Anime impiorum fremebant [℟.] 269, 286, 293
℣. Contumelias et terrores 286
Animam meam dilectam [℟.] 269, 286, 292
℣. Insurrexerunt in me absque 286
Annuntiate et auditum [℣. cf. Audite uerbum (℟.)] 231, 241, 245
Annuntiate et auditum [℣. cf. Canite tuba in Sion (℟.)] 243, 251
Annuntiate in finibus [℣. cf. Canite tuba in Sion (℟.)] 231, 243, 251
Annuntiatum est [℟.] 230, 231, 243, 250–1
℣. Aue Maria 230, 231, 243, 250–1
Ante diem festum [℣.] 296–7, 298
Apparebit [℣. cf. Ecce apparebit (℟.)] 242, 249

Appenderunt mercedem meam [℣.] 363 (**B55**)
Appropinquabat autem dies [℣.] 295, 297, 298
Armis diuinis [℣. cf. Hic est uir (℟.)] 338
Aspice domine infirmitates nostras [℣. cf. Concede nobis quesumus domine (℟.)] 331, 338, 386 (**D58**)
Aspiciebam [℟.] 230, 231, 235, 241, 244–5
℣. Ecce dominator 230, 235, 241, 244–5
℣. Potestas 231, 241, 245
Aspiciens a longe [℟.] 229, 230, 231, 235, 241, 244–5
℣. Excita 241, 244–5
℣. Qui regis Israel 229, 235
℣. Quique terrigine 229, 235
℣. Tollite portas 230, 235, 241, 244–5
Assument montes [℣. cf. Iuraui dicit dominus (℟.)] 243, 251
Astiterunt reges terre et principes conuenerunt [℣.] 373 (**B141**)
Attende domine ad me [℟.] 268–70, 278, 286, 292–4, 363 **B52**
℣. Homo pacis mee in quo sperabam 286
℣. Recordare quod steterim 286
Audite uerbum [℟.] 230, 231, 235, 241, 244–5
℣. Annuntiate et auditum 231, 241, 245
℣. A solis ortu 230, 235, 241, 244–5
Audisti opprobria eorum domine [℣. cf. In die qua inuocaui te (℟.)] 289
Aue Maria [℟.] 230, 231, 235, 241, 244–5
℣. Quomodo 231, 241, 244–5
℣. Tollite portas 235, 241, 244–5
Aue Maria [℣. cf. Annuntiatum est (℟.)] 230, 231, 243, 250–1

INDEX OF LITURGICAL FORMS

Aue Maria [℣. cf. Missus est Gabriel (℟.)] 230, 231, 235, 241, 244–5
Aue Maria [℣. cf. Suscipe uerbum (℟.)] 230, 231, 237, 242, 248–9
Auertantur retrorsum et erubescant [℣.] 368 (**B95**)
Beata dei genitrix [℟.] 123
Beati Laurentii interuentio [℟.] 323, 336, 342
℣. Floribus roseis 336
Beatissimus Christi martyr Hippolytus [℟.] 388 (**D74**)
℣. Ceco inluminato a sancto Laurentio 388
Beatus Laurentius clamauit deum meum [℟.] 324, 328, 336, 342–4, 377 (**C29**), 385 (**D50**)
℣. Mea nox obscurum non habet 336, 377 (**C29**), 385 (**D50**)
Beatus Laurentius clamauit et dixit deum meum [℣.] 346–7
Beatus Laurentius dixit [℣. cf. Quo progrederis (℣.)] 375 (**C10**)
Beatus Laurentius dixit [orabat, orabat dicens] domine [℣.] 333–4, 345–7, 375 (**C13**)
℣. Gratias tibi ago 347
℣. Quia accusatus 347, 375 (**C13**)
Beatus Laurentius dixit disce miser [℟.] 323, 337, 343
℣. Beatus Laurentius dum 337
℣. Carnifices 337
℣. Ecce miser 337
℣. Probasti 337
Beatus Laurentius dixit domine [℟.] 324, 325–8, 337, 342–4
℣. Gratias tibi ago 337
℣. Transiens autem 337
Beatus Laurentius dixit ego me obtuli [℟.] 324, 326, 327–8, 337, 342–4, 377 (**C35**), 385 (**D53**)
℣. Gaudeo plane quia hostia 337, 377 (**C35**), 385 (**D53**)

℣. Gratias tibi ago 337
℣. Quoniam ad te 337
Beatus Laurentius dixit mea nox [℣.] 333, 345–7, 375 (**C15**)
℣. Quia ipse dominus nouit 375 (**C15**)
Beatus Laurentius dum [℣. cf. Beatus Laurentius dixit disce miser (℟.)] 337
Beatus Laurentius dum in craticula [℣.] 345–7, 378 (**C41**)
Beatus Laurentius orauit et dixit [orabat dicens] gratias [℣.] 345–7, 376 (**C24**), 387 (**D63**)
Beatus Laurentius orauit et dixit [℟.] 377 (**C34**), 386 (**D56**)
℣. Gratias tibi ago domine 386 (**D56**)
℣. Gratias tibi ago quia ianuas 377 (**C34**)
Beatus Sixtus dixit [℣. cf. Non ego te desero (℣.)] 375 (**C12**)
Beatus quem elegisti [℣.] 346–7
Beatus uir benedictus [℣.] 384 (**D46**)
Beatus uir Laurentius qui post aurum [℟.] 301, 313, 324, 325–8, 331, 337, 342–4, 378 (**C37**), 386 (**D57**)
℣. Hic est uere martyr 337, 378 (**C37**), 386 (**D57**)
℣. Potuit enim transgredi 337
℣. Qui potuit transgredi 337
Beatus uir qui inuentus [℟.] 323, 338, 343
℣. Potuit enim transgredi 338
Benedicite deum celi [℟.] 226 n. 28, 227
℣. Ipsum benedicite et cantate 226 n. 28
℣. Tempus est ut reuertar 227
Benedicite deum celi [℣. cf. Te in omnem (℟.)] 226–7
Benedicite deum celi [℣. cf. Tempus est ut reuertar (℟.)] 226–7

INDEX OF LITURGICAL FORMS

Benedicta tu [A̸.] 379 (**C54**)
Benedictus qui uenit in nomine domini [V̸.(R̸.)] 362 (**B41**)
Bethleem ciuitas [R̸.] 230, 231, 237, 242, 248–9
  V̸. De Sion 242, 249
  V̸. Deus a Libano 230, 231, 237, 242, 248–9
  V̸. Loquetur 242, 249
Bonum certamen certaui [A̸.] 381 (**D12**)
  V̸. De cetero reposita est mihi 381 (**D12**)
Calicem salutaris accipiam et nomen domini inuocabo [A̸.] 372 (**B132**)
Canite tuba in Sion [R̸.] 230, 231, 238, 243, 250–1
  V̸. A solis ortu 230, 238, 243, 250–1
  V̸. Annuntiate et auditum 243, 251
  V̸. Annuntiate in finibus 231, 243, 251
  V̸. Congregate 243, 251
Cantemus in omni die [Hym.] 95 n. 63
Carnifices [V̸. cf. Beatus Laurentius dixit disce miser (R̸.)] 337
Carnifices uero urgentes [A̸.] 346–7
Carnifices uero urgentes [V̸. cf. Strinxerunt corporis (R̸.)] 341, 376 (**C28**), 385 (**D49**)
Carnifices urgentes [V̸. cf. Strinxerunt corporis (A̸.)] 376 (**C21**)
Ceco inluminato a sancto Laurentio [V̸. cf. Beatissimus Christi martyr Hippolytus (R̸.)] 388 (**D74**)
Cena facta dixit Iesus [A̸.] 280, 295, 297, 298, 299–300, 373 (**B138**)
Cenantibus autem accepit [A̸.] 295–7, 298, 299–300, 373 (**B139**)
Ceperunt eum omnes turbe [A̸.] 129 n. 193
Ceperunt omnes turbe [A̸.] 280, 295–7, 298, 299–300

Cepit Hippolytus tristis plorare [R̸.] 388 (**D76**)
Christus factus est pro nobis obediens [V̸.(R̸.)] 372 (**B137**)
Circumdantes circumdederunt me [A̸.] 361 (**B32**)
Circumdederunt me uiri [R̸.] 270, 287, 292–3
  V̸. Quoniam tribulator proxima 287
Ciuitas Ierusalem [R̸.] 230, 231, 236, 241, 246–7
  V̸. Ecce dominator 230, 236, 241, 246–7
  V̸. Ecce in fortitudine 231, 241, 247
Clarifica me [A̸.] 297, 298
Cogitauerunt autem principes sacerdotum [R̸.] 271–2, 278, 287, 294
  V̸. Testimonium ergo perhibebat turba 271–2, 287
Cogitauerunt impii et locuti sunt [A̸.] 369 (**B105**)
Collegerunt pontifices [A̸.] 297, 298
Compassus [A̸.] 384 (**D38**)
Completi sunt dies [A̸.] 180
Concede nobis quesumus domine [R̸.] 326, 327, 331–3, 338, 342–3, 386 (**D58**)
  V̸. Aspice domine infirmitates nostras 331, 338, 386 (**D58**)
Conclusit uias meas [R̸.] 277, 287, 292–4
  V̸. Factus sum in derisum 270, 287
  V̸. Omnes inimici mei aduersum me 287
Confessorum regem [Invit.] 383 (**D32**)
Confitemini ei coram omnibus [V̸. cf. Tempus est ut reuertar (R̸.)] 226 n. 28
Confundantur omnes inimici mei [V̸. cf. Noli esse mihi domine alienus (R̸.)] 290

INDEX OF LITURGICAL FORMS

Confundantur qui me persecuntur [℣.] 361 (**B35**)
Congregate [℣. cf. Canite tuba in Sion (℟.)] 243, 251
Congregauerunt iniquitatem sibi [℣. cf. Seniores populi consilium fecerunt (℟.)] 371 (**B119**)
Congregauit nos Christus [℣.] 297, 298
Considerabam ad dexteram et uidebam [℣.] 372 (**B136**)
Consilium fecerunt [℣.] 299–300
Consilium fecerunt inimici [℣.] 295–7, 298, 365 (**B76**)
Consilium fecerunt ut Iesum [℣.] 297, 298
Constantes estote [℟.] 241, 251
℣. Uos qui in puluere 241, 251
Continet in gremio [℟.] 123
Contritum est cor meum in medio mei [℣.] 372 (**B126**)
Contumelias et terrores passus sum [℣.] 367 (**B84**)
Contumelias et terrores passus sum [℣.] 268, 270, 277, 287, 292–4, 366 (**B82**)
℣. Iudica domine causam anime mee 287   ℣. Omnes inimici mei aduersum me 287, 366 (**B82**)
℣. Omnes inimici mei audierunt 287
Contumelias et terrores [℣. cf. Anime impiorum fremebant (℟.)] 286
Conuenerunt autem ibi multa [℣. cf.] Dominus Iesus ante sex dies (℟.)] 271, 288
Cotidie apud uos [℣.] 295–7, 298, 299–300, 367 (**B92**)
Credimus saluatorem [℟.] 128–9, 130 n. 198, 131
℣. Uox clamantis in deserto 129 n. 194
Cuius intercessio [℣. cf. Uir inclitus Laurentius (℟.)] 341
Cum accepisset [℣.] 296, 298

Cum angelis et pueris fideles inueniamur [℣.] 361 (**B34**)
Cum apud sedem [℣. cf. Leuita Laurentius (℟.)] 339
Cum audisset turba quia uenit Iesus [℟.] 271–2, 278, 287, 294
℣. Et cum appropinquasset ad decensum 272, 287
Cum his qui oderunt pacem eram pacificus [℣.] 372 (**B133**)
Cum sederit filius hominis [℣. cf. Uos qui reliquistis omnia (℣.)] 374 (**C3**)
Cumque audissent quia Iesus [℣. cf. Ingrediente domino in sanctam ciuitatem (℟.)] 289
Cumque [Cum] audisset populus [℣. cf. Ingrediente domino in sanctam ciuitatem (℟.)] 271–2, 289
Cumque sibi [℣.] 384 (**D40**)
Custodi me a laqueo [℣.] 372 (**B135**)
Da nobis quesumus omnipotens deus [Or.] 332
Dabit ei [℣. cf. Ecce radix Iesse ascendet (℟.)] 231, 242, 248
Dabo in Sion [℣. cf. Sicut mater (℟.)] 231, 242, 247
Damasci prepositus [℣.] 315, 374 (**C2**), 382 (**D14**)
℣. Deus et pater 374 (**C2**), 382 (**D14**)
De cetero reposita est mihi [℣. cf. Bonum certamen certaui (℣.)] 381 (**D12**)
De ore leonis libera me [℟.] 269, 270, 287, 292
℣. Erue a framea deus animam 287
De ore leonis libera me [℣. cf. Erue a framea deus animam (℟.)] 288
De reliquo reposita est mihi [℣. cf. Scio cui credidi et certus sum (℣.)] 381 (**D7**)
De Sion [℣. cf. Bethleem ciuitas (℟.)] 242, 249

Dederunt in escam [A̕.] 297, 298
Dederunt in escam meam fel [V̕.(R̕.)] 362 (**B37**)
Deponet [V̕. cf. Qui uenturus est (R̕.)] 231, 242, 249
Derelinquerunt me proximi [V̕. cf. Fratres mei elongauerunt a me (R̕.)] 289
Descendet dominus [R̕.] 230, 231, 237, 242, 248–9
V̕. A solis ortu 230, 242, 248–9
V̕. Et adorabunt 242, 248–9
V̕. Et dominabitur 242, 248
V̕. Ex Sion species 230, 231, 237, 242, 249
Desiderio desideraui [A̕.] 297, 298
Det tibi [R̕.] 210
Deus a Libano [V̕. cf. Bethleem ciuitas (R̕.)] 230, 231, 237, 242, 248–9
Deus a Libano [V̕. cf. Ecce radix Iesse ascendet (R̕.)] 230, 242, 248
Deus a Libano [V̕. cf. Egredietur dominus (R̕.)] 230, 231, 236, 242, 246–7
Deus a Libano [V̕. cf. Ierusalem plantabis (R̕.)] 230, 236, 242, 246–7
Deus a Libano [V̕. cf. Sicut mater (R̕.)] 230, 236, 242, 246–7
Deus a Libano [V̕. cf. Ueni domine et noli (R̕.)] 242, 248
Deus a quo et Iudas proditor reatus sui penam [Or.] 367 (**B93**)
Deus cuius dextera [A̕.] 316 n. 53, 374 (**C6**)
Deus deus meus respice in me [V̕. cf. Deus Israel propter te sustinui (R̕.)] 287
Deus deus meus respice in me [V̕. cf. In die qua inuocaui te (R̕.)] 289
Deus et pater [V̕. cf. Damasci prepositus (A̕.)] 374 (**C2**), 382 (**D14**)

Deus Israel propter te sustinui [R̕.] 268–9, 277, 278, 287, 292–4, 360 (**B24**)
V̕. Deus deus meus respice in me 287
V̕. Improperia improperantium 288, 360 (**B24**)
V̕. Intende anime mee 288
Deus meus eripe me de manu [A̕.] 368 (**B96**)
Deus meus eripe me de manu [V̕. cf. In die qua inuocaui te (R̕.)] 289
Deus meus eripe me de manu [V̕.(R̕.)] 369 (**B107**)
Deus qui peccati ueteris hereditariam mortem [Or.] 373 (**B140**)
Deus qui per crucem et passionem tuam redemisti mundum [Or.] 265, 285, 372 (**B131**)
Diffusa est gratia [V̕.(R̕.)] 379 (**C58**)
Diligamus nos inuicem [A̕.] 297, 298
Discerne causam meam domine [A̕.] 365 (**B69**)
Dispersit [V̕. cf. Leuita Laurentius (R̕.)] 339, 376 (**C20**)
Dispersit [V̕. cf. O Hippolyte si credis (R̕.)] 340
Diuiserunt sibi uestimenta mea [A̕.] 373 (**B142**)
Dixerunt impii apud se [R̕.] 268–70, 288, 292–4, 359 (**B19**)
V̕. Hec cogitauerunt et errauerunt 288
V̕. Tamquam nugaces estimati sumus 288
V̕. Uiri impii dixerunt opprimamus 288, 359 (**B19**)
Dixerunt impii apud se [V̕. cf. Uiri impii dixerunt opprimamus (R̕.)] 291, 361 (**B30**)
Dixerunt impii opprimamus uirum iustum [A̕.] 365 (**B72**)

INDEX OF LITURGICAL FORMS

Dixi iniquis nolite loqui aduersus deum iniquitatem [℣.] 370 (**B114**)
Dixit angelus [℟.] 210
Dixit Romanus [℣.] 333, 345–7, 375 (**C14**)
℣. Afferens autem urceum 375 (**C14**)
Docebit nos [℟.] 228, 230, 231, 237, 243, 248–9
℣. Domus Iacob 243, 249
℣. Ex Sion 230, 237, 243, 248–9
℣. Uenite ascendamus 231, 243, 249
Domine deus uirtutum [℣. cf. Non discedimus (℟.)] 230, 231, 238, 243, 250–1
Domine labia mea aperies [℣.(℟.)] 14, 62, 123
Domine uim patior responde pro me [℣.] 365 (**B71**)
Dominus deus auxiliator meus [℣.] 361 (**B31**)
Dominus dixit ad me [℣.] 123
Dominus Iesus ante sex dies [℟.] 271, 274, 278, 288, 294
℣. Conuenerunt autem ibi multa 271, 288
Dominus mecum est [℣.] 297, 298
Dominus mecum est tamquam bellator [℟.] 268–70, 288, 292–4, 364 (**B67**)
℣. Et uim faciebant 288
℣. Tu autem domine Sabaoth 288
℣. Uidisti domine iniquitates 288
Dominus sicut fortis [℣. cf. Ecce apparebit (℟.)] 242, 249
Dominus tamquam ouis ad uictimam ductus est [℣.] 371 (**B125**)
Domus Iacob [℣. cf. Docebit nos (℟.)] 243, 249
Donec ponam [℣. cf. Puer meus non timere (℟.)] 340
Dormite iam et requiescite [℣. cf. Una hora non potuistis uigilare (℟.)] 370 (**B113**)

Dum exiret [℟.] 210
Dum in hac terra [℣.] 384 (**D41**)
Dum iret [℟.] 210
Dum sacramenta [℣.] 382 (**D18**)
Dum tribularer clamaui ad dominum [℣.] 365 (**B70**)
Ecce aduenit [℣. cf. Nascetur (℟.)] 230, 243, 250
Ecce agnus dei [℣. cf. Rex noster adueni (℟.)] 230, 231, 236, 242, 246–7
Ecce apparebit [℟.] 230, 231, 237, 242, 248–9
℣. Apparebit 242, 249
℣. Dominus sicut fortis 242, 249
℣. Ecce dominator 230, 231, 237, 242, 248–9
Ecce appropinquabit hora [℣. cf. Tristis est anima mea (℟.)] 368 (**B101**)
Ecce completa sunt [℣.] 180
Ecce cum uirtute [℣. cf. Ecce dominus ueniet et omnes sancti (℟.)] 231, 241, 246–7
Ecce dico uobis [℣.] 297, 298
Ecce dominator [℣. cf. Aspiciebam (℟.)] 230, 235, 241, 244–5
Ecce dominator [℣. cf. Ciuitas Ierusalem (℟.)] 230, 236, 241, 246–7
Ecce dominator [℣. cf. Ecce apparebit (℟.)] 230, 231, 237, 242, 248–9
Ecce dominator [℣. cf. Ecce ueniet dominus (℟.)] 230, 231, 236, 242, 246–7
Ecce dominator [℣. cf. Egypte noli (℟.)] 230, 231, 237, 242, 248–9
Ecce dominator [℣. cf. Letentur celi (℟.)] 230, 231, 235, 241, 244–5
Ecce dominus ueniet [℣. cf. Sanctificamini filii (℟.)] 241, 251
Ecce dominus ueniet et omnes sancti [℟.] 230, 231, 236, 241, 246–7

431

℣. A solis ortu 230, 236, 246–7
℣. Ecce cum uirtute 231, 241, 246–7
Ecce enim transiuit [℣. cf. Meruit esse hostia leuita Laurentius (℟.)] 339
Ecce fulget clarissima [Hym.] 95 n. 63
Ecce iam uenit [℟.] 230, 231, 238, 243, 250–1
℣. Prope est ut 230, 231, 238, 243, 250–1
℣. Propter nimiam 243, 251
Ecce iam ueniet hora [℟.] 123
Ecce in fortitudine [℣. cf. Ciuitas Ierusalem (℟.)] 231, 241, 247
Ecce miser [℣. cf. Beatus Laurentius dixit disce miser (℟.)] 337
Ecce odor [℟.] 210
Ecce radix Iesse ascendet [℟.] 228, 230, 231, 237, 239, 242, 248
℣. A solis ortu 237, 230, 239, 242, 248
℣. Dabit ei 231, 242, 248
℣. Deus a Libano 230, 242, 248
Ecce sacerdos magnus [℣.(℟.)] 383 (**D22**), 383 (**D25**)
Ecce ueniet dominus [℟.] 230, 231, 236, 239, 242, 246–7
℣. Ecce dominator 230, 231, 236, 242, 246–7
℣. Et dominabitur 242, 246–7
Ecce ueniet dominus [℣. cf. Egypte noli (℟.)] 242, 249
Ecce uidimus eum non habentem [℟.] 369 (**B103**)
℣. Uere languores nostros
Ecce uirgo concipiet [℟.] 230, 231, 235, 241, 244–5
℣. Factus est 241, 245
℣. Super solium 241, 245
℣. Tollite portas 230, 235, 241, 244–5
Effuderunt furorem suum in me [℣. cf. Insurrexerunt in me uiri iniqui (℟.)] 290

Ego autem dum mihi molesti [℣. cf. Opprobrium factus sum nimis inimicis (℟.)] 290
Ego enim [℣. cf. Ierusalem cito (℟.)] 241, 246
Ego me obtuli [℣. cf. Gaudeo plane quia hostia (℟.)] 338, 377 (**C33**), 386 (**D54**)
Ego me obtuli [℣. cf. Meruit esse hostia leuita Laurentius (℟.)] 339
Ego sum dominus deus [℣. cf. Octaua decima (℟.)] 230, 231, 238, 243, 250–1
Egredietur dominus [℟.] 230, 231, 236, 242, 246–7
℣. Deus a Libano 230, 231, 236, 242, 246–7
℣. Et preparabitur 242, 247
Egredietur uirga [℟.] 230, 231, 243, 248, 251
℣. Rorate 243, 251
Egypte noli [℟.] 230, 231, 237, 242, 248–9
℣. Ecce dominator 230, 231, 237, 242, 248–9
℣. Ecce ueniet dominus 242, 249
Electus a fratribus [A.] 384 (**D39**)
Eram quasi agnus innocens [℟.] 369 (**B111**)
℣. Omnes inimici mei aduersum me 370 (**B111**)
Eripe me de inimicis [℣.(℟.)] 364 (**B59**)
Eripe me domine [℣.(℟.)] 362 (**B43**)
Erit mihi [℟.] 210
Erue a framea deus animam [℟.] 269, 270, 288, 292
℣. De ore leonis libera me 288
Erue a framea deus animam [℣. cf. De ore leonis libera me (℟.)] 287
Et adorabunt [℣. cf. Descendet dominus (℟.)] 242, 248–9

INDEX OF LITURGICAL FORMS

Et auferet [℣. cf. Qui uenturus est (℞.)] 242, 249
Et cum appropinquasset ad decensum [℣. cf. Cum audisset turba quia uenit Iesus (℞.)] 272, 287
Et dederunt in escam meam [℣. cf. Insurrexerunt in me uiri iniqui (℞.)] 290, 360 (**B28**)
Et dominabitur [℣. cf. Descendet dominus (℞.)] 242, 248
Et dominabitur [℣. cf. Ecce ueniet dominus (℞.)] 242, 246–7
Et dominator [℣. cf. Intuemini (℞.)] 230, 231, 238, 243, 250–1
Et preparabitur [℣. cf. Egredietur dominus (℞.)] 242, 247
Et tu exultabis [℣. cf. Ierusalem plantabis (℞.)] 242, 247
Et uim faciebant [℣. cf. Dominus mecum est tamquam bellator (℞.)] 288
Et uocauit per gratiam suam [℣. cf. Qui me segregauit ex utero (℣.)] 381 (**D6**)
Ex ore infantium deus et lactantium [℣. cf. Ingrediente domino in sanctam ciuitatem (℞.)] 273, 289
Ex Sion [℣. cf. Docebit nos (℞.)] 230, 237, 243, 248–9
Ex Sion [℣. cf. Radix Iesse qui exurget (℞.)] 243, 251
Ex Sion species [℣. cf. Descendet dominus (℞.)] 230, 231, 237, 242, 249
Ex Sion species [℣. cf. Qui uenturus est (℞.)] 230, 237, 248–9
Exaltata est sancta dei [℣.] 379 (**C52**)
Excita [℣. cf. Aspiciens a longe (℞.)] 241, 244–5
Excita [℣. cf. Ueni domine et noli (℞.)] 242, 248–9
Exortatus es in uirtute tua [℣.] 372 (**B127**)

Expandi manus meas [℞.] 269, 288, 293
℣. Qui dicunt recede 288
Exulta satis [℣. cf. Ierusalem plantabis (℞.)] 231, 242, 247
Exurge domine et iudica causam meam [℣.(℞.)] 368 (**B97**)
Exurge domine et iudica causam tuam [℣.] 369 (**B106**)
Faciem meam non auerti ab increpantibus [℣.] 363 (**B53**)
Factus est [℣. cf. Ecce uirgo concipiet (℞.)] 241, 245
Factus Iesus in agonia [℣.] 296–7, 298
Factus sum in derisum [℣. cf. Conclusit uias meas (℞.)] 270, 287
Festa dies mundo [℞.] 323, 338, 343
℣. Quo uirtute 338
Fiducia magna est [℣. cf. Memor esto filii quoniam (℞.)] 227
Filie Ierusalem [℣.] 297, 298
Floribus roseis [℣. cf. Beati Laurentii interuentio (℞.)] 336
Framea suscitare aduersus eos [℣.] 353 (**B54**)
Fratres mei elongauerunt a me [℞.] 268–70, 278, 289, 292–4, 363 (**B50**)
℣. Amici mei aduersum me 289
℣. Amici mei et proximi mei 289
℣. Derelinquerunt me proximi 289
Fuit uir uite [℣.] 383 (**D34**)
Gaudent in celis anime sanctorum [℣.] 387 (**D72**)
Gaudeo plane quia hostia [℞.] 324, 326, 327, 328, 338, 342–4, 377 (**C33**), 385 (**D54**)
℣. Ego me obtuli 338, 377 (**C33**), 386 (**D54**)
℣. Gratias tibi ago 338
℣. Probasti 338
Gaudeo plane quia hostia [℣. cf. Beatus Laurentius dixit ego me obtuli (℞.)] 337, 377 (**C35**), 385

433

INDEX OF LITURGICAL FORMS

(**D53**)
Gloria et honore [℟.] 387 (**D67**)
Gloria et honore [℣.(℟.)] 375 (**C16**)
Gloria laus et honor [Hym.] 273
Gloriosi principes terre quomodo in uita sua [A̍.] 380 (**D3**)
Gratia dei in me [A̍.] 315, 374 (**C1**)
℣. Gratia dei sum 374 (**C1**)
Gratia dei sum [℣. cf. Gratia dei in me (A̍.)] 374 (**C1**)
Gratias ago deo meo [A̍.] 345–7
Gratias tibi ago [℣. cf. Beatus Laurentius dixit domine (A̍.)] 347
Gratias tibi ago [℣. cf. Interrogatus te dominum (A̍.)] 376 (**C23**)
Gratias tibi ago [℣. cf. Beatus Laurentius dixit domine (℟.)] 337
Gratias tibi ago [℣. cf. Beatus Laurentius dixit ego me obtuli (℟.)] 337
Gratias tibi ago [℣. cf. Gaudeo plane quia hostia (℟.)] 338
Gratias tibi ago domine [℣. cf. Beatus Laurentius orauit et dixit (℟.)] 386 (**D56**)
Gratias tibi ago domine Iesu Christe [A̍.] 345, 347
Gratias tibi ago domine quia ianuas [A̍.] 345–7
Gratias tibi ago quia ianuas [℣. cf. Beatus Laurentius orauit et dixit (℟.)] 377 (**C34**)
Hec cogitauerunt [℣. cf. Dixerunt impii apud se (℟.)] 288
Hec cogitauerunt [℣. cf. Uiri impii dixerunt opprimamus (℟.)] 291
Hec dicit dominus conuertemini [℣.(℟.)] 356 n. 2
Hec dies [Grad.] 180 n. 119
Hec est dies [℟.] 123
Heu me fili mi ut [℣. cf. Sufficiebat nobis (℟.)] 227
Hic accipiet [A̍.] 346–7

Hic est martyr [℟.] 323, 338, 342
Hic est uere martyr [A̍.] 378 (**C46**)
Hic est uere martyr [℣. cf. Beatus uir Laurentius qui post aurum (℟.)] 337, 378 (**C37**), 386 (**D57**)
Hic est uir [℟.] 325–6, 338, 343–4
℣. Armis diuinis 338
℣. Iste est 338
℣. Iste sanctus 338
℣. Probasti 338
Hic est uir [℣. cf. Strinxerunt corporis (℟.)] 341
Hic qui aduenit [℟.] 123
Hoc est testimonium [℣. cf. Me oportet (℟.)] 230, 231, 238, 243, 250–1
Hodie illuxit nobis [A̍.] 380 (**D2**)
Hodie namque [A̍.] 297, 298
Hodie nobis celorum [℟.] 123
Hodie scietis [℣. cf. Sanctificamini hodie (℟.)] 241, 251
Homo pacis mee in quo sperabam [℣.(℟.)] 367 (**B91**), 370 (**B117**)
Homo pacis mee in quo sperabam [℣. cf. Attende domine ad me (℟.)] 286
Ierusalem cito [℟.] 230, 231, 236, 241, 246–7
℣. Ego enim 241, 246
℣. Israel si me audieris 230, 231, 236, 241, 246–7
Ierusalem plantabis [℟.] 230, 231, 236, 242, 246–7
℣. Deus a Libano 230, 236, 242, 246–7
℣. Et tu exultabis 242, 247
℣. Exulta satis 231, 242, 247
Ierusalem surge [℟.] 230, 236, 241, 246–7
℣. Leua in circuitu oculos 230, 236, 241, 246–7
Iesus factus in agonia [A̍.] 297, 298
Igne me examinasti [A̍.] 320 n. 66, 321, 333, 345–7, 376 (**C22**)
℣. Probasti 376 (**C22**)

Improperia improperantium [℣. cf. Deus Israel propter te sustinui (℟.)] 288, 360 (**B24**)
In caritate [℣. cf. Iuraui dicit dominus (℟.)] 243, 251
In caritate [℣. cf. Uirgo Israel (℟.)] 243, 251
In craticula [℣. cf. Meruit esse hostia leuita Laurentius (℟.)] 339, 377 (**C36**), 386 (**D55**)
In craticula sanctum deum [℣.] 378 (**C40**)
In craticula te deum non negaui [℣.] 387 (**D66**)
In craticula te deum non negaui [℟.] 324, 327, 328, 339, 342–4, 377 (**C31**), 385 (**D52**)
℣. Accusatus 339, 377 (**C31**)
℣. Probasti 339, 385 (**D52**)
In die magno festiuitatis stabat Iesus [℣.] 356 (**B2**)
In die perditionis seruabitur [℣. cf. Reuelabunt celi iniquitatem Iude (℟.)] 371 (**B121**)
In die qua inuocaui te [℟.] 268–70, 278, 289, 292–4, 363 (**B48**)
℣. Audisti opprobria eorum domine 289
℣. Deus deus meus respice in me 289
℣. Deus meus eripe me de manu 289
℣. In die tribulationis mee 289
In die tribulationis mee [℣.] 370 (**B116**)
In die tribulationis mee [℣. cf. In die qua inuocaui te (℟.)] 289
In diebus illis [℣.] 297, 298
In humilitate [℣.] 297, 298
In ipso [℣. cf. Nascetur (℟.)] 243, 251
In mente habito [℣. cf. Memor esto filii quoniam (℟.)] 226 n. 28
In monte oliueti orauit ad patrem [℟.] 368 (**B99**)

℣. Uerumtamen non sicut ego uolo In regeneratione cum sederit filius [℣. cf. Magnus sanctus Paulus uas (℣.)] 381 (**D11**)
Infirmata est [℣.] 279, 295, 297, 298
Ingrediente domino in sanctam ciuitatem [℟.] 270, 271–8, 289, 292–4, 362 (**B42**)
℣. Cumque audissent quia Iesus 289
℣. Cum [Cumque] audisset populus 271–2, 289
℣. Ex ore infantium deus et lactantium 273, 289
Ingressus Pilatus [℣.] 297, 298
Inposita manu puero [℣.] 382 (**D20**)
Inquire ut facias [℣. cf. Omne tempore benedic deus (℟.)] 226 n. 28
Insurrexerunt in me [℣. cf. Opprobrium factus sum nimis inimicis (℟.)] 290
Insurrexerunt in me absque [℣. cf. Animam meam dilectam (℟.)] 286
Insurrexerunt in me testes iniqui [℣.] 373 (**B143**)
Insurrexerunt in me uiri iniqui [℟.] 268–70, 277, 278, 290, 292–4, 360 (**B28**), 366 (**B80**)
℣. Effuderunt furorem suum in me 290
℣. Et dederunt in escam meam fel 290, 360 (**B28**)
Intende anime mee [℣. cf. Deus Israel propter te sustinui (℟.)] 288
Intende anime mee [℣. cf. Ne auertas faciem tuam a puero tuo (℟.)] 290
Intende anime mee [℣. cf. Saluum me fac deus (℟.)] 291
Interrogatus te dominum [℣.] 333, 345–7, 376 (**C23**)
℣. Gratias tibi ago 376 (**C23**)
Intuemini [℟.] 230, 231, 238, 243, 250–1

℣. Et dominator 230, 231, 238, 243, 250–1
℣. Precursor 243, 251
Inundauerunt aque super caput meum [℟.] 363 (**B56**)
Inuocabo nomen tuum [℟.] 296–7, 298 Ipsi uero in uanum quesierunt [℟.] 367 (**B85**)
Ipsum benedicite et cantate [℣. cf. Benedicite deum celi (℟.)] 226 n. 28
Israel si me audieris [℣. cf. Ierusalem cito (℟.)] 230, 231, 236, 241, 246–7
Iste est [℣. cf. Hic est uir (℟.)] 338
Iste sanctus [℣. cf. Hic est uir (℟.)] 338
Iste sanctus pro lege [℟.] 378 (**C49**)
Isti sunt due oliue [℟.] 316 n. 53, 374 (**C5**)
Iudica causam meam defende [℟.] 361 (**B33**)
Iudica domine causam anime mee [℣. cf. Contumelias et terrores passus sum (℟.)] 287
Iudica me domine [℣. cf. Synagoge populorum circumdederunt me (℟.) 291, 360 (**B26**)
Iuraui dicit dominus [℟.] 230, 231, 238, 243, 250–1
℣. A solis ortu 230, 238, 243, 250–1
℣. Assument montes 243, 251
℣. In caritate 243, 251
℣. Iuxta est 231, 243, 251
Iustificeris domine in sermonibus tuis [℟.] 371 (**B124**)
Iustorum anime [℣.(℟.)] 387 (**D71**)
Iustum deduxit dominus [℟.] 382 (**D21**), 383 (**D30**)
Iustum deduxit dominus [℣.(℟.)] 377 (**C32**)
Iustus ut palma [℣.(℟.)] 378 (**C39**), 387 (**D65**)
Iuxta est [℣. cf. Iuraui dicit dominus (℟.)] 231, 243, 251

Labia insurgentium et cogitationes [℟.] 363 (**B57**)
Laudate celi et exultet terra [℟.?] 129–31
Laurea Laurenti preclari [℟.] 323, 324, 339, 343
℣. Uictrici tota celi 339
Laurentius bonum opus [℟.] 334, 345, 347, 376 (**C26**), 386 (**D60**)
Laurentius ingressus est martyr [℟.] 386 (**D59**)
Letabitur iustus [℟.] 346–7
Letamini in domino [℟.] 387 (**D70**)
Letentur celi [℟.] 228, 231, 235, 241, 244–5
℣. Ecce dominator 230, 231, 235, 241, 244–5
℣. Orietur 241, 245
Leua in circuitu oculos [℣. cf. Ierusalem surge (℟.)] 230, 236, 241, 246–7
Leuita Laurentius [℟.] 324, 328, 339, 342-4, 376 (**C20**)
℣. Cum apud sedem 339
℣. Dispersit 339, (**C20**)
Leuita Laurentius bonum opus [℟.] 345–7
Libenter gloriabor in infirmitatibus [℟.] 382 (**D15**)
℣. Quando enim infirmor 382 (**D15**)
Libera me de sanguinibus deus [℟.] 366 (**B83**)
Liberabo te [℣. cf. Puer meus non timere (℟.)] 319, 340, 377 (**C30**), 385 (**D51**)
Liberasti [℣. cf. Protector tuus (℟.)] 340
Liberauit dominus pauperem a potente [℟.] 369 (**B104**)
Locuti sunt aduersum me [℣. cf. Opprobrium factus sum nimis inimicis (℟.)] 290

INDEX OF LITURGICAL FORMS

Loquetur [V̂. cf. Bethleem ciuitas (R̂.)] 242, 249
Magister dicit tempus meum prope est [Â.] 262, 359 **(B20)**
Magnus sanctus Paulus uas [Â.] 381 **(D11)**
V̂. In regeneratione cum sederit filius
Mandatum nouum [Â.] 297, 298
Maria ergo unxit [Â.] 297, 298
Martine misit nos [Â.] 382 **(D17)**
Mea nox [V̂. cf. Beatus Laurentius clamauit deum meum (R̂.)] 336, 377 **(C29)**, 385 ((**D50**)
Mea nox [V̂. cf. Strinxerunt corporis (R̂.)] 341
Me oportet [R̂.] 230, 231, 238, 243, 250–1
V̂. Hoc est testimonium 230, 231, 238, 243, 250–1
Media nocte surgebam [V̂.(R̂.)] 48 n. 122
Memento nostri [V̂. cf. Non discedimus (R̂.)] 243, 251
Memor esto filii quoniam [R̂.] 226 n. 28, 227
V̂. Fiducia magna est 227
V̂. In mente habito 226 n. 28
Memor esto filii quoniam [V̂. cf. Omne tempore benedic deus (R̂.)] 227
Meruit esse hostia leuita Laurentius [R̂.] 301, 313 n. 40, 324, 326, 327–8, 339, 342–4, 377 **(C36)**, 386 **(D55)**
V̂. Ecce enim transiuit 339
V̂. Ego me obtuli 339
V̂. In craticula 339, 377 **(C36)**, **(D55)**
Mihi uiuere Christus est [Â.] 381 **(D8)**
V̂. Per quem mihi
Minor sum [R̂.] 210
Misit dominus angelum suum [Â.] 387 **(D62)**

Missus est Gabriel [R̂.] 230, 231, 235, 241, 244–5
V̂. Aue Maria 230, 231, 235, 241, 244–5
Missus sum [Â.] 297, 298
Mittens hec mulier [Â.] 295–7, 298
Multa bona opera operatus sum [Â.] 358 **(B13)**
Multa turba [Â.] 297, 298
Nascetur [R̂.] 230, 243, 250–1
V̂. Ecce aduenit 230, 243, 250
V̂. In ipso 243, 251
Ne auertas faciem tuam a puero tuo [R̂.] 290, 293
V̂. Intende anime mee 290
Ne magnitudo reuelationum [Â.] 381 **(D9)**
Ne perdas cum impiis [V̂.(R̂.)] 359 **(B21)**
Ne perdas cum impiis deus animam [R̂.] 269, 270, 290, 292
V̂. Ne tradideris me in animas 290
Ne tradideris me in animas [V̂. cf. Ne perdas cum impiis deus animam (R̂.)] 290
Nemo tollit a me [Â.] 295–7, 298, 299–300, 365 **(B73)**
Nisi granum frumenti [Â.] 345–7
Nocte ac [et] die [V̂. cf. Ter uirgis cesus sum (R̂.)] 374 **(C4)**, 381 **(D13)**
Noli esse mihi domine alienus [R̂.] 268–70, 278, 290, 292–4, 364 **(B65)**
V̂. Confundantur omnes inimici mei 290
Noli me derelinquere [Â.] 333, 345–7
Non auferetur [R̂.] 230, 231, 238, 243, 250–1
V̂. Pulchriores sunt 230, 231, 238, 243, 250–1
Non discedimus [R̂.] 230, 231, 238, 243, 250–1

437

℣. Domine deus uirtutum 230, 231, 238, 243, 250–1
℣. Memento nostri 243, 251
℣. Ostende nobis 243, 251
Non ego te desero [A̠.] 333, 345–7, 375 (**C12**)
℣. Beatus Sixtus dixit 375 (**C12**)
Non haberes in me [A̠.] 295–7, 298, 299–300, 364 (**B60**)
Non [Noli] me derelinquere [R̠.] 324, 328, 340, 342–4, 375 (**C18**), D48
℣. Nos quasi senes 340, 375–6 (**C18**), 385 (**D48**)
Non me derelinquere [A̠.] 375 (**C11**)
℣. Quid in me
Non sis mihi [A̠.] 296–7, 298
Nos quasi senes [℣. cf. Noli me derelinquere (R̠.)] 340, 375–6 (**C18**), 385 (**D48**)
Nunc clarificatus est [A̠.] 296–7, 298
Nursie prouincia [A̠.] 384 (**D35**)
O bone Laurenti martyr [A̠.] 345, 347
O Hippolyte si credis [A̠.] 345–7, 376 (**C25**)
O Hippolyte si credis [crederis] [R̠.] 324, 325–7, 328, 340, 342–4, 376 (**C19**), 388 (**D75**)
℣. Dispersit 340
℣. Si dictis 340, 376 (**C19**), 388 (**D75**)
O ineffabilem [A̠.] 383 (**D28**)
O Ioseph quomodo credidisti [A̠.] 126
O Iuda qui dereliquisti consilium pacis [R̠.] 371 (**B123**)
℣. Os tuum abundauit malitia
O regem celi [R̠.] 123
Oblatus est quia ipse uoluit [A̠.] 372 (**B128**)
Obsecro domine [R̠.] 229, 230, 231, 235, 241, 244–5
℣. A solis ortu 230, 231, 235, 241, 244–5
℣. Qui regis Israel 241, 245

Occurrunt turbe [A̠.] 295–7, 298, 299–300, 362 (**B44**)
Octaua decima [R̠.] 230, 231, 238, 243, 250–1
℣. Ego sum dominus deus 230, 231, 238, 243, 250–1
Omne tempore benedic deus [R̠.] 226 n. 28, 227
℣. Inquire ut facias 226 n. 28
℣. Memor esto filii quoniam 227
Omnes collaudant nomen tuum [A̠.] 295, 297, 298, 299–300, 362 (**B40**)
Omnes inimici mei aduersum me [℣. cf. Conclusit uias meas (R̠.)l] 287
Omnes inimici mei aduersum me [℣. cf. Contumelias et terrores passus sum (R̠.)] 287, 366 (**B82**)
Omnes inimici mei aduersum me [℣. cf. Eram quasi agnus innocens (R̠.)] 370 (**B111**)
Omnes inimici mei aduersum me [℣. cf. Pacifice loquebantur mihi inimici mei (R̠.)] 290
Omnes inimici mei aduersum me [℣. cf. Sicut agnus ductus sum (R̠.)] 291
Omnes inimici mei audierunt [A̠.] 367 (**B86**)
Omnes inimici mei audierunt [℣. cf. Contumelias et terrores passus sum (R̠.)] 287
Omnia iudicia tua [℣. cf. Peto domine ut de uincula (R̠.)] 226–7
Omnipotens sempiterne deus da nobis [Or.] 362 (**B46**)
Opprobrium factus sum nimis inimicis [R̠.] 270, 276–8, 290, 292–4
℣. Insurrexerunt in me 290
℣. Locuti sunt aduersum me 290
℣. Persequar inimicos meos 290
Ora pro nobis [A̠.] 383 (**D23**)
Orabat sanctus benedictus [A̠.] 384 (**D43**)
Orauit Iacob [R̠.] 210

Orietur [℣. cf. Letentur celi (℟.)] 241, 245
Os tuum abundauit malitia [℣. O Iuda qui dereliquisti consilium pacis (℟.)] 371 **(B123)**
Osanna filio Dauid [℣.] 295, 297, 298, 299–300, 362 **(B39)**
Ostende nobis [℣. cf. Non discedimus (℟.)] 243, 251
Oues mee uocem meam audiunt et [℣.] 358 **(B12)**
Pacifice loquebantur mihi inimici mei [℟.] 269, 270, 290, 293
℣. Ego autem dum mihi molesti 290
℣. Omnes inimici mei aduersum me 290
Paradisi porte [℣.] 379 **(C53)**
Paries [℣. cf. Suscipe uerbum (℟.)] 242, 249
Pater sanctus [℣.] 383 **(D31)**
Per memetipsum [℟.] 216
Per quem mihi [℣. cf. Mihi uiuere Christus est (℣.)] 381 **(D8)**
Per quem omnes gentes [℣. cf. Tu es uas electionis sancte Paule (℣.)] 381 **(D10)**
Persequar inimicos meos [℣. cf. Opprobrium factus sum nimis inimicis (℟.)] 290
Peto domine ut de uincula [℟.] 223, 227
℣. Omnia iudicia tua 226, 227
℣. Qui regis Israel 226, 227
Petrus autem sequebatur [℣.] 296–7, 298
Pilatus dicebat ego nullam [℣.] 296–7, 298
Ponam arcum meum [℟.] 216
Positis autem genibus [℣.] 296–7, 298
Postquam surrexit [℣.] 297, 298
Posuisti domine [℣.(℟.)] 376 **(C27)**, 387 **(D68)**

Potestas [℣. cf. Aspiciebam (℟.)] 231, 241, 245
Potestatem habeo ponendi [℣.] 295–7, 298, 299–300, 365 **(B75)**
Potuit enim transgredi [℣. cf. Beatus uir Laurentius qui post aurum (℟.)] 337
Potuit enim transgredi [℣. cf. Beatus uir qui inuentus (℟.)] 338
Precursor [℣. cf. Intuemini (℟.)] 243, 251
Preoccupemus [℣. cf. Saluatorem (℟.)] 231, 235, 241, 244–5
Principes persecuti sunt [℟.] 269, 270, 291, 292, 361 **(B36)**, 364 **(B58)**, 367 **(B88)**
℣. Quasi qui inuenit spolia 291, 361 **(B36)**
Principes sacerdotum [℣.] 295, 297, 298
Probasti [℣. cf. Beatus Laurentius dixit disce miser (℟.)] 337
Probasti [℣. cf. Gaudeo plane quia hostia (℟.)] 338
Probasti [℣. cf. Hic est uir (℟.)] 338
Probasti [℣. cf. Igne me examinasti (℟.)] 376 **(C22)**
Probasti [℣. cf. In craticula te deum non negaui (℟.)] 339, 385 **(D52)**
Prope est [℟.] 230, 231, 237, 242, 248–9
℣. Qui uenturus est 230, 231, 237, 242, 248–9
Prope est ut [℣. cf. Ecce iam uenit (℟.)] 230, 231, 238, 243, 250–1
Propter nimiam [℣. cf. Ecce iam uenit (℟.)] 243, 251
Protector tuus [℟.] 323, 340, 343
℣. Liberasti 340
Puer meus non timere [℟.] 319, 324, 328, 340, 342–4, 377 **(C30)**, 385 **(D51)**
℣. Donec ponam 340

INDEX OF LITURGICAL FORMS

℣. Liberabo te 319, 340, 377 (**C30**), 385 (**D51**)
Puer quidam paruulus [℣.] 384 (**D44**)
Pueri Hebreorum tollentes [℣.] 279, 295–7, 298, 299–300
Pueri Hebreorum uestimenta [℣.] 280, 295–7, 298, 299–300
Pulchra es et decora [℣.] 379 (**C57**)
Pulchriores sunt [℣. cf. Non auferetur (℟.)] 230, 231, 238, 243, 250–1
Quando enim infirmor [℣. cf. Libenter gloriabor in infirmitatibus (℣.)] 382 (**D15**)
Quare detraxistis sermonibus ueritatis [℣.] 166
Quasi qui inuenit spolia [℣. cf. Principes persecuti sunt (℟.)] 291, 361 (**B36**)
Que est [℣. cf. Uidi speciosam sicut columbam (℟.)] 379 (**C59**)
Que est ista que ascendit [℣.] 379 (**C50**)
Quem uidistis pastores [℟.] 123
Qui dicunt recede [℣. cf. Expandi manus meas (℟.)] 288
Qui intingit mecum manum [℣. cf. Unus ex discipulis meis tradet me (℟.)] 369 (**B109**)
Qui me confessus [℣.] 378 (**C43**)
Qui me segregauit [℣. cf. Qui operatus est Petro (℣.)] 381 (**D5**)
Qui me segregauit ex utero [℣.] 381 (**D6**)
℣. Et uocauit per gratiam suam
Qui mihi ministrat me sequatur [℣.] 345–7
Qui odit animam [℣.] 378 (**C47**)
Qui operatus est Petro [℣.] 380–1 (**D5**)
℣. Qui me segregauit
Qui potuit transgredi [℣. cf. Beatus uir Laurentius qui post aurum (℟.)] 337
Qui regis Israel [℣. cf. Aspiciens a longe (℟.)] 229, 235

Qui regis Israel [℣. cf. Obsecro domine (℟.)] 241, 245
Qui regis Israel [℣. cf. Peto domine ut de uincula (℟.)] 226–227
Qui sequitur me [℣.] 378 (**C44**)
Qui sitit ueniat et bibat [℣.] 356 (**B3**)
Qui tribulant me exultabunt [℣. cf. Usquequo exaltabitur inimicus meus (℟.)] 291
Qui uenturus est [℟.] 230, 231, 237, 242, 248–9
℣. Deponet 231, 242, 249
℣. Et auferet 242, 249
℣. Ex Sion species 230, 237, 248–9
Qui uenturus est [℣. cf. Prope est (℟.)] 230, 231, 237, 242, 248–9
Qui uult uenire [℣.] 378 (**C45**)
Quia accusatus [℣. cf. Beatus Laurentius dixit domine (℣.)] 347, 375 (**C13**)
Quia ego tecum sum [℣.] 295–7, 298, 299–300, 365 (**B74**)
Quia ipse dominus nouit [℣. cf. Beatus Laurentius dixit mea nox (℣.)] 375 (**C15**)
Quid in me [℣. cf. Non me derelinquere (℣.) 375 (**C11**)
Quid in me [℣. cf. Quo progrederis (℟.)] 340, 375 (**C17**), 384–5 (**D47**)
Quid molesti estis [℣.] 296, 298, 358 (**B17**)
Quidam autem iudei dicebant [℣.] 357 (**B8**)
Quique terrigine [℣. cf. Aspiciens a longe (℟.)] 229, 235
Quo progrederis [℣.] 320, 333, 345–7, 375 (**C10**)
℣. Beatus Laurentius dixit 375 (**C10**)
Quo progrederis [℟.] 324, 328, 340, 342–4, 375 (**C17**), 384 (**D47**)
℣. Quid in me 340, 375 (**C17**), 384–5 (**D47**)

Quo uirtute [℣. cf. Festa dies mundo (℟.)] 338
Quomodo [℣. cf. Aue Maria (℟.)] 231, 241, 244–5
Quoniam ad te [℣. cf. Beatus Laurentius dixit ego me obtuli (℟.)] 337
Quoniam tribulator proxima [℣. cf. Circumdederunt me uiri (℟.)] 287
Radix Iesse qui exurget [℟.] 243, 251
℣. Ex Sion 243, 251
Recessit igitur [A℣.] 384 (**D37**)
Recordare mei domine [A℣.] 279, 280, 295–7, 298, 299–300, 364 (**B61**)
Recordare quod steterim [℣. cf. Attende domine ad me (℟.)] 286
Regem apostolorum [Invit.] 380 (**D4**)
Regem confessorum [Invit.] 383 (**D33**)
Regem martyrum [Invit.] 375 (**C9**), 388 (**D73**)
Regem sempiternum pronis mentibus adoremus [Invit.] 374 (**C8**)
Relicta domo [A℣.] 384 (**D36**)
Repleuit et inebriauit [A℣.] 296, 298
Reuelabunt celi iniquitatem Iude [℟.] 371 (**B121**)
℣. In die perditionis seruabitur
Reuertetur [℣. cf. Uirgo Israel (℟.)] 243, 251
Rex Israel [A℣.] 297, 298
Rex noster adueni [℟.] 230, 231, 236, 242, 246–7
℣. Ecce agnus dei 230, 231, 236, 242, 246–247
℣. Super ipsum 242, 247
Rogaui patrem [A℣.] 297, 298
Rorate [℣. cf. Egredietur uirga (℟.)] 243, 251
Sacerdos dei Martine [A℣.] 383 (**D26**), 383 (**D29**)
Sacerdotes dei [A℣.] 382 (**D19**)
Saluator mundi salua nos omnes [A℣.] 190

Saluatorem [℟.] 230, 231, 235, 241, 244–5
℣. Preoccupemus 231, 235, 241, 244–5
℣. Sobrie 241, 245
Saluum me fac deus [℟.] 268–70, 277, 278, 291, 292–4, 364 (**B63**)
℣. Intende anime mee 291
Sanctificamini filii [℟.] 241, 251
℣. Ecce dominus ueniet 241, 251
Sanctificamini hodie [℟.] 241, 251
℣. Hodie scietis 241, 251
Sanctus Martinus [A℣.] 382 (**D16**)
Scio cui credidi et certus sum [A℣.] 381 (**D7**)
℣. De reliquo reposita est mihi
Scriptum est percutiam [A℣.] 296–7, 298
Seniores populi consilium fecerunt [℟.] 370 (**B119**)
℣. Congregauerunt iniquitatem sibi 371 (**B119**)
Seruite domino in timore [A℣.] 173
Si dictis [℣. cf. O Hippolyte si credis (℟.)] 340, 376 (**C19**), 388 (**D75**)
Si dominus deus [℟.] 210, 350
℣. Uere dominus est 350, 351 n. 8
Si ego dominus [A℣.] 297, 298
Si male locutus [A℣.] 296–7, 298
Si quis mihi ministrauerit [A℣.] 316, 345–7, 374 (**C7**)
Sicut agnus ductus sum [℟.] 269, 291, 293
℣. Omnes inimici mei aduersum me 291
Sicut mater [℟.] 230, 231, 236, 239, 242, 246–7
℣. Dabo in Sion 231, 242, 247
℣. Deus a Libano 230, 236, 242, 246–7
Simon dormis non potuistis [A℣.] 295–7, 298, 299–300, 367 (**B89**)
Sinite mulierem [A℣.] 297, 298

INDEX OF LITURGICAL FORMS

Sobrie [℣. cf. Saluatorem (℟.)] 241, 245
Specie tua [A̞.] 379 **(C55)**
Strinxerunt corporis [A̞.] 320, 333, 345–7, 376 **(C21)**
℣. Carnifices urgentes 376 **(C21)**
Strinxerunt corporis [℟.] 324, 328, 341, 342–4, 376 **(C28)**, 385 **(D49)**
℣. Carnifices uero urgentes 341, 376 **(C28)**, 385 **(D49)**
℣. Hic est uir 341
℣. Mea nox 341
Sufficiebat nobis [℟.] 227
℣. Heu me fili mi ut
Super ipsum [℣. cf. Rex noster adueni (℟.)] 242, 247
Super solium [℣. cf. Ecce uirgo concipiet (℟.)] 241, 245
Surgens mane [℟.] 210
Surrexit dominus de sepulchro [℣.(℟.)] 180
Suscipe uerbum [℟.] 230, 231, 237, 242, 248–9
℣. Aue Maria 230, 231, 237, 242, 248–9
℣. Paries 242, 249
Synagoge populorum circumdederunt [℟.] 268, 277, 278, 291, 292–294, 360 **(B26)**, 366 **(B78)**
℣. Iudica me domine secundum iustitiam 291, 360 **(B26)**
℣. Tu autem domine susceptor 291
Tamquam nugaces estimati sumus [℣. cf. Dixerunt impii apud se (℟.)] 288
Tantam gratiam [A̞.] 384 **(D45)**
Tanto tempore uobiscum [A̞.] 295–7, 298, 299–300, 367 **(B90)**
Te decet laus [Hym.] 325
Te deum [Hym.] 206, 264, 325, 327
Te in omnem [℟.] 226, 227
℣. Benedicite deum celi 226, 227
Tecum principium [A̞.] 180
Tempus est ut reuertar [℟.] 226, 227

℣. Benedicite deum celi 226, 227
℣. Confitemini ei coram omnibus 226 n. 28
Tempus est ut reuertar [℣. cf. Benedicite deum celi (℟.)] 227
Ter uirgis cesus sum [A̞.] 316, 374 **(C4)**, 381 **(D13)**
℣. Nocte ac [et] die 374 **(C4)**, **(D13)**
Terra tremuit et quieuit dum resurgeret [A̞.] 370 **(B115)**
Testimonium ergo perhibebat turba [℣. cf. Cogitauerunt autem principes sacerdotum (℟.)] 271–2, 287
Tetradius [A̞.] 383 **(D27)**
Tibi reuelaui [A̞.] 296–7, 298
Tolle arma [℟.] 210
Tollite portas [℣. cf. Aspiciens a longe (℟.)] 230, 235, 241, 244–5
Tollite portas [℣. cf. Aue Maria (℟.)] 235, 241, 244–5
Tollite portas [℣. cf. Ecce uirgo concipiet (℟.)] 230, 235, 241, 244–5
Tradetur enim gentibus [A̞.] 297, 298
Traditor autem [A̞.] 295–7, 298, 299–300, 372 **(B130)**
Transiens autem [℣. cf. Beatus Laurentius dixit domine (℟.)] 337
Transiens autem per ignem [A̞.] 346–7
Tristis est anima mea [℟.] 368 **(B101)**
℣. Ecce appropinquabit hora
Tu autem domine miserere nobis [℣.(℟.)] 356 n. 2
Tu autem domine Sabaoth [℣. cf. Dominus mecum est tamquam bellator (℟.)] 288
Tu autem domine susceptor [℣. cf. Synagoge populorum circumdederunt (℟.)] 291
Tu es uas electionis sancte Paule [A̞.] 381 **(D10)**
℣. Per quem omnes gentes
Turba multa que conuenerat [A̞.] 295–7, 298, 299–300, 362 **(B38)**

Ubi fratres in unum [A̅.] 297, 298
Ueni desiderator bone [A̅.] 345–7, 378 (**C42**), 387 (**D69**)
Ueni domine et noli [R̅.] 230, 231, 237, 242, 248–9
V̅. A solis ortu 230, 231, 237, 242, 248–9
V̅. Deus a Libano 242, 248
V̅. Excita 242, 248–9
Ueniam dicit [V̅. cf. Alieni non (R̅.)] 230, 231, 235, 243, 244
Uenite adoremus regem regum [Invit.] 379 (**C51**)
Uenite ascendamus [V̅. cf. Docebit nos (R̅.)] 231, 243, 249
Uere dominus [R̅.] 210
Uere dominus est [V̅. cf. Si dominus deus (R̅.)] 350, 351 n. 8
Uere languores nostros [V̅. cf. Ecce uidimus eum non habentem (R̅.)]) 369 (**B103**)
Uerumtamen non sicut ego uolo [V̅. cf. In monte oliueti orauit ad patrem (R̅.)] 368 (**B99**)
Uictrici tota celi [V̅. cf. Laurea Laurenti preclari (R̅.)] 339
Uide domine et considera [A̅.] 280, 295, 298, 299, 365 (**B68**)
Uide domine infirmitates [Or.] 332
Uidi dominum [R̅.] 210
Uidi speciosam sicut columbam [R̅.] 379 (**C59**)
V̅. Que est
Uidisti domine iniquitates [V̅. cf. Dominus mecum est tamquam bellator (R̅.)] 288
Uigesima quarta die [R̅.] *see* Octaua decima die
Uir inclitus Laurentius [R̅.] 323, 327, 341, 342

V̅. Cuius intercessio 341
Uirgo Israel [R̅.] 230, 231, 238, 243, 250–1
V̅. A solis ortu 230, 231, 238, 243, 250–1 V̅. In caritate 243, 251
V̅. Reuertetur 243, 251
Uiri impii dixerunt opprimamus [R̅.] 268–70, 277, 291, 292–3, 361 (**B30**)
V̅. Dixerunt impii apud se 291, 361 (**B30**)
V̅. Hec cogitauerunt 291
Uiri impii dixerunt opprimamus [V̅. cf. Dixerunt impii apud se (R̅.)] 288, 359 (**B19**)
Una hora non potuistis uigilare [R̅.] 370 (**B113**)
V̅. Dormite iam et requiescite
Unus ex discipulis meis tradet me [R̅.] 369 (**B109**)
V̅. Qui intingit mecum manum
Uolo pater [A̅.] 317, 346–347, 378 (**C38**), 378 (**C48**)
Uos ascendite ad diem festum [A̅.] 357 (**B7**)
Uos qui in puluere [V̅. cf. Constantes estote (R̅.)] 241, 251
Uos qui reliquistis omnia [A̅.] 315, 374 (**C3**)
V̅. Cum sederit filius hominis 374 (**C3**)
Uox clamantis in deserto [V̅. cf. Credimus saluatorem (R̅.)] 129 n. 194
Usquequo exaltabitur [A̅.] 297, 298
Usquequo exaltabitur inimicus meus [R̅.] 269, 291, 293
V̅. Qui tribulant me exultabunt 291
Zelus domus tue comedit me [A̅.] 368 (**B94**)

Index of Biblical References and Liturgical Readings

As in the index of liturgical forms, texts transcribed in the appendices are referred to both by page number and paragraph number. Discussions of distributions of the whole psalter and of passages of scripture read throughout the liturgical year are noted in the general index (see under *Bible, canticle,* and *psalms*).

Exodus
   15:1–19 (canticle *Cantemus*) 372 **(B127)**

Deuteronomy
   32:1–43 (canticle *Audite celi*) 17, 19, 31, 117

1 Samuel
   2:1–10 (canticle *Exultauit*) 17, 19

Nehemiah (2 Esdras)
   9:3 119

Psalms
   1 375 **(C10)**, 383 **(D34)**
   2 373 **(B141)**, 384 **(D35)**
   3 375 **(C12)**
   4 384 **(D36)**
   5 375 **(C13)**, 384 **(D37)**
   8 375 **(C14)**, 379 **(C52)**, 384 **(D38)**
   10 375 **(C15)**, 384 **(D39)**
   14 376 **(C21)**, 384 **(D40)**
   16 376 **(C22)**
   18 379 **(C53)**, 380 **(D5)**
   20 376 **(C23)**, 384 **(D41)**
   21 372 **(B126)**, 373 **(B142)**, 375 **(C11)**
   23 379 **(C54)**, 381 **(D6)**, 384 **(D42)**
   31 381 **(D7)**
   33 381 **(D8)**
   44 379 **(C55)**
   45 379 **(C56)**
   47 379 **(C57)**
   50 371 **(B124)**
   54 381? **(D12)**
   60 376 **(C24)**, 381? **(D12)**
   63 376 **(C25)**, 381? **(D12)**, 384 **(D43)**
   64 376 **(C26)**
   68 368 **(B94)**
   69 368 **(B95)**
   70 263
   71 369 **(B104)**
   72 369 **(B105)**
   74 370 **(B114)**
   75 370 **(B115)**
   76 370 **(B116)**
   88:20ff. (as canticle) 384 **(D46)**
   89 371 **(B125)**
   91 384 **(D45)**
   115 372 **(B132)**
   118:62 33, 35, 48 n. 122
   118:106–7 159 n. 51, 160
   118:164 32–5
   119 372 **(B133)**
   139 372 **(B134)**
   140 372 **(B135)**
   141 372 **(B136)**
   148–150 (*Laudate*) 372 **(B128)**

Isaiah
   9:1ff. 122, 124

INDEX OF BIBLICAL REFERENCES AND LITURGICAL READINGS

12:1–6 (canticle *Confitebor*) 17, 19
38:10–20 (canticle *Ego dixi*) 17, 19
40:1ff. 122–4
41:28–9 121
42:3–4, 7 121
43:20 188
45:22 356 n. 2
49:13 130
51:9–10 121
52:1ff. 122, 124
63:5 362 (**B45**)
Jeremiah
2:9–12 356 (**B1**)
2:13–15a 356 (**B4**)
2:19–20a 357 (**B5**)
2:20b–22 357 (**B6**)
2:26–27a 357 (**B9**)
2:27b–28 357 (**B10**)
2:29–31a 357 (**B11**)
2:31a–32 358 (**B14**)
2:35b–37 358 (**B15**)
3:1 358 (**B16**)
4:16–19 358 (**B18**)
6:16–17 362 (**B47**)
6:18–20 363 (**B49**)
6:21–23a 363 (**B51**)
6:23b–24 364 (**B62**)
6:25–6 364 (**B64**)
6:27–30 364 (**B66**)
7:11–12 365 (**B77**)
7:13–15 366 (**B79**)
7:16–19 366 (**B81**)
Lamentations
1:1–2 368 (**B98**)
1:3 368 (**B100**)
1:4 368 (**B102**)
1:8–9 370 (**B112**)
1:10–11 370 (**B118**)
1:12–13 371 (**B120**)
1:14–16 371 (**B122**)
2:10 373 n. 11
Daniel
3:57–88 (canticle *Benedicite*) 17, 19, 113

Habakkuk
3:2–19 (canticle *Domine audiui*) 17, 19, 117
Matthew
11:29 159 n. 51, 160   14:44 129 n. 195
21:1–2 263, 359 (**B22**)
29:9 97 n. 67
Mark
10:15 129 n. 195
Luke
1:46–55 (canticle *Magnificat*) 17, 19, 38, 39, 113, 117,
1:68–79 (canticle *Benedictus*) 16, 18, 38, 39, 113, 114, 266,
6:16 26 n. 23
12:40 129 n. 195
19:37 272
John
5:29 274
6:38 26 n. 23
12:12–19 264, 271–5, 359 n. 5
Ephesians
3:9 99 n. 76
1 Peter
5:5–9 159 n. 51, 160
Ambrose
Expositio euangelii secundum Lucam, II (on Luke 2:15ff.) 124
Augustine
In Iohannis euangelium tractatus, 1 (on John 1:1ff.) 124
Sermo 194 121
Sermo 369 121
Bede
Homiliae II.3 359 (**B23**), 360 (**B25, B27**), 361 (**B29**)
Gregory the Great
Homiliae in euangelia, I. 8 (on Luke 2:1ff.) 124
Origen
In Lucam homiliae, 13 (on Luke 2:13–16) 124

General Index

Aachen 56, 60, 64–6, 74, 153–64
Abbo of Fleury 134
Abingdon 138 n. 26, 150, 152, 155,
   163–4, 165, 168, 173, 190, 194,
   283, 284, 349
   Chronicle 213, 284
Acca, bishop 131
Adalhard, Abbot of Corbie 60
Adelard, *Lectiones in depositione S.
   Dunstani* 194
Adhegrinus 74
Adhemar of Chabannes 107 n. 104
Admonitio generalis (789) 54
Adomnan 105 n. 97
adoptionism 265
Ælberht 101 n. 83
Ælfeah of Winchester 143, 194
Ælfred, ealdorman 140
Ælfric of Eynsham 4 n. 5, 103–4, 181,
   184 n. 135, 185, 195, 264
Ælfric, Archbishop of Canterbury 191,
   192 n. 173, 194
Ælfsige, bishop 221
Ælfwald, king 103, 108
Ælfwine, priest 192
Ælfwold 179
Æthelbald, king 99
Æthelflæd 140, 143
Æthelgifu 164
Æthelheard 88 n. 36, 90 n. 39
Æthelhelm of Canterbury 143
Æthelred of Mercia, ealdorman 140
Æthelred, king 89–90 n. 38

Æthelred, Archbiship of Canterbury
   89–90 n. 38
Æthelstan, king 143, 144 n. 64, 262
   n. 25, 232–3, 258
Æthelwine, ealdorman 179
Æthelwold, St, Bishop of Worcester 7,
   155–6, 161, 163, 165, 177, 181,
   307, 322, 328
   Benedictional of 159, 194,
   contact with Continent 153, 164–5,
      167–8, 183, 213, 234, 284, 327,
      329, 349
   expulsion of clerics 86, 150, 151,
      165, 173, 174, 177, 189
   houses of 11, 150, 152, 165, 171–2,
      179, 181, 186, 189, 195, 283–5,
      327, 329, 331, 334, 335
   monasticism of 7, 144, 150, 162,
      169, 171–3, 185–6, 187, 191,
      195–6, 234, 305, 327, 348–50
   writings of 156, 161, 174, 180, 183
Æthelwulf, poet 80, 97, 104–6, 108
Æthelwulf, king 140 n. 38
Agnes of Rome, St 315
Agobard of Lyons
   De antiphonario 55–6 n. 145, 57
Aidan of Lindisfarne, St 109 n. 114
Alan of Farfa 122 n. 163
Alba see feasts, Easter
Albi 83 n. 20, 146 n. 73, 218
Alcuin 33, 82, 88, 101 n. 83, 131,
   146–7, 225, 265–6
   correspondence of 80, 147 n. 76

446

GENERAL INDEX

De laude Dei 126–31, 146, 225, 266, 350
Aldhelm of Malmesbury 84, 95–7, 102, 108
Aldred, prior 221, 232
Aldfrith, king 84 n. 21
Alfred, king 10, 11, 89–90 n. 38, 133, 136, 137, 138 n. 25, 138 n. 28, 142–7, 148, 152, 156, 232–3, 350, 351
Altitonantis (charter) 187
Amalarius of Metz
   Pseudo–Amalarius 107 n. 104
   time of 44
   writings of 14, 30, 34–6, 37, 40 n. 76, 43, 48 n. 122, 51, 55 n. 145, 57, 107 n. 104, 123–4, 127–8, 163, 203, 225–6, 306 n. 25, 317 n. 57
Ambrose Autpert, abbot 121 n. 160
Ambrose, St, Archbishop of Milan 27, 122 n. 162, 123 n. 164, 131 n. 200
Ambrosian Rite *see* Milanese Rite
ambrosianum (hymn) 71 n. 190, 107, 118
Andrieu, Michel 49–50, 61
Angers 63
Angilbert, abbot 63, 64
Anglo-Saxon Chronicle 89, 133, 192, 260
Aniane *see* Benedict of Aniane
Annals of Lorsch 60
Anselm 214
antiphonal singing 93–5, 97
antiphoners
   Aquitanian 334
   Benedictine 20 n. 8, 72, 211, 213, 218, 348
   English 101, 126, 213, 217, 218, 285 *see also* York, antiphoner of
   Frankish/'Gregorian' 51, 146 n. 73, 226, 319

monastic 183, 190, 204, 209–11, 218, 269, 273, 314 n. 44, 317 n. 57, 322, 323, 329, 335
   Mozarabic 127
   'Old Roman' 43 n. 95, 47 n. 115
   Roman 62–3, 205–6, 211, 226
   secular 73, 183, 185, 190, 204, 209–11, 218, 269, 270, 273, 314 n. 44, 314 n. 45, 320, 324, 335, 350
Aosta 229, 239–40, 245, 247, 249, 251
Apostolic See 54, 83, 182
Arianism 131 n. 200, 265
Arles 23, 27, 108 n. 109
Arras 218
Asser 138 n. 25, 138 n. 28, 143 n. 54, 145, 146, 233
Athanasius, St 27
Athelney 142, 144–5, 196
Augustine of Canterbury, St 5–7, 10, 100, 106–7, 114, 184, 186
   mission 11, 86, 91, 149, 215
Augustine of Hippo, St 28, 122 n. 162, 123 n. 164, 124, 125, 311
   Sermones 121
Augustinian Order 230, 239, 245, 247, 249, 251
Aurelian of Arles 23, 27, 108 n. 109
Autbert, priest 147 n. 76
Autun 74
Bacon, Roger 136 n. 18
Baldwin, abbot 284 n. 68
baptism, rite of 30, 84, 99, 134, 145 n. 70
Barrow, Julia 187–8
Basilius, abbot 70 n. 187
   see also Hildemar of Corbie
Bath 144
Baume 74
Bäumer, Suitbert 31, 221
Bavaria 230, 231, 233, 239, 244, 246, 248, 250, 350

447

Bec 213–14, 215, 218, 274, 277–8, 279, 280, 294, 296, 325–6, 327, 334, 344, 345–6
Bede (Venerable) 6, 7, 10, 34 n. 50, 79 n. 3, 80, 87, 91–3, 101 n. 83, 104 n. 93, 105 n. 97, 108, 114–17, 119–20, 125, 131, 136, 171, 188, 224, 274–5
   Historia ecclesiastica 9, 88, 144
     Old English translation of 188, 220, 222
   Homiliary 264, 272, 275 n. 54
Bedrici-curtis see Bury St Edmunds
Benedict Biscop 6, 80–3, 91, 95, 107, 110, 114, 131
Benedict of Aniane 52, 60–1, 64–75, 77, 138 n. 30, 155, 156, 179, 181 n. 124, 265, 326
   Codex regularum 179
   Concordia regularum 179
   Regula S. Benedicti Anianensis (Collectio capitularis) 155, 157
Benedict of Nursia, St
   abbas Romensis 83
   biography of 5, 28, 84, 170
   depiction of 159
   disciples/followers of 6, 74 n. 205
   foundation of 29, 58 *see also* Monte Cassino
   liturgy at the time of 14, 30–1, 37, 38–9, 41–2, 43, 44, 45–6, 120
   language usage 67   reference to 172 n. 97, 176, 178, 189–90
   relics of 167, 168
   Rule of *see Regula S. Benedicti*
   teachings/writings/liturgy of 20 n. 8, 23, 24, 26, 28, 31, 33, 36, 41–2, 44–6, 58–9, 66, 68, 70, 80, 83, 96–7, 102, 118, 153, 157–9, 170, 173–4, 185 *see also* Benedictine Office; *Regula S. Benedicti*
see also Benedictine Office; feasts, St Benedict; *Regula S. Benedicti*

'Benedictine Hypothesis' 4–5, 7–8
Benedictine Office 27–8, 62, 75–6, 77, 152, 185, 194, 282, 285, 302, 322, 330–1, 348–51
   antiphoners 20 n. 8, 72, 211, 213, 218, 348
   breviaries 115 n. 138, 116, 213, 218, 252–300, 348
   books of 152, 163, 263, 269, 301–47
   customary 155 *see also Memoriale qualiter*
   distribution of psalms 64, 75, 116, 118, 158, 317, 348 *see also cursus*, Benedictine
   relation to Roman Office 28, 32, 37, 41
   observance/use of 5–8, 11, 52, 69–73, 85, 153, 154, 163, 179, 190, 193, 195–6, 253, 285, 330
   see also cursus, Benedictine; monasticism, Benedictine; *Regula S Benedicti*; Benedict of Nursia
Benedictine monasticism
Benedictine Order 5
Benedictine monasteries/houses 6, 14, 82, 144, 150, 169, 229, 277 n. 58
   reformed 190, 262–3, 282
Benedictine monks 7–8, 76, 150, 156, 187, 193
   reformed 69, 144, 152, 158, 179, 261, 277 n. 58
Benedictine Reform, tenth-century 4, 10, 143–4, 148, 149, 151–2, 162, 165, 167–9, 179, 214, 220, 227, 234, 261, 263, 264, 266, 302, 350–1
Benna, canon 231–2
Berhtwald, archbishop 84 n. 21
Berhtwulf, king 140
Berno, abbot 74
Bethlehem 32

GENERAL INDEX

Beyssac, Gabriel 200–3, 209, 217
Bible
   readings from throughout the year
      autumn (Tobit, Judith, 1–2
      Maccabees, Minor Prophets)
      222, 223, 226–7
      Holy Week (Jeremiah,
      Lamentations) 263, 271–5, 373
      n. 11
      summer (1–4 Kings, Wisdom,
      Job) 221
   recited from memory 119
   versions of
      Greek 99 n. 76, 110 n. 116
      Hebrew 110 n. 116, 111
      Hexapla 110 n. 116
      Septuagint (Greek) 110 n. 116
      Vetus Latina 109–10
      Vulgate 48 n. 121, 99 n. 76, 110, 263
   see also canticle; *cursus*; psalms
Bishop, T. A. M. 256, 304–7, 310–12, 330, 349
Blair, John 9, 83
Boethius 311
Boniface, St, Archbishop of Mainz 85, 99, 101, 231
Boniface II, pope 49
Bosa, bishop 88, 127
Breedon-on-the-Hill 140
Breviarium S. Albani (London, British Library, C.110.a.27 [printed book]): 278, 280, 281, 286–91, 294, 296, 325–6, 327, 336–41, 344, 346
Brittany 148, 156
Brooks, Nicholas 192
Brou, royal monastery 23
Budny, Mildred 223
Burgundy 74 Bury St Edmunds (*Bedrici-curtis*) 135 284 n. 68
Butler, Cuthbert 5, 6, 8
Byrhtferth of Ramsey 150–1, 165–6, 170–1, 175–9, 186–8

Byrhthelm 151
Caesarius of Arles 23, 27
Callewaert, Camille 30–1, 34, 37, 41
Cambrai 201, 218, 281
canon law 59, 79, 103 n. 92,
canticle, 44, 62–3, 70, 73, 113–14, 118, 120, 317, 335, 349
   Gospel 22, 38–39, 43, 113–14
   New Testament 113
   Old Testament 16–21, 31, 39, 71, 113, 117, 372
Canterbury 7, 81–2, 86, 89, 91, 98, 99, 110–11, 112, 118, 141, 147, 150, 151, 153, 165, 170, 192, 214, 223, 284 n. 68, 322, 351
   Æthelhelm of 143
   Osbern of 192
   scripts of 305–7, 310
   see also Christ Church, Canterbury; St Augustine's, Canterbury; SS. Peter and Paul, Canterbury
Carolingian Empire 65, 73, 155
Carolingian emperors *see* Charlemagne, Louis the Pious, Pippin III
Carolingian reform 26 n. 24, 65, 69, 81 n. 11, 87, 97, 129 n. 196, 146, 147 n. 76, 162, 184, 199, 234 *see also* Charlemagne, liturgical reform; Frankish monastic reforms; monasticism, Carolingian
Carthusian Order 14
Cassian, John 24-26, 28, 32, 44, 310
   Institutiones 26, 34 n. 50, 81 n. 8, 85 n. 26
Cassiodorus 33, 111 n. 127
Catalenus, abbot 49, 50 n. 131
cathedral Office 13, 34
Cautio episcopi 45–6
Ceolfrith, abbot 80, 92–3, 95, 119, 171
Ceolnoth, archbishop 89–90 n. 38
Ceolwulf II, king 140 n. 38
Chabannes 107 n. 104

GENERAL INDEX

Chadd, David 200, 213–18, 264, 274, 276, 284
Chalcedon 23, 79
chancery
  English royal 258
  papal 45
Charlemagne
  correspondence with 44, 55, 62, 76
  court chapel 137 n. 21
  liturgy, liturgical reform 33 n. 48, 52–60, 62–4, 125, 147 n. 76, 184 n. 134
  palace chapel, Aachen 56, 64
Cheddar Gorge 143
Chester-le-Street 134, 220–1, 231–2
Christ Church, Canterbury 86–90, 138, 140, 155, 159, 170–1, 191–4
  scriptorium of 191–4, 265, 302, 305–7, 310–11, 314 n. 42, 329 n. 75, 330, 332–3
Chrodegang of Metz 51, 52
Regula canonicorum 23 n. 13, 33, 65–6, 87, 89
Chronicon Moissiacense 60, 65 n. 178
Cicero 65
Cistercian Order 14, 203, 229 n. 34
Civate 69
Cluny 74, 201, 218, 275, 293, 296, 325–7, 333, 334, 343–4, 345
  Odilo of Cluny, abbot 75
  Odo of Cluny, St 74, 382 n. 16
Cnut, king 192
Codex regularum 179
Coldingham 105 n. 97, 277 n. 58
collectar 72, 145, 189, 190, 220, 223, 226, 265, 267, 318
Collectio capitularis (*Regula S. Benedicti Anianensis*) 155, 157
Collectio Dionysiana 59, 79 n. 2, 79 n. 3
Collectio Sanblasiana 79 n. 2
Colman, bishop 27
Columbanus 27, 28, 29, 53, 95 n. 63

Compiègne 72, 146 n. 73, 279, 280, 319
Concordia regularum 179
Constantinople 130
Constantius, bishop 83 n. 20
Continent
  English contact with 7, 11, 79 n. 2, 82 n. 12, 101, 132, 144, 147, 153–4, 164–9, 172, 191 n. 168, 231 n. 41, 233, 305–6, 329; *see also* Æthelwold, contact with Continent
  influence of/from the 11, 87–8, 99, 142, 145–6, 162–3, 168, 186, 226, 284, 315, 327, 348
  models/exemplars from 89, 141, 145, 162, 167, 234, 263, 305, 309, 349
Continental Synods 87
English foundation on the 110 n. 118
Irish observance on the 26, 128
monasticism of the 110, 141, 162, 166–7, 182, 195, 284, 335, 350
Office imitated from the 145, 284–5
practices, customs, tradition 10, 12, 13, 32, 33, 75, 77, 80, 100 n. 80, 104, 142, 144, 148, 153–4, 155, 184–5, 195, 213, 215, 217, 218, 220, 225, 254, 255, 269, 303, 305 n. 17, 312, 323, 335, 351 n. 8
reform movement on the 77, 146, 168, 172–3, 183, 325
Corbie 153, 165, 167–8, 213, 218, 226 n. 28, 234, 282, 284–5, 305 n. 12, 322, 333 n. 86, 335, 348–50
  Adalhard, abbot of 60
  'Corbie/Mont-Renaud' liturgical tradition 277–8, 279, 281, 284, 292, 294, 325–9, 331, 334, 343, 345
  liturgical exemplar in England 331, 334, 366 n. 9

450

Wala, abbot of 57, 62
see also Hildemar of Corbie
Corrêa, Alicia 145, 223
Corvey, Saxony 145 n. 65
councils and synods of the Church 23
  Aachen
    (802) 60, 65 n. 178
    (816) 64–8, 72–74, 75, 156, 157, 163
    (817) 64, 73–4, 75
    reform legislation of 155–6, 159, 161, 162, 164, 184 n. 134
    see also Institutio canonicorum; *Insitutio sanctimonalium*
  on Continent 87
  Chalcedon (451) 23, 79
  Chelsea (*Celichyth*) (816) 79
  Clofesho (747) 87, 92 n. 51, 98–102, 108, 112, 132, 137, 139 n. 33
  'Easter council', England (*Vita S. Oswaldi*) 175
  Ecumenical 129 n. 196
  in Francia 101
  Haethfeld (679) 130–1
  Lateran (649) 130–1
  Legatine, England (786) 131
  Mainz (813) 88 n. 34
  Nicaea I (325) 23 n. 13, 184 n. 135
  Ouestrafelda (*c*.703) 84 n. 21, 95
  Tours (813) 88 n. 34
  Trent (1545–63) 14 n. 1
  Vatican II (1962–5) 122 n. 162, 204
  Whitby (664) 27, 117, 132
  Winchester (*c*.970) 150, 175, 180, 184, 195
Crayke 81 n. 8, 108
Crediton 86
Crowland 195
cursus
  Benedictine 13–15, 27–8, 41, 58, 61–2, 64, 66, 69, 71–3, 76, 84, 108, 112, 114 n. 138, 116 n. 141, 117–20, 145, 153, 154, 157–8, 162, 163–4, 169, 171–3, 179, 181–3, 185, 186–7, 189, 190–3, 195–6, 221, 225, 229, 262, 317, 335, 349, 351 *see also* Benedictine Office, distribution of psalms; *cursus*, monastic
  Bethlehem 32
  cathedral 13
  Eastern 28 *see also* Eastern Office
  Irish 28 *see also* Irish Office
  monastic 13–15, 18–23, 31, 77, 87, 89, 112, 145, 184, 193–4, 199, 200, 203, 204, 206, 275, 302, 323, 325, 348, 351 *see also cursus*, Benedictine; monastic Office
  Roman 13, 28–9, 40, 57–8, 61–2, 64, 67, 76, 87, 102–4, 111, 113–14, 117, 120, 141, 148, 154, 157, 163–4, 174, 206 *see also cursus*, secular; Roman Office
  secular 13–17, 19–23, 31, 39, 41–2, 64, 72, 77, 87, 89, 91, 111, 113, 118, 145–6, 148, 174, 181–6, 193, 199, 200, 203, 204, 206, 212, 218, 221, 227, 234, 262, 269, 323, 324, 325, 348, 377 n. 9 *see also cursus*, Roman; secular Office
  of St Ambrose 27
  see also Ratio de cursus
customary 175, 272, 284
  Bec 274–5
  Benedictine 155
  Continental reform 183
  Fleury 168
  monastic 150, 169, 172 n. 97, 179, 181 *see also Regularis concordia*
Cuthbert, Archbishop of Canterbury 98–9, 101–2
Cuthbert, St, Anglo-Saxon monk 83, 106, 115–17, 134, 220, 232 *see also* feasts, St Cuthbert

Cwicwine 105
Danelaw 135
David, king 110 n. 120, 127 n. 182, 176
Deerhurst 284 n. 68
Denis, St, Bishop of Paris 72, 284 n. 68
Deshusses, Dom Jean 214, 265
De festiuitatibus anni 155
De horis peculiaribus 171–2
De laude Dei, Alcuin 126–31, 146, 225, 266, 350
Diadema monachorum 155 see also Smaragdus, abbot
Dijon 213, 215, 218, 277
Dionysius Exiguus 79 n. 2, 79 n. 3, 129 n. 196, 130 n. 198
Dominican Order 14
Doyle, Ian 121–2
dragons 188
Drauscius, Bishop of Soissons 29 n. 31
Dudoc, bishop 224
Dumville, David 143, 152, 256–61, 306–7, 332
Dunstan, St 5, 7, 11, 143, 150–2, 153–7, 163–7, 168, 169–71, 179, 186, 191, 192, 193, 195–6, 234, 261, 284 n. 68, 305, 307, 349, 351
  exile in Ghent 153, 165, 166–7, 168, 305 n. 15, 351
  Lectiones in depositione S. Dunstani, Adelard 194
  see also feasts, St Dunstan
Duplex legationis edictum (789) 60 n. 157
Durham 121, 135, 221, 277
  Durham Collectar 145, 200–51
Eadhæd, praesul 188
Eadred, king 152, 164
Eadmer 187
Eadmund, St, King of East Anglia 134–5, 143, 144, 149, 153
Eadwig, English king 152, 164

Eadwig Basan, scribe 191, 330
Ealdwulf, bishop 283
Ealhburg 140
Eanbald II, archbishop 147 n. 76
Eanmund, abbot 80–1, 104
East Anglia 103, 108, 134
Eastern Office 27, 28
Ecgberht, bishop 183
Ecgberht of York, archbishop 100–1, 127
Edgar, English king 143, 150–2, 162, 169, 172, 173–8, 187, 232, 261, 283
Edith of Wilton, St 232, 284 n. 68
Edward the Confessor, king 284 n. 68
Edward the Elder, king 143
Egyptian 'Desert Fathers', Office of 25–6, 37, 44
Ely 195, 327, 332
England
  Dorset 143, 282
  East Anglia 103, 108, 134
  Hertford 79 n. 3
  Humber 133, 142
  Kent 82, 139
  Leicestershire 140
  Mercia 99, 140, 265
  Northern 91, 121 n. 160, 131, 253
  Severn Valley 277 n. 58
  Somerset 143
  Southern 98, 109, 112, 133, 142, 145, 222
  Southwest 142, 191, 232
  Wessex 135, 196, 221, 232–233, 351
  West Saxon 140 n. 38, 142, 148, 223 n. 36
  Wiltshire 89–90 n. 38
  see also Northumbria, and specific towns
Euticius 74 see also Benedict of Aniane
Exeter 126 n. 178, 190, 222

Expositio in Regulam S. Benedicti 156, 157–8, 196 *see also* Smaragdus, abbot
Evesham 277, 350 n. 5
Eynsham
  monks of 181, 185, 195
  see also Ælfric of Eynsham
Farfa 122 n. 163
Farne 116
feasts and liturgical seasons
  Advent 99 n. 76, 121, 126–9, 210, 223, 225, 318, 350
    Old English Advent Lyrics (Christ I) 126
    Sundays in 200–1, 204, 206–7, 222, 226–31, 234, 235–51
  All Saints 171–2, 190, 202
  Annunciation 202
  Ascension 76
  Assumption 202, 301, 313, 314, 315, 318, 319, 320, 379
  Christmas 46, 47, 76, 121–4, 125 n. 171, 127–8, 146, 180, 223
    Christmas Eve 123
    Night Office 62
    Octave of 125 n. 171, 180
  Circumcision 124 n. 168
  Dedication of a church 125 n. 172, 193–4, 202
  Easter 63, 76, 83, 103 n. 91, 177, 180, 182–3, 281 *see also* feasts, Resurrection
    date of 27, 117, 135
    Easter Eve 252
    fortnight before 262
    Night Office of 47
    Octave of 51
    season 20 n. 8
    week after 70–1, 182–3
  Ember days 101
    Advent 204
  Epiphany 40, 76, 125 n. 171, 127–8, 180 n. 118

Night Office 41 n. 86
  Octave of 267
Exaltation of the Holy Cross 265
Good Friday 125 n. 171, 182, 202, 262, 265, 373 *see also* feasts, *Triduum sacrum*
Holy Saturday 42, 182, 202 *see also* feasts, *Triduum sacrum*
Holy Week 76, 184 n. 134, 201, 253, 263, 267–9, 275, 278–81, 295–300, 362–73
John the Baptist 223
Lent 42, 68 n. 185, 101, 128, 201, 210, 224, 262, 266, 267, 331–2, 350
Maundy Thursday 125 n. 171, 182, 202–3, 262, 267, 268, 280, 281–2, 295–300, 367–73 *see also* feasts, *Triduum sacrum*
Office of the Dead 125 n. 172, 172, 200, 202, 203
Palm Sunday 17, 97, 129 n. 193, 200, 262, 263–4, 266, 267–9, 272–81, 283, 286–300, 336, 358–62
Passion Week 252, 356–8
Passover 271, 274–5
Pentecost 40 n. 76, 70–1, 99 n. 76, 100–1, 182–3, 201, 223
Purification 128
Resurrection 42, 44 *see also* feasts, Easter
Sanctorale 99, 125, 200–1, 313–14, 318
Septuagesima 17, 40, 42
St Benedict 76, 146 n. 70, 189
  Translation of 72, 313, 314, 330, 383
St Cuthbert 221, 232, 233 n. 50, 255
St Dunstan 193
  Deposition of 194 n. 186
St Hyppolitus 330, 387
St James the Apostle 313, 314

453

St John 223, 283
SS. John and Paul 223
St Lawrence 189, 200, 301, 313–18, 319–22, 323–9, 330–5, 336–46, 349, 350, 374–8, 384–8
St Martin 76, 223
  Ordering and Translation of 330, 332, 382–4
St Oswald, king and martyr 313, 314
St Paul 315, 316
  Beheading of 315, 374
  Commemoration of 223, 301, 313, 314–16, 318 n. 60, 330, 380–2
St Peter 76, 125 n. 171, 315
SS. Peter and Paul 171, 223, 313, 314–15, 316, 374
St Stephen 223
Temporale 99, 125, 318
Triduum sacrum 51, 129, 182, 200–1, 202, 281 *see also* feasts, Maundy Thursday, Good Friday, Holy Saturday
Virgin, Little Office of the 200
Virgin, Office of the 171–2
Fécamp 274, 320, 321 n. 68, 325, 326, 327
Ferrari, Guy 30
Ferrières 126 n. 177
Ferreolus of Uzès 25
Flanders 232 n. 42,
Fleury 72, 134, 153, 165–6, 167–9, 184, 191, 195, 218, 305 n. 12, 305 n. 17, 346
  Abbo of Fleury 134
Florence, 316 n. 53
Foot, Sarah 9, 10
Foyer Saint-Benoît à Port-Valais 202 n. 8
France
  northern 279, 281, 282, 295, 377 n. 9

Francia 53, 57–8, 73, 74, 79, 101, 195
  see also Gaul
  northern 73
Franciscan Order 14, 136 n. 18
Frankish Office 10, 40 n. 76, 43, 47 n. 115, 125, 184, 265–6, 348
  books of 14 n. 2, 47 n. 115, 51, 123, 184, 318–19, 335
  antiphoners 51, 146 n. 73, 226, 319
  Eastern Frankish ordo 228–9, 231
  liturgical reform (imposition of Roman Office) 13, 33, 49–51, 52–64, 66, 206
Frankish clergy 87 n. 28
Frankish monasteries 52, 54, 58, 61, 64, 67, 76, 138 n. 30, 154
Frankish monastic reforms 152–3, 154, 156, 179 *see also* Carolingian reform
Frankish monastic texts 164, 190, 195
Frankish monks 13, 157
Franks 77, 124
Froger, Jacques 72, 205–8
Gall, St, Irish missionary 50, 73, 81 n. 11, 211, 212
Gallican Office 27, 29, 53–4, 78, 128, 149
Gallican monastery 36 n. 59
Hiberno-Gallican Office 128
Ganz, David 261
Gaul 27, 107
  Carolingian 30
  liturgical traditions in 26–7, 54, 97, 149, 184, 234
  Frankish 149, 234
  southern 101 n. 85
Gazaeus, Alardus 34 n. 50
Gelasian sacramentary 101, 147 n. 76
Gelasius I, pope 49
Geneva 239, 240, 245, 247, 249, 251
Gerard of Brogne 74, 144

Germanus of Winchester 165–6
Germanic Office 229–31, 233, 234, 350, 351
Gervase of Canterbury 192
Ghent 153, 165, 166–7, 168, 184, 218, 305 n. 15, 351
Giso, bishop 224
Glastonbury 143, 150, 153–7, 163–5, 168, 180, 181, 192, 196, 224, 232, 234, 305 n. 15, 345, 350, 351
Glosses
  Old English 81 n. 8, 81 n. 11, 109 n. 111, 110 n. 115, 137, 141–2, 220
  of *Regula S. Benedicti* 82 n. 11, 102, 118, 157–158
Glossary
  'Abavus' 55 n. 145
  Leiden 81 n. 8, 81 n. 11
Gneuss, Helmut 107–8, 252, 264, 301–2
Gorze 74, 282
Goscelin of Saint-Bertin 232 n. 42
Gozbert, abbot 73
Grand-Saint-Bernard 239–40, 245, 247, 249, 251
'Gregorian' Office (Romano-Frankish 11, 127–29, 131, 146–7, 225–6, 234, 316, 350
  antiphoners 51, 146 n. 73, 226, 319
  chant 6 n. 17, 50 n. 131, 94, 127–9, 146
  sacramentary 59, 147 n. 76, 184 n. 134
  see also Frankish Office
Gregory the Great (Pope Gregory I) 7, 10, 28, 34 n. 49, 43 n. 92, 45, 49, 83–4, 86, 106, 122 n. 162, 123 n. 164, 174, 182, 183–4, 186, 195, 311
  liturgical books attributed to 100–1, 184, 203
  Dialogi 5, 24, 28, 29, 84, 170

  monastery of (St Andrew on the Coelian Hill) 5
  writings of 5, 135–6, 158 n. 44, 184 n. 134, 186
Gregory III, pope 30, 44 n. 96, 49, 98
Gretsch, Mechthild 155–6, 159, 160, 191
Grimbald of Saint-Bertin 144–6, 156, 233
Guthrum 142 n. 46
Gy, P.M. 211–12
Hadrian, abbot 81, 119
Hadrian I, pope 59, 98
Hadrianum 147 n. 76, 355
hagiography 9, 20, 40, 122
Hanssens, Jean-Michel 34, 57
Hartker 73, 190, 210, 322
Hartzell, K. D. 302
Herefrith 116
Helisachar, abbot 62, 146 n. 73, 319
Herewulf, priest-abbot 139 n. 32
Hertford 79 n. 3
Hesbert, Dom René-Jean 190, 200, 203–11, 213, 216–18, 227–31, 239, 241, 251 n. 51, 268, 270, 314, 318, 355, 375 n. 5, 385 n. 9
Hexapla, Origen's 110 n. 116
Hexham 131
Hilary of Poitiers 129 n. 196, 130 n. 198
Hildemar of Corbie 35, 67 n. 183, 69–71, 92 n. 49, 107 n. 104, 158, 184 n. 134
Hilduin, abbot 72
Hiley, David 213
Hippolytus of Rome, St 309, *see also* feasts, St Hyppolitus
Historia de Noe 215–16, 274
Historia ecclesiae Abbendonensis 167, 169, 349
Historia ecclesiastica, Bede 9, 88, 144
Hohler, Christopher 214–15, 224–5, 232

GENERAL INDEX

Holdsworth, Christopher 84–5
Holy Nails, relic 232
homilies 54, 72, 80 n. 6, 122, 123 n. 164, 124 n. 170, 224, 263–4, 272
Homiliary
  of Bede 264, 272, 275 n. 54
  of Paul the Deacon 55 n. 144, 125, 264, 284 n. 68
Honorius, pope 45, 98
horarium 31, 32–6, 78, 99, 101, 102–8, 109, 119, 132, 182
Horningsea, Cambridgeshire 134, 139
Hrabanus Maurus 34 n. 50
Hugh of Autun, St 74 n. 205
Humber 133, 142
Humberht, prince 140
humility 26, 67–8, 70, 158 n. 44, 159–61
Hyde Abbey 210, 320, 327
Inde 75, 181 n. 124
Institutio canonicorum 65, 66, 156, 163
Institutio sanctimonialium 156
Invitatory 16, 18, 39, 41, 62, 123–4, 202, 317, 318, 319
Ireland 265 *see also* Irish Office
  sources from 128, 129 n. 194, 191 n. 168, 224
Irish missionaries 7, 95, 109
Irish observance 26, 132
Irish Office 10, 27, 53, 78, 95 n. 63, 110, 111 n. 127, 149
Isidore of Seville 34 n. 50, 65 n. 177, 92 n. 49, 95 n. 63, 311
Ivarr 'the Boneless' 134
Jarrow 9, 80, 82, 93, 104, 108, 117, 119, 136, 171
  Wearmouth-Jarrow 7, 111 n. 125, 135
Jeffery, Peter 128–9
Jerome, St 24, 46, 110 n. 115, 110 n. 116, 123 n. 164
Jerusalem 44, 56 n. 147, 271–272

Jesse, father of King David 175
John, Eric 187–8
John I, pope 49
John of Gorze 74
John of Salerno 74
John of Worcester 192
John the Archcantor 50 n. 130, 91–8, 117, 127, 130–1
John the Baptist, St 86 n. 27
John the Evangelist, St 27, 86 n. 27
John 'the Old Saxon' 144, 156, 233
Joshua 176
Jumièges 215, 332
Keefer, Sarah Larratt 223
Kent 82, 139
Koenwald of Worcester 143, 169
Ker, N. R. 222, 256, 301
Knowles, David 6–7, 173, 233
Krakow 240, 245, 247, 249, 251
Lambeth Palace Library 282
Lanfranc 214, 332
  Decreta 273
Langefeld, Brigitte 88
Lapidge, Michael 136, 170, 171–2, 173, 187
Lateran Basilica, Rome 49 n. 123, 86, 98, 122, 124, 135 n. 14
Laudes regiae 63
Lawrence of Rome, St 315 *see also* feasts, St Lawrence
Lazarus 271–2, 274 n. 50
Lectiones in depositione S. Dunstani, Adelard 194
Leicestershire 140
Leidrad, Archbishop of Lyons 55–6, 64, 147 n. 76
Leo the Great (Pope Leo I) 49, 122 n. 162
Leofric, Bishop of Exeter 126 n. 178, 222
Leofsige, abbot 232
Le Roux, Raymond 40, 47–8, 281–2
Lérins 23, 107–8

Leroquais, Victor 200–3, 209, 217
Liber diurnus 45
Liber pontificalis 30, 50–1
Limoges 240, 245, 247, 249, 251
Lindisfarne 83, 106, 109, 110, 112, 115–17, 121, 132, 134, 135, 221
 Gospels 221
Linenthal, R. A. 302, 313 n. 40
Logeman, Henri 5
Lombards 29, 53
London 143, 165
Lorsch 60
Lotharingia 232 n. 42, 350
Louis the Pious 52, 63, 64–9, 72–5, 77
Low Countries 233 n. 50
Luxueil, use of 36 n. 59
Lyminge, Kent 139
Lyons 26, 55–6, 64, 201
 Agobard of Lyons 55–6 n. 145, 57
 Leidrad of Lyons 55–6, 64, 147 n. 76
Maban 131
Mainz 99, 229, 240, 244, 246, 248, 250, 282
 St Alban's, Mainz 183 n. 132
Malmesbury 108
 Aldhelm of Malmesbury 84, 95–7, 102, 108
 William of Malmesbury 143 n. 48, 143 n. 51, 192 n. 173, 233
Mark the Evangelist, St 27
marriage, rite of 145 n. 70
Martin I, pope 49, 130
manual labour 36, 85, 105, 181, 187
 see also Opus Dei
marriage, rite of 86 *see also* secular clergy, marriage of
martyrology 72,
 Old English 147 n. 76
 Roman 99–100
 of Usuard of Saint-Germain-des-Prés 155
Maurianus, abbot 49, 50 n. 131

Maurus, St, disciple of Benedict 74 n. 205
Maximin of Trier, St 233 n. 47
Medeshamstede *see* Peterborough
Mediator dei et hominum, homily 272, 275 n. 54, 359 *see also* Homiliary, of Bede
Memoriale qualiter 155, 157, 161
memory 67, 81, 103, 127, 165–6, 191, 195, 255, 319, 355
Mercia 99, 140, 265
metrical hymns 71 n. 190
Mettlach, Trier 232
Metz 51, 52, 56–7, 146–7, 229 n. 34
 see also Amalarius of Metz, Chrodegang of Metz
Milanese Rite 27, 28, 44, 94, 127–8
Mildrith, St, Anglo-Saxon abbess 134
Milton Abbas 143
minsters, mynsters 8, 143–4, 147, 151, 164–5, 175, 195, 348, 349
 'Minster Hypothesis' 8–9
 Office of 9–10, 78–90, 104, 132, 220, 224
 secularization of 134, 138–139, 148
Modestus of Trier, St 233 n. 47
Möller, Hartmut 204, 208
monastic Office 6–7, 9, 11, 13–29, 58, 62, 64–9, 77, 91, 94, 183, 185, 196, 213, 218, 231, 281–2, 284, 320, 322, 348 *see also cursus*, monastic
monasticism
 Benedictine 7, 29 n. 32, 61, 69, 74, 85, 173, 187, 307
 reformed Benedictine 144
 Carolingian 69, 73, 211
 reformed Carolingian 74–5
 Continental 110, 141, 162, 166–7, 182, 195, 284, 335, 350
 Frankish 66
 reformed English 164, 284
 Roman 30

monastic reform, tenth-century 5, 11, 77, 104, 167, 195, 282
monastic rules *see Regula canonicorum*; *Regula Magistri*; *Regula mixta*; *Regula monachorum*; *Regula S. Benedicti*
monastics, contemplative 79
Monothelitism 130, 131 n. 200
Monte Cassino 29, 43, 44, 58–59, 70 n. 187, 75–6, 201, 211
Mont Saint-Michel 215
Mont-Renaud 73, 212, 226 n. 28, 277–9, 281, 284, 292, 294, 325–9, 331, 334, 343, 345, 351 n. 8
Moses 34 n. 48, 117, 176
Mozarabic antiphoner 127
Muchelney Abbey 143, 196, 230–1, 233, 350, 351
Nicaea 23 n. 13, 184 n. 135
Nicene Fathers 27
Nicene Creed 56 n. 147, 129, 130 n. 198
Nigellus, Ermoldus 65–66
Nightingale, John 151, 168
Norman Conquest 11, 89, 143 n. 49, 160, 187, 214, 217, 277 n. 58, 323, 326, 327, 329, 333, 350, 351
Northumbria 7, 83, 95, 109, 111 n. 125, 112, 125
  abbots 83
  monasteries 6
  unknown scribe from 79 n. 2
notation, musical 146 n. 73, 147, 252, 255, 330, 377 n. 9, 380 n. 2, 385 n. 10
  neumatic 166, 172 n. 97, 226, 301, 331, 381, 385 n. 11, 386 n. 12, 386 n. 14, 387
    'Breton' neumes 148, 223, 227, 313 n. 40
    Insular neumes 313, 329, 377 n. 10

Northern French neumes 377 n. 10
Notker Balbulus 137 n. 21
Notre-Dame, Paris 218
Notre-Dame de Bonne-Nouvelle, Rouen 274
Notre-Dame de Soissons 29 n. 31, 110 n. 118
novice 80, 82, 182
Nunnaminster 143
Nursia 74 n. 205
obedience 23, 26 n. 23, 69, 79, 82, 85, 154, 159–62, 163–4, 178, 195
Oda, Bishop of Ramsbury, Archbishop of Canterbury 143, 165, 169
Odilo of Cluny, abbot 75
Odo of Cluny, St 74, 382 n. 16
Old English Advent Lyrics (*Christ I*) 126
'Old Hymnal' 107–108
'Old Roman'
  antiphoner 43 n. 95, 47 n. 115
Opus Dei 102, 181 *see also* manual labour
Orchard, Nicholas 193, 315
Ordines Romani
  XII 38, 46 n. 112, 51, 123–4
  XIIIA 122–3, 125, 135 n. 14
  XIIIB 47 n. 118, 125 n. 171
  XIV 122 n. 163, 135 n. 14
  XV 46 n. 113
  XVI 40 n. 78, 61–2
  XVII 61–2
  XVIII 35–6, 49, 62, 104, 106
  XIX 49–50
  XXXA 51, 128–9
  XXXB 128–9
  L 183 n. 132
ordo canonicus 65, 69, 76
ordo equester 65
ordo monasticus 65, 69
ordo officiorum 124
ordo scribarum 65

ordo senatorius 65
Osbern of Canterbury 192
Oscytel of York 165
Osgar 165, 167–8
ostriches 188
Oswald of Worcester, St 7, 150, 151, 153, 165–7, 169, 175, 177, 186–9, 190–1, 195, 283, 349 *see also* feasts, St Oswald
Oswulf 139
Otto I, emperor 232, 315
Oxford 136 n. 18
Oundle 115 n. 138
pallium 154, 165, 170
papal bull *Quod a nobis* 14 n. 1
papal Curia, thirteenth century 43
Paris 201, 218, 284
Pascher, Joseph 37, 41
Passau 231
Patrick, St 95 n. 63, 224
patristic texts 20, 40, 54, 122, 124, 135, 264, 348
Paul the Apostle, St 176 *see also* feasts, St Paul
Paul the Deacon (Paul Warnefrid) 54, 58, 59 n. 154, 70 n. 187, 125
Homiliary 55 n. 144, 125, 264, 284 n. 68
see also Theodemar
Paulinus of Trier, St 233 n. 47
Passio S. Eugeniae 35
Pentateuch 111
Peter the Apostle, St 26, 27, 315 *see also* feasts, St Peter
Peterborough (*Medeshamstede*) 134, 195, 283, 327, 332
Petronax of Brescia 29
Pfaff, Richard 118
Philippus Presbyter 135
Pippin III 52–4, 58, 62
Plegmund 146, 351
Plummer, Charles 6, 114, 116
Poitiers 64

Hilary of Poitiers 129 n. 196, 130 n. 198
positurae 255
psalms
 chanting of, singing of 20 n. 7, 22, 34, 86, 91–5, 97, 137, 170, 180, 316
 antiphonal psalmody 94
 choral psalmody, two-choir psalmody 94–8
 'direct psalmody' 93–4
 responsorial psalmody 94
 'current psalmody' 38, 41–2, 43 n. 93, 320
 distribution of 14–20, 31–2, 37–43, 44, 56–9, 64, 68, 70, 73, 75–6, 78, 91, 112, 116, 117, 132, 142, 157–9, 191, 195, 199, 320–2, 348 *see also cursus*
 monastic psalmody 93–4, 100, 101–2, 112 *see also cursus*, monastic
 perpetual psalmody 29
 psalmic responsories 40, 47, 48
 recitation of 25, 40, 57, 105, 181
Psalter, Latin versions, *see also* Index of Manuscripts
 Gallicanum 63, 109–11, 152, 191, 195, 263, 320
 Hebraicum (*iuxta Hebraeos*) 110 n. 116
 Romanum 98, 109–11, 112 n. 128, 114, 141 n. 41, 152, 191, 262–3, 285, 320, 348
 of St Jerome 110 n. 115, 110 n. 116
Psalterium Augustini 106–8, 110
Pseudo-Amalarius 107 n. 104
Pseudo-Fulgentius 155, 157, 185
punishment 67, 174
Ramsbury 143
Ramsey 150, 166, 179, 190–1, 195, 283 n. 64 *see also* Byrhtferth of Ramsey

Rankin, Susan 126–8, 131, 318–19
Ratio de cursus 26–9, 53–4
Regula canonicorum 23 n. 13, 33, 65–6, 87, 89 *see also* Chrodegang of Metz
Regula Magistri 24, 26, 30, 33, 35, 36, 38, 41, 42, 44, 45, 46 n. 110, 48, 94, 97, 105–6
Regula mixta 28–9
Regula monachorum 27, 28, 29, 53, 95 n. 63, 108 n. 109
Regula S. Benedicti
 authority of 24, 28, 77, 83–4, 108, 150, 158, 168, 179, 184
 commentary on 35, 68, 184 n. 134
 copy of 72, 74, 155, 159, 162, 312–13
 autograph of 58, 190
 influence of 58, 88, 118, 120, 178
 language/text of 5, 92, 94, 98, 116 n. 141, 157–62, 178, 179, 185
 observance, obedience to/use of 4–6, 8, 11, 29, 58, 59–61, 62, 64, 75, 82–3, 85, 104 n. 94, 119, 150, 154, 157–9, 163–4, 172, 179, 192, 195, 317, 335, 348, 351
 Office according to 7, 13–15, 25, 27–9, 30–1, 33, 35, 38, 41, 42, 48, 58, 70, 73, 78, 94, 102, 106, 107, 119–20, 149, 157, 174, 183, 185, 187, 348 *see also* Benedictine Office
 distribution of psalms 41, 157–9, 191 *see also* cursus, Benedictine
 promotion of 52, 58, 60, 77, 155, 180
 reading of 60, 62, 136
 study of 11, 81, 118–19, 154, 155, 159, 195
 textus interpolatus 81, 162
 textus purus 81 n. 11, 158
 textus receptus 81 n. 11, 158, 162

 translation (Old English) of 156
Regula S. Benedicti Anianensis (*Collectio capitularis*) 155, 157
Regularis concordia 103–4, 140–1, 150, 153, 161–2, 171–2, 179–86, 192, 195, 262, 264, 273, 283, 359 n. 5
Reichenau 81 n. 11
Reims 214
Réôme 23
Richard, duke 213
Ripon 104 n. 94, 117, 188
 Stephen of Ripon 104, 111, 115 n. 138, 188
Robert of Jumièges 332
Rodolphus Glaber 74 n. 205
Roman Office 11, 15, 26, 28, 30–68, 69–71, 75, 77, 91–2, 95, 101–2, 122–3, 132, 135 n. 14, 141, 145, 148, 149, 154, 211, 225–6, 234, 269, 315, 327
 antiphoner 62–3, 205–6, 211, 226
 breviary 115 n. 138, 116, 122 n. 162, 204
 cantus Romanus 53, 54
 distribution of psalms 37–43, 44, 58, 70, 73, 78, 91, 109–20, 132, 142, 159
 first description of 30, 37
 horarium 31, 32–6, 78, 101, 102–8, 109, 132
 imposition of 13, 51, 52–8
 Roman Curial Office 17
 Roman monastic Office 30, 33, 34, 35, 38, 78, 91, 97, 98, 105–6, 108 *see also* cursus, Roman; Rome, practices/traditions
Rome 28, 43 n. 95, 57, 63, 65, 74, 79 n. 2, 81, 83, 95, 98, 100–1, 110–11, 117, 120, 123–4, 125 n. 171, 128, 129 n. 196, 131, 147 n. 76, 149, 154, 165, 170, 184, 225, 315, 316
 missionaries 87 n. 28, 108, 149

monasteries in 5, 13, 30, 31, 36, 42, 49–51, 91, 120, 139 n. 33
basilicas in 11, 30, 36, 49–50, 86, 98, 107, 139 n. 33
practices/traditions 14, 31–2, 34, 35, 40 n. 76, 41, 42, 45, 46 n. 110, 48–50, 51, 68, 77, 84, 100, 107, 120, 122, 125, 127–9, 132, 204, 316, 317 n. 57, 373 n. 11
see also St Andrew on the Coelian Hill, SS. John and Paul, Rome; St Lawrence, Rome; St Martin, Rome; St Mary Major, Rome; St Paul, Rome; St Peter's Basilica, Rome; St Stephen Major, Rome; St Stephen Minor, Rome; St Pancratius at the Lateran
Romsey 143
Rouen 274
rubrication, rubrics 55 n. 145, 106, 108, 200–201, 256, 262, 263–264, 283, 304, 315, 316, 317, 319, 320, 353, 354, 360 n. 6, 382 n. 5
rules, monastic *see* Regula canonicorum; Regula Magistri; Regula mixta; Regula monachorum; Regula S. Benedicti
Saint-Aubin, Angers 63
Saint-Bénigne, Dijon 213
Saint-Bertin 144, 156, 232 n. 42, 233
Saint-Denis 51, 52, 72, 75, 226 n. 28, 282, 284, 316 n. 53, 318–19, 351 n. 8
Saint-Germain-des-Prés 155
Saint-Martin, Autun 74
Saint-Maur-des-Fossés 316 n. 53
Saint-Mihiel 68, 155
Saint-Riquier 62–4
Saint-Savin, Poitiers 74, 75
Saint-Vaast, Arras 218, 281, 284 n. 68
Sankt Florian, Linz 230, 231, 233, 240, 244, 246, 248, 250
Sant Sadurni de Tavèrnoles 334

Sawyer, P. H. 187–8
schola cantorum 147
Sechnall, St, hymn of 224
Second Coming 129
second sleep 35–6, 105
secular clergy 8, 11, 13, 30, 33, 52, 62, 65, 71, 78–9, 87, 100, 102, 126, 151, 156, 163, 170, 172, 173, 174, 196
cooperation with monks 78–79, 86–7, 89, 163, 220, 227
distinction from monks 65, 69
expulsion of 86, 150, 151, 165, 173, 174–5, 177–8, 187–9, 191–2, 195
marriage of 86, 173
secular Office 11, 13–17, 20–3, 38 n. 73, 40, 45–6, 48, 52, 62, 76, 116, 118, 225, 262, 335 *see also cursus*, secular
Sedulius, hymn of 170
Senlis 318
Septuagint 110 n. 116
Severn Valley 277 n. 58
Shaftesbury 143–5, 191
Sherborne 172 n. 97, 184 n. 135, 223 n. 16, 224 n. 20
Sigbald 104
Sigeric, archbishop 192, 315
Sigulf 146, 147 n. 76
Sigwine 97
Silos 226 n. 28
Simeon of Saint-Ouen 332
Smaragdus, abbot 68, 155, 156, 157, 162, 167, 179 n. 112, 196, 264 n. 37
Diadema monachorum 155
Expositio in Regulam S. Benedicti 156, 157–8, 196
Somerset 143
Soissons 29 n. 31, 72, 110 n. 118
Solomon 176
Spain 265
Spanish liturgy 10, 265
St Albans, Mainz 183 n. 132

St Andrew on the Coelian Hill 5
St Augustine's, Canterbury 17, 19,
    106–8, 109, 139 n. 32, 140, 170–1,
    196, 312, 314–15, 319, 322, 334–5,
    345, 349, 351
    scriptorium 193, 302, 305–7,
    310–13, 315, 330, 349
St Chrysogonus, Trastevere 49
St Cuthbert, Chester-le-Street 134, 220
St Jacquême, Aosta 239, 245, 247,
    249, 251
SS. John and Paul, Rome 49
St Kylian, Würzburg 240, 244, 246,
    248, 250
St Lawrence, Rome 315
St Martin, Rome 49, 91
St Martin, Tours 69
St Martin, Trier 73
St Mary Major, Rome 49 n. 123, 123
St Mary's, Worcester 186–7
St Mary's, York 278, 350 n. 5
St Maximin, Trier 229, 282
St Medard, Soissons 72
St Neots 195
St Oswald, Gloucester 143
St Pancratius at the Lateran 49, 98
St Paul, Rome 49 n. 123
St Paulinus, Trier 232
St Peter, Fritzlar 239, 244, 246, 248,
    250
St Peter's, Abbotsbury, Dorset 282
St Peter's, Worcester 187–8
St Peter's Basilica, Vatican 44 n. 96,
    49–51, 53, 91, 98, 117, 122 n. 163,
    123, 135 n. 14
SS. Peter and Paul, Canterbury 86,
    107, 315
St Stephen Major, Rome 49
St Stephen Minor, Rome 49, 50
Statuta Murbacensia 66–9, 71
Stephen II, pope 50–1, 52–3
Stephen of Ripon 104, 111, 115
    n. 138, 188

Symeon of Durham 221
Symmachus, pope 49
Symons, Thomas 141, 154, 168, 180,
    273
synods *see* councils
Talbot, C. H. 85
Theodemar, abbot 44–5, 58–9, 61–2,
    75–6, 185 n. 158
Theodore, archdeacon 34–5
Theodore, archbishop 79 n. 3, 81–2,
    119, 131 n. 200, 136
Theodoric, *comes* 76
Theodred, bishop 143
Thomas of Elmham 106–7, 108, 110
Thorney 195
Tours 33, 69, 74
Trebič 240, 244, 246, 248, 250
Tridentine Breviary (1568) 14 n. 1, 17,
    31, 43, 48 n. 122, 122 n. 163
Trier 229, 231–3, 239, 240, 244, 246,
    248, 250, 282
    St Martin, Trier 73
    St Maximin, Trier 229, 282
Trina oratio 181
Turpilius 176
Usuard of Saint-Germain-des-Prés 155
Vallombrosa 316 n. 53
Van Dijk, S. J. P. 301, 318
Venerandus, founder of Altaripa 83
    n. 20
Viking attacks 6, 10, 11, 73, 133–5,
    139, 142, 148
Virbonus, abbot 49, 50 n. 131
Vogüé, Adalbert de 37, 67
Wala, abbot of Corbie 57, 62
Walahfrid Strabo 53
Walcher, bishop 221
Wallace-Hadrill, J. M. 6
Wearmouth 6, 80, 82, 91, 104, 108,
    114 n. 138, 117, 127, 136
    Wearmouth-Jarrow 7, 111 n. 125,
    135
Wells 224, 232

Wessex 135, 196, 221, 232–3, 351
Westbury-on-Trym 165–166, 186–7, 195
Westminster 193, 196, 284 n. 68
Whitby 27, 117, 132
Wilfrid, bishop 5, 82–4, 95, 98, 104, 110–11, 114, 115 n. 138, 117, 131, 132, 188
William of Dijon, abbot 213, 215, 274–5, 278, 279, 280, 281, 294, 296, 325, 334, 342, 345–6
William of Malmesbury 143 n. 48, 143 n. 51, 192 n. 173, 233
Willibald, 29, 85
Wilton 143, 232
Edith of Wilton, St 232, 284 n. 68
Wiltshire 89–90 n. 38
Winchcombe 166, 215–16, 350 n. 5
Winchester, 141–3, 150–2, 165, 168, 171, 172 n. 97, 173, 175, 177, 187, 189, 190, 194, 212 n. 34, 222–3, 233, 283, 303 n. 7, 305 n. 12, 330, 332, 349
Ælfeah of Winchester 143, 194
Council of Winchester (c.970) 150, 175, 180, 184, 195
New Minster 143, 150, 171, 173, 174–5, 224 n. 20, 327
Old Minster 86, 150, 167, 171, 172–3, 254 n. 3, 283, 349
Witiza 74 *see also* Benedict of Aniane

Worcester 6–7, 81 n. 10, 140, 142 n. 46, 150, 151, 165–6, 175, 180, 184 n. 135, 186–90, 191 n. 166, 195, 226 n. 28, 277 n. 58, 281, 282–3, 285, 327
John of Worcester 192
Koenwald of Worcester 143, 169
St Mary's, Worcester 186–7
Wormald, Patrick 154, 167
Wright, David 113, 114
Wulfred, archbishop 79, 87–9, 138
Wulfric 154
Wulfsige III, Bishop of Sherborne 184 n. 135
Wulfstan II, St, Bishop of Worcester 188
Wulfstan of Winchester 155, 161, 168, 173
Wulfstan the Homilist, Archbishop of York 103 n. 92, 184 n. 135, 283
Würzburg 229, 240, 244, 246, 248, 250
Wynfrith 85 *see also* Boniface, St
York 81 n. 8, 88–89, 100, 106, 126–7, 147 n. 76, 147 n. 76, 150, 184 n. 135, 225, 282
antiphoner of 126–8, 131, 225
Ecgberht of York, archbishop 100–1, 127
library of 135
Oscytel of York 165
St Mary's, York 278, 350 n. 5

Lightning Source UK Ltd.
Milton Keynes UK
UKHW010808100219
337015UK00006B/11/P